CITY

of LIES

CITY
of LIES

SAM HAWKE

TOR

A TOM DOHERTY ASSOCIATES BOOK

NEW YORK

CITY OF LIES

Copyright © 2018 by Sam Hawke

A Tor Book
Published by Tom Doherty Associates
175 Fifth Avenue
New York, NY 10010

www.tor-forge.com

Tor® is a registered trademark of Macmillan Publishing Group, LLC.

The Library of Congress Cataloging-in-Publication Data is available upon request.

ISBN 978-1-250-30668-5 (hardcover)
ISBN 978-0-7653-9689-1 (trade paperback)
ISBN 978-0-7653-9691-4 (ebook)

Our books may be purchased in bulk for promotional, educational, or business use. Please contact your local bookseller or the Macmillan Corporate and Premium Sales Department at 1-800-221-7945, extension 5442, or by email at MacmillanSpecialMarkets@macmillan.com.

First Edition: July 2018

Printed in the United States of America

0 9 8 7 6 5 4 3 2 1

For my boys, the other three parts that make me whole. I'd be a one-legged chair without you, my loves, and I think we can all agree that would be a pretty terrible chair.

Acknowledgments

A book is very much a big team effort (or at least this one certainly was), so my sincerest thanks to everyone who helped in large ways or small. In particular, but in no particular order:

Thanks to the two women who took a chance on this book and made it a reality: my agent, Julie Crisp, who brutally pulled all the stuffing out and made me put it all back in in a different order, and my editor, Diana Gill, who did the same, only this time with magical stuffing. Epic, magical stuffing. You both saw the better shape the book could be in, and I take back all those things I muttered under my breath as I typed, I swear.

Thanks to Greg Ruth and Irene Gallo for the magnificent artwork on the cover. One day I'll stop squealing when I look at it. Maybe.

More generally, I am so grateful to everyone on the amazing Tor team (including Gifmaster Kristin Temple, and my own personal Finnish road safety consultant, Jen Gunnels) for their hard work on the book behind the scenes and for nursing a bumpkin Aussie through the realities of NY publishing. Thank you all!

But before *City of Lies* was a book it was a project of many years that was supported not only by my household (love of my life, K, partner in all things, encourager, supporter, and—where necessary—prodder, who re-read a book for the first time in his life for me; and my beautiful sons, who shared my attention with the computer and notebooks for their entire young lives without complaint and with fullhearted cheerleading) but by my entire extended clan, most of whom read at least one draft and all of whom gave their unwavering support. In particular:

Sis the Younger, Gemma, who gave her time and attention to every word I sent her (day or night, as many times as I asked), helped me brainstorm, invent nouns and solve problems, and engaged in countless annoying moaning phone call/text walls over the space of at least ten years. Meg, you put up with my crap surrounding this book with a degree of patience, support, and good humor that should qualify you for some kind of award, but doesn't, so sorry, it will just have to be my thanks.

Sis the Elder, Annette, fictional plant-and-symptom-makerupperer-extraordinaire, whose eagle eyes proofread this sucker more times than they could possibly enjoy, who sneak-printed manuscripts for me in the wee hours of the morning, and who even wasted time on a well-earned holiday on a cruise rereading and sending me notes during sporadic patches of Wi-Fi on Pacific islands. I'm sorry for contributing to your sea sickness, Nettie!

Elder Bro, Chris (even though he had a maddening habit of texting me his 100-percent accurate predictions while he was reading and therefore generating a deep fear that I had written the most predictable story ever, goddamn it, Bro), and my lovely sister-in-law, Di, who dabbled well outside her preferred genres for my sake.

Mum and Dad, Robyn and Bob, the most loving and supportive of parents, who never faltered in their unrealistic and unwavering belief that I would make this happen.

My beloved uncle Chiz, who is always there for me, and with whom I will absolutely have an argument at some stage in the future about something that happened in the book. The trifling fact that I wrote it will not sway his opinion.

Oh, and Younger Bro, J, who hasn't read this yet but promises he will at some point. I believe you, kiddo, I really do. (And Reeny, who hasn't, either, but I DO actually believe).

Love you all so much.

Thanks also to my many lovely friends who generously gave up their time to read drafts and/or generally talk shop: Tammy Jones, Anna Mc-Nair, Aiden O'Hehir, Cath and Ian Sainsbery, Jane Abbott, Jacinta Geaghan, Jeff Fisher, Robin Hobb, Fleur Roberts, Damon Taylor, and Jess Cleaver. Your advice and comments were invaluable.

Also a shout-out to the ACT Writers Centre HARDCOPY program, especially its mastermind Nigel Featherstone; QOTKU Janet Reid and the Reiders on the Reef; the Forward Motion writers community; and the Canberra Speculative Fiction Guild. It feels like a small and kind world hanging out talking writing with you all.

Oh, and finally, thanks to my year one teacher, Mrs. Lyn Sheils, because I promised I would acknowledge her in my first published book when I was a (probably quite obnoxious) six-year-old, and by jiminy I'm keeping that promise.

CITY

of LIES

Laceleaf

DESCRIPTION: Attractive wide-ranging plant with delicate green leaves and clumps of small white flowers.

SYMPTOMS: Dilated pupils, rapid weak pulse, and a peripheral numbness that spreads inward, resulting in respiratory paralysis and heart failure.

PROOFING CUES: Mild, musty smell and pleasant flavor, often mistaken for harmless cousins.

1

Jovan

I was seven years old the first time my uncle poisoned me.

He served me the toxin in his signature cheese stew. It gave me waves of stomach cramps and hallucinations of every horror my young mind could conjure, but left no lasting damage. I learned that day to trust nothing on my plate or in my cup, not even something prepared by my beloved uncle Etan, my *Tashi*, the most honored and trusted person in my world. *Especially* not him.

By ten, I could identify the ingredients in most dishes set before me, from the spicy baked fish served year-round in Sjona's farms and estates, to the flat black bread cooked in clay ovens in every kitchen in the city, to the delicate cheese-and-honey pastries favored in the highest circles of society. I could detect any of the eleven greater poisons hidden in those dishes. Most by taste, some by smell, and one by its unique mouthfeel. I could also, should the need arise, use them myself.

Before his own Tashi died and my uncle Etan inherited his seat on the Council, he had trained as a cook—something of an oddity among the six

Credol Families, but not unheard of. No one thought it amiss that he should instill in me the same dedication to the craft. Under his tutelage, foreign dishes and imported spices ceased to be an obstacle to my tongue or nose, and I learned all that had ever been written about the natural and crafted poisons of our land.

Over the next ten years, and hundreds of poisonings, Etan gave me many gifts: immunities, scars, an appreciation of our family's honorable and secret role, and a memory and mind trained in our craft so I could one day protect the ruling family of Sjona as he did.

As he lay dying before me, none of it seemed enough.

A well-trained memory is a fine thing, an essential skill for learning and of critical importance to a proofer. Today mine, once a source of pride, revealed itself as a useless trick. I could recall the whole day, an unwilling audience to my own play, but what good could I do, reliving a day of mistakes and inaction? I had gone over it again and again, and still I did not see our enemy. Over and over, I did not save my uncle.

We had sailed home only yesterday morning, not knowing it for the last day of our old lives, smuggled like thieves in the back of a fat little transport ship bringing wood from the Talafan Empire south to the capital. Tain Caslavtash Iliri, the Chancellor's nephew and heir, future ruler of the country and equal parts my dearest friend, solemnest duty, and pain in my rear, nursed a sore head with infuriating good humor. I nursed a bad temper and a dose of relief. Several days earlier than planned, Tain's retinue abandoned long behind us in the northern border city, we had both hoped to slip back into Silasta without remark.

A month of meetings and social engagements had left me exhausted and irritable, longing for the familiar comfort of routine. In Silasta, I knew everyone who might interact with my charge, highborn or low, and what they stood to gain or lose. Or at least, so I had naively thought. But in Telasa I had been forced to rely on my judgment alone in assessing new threats and challenges. Who might be tempted to dose the Heir's kavcha with beetle-eye to fuel careless tongues, or bake hazelnode into his bread to cause a stomachache and absence from a key event?

The boat passed under the north river gate and through familiar white walls, breaking the force of the wind and bathing us in the emerging smells and sounds of our city. While the captain handed over weapons and nego- tiated passage in a confusing jumble of broken Sjon, Talafan, and simple Trade, I nudged my friend from a doze. He came alert and stood without apparent stiffness. No matter how luxurious his ordinary accommodations, Tain could relax in the most awkward of places. "That didn't take too long," he said cheerfully.

I rolled my eyes as I gathered the last of our belongings. "Sure, for some- one who slept through most of it, and spent the rest drinking with the crew." He'd loved socializing with men and women who couldn't read our tattoos and thought us merely wealthy wastrels from the capital. I had to admit I'd also enjoyed the anonymity and the break from worrying about anything untoward in his cups.

He turned his easy grin on me. "Practicing diplomacy, my friend."

On deck, we leaned over the rail as the boat negotiated the channel through the marshy north end of the Bright Lake, enjoying the sun's warmth. The fierce breath of the Maiso had kept us mostly belowdecks on the trip, but Sjona's harsh winds couldn't penetrate the walls of the city. I felt comfort- able for the first time in weeks.

The magnificent arch of Trickster's Bridge loomed before us, a grand win- dow into Silasta, the Bright City, with its white stone brilliant against the late summer sky. To the east, domed roofs and zigzag streets rose from the bank, a pale honeycomb against the slope of Solemn Peak. On the western shore, a merry jumble of boats, foreign and local, spilled traders and visitors of all descriptions out to the docks of the sprawling, industrious lower city. Yellow-sashed officials from the River Guild weaved through the crowds. Blackwing gulls swooped unwary workers unloading barges, and their shrill squawks mingled with the distant hoot of oku being unloaded from a barge and the lively orchestra of commerce. It felt like waking from an uneasy dream as we passed under Trickster's and back into our reality.

We paid our host and joined the mixed and colorful soup of merchants, workers, and tourists moving from the docks into the lower city. Silasta's younger and less cultivated side was three times the size of its older sibling, a hodgepodge of industry, trade, and residences of varying levels of re- spectability. The smell of a dozen different spices and frying oils assailed us. Tiny canopied stalls were wedged between elegant old teahouses and subtle gambling dens, and hawkers melted in and out of the shadows with cunning spreads of goods ready to fold up and disappear at the first sign of a Guild official. By the nearest canal, a swaying tourist bickered with a preacher kneeling by an earther shrine crafted of rock and bird bones.

I longed for the peace and space of our family apartments, a pot of proper Oromani tea, and the calming presence of my uncle and sister. "I'll call us a ride." I caught the prowling gaze of a litter carrier, but Tain interrupted.

"What's going on there?"

I followed his gesture. The confrontation between the drunk and the street preacher had escalated. The foreigner had a hold on the earther's wrist and was shaking his arm, shouting, while the smaller man clutched prayer charms around his neck and half-sung, half-moaned some kind of chant. "It's a bit early for that, isn't it?" I muttered. Our local merchants should have known better than to sell kori to a tourist at this time of day. Though from the look of him, he'd perhaps been out all night. He wore a crumpled jacket and wide trousers in a fabric too heavy for our climate, and an air of belligerence far stronger than the smell of alcohol and gaming house smokes.

Tain moved closer and I caught his arm. "Leave it to the Order Guards." I looked through the crowd in vain; no red-and-blue striped uniform in sight. "Or a Guild official."

The drunkard had taken offense at the preacher's rantings and his accented Trade tongue grew to a roar. "—eh, eh, I'm talking to you, bloody street scum! Look at me when I talk to you!" He kicked out roughly at the shrine, toppling one of the balanced piles of stone.

The preacher, who until then had been avoiding eye contact and allowing his arm to be shaken like a loose streamer on a festival day, stopped his warbling chant and snapped his gaze to the bigger man. He said something I didn't catch, but whatever it was enraged the tourist. He reached into his billowing pants and the glint of a weapon flashed in the morning light. Someone shrieked and the surrounding crowd drew back from the altercation.

"Guard!" I yelled, but as I turned to usher the Heir back to safety, Tain lunged for the man's knife hand. He grabbed the wrist two-handed and pivoted in a half turn back toward me. The drunkard dropped the preacher and fell backward with the pressure on his elbow and shoulder, and the knife clunked to the ground. "Lem—lemme go!" he bellowed, struggling as much with confusion as pain.

I cautiously shuffled in and kicked the blade out of reach. It was illegal to carry weapons in the city, but fools will be fools, and sometimes the confiscation process at the gates wasn't as rigorous as it could be. Still no sign of an Order Guard. I edged closer to Tain. My duty was to protect him, but from hidden threats, not violent idiots in the streets. Why he had to make everyone's duties harder was another matter. The crowd looked on in embarrassed fascination, and a few people had recognized Tain. "We should—" I started.

"Are you finished here?" Tain rested his own knee on the man's bicep.

"Finished! Finished!"

His arm released, the man rolled onto his side, shaking his wrist and moaning. Tain turned to the preacher, who was hastily restacking stones and muttering. "Are you all right?" He crouched beside him. "Can I help?"

"The spirits are displeased," the man muttered, scowling without taking his eyes from the shrine. "This city is corrupt and the spirits are angry. We will be punished." He shrugged Tain's hand from his shoulder. "We will *all* be punished."

"Let the Guilds handle this, please, Honored Heir," I said. If hearing the title meant anything to the earther, he hid his reaction, continuing to reassemble his shrine and mutter dark warnings and curses. I sighed. Technically the man shouldn't be bothering people by the harbor but usually earthers were no more than a mild annoyance. He'd probably cursed the foreigner for drunken behavior or otherwise offended him. Where were the Guards, though? On a busy trade morning the place should have been swarming with them as a deterrent. Silasta was a famously nonviolent city but the Order Guards were a necessary precaution to prevent escalation of any heated trade or tariff disputes, especially with an influx of foreign merchants and visitors who did not necessarily share our peaceful outlook.

I took Tain's arm and pulled him to his feet, trying to steer him away. "Do I really need to tell you not to—" With a *whoof* the air was punched out of me as the foreigner plowed into us from the side, sending me to the ground and Tain scuttling back from the man's tackle and crashing into a canopied stall selling fried glintbeetles. Bright beetles and paper cones

crashed everywhere and the woman running the stall shouted in annoyance. By the time I'd regained my feet and my breath, Tain had scooped
behind one of the man's knees and with a kind of awkward shuffle-hop he
overbalanced his opponent. The drunk fell into the leg of the stall with a
loud curse in a language I didn't recognize, almost toppling it entirely.
Tain fell with him and the two scuffled and wrestled in the pile of spilled
food.

I cursed under my breath and circled the pair, looking for a way to help.
When the bigger man pinned my friend underneath him, I launched in and
locked my arms around his neck. "This is *not* what I call a homecoming," I
panted as I tried to pull him off. Honor-down, it had been a long time since
I'd had to do any martial training. Where were the *bloody* Order Guards?

The man released Tain and struck me in the solar plexus with his elbow.
Winded, I loosened my grip and he pulled free, shaking me off like a bug.
He roared, his intoxicated rage-presence making him seem at least twice
our size, and swung a fist clumsily at Tain, who ducked it and delivered
two short hard punches to the man's stomach before dancing back out of
reach. "He's full of kori," Tain said. "Hit him in the guts!"

I felt like giving my friend a whack instead when I saw the enjoyment
sparkling in his eyes. I didn't want to get anywhere near the man's guts.
Around us the crowd continued to scamper back out of the way. The spectacle
was either making or ruining their morning, but no one seemed inclined to
assist. I dodged a stray blow in my direction and as the man launched himself heavily at Tain again, his drunken focus on this new target of his rage,
I chopped into his stomach as hard as I could with the side of my hand. "I
just want a cup of *tea*," I told him bitterly.

Tain actually laughed. He sidestepped the attack and hit the man one
final time; with that last blow he folded in half like a deflating waterskin
and sat on his backside by the canal with a sickening groan. "Get back,"
Tain warned me, and we skittered out of range just in time to avoid the
sudden torrent as the man's overfull body gave up its contents.

And finally—*finally*—an Order Guard appeared at a run, errant hair
springing out of her Warrior-Guild braid and a sheen of sweat on her brow.
She pulled up to a stop and her terse expression melted into shock as she
took in the participants. "Honored Heir! Credo! I—my apologies, there
was an altercation with a herd of oku and some lutra at the south end of

the pier, and . . . Honored Heir, are you all right?" She looked around us, presumably searching for the servants who should have been there preventing this sort of thing, but who were in fact days away down the river.

"We're fine," Tain assured her with a broad smile. "This fellow couldn't handle his kori cups and was disturbing the poor gentleman by the shrine, there."

"He had a knife," I said, and gestured to the area where I'd kicked it.

"No weapons in our city," the Order Guard barked at the man by the canal, but he was still slumped over and heaving, so I doubted he heard. She looked anxiously at Tain again. "Again, my apologies for the delay, Honored Heir. We've limited staff at the moment."

"Not your fault." Tain, still all smiles, knelt and straightened the bent leg of the stall they'd crashed into, while I helped the merchant pick up her paper cones and sweep up the ruined beetles. Her earlier agitation forgotten now that she realized who we were, she tried to shoo us away.

"We'll pay for the food," I told her as I scooped up the last of the mess.

"No, Credo, that isn't necessary, not necessary at all," she said, but I pressed my family chit into the wax tablet on her now-wobbling tabletop with a weary glance at Tain.

"It was entirely our fault getting involved," I said firmly.

Tain helped the Order Guard haul the big drunk to his feet. As if his stomach contents had been the source of his aggression, he slumped meekly on the spot and let the Guard fix his wrists behind his back with the wire-centered cord hanging from her tunic. "I'll take him to the Guildhall with you," Tain offered.

"Of course that's not necessary, Honored Heir," the Guard said, her tone anxious. "This's been quite enough bother as it is."

"Nonsense!" Tain beamed at her. "I wouldn't mind a word with the Warrior-Guilder in any case."

Like a room doused in sudden sunlight I finally recognized his idiotic behavior for what it was. It was very bad manners to roll one's eyes at the second most powerful man in the country, so I settled for a sigh. A month or so downriver and I'd quite put out of my head my friend's recent obsession with the Warrior Guild and, more importantly, its coarse, disreputable leader, Credola Aven.

He'd spent the better part of summer training with the Guild, much to the bafflement of his peers and the irritation of his uncle the Chancellor. Unlike them, I knew why. Aven was twenty years his senior and the leader of the least honored and respected of the Guilds, disinterested in art, music, or cultured discourse. Tain's fascination was unfathomable, considering Silasta was full of interesting, talented women and men, beautiful and clever and contributing far more to civilization than someone whose main skill was the effective use of violence.

But the Guard deflated his hopes in any case. "The Warrior-Guilder's not in the city, Honored Heir. She's with the army out near Moncasta, fighting Doranites over the mines again. That's why we're low on bodies here." She ducked her head, her discomfort obvious. "Please, allow me to deal with this. My apologies for your involvement."

After she left, we rinsed our scraped hands and shins in the canal and Tain took my berating with good humor but no apology. "No one else was helping him," he pointed out.

I frowned. "No, but that doesn't mean—"

"Would you prefer the old man got stabbed?" He stood, distracted. "We should check on him. I think I offended him somehow."

But several yellow-sashed Guild officials now moved about the area, directing the cleanup, and the preacher had long since disappeared either voluntarily or at their direction. It wasn't illegal to preach the old religion, of course, but it was common to see earthers moved along for disturbing trade or obstructing traffic.

I checked the position of the sun. "We'd better head up. The Chancellor will probably hear about this soon enough."

He gave me a mournful look. "Let's walk, at least. Enjoy the last of the peace while we can." I raised an eyebrow, unsure our morning could be described as peaceful anymore, but then he grinned. "We can have that cup of tea at least."

We walked south and crossed the pedestrian bridge to the east side of the lake. A calm contrast to its commerce-driven sister, the east shore was all long silvery grass and white sand, dotted with groups of Silasta's wealthier classes enjoying the morning sun. Bathers splashed in the shallows and daring gulls snatched at unattended food. As we came off the bridge we dodged a stack of squealing children playing "old wooden" on the grass; tottering on one another's backs and shoulders as they sang the rhyme, they almost collided with us as they shouted the last line: "The great old wooden saved us *all*!" and came tumbling down in a heap of giggles and cheerfully squashed limbs. Behind them, a knot of men and women lounged about, casually betting on informal footraces on the grass.

This side of the lake was more homogeneous and we blended in easily among crowds of dark heads and bare brown limbs under white tunics or palumas. But our anonymity didn't last; first we were waylaid by earnest young Credo Edric, eager to share with us his latest song for my sister (called, imaginatively, "Kalina Kalina") then by a wily couple of jewelers who were working the crowd of young Credolen in the hopes of securing a commission. I was grateful when we finally made it to my apartments.

The tinkle of the tiny hanging bells in the doorway rang out into emptiness. No movement stirred the green necklace of plants framing the curved walls (some decorative, some medicinal, some lethal). A suggestion of Etan's earlier baking or experimentation hung in the air by way of a faint smoky scent. No sign of him or Kalina.

I changed, grateful for clean clothes—Tain waved off my offer of the same, unfazed by his rumpled state—and had begun to prepare the tea when my sister arrived home.

She froze as she saw us, furtive. Or perhaps it was just an involuntary flinch, as she followed it with several successive sneezes. Tain laughed and sprang to his feet. "There's a sound I've missed!"

"Are you all right?" I blurted out.

"Hello to you, too, Brother." She smiled to blunt the rebuke and squeezed my hands in greeting, then Tain's. "Welcome home, both of you."

"It's a relief to be back," I said by way of apology. Up close, her hair was damp and springy, and her skin prickled faintly with cold. "Where were you? Are you well?"

"Just walking. And I'm the same as usual." Soft voice hoarse, she didn't meet my eyes as she slipped past us to settle on a cushion by the table.

I checked the color transition of the brew and found it a satisfying rich gold. I settled the pot among the three of us and listened to my sister's breath over the comforting warm *gur-gur-gur* sound of the tea pouring into each of our cups. No telltale squeak or rasp. Nothing to be anxious about.

A few sips in, the blanket of routine wrapped around me, it was as though

we had never left. Tain entertained Kalina with tales of our trip, somehow
turning weeks of monotony and stress into amusing escapades. I mostly sat
in peaceful silence. The tea was a new one our mother had sent in my absence; delicate in aroma, but surprisingly pungent and earthy. Mother had
never been a proofer, or much of a mother, but the genius of her palate for
tea was undeniable.

"Enough about these two idiots," Tain said at last. He left the table and
began rifling through our bags. "Gifts! And you tell us your news. You
haven't been working too hard, I hope?"

"Oh, much of the same," Kalina murmured vaguely. He'd bought her a
set of polished wooden beads. I'd found a Talafan book of children's stories
with gorgeous painted illustrations. "Now you didn't choose this just so
you could scrape samples of the paint colors, did you?" she asked me se-
verely, and Tain laughed at my attempts at bluster, having heard me enthus-
ing in the market about the shade of blue.

"Well, your heart was half in it," she teased, but her cheeks dimpled
with pleasure just the same. Tain wound the beads through her dark cloud
of hair—the wood was same warm brown as her skin, and gleamed like
dewdrops in her curls—while she pored over the book. Talafan looked
nothing like our written language and not much like Trade; indecipherable
to me, but no obstacle to my sister. Her fingers stroked the pages and she
read hungrily.

"I wish you could have come," I said quietly, and her hands quivered a
moment on the page before she shrugged with artificial nonchalance. I
cursed myself for saying it and hastened to change the subject. "Etan's
notes were very short. Has he been busy?"

"I've barely seen him," she said. "First there was the mess with the raids
on the mines, then I think there was some kind of problem getting the
summer harvest deliveries. Oh, and there was an earthquake that damaged
a quarry, and the rains still haven't come to the rice fields so everyone has
been worried about yields."

"What happened with the mines?" Tain's voice was a touch too casual.
We had longstanding disputes with various Doranite mountain tribes about
ownership of some of the mines near the southern border; it wasn't unusual
to see raids in summer, but these had been larger and better organized

than in previous years. Tain's interest, though, had nothing to do with the military implications.

"Some of the attacks started getting close to Moncasta," Kalina said, and twisted ever so slightly so that Tain's hands fell away from the beads in her hair. "One of the outskirt villages got attacked. The Council sent the whole army to force the Doranites to either retreat or move to a full confrontation."

"That's why Aven's gone with them," he said, disappointment rich in his tone.

My sister's lips tightened around the fine porcelain of her cup, midsip. "Yes, the Warrior-Guilder led the army."

Tain sighed, and now that we were in the privacy of my own home, I rolled my eyes freely. "Come on, Jov," he said, catching my expression and giving us an innocent grin. "I'm the Heir, aren't I? My uncle's always saying I need to have relationships with all the Councilors."

"I'll look forward to you spending the next few months in the Craft Guild practicing your leatherwork, then." It was unclear whether taking up sparring and weapons lessons at the Warrior Guild, much to the consternation of many of his peers, was the cause or a consequence of his infatuation. I glanced at my sister, who stared down at her cup, the Talafan book pushed aside. "Did the Doranites retreat?"

"I haven't heard anything." Her tone had cooled.

Feeling the peace of our reunion breaking away from me, I tried again to reel it in, topping up our teacups with a forced smile. "What did Mother call this blend? It's very good. In Telasa they said the Talafan Emperor himself is drinking our tea now."

"It's called pale needle." She cleared her throat. "Actually, Mother asked me to come to the estate for a while."

"What for?" Like all the six Credol Families, our estates in the country were the lifeblood of our family business and the source of food to support the capital, but they were hardly interesting to visit. Nor was there any great compulsion to visit our mother, whose fascination with and ambition for our family's tea production outweighed any desire she'd had to help her brother raise us. She'd left the city when I was barely walking and we saw her perhaps once a year, if that.

Kalina shrugged, swirling her tea and avoiding eye contact. "I suppose she thought I might be useful there."

I might have imagined the slightest emphasis on *there*.

Kalina was the eldest and should have been Etan's apprentice. She was bright, quiet, unobtrusive, and desperate to please. But when she had not been able to fulfill that role I had replaced her, and neither of us could ever forget that sore spot between us.

I remembered lying awake in bed as a young child while she sat in the corner of our room with a candle, face screwed up in concentration. She studied so hard, memorizing quantities and names and drawing elaborate labeled pictures of plant leaves, trying to impress our Tashi with her devotion to her duty, hoping it would make up for her body's weakness. I didn't understand, back then. I'd had my own problems—as a child my compulsions had been overwhelming, and I had lacked tools to fight them. The thoughts I couldn't stop dwelling on, the seemingly meaningless things that bothered me . . . My sister had been my anchor, calming me when the anxiety drove me to fits, and helping me develop the patterns and order that would eventually help me manage the problem.

Kalina taught me our family's secret code of lines and dots almost before I learned to read ordinary language. We left secret messages for each other not just in print but on any tactile surface that could be marked—wax tablets, a beaded necklace, even baked on bread—practicing reading it by feel as well as sight. Sometimes we also left messages in geraslin ink, which would disappear if you sprinkled a certain powder over the text, then reappear under heat and light. Through her I inadvertently learned early the many varied fauna of our country as I held up pictures of plant parts she'd drawn and she named them in turn. I'd loved that game, its methodical calming repetition. I didn't realize until years later that for her it was no game. She was constantly pushing and testing herself.

But no matter how hard she worked, it wasn't hard enough.

The first and only time Etan poisoned her, she almost died. Even after years of immunization, her frail body, ever susceptible to every cough and fever, couldn't cope with the dose. I was so young, then, but I never forgot the loneliness of those dark weeks when I wasn't allowed to see her, and there was no one to play games and keep my mind operating smoothly. She recovered weaker than ever, her skin tinged gray, her hair dull, her eyes fever bright. Though we still left each other coded messages for fun, never again did we play the card game. She told me years later, in a stiff voice, that she had burned the cards. She had failed, and I had taken the place that should have been hers.

My tea was cold and the conversation had fallen away. The comfort I'd found in the three of us back together had been spoiled, and I could think of nothing to bring it back.

A messenger arrived soon after, sparing us further awkwardness. Our return had been noticed and passed on; Chancellor Caslav respectfully requested his nephew's presence at a formal luncheon at Credo Lazar's apartments to welcome a visiting Talafan dignitary. Presumably the nobleman was the passenger on the ornately decorated Talafan boat we'd seen in harbor when we arrived. Tain immediately set to wheedling to convince me to come with him. Back to normal, indeed.

Looking back, I could have gotten there faster. Entered differently. Spoken to different people. Perhaps I would have seen something different. But all I had was what was done.

The apartments for the six Credol Families were built on the great sweeping drive at the top of the hill, so it was a short walk to the Reed family's from our own Oromani apartments. The sound of the gathering leaked out into the streets and a retinue of stony-faced Talafan servants waited outside the grounds by an elaborately decorated litter. The visiting nobleman must have been an important man, but it was the height of poor manners—even for a foreigner—to take your own servants into another person's home, so outside they remained.

Servants dressed more expensively than I ushered us into Lazar's entertaining suite. The Performers' Guild's most celebrated musician played delicate strings in a corner. Hanging silks in the unmistakable hand of the Artist-Guilder herself fluttered in the light breeze from the gardens, and tall spears of blue flowers imported from the Great Wetlands filled cunning alcoves in the walls. All new since I'd last seen this room, all worth a fortune.

"Honored Heir!" Lazar grasped Tain's shoulders in welcome and beamed. "You've returned! Why, we weren't expecting you for days! I was going to throw you a party." Our host's head was a shiny, wobbly teardrop glistening with expensive oils and ending in a weak chin. Extravagant fabric garbed his obese frame. He looked me over, soft face scrunched in polite confusion as he assessed the appropriate response; I wasn't invited, but I was heir to Etan's Council seat, and my family outranked his. "Credo Jovan. How pleasant to see you also. Welcome home, lad."

"My apologies, Credo Lazar." I shot a glare at Tain, who ignored it complacently. I shouldn't have given in to his pleading. "I know this is a Council function. I wanted a quick word with my uncle. I'll just be a moment."

"Of course, of course, my boy." Lazar ushered us in, his attention already fading. "You wouldn't have heard this piece yet, would you? Exquisite. The Performers' Guild is calling it the composition of the season, you know. *I* think—" He broke off at a crash across the room; the Stone-Guilder had collided with a servant. Vivid orange soup splashed onto the white tiles like a spray of blood. "Not again!" Lazar's voice jumped an octave higher. "Please excuse me, Honored Heir." His perfume didn't mask the reek of panicked sweat as he darted away. Tain and I exchanged amused glances.

The heads of family and Guilders who comprised Silasta's ruling Council milled about in small groups, servants weaving expertly between them. We passed the Theater-Guilder, Varina, conversing with a servant carrying cups of cloudy kori, and identified the thin, sunken-eyed Talafan nobleman, a gleaming pale ghost in a bright silk jacket as he stood listening to the musician with Credola Nara and Credo Javesto. At the other side of the room, Etan and Chancellor Caslav spoke with a few other Councilors by the food table.

The Chancellor caught sight of us and beckoned, lips tight. He and Tain could have been brothers, sharing the same slight build, broad nose, and dark curls worn long enough to mask what Tain called "the family ears." The tattoos circling Caslav's bare arms were a more elaborate version of Tain's, signifying his role as Chancellor. He was a handsome man, but unlike his nephew's his face was solemn and humorless. Beside him, Etan faded into the background: a plain, bearded man in his fifties, shorter and stockier, with gentle eyes. I'd heard him called meek. I knew better.

Tain breezed up to Caslav, ignoring his uncle's frown, and gave the older man a warm squeeze of the shoulders. "Glad to see you. I'm starving. Are those fish cakes?"

"You are three days early," Caslav said, and I could have sworn the temperature dropped. "And am I to understand that you have returned without your retinue? I received a rather distraught bird from your cousins."

"Well, it's a very long journey, Tashi, so I imagine the poor thing got tired." Failing to generate an answering smile, Tain switched to his most sincere manner. "I'm sorry, Uncle. They were a little over-zealous and I saw a way to come home a fraction early without the fuss. But at least it's given me a chance to help greet our guest. I learned a little Talafan in Telasa. Shall I go and introduce myself?"

I shuffled back to stand beside Etan as they continued their conversation.

"Jovan," Etan said, raising a brow.

"Tashi," I replied with a shrug. A corner of my uncle's mouth twitched.

In front of us, a big man in an ill-fitting paluma who had been waiting for food also stepped politely backward, trying not to intrude on the conversation between the Chancellor and his nephew. So out of context was his presence here that it took me a moment to recognize Marco, the head of training at the Warrior Guild. He'd taught me in compulsory classes years ago, and had been tutoring Tain for his recent sessions. He was not on the Council, but he must have been assigned temporary Warrior-Guilder status while Aven took the army south. Like a great tree stuffed into an ornamental pot, the soldier stood out in the refined company, his balding head well above the rest, muscular chest and shoulders straining the normally loose paluma. The garb constricted his movements as he tried awkwardly to accept from an unsympathetic servant a bowl for soup with one hand and a flat circle of bread with the other.

"Guilder Marco!"

Credo Bradomir—second only to the Chancellor's family in honor and wealth—swept past in a cloud of fragrant oil and folds of white silk to accost Marco before he could be served any soup. "My dear man, my dear Guilder." Bradomir snatched the soup bowl and held it between manicured fingernails as though Marco might have infected it. "Doubtless there are no such niceties in the army, but here there is a certain standard of behavior. The Chancellor is *always* offered the first serving at a gathering."

Bradomir replaced the bowl with a *chink* of expensive ceramics. Marco wiped his forehead and took another step back, head down and eyes searching for an exit. I gave him a shrug in solidarity. I had little in common with Marco or his ilk; though they provided a necessary service to the city and the country more broadly, their skills and values were at odds with the rest of peaceful, cultured Silastian society. On the other hand, Bradomir was indisputably a sanctimonious ass.

"I'm sorry, Credo Bradomir," Marco said, his voice an uncultured rumble, faintly accented despite his many decades in the city. He extended an uncertain hand, offering his bread to Bradomir as well.

At that, Tain stepped between the two men. "Don't be ridiculous," the Heir said. "Please keep your bread, Warrior-Guilder." He raked Bradomir with a contemptuous glance and nodded to the sweating servant, who served two bowls of the bright soup. Tain made a show of handing one back to his uncle and smiled apologetically at Marco. "There, no harm done."

Marco moved away, clumsy and silent as he pushed his way to the back of the group. Bradomir's heavy-lashed gaze lingered on the back of Tain's head as he allowed himself to be served. I stepped closer to Etan and we took our turn next. "Anything I should be worried about?" he murmured.

I shook my head. "You?" We were close to, but turned at an angle from, the Chancellor, who was now engaged in a discussion with the Stone-Guilder about road paving materials in the lower city.

"No. Well. Later." Etan set down his bowl of soup next to the Chancellor's to adjust the cording on his paluma, then, moments later, seemingly picked it up again. The switch of the bowls was so subtle, so effortless, it was all I could do to keep my eyes averted. Hard as I trained, I couldn't imagine matching his skill as a proofer.

I wanted to ask him about Kalina, and Mother's invitation, but a screech from the other side of the room interrupted my thought.

"What *now*?" Credo Lazar pushed through to the source of the disturbance: a servant dancing about on the spot, engaged in some kind of weird spasm with her arms slapping her own back. When her strange hopping spun her about to face us a few more people let out shrieks. A creature clung to her hair, gray and about the size of her head, and nimble enough to avoid her panicked slaps. As several other servants moved in to help her, the animal sprang from her hair onto one of the painted hanging silks dangling nearby and scrambled up it as effortlessly as a large spider.

"Not the silks!" Lazar moaned. "Get it down! Someone get it down!"

"What in all the hells is that thing?" Tain's voice was a blend of horror and fascination as the animal sprang like a tiny acrobat between the fluttering silk panels. "Is it *flying*?"

It was, almost; with each leap of the lengths between panels a concertina of dark skin stretched out like wings between the creature's front and rear legs then folded back to nothing as it landed. We were treated to an excellent view of gleaming black underwing as it flung itself from the silks onto a nearby cushioned stool.

"A gift for the Chancellor from our most generous guest, Lord Ectar," Etan said, and added in an undertone, "It's called a 'leksot,' I believe. It's some kind of Talafan pet. It wasn't received quite as well as Lord Ectar might have hoped; one of the servants fainted when he took it out, and another was convinced it was some kind of bad spirit given form. Oh, and it drooled on Credo Lazar."

Herded by our anxious host, three servants closed in to capture the animal, while the Talafan nobleman Lord Ectar protested from the side. "It is just playful," he was saying. "It does not hurt anyone. Please, allow me, allow me. . . ." Beside him, a servant moaned and mumbled as her gnarled arthritic fingers caressed the earther pendant she wore. Through it all, the leksot bounced on the cushion on light paws, tail coiled in a spring, like an athlete about to begin a race. It cocked its squashed head and regarded us speculatively.

"Perhaps our new Warrior-Guilder could dispose of it for us." Bradomir's sly tone raised a few titters in response.

One of the servants, prodded by Lazar, sprang forward to grab at the leksot, but it was far too swift, flattening itself to duck under grasping hands and scrambling up through the sea of legs, right into our group. Amidst shouts and a sudden crush of fleeing bodies, and the rising volume of the earther servant's prayers, the creature emerged suddenly on my uncle's bare legs. It scaled him as easily as the silks, faster than he could snatch at it, then leaped from Etan's shoulder to the Chancellor's. The flurry and panic intensified as the leksot hitched itself to the back of his paluma and let out a guttural grunt. The absurdity of the city's wealthiest and most powerful men and women all attempting to rid the Honored Chancellor of the animal plaguing him while also being too afraid to touch it themselves might have been funny in other circumstances.

Lord Ectar himself extracted the creature in the end. The Talafan stammered apologies as he pushed through the crowd and scooped the leksot from the Chancellor's clothing. "Forgive me, Honored Chancellor," he said. "I do not know what happened. The cages should have been locked." He looked about helplessly and then, perhaps remembering that his own servants had been forced to wait outside, carried the leksot himself back to the gilded cage from which it had escaped.

Once clear, Lazar's army of servants swooped in to fuss over the Chancellor and brush hairs from his paluma while the sweating host himself panted behind them like an overfilled sponge. Honor was as important a currency in Silasta as wealth, and embarrassing the Chancellor would cost Lazar deeply in Council politics. Credo Bradomir and the Theater-Guilder, Credola Varina, made a grand show of dusting themselves off, and Credola Nara took great delight in pointing out the damage the creature had caused to Lazar's hanging silks with its claws and drool. Marco, free from Bradomir's scrutiny and unfazed by the commotion, had taken the opportunity to tuck into his soup and bread at last.

The cause of all the excitement, the leksot, shrunk to docility now that its adventure had ended, grunting happily and nestling up against the Talafan's arm as he put it back in the cage. "It is just excited," he tried to explain, to nobody in particular. "They like play. They are the most beloved pet in the Emperor's court."

Tain elbowed me, deadpan. "Think it'll catch on here?"

I did my best not to laugh.

The family ears apparently conferred additional functionality, because Chancellor Caslav's gaze snapped over to his nephew. His tone was unamused as he said, "Credo Jovan, I wonder, would you be so good as to take my fine gift to the Manor? I think perhaps we've had sufficient excitement for one gathering, and you did mention you were heading back that way shortly." Over his shoulder, Tain made a pained expression.

"Certainly, Honored Chancellor."

"The glass garden will do."

I inclined my head. A job for a servant, perhaps, but given the reaction most of Lazar's were having to the animal it probably wasn't wise to leave it to one of them. I masked a shudder. The thing might have been harmless, but it was messy and smelly, and my skin itched just looking at it.

Etan patted my shoulder. "I'll see you at home later."

Across the room, Tain gave me a mournful wave as I struggled out the door with the unwieldy cage.

At home, I washed my stinking, fur-sprinkled paluma and scrubbed myself clean in the bath. My back ached. I'd left the leksot leaping around the glass-walled garden in the Manor to wreak its mischief, and sent a silent apology to the gardeners there.

I'd finally settled down to a pot of tea and a book when Etan came home. The wooden beads hanging from my doorway clicked as he entered; I glanced up and my chest compressed as I took in my uncle's swollen lips, shiny skin, and puffy eyes.

"Time to go, Jovan," he said.

I sprang to my feet.

Etan shuffled gracelessly into the kitchen and pressed the underside of the stone bench, activating the mechanism that moved a section of cupboard and revealed our hidden proofing room. My heart rate increased as we packed a satchel full of antidotes: charcoal, sea snake scale powder, atrapis, panshar balls from the digestive tracts of wild lutra. "How long since you noticed?"

"I came straight here from the wharfs," Etan said. I marked how many bottles and jars he took, and the lack of precision made me anxious. "Less than an hour. Dizziness first, then swelling, then perspiration. No stomach pains or nausea, but pressure in my chest."

My throat dried. "The Chancellor?"

"At the Manor."

"Sit down," I told him, and took over packing the satchel, my stomach knotting. There had been other attempts to dose the Chancellor with various substances over the years, but never had I seen my uncle this way.

"Have you eaten since lunch?"

"No."

"You proofed everything at Lazar's?"

He might have been feeling ill but it hadn't dampened his spirits entirely; the look he fired at me stung.

"Sorry, Tashi. I just know these functions are difficult." Etan himself prepared the majority of the Chancellor's food, or else proofed it long in advance. But functions like today's were the bane of our profession: shared food, someone else's kitchens, staff we didn't know, and the scrutiny of canny eyes under which we must secretly test. Visibly proofing would expose open distrust and weakness—much like bringing one's own servants to another's home, or being surrounded by openly armed guards—something custom and honor dictated that the Chancellor must never do. Etan had to proof everything on the spot, before the Chancellor, without being noticed.

Etan tilted his head in acknowledgment. "I got into Lazar's kitchens this morning and tested everything they'd prepared. I noticed nothing, and there were no masking flavors." Food with a naturally bitter, sour, or acidic taste, or food so heavily spiced as to hide subtler flavors, would never be passed on to the Chancellor unless it had been proofed well in advance. "I don't know much about Lord Ectar the Talafan, so I took no chances." We knew of only two toxins that were effectively undetectable in food, even to a trained proofer; petra venom and a complicated compound known as Esto's revenge. If Etan had consumed either of those, he'd be dead already.

I waited while he purged his stomach contents into a basin, and gave him two of the most generalized antidotes—charcoal and a panshar ball—after he had cleaned himself. "Without any stomach pain, the only thing that matches your symptoms is maidenbane, but obviously you'd have tasted that," I said. That plant was so bitter even an untrained person would detect something amiss. "It might be an illness?"

Etan shrugged. He suddenly seemed so diminished. Older. Frailer. "I hope so."

We hailed a litter but asked the men to move slowly. Up here, between the Credol residences, the streets were the original unpaved pathways, with no heavy wagon traffic to drive ruts into the packed surface. It made the journey smoother, but still fear and concern dogged me as we traveled in silence. The white azikta stone walls of the buildings around us glowed warmly in the afternoon light as we made our way up the heavy gradient pathway to the sprawling Chancellor's Manor.

Argo, the Manor doorkeep, noted our passage in his visitors' tome in silence, solemn as he stared at us through spectacles in need of repair.

"We have urgent business with the Chancellor," Etan told him.

Argo pulled a cord hanging from the wall behind his desk and a middle-aged woman appeared through the beaded arch to escort us beyond the entrance hall. She had served the Chancellor for years and knew not to question the purpose of our visit. Her eyes followed me as she left the study, brows drawn together; it was rare for me to accompany my uncle here in daylight hours.

The Chancellor came soon after. His dark gaze swept over Etan, and I fancied a little color left his face. A slow-acting, undetected poison was our greatest fear: more than one Chancellor had lost his life that way.

Etan strode forward with renewed energy. "How do you feel?" He checked Caslav's skin, eyes, mouth, and nose in turn. The Chancellor sat, mute, as Etan checked his temperature and smelled his breath. My mouth felt dry. No poison attempt had ever passed my uncle. Not one.

"I feel well," Caslav said slowly.

I finished my own visual scan, and my breath—unconsciously held—hissed out. The Chancellor looked fine. Rattled, maybe, but healthy. Etan settled back on the desk and regarded his old friend with open relief.

"Take these, in case." He handed the Chancellor a few small dark squares of charcoal to block the absorption of poison through the system. "But it looks like I'm just ill."

"I'll send someone to fetch a physic," Caslav said. "I'd rather you didn't go to the hospital."

Etan nodded. Privacy and secrecy were the cornerstones of our role.

"Thank you." The Chancellor rocked back on his chair and folded his hands into his armpits, a gesture that reminded me strongly of his nephew. We left him there, but the feeling of unease stayed with me.

Etan stayed behind in a guest suite at the Manor in the care of Thendra, a square-jawed physic with the gleaming black skin of a western wetlander, who often treated Kalina. She knew my need for order well, and watched without comment with her slanted, unblinking eyes as I checked over Etan one last time. She even moved carefully so as not to disturb the arrangement of cloth, drinking glass, and book I had set on the bedside table.

My compulsions always grew in proportion to my anxiety, so sitting in a room berating myself and becoming increasingly erratic would help no one. Instead, I borrowed a Manor messenger and sent for my sister to watch Etan. Our family duty was our greatest honor and my first responsibility. Etan might merely be ill, but we could never assume that. Walking, I pictured the Council lunch, recalling the room, the food. There had been two courses I had seen—fish cakes eaten by hand, and the soup and bread. Etan had mentioned two more, plus drinks: pre-poured cups of kori and kavcha and, at the end of the event, tea served individually from the pot. He'd proofed it all. I counted my steps down the corridor—left, right, left, longer step right to dodge a crack in the stone, longer step left to compensate—out of the visitors' wing and back through the entrance, nodding to Argo on the way past. There had been no seated meals and no plates designated for a particular person. Unless everyone at the lunch had been poisoned—and Etan was the first to show symptoms because he had proofed the food earlier in the morning—then any poisoner must have been there personally to directly tamper with the Chancellor's food once he had selected it.

The Talafan nobleman was the obvious starting point. While the Empire was a valued trade partner, partners maneuvered against each other all the time, and Etan had said he knew little about Lord Ectar personally. Certainly the nervous, embarrassed man I had seen didn't appear a likely poisoner, but looks, of course, meant little.

And if a poison attempt was targeted only at the Chancellor, our Talafan visitor wasn't the only possible enemy. Most of the Council had been there—all six Credol Families had been represented, as well as four of the six Guilders. Beneath the overt civility of the Council always rippled quiet plays for power and influence; while the rules of honor kept ill feeling masked, the Chancellor had as many enemies as friends, particularly among the Families. A diminution of influence in one family left an opening for another, and this wouldn't be the first time a subtle poisoning had been attempted. Indeed, our family's historic role had developed out of a past with more aggressive maneuverings, when the Families jostled for power and quiet, civilized murder was a common tool. These days such things were far rarer, but not unheard of. I was a month behind on current politics, but Etan would know who stood to gain and lose if the Chancellor were harmed.

And of course, Lazar's servants would bear closer examination; at least one was foreign born, because I remembered seeing a Doranite man in house colors serving kori to the Theater-Guilder. For Silasta's wealthiest families, invisible servants had better access than the closest friend or lover.

I stopped outside the Reed apartments. The buildings loomed aggressively over the promenade, crowding the land. Unlike the elegant, classically-designed neighboring apartments, Lazar's expanded buildings were the product of his considerable fortune and his grandiose and, in places, garish taste. Around the side of the narrow garden, my head ducked low, I crept past the veranda where several singers and two pale northern jugglers were entertaining the Credo and his family for the afternoon. Explaining my presence here would create unwelcome issues. Instead, I used the kitchen entrance at the back of the property. Etan's well-known love of cooking gave me a pretext to study techniques and the opportunity to visit every kitchen entrance of the Families' apartments, the Guildhalls, and every building the Chancellor might conceivably enter. So although the serving staff looked up, quizzical, upon my entrance, no one seemed displeased.

Lazar's head cook greeted me jovially. "Credo Jovan!"

Cardamom and honey hung in the air, and something thick and sweet boiled on the great stove. "Nice to see you again."

The little woman returned my smile. "I am at your service."

"I've come to ask a favor," I told her. "My Tashi complimented your luncheon and wants to use it as a lesson for me. I was wondering if there were any leftovers—a small sample of each course?"

The cook looked over her shoulder at the swarming kitchen. A stack of clean bowls stood beside several large kori bottles on a bench, and a crumb-scattered platter and two empty soup tureens waited to be washed. In the corner, a long clawed kitsa prowled around underfoot, snatching up spills and crumbs with its quick pronged tongue. "We've packed up from lunch, I'm afraid, though there might be some of the sweet left—I was going to leave it for the staff." She clicked her fingers and a servant sprang to her side. "Boy, serve a sample of the goa confection for Credo Jovan, here."

I thanked her and accepted the small bowl. "The Credo's been keeping you busy," I said, casually stepping out of the way of some of the workers and closer to the tureens. "I stopped by the lunch on an errand for the Chancellor and it looked like the whole staff was in there. Did you have to bring in extra people?"

"No, but the Honored Credo pulled every member of his staff for this lunch," she said. "And the family has had guests and entertainment out on the porch all afternoon—no one will be allowed a break until tonight." She added hastily, "Hard work for an honored family is the path to our own greater honor, of course."

I smiled. Behind my back, I scraped a spoon across the edge of the inside of the tureen. "The Credo is lucky to have you. Thank you for the sample. My uncle will be delighted."

"Please thank Credo Etan for the compliment. I've the recipes, too, if that would assist." She turned to find the papers and I slipped an empty kori bottle into the folds of my paluma. Then, sample and recipes in hand, I excused myself and returned up the road to my family apartments, where the dessert sample, kori bottle, spoonful of soup, and handful of fish cake crumbs joined Etan's saliva and vomit. However unlikely, I would test it all for poison.

Some basic things I could do immediately. I made a solution from a lichen powder and tested the food samples; the presence of some corrosive poisons would turn the solution red. Etan's saliva generated an extremely pale pink, which was to be expected, but there was no response with any of the food. I examined his partly digested stomach contents; the color and smell, while unpleasant, seemed normal. Thendra had taken blood and urine from him and I would need to do the same.

After a thorough visual examination under Etan's best glass—nothing looked abnormal—I tasted the food samples myself. The soup was a well-made but simple root affair, the only detectable additives salt and two seed-based spices. The dessert was crushed nuts and bindie egg, whipped with goa berry syrup. Only crumbs remained of the fish cakes, but the ingredients list provided by Lazar's cook matched the smell, texture, and taste of the sample I had. The kori was standard cloudy liquor from the southern Losi region, with no additives that I could detect.

Replacing the sliding panel in the kitchen wall that hid Etan's workroom, I shook my head. Etan had trained me too well. There was no call for me to be more worried than my uncle. But then the front doors thrust open and Kalina darted in, sweat sticking her hair to her face and her eyes wide. I stopped, unable to take my next breath.

"Jov," she said, and before she could say another word, I knew my sister's news.

My uncle was dying, and so was the Chancellor. For all that my entire life had been built around this very scenario, faced with it I now felt incompetent. Unprepared. Unworthy.

When the Chancellor fell ill, the physics shifted their attention from Etan to Caslav, and Kalina and I made it through the burgeoning chaos in the Manor without difficulty. Half the Council flocked about and the Manor staff looked fearful. No one paid us any heed as we were escorted to the suite adjoining Caslav's.

We sat there now, silent, trying to get fluid through our uncle's puffy lips. The physic Thendra darted in occasionally, her voice sharp as she barked instructions at her apprentices. Tain broke from his uncle's bedside only once, to briefly check on the three of us. None of us spoke of poison, but with the physics feeding both men purgatives and emetics it must have been suspected. All we knew for certain, though, was that with every moment that passed, they grew worse.

"Home," Etan murmured. "Go home."

"*Shh*, Tashi." Kalina patted his hand gently. "Just rest. We'll take you home when you're well."

"You . . ." His lips worked silently, then he slumped back again. "Home. So—sorry."

I could not bear to make eye contact with my sister. My sense of failure was so intense I could barely breathe.

Our family's great proofing tome lay under the bed, hidden from immediate sight, and the satchel of antidotes we'd brought earlier now bulged with every remedy we had. We had tried ingested antidotes and absorbing creams, sometimes the same ones in powder, liquid, or raw plant form. When Etan could no longer swallow, Kalina propped his weak body up against her while I poured teas down his throat. While the physics were occupied with the Chancellor, she stood guard by the door as I used a hollow needle to inject our only blood-borne antidote.

Nothing stemmed the tide against him.

As evening deepened, Etan was conscious less and less, his breathing weakening. Earlier, he had detailed his day for us as best he could while Kalina took notes. Even then he had struggled to force the words from his thickened tongue. Having spent much of my life drawing calm from my Tashi when the compulsions seized my body and my brain, the sight of unflappable Etan swearing in frustration at his lack of control over his own body set me off.

My problems were manageable in everyday life if I kept things in order, stuck to a routine, stayed calm. But in times of high stress, a storm of panic and fear and speculation built in my head. My usual physical calming exercises—breathing, pacing—themselves became part of the problem, and I ended up stuck in a recurring pattern. After we'd tried the last of our antidote options, I'd paced in sets of eight until my legs wobbled with exhaustion. I'd never resented my weakness so much as today, when my uncle and my sister needed me the most.

Thendra, too, grew visibly frustrated as the hours passed. "Both men say they were in perfect health this morning, yes," she had told us. "Their symptoms are the same. Credo Etan's manifested sooner, but the Chancellor's are escalating faster. I fear their bodies cannot continue with this pressure, no, but since I do not understand what ails them, I cannot treat it."

She had suggested maidenbane as a possible poison and Kalina and I feigned ignorance, but the antidote had had no effect; we knew it would not, not only because Etan would never have missed such a basic poison, but because we had already tried it, just in case. Nor did any other remedy offer any improvement in either man. In private, we had attempted every antidote for the greater and lesser poisons in our secret stores, to no effect. Ideas thinned, as did our hope.

Kalina leaned against me now, her frail form a light, even weight against my back and her hair a dark shroud between us. "What are we going to do?" she asked, her voice bleak, and though I wanted to reassure her, no words came to me. The weight of my failure crushed me.

"We'll manage it together," I assured her.

She stayed silent.

Etan stirred and we both started. Kalina rose and leaned over our uncle, touching his hand with hesitant fingers. "Tashi, can you hear us?"

I stared at Etan, mute. What could I say to the man who had raised us? Something lighthearted, to take his mind off the inevitable, or something sincere and thoughtful that represented all we had shared? Instead, my mind cranked through its usual gears, noting pointless details, counting breaths, evaluating symptoms.

We are who we are, I told myself. It wasn't a comfort.

Etan coughed, making a sound like water sucking down a drain, and blinked furiously. His lips moved.

"Tashi?" I leaned close. He was trying to say something.

Etan's gaze moved between us and he clutched at his chest. I turned to grab the cup of water from the table but, at Kalina's gasp, the cup fell out of my hand and spilled water over my lap.

Etan's dark eyes were still open, his lips parted, but some spark, an animation that had been there before, was gone.

Whatever knowledge our uncle had wanted to impart, he'd taken it with him.

Zarnika

DESCRIPTION: Naturally occurring mineral, brittle and gray, often with a colorless, odorless crystalline coating, soluble in water. Poisonous to ingest directly or through plants or water supplies in high concentration areas. Poison can also be absorbed through skin.

SYMPTOMS: Facial swelling, acute abdominal pain, vomiting, diarrhea, leading into coma and death.

PROOFING CUES: Subtle, sweet, and slightly metallic flavor, difficult to detect at low levels or in sweet dishes.

2

Kalina

Duty takes precedence over all else, and I knew what it meant to fail at it far better than my brother ever could. There had been no time spared to comfort me all those years ago when we all realized my body couldn't tolerate the life of a proofer; I'd simply recovered from another health crisis to find my Tashi's time devoted instead to my small brother. The same honor and duty that was taken from me still bound our family to the Chancellor, and while he still lived we couldn't pause to grieve for our own uncle.

But already it seemed hopeless. Jovan and I stole moments where we could talk out of hearing of the physics, whispering thoughts and theories, reaching dead ends. It had to be poison, surely, for all the physics' talk of unknown diseases—and I knew as well as anyone their fascination with unexplained ailments—because no one else had fallen sick. But if so, it was one Jovan didn't know. And he knew all of the poisons. Or at least we'd thought he did.

Jovan leaped to his feet, pacing again. I sat on the floor, back to my uncle's body, knees drawn up to my chest and arms wrapped around my bare shins. He took his measured steps: left, right, left, right, spin to the left, left, right, left, right, spin to the right. The impeccably timed sound of his feet on the floor, in precisely equal steps, tapped out the rhythm of my childhood. Always balanced, no movement with one side of his body failing to be echoed by an equal one on the other. I rested my head back on the bed, watching him. Although average in his dark coloring and his medium height and build, my brother was striking in his symmetry and precision, even at his most anxious. Perhaps *especially* at his most anxious. His breath released slowly as his pacing calmed him. It calmed me, too.

Etan had given us a detailed description of his day, including everything he ate and drank, and every person he saw. Nothing unusual. First thing in the morning he had proofed the kori, kavcha and tea, cheese and dessert at Lazar's kitchen and then spent the morning with Chancellor Caslav, eating only food he'd prepared himself. They hadn't left the Manor until Lazar's lunch, and afterward Etan had gone alone to the docks to check on a late tea delivery while Caslav had returned to the Manor.

The symptoms had begun at his mouth; likely whatever had triggered the attack did, too. "Eat, drink, breathe, kiss," I murmured. At my words, Jovan finished his set of eight and visibly resisted the urge to begin another set. I offered my hand and he sat beside me. Together we thumbed through the pages of my notes.

"He ate two courses with his fingers," I said. "So he could have touched something and passed it to his mouth. But it would have to be something only he and Caslav touched." I looked back at the notes. Etan had kissed every Councilor and recalled touching the shoulder of the musician who had performed, a man called Hasan. The Talafan nobleman had shaken his hand in the manner of the Empire. Etan had also handled the leksot briefly when it had crawled over him during its brief escape, but he had washed his hands after doing so because of the smell and the shed fur. And although the Chancellor had also touched the animal, so had Lord Ectar, Jovan, and Credo Lazar, as well as at least one of Credo Lazar's servants.

Jov stopped at that place in my notations. "Have we checked his skin where the leksot crawled on him?" He thrust back the bedclothes from our uncle's body. Several red scratches marked his calves and knees. Jov touched the skin around the markings, but they were ordinary scratches and showed no sign of special irritation.

"I looked at those already," I reminded him. "Didn't we agree this was something oral?"

The beads at the door rattled. "I am sorry to disturb you, Credo, Credola," Thendra said. The sight of the physic triggered a wave of nerves in me. Though never anything less than courteous, Thendra looked at me like an interesting puzzle that she hungered to solve, and I'd grown to dislike her assessing, dispassionate face for all that I relied on her.

Jov stood. "We were just looking at these." He indicated the scratches. "The Chancellor will have some too . . . ?" But she was already shaking her head.

"I asked your uncle about the marks, Credo. If the animal had a toxic scratch we would see symptoms surrounding that area." Her gaze dropped. "I do not know what is causing this. It is no poison or disease I know of."

Jovan looked back at the scratches, desperation apparent in his shaking voice. "The animal drooled a lot. What if it had some foreign disease, one we've never seen here, and passed it through its saliva onto an open cut?"

Her sleepy gaze sharpened as she regarded him. "I could examine the animal," she said. "I do not know if it will help, but I am happy to do so if you wish." She left unspoken our lack of remaining options.

"I'll go," I said quickly, before Jovan could move. His experiments would be outside my knowledge and understanding to conduct; I wanted to do something, anything, that might help. Though the tension in my brother's expression signaled his objection, the desire to examine the scratches more closely won out and he didn't argue.

"The glass garden," he said. "Be careful."

Dozens of staff members and even a few Councilors crossed my path on my way to the gardens; word had spread. I didn't stop to hear commiserations. Every time I pictured Etan lying still and empty, my chest squeezed in on me and my throat and eyes burned. But Caslav lived, still. We'd lost our Tashi, but maybe we could redeem our family's honor. Maybe I could help, for a change.

The glass-walled gardens were small, so even in the darkness it didn't take long to find the leksot. I wouldn't need the cage after all.

The creature lay prone on a patch of dirt underneath a crying fin tree, its tail spread limp across the ground like a snake. Jovan had been right. Here was the architect of our uncle's downfall; not some shadowy foreign poisoner or a treacherous colleague, but a pitiful dead animal, its paws and face still and wilted, tongue protruding from its little mouth. My hand shook, wobbling the light. Losing our uncle to something so stupid and random as a foreign disease was so *unfair*, so unworthy of all he'd been. But at least I could hope something in its body would help Thendra and the others treat the disease. The Chancellor was running out of time.

I crouched, about to scoop up the body, when something made me pause. I swept the light around slowly. Something looked wrong.

The dirt surrounding the body was unmarked. I pressed a light finger in and noted the easy impression it left. The leksot hadn't walked or crawled here; it must have fallen from the tree. A low branch of the crying fin formed a green fan just over the animal. I ran a hand down its flexible length. It was no wider than my wrist.

An odd place for a sick animal to sit. Etan had suffered for hours. Why would an animal in distress have perched on a branch too narrow to lie down on? The swollen, protruding tongue suggested it had died the same way as my uncle. But it had been in apparent good health when Jovan left it here. How had it come into the city carrying a disease but then sickened and died so quickly? That was odd even accounting for differences in anatomy.

My sweeping lamplight, scanning the garden, illuminated a flattened patch of the toxic weed feverhead by the pond. Tracks marked the grass around the entrance and through the center of the garden. Not just my own footprints, marking a path toward the crying fin, but also a second set, from the pond. Someone had been in here recently, perhaps even this afternoon.

I wasn't sure what it meant. Maybe nothing.

I gathered the leksot with a fold of my paluma. We could still hope Thendra could learn something from the body and help the Chancellor. An image of my Tashi's distorted face sliced through my mind. Either way, we'd failed him.

As I passed through the arch and back into the Manor, my brother came around the bend. Our eyes met for a moment, and he shook his head. I lowered my gaze.

We'd failed the Chancellor, too.

They took Etan's body away in a covered litter, a flock of physics trailing it, solemn-faced. I pretended to need to relieve myself so I didn't have to watch. Keeping the mask of calm—don't be fragile, don't be weak—had taken a toll. Alone, cracks widened into chasms, and I cried for my uncle until my sobs turned to hiccups. Leaning my forehead against the cool stone wall, I listened to the sound of my brother's footfalls, back and forth. The familiar sound gave me no comfort now.

I scrubbed my eyes and returned, my legs shaking. Desperation to save the Chancellor had invigorated me, but without that task the energy had seeped out. We made a fine pair, me too tired to stand and my brother unable to stop pacing. When he spoke, his words were rushed and mumbled.

"We have to tell Mother and the rest." Pure Jovan, always focused on the practicalities. It helped him, but still rankled at me.

"It's too late to send anything tonight," I said. "We'll send a bird to the estates and to Telasa first thing in the morning." *Along with everyone else in the city.* Breathing slowly, I wobbled to my feet. Engaging Jov's memory and the rational part of his brain would help him calm down, so I asked a question to which I knew the answer. "There was feverhead in the garden. There's no chance the leksot just ate some of that, is there?"

"No," he said. "You'd have to eat your own weight in feverhead to kill you in the short term. It damages your system over time." His pace slowed a little. "There shouldn't be feverhead in the garden, though. We should tell the gardeners." I nodded along with the pretense that such a thing mattered.

Thendra interrupted us from the doorway, and Jovan fell silent. "Credo, Credola," the physic said. She wrung her hands and glanced at Jovan. The concentration on my brother's face intensified as he tried to stop pacing. "Considering what has happened, I am going to recommend to the Honored Heir that all those who came in contact with the diseased animal be quarantined. Neither of you are showing symptoms, no, but since we do not know how the disease was transmitted . . ."

"Of course," I said quickly, drawing her attention back to me and away from Jov. "We understand." My heart beat faster. Whatever had happened to the Chancellor, it had involved that animal somehow. Whether Lord Ectar had brought a diseased animal deliberately or inadvertently, we needed to know. Physically weak I might be, and a proofer I was not, but Etan had not left a potential tool lying about his household unused for long; behind my diplomatic career I had my own training and my own skills in less genteel arts.

Thendra let out her breath. Perhaps she'd been expecting arguments. "I have arranged a litter to the hospital. Who else handled the creature?"

"Credo Lazar, and a few of his servants," Jovan said. His steps had slowed, signaling he was gaining control over the pacing. "The Talafan nobleman who brought it, of course—Lord Ectar, I believe is his name—and any of his servants who handled it on the way here, I suppose." He slowed his pace further, finished his eighth step, and stopped with his own relieved sigh. "You might want to send an Order Guard or two," he added. "I've no idea how they'll react to the quarantine." He shot me a sidelong look, quizzical but trusting in my plan.

"Care will need to be taken with Lord Ectar," I said. "There's no centralized medical care in the Empire. No hospitals. Their physics are hired privately by those who can afford them. Our visitor may not understand what you're doing."

"I see." Thendra frowned. "I do not want to cause panic. News is already spreading of the Chancellor, and the last thing we need is a public scene."

"I know their culture," I said. "And I can speak some Talafan. Perhaps I could accompany the Order Guards and help smooth relations?" I used my meekest, most obliging tone. One of my most-practiced. Quiet, shy little Kalina; everyone knew her so well.

"And I could assist with Credo Lazar," my brother added.

She seemed grateful to have something to do with us. "I will ask the Honored Heir to approve this, yes?"

We hadn't seen Tain since the Chancellor died. He'd been closeted in his uncle's room with the body, and though sounds could be faintly heard through the wall, no one had been in since. We tapped tentatively and the muffled sounds stopped. The jangle of beads of the inner door sounded, then the outer door opened a fraction. Tain looked out, his eyes red and his mouth set in a hard line of contained emotion. My heart hurt for him.

"Honored Heir," Thendra said, "I am proposing to quarantine Credo Jovan, Credola Kalina, and anyone else who touched the diseased animal, yes? May I have your permission to do so, at least until tomorrow?"

Tain frowned, starting to speak, but a hard look from Jovan silenced him. Thoughtfulness chased the confusion from his face as he looked at us carefully. "That would be best, I suppose," he said, his voice raw. "Please ensure they have every comfort. They've lost their Tashi, too." A pause. Even in grief, Tain was still thinking. "We don't know whether that animal came here diseased on purpose or not. Please take Order Guards and make sure the Talafan does *not* leave."

As Thendra murmured her agreement and turned away, Tain's hands shot out of the gap and grabbed one of each of ours, wrapping our fingers together and squeezing, just for a moment. I blinked away tears and squeezed back.

The Manor had been a hive before, buzzing with anxious servants and serious-faced physics, Councilors and messengers pounding the winding internal corridors. After the announcement it had emptied like water from a basin, all the noise and energy sucked from the building that had become a tomb. We met four Order Guards at the entrance, uniformed in red-and-blue striped leather vests over their tunics, short swords dangling from their belts. Thendra insisted on a hospital litter for me, and I didn't protest. It felt easier to close the cloth sides and my eyes as we made our way down the zigzag, hilly streets of the upper city, shutting out the bright merriment of the evening. But voices and laughter and the *chink* of teacups, music from street corners, and even the faint sound of applause from the closest theater bled through into my dark, cushioned world, an oddly merry background to the grim *clump-clump-clump* of the Order Guards and the practiced smooth shuffle of the litter carriers. One last night of oblivious normality. In the morning the great bells would ring and the whole city would be in mourning.

We crossed over Trickster's Bridge to the lower city. The massive bridge, an inspiring feat of architecture, spanned the north end of the lake where it thinned into marshes. On the east side was the bridge tower, nicknamed the Finger for its height and bulbous middle, and all that remained of the lakeside fortifications of the original city. Now, most of our wall circumference lay on the west side of the lake, where the newer part of Silasta sprawled, less elegant than the old but equally important. If the old city was the face of Silasta—beautiful, with its glimmering buildings, graceful archways, and famous flowering vines—then the lower city was the internal organs, pulsing with commerce, learning, and enterprise.

The Talafan nobleman was staying in one of the best guesthouses in the city, near the school complex just near the northwest bank of the lake, only a short walk from Trickster's. The proprietor visibly struggled with her competing urges to protect her expensive guest and to stay on the right side of the grim-faced Order Guards, but in the end she directed us to the gaming room across the street where the Talafan was deeply embroiled in a game of four-strike. He sat cross-legged opposite three local opponents, a small pile of polished bird bones in front of him and a frown of concentration on his thin, clean-shaven face. It was hot inside, the room lit with scented oil braziers and urns of steaming sweet tea constantly refilled by servants as the guests played.

The other players noticed us before the Talafan. One was well born, wearing Credo Bradomir's haughty nose and brow. The others I didn't recognize, but the sumptuous fabric of their clothing and the jewels in their hair suggested wealth. All three gave a start at the sight of us. In the corner, the musician stopped playing.

"Lord Ectar, may I beg a moment of your time?" I spoke in my best Talafan, inclining my head.

He stood gracefully, gray eyes taking in the tattoos on my arms, and bowed low. His cosmetics were skillfully applied and his fair hair floated lightly into its clasp at his nape, unoiled. "Credola," he replied. His voice surprised me; it was young, rich, and pleasant, at odds with his rather ascetic visage. "Of course. What may I do for you?"

I led him outside and introduced myself. His eyes widened at my family name, flashing quickly to my arm and then back again. I could practically see the vying forces of opportunism and cultural bias warring across his face, though he moved little more than a fraction. "I hoped to meet you,

Credola Kalina," he said, speaking now in our language. "I have a business proposal for your family. Perhaps—"

"Lord Ectar," I interrupted him, but as politely as I could. "We must speak about the gift you brought the Chancellor earlier today."

"The leksot? A marvelous animal. Maybe your family enjoys one as a pet as well? I feel it will soon be the fashion." He looked immediately more comfortable. Gifts and bribes for women were far less challenging for a Talafan than directly doing business with one. He spoke good Sjon, not just the simplified Trade tongue that most merchants shared across borders. He must have studied us, and he'd have been a fool to come to Silasta expecting to deal only with men. But the habits of home are hard to break. I would make it as easy for him as possible. For all the talents I might lack, appearing less than I could be wasn't one of them.

"I'm afraid the creature appears to have carried a disease," I told him, watching his reaction closely. "Our physics need to examine everyone who came in contact with it, for everyone's safety."

"A disease? Nonsense!" Ectar folded his arms, his tone indignant, but the light spilling from inside the gaming room was too good to hide the draining of color from his already pale face. "I traveled with it for two weeks."

"The creature sickened and died, Lord Ectar," I said, lowering my gaze and spreading my hands, helpless. "And it infected several others. I, too, have been summoned to the hospital." He didn't need to know, yet, who had fallen victim to the disease.

"Just a precaution, Lord Ectar," one of the Order Guards chimed in. "We take public health seriously in Silasta. You'll need to bring any of your servants who handled the creature, as well."

The line between his eyes deepened. Before he could protest, I added in Talafan, "Please, Lord Ectar. I asked to accompany you. I am fascinated by the Empire, and hope to visit someday. Perhaps we could pass the time in quarantine together?"

He looked me over. Talafan and their expressionless faces! But this, this I was good at. I read hesitance but also curiosity in his eyes. Perhaps it was not just business that had driven him here, far from his pampered existence in the Empire. Behind me, the Order Guards took a leisurely step closer.

Across the street, several passersby stopped to watch. A couple of women kissing enthusiastically in front of the next building stopped their fun to stare. An earther preacher rambling on the nearest corner mumbled off into silence. The silhouettes of Ectar's gaming companions were visible from where we stood, as they hovered, listening, on the steps inside. Ectar's gaze traveled back to the Oromani family tattoo on my arm.

Opportunism, curiosity, a desire to avoid a scene; whatever it was, it won. He bowed deeply. "Of course, Credola Kalina. How do you say it? There would be . . . much honor?"

I smiled. "Thank you. We have a litter for yourself and one for your servants."

He waved a dismissive hand. "They can walk. They have never been carried before; let us not begin now. Maybe I can share with you?"

The Order Guards blocked his impertinent step toward the litter, but I nodded. "It would be my honor."

It was a short but strange journey to the hospital, which was back on the other side of the lake, not too far from the Finger. Ectar seemed both fascinated by me and slightly repulsed, as if I were a strange animal who had inexplicably learned to speak. Here, family was the cornerstone of our culture and our honor. Women contributed to families with our learning and skills, just as any other adult, and when we wished to have children we chose our most trusted male relative—a brother or an uncle, usually—to help raise them within the family. In the Empire, women were forced from their own families and expected to live as a kind of pampered ornament in the home of an unrelated man, who would then take the woman's children as his own. They lived what seemed to me a bizarre, intolerable existence, unable to choose their own lives, careers, or the number, gender, or even specific identity of their romantic partners. So we spoke tentatively, politely, but always conscious of the undercurrent; I was as peculiar to him as he was to me.

The physics at the hospital escorted us to a well-lit upstairs room, where Jovan and Credo Lazar waited. Lazar looked frantic, a wreck of a man. Sweat drenched his tunic from armpit to waist, his manufactured curls wilted sadly about his bulbous face. Two of his servants sat quietly in the corner. Jovan, given new lease by a fresh task, looked as impeccable as ever as he sat straight-backed and cross-legged on one of the pallets, watching the Credo wobble around the room. The smell of fortified kavcha assaulted us. The tiny, spectacled physic with us wrinkled his nose in disapproval. "Credo Lazar," he said, his voice deep and authoritative for such a diminutive figure, "there is to be no food or drink in this room. We need to observe you unimpeded."

Lazar noticed us at last. His face went through a few contortions as he tried to balance his outrage and fear with his instinct to flatter potential business partners. "Lord Ectar," he said at last, in a passably neutral tone.

I introduced Ectar to Jovan, watching the jump of interest in the man's face as he realized he'd been quarantined with two members of the Oromani family he'd traveled here to bargain with. Lazar's obvious panic and discomfort seemed to have a steadying influence on the Talafan; any tension he had harbored toward the process seemed to dissipate. His gray gaze swept the austere hospital room without apparent judgment, and he took a pallet and endured the physic's examination as politely as I did. His servants spoke only in direct response to the physic's questions, with Ectar translating from the pallet in a lazy tone.

Lazar, uncharacteristically, seemed too distraught even to talk. He lay down on the farthest pallet, his back to the rest of us, and his drunken snores soon filled the room. Jovan, too, lay still, though to someone who knew him well it was clear he was concentrating deeply rather than relaxing. We were trapped in a room with people who might have caused the Chancellor's death; here was our chance to learn whatever we could from their reactions.

I was exhausted, but so well-practiced at masking it that it was no trouble to pretend enthusiasm for a late-night conversation. For his part, Ectar seemed genuine. If he knew about our uncle's death, he was an excellent liar, because he spoke readily and easily about Etan as he relayed his excitement to supply the Emperor with our tea. For a time, I could pretend I didn't know, either.

"You are related to the Emperor, I understand?"

"He is my . . ." He paused, searching for the word, then must have remembered there was no equivalent term in our language. "Grandfather," he said in Talafan. Then a smile warmed his face, making him seem younger. "But I am very far from the throne. The youngest son of a youngest son is not likely to inherit."

"How many brothers do you have? One seems sufficient to me," I said, shooting a sidelong smile at Jovan.

Ectar laughed. "One would be sufficient to me, also yes! Alas, I have eight older brothers."

"Eight!" Jovan exclaimed. "What bad luck for your family."

I glared at him. The only thing he studied about other cultures was their use of poisons; I doubted he'd understood the reference to Ectar's "grandfather." Here, to have sons instead of daughters was indeed bad luck. Women could continue the bloodline and family name, while sons had to find some other way of distinguishing themselves and adding value to the family. In the Empire, parenthood was illogically granted to men, and bloodlines supposedly—and probably inaccurately—followed through males.

I reframed my brother's clumsy comment. "It must be challenging to distinguish yourself among so many. You've obviously become a trader of some esteem."

Ectar puffed up. The more we spoke, the more expression seeped through his careful Talafan mask. "I . . . er, cultivate my grandfather's taste for foreign goods. When I was a child, you may not consume a food product in the Imperial City that was grown outside the Empire. Now, I bring him Sjon tea for his cups, and Doranite furs for his bed. He wears a bloodstone necklace from Perest-Avana! He hungers for new things to surprise him. It is a new world. A good world for a man like me." He leaned closer to me, eagerly, his gaze darting to Jovan and back. "I desire much to make a most beneficial deal with Credo Etan. Oromani tea is the very best, and my grandfather hungers only for the best."

I seized the moment. It took little effort to summon tears; the mention of my Tashi's name had burned anyway, and the memory of his body being carried away from us was enough. I let them splash down my cheeks and dropped my head. Though he was behind me, Jovan was doubtless watching Ectar closely as I said, in a tiny voice, "Oh, Lord Ectar. I . . . I have tried to be brave, but . . ."

He knelt closer to me. "What is it? What has happened?"

"Credo Etan. My uncle. I didn't want to frighten you, but I'm afraid he was infected. It was fatal."

"*Fatal?*" Ectar scrambled to his feet, reverting to Talafan as he spluttered, "You mean we are infected with something that might *kill* us? Why did no one inform me of this? This is *unacceptable*!" Now he was shouting. The solicitous merchant persona abandoned, he reverted to pure nobleman. His servants hovered about him like bobbing flies, convincingly fearful and unsure. "This is an outrage! I will not be treated like this. Call your physics, woman, and summon me a messenger at once! My grandfather will hear about this."

Exchanging glances with Jov—he would understand the sentiment if not the words—I tried to calm the Talafan. "Lord Ectar, please."

But he was having none of it. Lazar woke, spluttering and red-eyed, and stared at the furious Talafan. Jov stood. "Lord Ectar," he said firmly, "you should also know that the disease that apparently killed your animal was passed to the Honored Chancellor himself."

Ectar broke off midrant, and his already pale skin went alabaster. Tiny muscles around his mouth worked. Rage subsided into the bone-deep politics of nobility; he was from a different world, but politics were not so different all the world over. He knew what the death of the Chancellor meant. "I am . . . deeply grieved to hear this," he said in Sjon, bowing his head. "Please forgive me, Credola Kalina, Credo Jovan, Credo Lazar. The Chancellor! I . . . I did not know." Still shaking, he stepped back a few paces. "How could I know? The leksot was perfectly healthy, you believe me. I bought her from the best breeder. I beg you, please understand. This was not my doing."

"It doesn't matter," Credo Lazar said tearfully. "Word is already spreading. The whole city will know by the morning. I brought you into my home! My family's honor will never recover. To have had a role in the death of our most beloved Chancellor and his closest adviser . . . the *shame* of it."

"It was healthy," Ectar insisted. "I would never have gifted an animal that had so much as sneezed in my presence."

"Yet the creature scratched our uncle and the Honored Chancellor," Jovan said, his tone cold and his face still. "Now they are dead."

"And we are going to die also?"

I suddenly realized he was not much older than we were, and not nearly as controlled as he'd appeared. If this fear was not genuine, he'd best make an appointment with the Performers' Guild, because I believed it. "I'm sure we are not in true danger," I reassured him. "The symptoms came on fast, so we are only here as a precaution."

But the Talafan, still white and shaking, closed himself off once more.

He mumbled another apology and then lay down with closed eyes. I would get no more from him. Jovan and I shuttered the lamps without speaking, and we lay down on our pallets in the darkened room, holding on for just a bit longer in the darkness to the illusion that this was all a terrible nightmare. He held my hand as I fell asleep.

Morning dawned without symptoms and the physics cleared us to leave. Lord Ectar was asked, in the politest possible terms that could be backed up with a sword, to accompany the Order Guards who had guarded our room to the Manor.

"I'll go with them," Jov told me. The creases around his eyes and brow and the redness of his irises gave away his lack of sleep. My heart ached for him. Sleep had been a brief escape for me; my brother would have spent the whole night trapped in his own head, imagining things that he could have done differently, berating himself for the path of his own thoughts. "You go home and rest."

As if home, empty of our Tashi, would bring rest for either of us. "I'll send a message to the estate," I said instead. "If I go now I might not get trampled." Most, if not all, of the Council would have heard the news last night. All the Credol Families owned birds to communicate swiftly with their family in the other cities and their estates; it would be crowded at the cote before long.

"Take a litter," he said, frowning at me even as I slipped off. Well out of anyone's earshot, I let out the cough I'd been smothering. My chest hurt and my breath came shallow and fast. Thendra crossed my path on the way out of the hospital, and the dark creases fanning out from her eyes deepened as she looked me over with swift appraisal.

"Go home and rest properly, Credola," she warned me. "You should not push yourself so hard. The last thing you need right now is a relapse, yes?"

She was right, of course, even if I resented her for it a little. The cote was at the southern base of Solemn Peak, a fair walk from the hospital. Though I'd been working on my strength, it seemed spent today all the same. It was barely dawn, but the hospital was good business for the litter carriers and I found a pair easily. They were fit men who sang old religious songs in harmony as they jogged me south along the lake path. I envied their lungs.

As we passed Bell's Bridge, the great bell tower by the Manor rang out a solemn peal, and kept ringing. The carriers slowed in surprise, speculating in anxious tones. "It's the Chancellor," I told them quietly. The man in front twisted to stare at me, shock stopping him in place. "To the cote, please," I reminded him, and he gripped the edges of the litter tightly and took off at pace.

The cote was a rough tower built into the stone so the birds could nest naturally in crannies in the rock. If not for the orderly spacing of the nests it would almost seem like a natural breeding space. Some of my peers in the Administrative Guild hated coming here with missives, preferring to send messengers or servants. I liked it: the strong, earthy smell, the streaks of bird droppings that striped the insides black and white, the chorus of the birds' raucous chatter echoing around. It was quiet—I'd apparently beaten the other Credolen here—but the door was open. "Hello?" I called, approaching the opening. Unease settled over me. I cleared my throat. "It's Credola Kalina. From the Administrative Guild."

The bird keeper edged out, slablike arms encircled with heavy claw-scratched leather bands, her trepidatious mannerisms at odds with her rectangular chunk of a body. "Credola," she said, wringing her hands. "I heard the bells, and I knew people would come. I didn't know the tower was weak, honor-down, I swear it was sound. . . ."

Following the keeper into the cote, the blood pounding in my ears was the only sound to be heard. Through the jagged mouth of a hole in the top corner of the tower a pale blue patch of wrongness gleamed. Scattered beams of light sprayed down into the cote, long white fingers pointing at empty hollows where the gray-and-white birds should have nested. "The birds . . ."

"They've flown," the keeper finished. "All the tourists. They've all gone home, and no messages on them! Today, of all days."

Tourists were birds not from this cote; released, they would fly to their own home cotes. "All of them?" I asked, dismayed. There should have been dozens of tourists here; the city birds, for official use, as well as the private flocks housed here for a fee and owned by some wealthy merchant families and all of the Credol Families, including mine, for messages between Silasta and the other main cities, and to the country estates. But the only birds to be seen were marked with white tags on their legs, indicating they were trained for this cote, and the locals were no use at all. They wouldn't fly anywhere but to their own familiar nests located right here.

"All of them." The keeper pointed one thick finger at a pile of collapsed rock and root-bare shrubbery. "It must have been a rockslide during the night. I came in to feed them this morning and found it like this. A few of the locals went out to explore, but most have come back. The Oromani bird is fine," she added, quickly pointing out the gray-chested bird, which had arrived with a message from our steward a few weeks ago and was waiting to be taken back with a courier.

Fat lot of good the locals will do us, I thought, but the poor keeper already looked distraught enough. Probably afraid of losing her job. And with good reason, too; I doubted the Credolen would take well to the news that they'd have to inform their families about the death of the Chancellor by courier instead of bird. While boats could reach Telasa downriver in a day, the journey upriver to Moncasta would take far longer, and West Dortal even longer, by road. For those who had close family on their country estates, the delay would be substantial, even with the best couriers.

The feeling of unease strengthened as I stared up at the hole again. It was just an inconvenience, I supposed, but it somehow felt like more than that.

"Stay here," I said, trying to sound authoritative. "We'll get someone from the Builders' Guild here to patch the roof so no predators get to the rest." And my own Guild would need to be informed that there was going to be a sudden demand for couriers. Maybe there would need to be some kind of central organization for how we spread the word. We'd have to inform our neighbors and trading partners, and there were only so many messengers in the city.

I'd wondered yesterday how we would get through life without our Tashi. Perhaps this was how people did it; letting themselves be pulled to and fro between things that must be done, obligations and decisions and more decisions. It was easier than thinking. Definitely easier than feeling.

Inherently suspicious, my brother took the news of the damaged cote with unease. *What's the difference between a coincidence and a pattern?* Etan used to say.

"What happens next . . ." Jovan murmured, as if answering my thought.

We had been allowed in the Manor, though our time was limited. Tain had called a Council meeting and even now the others would be gathering in the Council chamber. The three of us sat in the mess of his sitting room—the surfaces bare, the floor strewn with belongings he'd hurled in his rage and grief—clinging to the last few moments we had. Tain looked a wreck; I doubted he'd slept at all.

After hearing my report on the birds, Tain had spoken to the Stone-Guilder, Eliska, and she'd sent builders and an engineer from the Builders' Guild both to repair the cote and to report on whether the rockslide had been natural. There was no specific reason to connect the damage to yesterday's events, except timing, but it was enough to concern Jovan and me. Tain seemed dazed, willing to take our advice on what to do next, and I worried how he would cope with the Council meeting.

"You'll need to talk to the Scribe-Guilder," Jov said. "To manage the priorities for who gets informed when. We can send a boat in each direction, and a messenger by road west, perhaps one messenger per estate, one for the army, as well—do we wait to inform other countries?"

"I'll consult with Budua," Tain agreed. "I don't know enough about our international relations. About anything." He stared at the wall, face shadowed. He hadn't expected to replace his uncle for decades or longer. We'd all thought we had so much time.

One of Tain's servants interrupted us politely with a tray of food. Once he left, Jovan pulled the tray out of Tain's reach and examined the plate of fruit and three bowls of baked fish. "From now on, you eat nothing I haven't prepared."

Tain regarded him with a strange look and tense shoulders as Jov started his process, sniffing everything, separating the components of the food with his fingers. This was the inevitable progression of their friendship, and hardly unprecedented, but from the range of emotions tugging at his expression it seemed Tain had avoided thinking about that. Undeniable, too, was the kernel of dread in my stomach. Yes, this was our family's duty, and protecting Tain was an honorable task. But could Jov protect Tain if Etan had failed to protect Caslav?

"What do I say about what happened yesterday?"

Tain's question forced us to an uncomfortable place, and we were silent a moment. "I suppose you have to say it seems to have been a disease or toxin carried by the leksot," Jov said at last. "You can tell them you have Lord Ectar in custody for questioning as a precaution, but that at this stage it doesn't look deliberate."

"*Was* it, though?" Tain looked between us, eyes red. "Was this just an accident?"

"I don't know," Jov said. "Honor-down, it wasn't a poison we know of, but Thendra said it didn't act like any disease she knew of, either. If Ectar's telling the truth about the animal being healthy during the trip here, why did it only die yesterday, without sickening?"

"I don't even know what to do with Ectar. He's related to the bloody Emperor; I can't accuse him of anything without good evidence."

I cleared my throat. "I'm not even sure the leksot was connected. Someone could have poisoned it, too, to throw suspicion on Lord Ectar." When Tain looked surprised, I elaborated. "I found the leksot in the glass gardens, but someone else had been there, too. There were crushed weeds by the pond, footprints, and the way I found the body didn't look right. I think . . . I think it's possible someone laid it out for us to find."

Even as I said it, I wondered if it sounded paranoid. My brother looked at me strangely, not in condescension or judgment but rather, an uncertain reevaluation. He trusted me, but he didn't understand everything about me. He wasn't the only one who had been trained to a duty.

"Plenty of other people were at that lunch," Jov agreed slowly. "I don't think we should ignore other options at this stage. Don't tell the other Councilors you suspect anything but a disease. Thendra is examining our uncles' bodies this morning. We might know more after that."

"So I just have to hold off that baying pack in the Chamber in the meantime." Tain managed a weak grin. "Should be no problem."

The two of them sent me off home, again, when time came for the meeting. I couldn't deny my exhaustion, but their well-meant concern stifled me. I had lost my uncle, too, and that same family honor tied me to protecting Tain as much as my brother. So I nodded meekly and exaggerated my weariness so as to be outpaced. When they'd passed from my sight down the spiral corridor, I slowed further, waiting until their footfalls pattered away.

I removed my sandals and tucked them into the cording of my dress. Evading servants was easy enough. They were distracted and unsure, and I was a silent ghost, moving barefoot through rooms and corridors I'd not visited in years. My heart beat fast as I wobbled on top of the cupboard in the dusty storeroom at the end of my journey. Ghost or no, I'd be in trouble if anyone disturbed me now.

The panel stuck and I had to pry it open; no one had used it in years. Inside was a tighter fit than I remembered, and the darkness and heavy air more intimidating. Though perhaps that was because my memories of this place were as a young woman desperate to impress an uncle she'd long thought was shamed by her failures. It had been a game I was good at—at last, something I could do well!—being quiet, being underestimated, and listening, always listening. My throat constricted again as I remembered the warmth of my Tashi's praise. A secret only he and I had shared, and something no one else ever knew about me. Not even my little brother. The loss of Etan beat inside me like a hammer, but I crawled on.

The murmur of voices alerted me that I'd reached my destination long before my fumbling fingers found the latch in the dark. It opened soundlessly, giving me a sliver of a view down below. I settled into the small alcove and pressed close.

The chamber was a comfortable room, designed for long hours of discussion, with soft thick carpet and plush chairs around a circular polished stone table, and cabinets stacked with expensive ornaments and artifacts. All the great and terrible decisions of Sjona's past had been made right here beneath the enormous glass-and-metal dome roof. How many had been observed by someone in this hiding place, all but invisible between carved panels depicting the histories of the peoples who had come together to form a country of peace and prosperity?

Jovan sat in my uncle's chair; behind him hung Etan's portrait, his gentle face inclined slightly downward as though watching over his nephew. Between him and Tain was an empty seat, Chancellor Caslav's solemn face above it, gazing off to the side in contemplation. To Jov's left were the other four Credol Family seats, organized in order of the strength of their relationship to the Chancellor. I catalogued them now as Etan had required of me in the past: Bradomir, impeccable from fingernail to groomed moustache; Lazar, shrinking into his seat, a disheveled ghost of his usual self. The other two—plump, handsome Javesto and shriveled Nara—an exercise of contrasts; one bold, careless, squandering family fortune and sometimes honor in dubious business arrangements, the other bitter, miserly in her protection of power and money.

To Tain's right, the six Guilders: Warrior, Craft, Artist, Stone, Theater, and Scribe, the difference in their levels of haggardness marking who had heard the news last night and who had woken to it this morning.

"It is imperative that I be able to send the best couriers immediately, Honored Heir," Credo Bradomir was saying, leaning past Jovan toward Tain. "Much of my family is in Moncasta at this time of year. It will be difficult for them to return for the funeral if I am forced to—"

Credo Javesto snorted. "We can't wait for everyone's family, friend, or the funeral won't be for a month."

"Forgive me, Credo, but as someone who is terribly *young*, and new to the Council, perhaps you're struggling to understand the depth of relationships that some of us had with our beloved Chancellor." Credola Varina, the Theater-Guilder, was Bradomir's cousin, and shared both his good looks and his supercilious attitude. Despite the circumstances, she'd found time to immaculately style her hair in a fashionable structure of braids, curls, and beaded sections. "I understand it possibly doesn't mean as much to *your* family to be present, but some of us were very close."

They continued to argue, always within the bounds of strict politeness but voices growing shrill and honorifics delivered with increasing sarcasm as it escalated. Tain looked bewildered, his arms tucked across his chest and his eyes glazed. Jovan kept shooting concerned glances his way, sharing my worry that Tain was being talked over by his own Council. These early days would be critical for his reign. He was at least ten years younger than the nearest Councilor in age, and his fluctuating interest in his duties as Heir had taught the rest of them to disregard him. If he didn't assert himself, that would set the pattern for his leadership.

Then he surprised me, and everyone else in the room, with a sudden *bang* on the table as he brought down his fist. "We're not delaying the funeral. The Scribe-Guilder will prioritize which messengers are sent where. Next issue?"

Everyone stared. Bradomir stroked his moustache, his eyes cold and evaluating. Credola Nara scowled, her bitter slash of a mouth working as if restraining the urge to criticize an impertinent child. I thought I glimpsed the acting Warrior-Guilder, Marco, burying an approving smile. Budua, the elderly Scribe-Guilder, regarded him with pursed lips. One half of her deeply lined face from eye to chin bore a slight slump, the mark of a long-ago illness; the asymmetry made her resting expression as inscrutable as ever. "Of course, Honored Heir," she murmured. "I think that—"

"With *greatest* respect, Honored Heir," Bradomir interrupted smoothly, once again leaning in front of Jovan as if he were invisible, "that may be a mistake. There are many important people who will need to travel for the funeral. I am aware that custom is to hold it within three days, but only for outdated religious reasons. In our modern times, few would object to a sensible delay for reasons of state."

"My uncle may not have been a religious man, but he was a great believer in custom and tradition," Tain said. "Every Chancellor since we built this city has been buried in the Bright Lake. I don't think he'd have wanted an accident at the cote to delay an important ritual. The city will be in mourning until we farewell the Chancellor properly. Do you expect every merchant in the city to stop business for weeks while we wait for our relatives to arrive?"

"But—"

"Next issue, please," Tain said.

I winced. Bradomir's family was one of the richest and most honored of the Credol Families and easier to manage as an ally than an enemy, regardless of his difficult personality. Tain needed to assert himself, but he didn't need to be combative.

"Is anyone going to tell us the risk of this illness, whatever it is, spreading to half the city?" Credola Nara asked, not bothering to wait to be invited to speak. "And what's being done about this Talafan fellow?"

Tain rubbed his forehead, looking drained. "The hospital cleared everyone else who touched the animal. Whatever it was seems to have died with the creature. As for Lord Ectar, he's our guest at the moment."

"Lock him up! You can't trust those Talafan. Probably here on the Emperor's orders."

"Now, now, Credola," Bradomir said. "The Honored Heir has said there is no indication—"

"They've been complaining about paying our duties for years. Whinge-ing, cunning bastards. They'd cut us out of the equation altogether if they could, I'll give you the drum."

"No doubt this animosity has nothing to do with your business competing with the Empire, Credola," Javesto said, eyebrows raised. "Just a coincidence, I'm sure."

I adjusted, trying to restore blood flow to my lower legs and beginning to regret my impulse to use the spyhole. Transparent self-interest seemed to be the only thing motivating the childish squabbles below. Perhaps we *were* being paranoid.

"We'll have a report from the hospital after they've . . . after they've fin-ished examining the bodies," Tain said. "We'll know more then. For now, there's nothing much we can do." He looked around the table. "Is there anything else pressing that needs to be discussed today?"

Eliska, the Stone-Guilder, cleared her throat, twirling her simple neck-lace between nervous fingers. In her forties, she was one of the youngest Councilors. Her tone and expression were tentative. "If I may, Honored Heir? I know this is not an important matter by comparison, but you may not have heard that we've been having trouble with harvest and other de-liveries failing to arrive to the city in the past few weeks. I believe a num-ber of the Credol Families' stewards have sent word that deliveries have left the estates, but they've yet to arrive. While no one has reported trouble on the main roads at the gates, I'm concerned that there may be bandit activ-ity on the estate tributary roads."

A few heads nodded around both sides of the table. Etan had been in-vestigating that very thing on the day he died. Clearly our own deliveries weren't the only ones that had been affected.

Marco cleared his throat. When he spoke, his soft voice came out a gen-tle contrast to his grizzled exterior. His foreign background was more ap-parent in his physical appearance than in his faint western accent. "I could send some men out to look into it, Honored Heir, but with the army away, we have a very limited garrison in the city."

"Well, what about sending some Order Guards, then?" Credo Javesto asked. "Surely they can deal with bandits if that's the problem."

Marco's visible uncertainty increased. "Silasta does not maintain the army at full readiness all the time," he said. "We could not afford to. Our soldiers have ordinary jobs in the city and one of the most common occupations is Order Guard. When the Council sent the full army away, most of our Order Guards were required to go with it, as soldiers.

"Rather than send Order Guards we need here, if the Council agrees, I could send word to Warrior-Guilder Aven and ask her to siphon off a small force to investigate. The army is south near the spice mines, not too far from Moncasta or the Ash estate. When we inform the Warrior-Guilder of the death of—of the tragic news, we could also ask the army to send a force to check the roads and surrounding countryside."

Credola Nara, head of the Ash family, gave an indignant snort and exchanged a look with the Craft-Guilder, her nephew Pedrag. "No bandits on *my* estates. My steward runs a tight operation out there. She'd know about it if there were trouble on my roads."

"Not if messages are being intercepted or delayed on those very roads, my dear Credola," Credo Javesto said. "That's rather the point."

Jov's fingers tightened in sequence. This was his first Council meeting, and he must be hating the assessing gaze of all those men and women. "What about the safety of our messengers to the estates, then?" he asked. "If there might be bandits preying on the roads, do we need to send an Order Guard with each courier for protection?"

"I do not know if we have sufficient Guards in the city to spare so many," Marco said with a frown. "We will still need to keep the peace in the interim."

Budua, the Scribe-Guilder, was the formidable stick insect queen of my own Administrative Guild, but she had once been a teacher and it still showed; she might even have taught some of the men and women around this very table. The ailment that affected the right half of her body had not noticeably limited her movements or her charisma. When she rapped a bony hand lightly on the table, the whole Council snapped to attention. "Since the safety of the couriers is my responsibility as their Guilder, it is my opinion that they should be adequately protected. It would only be for a few days."

"I agree," said Bradomir. "Our city—and ourselves, of course—may be in mourning, but we cannot neglect our duty to keep our own roads safe, not when our country's reputation is built on safe trade."

"While you're sending messengers to your steward, you just make sure she's not burning that south field we spoke about." Nara pointed a thin finger at Javesto. "I could swear I saw smoke on the horizon in that direction this morning, and we *agreed* that would have to wait until all the summer winds were past. If that smoke affects the taste of my kori crop this year you'll be hearing about it."

"Smoke? I don't think so. If you're having trouble with your eyesight again, Credola, there's a very fine spectacle shop not far from your house. I'd be well pleased to escort you."

I stifled a yawn as they continued, once again the Families dominating the conversation while the Guilders held back. Even the two Guilders who were also Credolen—Varina and Pedrag—had earned their positions on merit, and had less to gain from the scramble for position and influence than the Families, whose relative honor and status might shift depending on their relationship with the new Chancellor.

The new Chancellor. The reality of it pressed like an expanding stone in my chest.

As though connecting to my thought, the meeting below drew to its most important conclusion. His handsome face grave, Credo Bradomir sat up straighter. "Honored colleagues, there is of course one more matter to address today. Tradition dictates that we formalize our new Chancellor before we farewell our former." His voice dropped, becoming gentler, solicitous. "But this has been a terrible shock to us. The Honored Heir has not had sufficient time to prepare for his ascension. I, for one, would be happy to support a longer transition period, if this Honored Council is so generous." He smiled at Tain, a benevolent elder offering a gift.

"Of course," Varina jumped in immediately. "It's only sensible."

"Yes, yes, a fair point," Javesto agreed.

"Indeed, indeed," said Pedrag.

Nara hesitated a moment, her skeletal face twitching as she attempted warmth. "That sounds reasonable to me."

The stone in my chest pressed harder. A tiny hint of weakness and they were circling. Tain wore the same wide-eyed expression as last time they'd talked over him; Jov looked doubly tense as his eyes flicked around at all the Councilors, but he stayed silent. Had he forgotten he was no longer an observer, but a voice in the Council on his own?

The lowborn Guilders mostly sat in cynical silence—a delay in formally elevating Tain to Chancellor didn't affect them one way or the other, but they weren't oblivious to the opportunities it afforded the Credol Families. Marco, though, cleared his throat, looking uncomfortable. "Forgive me, honorable Councilors. Perhaps I do not understand this issue. Was the Heir not presented by the Chancellor and endorsed by the Council years ago? Unless there is to be a new vote, what gain is there in waiting?"

Uncomfortable silence fell. Bradomir continued to stroke his moustache, but a vein in his neck pulsed as he stared at the Warrior-Guilder. Jovan, on the other hand, gave Marco a look that suggested he'd rather like to hug him.

"Of *course* nobody is suggesting a vote," said Credo Lazar, whose presence I'd almost forgotten due to his uncharacteristic reticence. "Honored Heir, I stand ready to advise and guide you as you lead us into your most honorable reign."

Once a few Councilors had echoed the sentiment, they all followed in turn, falling over themselves to offer support; if they couldn't supplant Tain, they'd seek to make him reliant on them instead. But I didn't miss the cold calculation in Bradomir's eyes, or the naked resentment in Nara's, as they watched their new leader. It was stuffy up in my perch, and far too hot. I shivered all the same.

The day passed in a kind of busy tedium. Jovan and I both avoided our empty, quiet apartments, where the absence of Etan was most apparent. I crafted a message for Mother and our steward, our third cousin Alozia, in the buzzing anonymity of the Administrative Guildhall, wondering as I did how they would react to the news. Mother and Etan had had such a complicated relationship, brittle from the strain of their mirrored resentments, yet deeply moored in shared respect and history. The extended family, too, would feel the strain not only of the loss of their ceremonial head, but the knowledge that one of the younger generation would need to come to the city to be Jov's apprentice. Everyone had assumed I would provide him with an heir in time, but no one had expected him to need one so soon.

Just what I needed; another reminder of my limitations. Unconsciously, my hands pressed against my abdomen. I could find a willing partner in the curtain rooms of the bathhouses as easily as anyone, but Thendra had warned me that pregnancy would be dangerous and likely unsuccessful. Perhaps it was for the best that one of our cousins' children move to our apartments and take my child's role.

I finished the letter and left it with the assigned messengers. Our family would never make it back for the funeral—it'd be over before they even got the message, probably—but they'd have time to prepare for Jovan and me to return home with Etan's body, at least.

And, it transpired, part of the reason Tain had insisted on pressing ahead with the funeral was to avoid families returning in time. "He didn't want to have to deal with his mother," Jov told me when we met later. "He wasn't sure which would be worse—her turning up or her staying behind."

"I'm sure she would have wanted to see Tain," I said. "And wouldn't his brothers and sisters have come, too?"

He shrugged. "She made her decision a long time ago. Coming back now, it'd bring the whole thing up again."

I'd only been ten or so, but it was impossible to forget the intensity of the scandal when Credola Casimira, Tain's mother and the Chancellor's only sister, had left Caslav and her eldest son to abscond with a romantic partner, a man of another family. The dishonor to Caslav, and the stain she had left on the remainder of her children by raising them outside the reputation, safety, and security of their own family unit, echoed through society even now. Still, I knew enough about foreign societies and their different conceptions of family to understand Casimira, at least a bit.

"She was in love," I couldn't resist pointing out. "Can't people forgive her for that?"

My brother looked genuinely baffled. "What's romantic love got to do with family? Casimira abandoned her family and honor, and she cost Tain his siblings. No one would accept them here, when they've been raised without a Tashi and without honor."

"*Shh*," I quieted him, as Tain appeared from within the passing crowd.

He had covered his tattoos and was unaccompanied by servants. Not

wanting to draw attention, we kept to the busiest streets, sharing the bread
Jovan had brought from our own kitchens. Thendra had promised a report
by this afternoon, and I doubted any of us would be able to think of much
else until we heard what she'd learned from her examination. Our nondescript clothing and hidden family markings seemed to work, because on
Red Fern Avenue even Marco walked past, in conversation with two Order
Guards, without noticing us. We were almost at the hospital when Jovan
touched Tain's shoulder and gestured behind us with a quick tilt of his
head. "Someone recognized you."

A man I did not know, middle-aged, not distinctive in any way, stood
out from the crowd down the street only because of the directed intensity
of his gaze. He moved toward us, lifting a hand in a kind of low wave, as if
he meant to cry out for our attention.

"The petitioners are starting already," Tain sighed. "I had to dodge a
whole crowd of them getting out of the Manor. He's going to have to wait,
like everyone else. Come on, before I get stuck."

"Honored Heir!" Instead, the voice came from the other direction, and
we spun to see Thendra, her tired face wearing a worried frown. "I would
have brought you the report." She ushered us into the hospital and into a
private side room. At her instruction we wiped a waxy substance under our
noses. My palms felt hot and sticky and my breath tight in my chest.

As ever, the physic wasted no time. "I do believe the creature and your
uncles died of the same cause," she said. "If you care to look?" She drew
back a thin cloth. I squeezed my eyes shut and turned away, instinctively,
at the flashed sight of layers of peeled-back skin and fur, and neat piles
of slimy organs. I did *not* care to look, as it turned out. I forced my eyes
open but my stomach bucked in revulsion. Tain, looking equally horrified,
squeezed my shoulder. Jov stepped closer.

"The stomach," he said, and Thendra nodded, pressing into one of the
gleaming white blobs beside the animal's corpse.

"It had two stomachs. You can see the damage to the first, but not the
second, yes?"

I leaned close enough to glimpse what looked like heavy corrosion of the
pale stomach lining, then had to turn away again. The thought of this happening to my Tashi . . . My eyes burned again. I envied Jov's dispassion.

"And my uncle?"

Thendra's face froze, her gaze jumping to Tain and back again. We'd never have progressed beyond primitive medicine without internal examinations of human corpses, but it was neither discussed openly, nor performed on the bodies of important citizens. Although the old religion was no longer commonly practiced in the cities, especially Silasta, death rituals remained an important part of our culture. Word could never get out that a Credo or, worse, the Chancellor himself, had been so desecrated. Jov gave her a wan smile. "He knows we gave you permission, Thendra," he said.

"Credo Etan was one of the most learned minds in the city," Tain said. "And he was the most honorable Councilor and adviser that my uncle could have asked for. He would have wanted us to use anything that could help protect us."

She nodded stiffly. "I did examine Credo Etan, yes. Most respectfully."

"Of course," Jov murmured.

"I saw the same damage to his stomach and to part of his intestines, but also damage to his lungs and some other organs. I believe his heart failed, in the end." She shook her head, looking back at the leksot's stomach. "I would have expected complaints of abdominal pain," she said. "The damage is most obvious in that area. There must have been some kind of numbing agent that prevented them from feeling the pain."

"So what caused it? Was this a disease?"

Jov and Thendra exchanged looks. I wondered how much of our role she might have guessed. "No," she said bluntly. "No, Honored Heir. The stomach is the area of greatest effect, and there was likewise some damage to the mouth and throat. There is no sign of corrosion in or around the scratches Credo Etan received from the creature. This was an ingested poison, consumed by both this animal and the Chancellor; of what kind, I do not know."

Tain exhaled like he'd been struck. Jov merely nodded. I supposed I had known, too.

"Someone poisoned them." From the dull resignation of his tone it was clear Tain had convinced himself it had been accidental. How much I had hoped the same.

Jov glanced at the dead animal then pointedly at me. His thoughts bled through his quick frown. My unease about the leksot's placement in the garden, and the trampled feverhead, returned. Someone had deliberately poisoned the animal. To throw suspicion on a visiting noble, or Credo Lazar? Or in the hopes of disguising a murder as an accidental infection from an exotic pet?

"Thendra, did your apprentices help with the autopsy?" Tain asked suddenly.

"No, Honored Heir. Credo Jovan asked me to do this, but it is . . . unorthodox. I thought it best to—"

"Yes. Yes, it was best." Tain squeezed his arms across his chest, tucking his hands into his armpits. His head made a little bobbing motion, like a constant affirmation of some inner thought. "Thendra, please promise me something."

The physic gave a tense nod and regarded us, unblinking.

"Tell no one what you found. In your hospital records state only that you observed the leksot's body and noted similar symptoms as Credo Etan and the Chancellor. Don't tell anyone that you performed an internal examination, not of the animal and certainly not of Credo Etan. Just conclude it was likely the carrier of an exotic disease."

We needed to know more. If whoever had poisoned the leksot believed we had been taken in by the ruse, we might have an advantage.

"Yes, Honored Heir," Thendra said. "I understand. The city is reeling from this horrible tragedy, yes? It does not need to panic further." She paused, a shake of her hands marking her transition from tension back to her usual gruff concern. "I must advise that you be careful, Honored Heir. If the Chancellor was indeed murdered . . ." She trailed off, but the unspoken end of the thought echoed around my head as if she had shouted it. Poison meant someone had targeted the Chancellor, with a poison Etan had failed to detect and we could not identify. Poison meant Tain could be targeted next.

And my brother with him.

The longhorn rolled out in grieving notes over the still lake, the sound racing across the water until it echoed into nothing on the far shore. Jovan stood in front of me, lined up with the other Councilors, his measured breathing punctuating the slower notes of the longhorn.

Earlier, Tain had performed the ceremonial release of Caslav's body into the Bright Lake, to join his ancestors in their final rest. As the longhorns now played the traditional mourning music, he accepted personal condolences from those gathered as he moved down the line of Credolen and other prominent citizens. There only remained the final song, and then we could slip away. The public display of grief was part of our duties, of course, but oh, to be allowed to just take Etan and bury him in our homelands, instead of suffering through more scrutiny! Perhaps then we could say a proper goodbye to our Tashi, free of obligation and duty for at least a few days.

Just as Tain reached us, a commotion broke out down the shore. A messenger, right arm tattooed with the stylized pen of the Administrative Guild, same as my own, scurried toward us, his legs a frenzied staccato against his rigid body and bowed head. Everyone stared. The entire city had been shut down today for this ceremony; what could be important enough to interrupt it?

"Crowds are approaching the city from the west, Honored Heir—I mean to say, Honored Chancellor," the messenger panted, voice low. "The guard at the west gate was afraid it was some kind of invading army, but she looked through the spyglass and it's countryfolk. Peasants."

"What do you mean, crowds?" Tain asked, picking up on the messenger's undercurrent of unrest. The nearest Councilors edged closer to eavesdrop. The musicians playing the ceremonial music faltered and petered off.

"Hundreds of people. They've got something over their faces, wrapped around their heads."

"Headscarves?" Jovan said, hesitant. Though rare in the cities, most countryfolk tied their hair with scarves because of the winds.

"More like masks, or veils, Credo."

"Is it a religious thing? Lots of people in the country are still earthers."

Jov looked over his shoulder to me for assistance, but I studied foreign cultures, not our own population. Earthers, a slang term for believers in the old Darfri religion, weren't terribly common in the city, and less so in the higher classes; no one in our family or any of the other prominent Silastian families had been religious in generations, that I knew of. Belief in spirits was generally regarded as an embarrassing relic of the past, unfit for a modern and civilized society. Still, we'd all been believers in the beginning; someone likely remembered more about the old rituals than I.

"May I ask what is happening, Honored Chancellor?" Bradomir sidled up, oily and obsequious.

Tain hesitated, glancing at the group of Councilors who had floated into hearing range like silent wraiths. One hand stole up to his upper arm, where bandages still covered the Chancellery tattoos. After a moment, he gestured to the messenger and the man repeated his news.

Marco snapped to immediate attention, shedding his shrunken demeanor. "Honored Chancellor, we need to secure the gates immediately until we know who or what is approaching."

"It's not an army, Warrior-Guilder, don't worry," Tain said. "That's what the Guard thought at first, but it's our own people. Farmers, estatefolk."

"But they're wearing masks?" Varina, the Theater-Guilder, said. She stood too straight and spoke too loudly, with the exaggerated care of an intoxicated person trying to appear sober.

Another messenger, this one behind us, suddenly stepped through the gathering crowd and clarified. "Not masks. They've veiled their faces below the eyes, Honored Chancellor. And they're coming from all directions, not just west. Across the plains and on the roads. They're singing, we think. Can't make it out, but old hymns, or something."

"Our messengers obviously reached the estates, then," said Credo Javesto. "I expect the workers have been given permission to stop work on their farms to show respect for the late Chancellor. I've seen a Darfri funeral before. I think they cover their faces as some kind of mourning ritual."

Credo Bradomir whispered something to Credola Varina about Javesto's upbringing; I didn't hear it properly but the scornful tone was clear enough. He'd spent some of his childhood on his family's estates rather than in Silasta, and no amount of expensive city living could erase that humble past in the eyes of some of his colleagues. He was also very new to the Council, only recently having taken his great-aunt's seat.

"Peasants don't respect anything." Credola Nara's tone was acidic as always. "They don't even understand honor. Probably just want a day off work."

"You know, I can't imagine why workers on your land don't respect you. It's a real mystery, Credola." Javesto turned to Tain. "We should give word to open the gates for the crowds. Chancellor Caslav was their Chancellor, too, and they've just as much right to mourn as us."

"My dear fellow, it's a matter of *practicality*," Bradomir said. "The gates to the city are shut today and must remain so. There is no room around the Bright Lake for thousands more mourners."

As in Council, Tain's vague bewilderment at the argument abruptly vanished; he cleared his throat aggressively until the cacophony quieted. "We'll finish the ceremony," he said. "But afterwards, I'll go out to the walls and personally thank our people for coming to honor my Tashi."

Councilors exchanged calculating looks. The man they had regarded as a good-humored but somewhat irresponsible young relative rather than a player in Silastian politics was unpredictable, and forcing changes in their game.

Tain gestured to the musicians and the ceremony continued, culminating with us all singing along to the end of the mourning song. He left, head low, before the rest of us, but once we were free to move I followed Jov through the dispersing crowd to catch up with Tain as he headed west toward the city gate.

He caught sight of us. "I'm going to wait at the gate. Come with me? Unless you're not finished doing whatever it is you're doing." The last was directed at my brother, who wore a frown of concentration and knotted his fingers tightly. "I can tell when you're obsessing over something."

"Hardly a brilliant insight," I said. "You could say he was obsessing over something every couple of minutes and you'd be right most times."

He grinned, if halfheartedly. "What's the matter?"

Jov looked between us, his anxiety apparent. "Don't you think this is odd? Yes, we sent messengers out, but everyone just, what, dropped tools and started walking? How are they all arriving at the same time? It's just . . . it's odd, is all."

I nodded. "It is. Are we absolutely sure that it's actually our people? I'm still not sure about the veiling."

"Maybe if we could hear what they were singing, as well," Jov said. He stopped and looked over the small group of servants tailing us. "Are any of you believers? Or do you have family out in the country who are?"

All four servants shook their heads. "We were all born here in Silasta, Credo Jovan," one said. "I've got distant family out in the Losi valley who're probably earthers, but I don't know much about it."

We crossed Bell's Bridge, following the main road through the lower city to the road gate in the outer west wall, a thick and imposing testament to a violent past that modern Silastians didn't like to remember. A repetitive crunch of gravel from outside marked the grim shuffle of the people approaching on the road. Tain started up the external steps of the tower by the gate.

"I'm going to go up and see how far they are," he said as he ascended. "If you can think of anything about Darfri mourning customs, any tips you could give me about something I can say, so I don't accidentally insult some spirit or something, let me know. They've come all this way, I don't want to look like an insensitive prick."

Jovan leaned against the wall, closing his eyes. He might not have studied other cultures as I had but he had an amazing memory. He'd once tried to describe to me how he could take a familiar book off a shelf in his mind, recalling the feel of its pages, the smell of the ink, the illuminations and words. He'd read every book in the Manor and school libraries and, thanks to his compulsions, a lot of them more than once. Sometimes his obsessiveness could be an advantage.

Watching from the guard post as Tain made his way slowly up the tower was a strapping Order Guard with long braids. Her bicep was marked with the Warrior Guild's knife, and her broad face wore a worried scowl.

"Ancient mourning practices," Jov murmured, his eyes still closed, as if he were reading aloud from a book behind his eyes. "People used to—I mean I guess they still do, out there—think that death could be an offering to the spirits. Burying bodies near the person's birthplace was about offering their essence back to the earth spirits. But there's nothing about veiling as part of a funeral ritual."

Jov opened his eyes. "Veiling, there *was* something about veiling I remember. . . ." His eyes widened. "Oh, *shit*. Tain!" he bellowed, scrambling up the steps.

A whistle and a high-pitched whine, then something made contact with the walls. The pale stone shuddered. I started after my brother, breath catching in my throat. "What's happening?"

Tain, open-mouthed, burst through the tower door above. "They're armed!" he yelled, disbelieving. "They're attacking us!" Behind him, through the open tower door, the Order Guard tugged at the old bellpull, which labored and jerked under her strong grip.

Jov sprang up the last few steps and I followed, chest tight, to see the view for myself through the thin slit in the stone tower—rows and rows of eerie masked figures, stretching out beyond the walls in every direction. Bows in their hands revealed their intent. Not mourners but an army, marching straight toward us. Arrows struck the wall and the ground like pelting hail. After the volley, a roar drowned out the sound of the bell.

"They're not mourning," Jov said, breathless, as though the climb had been ten times as long. "Tain, it's not veiling for mourning. Earthers veil for *vengeance*."

As I watched, frozen by the sight—a scene that belonged in history books and tales of warring cultures, not assembled outside the walls of Silasta—the crowd released another volley. The weirdly attractive formation sailed toward us like a flock of pale, deadly birds. The Order Guard snapped down the shutter across the tower viewing slit.

All around us, the wheezy old bell pealed out an alarm the city hadn't heard in living memory.

Paralysis lifting, I grabbed Tain's shoulder, shaking him out of a similar stupor. "We have to get back to the city," I said. Beside me, Jov twitched madly, his hands spasming. By my reckoning, this time, it was the right situation for some good old-fashioned panic. "Come on!"

"Keep the bell going and stay safe," Tain told the Order Guard. She nodded grimly, drawing her sword—useless against an army outside a massive thirty-tread wall—and continuing to ring the bell with her free hand.

We half-ran, half-slid down the steps.

"We've got to let everyone know what's going on, and get you away from these damn walls," Jov said.

"What did you mean, *vengeance*?" Tain looked confused. "For my Tashi? Who do they want revenge on?"

Jov shook his head, shuddering. "I don't know. But it's about justice. There was a picture—I remember the picture. A beaten man, and relatives surrounding him, with spears, and their faces veiled below the eyes. Spearing the attacker. Skewering him."

"Honored Chancellor!" A group of three Order Guards met us. They clasped their hands together and raised the grip to Tain in respect. Silence fell as we looked at each other. I barely knew what to say or think. Jov looked on the brink of a meltdown, his hands and thigh muscles tightening and loosening and his face losing color. I put a hand on his shoulders, hoping to calm him, but he jolted under the touch and moved away.

"Tain," he said, his voice choking out. "Tain, the *army*."

And only then did true dread seize me, too, as I remembered where our actual army was.

"I'll send a bird—" I started to say, then fell into silence, meeting Jov's horrified expression. No birds to send, and clearly no accident.

Tain didn't blink. "All right," he said, scanning the gathered group. "We need to get organized. There's a force out there, and they're coming in fast. How many of you are there in the city?"

Silence. I remembered what Marco had said in the meeting: most of the Order Guards were in the army, leaving us under-garrisoned. The guard in front looked young and frightened beneath his shining helmet. I didn't blame him. Order Guards kept peace and order within the city; they dealt with the occasional unruly crowd or un-Guilded street seller, carried the odd drunk tourist back to their guesthouse. For those who weren't already in the army, they probably never expected much more than that. Who would ever have expected to face an attack on the city itself?

Tain asked again, "How *many*?"

The man swallowed. "Twenty-two, Honored Chancellor," he whispered.

"Twenty-two?"

We exchanged dull looks of horror. Not even two dozen Order Guards and a city full of civilians. And the army was upriver in the southern mountains, days away.

Maidenbane

DESCRIPTION: Water plant with large, attractive floating flowers abundant in marshy areas—pulpy floating roots are toxic if ingested. Corrosive poison but contains a pain-numbing agent that prevents the victim from feeling the stomach damage. Used in small quantities as a relief for painful stomach cramps and women's bleeding cycles.

SYMPTOMS: Dizziness, swelling of the face and extremities, excessive sweating, fever, chest pain, heart failure.

PROOFING CUES: Strong bitter flavor and smell, difficult to mask in food, noticeably thickens liquids.

3

Jovan

Everything got loud and frantic. The tolling alarm bell went on and on, and behind it built the swell of noise from the thousands concentrated around the lake, reacting to the warning. People streamed up the main road toward us, drawn by the bell, their curiosity visibly melting into panic as word spread.

The great west road gate we stood before was closed for the funeral, but I had no idea what it could withstand. "Is there anything else that can be done to secure the gate?"

"There's a second gate and portcullis on the inside entrance," one of the Order Guards said, her voice shaking. "We never use it but I know how to operate it."

"Do it," Tain said. "What about the others? Someone needs to go to the north and south road gates and the river gates. No, not you—" He caught the arm of the Order Guard who had started to spring away. "Grab someone, anyone. Two to every gate. Make sure the Guards there get them secured."

The Order Guard nodded. "Honor-down, someone get word out to the army!"

"Marco," Kalina said, and pointed. Marco had at last appeared in the crowd, the big man pushing his way through the throng toward us. Tain gave a relieved cry.

"We're under attack! They're attacking us." Tain clasped Marco's forearms, eyes wild. "Marco, what do we do?" Tain's demeanor had fooled me; now his fear was obvious. People around him heard his words and repeated them, the confirmation of our situation passing like a grassfire through the crowd.

"Keep them back," I told the Order Guards, and they formed a tentative ring around the four of us. Kalina pressed close against me.

Marco, grim but calm, listened to Tain's quick summary and leaned in close, talking into the Chancellor's ear. I couldn't hear above the tide of blood in my head and the increasingly shrill and desperate questions and cries. But Tain nodded, said something, nodded again. Marco strode a few steps up the wall and held his arms up for attention.

"Quiet!" he roared. The Order Guard in the tower stopped ringing the bell, and slowly the crowd below quieted to an anxious murmur. "There is an army outside, and we are without our own. We have *no time*. If you are between fifteen and fifty years old, and physically capable, you will stay here and wait to be given a weapon. You are our line of defense if the gate is breached. If you are younger or older, you will go back to your home right now and pull together anything that can be used as a weapon. Knives, tools, anything you can hold and swing. You will bring it back to the nearest road gate." He raised a hand again to the increased shouts and cries in response. "Take children who are too young to be alone and the elderly who cannot run to the school. Get them inside and keep them together. *Now!*"

Someone nearby started sobbing. Kalina's hand shook in mine. "You heard Marco," I told her, stupidly, desperately grateful for his words. "Etan's knives. Whatever else you can find. Then get to the school."

She yanked her hand free, her eyes teary as she glared at me. "I'm capable enough. I've been swimming, running. . . . I'm stronger now."

There was no time to argue. Marco was back down to our level now, his eyes sweeping over us all, seeing resources, making calculations. He barked orders at the Guards around us. "You two, go to the other road gates and give the same instructions there. There is a weapons storeroom in every gate tower containing confiscated weapons from visitors to the city. Hand out what we have. Prioritize people who have held a weapon before. Take a few youngsters to be your messengers and you keep me informed. Yes? You, there, you take a dozen citizens with you and get back to the Guild-hall. Take my chit"—he yanked a thin chain from his neck and pressed it into the Order Guard's hand—"and tell the clerk at the armory you're tak-ing everything they have. Confiscate the first carts you come across and get those weapons back to the wall."

Tain stared out at the crowd. "They're not moving." He squared his shoulders and pushed past me, back up to the stairs. "Silastians!" he cried. "I am your Chancellor! This is our home, and it is under attack. For the honor that we all live by, do as the Warrior-Guilder says and protect our home!" My friend's voice shook. He was no natural orator, and he'd been thrust into a new role he'd not expected to shoulder for a long time. He wasn't prepared. None of us were.

But Silastians lived by a system of honor, and they loved their Chancel-lor. They listened. Marco repeated his directions and the crowd dispersed, though wails and shouts still filled the air. I felt their confusion and terror reflected in me. We were merchants, craftsmen, students, and artists, liv-ing rich and sheltered lives in the most beautiful and cultured city in the continent. We knew nothing of the war and tyranny our ancestors had fled long ago; it had not followed them. Only the Warrior-Guild remained of that lifestyle, least respected and honored of the Guilds; and now, when they could have proven their worth, they weren't here.

"Will the gates hold?" Tain was asking Marco.

The big man rubbed his close-cropped hair, frowning. "I do not know, Honored Chancellor. I am not . . . I teach weaponry, you see. I do not know much of walls."

"Where's Eliska?" Tain asked. "Someone find the Stone-Guilder!" He looked up at the Order Guard hanging out of the tower. "How far, Chen?"

"Two hundred treads, Chancellor, maybe less. Coming steady."

"Honor-down, we have to be able to talk to them." Tain stared up at the walls with a kind of fascinated horror. "What if I—"

"You can't go up there again," I said.

"We can't let them attack without trying."

"I agree," said Marco. "But you were shot at before, Honored Chancellor. We don't know who those people are. They may have disguised themselves as peasants in order to gain access to the city, and only when they realized the city was closed down and the gates shut did they decide to attack. We have to assume this is a well-provisioned army. So we have a short window to send out a peace negotiator before it is too dangerous to open the gate."

Tain hesitated, then nodded. "Set it up."

It seemed to take an eternity to find a diplomat from the Administrative Guild. A rounded, elegant woman, she visibly trembled as she took the hastily made negotiation flag, green fabric torn from a commandeered litter and a black sigil for peace in standard Trade, drawn with purloined makeup. Tain murmured encouragement, holding her shoulders, and his words seemed to calm her.

"We have no quarrel with anyone, and certainly not our own people if that is them out there," Tain said. "Remember, we want to talk, and we'll hear any grievances."

As she ducked under the partially raised portcullis and through the lonely dark tunnel toward the gate, a shiver came over me. Grievances from our own people could have been brought to a determination council in any town, or appealed directly to the Council. This was something else entirely. A rebellion, or an attack from a foreign power?

The clank of the metal gates closing behind her reverberated in my chest.

An Order Guard handed out weapons from the tower as Marco scurried about, pointing and shouting, trying to organize the crowd. I was no strategist but I knew the layout inside the city didn't favor us for any kind of battle. There was too much open space around the road and the buildings were set too far back from the wall. There would be no way of containing the spread of attackers if they made it through the gate.

I accepted a simple shortsword from the Order Guard then followed Tain up into the top of the tower with the unfamiliar weapon. We peered together through the slit window.

Below, the lone messenger, flag dragging her crooked in the wind, teetered into view. I crouched lower, watching the progressing army, hoping with everything in me that an answering green flag would emerge. The cocoon of the tower room insulated us from the panic below. Every sharp breath Tain took rasped like a scratch in my ears. Why was it taking so long?

"There!" Tain grabbed my arm.

A small contingent advanced from the army. From the distance I could make out little about the veiled figures. Were they leaders? Negotiators? Real peasants or soldiers disguised?

Closer they drew together. A vein in my lip pulsed against my gums. I tried to ignore it. The figures stopped, then . . .

"No!" Tain screamed in the same instant I did; the smooth draw of bows from their billowing clothes, the nocking of arrows, and it was over in a moment. "Fuck, *fuck*!" Tain pounded the stone, useless, hopeless, thirty treads in the air and fifty from her body, punctured with arrows, green peace turning brown with her blood.

I squeezed my eyes shut while Tain raged around the room. The shock had stolen my breath. There was to be no honor and no negotiation, then. "We need to prepare," I said, finding my words at last.

The first of the wall defenders streamed up the external stairs on the other side of the gate, some carrying bows, some rocks, as we passed the news to Marco. He took it in stride. "They do not wish to give us time to prepare. You must get across the lake if the gate falls, Chancellor." Outside, the thunder of feet seemed to shake the very ground. "I will check that the other gates are ready," he said. "Chen, call the volleys."

"In range!" someone cried from the wall moments after Marco disappeared. Tain charged down the steps and I was left scrambling after him. "Honor-down, Tain! You can't go out there."

He didn't even turn around, just slipped from my grasp and leaped out onto the battlements. I swore and followed.

People lined the wall, fumbling awkwardly for spaces and tripping over dropped items. Some had bows and shot downward through the crenellations, seemingly at random, despite Chen's timed commands in the background. Many hurled rocks and pottery and metal utensils over the edge. Others had scrambled back to the far side of the battlement, too fearful to act at all.

A crash sounded as the army collided with the gate. An arrow whizzed past me and sailed into the empty space behind the wall, dropping with deceptive softness and grace. My heart in my throat, I hunched, trying not to get in anyone's way as I followed Tain. He moved fearlessly through the chaos, pressing to the edge of the walls to get a view below. Breathless, I finally caught up, grabbing his shoulder as I joined him between two men with bows.

"You have to get away from here!"

I snatched a glance below. I could see straight down but the blinding western sun obscured much of the movements below. Close to the wall, what looked like a great overturned boat, covered in leathers, sheltered attackers working with axes on the gate. One of our arrows found the side of a man supporting the device and he staggered and fell. I pulled back from the wall, feeling nauseous.

Faint tremors rumbled through the wall as axes struck the gate. I reached over and yanked Tain's paluma. He stumbled and dropped back beside me.

"They can't really be our own people," he said in my ear. "What if—"

Before he could finish, the man next to us fell backward with a grunt, colliding into several other people, an arrow protruding from his neck. Blood pulsed through his scrambling fingers, and his mouth worked silently, like a fish.

I crawled over and caught his hands, putting pressure on the wound to slow the bleeding. "Don't pull at the shaft," I told him. "You'll make it worse." Part of me wondered how it could possibly get worse. "Are there any physics here yet?" I yelled.

Tain knelt on the other side. My eyes fixed on the bone shaft jutting out from the poor man's throat. I measured his struggling breath, the pallor of his skin, the speed of the blood from the wound, seeking the familiar dispassion of analysis while beside me Tain comforted him, holding him still at the shoulders and speaking slowly and calmly. The wall shuddered as the attackers pounded at the gate.

Finally, a man in a physic's blue sash scrambled up the stairs and over to us, a bag in hand. I moved out of the way as he took charge, checking the man's pulse and breathing and then padding around the arrow with cloth from his bag. "Good—you didn't move the shaft. Hard enough to get an arrowhead out without having to scramble around to try to find it. Here, give me a hand with this fellow."

The physic hadn't recognized Tain in the confusion. I hid my relief by assisting with the injured man's legs and the three of us carried him back down into the city grounds. We had barely reached the bottom step when others hurried forward to help with our burden. I scarcely had time to breathe before Marco found us.

"This is the weakest gate, Honored Chancellor," he said. "It replaced the original gate some decades ago and it is not built to withstand this kind of force. They are attacking the joints between the panels."

"We can't sustain this," Tain said. "We've barely any weapons and our people don't know how to use the bows they've got. We're relying more on luck than anything else. Where's Eliska?"

Marco collared a nearby Credola. "Find the Stone-Guilder," he ordered, and though her mouth twisted with affront, she sprang off quickly enough. Yesterday Marco had been the least important Councilor—the temporary substitute leader of the least respected Guild. Now our lives depended on his leadership as much as Tain's. The fortunes only knew whether either would be up to the task.

Eliska found us soon after. Her well-muscled arms and broad, strong hands bore some scratches and dirt marks, and her round face seemed to have gained ten years in the past hour.

"We need this gate reinforced," Tain said. "Can you get your best people—pull them off the walls if they're up there—and do something from the inside that will help it hold?"

The Stone-Guilder frowned, calculating in silence. Eventually, she nodded.

"I can secure it—it'll make a mess of the gate for the future, but I can stop anyone getting in there."

"Do what you can." Tain clasped Marco's shoulder. "Can we pull all the Order Guards here? We need people who can actually use bows to protect the gate."

"We need to break that contraption they're sheltering under," I said. "What if we dropped something seriously heavy on it—statues from the wharf street gardens, maybe?"

"That should buy Eliska time," Tain said. The Stone-Guilder already had a small group of Builders' Guild members around her, scurrying to her quick orders. "I just hope it holds."

It held. As Eliska said, it wasn't pretty, but the reinforcements strengthened the gate where the metal had bowed and chipped from the force of the attacks. Eventually, after having lost their upturned boat to some of our fine marble sculptures, the attackers abandoned the attempt and fell back to a position away from the wall. Though it had felt like hours, the whole attack and retreat had been swift.

We had left the Order Guards and senior Guild officials in charge while we held the emergency Council meeting. I wasn't sure they would be able to contain the panic; some terror-driven scuffles had already broken out as people streamed in every direction through the lower city and across the lake. The gate reinforcement had given us some time, but likely not much. How fast could we fit untrained citizens with our light stores of armor, and show pampered scholars and merchants how to use weapons they'd never even held?

The Council chamber had been tense and unruly a few days ago at my first meeting. Now that seemed tame by comparison. The comfortable setting contrasted sharply with its disheveled, quarreling inhabitants.

Marco, his earlier authority swallowed by politics, sat like a nervous child in school while Councilors loomed over him on either side, peppering him with question after question. A few Guilders were engaged in heated words with the Credolen about whether the landowners ought to have known there was trouble on their estates. Tain's gaze and attention flew back and forth, trying to listen to multiple conversations at once and contributing to none of them. I watched, anxious, willing him to take control.

"Why haven't our spies reported an uprising on the farms? We do *have* spies, don't we?"

"Why would we need spies when the landowners are right here around the table? I know none of you like to actually *go* there, but you all have stewards. Don't you get reports? Rebellions don't come from nothing."

The Credolen around the table looked uncomfortable; lots of shifting eyes and wringing hands. Some of it I shared; after all, what attention had I ever paid to our estates? Etan and I had always been focused on our duty to the Chancellor's family, and left the management of our family's business largely to our steward, Alozia, and my mother. Tain, too, knew next to nothing about how his estates worked; it was the usual practice for the Chancellor and Heir, who had to look to the health of the entire country and not just to their own businesses and affairs. "Farmers, miners, workers, they always grumble," Credo Lazar blustered at last. "No one could expect things to come to violence."

"No point wondering where it came from for now," the Craft-Guilder, Credo Pedrag, said. "We just need to stop it, quick smart. We need more archers up there to shoot them down."

Marco rubbed a hand over his close-cropped hair, sighing with the frustration of a man relaying information for the fiftieth time. "We lack the people and the weapons."

"What I cannot understand is *why*," Budua, the Scribe-Guilder, the calmest at the table, balanced her wrinkled chin on her hand with the air of an academic studying an interesting problem. "Yes, I know the Council voted to send the army south. But no one asked me to vote on the understanding that there would be no protection left for the city. We skirmish over those mines every few years. Why did this necessitate leaving the city unprotected?"

"I was not party to all your deliberations," Marco reminded her. "But it is my understanding that Chancellor Caslav sent the full army as a deliberate show of force to prevent these skirmishes in the future. As for our own garrison, well, Silasta sits in the center of the most protected country in the continent, Scribe-Guilder. Between the mountain ranges and the marshes, no external force could realistically enter Sjona other than through the three border cities, which *are* garrisoned. An attack on the city has not been a realistic possibility in decades."

"And yet here we are."

"Here we are," Marco repeated. His gaze sank to the table. A few days before, the worst part of this role must have been the prospect of being forced to listen to spoiled, wealthy old men and women insulting him; now here he was suddenly in charge of a defense plan no one had even contemplated us ever needing, and having to defend decisions made well above his level of seniority.

"It's not the Warrior-Guilder's fault. No one could have foreseen this," Tain reassured him. Irritation flickered inside me; of course in Tain's eyes

Aven could not have been responsible for a misjudgment. The fact was, she *had* misjudged, and perhaps it was her error that cost us everything.

"Do we even know what *this* is?" Varina asked. "Forgive me, Chancellor, but is this really some kind of rebellion?"

"Of course it's a rebellion," Nara scoffed. "That's our own bloody peasants out there."

"We don't know yet what—" Marco began, but his soft voice was quickly lost in the increasing din.

"Rebellions are for tyrannies! What's there to rebel against here? Too wealthy? Too much food? Good work, safe homes, medicine, what am I missing?"

". . . out there in their veils, chanting like primitive bloody lunatics— too soft we've been on the estates, letting people run wild, this is what happens when you let these people do what they want . . ."

"Obviously we *weren't* letting them do what they want," Javesto said, his tone acid, "or they'd hardly be attacking us now. If we could understand *why* this happened, we might be able to stop it before it gets too serious."

"There is an army at our gates, Credo," Bradomir said, a sharp slope to his eyebrows. "I rather think it's as serious as it could be."

"If we just listen to them—" Javesto began.

"With respect, Credo, we have tried listening," Marco interrupted him, big hands spread palms up. "They shot a peace emissary. They don't want to talk. There's nothing to listen *to*. I agree we cannot be certain this is a rebellion, and we should not underestimate these attackers on the assumption that they are mere farmers. We do not know what is hiding behind those veils; all we know is that they are well armed and disinclined to negotiate."

"What should we do first, Honored Chancellor?" I made my voice as loud as I could without shouting, and shot a thankful glance at Marco when he stopped talking and stared attentively at Tain. Budua, Eliska, and the gentle-eyed Artist-Guilder, Marjeta, did the same, and the chamber settled into uneasy silence. Tain pulled the map across the table, and I hoped only I caught the tremor in his hands as he did.

"I see two priorities," he said. "Getting word out to the army directly or via one of the cities, and holding Silasta until help can get here. I'd like suggestions for both."

Marco spread his hands over the map, smoothing it and knocking aside the other Guilders' hands like crumbs. Our city, reduced to flat shapes and colors. "They have us surrounded," he said. "The biggest forces are here, on the west side of the city." He gestured around the semicircle of the west side, split by the three main roads running roughly south, west, and north. "But my Guards have confirmed there is a small force this side of the river on the north and south, here and here." The east side of the city, Silasta's original footprint, stretched from the lake to the mountain, bordered on either side by the old city walls. No gates or roads remained on that side of the lake, but if the army outside had neglected those sections we could have sent messengers over the wall and through the countryside to bypass them altogether. Marco's fingers lingered at the south end of the map. Well past its borders, our impeccably trained army waited, out of reach.

"Send birds," Lazar suggested, then his eager expression crumpled like paper as he remembered: *no birds.*

"When does the Warrior-Guilder expect to return?" I asked Marco. "How long will it take her to realize something's wrong?"

Marco rubbed his forehead. "Warrior-Guilder Aven will not return until the conflict with the Doranite groups is resolved. She will send progress reports, but she would not expect a return bird from us as a matter of course. Unless someone alerts her directly, it could be weeks or more, depending what the Doranites do."

Tain sighed. "So we need to send someone in person."

"We've only two dozen trained fighters."

"More than that. Certainly a proportion of my servants are also trained for my protection." It was easy to forget; although the Chancellor required protection as a matter of practicality, tradition dictated that such protection be subtle, almost invisible, so as not to suggest distrust or fear. "That must be true for some of you, too."

"Even so," Bradomir acknowledged stiffly. "We need them all here."

"I could go," Marco suggested.

"Not a chance," Tain said.

"I may be older than the Guards, Chancellor, but if I run into any trouble, I can handle myself."

"I know." Tain gave him a wan smile. "But we can't afford to lose you from our defense. My Warrior-Guilder is far from here and no one around this table, me especially, has seen anything of war. Who but you can help defend the city?"

"With respect, Honored Chancellor, *you* must learn. Silasta will look to you to save her."

"It might," Nara said, acerbic. "But he won't have much chance at that if our only military mind leaves the city."

"What about one of the runners?" The others stared at me. "An athlete, I mean."

"Excellent thought, Credo," Marco said. "A swift runner could reach the army quickly, without costing us a Guard."

Tain shook his head. "That doesn't answer how they get past the army in the first place."

"They haven't completely surrounded us yet. The contingent east of the river is farther away and they're still organizing into formations. A quick person using the mountain paths might find a way to get through without engaging."

Marco nodded. "If we do not send someone quickly, while our enemy's army is still preparing, then they will never make it. Our only chance is to risk it now, before we are in a full siege."

"I can't send some poor sod out where people will try to kill them," Tain retorted, crossing his arms.

I swallowed, remembering the sight of the peace emissary riddled with arrows. I knew many of the best athletes in Silasta, and I didn't much care for the thought of any of them in that situation. But I was nothing if not adept at appearing calm while pushing down horrific mental narratives. "They'd be doing their duty to Silasta," I said. "Just like all the other people who aren't fighters but are going to be stuffed into armor that doesn't fit them and told to use weapons they can barely lift."

"There's a difference between helping people defend themselves and sending them out into half-certain death."

"Perhaps ask them, then, Honored Chancellor," I said, dropping my head. Undermining Tain's fledgling authority now was the worst thing I could do. "Ask for volunteers."

Tain glanced at me with reproach, but around the table the other Councilors nodded. "Volunteers, then," he said stiffly.

Eliska tapped the south end of the map. "Let's send several. If even one runner makes it through the perimeter they could stay off the roads and make their way to the army or at least to the closest city. Whoever it is out there, they can't be patrolling the whole country."

"Well there are bloody peasants all over the country, aren't there?" Nara said. "That's rather the point of them."

"If it's a rebellion, which we still cannot say. It's still possible this is a fast-moving invading army and it's gone through one of the border cities already."

Lazar sat forward. "*Through* one of the other cities?" he croaked. "What of our families?"

Cold hands squeezed around my ribs, and the air seemed to get very heavy. We had been in Telasa only a bit over a week before and seen family there; could that lively place have been overwhelmed by invaders only days later? In the shock of the attack, I hadn't thought about who else might have been a victim of it already. "We sent messengers to the cities and estates," I said. "Has anyone heard back? Credo Javesto? Anyone?"

Heads shook around the table.

"You saw smoke," Javesto murmured to Nara, stricken. "The other day. In the direction of my estates."

Whichever way we looked lay grief. Had we lost a city, or had our own estates risen against us? All the Credolen had family in the other cities, and often out on the estates as well, albeit generally more distant relatives. If, indeed, the people had risen in rebellion, what had they done to the stewards and other estate managers? Or if a city had fallen—though surely, surely, some word would have reached us—that could mean even more dire consequences. I thought of Mother and Alozia and all our cousins, growing tea and living a peaceful life absent intrigue. . . . What had become of them?

A high cry escaped Nara. "My little ones," she whispered, her face a rictus of pain. I'd never pitied the old bastard before, but sympathy ran over me now in a hot wave. The Ash family, diminished through years of producing mostly male children, all doted on the little twin girls finally born well past when the last childbearing heir had expected it. I'd seen bitter old Nara around those girls, and she was an entirely different woman, caring and playful. Lazar, too, quivered with silent emotion; he was famously close to his enormous family, who spent the year trudging between

Silasta, Moncasta, and one of his estate plantations. We all felt it, to varying degrees, and the shared emotion around the table smoothed some of
the lingering tension between us. We were all in the same position here.

"We can't do anything for our families if we can't defend ourselves,"
Tain said, and this time everyone responded to the quiet authority in his
voice. "Marco, Eliska, can we hold the city?"

"The perimeter walls are sound," Eliska said. "Thirty treads high; forty
on this side of the lake. And I'll have that gate permanently secured."
Silastians liked to pretend that we had always been a beacon of peace,
trade, and tolerance, but our ancestors had built a country and its capital
expecting to have to defend it with force. We'd forgotten that, over the
years, but perhaps the rest of the country had known better than us after
all. "Unless they have full siege weaponry, they'll have to resort to coming
over the walls."

Marco nodded. "Today's attack was opportunistic, hoping to catch us
off guard. But this is no spontaneous attack. Whoever is out there is organized. They took out our communications, and they may have . . . neutralized . . . our settlements outside the city to reduce the chance of someone
getting word to our army. We must assume they could be working with
one of our neighbors; I do not wish to speculate, but if the Doranites are
involved, it is possible the intention is to keep our army busy in the south
with these small raiding forces while they take the city." He looked at the
shocked faces around the table. "I . . . I do not mean to alarm you more.
This could be a benefit. If they are confident that no help will be returning
for some time, they may intend to try to starve us out rather than storming
the walls."

"The harvest," said Marjeta, the quiet Artist-Guilder. "We thought it was
bandits but they delayed the harvests. We are at our lowest in food supplies."

"We've barely any weapons, not enough food, no soldiers. . . . What's
going to happen to us?" Fear quivered behind Varina's haughty tone, the
stiff toss of her braided hair, and the shake in her shoulders.

"We can make weapons," Eliska said. "We have stockpiles of peat fuel,
oil, metal, and stone. I've got workers in my Guild who can craft a stairway
out of metal that looks like it's made of lace. If the Warrior-Guilder will
work with me, I'm certain they could fashion whatever defensive weapons
or machines we need."

"I have a number of sculptors in my Guild who could assist," Marjeta offered.

Practical suggestions seemed to lift the mood.

"The Craft Guild can help with leather work and armor."

"It's not just Order Guards who can shoot a bow. Athletes, anyone who's been hunting, anyone who took military classes at school."

"So we'll need bows, slings, and anything else we can shoot at them."

"And shortswords to use for when they breach the walls," Marco added. "Not too heavy, just something everyone can swing and stab."

I wondered if I was the only one to mark how he said *when*, not *if*.

Night fell fast, spreading its shadows over the buildings and gardens with a sudden chill uncharacteristic of the season. Or perhaps it was just in my head. The hours blended together in a mass of huddled conferences, scrawled plans, and suppressed panic. The army outside our walls had taken no further action, which heightened the tension as we waited to see what it would do.

The air felt heavy around us. It was the darkest part of early morning, and Tain and Marco were giving the five brave volunteer runners their last instructions. Tain spoke to them all individually, thanking them and wishing them luck. He looked much better than I felt.

The two smallest had the unpleasant exit through the sewer tunnel that opened up downriver in the marshlands to the north. Though they perhaps had a greater chance of emerging unseen, their path to our army would be far longer. I would assist the other three, lowering them over the southeast wall where it met Solemn Peak, and they would use the mountain itself as cover. The south side of the city was riskier, but if they got out undetected they could reach the army in days rather than weeks. My sister's admirer Edric was the only Credo among the five, and guilt suffused me as I regarded him; cocky but warm-hearted, he was a truly decent young man. The others I didn't know well but recognized from sporting events. Their families would rise in honor and recognition of this feat. Their loyalty to their city and country made my throat tight with emotion. Silasta was a place worth loyalty, worth risk. Such a visceral reminder of its importance was a balm at a time when everything in the world seemed to have fallen to despair and treachery.

We had done our best to disguise them, though not knowing exactly who made up the attacking army, we were only guessing. We had dressed them as ordinary farmers and hidden their tattoos with cosmetics from the Performers' Guild. Under the country-style baggy pants, scarves, and shirts, all in pale, nondescript colors, our runners wore hardened leather breastplates and thigh-guards. Enough, perhaps, to give them a chance of getting through alive. We dared not armor them more heavily for fear of attracting attention and weighing them down.

I scanned their nervous, solemn faces and tried not to imagine the worst. The disguises would not pass close scrutiny, but if they could slip through the heavy shadow of Solemn Peak in the dark, we had a chance.

Eliska had spent all night with her engineers and builders crafting a giant weapon that looked something like an oversized sling. She would stage an attack at a different location to draw the army's attention while our runners crossed that crucial open space between our walls and the army. When I'd last seen Eliska she'd been poring over the device, sprung with nervous energy. I admired her composure and capabilities; she was one of the youngest Stone-Guilders in generations and she was demanding things of her Guild no one had considered for centuries. Silastian builders and engineers were lauded across the continent for beautiful buildings and cunning technologies to enhance our lives, not weapons. Yet she hadn't faltered.

And we needed her not to falter, because distracting the patrols outside depended on the success of that machine.

"The hopes of the city lie upon you. Be swift and fearless," Marco said. He gripped the shoulders of each runner in turn as he walked before them. They straightened, renewed in their resolve by the big man's quiet words.

"You three are with Credo Jovan at the southeast wall," Tain said, dividing the volunteers between me and Chen, the Order Guard who had first rung the attack bell earlier today. "You two are with Chen. Marco and I will lead the diversion attack. Timing will be everything." That last he directed at me, and I nodded. I disliked the idea of being away from Tain during this first strike, but someone needed to judge the moment to send the runners, and I didn't want to leave this most vital task to anyone else. If the runners didn't make it . . . well, I didn't want to think about that, either.

"We should begin, Honored Chancellor," Marco said.

I silently wished them luck as they melted away through the predawn dark; Chen and her runners to the north, Tain and Marco across the bridge to the western tower, where Eliska's catapult waited. "Our turn now." We stuck close to the walls, avoiding the streets, and came eventually to the partially repaired cote, its jagged white shape silent in the dark. Temporary laddering for the repairs made it easy to get to the roof, but we needed ropes and tools to scale the mountain face up to its connection point with the city wall. The runner ahead of me shimmied up, barely needing the climbing tools, while I scrambled between handholds, sweating and suppressing grunts.

Edric grabbed my arm to help me up the last section, and gave me his familiar earnest smile. "If I don't survive, tell your sister to remember me fondly, won't you?" False reassurance seemed like an insult; the words jammed in my throat, so I merely nodded.

Outside, a few fires twinkled in the predawn and figures shifted about in the dark mass of the sleeping army. The smaller force this side of the river had only three watchers. We needed their attention anywhere but this dark southeast corner of the city. Faces pressed to the edge of the parapet, rope tied and ready, we watched and waited.

A crash splintered the night. Even expecting it, I jumped. Shouts and cries broke through the silence as the first projectile landed. We had bound containers of oil around the rock and now flaming arrows would follow, intended to catch the spills alight. Sure enough, a burst of red flared up to our right. I kept my eyes on the black mass ahead, scouring it, following those tiny black sentries. One, two, moving off to the west, trying to see, no doubt; the other back in to the mass, perhaps to report. *Now.* On my whispered signal, we dropped the rope over and the runners followed it in silence. One, two, three, they went over.

Time trickled, and still the rope jerked and wobbled in my hands as I steadied their descent. I used the burn of the rope against my palms as a distraction from the doubts bubbling inside me. Eventually, the rope shook one last time and the pressure suddenly fell away as the last runner transferred from rope to mountain face. I pulled it up swiftly, then waited, pulse pounding in my ears. It was hard to resist peering over the wall to check on their progress, but the less movement I made, the better. Mouth dry, I searched the darkness, listening hard. My nails cut into my palms waiting for some sign a sentry had seen them, but the stirring forces cried no alarm in our direction.

I stayed there a while longer, but as the light slowly improved, no movement was visible along Solemn Peak or anywhere else. I opened my palms and shook my hands to loosen knotted forearm muscles. I barely dared say it to myself for fear of somehow jinxing it, but maybe, just maybe, help was on its way.

Bluehood

DESCRIPTION: Herbaceous perennial in mountainous regions, with a hood-shaped blue flower. Flowers believed to be a sign of a spirit's blessing; used extensively in Darfri rituals. Green parts of the plant poisonous if ingested.

SYMPTOMS: Nausea, vomiting, and diarrhea; burning, tingling, or numbness in the mouth and face, developing into motor weakness and numbness in limbs; paralysis of the heart or lungs, causing death.

PROOFING CUES: Detectable bitter, acrid taste and pungent smell.

4

Kalina

I woke my brother with tea, made more out of habit than desire. Our diversion attack had petered out by dawn, after the new catapult had broken, and everyone sought their beds for some rest. Confined to our apartments long before then, I'd slept too deeply to even hear the commotion. Though guilt lingered for having rested in those circumstances, there was only so much my body could do, and now at least the gray fog of exhaustion had lifted from my head, and the worst of the soreness from my joints. Outside, daylight had progressed over our groggy city; there had been no more alarm bells throughout the night or morning.

While Jovan had taken a few hours of rest, I had searched our proofing tome and reference books in the hopes of finding something we had missed. Jov was convinced the poisoning and the attack on the city were linked, and until we had better intelligence about the motivations for this apparent rebellion, the only mystery to which I could put my mind was the murder. But all I had accomplished, besides some thin distraction, was confirmation that we knew nothing of the poison that had killed Etan and the Chancellor.

My brother's initial conclusions were right; none of the known poisons could have produced the symptoms Thendra presented in her report. This poison was corrosive but incorporated some kind of pain-numbing component, like maidenbane, and left no trace in the vomit or excrement. Unlike maidenbane, though, it was capable of killing in a single dose and sufficiently odorless and tasteless to have gone undetected in Etan's food. The only two single-dose, fatal undetectable poisons in our book were rare and complex substances that hadn't been used on a person in all of Silasta's recorded history, and both caused immediate and dramatic symptoms. Nothing fit. Whatever had felled our uncle was outside our knowledge.

Jovan emerged immaculate with his habitual air of precision and symmetry, but for the puffiness and scabs from his still-new extended tattoo on one arm. We drank our tea swiftly and without ritual at the table, beside the food prepared last night and meticulously laid out ready for Tain. Even after the night he'd had, Jov had not neglected his duty.

"Is there a Council meeting?"

He nodded. "Midmorning, if things stay quiet. Gave us all enough time for some rest. I don't think the army will wait long to attack again; the longer they give us, the more time we'll have to build defensive weapons and get organized."

"I read Halka's account of the great siege of Katan last night." Katan was once an independent southwestern city state, now part of the Talafar Empire, famously attacked by the now-dispersed warrior clans of Bari for three straight months. Halka was a scholar who had survived it and immigrated to Silasta. Thankfully, she had learned our written language and published in it; I would never have made it through the tome with my Talafan. "No weapons broke its walls, but they'd have been starved out if the Empire hadn't arrived when it did." The book had been a sobering read, with its tales of internal rioting and disease. The Bari clans hadn't realized how close Katan had come to destroying itself while they waited outside. "Without the harvests, we don't have the food to hold out for three months."

"We won't have to," he said. "Aven will be back long before then. Within days, we can hope. We just need to sit tight."

"And protect Tain," I added, handing the parcel of prepared food to him as he tied his paluma.

He nodded, grave. "I think this engages Etan's rules of coincidence. The poisoning and the rebellion are connected; I just don't know yet whether Tain's in danger or if it was only an attempt to destabilize us before they attacked. No one poisoned Tain, and he was there at that luncheon right along with Caslav."

"But he wasn't meant to be," I pointed out. "You turned up days early. The Chancellor basically forced Tain to go so he could berate him—no one was expecting him." To that reassuring thought, I added, "And poison isn't the only way to get to him. He has servants who can protect him from direct attacks, but can we trust them?"

We shared an uneasy look. We were under siege, apparently from our own people; it was hardly unthinkable that they might have agents working in service roles in the cities.

"Until we figure out what's going on, we can't do much about that," Jov said, but he looked uncomfortable. "One of us should be with Tain as much as possible. Speaking of which, I'd better get to the Manor."

I let him go, finished my almost-cold tea, then slipped out myself. I too wanted to go to the Manor, but for a different purpose. I couldn't attend a Council meeting, fight in a battle, or protect Tain from poison, but I had my own skills, and perhaps they were more suited to finding an enemy than even my brother's. Someone had poisoned the leksot as well as the Chancellor, whether to falsely divert suspicion to the Talafan noble—I stopped suddenly, realizing Lord Ectar was probably still under guard at the Manor; had someone even told him what was happening?—or to disguise the murder as an accident. But Jov had taken the leksot to the Manor straight from the lunch, which meant either the poisoner had dosed the animal earlier as part of a plan, or he or she had gained access to it at the Manor.

Rather than follow my brother's path up the great drive and to the main entrance, I took the back roads around to the servants' entrance. The Manor had three wings: the servants' wing, which contained the kitchens, laundries, and living quarters for the Chancellor's household staff; the official business wing, containing the Council chambers, library, meeting and entertaining rooms, and the gardens; and the private wing, with the living rooms for the Chancellor and his or her family. The servants' entrance, normally bustling with deliveries and activity, was closed up, eerily quiet.

The door was latched but opened to my tentative knock. A pockmarked man asked my business, rudely at first and then with greater deference when his gaze caught my tattoos. "Chancellor's business to the main entrance, Credola," he told me, confused. His crooked teeth made a whistling sound when he spoke.

"I need to examine all access points to the Manor," I told him, trying to sound official. I pushed in, channeling someone more confident than myself as I breezed past. "We're in a siege, man. We need to know how secure every building is if the city is stormed. And we might be facing thefts of food or supplies in the meantime. Who can get in here?"

He scurried after me. "Well, we take deliveries here, Credola. And anyone with a Manor chit could come through, of course. But the Chancellor stood down most of the staff because of the emergency; it's only the kitchen on today." A hum of noise and the spicy smell of baking fish wafted out as we passed the kitchen entrance.

"What about access to the other wings? Where's the internal connection?"

He gestured ahead to a door at the top of a short set of steps. "The connecting passage is through there, Credola. It is always locked. The duty servant for the day only gives keys to staff assigned in the personal and business wings. All keys are returned at the end of the shift."

I examined the door casually. Locked, as he said; nothing so sophisticated that it would be impenetrable to a skilled lockpick, but nothing that could be done too quickly, either.

According to the head cook in Lazar's kitchen, none of the staff had been excused for a break all afternoon. Even if someone had slipped out unnoticed, it would have been difficult to come in through this normally busy area unseen, or to get through into the Manor proper without authorization. I supposed it was possible that servants working together, one in the Manor and one in Lazar's, could have managed it, but if one of the Manor servants with access to the Chancellor's personal wing was involved, why bother to poison Caslav at Lazar's? There would have been easier opportunities in his own home.

I thanked the confused servant still trailing me, and retraced my steps
back to the road. Stopping beside the gates to rub my aching wrists, I
looked up at the main entrance. If the poisoner hadn't come in through the
servants' wing, there was really only one other option.

Argo had kept the front entrance of the Manor for the better part of five
decades. His heavily lined and folded face seemed perpetually stuck in a
solemn frown, and his movements had a slow, fluttery quality that called
to mind a moth. He sat at his usual post by the door as if nothing had
changed.

"Credola Kalina," he said. "Have you come to see the Chancellor? The
Council meeting is still going, I'm afraid."

"No," I said. "I've come to see you, Argo."

His mouth dropped open a little, showing the gaps in his teeth, and his
eyebrows rose.

"I was hoping you'd be able to help me. You keep a log of everyone who
comes to the Manor, don't you?"

He nodded. "I record all comings and goings, unless I'm otherwise instructed by the Chancellor."

"And you always keep it? What about nighttime?" It seemed stupid to
ask, but I needed to be thorough. I'd never seen anyone but him at the
entrance.

"I've a room behind here," he huffed, gesturing to a door. "If anyone but
the Chancellor wants admission after I lock up, they have to ring the bell
and wake me."

A great tome rested beneath Argo's closed fists. "Do you think I could
take a look?"

He stared, hands frozen on the book, dark eyes suspicious. His protectiveness decided me; this was a time for honesty, not deception. "I need to
know everyone who was in the Manor the day Chancellor Caslav died," I
said. "You're the only one who knows that. Please, Argo. It's important."

A long silence, then Argo slid the tome across the desk to me. "Wasn't
like any sickness I've ever seen," he said, so quietly I barely heard it. Our
gazes met before he dropped his and resumed his usual impassive expression.

Argo's neat handwriting recorded orderly lines of dates, names, and even purposes in the well-kept book. I turned the stiff pages back three days. I skimmed through the times, my finger lingering on my uncle's name for a moment.

The list of visitors between the time Jov had brought the leksot to the Manor until the time when the Chancellor had shown symptoms and rumors had begun flowing around the city was longer than I'd expected. It included accountants, the librarian, and Thendra the physic, all before the time I had found the leksot. I looked for names of people who had been at the lunch: there was Jov, bringing the leksot; the Chancellor returning from lunch; later Etan and Jovan again; and me. But interspersed were other Councilors: Credo Bradomir for a meeting with Caslav in the early afternoon; Credola Varina, the Theater-Guilder, to inspect the indoor theater for the upcoming concert for the Chancellor's birthday celebrations. My own Guild leader, the Scribe-Guilder Budua, had met with Caslav's personal scribe, and both Marco and Eliska had separately visited the library. Credo Javesto had "sought the Theater-Guilder on personal business."

Six Councilors had been in the Manor the afternoon of Caslav and Etan's deaths with enough time to have poisoned the leksot. I looked back down the list. Each notation included the arrival and exit time. The longest visits had been Marco and Eliska, then Budua and Bradomir. My gaze lingered over Javesto's name. He had been in the Manor only a short time, and had left with the Theater-Guilder. So he had, as claimed, met up with Varina. Still, a conveniently vague reason for a visit.

I borrowed paper from Argo and made some quick notes. "Thank you," I said, smiling at the old man. I clutched the paper to my chest. Its insubstantial weight belied its contents. It might not have the answer we needed, yet, but it was a step forward. "I'm going to go to the library now," I told him.

"I hope you find what you're looking for, Credola," Argo said.

I did pay a short call to the library; the librarian was absent, but I found a Talafar history book worth investigating—the Empire had been involved in several sieges over the past few centuries, and there might be something of value to learn in there. But soon after I was nestled up in my spy hole above the Council chamber. Jov would report everything that happened, of course, but this gave me the chance to observe the Councilors myself, and I wanted to do so armed with my new knowledge about who had had direct access to the leksot and to the Chancellor that day.

They had converted the great Council table into a giant map. Chalk lines on the surface marked out the two halves of Silasta, separated by the lake in the center and the whole circumference surrounded by walls. Both bridges—Bell's to the south at the river mouth and Trickster's to the north at the marshes—were indicated, as well as the road and river gates and their accompanying towers. Remains of the old fortifications on the east side of the lake had also been set out, though those walls had been largely dismantled after the city expanded and only the Finger, the tower at the east side of Trickster's Bridge, remained of the old west wall.

Lighter chalk marks divided the rough circle of Silasta into wedge-shaped sectors, each marked with a family or guild symbol. The Oromani symbol lay over a section of the upper city on the north side.

The mood in the chamber was somber. I had missed the inevitable bickering that must have accompanied the division of sectors, but after listening for a while Marco's plan became apparent. Each Councilor would be responsible for an area of town and a section of the walls, with the Order Guards and messengers split between the sectors to help coordinate the defense of that area. Citizens would be allocated to each sector to ensure each had enough bodies patrolling the walls and preparing weapons and machinery.

"With careful management of our food and weapons, we can withstand this siege," Marco said. He looked too big, perched on the edge of the Council chair as though he couldn't settle into the plush furnishings. He sweated under the scrutiny of the rest of the Councilors.

"And then what happens?" Credola Nara asked, scowling. Was there extra venom in her tone? Her family hated Tain's. For a short period the Ash family had been the ruling family, but it had been decimated by the sleeping sore sickness and thereafter had such a dearth of female heirs that its very survival had been in doubt. The Council had voted the Iliri family back to the Chancellery generations ago, but I saw the way she looked hungrily at the chair Tain now occupied.

"Our army will come back, hopefully within days, and theirs will be trapped between Warrior-Guilder Aven and our walls," Tain said. "At which point they may be inclined to honor a peace flag and negotiate."

Credo Lazar scoffed. "Why would we bother? Let Aven crush them and be done with it." He seemed to have regained some of his diminished confidence.

"I agree," Eliska said, vehement. She rubbed the back of her neck with one hand as she spoke. "They're either invaders or traitors to their own country."

Several other Councilors nodded or murmured agreement. Javesto caught my attention, tightening his lips and following the conversation in silence, his eyes expressive. Something lay beyond the surface there. If this really was a rebellion, was Javesto's recent ascension to the Council part of some broader plan? He had grown up outside Silasta, after all, and was the only Councilor to have done so other than Marco. His excuse to visit the Manor on that fateful afternoon had also been the weakest.

"If we can spare more bloodshed, on either side, that's the best outcome," Tain said.

"*Pah!* If we wipe out the treacherous lot, *that's* the best outcome," Nara said.

Javesto shrugged. "And who do you suppose will work our estates and grow our food then, Credola Nara? I know you're in excellent condition for your age, but I can tell you I don't particularly want to farm my own lands, that's for certain." The image of the extravagantly dressed Credo tending a field garnered a few awkward laughs.

"Warrior-Guilder, what about the food rationing? Shall we coordinate a central distribution to ration stations?"

As talk moved on to food management, I gazed about the room, noting who agreed with whom, who stayed silent, who deferred to Tain, and who hesitated. Tain wielded greater control than he had the other day, but still the Families jostled to be seen to "guide" him. I caught both Budua and Marjeta, the Scribe and Artist Guilders, glancing at Jovan when Tain emphasized that all Silastians, including the Council and the Families, should partake in the rationing. Caslav had eaten in private as much as possible, but events like that last fatal lunch had always been a challenge to secrecy.

There was no telling who might have noticed Etan and Caslav's relationship, and drawn inferences. If the poisoner knew Jovan was more than just a close friend and adviser to Tain, we had lost one of our biggest advantages. Of course, Budua and Marjeta might simply have glanced at my brother by chance. I doubted someone of Marjeta's legendary warmth and gentleness could be a murderer, and she and Budua had been lovers for so long it was hard to imagine one being involved without the other.

I blinked. Talk had moved on and I had lost it.

". . . would help if you could arrange access for me," Tain was saying, his dark gaze fixed on the Scribe-Guilder.

Budua tightened her spidery lips and shrugged. "Of course, Honored Chancellor," she said. "However, the city has never been under siege, so I can't imagine why a previous Council would have had any useful discussions."

"We didn't start out as a peaceful people," Tain reminded her. "Our ancestors were warriors, and they built this city expecting resistance. I can't imagine everyone took kindly to us settling here and securing the best trade route in the continent. There must have been extensive conversations about defense from the Council in our early history."

Budua lifted her shoulders again.

"In any case, I wish to review them," Tain said, and this time he used his best Chancellor voice.

"As you will, Honored Chancellor," Budua said. "I will arrange for you to be shown the archives when it is convenient." She glanced at Marjeta, and when she moved one hand from the tabletop it left a tiny smear of sweat behind. I wondered what was in those records to cause her nervousness, and my earlier confidence about Budua and Marjeta's involvement evaporated.

Tain checked the position of the sun through the dome roof. "It's time we were back to our tasks," he said. "Thank you all."

Budua and Marjeta hurried out first. Varina and Lazar trailed after, both looking absent. Eliska, Marco, and Pedrag conversed as they left, each Guilder clasping a sheet of notes. Nara pushed through them all, elbows flared like a rude patron seeking the front row at the theater. Bradomir walked close by Tain, his ringed hands flashing expressively. Javesto stepped after Tain, reaching toward the Chancellor's shoulder, his breath held as if steeling himself. But he dropped the hand before it reached Tain, and instead left, his head bent.

Jovan and the other Councilors spent the better part of the day in their own sectors, sorting out tasks and allocating responsibilities within their own little structures. I'd only had short moments with my brother and Tain after the Council meeting to share the list of names.

"Someone poisoned the leksot for a reason," I said. "Lord Ectar had no reason to do it; it only increases suspicion over him. So either someone is working with a member of your household or administrative staff, or someone on this list is the poisoner."

"I agree," Jov said. "I suspect the poisoner saw the leksot on the Chancellor and took the opportunity to cover their tracks. It either looks like an innocent accident or a convenient visiting noble is blamed. Much easier than dealing with the aftermath of a poisoning."

"So you're saying someone on my own Council killed my uncle? And is working with the army out there?"

"There were a few administrative staff at the Manor that afternoon, too. Accountants, a scribe, the librarian. They weren't at the lunch, but they could be working with one of Lazar's staff, or could have been paid by someone to poison the leksot. But, yes, I think you shouldn't trust your Council."

Tain looked unconvinced. "I know this is your family's job, but maybe you're overthinking this. What on earth would a Councilor have to gain from a rebellion? The Credolen have already probably lost family members out on the estates. This isn't just a power scramble within the city. People are going to get killed, on both sides. Have already been."

It was true that the idea of, say, Bradomir working with ordinary workers and farmers to overthrow a system from which he benefited lavishly was absurd. And though Tain detested the man, he had been a strong ally of Caslav's for decades. "The Families have all got trade relationships with other countries," Jov said, as if in answer to my thought. "Who's to say that hasn't developed into some more sinister alliance? Or someone could have been blackmailed; we all have family and property in the other cities and on the estates that could have been used as leverage."

Tain rubbed his forehead and sighed. "I love you both, you know that. And I know you're looking out for my best interests. But listen, Lini, Jov, I've got to defend the city. I can't be dredging through my advisers or trying to solve a mystery here. We're all stuck in the city together and it's in all our interests to get out of this siege alive, so can I just concentrate on that?"

"Forgive me, Tain, but no," Jovan said firmly. "Sieges have been lost because of internal traitors." He gestured to the book in my hand. "The Talafan lost a northern border city sixty years ago because someone inside poisoned the wells."

Tain shifted about uncomfortably on the cushion. "Then I'm leaving that part of it to you, all right? I trust you two, I won't trust anyone else completely, but I have to be able to run the defenses without second-guessing everything I'm told."

I wanted to argue. Tain always thought the best of people; it was a great strength and an equally great weakness. I recognized the stress in his expression and Jov must have, too; unspoken, we dropped the subject. But I worried for him.

The afternoon light turned golden, splashing over the white azikta stone buildings like gilt paint, and the warm glow made my eyelids heavy. There had been no further attacks. All day we had waited uneasily for any sign that the army would strike again, but perhaps they needed time to build weaponry. I'd alternated between further research of sieges and performing odd jobs in the Oromani sector. I couldn't operate machinery or transport heavy goods, but I could help coordinate people and send messages easily enough. When I mentioned to my brother that I might try training with the archery groups Marco was assembling, he gave me a blistering lecture about triggering a relapse. I blanked out, the picture of meekness, all the while thinking how to time my attendance to avoid my overprotective brother. Archery, after all, required strength, but not the same kind of sustained energy as other martial areas.

Late in the afternoon, I sought out the Theater-Guilder, Credola Varina, finding her at the expansive Leka family apartments she shared with her cousin Bradomir. A younger family member let me in and directed me to a sitting room where Varina talked with a young Order Guard, marking items off a list. She glanced up with narrowed eyes. Like a smooth, elegant reptile, she wore the deepening lines of her advancing age with grace.

"I've sent a whole group to act as the Chancellor's runners, if you've come to remind me," she said, brusque. "But that's the last lot—Marco's given me enough to do with my little population here as it is."

I addressed the Order Guard, keeping my tone polite. "May I have a moment with the Theater-Guilder?"

"Of course, Credola," he said, but he waited upon Varina's sharp nod before he left. I settled myself down at the table.

"This isn't about runners," I said. "I'm trying to get some information."

Varina stiffened. "About what, dear?" She pretended to consult the list in her hands. Up close, she looked peaky; her eyes and nose were red, as if she'd been crying, and her face looked thinner than usual.

"The day the Chancellor died," I said. She looked up, eyes widening. I'd surprised her—whatever she had worried about me asking, it wasn't this. "You were at the Manor. . . ."

"What of it?" Defensiveness made her drop her manners. I made my tone more conciliatory.

"While you were there, did someone else come to see you?"

She sniffed, indelicately wiping her nose. "I don't . . . Oh, yes. Credo Javesto found me when I was looking over the theater. It was something silly, I can't remember. . . . No, that's right. His niece was desperate for a part in one of the autumn plays, and he was trying to get me to talk to the producer." She tossed back her hair. "I told him no, naturally. You can't interfere with the artistic vision."

"Of course," I murmured. So Javesto had indeed sought her out, but not about anything urgent. He could have made an appointment at the Guild-hall, or asked her at the lunch, without needing to get into the Manor.

"What does it matter? What has Javesto's niece got to do with any-thing, and since when is my Guild your business? You work for Budua, don't you?"

Her confidence was back, but the rudeness remained. The arrogant curl of her pretty bow mouth and the tilt of her jaw grated like sand in my shoes. "Of course," I said, ducking my head and allowing myself to look younger, embarrassed. "It's only that the Chancellor is thinking of releasing Lord Ectar, you know, the Talafan? That unfortunate animal . . . It was *probably* an accident, but he's trying to be sure. And I don't want to spread rumors," I dropped my voice conspiratorially, "but we had heard Credo Javesto is awfully invested in trade with the Empire."

Varina considered me, her face still. "I see."

"It's probably nothing, but we were just trying to account for the Credo's movements that day. Just to be certain. We lost a Chancellor and now this siege. . . ."

"We have a new Chancellor, and he must be protected, I agree," Varina said.

"Please don't say anything to anyone." I tried to sound a little breathless. Easy for me, since it was my natural state half the time. "It would be most indelicate."

"Of course, dear." She settled back in her chair, relaxed again. I dropped from her concern as easily as that.

And just like that it annoyed me, so I pushed a little more. "You know I'm really an admirer of yours, Credola Varina. The productions this summer were some of the best shows I've seen. Oh, I meant to ask. Is that Doranite servant of Credo Lazar's an actor? Jov noticed you talking at a lunch a few days ago and thought he looked rather familiar."

"Just an aspiring one," Varina said, all poise. "Don't you think we have more important things to concentrate on right now?"

The smoothness of her response rang falser than her earlier hesitation. I'd surprised her before; this one she'd been ready for.

"Of course. Thank you for your help. I'll leave you to your work."

Varina sniffed again, and didn't look at me as I left.

Another night of relative safety. No alarm bells or other emergencies. Jovan had already left without waking me; I tried not to feel annoyed about it, but failed. He had come in too late to disturb me last night, too. I suddenly wondered if he had come home at all. I had wanted to show him my sewing efforts from last night, but it would have to wait.

I visited our sector first. It already seemed more organized than yesterday, though I despaired at how young many of the wide-eyed men and women seemed. Too young for their lives to be in jeopardy, not that there was ever an ideal time for that. Chen, our assigned Order Guard, showed me the camp through a spyglass, pointing out their tents and fires.

"We think they're getting supplies carted in," she told me. "See those wagons, there? They arrived overnight. Looks like swords and bows to me."

"From what direction?"

"The west road, least it looks that way."

They were being supplied from somewhere. So much for any hope that this was a hasty and unsupported rebellion. And did this mean West Dortal—the smallest and least defensible of the three border cities—had fallen, if supplies could be so easily brought in? I made my way to the Manor slowly, in deference to my aching joints.

Argo let me through to the private wing; it felt odd walking through unescorted by servants, but all nonessential staff had been assigned other duties. Only those trained to protect Tain remained. My brother let me into Tain's chambers and offered me tea. The playing pieces from a Muse board and other assorted ornaments were set up in formations on a large paper map on the floor, like a great game. Tain, kneeling beside it, looked up and smiled his slow smile. Even in the worst of situations, the force of his warmth turned on me was like the sun on a cold winter day. I smiled back.

"Did you get any sleep, Lini?"

I'd had a little, but not enough to satisfy my brother; I shrugged and changed the subject. "I called by our sector on my way here."

"I'd prefer you stayed away from the walls," Jovan said, frowning.

My breath came out and my frustration rose. I was stronger now than ever before, but my brother couldn't see that, or didn't want to. I started to respond, then took a sip of tea instead. Now wasn't the time to pick a fight.

Instead, I told them what I'd learned about supplies from the west.

Tain pushed a few of the stones representing the army around with one finger. "Do you think it means anything?"

"It means they're being supplied externally. And that they could get weapons in through our borders in quantity." Our neighbors were marked on the paper: Doran to the south, the Talafar Empire to the north, and an assortment of smaller nations past the wetlands to the west: Tocatica, Perest-Avana, Maru, and Costkat, some bordering us and some not. Though we had almost exclusively peaceful relations with our neighbors, Silasta's wealth and trade dominance made us a potential target. The Doranites were a hard, aggressive people, fractious and bound together only loosely by the man who called himself king. Their lack of genuine centralized leadership made it difficult to secure meaningful peace—hence the occasional raid or dispute over resources in the mountains—but likewise it was hard to imagine them staging a siege of an advanced city. Talafar had the resources and organization to plan an attack, but we'd had longstanding and mutually beneficial treaties in place for over a century. I followed Tain's gaze to the west. Doubtless any of the small nations comprising the great western wetlands, who had once shared the trade routes north and south—albeit in a fragmented and inefficient manner—coveted our secure, fast route for themselves. Perhaps they'd put aside eons of conflict and decided to act collectively for once.

Had they seized on grievances from our people that we had failed to notice? Or had the rebellion sought its own supplies from a neighbor who supported the downfall of Sjona's rich capital? We needed to know the causes of this rebellion or we would find no way to undo it.

"Has the intelligence master reported?" Silasta's official spy networks were run by cooperation between the Warrior Guild and my own Administrative Guild. I had no such official role; as far as my Guild knew, my training in diplomacy was never intended to be anything more than that. Etan had only ever wanted me as a private source of information to serve our family's duty and protect the Chancellor. I didn't even know the identity of the intelligence master.

"She'd nothing to offer," Tain said, drawing a chalk line with rather more force than necessary. "We don't spy on our own farms, generally, but no unusual activity has been reported from any sources at all. Some reports due that haven't arrived—but that's not surprising if the rebels have been intercepting messages, or if one of the border cities was taken."

"All of this is connected." Jov traced an idle finger around the rim of the empty bowl beside him. Undistracted by the siege, my brother repeatedly circled back to the poisoning; he felt Etan's failure to protect the Chancellor as his own, and feared he would likewise fail Tain. "This is a planned attack and your uncle was murdered. If we can figure out the why of one, we might find the who of the other. Or the other way around."

"That reminds me," I said. I produced the product of my late-night sewing; two converted old purses, stitched carefully onto bands that could be worn under clothing. Not comparable to a proper Craft-Guilded seamster's work, but I was decent enough with a needle. "I think you should have these with you. You're not going to be able to prepare all of Tain's food, and he won't have the luxury of only eating in your apartments or the Manor."

Jovan was already nodding. He took the connected purses, delving into the small compartments and straps within with obvious interest. "Why two?"

I glanced sideways at Tain. "We can be with you most of the time, but neither of us would be much use in a fight, if someone attacked you directly." Outright violence in Silasta at all, let alone within high society, was so socially unacceptable it was hard to imagine. So many things that had been hard to imagine only weeks before were becoming our new reality.

My brother let his breath out in a hiss, his gaze troubled as he understood my meaning, but he gave me an approving nod. "One for antidotes, one for . . . the opposite."

"If you can be a proofer, you can be a poisoner," I said. After all, our family's secret role had developed for a reason. Once each Family would have had their own secret poisoner, and it was foolish to believe our own ancestors had been too noble to participate actively in the squabbles for leadership. I doubted the proofing role had always been entirely reactive, even if our records spoke only of defense. My gaze dropped to the scars on Jovan's arm; not his only ones, but the most visible. Even if the role of proofer had been a silent and purely defensive one for generations, Etan's experiments had always been wide ranging, and some of our resources could be turned to weapons in an emergency. Jovan knew that, at least intellectually, but he had never harmed anyone with his knowledge before. We were protectors, not assassins. As someone prone to quadruple-guessing and harshly judging his every decision as it was, he might struggle to cope with such a change. But what choice did we have?

Tain looked uncertainly at the pouch. He had always avoided discussing

Jovan's work, and confusion and concern flickered over his face. My brother tucked the pouches away out of sight and by unspoken consent we let the subject fall away.

"Are you going to release Lord Ectar?" I asked.

"I think so." Tain stretched, looking down at Talafar on the map. "He isn't likely to be our poisoner, is he, unless he's hoping he's so obvious a suspect we'd disregard him? And Talafar has ridden to the rescue of besieged cities before. If we're so lucky I wouldn't want to explain why I've got the Emperor's grandson locked in a room in my house."

"We can keep an eye on him as best we can," Jov said. "Assign him to my sector, perhaps—then we can see what he's doing and keep him away from the other Councilors."

Tain let his fingers drift to the outer edges of the map on the model. "I wonder."

"What?"

"What are they doing about the traffic?" He traced his fingers along invisible roads to the city. "Scores of people usually come in and out through the road gates every day. How are the rebels stopping them? If they're turning around when they see the army, word is going to reach outside our borders pretty soon."

"So even if our runners didn't get through . . ." Tain broke off and looked at me, chagrined. "They will, of course," he said. "Edric will be safe."

I avoided his gaze, letting my hair obscure my face. I'd not told them about the short note Edric had left me, not liking the combination of guilt and irritation and worry that uncurled in my stomach when I thought about it. He had a good heart and an entirely unrealistic picture of dear, sweet Kalina, fancying himself heroically caring for such a frail little thing as me. I wished him all the best, but there were only so many times I could take people trying to thrust him into my bed. I raised my chin. "Of course he'll be fine. But while he's away I could use the break from hearing 'Kalina Kalina.'"

Tain laughed, and Jovan's lips twitched even as he gave me a reproachful look. "I didn't realize you'd heard it."

"Who hasn't? He sprang out at me last week with about twenty of his friends from the Performers' Guild to sing the whole thing. And now it's spread—I even heard someone humming it on the wall this morning."

A knock at the door startled us from the momentary levity. Marco stood there, looking oddly cowed for a man his size. He held a sack in one hand and rubbed the other over his head.

"I'm sorry to interrupt, Credola Kalina," he said politely. He came inside and sank into one of the cushions, setting the bag beside him, then cleared his throat and cracked his knuckles as though unsure where to begin. When Jov offered him tea he took it eagerly, twisting the cup around and around in his big hands and sipping far too often. There was something he didn't want to tell us. My heart rate picked up, but still the soldier stayed silent, staring at his tea.

"How are the Builders doing with the new catapults?" Tain prompted.

"Well, I believe, Honored Chancellor. The Stone-Guilder promises they will be sturdier this time, and have better accuracy. However." He cleared his throat again. "I have some new information about our enemies." He fell into silence again, and I tensed with frustration. Tain, ever the most patient of the three of us, set down his teacup and cleared his throat politely. As if waking from a momentary stupor, Marco shook his head and continued. "The army appears to be constructing siege weaponry as well, and is being supplied with materials and weapons by boat and by road. It appears they will not be attempting to merely wait us out."

Tain nodded. "They can't know how long Aven will be, and they can't risk being trapped between our walls and our army. They have to attack soon. What else?"

"We received a communication from them in the night."

We all sat forward. Blood pounded in my ears—at last, some indication of what they wanted?—but no relief showed on Marco's face.

"A single man left it outside the west gate. I sent one of ours over the wall in a harness to collect it—I had thought it might be a trap to trick us into opening the gates." He opened the sack tucked away beside him and re-trieved a folded green cloth; our hasty peace flag, now crusted dark with the emissary's blood. The smell of old metal filled the back of my throat. Jovan hastily moved the teacups as Marco settled the fabric on the table and un-folded it with slow, precise movements until it took up the entire surface.

They had written on the unmarked side, angry bold words in our own written language, setting out our sins.

"*No peace for murderers*," I read, my voice sounding squeaky and shrill. "*No peace for the unfaithful. No peace for spirit killers. The rotten city will fall and the*—what does that say? *The* something *will be restored*?" I squinted at the mark I didn't recognize in the last line. It was not a word, but a symbol of some kind.

"I do not know," Marco said. "I have been in your country for nearly twenty years and still I cannot read your language well."

"It's not in our language." Unlike Trade, or Talafan, or the various related wetlander tongues, written Sjon bore no relationship to spoken; the latter was the oral language spoken by modern Sjona's tribal ancestors, the former the written language brought by refugees over the Howling Plains from Crede—including my great-great-however-many-times grand-mother. The assimilation of the two peoples over time meant Sjona effectively had two entirely disconnected languages, one verbal and one written. And the symbol in that final sentence on the crumpled flag was not ours.

"Could it be a religious symbol of some kind, I wonder?" Its shape looked vaguely familiar, like something on a festival costume or a Darfri shrine. "Spirits, unfaithful . . . it does seem to fit."

"What does that *mean*? *Spirit killers*? *Murderers*? What are they talking about?" Tain, rubbing his forehead, read the flag over and over. "It doesn't make sense."

Only then did I notice Marco's silent, grim face, and my hand shook as it touched Jov's shoulder to get his attention. He followed my gaze. "Marco?" my brother asked, his whole body going still even as mine shook harder. "What else?"

Marco dropped his gaze. "The flag was not the only message." He picked up the dark cloth sack, still hanging heavy with unseen contents, and slowly held it out toward Tain. "Please . . . I know this is upsetting, Honored Chancellor, but I believe you need to see this."

My lungs drained of air and my eyes burned, as Tain, stricken, opened the sack, the size and shape of which I abruptly and unwillingly recognized. He winced and looked away. Jovan took one quick glance, his face tightly controlled, and slowly met my gaze with a small shake of his head. I opened my mouth but nothing came out. My head spun.

"I'm afraid that no word will be reaching our own army," Marco said quietly. "That is the second part of their message. They know we tried, and they are showing us that we failed. There were five other examples, Honored Chancellor."

"The runners?" Tain whispered, and at Marco's tense nod he pressed his hands into his face. I tried to swallow and found my throat too dry. Tain gestured sharply and Marco closed the sack, slipping it under the table again. Though hidden from my view, its dark presence still radiated like a baleful spirit. My head spun as the horror and enormity sank in. I couldn't get my breath.

"They did this to all our runners?" Tain's voice was a pale echo of its normal timbre, but as he spoke his words came out faster and faster. "*Why*? Why would they do something so monstrous? I think I'm going to be sick. They could have just captured them. Why would they do this? What am I going to say to their families?"

Everything seemed to be swirling around me in a very faint haze. Was I breathing? I couldn't remember how to make my lungs work. What *could* Tain tell their families? He could not possibly show them these remains. Silastians might no longer be terribly observant of the old religion, but respect for our dead was something that bound us all together no matter what. To do . . . what had been done, was to dismember a person's very essence so that they could not travel safely beyond. It was a deeply dishonorable, cruel act.

Jovan, still motionless, swallowed hard. He looked at Marco. "But who . . . ?" His eyes trailed back to the grim sack. "I thought I recognized him, but that wasn't one of our runners."

Marco sighed. "He was one of our spies along the south border. I doubt you had met him, Credo, but the best spies have the most ordinary and familiar of faces. I have no involvement in our spy network, so I was as confused as you to find a stranger among our runners. The intelligence master identified him, though. He had failed to report in for some weeks. She suspects he may have learned of and infiltrated the rebellion but been discovered." Marco inclined his head. "I chose the . . . what I just showed you, because I remembered that you knew some of the runners personally and I did not want you to see a familiar face."

Jov squeezed my shoulder gently before answering. "Thank you. We appreciate that." Oh, by the fortunes, he'd gotten there before me. If possible, everything grew darker still, and like Tain I suddenly wanted to vomit. Poor persistent, daft, likeable Edric, with his head in a bag somewhere. I couldn't bear it. I tried to stand up and almost fell, but pulled away from Jovan when he tried to comfort me. I suddenly couldn't handle the thought of anyone touching me. Tears blurred my vision. Without looking at anyone, I turned and fled.

Hazelnode

DESCRIPTION: Brown growth on rocks in particular conditions that hardens into glossy circular formations which can be removed and crushed into a toxic paste.

SYMPTOMS: Intense abdominal cramping, diarrhea, severe internal bleeding, eventual collapse and death.

PROOFING CUES: Taste is strongly metallic and lingering, smell faintly fishy.

5

Jovan

The news sucked what optimism we'd had away in one powerful stroke. Back to the beginning, only now we had fewer options, and less hope. Whenever I paused in any task, my brain tortured me with the faces of the runners we'd sent to their doom. They had died, alone and afraid, murdered by their own people in the most brutal, dishonorable way. Had it been my fault? Had I let them out too soon, or too late? Should we have opted for secrecy rather than distraction? We'd gambled, and they had paid for the mistake.

"We need to try again, sooner rather than later," I told Tain. We waited in the Manor for Bradomir and Lazar, Tain still ashen but composed, me pacing and counting my steps in my head in equal sets of eight. Kalina hadn't returned and though I worried for her, part of me was relieved. I had no words of comfort for her. "We can't hold the city indefinitely, especially if they're building siege weapons."

Not to mention that there remained danger to Tain within the city. I patted my paluma, feeling the weight of my new purses disguised under the folds, and accessible through an unpicked slit. I'd diverted to our apart-ments and filled one with a selection of general antidotes and treatments, from simple charcoal and vinegar to zensu shell paste and river snake scale powder. The other now bore more dangerous fare: hazelnode powder, Malek's acid, lavabulb seeds, and flare oil. Things I could use quickly in defense if necessary. At least one enemy was still in the city with us, and I'd not be caught without options, if it came to it. I wondered if my ancestors, back in more treacherous times, had carried such things with them as a matter of course.

I'd had to quiet the new worries this raised inside me. New situations called for new behaviors, I told myself, and if the core of our responsibility was to protect the Chancellor, was I not better to do so by more actively preventing harm from coming to him? After all, I was not proposing to use my tools like an assassin would, sneaking about to harm others in secret. I would just be providing one more kind of shield, one more layer to my duty. Duty and honor were everything. If I couldn't meet my responsibili-ties, then what good was I to those I loved?

Tain let out his breath in a huff of air and gazed at me with the wounded expression of an animal kicked to the side of the road. "Are you joking? After what happened? I'm not risking anyone else that way. If I'd known what would happen if they were caught I wouldn't have allowed it in the first place."

We had no time to discuss it further, as Bradomir and Lazar soon joined us, their manners somewhere between concern and smugness that they had been called privately.

Tain wasted no time, thanking them for coming and speaking plainly. "I'm afraid it doesn't appear any of our messengers made it through." The Credolen sucked in their breath—genuine surprise, I thought. "Which means we can't assume help is on its way." We had decided not to reveal the de-tails of how the runners had died. The truth would bring nothing but grief and turmoil to the families, and since presumably the army outside had wanted their brutal act to raise terror among our people, we would not give them that satisfaction. Marco had promised to arrange a private and respect-ful burial for the remains.

Bradomir stroked his moustache. "And they have cut off our supplies, so we cannot afford to wait here indefinitely."

"We must send out more messengers." Lazar looked between us, his voice edged with wildness. "At once!"

"They're waiting for us to do it," I said.

"Surely we could slip some men over the walls in the dark?"

"We will find a way of getting help," Tain said. "No matter how widespread this rebellion, they can't have taken all of our border cities. Very soon I'm confident the siege will be noticed and word sent to our army. In the meantime we have to buckle down and hold our defenses. I need to try to communicate with the army out there, to find out if we can negotiate our way out of this." He leaned in closer. "I have a few favors to ask. First, can you check with your household staff whether you have any Darfri believers? I want to find out more about how that's tied into the rebellion, but I don't know enough. You two have the two biggest staffs in the city. Can you send me someone to help?"

"Of course, Honored Chancellor," Bradomir said, and Lazar echoed the same.

"Second, can you use your contacts, any of the merchants you deal with, to find out if there is any way to get in and out of the city undetected?"

When both men looked guarded, Tain laughed. "I'm not stupid. I'm aware smuggling goes on. Not that I'm accusing either of you of profiting from it, of course."

"I can certainly ask some of my people to look into it," Bradomir said, inclining his head politely.

"I'll have an answer for you by the end of the day," Lazar boasted. "I know the merchants of this city, Honored Chancellor." The poor man practically salivated in his eagerness to impress Tain.

"Much honor to the both of you, then," Tain said. "I appreciate your help and your loyalty." He clasped each man by the shoulders.

Lazar caught Tain's arm as he did so. "Honored Chancellor," he said, and his voice quavered, "I must thank *you* for this opportunity to help you. I so desperately want to restore my family's honor and your trust in me. I was so ashamed it was in my home that Chancellor Caslav . . . that I hosted the man who gave that . . . terrible gift . . ." He seemed to choke on the last few words.

Tain patted him on the shoulder, his face bleak. "I don't doubt your intentions, Credo," he said. "You weren't to know Lord Ectar's gift was dangerous. And your servants did their best to capture it."

I felt cruel watching Lazar supplicate himself, guilt and shame leaching from his pores like sweat. There was no way to comfort the poor man and let him know he had not contributed to Caslav's death, not without admitting it had been poison. We had agreed to tell no one we did not accept the illness theory.

As Tain and I had planned in advance, I walked the two Credolen out of the Manor. The older men seemed unsure how to deal with me; Bradomir in particular alternated between condescension and flattery, making it clear he did not respect me but was willing to pretend to do so in order to ingratiate himself into Tain's closest circle.

"You mentioned Lord Ectar, Credo Lazar," I said as I escorted them through the grounds. "I wanted your opinion on something, as two of the most learned statesmen on the Council." My attempt at flattery seemed clumsy and transparent to me, but both men puffed up at the compliment. "The Honored Chancellor doesn't think he has cause to hold him, and Lord Ectar is understandably frantic at being confined and unable to follow what is happening in the city."

Bradomir, settling with relish into the role of trusted adviser, nodded. "He is a well-connected fellow. It could have political ramifications."

Lazar wrung his hands. "I do believe it was a horrible accident only," he said. "But . . . if he were such a villain as to deliberately gift an infected creature to the Chancellor, how can we be safe with him loose in the city?"

"I agree, it's a risk," I said. "And certainly I—and the Chancellor—would be more comfortable if trustworthy eyes were on Lord Ectar, if he were free."

Both men nodded vigorously.

"We trust the two of you," I said. "But some Councilors have very strong relationships in Talafar, and I'm just not sure they would be quite so capable of being objective."

Bradomir frowned. "I, too, would be cautious." He paused. "We cannot overlook the timing of our beloved Chancellor being attacked only days before the city itself. I would never suggest anyone from the Families would be involved directly in any kind of plot, but there have been . . . *interesting* . . . words spoken in defense of these traitors. Credo Javesto . . ." He trailed off delicately.

"Just so," I agreed. "I don't like to suspect anyone, least of all fellow Councilors from the honored Families, but we're vulnerable here."

"You can count on me, Credo Jovan," Lazar said, wetting his plump lips and bowing his head. "I would sooner forsake my family's fortunes and honor than betray our city or our country."

"Likely I'm being overcautious, and the rest of the Council shares our dedication. But until we can be certain, can we count on you to say nothing of this to anyone else? Just if you happen to observe any . . . odd behavior from Lord Ectar or from any of your fellow Councilors . . . ?"

"Of course," Bradomir said. "I will take an active interest in the activities of my colleagues."

Lazar's head bobbed. "You can rely on us."

I watched them go, wondering if we had done the right thing. Bradomir had been right near the Chancellor at the lunch, and had visited the Manor later according to Kalina's list. But he owned half the city; it was just impossible to imagine he could be involved with a rebellion from our common workers. Still, I did not trust him.

A crowd of petitioners, ever present outside the Manor, called out to the Credolen as they tried to leave, and Bradomir hastily urged his waiting handservant to prepare his litter. One of the petitioners, though, a tall woman in gray, focused her attention not on the two men struggling into the litter but me. I looked back, disconcerted by the intensity of her gaze, but she made no move to approach. This new world of being a Councilor and being recognized widely outside my normal circles was unsettling. Given she seemed only interested in watching, not calling out or crossing the street, I turned to return to Tain.

But the faint blast of a distant horn made me pause, and then the warning bells tolled, first in the distance and then closer as all of the watchtowers picked up the signal. It could only have one meaning. The army was attacking again.

It had come without warning. One minute the attackers seemed at ease, the next a wedge of them had charged out of the falling afternoon sun. The woman reporting this to me sweated in her ill-fitting armor and gulped mouthfuls of air between sentences. A week ago she'd probably never seen violence of any kind. I listened, shoving a pointed helmet on my own head while someone buckled a resin-hardened plate around my chest, unable to pretend I was any less scared than she.

The sun had been in our sentries' eyes, and none had noticed the ladders until the army had rushed across most of the gap. They had simply emerged, rising from the ranks like magic.

"We've sounded the alarms, but it's mad up there," the woman said, her voice high and shaking. "They're coming up the ladders so fast." Pulse drumming in my head, I accepted the sword handed to me and joined the stream of makeshift defenders scurrying up the stairs onto the wall.

The walls were a press of bodies and fear. We weren't soldiers, only ordinary men and women poorly armed, clotted together in a panic, clutching swords or daggers or firing bows over the walls.

Rebels swarmed like insects up a tree, protecting themselves from our arrows and pitch with small bucklers strapped to their arms. The sight of them so close, so determined, sent my stomach churning in a wash of cold fear. They still wore veils, and it gave their faces a frightening, sinister air. I could face being poisoned a hundred times over this. Though our precious arrows flew like rain in a windstorm, few seemed to hit their targets. I pushed away from the parapet to make room for an archer and headed into the press above the nearest ladder. My hand, wrapped around the hilt of the unfamiliar sword, felt hot and weak.

In the thick of clumsy, desperate fighting it was hard to see through the crowd, but as many attackers seemed to be scrambling over the wall as were stopped. The horrible sound of screams as rebels fell or were pushed from the walls rang through my ears. The man in front of me staggered to his knees, crying out, and a sword thrust toward me. I leaped back and to the side, just avoiding the blade, and stabbed forward. Only as I pulled back my strike did I realize with shock that it had found its mark. Our eyes met. He looked as surprised as me, and as scared. Then he collapsed to his knees on top of the fallen Silastian.

My throat clenched and my stomach turned over. I'd killed someone. Blood rushed in my ears but there was no time to think before someone jostled me from behind and I stumbled over the bodies toward the wall. A clumsy attempt at a block earned me a burning slice on my arm. The big

Silastian to my right hacked my attacker's arm clean off with a huge axe blow, and the blood spurted over me in a sickening burst of red and the overpowering metallic smell of blood. A mass of bodies surrounded me, screaming, shoving, with seemingly no direction or focus to the attack.

Stumbling forward again, I found myself at the wall, faced with a rebel scrambling over the edge. I met his howling lunges with slow and unresponsive arms, my breath in short gasps. Somehow I blocked one strike after another, then our swords came together and mine slipped down into the man's chest. He fell, nearly taking my sword with him, and I couldn't look down at his body.

Panting, I slashed at anything trying to come over the wall; an emerging arm, legs, a questing hand—trying not to think of the people to whom the appendages were attached. I drove the butt of my sword into the face of another attacker as she tried to vault up. They had the advantage of numbers but our positioning was strong; it should have been easy to stop the climbers or to dislodge the tops of the ladders and tip them. But in the mad cluster and overpowering noise, the rebels kept managing to get over. Everything was so close it was hard to distinguish between Silastian and rebel, especially since in the close quarters of battle veils were torn or had fallen from their faces, making it all too obvious that we fought our own people.

I found myself caught between foes—my right arm entangled with one woman, our shortswords locked together, my left shoving back a man with an arm and a knee up on the edge of the parapet and a long knife in his free hand. I wavered, my attention split, panic choking me, until someone else shoved into the woman and knocked her away from me. I pulled my arm free and spun back, throwing my weight against my left forearm to tip the climber back over.

I was already turning to find another opponent when a sudden tug knocked me off my feet and my body was jerked like a puppet to the wall. My hip smashed into the stone and my feet bounced off the ground. Nausea, dizziness, then sheer terror took over; my attacker had latched on to my arm and dragged me with him, over the edge. Light and sky and stone and ground spun in my vision as I plummeted.

Sheer luck saved me. I tumbled into another climber and the impact, hard enough to knock the wind out of me, broke the speed of my fall. Tangled together, both of us managed to wrap limbs around parts of the ladder, crying out as desperate, grasping hands lost skin in the attempt. I squeezed my knees around the side of it and clung, upside down, but lacked a decent purchase. I half-fell, half-slid down the rest of the ladder and landed on my side, dazed. But not dead.

At least not yet. A glint of steel flashed in the corner of my eye and I rolled instinctively away as a sword smashed into the spot I'd vacated—which was the body of the man who had fallen with me, I realized with horror. Gasping for breath, I scrambled to my feet and backed away from my assailant as he pulled his sword from the body. My own weapon was long gone. He rushed at me and I dodged, clumsy and dizzy, barely avoiding his lunge and almost tripping over yet another body. He was much bigger than me but looked, from the way he held his sword, as uncomfortable with its use as I'd been. His veil had fallen around his neck and his face was twisted with hatred. The image of the head in the sack flashed before me, and for a second fear paralyzed me. People who could do that to a messenger were capable of anything. I backed up, scanning the ground. There must be weapons on the bodies scattered about. But even as I ducked to try to pry a knife from a dead man, the swordsman lunged again and I just barely stayed on my feet.

"Heretic!" the man yelled, gesturing toward me with his sword. His cry attracted the attention of several others who peeled off from the throng heading for the ladders and circled around me as I backed toward the wall. They wore little armor. Two wielded farming tools, another a crude spear, the last an axe. "Spirit killer," one spat, and all five advanced, their eyes dark with fury.

Five to one were bad odds even if I'd had a weapon. My helmet had come off; nothing protected me but a leather vest, half-hanging with a broken strap, which would hardly slow down even their farm implements. But my broken armor had given me another option. My hand fumbled through the purse strapped to my side. As the men closed in I spread my arms wide. "Wait!"

They didn't, and neither did I.

I sprang right, lunging toward the man with the spear. He hadn't expected it; his eyes widened and he stumbled backward. Too close for the range of his spear, I used those precious moments to fling the contents of one paper packet at him. He swatted at his eyes, momentarily distracted.

The man beside him caught the spray of an open phial; acid peppered his hands and forearms and he screamed, dropping his axe and spinning backward, shaking his arms like a madman. The first man had rubbed the lavabulb seeds into his eyes in his attempt to clear his face, and as the burn set in I grabbed his spear and pivoted, easily breaking his grip as he fell, blinded and screeching.

The other three edged back, eyes darting between my new weapon and their moaning companions. Suddenly they didn't seem so keen to engage. Spear trained on the swordsman, I edged sideways, the ladder in my peripheral vision. My fingers found the purse again, and as the swordsman charged past my clumsy one-handed spear thrust, I blew the contents of the paper twist at him. He blanched, stumbling enough for me to dodge, but the other rebels came at me at once, and I collected a fiery slash to my upper right arm with a scythe even as I clumsily blocked a hoe, losing my grip on the spear in the process.

The swordsman raised his weapon again, then started to cough, then gasp, then choke. The man with the scythe stared at his companion in horror as he sunk to his knees, clutching at his throat and chest. *"Summoning!"* he hissed, like an accusation, and for a moment I just stared, confusion overwhelming my fear. Then he raised his voice and bellowed, "We need a Speaker!"

Survival instinct took over once again. Whatever they thought I was doing, they feared it. I rummaged in the purse and shook my fist at them menacingly as I edged sideways. I only had flare oil left, and nothing to ignite it. I needed to get to the ladder. My heart pounded so loudly I thought it might be failing before I realized it was not my heart but a real drum somewhere nearby. One of the men glanced over his shoulder just as a figure emerged from the crowds of rebels. Walking deliberately, she was unveiled, face and bare chest streaked with pale mud forming symbols I didn't know, and tailed by a child beating a skin drum, his song lost to the roar of the crowd. Clouds of dust beneath the feet of the rebels seemed to part around them. There was something *wrong* about her, something old and otherworldly, like a creature from a nightmare. I suddenly very intensely did not want to know what a "Speaker" was.

Where the sight of the approaching woman had increased my fear it had the opposite effect on my enemies; buoyed by her approach, and seeing through my bluff, the remaining two men approached cautiously again. Though I feinted to gain a few steps closer to the ladder they figured me out soon enough and moved to block my exit, weapons raised. All the while the woman approached slowly, the beat of the child's drum matching her footfalls as though she shook the very earth.

This was it. I had nothing left. I met the eyes of the man who was about to kill me—with a hoe, of all things—and he lunged, driving it toward my throat.

Then feathers sprouted from his chest. His eyes widened with shock as he fell. The man with the scythe stopped midstrike, staring at his fallen companion, then he, too, was hammered down by the force of an arrow plunging into his shoulder. I looked up. A figure—no, two figures—hung dangerously off the edge of the wall, shooting down at my opponents. A louder pounding sound broke my stupor; I spun to see the child with the drum only a few treads away, and the woman crouched to the ground, fists full of dirt, burning gaze on me.

I ran for the ladder, clambering over bodies. A hiss and cry sounded behind me as another arrow found its mark. Grabbing a rung with my slippery left hand I hauled myself up, clinging three-limbed to the underside of the ladder. Rebels surged up its front side, face-to-face with me but oblivious to my identity as they climbed past.

From the ramparts above came a cry that might have been my name, then a hoarse scream of a woman falling off the ladder. My rescuers above were clearing me a path. Gritting my teeth with the effort, I scrambled a hand around to the top side of the ladder and pulled myself over.

Screams, shouts, and the twang of arrows bloomed around me, but I shut them out and concentrated on the rungs, counting them in eights as I climbed. At one point a horrible crack broke my concentration and terrified screaming cut through the battle noise as one of the other ladders burned and broke, dropping dozens of rebels to their deaths. My breath came out in wheezy little puffs and gasps, and several times my bleeding hands weakened and slipped, but none of the arrows struck. The soldiers above didn't notice I didn't belong, and those below didn't catch me. *Left, right, left, right, five, six, seven, eight* . . . How was it taking so long?

Then a jolt as someone below me grasped at my ankles, yanking one leg free from the rung. I slipped and cracked my chin, but hung on and kicked down hard, trying to knock them away. The grip only tightened; it felt abrasive, grainy, like a glove made of crushed shells. I dared a look down but in the confusion and with the other climbers I could not see who held me, only a glimpse of hard brown fingers around my shin, tightening, tightening, with each beat of the now-distant drum below, crushing the bone. . . .

Then the drum stopped, and the pressure was gone, like that. I peered down but saw no sign of my pursuer; no one was looking at me or appeared to have fallen suddenly. Discomforted, I paused, but then I heard "Jovan!" and shaking my bruised leg I hurried after the man above me. We were almost at the top. Tain was there, leaning too far out a crenel, Marco on the other side with a huge curved blade, slashing down at the men trying to scramble up over the wall.

"Hang on!" Tain called. The man above me surged up the last few rungs and sprang over the top. I heard him grunt as Marco's blade took him, then he half-slid, half-fell, his foot scraping over one of my hands. He hit my shoulder and tumbled off the ladder, but I clung on. Below me his body hurtled to the ground, and as he landed I saw the body of the strange woman beside him, felled by an arrow.

"Get up here!" Tain yelled, and I forced my half-numb body to obey, working my way to the topside of the ladder then scrambling up the last few rungs. Strong hands gripped my forearms, helping me, dragging me over the cool stone and into the safety of the ramparts. I slumped against the wall, curling my knees up to my chest. I didn't have the energy or the balance to stand.

"Now!" Marco bellowed. "One . . . two . . . over!"

A huge rock went over the edge, and a massive *crack* signaled the destruction of the ladder. I shut my eyes, breathing hard, and tried not to listen to the screams of the falling and crushed people below. Having just been below the wall, with its immense height and weight looming above like a malevolent giant, I empathized too easily.

"That's the last one," Tain said, dropping a hand on my shoulder. His voice sounded raspy, hollow. "The last ladder. They're falling back."

"Arrows after them!" Marco yelled, and I summoned enough strength to crawl across the ramparts so our archers could move back to position. Tain crouched in front of me, pulling off his battered helmet. His face was drenched in sweat and splattered with blood. "How badly are you hurt?"

I blinked, trying to catalogue my various injuries, but unable to focus. "I'm fine," I managed. My tongue felt thick in my mouth and when I tried to thank him my words didn't come out, my head swam, and then black spots in my vision became black clouds and took over altogether.

Clouddust

DESCRIPTION: Spray released by the cloud lizard, a highly aggressive white/gray alpine reptile. Inhalation of or exposure to the spray is extremely dangerous. Can be harvested into a highly corrosive serum, which is deadly if undiluted.

SYMPTOMS: Topical, manifesting in reddening and blistering of exposed skin, usually causing permanent damage if not immediately treated. Ingestion of the serum causes immediate painful burning of mouth, throat, and stomach and intense abdominal pain; inhalation of the raw spray causes lung failure and can be fatal.

PROOFING CUES: In high quantities burning sensation in mouth is obvious and the smell rancid and pungent.

6

Kalina

When I finally burst into the hospital, it was barely recognizable. Pallets filled the cool, spacious entrance hall, physics and assistants threading between them in moving lines like great serpents. People bustled past and I tried to dodge but ended up jostled, always in someone's way. I backed up against a wall to escape the chaotic mass for a moment, trying to see through the crowd.

"Lini?"

Tain slipped through the crush, people flowing around him effortlessly, and as he put his hands on my shoulders I grabbed one, relieved. "Have you seen Jov? Someone said he was here, but I can't find him."

He squeezed my hand, brushing my disheveled curls off my face. "He's all right," he said. "Jov's all right."

My breath fell out, relief drenching me like a sudden shower. "Where is he? How badly was he hurt?"

I was looking right at Tain, our faces close, and I knew his tells as well as my brother's; the tiny glance to the side, licking his lips before he spoke.

Though his words were reassuring—Jov was not badly hurt, no permanent damage—he was hiding something.

"We broke the rest of the ladders after that," he finished. "And we got Jov to the hospital straight away. Thendra says he's going to be all right." He smiled wanly. "Come on, I'll take you to him."

He held my hand across the room and the noisy path gave me no space to speculate further about what was wrong. Once I saw Jovan, it no longer mattered. I dropped Tain's hand and ran to my brother.

Jovan sat on a stretcher pallet, his head bowed so his hair fell over his eyes, his legs crossed, while the physic Thendra stitched a wound on his right shoulder. Purplish black shadows and zigzags of blood and dirt dappled his entire torso. At my approach, he looked up.

"Thank the fortunes," he said. "You stayed away from the fighting."

"You were worried about *me*?" My laugh caught in my throat. "Tain said you fell off the wall. Thank the fortunes you're alive, you clumsy oaf."

I perched next to him, taking his hands. His tight smile turned to a grimace as the physic pulled together ragged pieces of skin. "Thank Tain and Marco," he said. "They're the ones who rescued me."

It was only then I realized Tain hadn't followed me.

"Hold still," I murmured as the physic worked her way down the wound. An ugly, jagged gash began with a burst of torn flesh a handspan below his shoulder and traced around to finish under the point of the joint like macabre bloody jewelry. I felt sick looking at it. Jovan's face was drawn and his eyes unfocused, signaling that he had retreated into his mental space to try to stay calm. His whole body thrummed with tension as he suppressed whatever compulsion plagued him. I cleaned the blanket of grime, blood, and sweat from my brother's arms with damp linen.

Thendra tied off the end of her stitching, neat and precise. "How many people got hurt?" I asked, trying to avoid looking at the ruin of my brother's shoulder.

"I do not know for certain," Thendra said. She rubbed the heel of her hand over her tired eyes. "At least two dozen dead, perhaps more." She gestured to the far corner of the room. I followed her arm and winced at the sight of the covered, still figures, laid out on the floor together like dolls.

"They were ferocious," Jovan murmured, scrutinizing the newly puckered flesh on his arm with dispassion, a look reminiscent of Etan. "Even with the ladders, I didn't think they'd do much damage—we should have been able to hold them off. But they fight like . . ." He blinked, and his face turned thoughtful. "Like it's more important than anything. When I was down there, they *wanted* to kill me. They hate us, and they'll give us no peace, just like they said. They called me *spirit killer* and *heretic*. It's religion driving this, I think, but I don't understand *why*."

I felt a strange sensation deep inside me, like an ancient but familiar wound. Religion had been part of what drove many of our ancestors to flee here centuries ago. That group of misfits and, yes, rebels had escaped a brutal religious state and sought refuge here. Doubtless those old fears had created a certain reluctance by some to mix the governance of a country with its spirituality, and perhaps led the gradual move away from religious practices in the cities over time. But Silasta had so much to offer. Designed as a testament against the worst civilization had to offer—violence, oppression, cruelty, and ignorance—it stood as a beacon of peace, learning, and grace. Perhaps the city had few temples and shrines, but a lack of shared belief couldn't justify a violent rebellion. We were still the same people, and how could our supposed heresy harm believers out on the estates?

Jov drew his left leg up and rubbed the bottom of his shin as though it pained him, though I saw no wound. "There's something more. Something . . . something happened down there. I can't really . . ." He trailed off, tone turning embarrassed. "No, it's nothing."

"There," the physic said, daubing the stitching with a pale ointment. "If the flesh turns red and hot, you must come back, yes?"

Jovan thanked her and stood gingerly. "Where's Tain, do you know?"

I helped refasten the cording on his paluma, which had been pulled down to expose his shoulder. "There." I pointed to a familiar dark, curly head by the main doorway. We wound through the throng, trying to block out the heartrending cries and moans from all around.

Tain was comforting a sobbing young man beside a woman's body. Long corkscrew ringlets obscured her face and chest, but left exposed the ragged hole in her belly. Perhaps his mother, or aunt? His grief was infectious. My own breath hitched in my throat and my eyes burned. Etan would never comfort us again, or offer us wisdom. All we had was each other, and I could have lost Jov today.

Outside the hospital, the evening lay heavy around us, moonlight skimming the thick shadows. We sat on a bench by the canal in silence, listening to the *lap lap* of the water and the sigh of the breeze in the bushes. Tain's posture was rigid and he avoided looking at Jovan.

"Honored Chancellor," someone said, and we looked up. A boy wearing a messenger's sash and carrying a bottle and a cloth parcel, hopped from foot to foot. His hair stuck up in the middle of his head like a little crest. He looked vaguely familiar—possibly a child of one of the Families, though he was only ten or twelve, too young for identifying tattoos. "Credo Marco asked if you could come to the Warrior Guildhall when you are available."

"Thanks, Erel," Tain said. "Did he say what it was about?"

"Yes, Chancellor. It was to do with the deserters, he said."

"Deserters?" Jov asked, frowning. "We're in a siege! Where can anyone desert to?"

"Marco's trying to work out what to do with people who aren't showing up to their sectors for their duties. I imagine he's worried about how many people didn't respond to the call today. He's calling them deserters, for want of a more appropriate word."

"What are you going to do?" I asked.

Tain sighed, running a hand through his hair. "Honor-down, I don't know. It's hard to blame them, but we need every person we've got if we're going to make this work." He stood. "I'd better go, anyway."

"Have something to drink and eat first, Honored Chancellor," Erel said, thrusting the bottle and parcel toward Tain. "I picked it up for you on the way."

Jov intercepted the items. "I'm thirsty," he said, taking them off the bemused boy. "And hungry. The wound and all. You don't mind, do you, Chancellor?" When he caught the messenger boy staring at him, slack-jawed, he added dryly, "Nor you, Erel?"

The boy mumbled something about "not my place," but I was looking at Tain, and saw his frustrated gaze dart from the bottle Jov raised to his lips to the angry wound on his shoulder, and back again. I suddenly understood the awkwardness between them.

Jov passed him the bottle once Erel had left. "It's just water," he said. As Tain took the bottle, the glance they exchanged, the torment in Tain's eyes, made my chest hurt.

"You saved my life today," Jov said, reading Tain as easily as I had. "If you and Marco hadn't shot those men when you did . . ."

"You offer yourself in my place *every* day," Tain replied.

"That's my duty." Of all the things my brother held dear, his honor, our family's honor, was always at the forefront. The duty that should have been mine had always ruled our lives. A wave of bitterness and failure swamped me, familiar as an old friend.

"Yes," Tain said, but his mouth twisted. "I have to go."

We watched him leave, silent, neither looking at the other. I felt like crying. Between Tain's guilt, Jovan's fears, and my resentments, this war was making strangers of us all.

"How many deserters are there?" Nara's heavy eyebrows were drawn together in her wrinkled face, giving her the look of a very angry papna fruit. It had only been a day since the attack but the shock had worn off and everyone seemed ready to assign blame. Jov was holding his injured side awkwardly and his expression suggested he was fantasizing about poisoning half of the whining, self-important men and women around the table.

"So far, we have rounded up thirty-two," Marco replied. He rubbed his head. "As I was saying, the Honorable Chancellor—"

"Honore*d*," Bradomir corrected, his well-manicured hands folded primly on the table. Tain frowned, his patience for dealing with authoritarian condescension clearly stretched thin.

Marco had thicker skin, because he continued without a change in tone. "The Honored Chancellor has determined that these deserters will not be punished now, but will be assigned duties reporting to Order Guards directly, and will pay fines after the siege is over." He gave Tain a look that, while not precisely disrespectful, conveyed his disapproval.

"These are our people. They're afraid," Tain said. "Can you blame them? And locking people up won't alleviate that fear, it'll just cost us extra bodies we desperately need. This is the best solution for now." As one or two other Councilors began to speak, Tain overturned the paper in front of him and continued on in a firmer tone, making it clear the discussion was over. "What's next?"

"We need to prepare for the next attack," Marco began.

"We swatted them away easily enough yesterday," Lazar said, waving a plump hand confidently. "I daresay we'll do so again!"

There was a sudden silence as many faces regarded the Credo with something close to disgust. Even among this crowd, yesterday had been a confronting day, not a triumphant one. "We lost people we could ill afford to lose," Marco said. "We were lucky to withstand it. Next time, I believe the rebels will make a stronger attack at our infrastructure, since they failed to come over the walls." He turned to address Eliska. "Stone-Guilder, we will need to redouble our efforts to build our own range weaponry. I propose we reduce our presence on the walls and supply additional people to assist your Guild to build siege weapons."

A few murmurs rose up around the room and even Eliska frowned. "I appreciate the gesture, but I don't think unskilled workers will assist much—even my best Guild members have never made anything like this. We're working from drawings and diagrams in books."

"Use the help to delegate the less-skilled parts," Tain said. "Searching the city for materials, shifting them, melting metals down—anything to make it easier for your Guild workers."

"Isn't it too risky taking our people off the walls?" Varina asked. "Won't they see that and respond?"

"Our supplies of cane and wood for arrows are limited and they outnumber us ten to one. We will not be able to hold them off if they can come through our walls." Marco shook his head, grim. "If we don't have proper weapons to defend a full attack, we will lose the city."

Everyone fell silent. Both Varina and Marco made fair points. We didn't need people on the wall wasting their time if there was no attack, but we couldn't risk the rebels exploiting any decrease in manpower should they detect it. I shifted, starting to feel the discomfort of crouching hidden up here again. My joints had started to protest these frequent visits.

"I have an idea." Jov cleared his throat. "Credo Pedrag, your Craft Guild members are assisting with making armor, but do you think you could set some to sew false sentries? Like the dummies we use to practice archery. If we dress them in armor and set them at intervals around the wall, between our real sentries, wouldn't they look the same from a distance? The army is staying out of range for now, and if we show the rebels the appearance of a full defense, maybe it'll discourage them from doing anything rash until they've built their rams and catapults."

Pedrag's crinkly little eyes disappeared when he smiled. "I could do that, Credo," he said. "I daresay it'd be easy, in fact. We've plenty of straw and we can make giant moppets that'll look as good in silhouette as any man."

"I agree," Tain said. "Let's take fifty extra people from wall duty to be laborers for Eliska, and get replacement dummies made as soon as we can." He turned over another paper and I caught a suppressed sigh as he continued. "Now, you all saw the message the rebels sent us a few days ago, and you've probably heard rumors about the sorts of things they were shouting during the attack. We know from the bodies of those who made it over that they are indeed Sjon. We now know for sure it's a rebellion. Our countryfolk are aggrieved at the city, possibly for some reason connected to religious beliefs."

"I've always said those earthers are practicing a primitive belief system," Varina said. "And apparently it's a violent one, too."

"The proper name for it is Darfri," Javesto corrected. "And I never saw any sign that they were violent until now. Did you? Has something been happening out on the Leka estates, Credo Varina? Credo Bradomir?"

As with every previous time the subject had come up, this question turned the mood immediately defensive, as the other Credolen hastened to express their ignorance of what could have spurred an uprising. "You must understand, Honored Chancellor, these matters are handled by our stewards," Bradomir said. "That's what they're for. Like yourself and your most Honored uncle before you, we lack the time to personally oversee these kinds of operations."

And once again, Tain was left unable to press the issue. Chancellor Caslav had indeed had little involvement in the Iliri estates, partly because it was inappropriate for the Chancellor to be too concerned with his personal wealth, and partly because of the scandal associated with his sister Casimira and her unconventional "family" out there. Likewise, Jov and I knew little of the Oromani lands and affairs. We had other responsibilities, and my health and his compulsions and anxiety made traveling difficult. It was hard to demand answers when we could offer none ourselves.

"There were only three survivors among the rebels, and none are yet conscious. In the meantime, I've checked my household staff," Tain said.

"A few are believers, but they were all raised here in Silasta. They didn't know why the countryfolk, Darfri or not, would have a grudge against the city and certainly not why they'd be calling us heretics."

Javesto shrugged. "The Darfri religion isn't about gods or worship or recruiting followers. I knew plenty of believers growing up and they were never bothered by whether someone else believed or not."

"As for calling us spirit-killers, my staff didn't know what that could mean. They'd never heard of anyone talk about killing spirits. To them, spirits are a part of the landscape, just as natural as a mountain or a river." Tain's tone rang with the same frustration I felt. His servants had been genuinely baffled, unable to help unravel the mystery at all. One of them, who was both servant and, surreptitiously, a personal guard, had been raised Darfri but said other than paying his respects if he passed a shrine, he barely thought on it. Another had been more devout, showing us her Darfri charm necklace and explaining each sigil on it as belonging to spirits that her mother and Tashi had hoped would bless her with good fortune and strength—one for the great spirit of Solemn Peak, one for the great spirit of the Bright Lake, another for the spirit of the land her mother had been born on. To the servant, they were symbols of a connection to the earth and a source of comfort. She had cried as she showed us. I hated that we had made her afraid.

"How can you kill a spirit, anyway?" Pedrag grumbled. "It doesn't make any sense. Either we're heretics for not believing in their silly spirits or we're killing them with our supernatural powers. It can't be both."

"Forgive me, Honored Chancellor, but is there any point delving into these daft beliefs?" Eliska asked wearily, rubbing the back of her neck as if it pained her. "They murdered our peace emissary and sent back a message saying they want no peace. There's no prospect of negotiation. They've established themselves as the enemies of our capital and our Council and therefore as traitors to Sjona. That's good enough for me."

I couldn't see Tain's face properly but the conflict inside him came out through his long pause and hesitant tone. He wanted so badly to protect the city, but struggled to believe his own people could be his enemies. He was a grown man now, but in him I still saw the boy who never wanted anyone to be unhappy or upset. Who wanted to be loved. Perhaps he had finally come across a game he couldn't win without cost.

"I want to understand," he said eventually. "I need you all to ask among your staff as well. Someone must know something that could help us."

"I don't know about the rest of you, but I'm almost servicing my own home as it is—my entire blasted household staff have disappeared," Pedrag said. Other Councilors added their agreement.

Credo Lazar shifted in his seat. "Gone without so much as a word. Employed mine for years, ungrateful things."

"Yes, I can't *imagine* why they're not putting your chores first," Credola Varina said, curling her lip in scorn. "The city's under attack. I doubt anyone expected they were still required to turn up to work."

Tain let out his breath, his patience visibly thinning. "I don't expect staff to still be working in our houses, but presumably you have a way of contacting them? And some probably live on your properties, don't they?"

"Yes, Honored Chancellor," Bradomir said. He cleared his throat. "However, what I meant is that many of our staff have fled our home altogether. Perhaps to stay with relatives in the lower city."

It was almost like our plans were laid out before us like pieces on a game board, and someone was there, in front of us, knocking them over one at a time. Every time we got an answer, it led to more questions.

By the time I headed back to our apartments I was exhausted. The road seemed endless. I had let myself go too far past my energy limits, and now the way home felt like an arduous trek. Worse, one of the crowd of petitioners lined up along the street outside the Manor caught sight of me, and the disheveled woman peeled off to follow me as I tried to walk away.

"Credola! Credola!" she panted, hobbling after me. She walked with an obvious limp and apparent pain. Guilt made me slow down, though I knew I couldn't help.

"I'm sorry, but I'm really not able to take petitions," I told her. "You can report matters to the Order Guard in charge of your sector, or you can leave your issue with the clerk at the Manor at the end of the week. Please—"

Though she moved slowly, when her hand snaked out and grasped my elbow the grip was firm. Too firm, in fact. I tried to pull it back but it was as if she couldn't even feel it. "You must help me." She looked back and forth on the street, edgy. "I tried to talk to the Chancellor, but it's impossible to get time with him, you see."

"He cares about all of you," I said, "but you must understand how much there is to do in a besieged city, auntie. Which is your sector?"

"The Order Guards run the sectors, Credola!" The old woman's grip tightened on my arm. The smell of cheap spirits and soiled clothing wafted from her. "They're everywhere, and you must stop them finding me. They're killing us off! Taking us for food! Everyone knows you can starve in a siege!"

I patted her arm gently as I pulled my own harder, trying to free my elbow. "I promise no one is taking any people for food, auntie. I know you're frightened, but I really do promise you—"

"They come in the night! Only last night, five of us streetfolk vanished, *poof*!" Her fingers were trembling. Something had certainly terrified her. "I saw the Guard checking on us earlier, in the evening, looking us over like he was measuring us. I hid under my blankets, Credola. I didn't like the way he looked at us, no I did not. No mistake, in the morning, gone, five of us!"

"He was probably looking for recruits," I said. "We need all the help we can defending the city. If an Order Guard talked to your friends and now they're gone, they were probably assigned duties."

"Or spirits!" she cried, changing tack as if she hadn't heard me at all. "It might not have been the Guards! There's talk of wicked spirits coming alive down by the canals. People didn't believe before, but there were darker than usual shadows last night, you mark me."

"Please let go of my arm, auntie. You're hurting me."

She dropped it like a coal and looked me up and down, terror morphing into scorn. "You don't care! None of you care. This city's doomed and no one sees it!"

Before I could respond, she ran, limp and all, and I stared after her, not knowing whether I wanted to follow or not.

Days piled on top of each other, bleeding together into a stream of wearying tasks and increasing worries. None of the injured rebels survived to be interrogated. The army had retreated and the smoke and sounds from their sprawling camp suggested they were building more serious weaponry after their first failed attempt to scale the walls. I didn't see the streetwoman again, but it was hard to move through the city without someone approaching me, seeking favors or audiences with Tain. I stayed inside much of the time, and covered my tattoos when I went out.

Within the city, tensions ran high as we settled into a strange new routine. Some businesses remained open; others had been redirected to perform citywide tasks. Hourly, it seemed, Jov was petitioned by someone in our sector, seeking instruction about how best to use a resource, or exemption from duties. We feared such rulings were being applied inconsistently across the city, but none of us had ever had to reorganize ten thousand people before, not even Marco, and mistakes would be made.

I slipped through the gate of the tournament grounds, entering the arena along with the dawn shift. Here, Marco and the stretched Order Guards taught rough classes in basic martial skills that we could use from the walls and, if they were scaled again, face-to-face. Technically, only those able-bodied enough to be up on the walls were supposed to attend, but enough Credolen were mixed among the common folk that I could join the archery practice squads without anyone taking notice. Just one more Credola, unskilled and weak, but determined. Jovan knew nothing of my plans; he had been sleeping at the Manor in any case, too worried to leave Tain alone in the company of only servants of whose loyalties we could not be certain.

It had become a routine. For months, well before the siege, I had been building up my physical strength. Swimming in the lake in the early morning, walking and even running on the tournament grounds, trying to slowly work past some of my limitations. Etan and Jov wanted me to rest, always to rest; I knew the root of their concern was love, and knew, too, I would never have a fully healthy body. But though the work had exhausted me, and sometimes left me unable to properly fake good health the following day, I had also seen signs of improvement that gave me hope. So why should I not learn some skills that could help my city?

I had tried to avoid shifts run by anyone who knew me. This was one of Credo Javesto's sector's shifts, a sector far from ours. But today luck hadn't favored me and Marco himself was directing the training. He saw me immediately.

"Credola," he said. Not quite a question, but the conflict in his expression was drawn in his thick eyebrows, bunched together. Was there anyone who didn't know my limitations? "You are practicing?"

"Yes." It was an effort not to add anything, not to explain or excuse.

He hesitated. I made myself meet his gaze, calm.

"The lightest bows are marked with white paint."

"Yes, I know. Thank you." Held my head up until he moved on.

I joined the line, standing in sequence with the others, just one more anonymous citizen. Stand side on. Body still. Head to the target, lift the bow with my left, grip the string with my right. . . .

"You grip it too tight."

I loosened my right hand, bristling inside, and drew back. Apparently today peace would elude me. "Thank you, Lord Ectar. I always forget that." Release.

The Talafan noble and his servants had been freed weeks ago with little fanfare and great embarrassment on both sides. Being locked in the Manor while an army attacked the city wasn't exactly proper treatment of a noble guest; on the other hand, Ectar had still, as far as he and anyone else knew, brought a gift that had resulted in the death of the ruling Chancellor and his closest adviser.

Tain had escorted him from the Manor, awkward and stumbling over his words. Ectar had spoken little, and clutched his servant's arm, fingers like the grip of a great pale bird. Since then, though he had faithfully turned up to our sector as agreed, he had avoided being anywhere near Tain. It had been a mistake to handle it personally; the Council had urged Tain to let our best diplomats handle the release, but he had refused. More reasons for resentment and frustration where he should have been building accord. He needed their respect if not their trust, but instead they feared him, feared his sudden shifts between malleable and stubborn.

"Your technique is improving, Credola."

"Thank you," I said again. Forcing a smile, I lowered my bow and turned to him. "Surely you don't need any extra practice?"

"I am helping the Warrior-Guilder with training," Ectar said. He looked different; it took a moment to realize it was his bare face. Usually heavy powders made his face pale as snow; today cosmetics still decorated his eyes and brows, but his skin looked natural. Pale, but pinkish-brown rather than alabaster. It made him seem less alien. "May I?" He helped me adjust my draw. "Relax your shoulders. You hurt your neck elsewise, see?"

"It's kind of you to help Marco," I said. "All of us."

He shrugged, his eyes scanning the distance. "What am I to do? I wish to go home. That army of savages will not care who I am."

True enough. We were all in this together, like it or not. "When will the Emperor become concerned and send for you?" Ectar had blustered to that effect upon his release, but been oddly quiet about it since. Perhaps he thought already to have been rescued. Perhaps, like me, he merely hoped some external ally had seen the siege and returned to Talafar to summon our allies for assistance.

"It is hard to say," he said, then quickly deflected. "Has the Honored Chancellor made any progress toward peace talks?"

"I'm afraid not." Ectar pressed me for information often, and I played a delicate game attempting to win his trust without risking revealing anything important. The more youthful, innocent version of myself needed to be flattered by his attention, but not suspiciously so. "If we only knew more of what they wanted."

"There are some of these 'earther' people in your city," he said, silently adjusting the stance of the person beside me. "Why does the Chancellor not require them to answer? My grandfather would force them to tell him what they know. And if he did not get the answers he would hang them outside the walls one by one until they talked, or the rebels did."

It was impossible to hide my shock. One moment Ectar could appear vulnerable: a young man in a terrible situation, far from home and in a culture he didn't fully understand. The next he seemed so casually cruel it turned my stomach. I found my voice at last. "What a thing to suggest, Lord Ectar." Gentler than I felt. "We do not do such things in Silasta."

"Perhaps that is why you are under attack," he pointed out, but even as he said it he seemed to realize he had erred. He gave a false laugh. "I joke, Credola. It is frustration. We are stuck here, not knowing when they will strike. Your people are not prepared. I am afraid. Are you not afraid?"

"Of course I am," I said, honestly. My arm, already weakening, shook as I drew again.

"I must help others, Credola. I will see you on assigned duties later?"

I nodded, returning to my practice. Ectar's constant presence and watchfulness made a difficult task harder. Worse, I hadn't missed some of the supportive grunts of people around me who had overheard his suggestion. It echoed the same sentiments increasingly muttered about the city since it had become apparent our attackers were Darfri; no matter how much Tain attempted to soothe such talk, his fledgling authority was insufficient to dampen it entirely.

When I finally packed up, dripping and drained, it felt doubtful I'd achieved much.

A quick visit to the bathhouse on the way home masked my morning efforts externally, but they had cost me. Even making tea felt like too much. I settled at the main table, surrounded by weeks of accumulated piles of paper, and tried to distract myself from physical exhaustion by reading.

I sifted through various complaints sent to Tain, most of which seemed to be increasingly hysterical accusations. Though word had quickly spread that the attackers had a religious motivation, there was an underlying assumption that the rebellion had at least been funded if not actively encouraged by some foreign power; accordingly, any sign of what was deemed "suspicious" behavior from any poor soul with the wrong name or outfit or skin color was reported as if it were high intelligence. And while the majority was nonsense, we couldn't afford to let real information slip through unnoticed. The Darfri *were* being aided by someone outside the country. Not only were supplies still arriving from multiple directions, but our watchers had seen signs of military leadership from people who did not appear to be Sjon; people garbed differently, mounted on graspads and moving through the camp like inspectors. Given the risk to the city of betrayal from the inside, the Council had made subtle, quiet restrictions on how wall defense allocations were to be made, limiting the numbers of foreigners who could be set to a particular task or given particular responsibilities. It was easy to see potential enemies or traitors. What had once been harmless, decorative expressions of our diverse city—different colors and clothes and the sounds of different languages and accents—had become something to mistrust.

The letters blurred together to my tired eyes. Suspicions and worries and risks . . . these names and numbers didn't bring us any closer to understanding what was happening, let alone solving it.

I turned to another pile. Jov and I had likewise had no further luck in our investigations into the poisoning. Without the missing piece of the puzzle—what precisely was motivating the rebellion—we couldn't know who was involved or how—even *if*—it was connected to Etan's and the Chancellor's deaths. The other side of the table was piled with bound rolls I'd collected from the Guildhalls. In them I hoped to find names of successful, even influential, people in the city who were Darfri. Out on the estates, people named their children in the old style, with the prefixes An- and Il-, so looking for those styles of names in the rolls should at least tell me who might have been raised Darfri. Despite our requests at every sector, few believers had come forward to help, and none had expressed insight into any religious cause for an uprising. I understood ordinary folk might be reluctant or fearful to come forward in the current atmosphere, but perhaps if we quietly approached prominent members of the Darfri community, we could learn something useful.

But to no avail.

"There's nothing in here," I said to my brother when he eventually came home in the late afternoon. My words distracted him from scrutinizing me. I had propped myself with pillows to help me sit straight but I couldn't mask my pallor. I pointed at the page in front of me and he frowned down at it.

"Nothing where?"

I turned another page, gesturing at the list of names and profiles. "Look at these names."

His eyes tracked the paper, taking in the Performers' Guild sigil marking the top corner of the page, listing names, joining dates, and short profiles of members. He blinked, staring blankly at the neat text. "I don't see—"

"Where are the Darfri?"

I gestured to the rolls spread out before us. Page after page of names and profiles, but no Darfri prefixes on any of them. Jov sat, rubbing his head, his frown deepening as he understood.

"It's the same for all of them."

"But there have to be *some*. People move from the estates to the city, surely? And while some of them probably take servant or un-Guilded jobs, they can't all be doing that."

"Presumably," I said. "But if so, they're dropping their full names when they do."

He frowned. "Can we cross-check from school rolls from the estates, and look for names of the highest-achieving students? Then we can find them, prefixes or not, on the Guild rolls."

I shook my head. "That's what I thought, too. But I asked Budua for the school records from the estates and she said they haven't been collected for decades."

"Doesn't your Guild have any supervision over the local schools, then? How—" My sharp cough cut Jov off. He winced and put a hand on my shoulder; I shrugged it off. "It looks like the Guild used to, but hasn't been interacting much with them in years."

Before I could say anything further, a knock made us jump. Tain's messenger, Erel, waited there. "The Chancellor called for you, Credo Jovan," the boy said. "He wants you at the Manor."

The original Silastian school was in the upper city, a beautiful old building not far from our apartments. For the last half a century now, Silastian youths had studied in the lower city, in not one building but many. The school complex was an entire section of the city. It felt like returning to the past to walk that passage across Trickster's Bridge and toward the administrative tower, the tallest building in the school. I could have found it blindfolded.

Though I couldn't have articulated why, I'd found the Scribe-Guilder evasive when I asked her about the records. Perhaps Budua had just been defensive about having limited control over the nation's education, but though Tain didn't want to hear about it, and there had been no attempts on his life, Jov and I still remained on alert for a traitor on the Council.

I descended the narrow staircase into the bowels of the administrative building, the rhythmic taps of my footsteps echoing around me like a drumbeat. The air felt cool on my cheeks, still and lifeless, and the light from my small oil lamp struggled to part the thick cloak of darkness.

The door to the records room was locked, but of all the things I'd struggled with in my Tashi's training, lock-picking had not been one of them. I made short work of it, the mechanism moving into place with a satisfying *snick*. High-ceilinged and cavernous, the room loomed around me, silent and austere with its rows and towers of metal shelves and cabinets. I walked its length, drawing my light across the neat, etched labels, searching for some references to schools outside Silasta. There were multiple cabinets marked for Moncasta, Telasa, and West Dortal, and when I searched through them I found not just rolls but extensive correspondence between teachers, reports on performance, and even work samples and recommendations from the school administrators. Meticulous records of students who had passed every course run at the school. All ranges of subjects—academic, physical, specialist. But of Sjona's broader regions: nothing. No cabinets, no files, no sign of any Darfri-style family names.

I finally found reference to estate schools in the poorly labeled files and cabinets at the back of the room. Poorer quality materials, with faded lettering, and only very roughly organized into regions, but better than nothing. There was nowhere to sit and read, so I squatted on the cold stone floor, much to the protest of my knees and back.

By the time the oil in the lamp ran low, I couldn't feel anything much below my waist, and a heavy sensation filled my chest like I'd breathed in the wrong kind of air. Some of these papers were a hundred years old, and the quality of the information recorded dramatically diminished by the time I'd reached the "newest," which was still over forty years old. Over time, the city's interest in the estate schools had clearly faded, leaving us with the frustrating modern state. I couldn't tell from this what condition estate schools were in, or what they were teaching. I had no way to track their students. But I found the idea that the Council had let stewards of the Families determine the standard of services provided to their residents deeply troubling.

The rush of blood back to my lower limbs as I stood made me gasp, tiny flares of nerves flooding my senses, and my movements scooping up and returning the documents were clumsy.

I was due to begin a shift in our sector in a while, but the thought of the long walk back up the hill was daunting. Instead, I followed a different idea and walked farther north, heading into the residential areas surrounding the sprawling school complex. Even in this subdued atmosphere, people still went about their daily business, particularly the young and elderly, who had not been assigned duties on the walls or elsewhere. The area ahead looked to be a poorer neighborhood. I wandered in, listening for sounds of activity. It was quiet, even for the circumstances; no open windows, no pedestrians, just bare streets and narrow, unfriendly houses looming overhead.

A group of young women crossed the road in front of me, carrying baskets on their broad shoulders. They walked past without chatter, disappearing into the maze of crooked stone housing on the left.

Unlike in the upper city, these houses snuggled close together, tottering up to four or five stories and stacked back from the road. Some shared tiled roofs and had small, communal walled gardens. From the edge of one roof on the corner a few wilted bluehood wreaths dangled, perhaps left over from the Children's Festival earlier in the summer. Tiny alleyways connected the maze, and many of the walls had steep, external stairs built into the stone. The muffled sound of the girls' footfalls carried strangely among the tightly packed buildings so I wasn't sure in what direction they'd gone. I must have walked past these little communities a thousand times before, but until now had never paid any heed to them, or noticed how different these homes were from the spacious apartments of the upper city or even the neat housing closer to the school.

I noticed another faded wreath, then another. I found myself following them, a thought forming in my head. If countryfolk moving to the city were taking lower paid, un-Guilded work, this would be the kind of area where they would live. An area with prominent decorations for a celebration that had its roots, like so much of our culture, in the spiritual beliefs of the past. If no Darfri would come to us, perhaps I could go to them.

When I squeezed down a tight alleyway, the heads of two women rose above one of the walled gardens, one with hair in a tight tail and something familiar about the profile. I called out without thinking. "Eliska?"

They were a distance away, and the tall buildings limited the sunlight, so even when both faces jerked round, I couldn't tell if the woman was the Stone-Guilder. Her companion's face was unobscured as it stared at me, suspicious. Both turned and vanished from my sight, and I suddenly felt foolish; there was no reason for Eliska to be here, and I'd probably just scared off residents I'd hoped to talk to.

"Hello?" I called out. The gardens I passed by were sad things, overgrown with weeds and strewn with the hollow shells of rotten vegetables. I could no longer hear the women I'd originally followed. I walked down the alleyways, my footfalls intrusive in the silence. The buildings all looked much the same, with a single door on the ground floor, a window barred and oil-papered, and a frighteningly narrow stone staircase leading up the outside of the building to the upper floors. Clothing, laid out to dry in the sun, draped the iron balustrade of the equally narrow second-story landing of the nearest house.

And opposite, in a tiny alcove, a Darfri shrine.

They were common enough, especially around festival times: usually a small stack of rocks, clusters of herbs and flowers, artfully arranged, to which believers sometimes brought their young ones for blessings, or to wish someone good tidings. They were harmless little things, decorative and unobtrusive.

This one had been smashed, the rocks scattered and faded greenery flattened. The intense smell of old urine assaulted my nose. Uneasy, I backed away. "Is anyone here?" I called out again and bumped into the gate of the garden behind me. I tried knocking on the door of the house, but it swung open on its rickety hinges at my touch. "Hello?" Something felt wrong about the house; the silence, the stillness. . . . It was too intense. I stepped inside.

"Hello?"

Poorly lit though the room was, it was obvious no one would answer.

Cupboards lining the walls gaped like sad, empty mouths, and a blanket of dust and grit covered most of the surfaces, broken only by scattered foot tracks. On the back wall, someone had painted a single word: *traitor.*

The house was abandoned. More than that; abandoned and ransacked. I stepped through, queasy. *By Silastians. Our own citizens did this.* Stepping over smashed crockery and discarded clothing, I ran my hands over the stripped pallets in the corner, bending to pick up a toy wedged beneath an overturned stew pot. It was a child's moppet, dressed in traditional country-style clothing with bright layered skirts and a scarf over its head. It was crudely stitched but its clothes were worn from hugs and the ink markings of its face had been loved off. Its hair stuffing poked out in places where the stitching had failed. Around its neck hung a miniature charm necklace like the one Tain's Darfri servant had worn. I could almost picture the child who must have owned it. That a beloved toy had been abandoned left me almost as disquieted as the sacking.

Even as I knocked at the door of the neighboring building, which shared the yard with the first, I suspected the result would be the same, and it was. Any valuables that had ever been in these poor homes were long gone, just like their residents. The same layer of dirt and dust covered the remnants of the life the family had left here. It was the same thing in the stories above, and in every house on the small block.

I held the doll, transferring it between my hands. Where had the people gone, after their shrines were desecrated and their homes vandalized? Had they been driven out by fear of their fellow citizens, or forced to leave?

I climbed down one of the thin, stone staircases, pressing the side of my body and both hands close against the wall for balance. I felt like I'd just visited a different city from the Silasta we knew, a city within a city. I needed to talk to Tain.

Lendulos

DESCRIPTION: Decorative, flowering, warm-climate perennial, with plentiful bright orange flowers. Leaves used to treat headaches and joint pain, flower extract combined with alcohol used to treat bleeding wounds.

SYMPTOMS: Injection of flower tincture causes blood clotting, manifesting in localized pain and swelling, tenderness, muscle cramps, red or blue skin discoloration and heat, organ damage, death.

PROOFING CUES: Strong, citruslike taste with a rancid edge, extremely unpleasant and difficult to disguise (unlikely to be used as an ingested poison).

7

Jovan

I dreamed too much.

First it was fragments: lessons with Etan, tomfoolery with Tain. Then detailed, vibrant dreams, rich in memories, as though I were living those times again. One took me through my first poisoning and then my worst, and I woke clutching my throat and coughing, the caustic feeling still burning in my lungs as if I had freshly inhaled the deadly powder. I turned over in my bed, skin slick and muscles clenching. I tried breathing exercises to calm my mind, but the cough kept erupting and destroying my concentration. *Sleep, you need to sleep.*

Upon waking yet again, my heart raced and my brain swam with stress and fear. I couldn't remember details—just a sense of threat. Tain and Kalina had been in danger, and I had been unable to get to them, but somehow knew they were going to die, and it would be my fault. I had to protect them both, and I was failing.

It had just been a dream. Not a premonition, or even a memory. Just my mind tormenting me. *Nothing new there.* But it had left me with a shameful desire to flee the city, forget risking our lives defending it, forget about poisons, assassination attempts, political machinations, and everything else. Kalina and Tain and I together somewhere else, somewhere safe. . . .

Unable to tolerate stewing in bed anymore, I dressed and went outside into our grounds. We had buried Etan here on our own property, but visiting the spot gave me no peace; I felt my failure of our duty too intensely, as though he reproached me from the earth. Still, I could imagine I felt his presence and try to speculate about what he would do if he were here.

It had been a frustrating evening, going over supply lists and sewage management with several Councilors and then preparing the next day's food for Tain in the Manor kitchen after everyone else had left. I'd found Kalina deeply and troublingly asleep when I finally returned. Carrying her to her bed had not even woken her, and the heavy lines around her eyes and forehead had not eased even in her supposed rest. I felt helpless in my worry for her.

Something had bothered me at the meeting, and if it had taken anxious dreams to rouse me then so be it.

There had been no attack on Tain, and I had kept my word that I would not bring up my suspicions about his Council. Either he did not truly believe there was a conspiracy or he did not want to be burdened with the doubt and suspicion that haunted me. I understood the desire to believe those in power could be trusted. Sniping and self-interested though they were, and while they still jostled to influence or manipulate their new Chancellor, it would make all of our lives easier if we at least knew they were not working with an enemy of the city. Yet while Tain had ever been capable of abandoning grudges and hurts and ill thoughts of any kind, I did not share that skill. Every instinct I had told me one of the Councilors, or more, was working against at least Tain's family, if not the entire city.

Tonight it was Javesto who had troubled me, even if it had taken some time to process why. His keen interest in the food store levels could simply have been the same interest and concern we all shared. But his gaze had lingered too long, and too often, on the roster pages and distribution lists Marco had been sharing with Eliska, whose sector included the warehouses. Perhaps it was paranoid to worry, but perhaps not. As if the silence from my uncle's grave were an endorsement, I decided I would go. At worst, visiting the warehouses would be a good stretch of my legs and a chance to think.

The darkened streets, empty except for the hollow, distant sounds of the night patrols on the walls, were gray ghosts without merry revelers, acrobats, or poets. The teahouses and kori bars were silent shells, the theaters empty of crowds that should have spilled from their doorways. Now, the late summer air close around me, I passed under archways absent lanterns and shop doorways locked tight. Those few people who were around scurried past without raising their faces in greeting. The smooth, silver-veined azikta of the elegant buildings glowed softly in the moonlight, lighting my way as I walked down the streets past the great theater, the old academies, the original Guildhalls . . . three hundred years of history speaking to me through the architecture.

As I worked my way down toward the lake, my anxiety slowly calmed. I walked faster, steps punctuating my breathing. Sound carried oddly across the lake as I crossed Trickster's Bridge, so the crunch of pacing footsteps echoed down from the wall and muffled activity sounded from the lower city. The Builders' Guildhall and some of the surrounding buildings rang with the distant song of industry.

I traced the path of the lake, past the harbor, by the great warehouses. This close to the deep, still waters, the air temperature had dropped. Rubbing the raised hairs on my arms, I steered between one of the granaries and a warehouse, heading toward the center of town. During the day this area was bustling; now, only a few people trailed between the warehouses and the road, delivering supplies to the stations in each segment. Soon, wandering through the maze of alleys between the buildings, I lost sight of any other life.

I had taken two steps into the next passage when a sharp sound startled me. Tile fragments shattered on the floor a few paces away. I looked up. There, on the roof of the warehouse, silhouetted against the night sky, a figure froze, half-crouched. For a moment neither of us moved. Then the figure sprang to its feet and ran.

Without thinking, I followed.

The moon gave enough light for me to track the figure as it scrambled across the roof and then leaped to the next. I sprinted down the alley, my eyes fixed on the rooftops, and skidded around the side of the next building in time to see the person nimbly dropping from the eave. The jump slowed him enough to close the gap and by the time we rounded the next corner I caught him. My first thought on grabbing his shoulder and spin-ning my quarry around was that the shoulder was quite a bit higher than mine.

The second was, *Oh shit*.

He struck me in the stomach before I could react, and the blow sent me flying backward with a grunt. Luck more than instinct helped me duck under the follow-up punch to my head, though it came close enough that his forearm scraped my hair as it hooked past. I'd no hope in a fistfight with this man, so I stayed low and launched myself at him instead.

I hit his midsection with my shoulder and scooped up his legs with both my arms, driving in and up. We both hit the ground, me on top. But my opponent was a far superior fighter, and bucked and twisted, so suddenly it was me on my back. I tried to protect my head as the blow came down, but instead his mallet hands struck either side of my ribs with force enough to knock the wind from my lungs. He grabbed me by the hair and pounded my head back. In that one moment before my head made contact with ground, I saw the charm necklace dangling from his neck.

It seemed like only moments later my eyes opened, but even as my shak-ing hands checked the damage to my head I knew time must have passed. The sky above me had turned the rich indigo of predawn. I tried to sit up, but the attempt sent waves of nausea and pain down my body. Breathing in, my chest exploded with fiery splinters as though my ribs had been shat-tered. I lay still, trying not to move any part of my body, and looked around me as best I could. At least my eyeballs didn't hurt.

The low branches of a tree hung over me from one side, the broad flat leaves forming patterns over about a quarter of my vision. At the other side I recognized the edge of the tiled warehouse roof. Grass tickled the sides of my cheeks and the greasy scent in the air suggested proximity to the docks.

Moving slowly, I tried again to sit, and made it about halfway to vertical before the nausea hit again. There was just time to turn my face before throwing up, to avoid ending up covered in vomit. Minor victories.

After a while, I managed to get to my feet with help from the overhang-ing tree. It looked as if my attacker had dragged me to the grassy embank-ment on the lake side of the road, near the food storage warehouses, and left me there. Why beat me unconscious then take me somewhere to re-cover safely?

My gaze rested on the storeroom roof I'd first seen him on. The door was locked. Obviously the first load of deliveries hadn't started for the morning yet. Clutching my head as a wave of dizziness made my legs wobble, I walked toward the nearest ration station, where a thin man regarded me warily with bulging eyes. I must have looked a sight, battered and dizzy, but once his fishy gaze took in the tattoos on my arms he agreed to follow me back with the key to the warehouse.

"It's not meant to be opened yet, Credo," he told me for the third time, as we approached the door.

"I know," I muttered.

I had been here only yesterday and saw the difference immediately. The sacks of grain stacked by the door for delivery to the bakers' district were diminished; so too were the casks of beans. I circled the room, stepping among the vats, casks and cloth sacks of grains, vegetables, and fruit, the small precious bags of salt and other spices, my eyes constantly scanning. Toward the back of the warehouse the loose tiling and scuff marks in the beams showed where my attacker had broken in and cleared out a portion of our precious food.

"Does this door need a key from the inside?" I asked the man.

"No, Credo, you can lift the latch from here." He indicated the mechanism.

"This is the Stone-Guilder's sector, isn't it? Please tell her to arrange a check against the inventory." One man to enter the warehouse and let others in. He'd had help. We would need guards on here at all times now—day and night.

I started the long trek back the Manor, considering the theft. We were weeks into a siege and citizens might be driven to panicked hoarding. Businesses could try to exploit the shortages and run a black market in supplies. And Silasta had thieves, like everywhere else. But I'd recognized the charm necklace that had fallen out of the thief's clothes as he bent over me; he'd been Darfri, I'd have staked my honor on it.

The physics were more concerned with my shoulder wound reopening than the new injuries. "Nothing broken," one woman told me briskly. "But your head's had a bit of a bump. If you can keep off physical duties for a few days, that'd be best." We exchanged a look. "Well, as much as possible, anyway."

The lump was like a small fruit sprouting out of the back of my head. I rubbed it gingerly as I returned slowly to the Manor, the walk up the hill far more taxing than usual. Several times I thought someone was following me, but no matter how suddenly I glanced around, or paused to adjust the cording on my paluma, there was never anyone there. Probably just leftover fear from my nightmares, but it was unsettling enough that I was unusually grateful to see Bradomir as I passed the Leka apartments, smoothing his moustache and giving me his usual charming, empty smile. "Has the Honored Chancellor summoned you too, Credo? I seem seldom to see him without you."

"Our families have always been close, as you know, Credo," I said, tone neutral as I could make it.

"Indeed, indeed." He looked me over in a calculating fashion. "But you and the Chancellor, why, you practically grew up as brothers. Two motherless boys, drawn together. . . ."

I stiffened, and he patted my shoulder like a concerned Tashi. "Oh, my boy, my boy, I mean no offense. Of course you both have mothers. I just meant perhaps the fact that your mothers were so *unavailable* during those crucial early years strengthened your bond. And now, why, now you're terribly fortunate to have his ear and his trust. Who could have known that he would become Chancellor so young, with so little time to prepare?"

This time I masked the stiffening and nodded blandly, though I longed to study his face the way he was studying mine. Was this meant to be intimidation, or an accusation? Did Bradomir suspect *me* of something?

Before I could think of how to phrase a reply, a litter approached from behind. Credo Lazar struggled out of it and dismissed his two manservants as he hastened to join us.

"Credo Jovan!" he said, patting my shoulders with sweaty hands. "Glad to see you! I had hoped to speak to you."

"Yes?" I said, my interest picking up. "Have you learned something about Lord Ectar? Or someone else?"

He shook his head, regretful. "I fear not, Credo. I'm sure you have seen Lord Ectar working in your own sector. But when he is not there, I have observed the Talafan lord frequently at the training grounds, assisting the instructors there. Talafan are fine archers and I believe he has quickly become rather well regarded there. Oh, he is enjoying what pleasures Silasta still offers, of course, as well. He has become acquainted with the bathhouses and the last of the gaming establishments that are still open. But honestly, Credo, he appears no more than a tourist at worst."

I nodded, continuing to walk toward the Manor entrance. I had not really suspected Lord Ectar in any case, but it was good to see that Lazar had put no insubstantial amount of effort into helping me. I could certainly believe that the spoiled Credo might have inadvertently contributed to the rebellion, perhaps by letting conditions on his land deteriorate, or by the common worker resenting his obvious and extravagant wealth. But actively assisting the rebels, or murdering the Chancellor, would be beyond him. Perhaps we could use him further to assist.

"I've also been sending runners with messages to Credo Javesto on and off the past few days," he continued, huffing and puffing as he trotted beside me even at my substantially reduced pace. Unlike Bradomir, he hadn't seemed to notice anything unusual about my disheveled appearance. "And always they found our fellow Councilor in his correct sector, instructing his people and taking reports. My runners said he was always easy to find, and had been prominent around his sector through the day." He clicked his tongue, frowning, as though his target's diligence were itself some character flaw.

Bradomir coughed. "I spoke to the Order Guard assigned to Credo Javesto's sector personally," he said. "She reported the same, that the Credo has been helpful and active in his sector each day, and takes no unusual meetings." He waved a hand lazily at me. "Don't worry, young Credo, I concocted plausible excuses to be asking. The Guard didn't think it suspicious."

"Thank you, both of you," I said. "The good Credo is probably just outspoken, not a villain." As I said it aloud I wasn't convinced myself; after all, I had been right to act on my suspicion regarding the storehouses last night.

Tain waited for us in one of his Tashi's favorite audience rooms; a quiet, curved space at the back of the Manor, built into the side of the mountain itself and lit by elegant blown-glass lamps suspended from the ceiling. He started to rise with immediate concern at the sight of me, but I shook my head quickly from behind Bradomir and he took the signal, diverting to clasp the Credo's hand instead. "Thank you for coming," he said. "I'm afraid I have further news about matters within the city. I've just been informed by the Stone-Guilder that thieves raided one of our storehouses last night."

Bradomir froze and Lazar gasped. "How much was taken?"

"Enough to damage us," Tain said. Even at prior levels there had been grumbling in the lower city about the rationing system, rumors others were hoarding, storing up for their own families or for trading if things got grim. If the rations had to be spread more thinly, things might flare up.

"And do we know who—"

"I'm afraid not." Tain ushered the Credolen to a seat among the fat little chairs of which Caslav had been so fond; not quite the familiarity of sitting on cushions on the floor, but less formal than a full meeting room. He poured the tea carefully. "Was it opportunistic, or intended to weaken our position?"

"I rather think we should assume we have traitors within the city looking to assist their brethren out there," Bradomir said. "After all, this theft confirms what we already suspected, that those in the country resent the wealth and power they see here in the city, and want to take it for themselves. It is no surprise that they would steal food, when this uprising is really at its core about taking what is not earned."

It was then I noticed a strange look on Tain's face, a kind of bright-eyed intensity as he looked between the men. "And we've earned our wealth, haven't we?" he asked, with such false mildness that I almost wanted to shout caution at blustery, oblivious Lazar as he nodded in fierce agreement.

"Precisely! Our ancestors, the first Council, made this city and this country what it is!"

"Aren't we finding out right now how dependent we are on the rest of the country to sustain us here, though? For food, for labor, for the supply of trade goods that make us rich?" Tain still spoke levelly, but this time Bradomir caught the undercurrent; he shifted back to solicitous-uncle mode in a heartbeat.

"You are right, of course, Honored Chancellor. So wise for your years! The country does depend on all of us doing our part. We are a great engine, are we not? And our farmers and miners and estate workers have all contributed to that greatness. As have we! We provide education, justice, the finest healthcare in the continent, and countless opportunities to learn the fine arts and crafts and skills of our Guilds. All are welcome in Silasta. But this?" He spread his hands in the manner of a disappointed tutor and clucked his tongue. "This violence and brutality? This is not what our country stands for. Though it saddens me to oppose my own countrymen, we are bound by our honor and loyalty to our country and they have betrayed that loyalty. I believe we must stand up and defend this city."

I thought of the head in the bag, and my own beating, and the murder of our uncles. There was no easy answer to this, but I found myself not in disagreement with Bradomir, which was an odd sensation.

Tain stared at the wall, a muscle in his jaw working, and said nothing for a very long time. The Credolen shifted, uncomfortable; even Bradomir seemed to have run out of things to say. Abruptly Tain got to his feet. "I've got some important things to take care of, gentlemen," he said.

"But, you summoned *us*, Honored Chancellor," Lazar stammered, looking confused.

"I don't think you can help any further, Credo," Tain said coldly. "Attend your duties. I have a lot to think about."

Lazar mumbled a hasty apology, but the shutters came down on Bradomir's smooth expression, and I knew Tain had made a mistake, maybe even an enemy.

I told him so, once we were alone, along with my theory that Javesto might have tipped someone off about the best time to break into the storehouses. "We need to seriously consider the possibility that Javesto is actively working with Darfri rebels inside the city."

The anger was gone as abruptly as it had erupted. "I'm just tired. I want a solution, not rhetoric about traitors and loyalty." He looked up at me, bleak. "Lini was up here last night. Did you see what she's found about the Guilds? And the school? We've let the estates go, Jov. We're not treating people outside the cities as part of Sjona—we might as well be two separate countries, where we're taking everything and it's not clear that we're giving anything in exchange. We don't know what education their children are getting, or what quality of judicial services there are in the villages. Money goes from the Administrative Guild to the Families for determination councils and schools in the estates but the amounts have dwindled and we're not getting any accounting for the funds. I asked Budua when we'd last had an appealed decision from an estate determination council to the city ones, and she blustered and couldn't tell me. I went through my family's steward's reports and there's never a mention of any of these services. I was going to ask Bradomir and Lazar to explain how it works on their lands, but what's the point? They just tell me they don't know precisely, that their stewards take care of these things. And I can't even argue because that's what mine does, too. And yours.

"We call the Darfri outside traitors for rising against us, but what reason do they really have for loyalty? What proof is there that we've been any kind of proper government for them?"

I let out my breath in a puff. "Look, I won't pretend this isn't all troubling. Maybe services have been run down out there. But there's a big jump between resentment about living conditions and pitching a siege on the capital. If things are bad out there, why not petition the Council directly? Or write to the Chancellor? Why raise a bloody *army* as a first step? And honor-down, Tain, look what they did to our messengers. I know you've been obsessing over the Warrior-Guilder, but I never thought you'd think violence was the way you solve difficult problems."

He scowled. "Aven's not violent. She's brave, and she's a fighter of course, but she—"

"Tain, I don't want to hear a treatise on the virtues of Aven the precious Warrior-Guilder, all right? I don't trust our Council and I'm not convinced they wouldn't enslave the population of the estates if they could get away with it, so I don't believe people rebelled for no reason. What I *do* believe is that murdering people for living in a city and trying to destroy our entire civilization is not the right course of action, and we don't deserve to be killed for whatever grudge they might have, valid or not."

He looked at the floor, sails drooping. "I know," he said at last. "I do know. But you should read some of the Council records. Did you know there've been motions to get additional Guilds—for years they've tried to get a farmers' guild, and a miners' guild. . . ." Animated again, he sprang up. "The deaths in our gemstone mines, Jov! I never knew how many people died in there, and there's no Guild to look after them, or change the way things are done. But every time it comes up, it gets crushed. And these people who were my Tashi's closest allies, and who we're meant to trust with our lives here, they're the ones who were always arguing how the Guilds are part of our traditions and we can't go adding new ones. They don't care that people die out there."

"Well," I said, fidgeting, "we can't have a Guild for every job there is, or the Council would be hundreds strong. It's hard enough getting twelve people to come to a decision on something."

Tain's mouth twisted as he looked at me, like he'd discovered something unpleasant he'd never noticed before. He shook his head and spoke slowly. "Jov, we've got two different Guilds just for kinds of art. Surely *one* Guild which looks after the people who aren't in the cities is warranted, at least, given we couldn't even feed ourselves without them. Did you know there are ten times as many people who live outside the cities as in?"

I thought of the camp outside our walls, an ocean of tents and figures trying to swallow us whole. "Yes, actually, I did." When he fell silent, staring at the wall with his hands jammed under his armpits, I levered myself up and stood beside him. "I do understand, and of course you're right." Etan's kind, serious face flashed across my eyes then, and my throat tightened at the wave of emotion—the love, respect, and trust I'd shared with my uncle, soured by grief at his loss, and shame at my failure to save him. "It's just hard to think about these things when we've lost so much."

"We have to, Jov." Tain's face was still serious, but without judgment. He picked up a paperweight from the table and passed it from hand to hand, his gaze distant. "We have to find out why this happened before we can stop it."

He was right. I needed to put aside the illusion of Silasta as a perfect place, a beacon of illumination and progress. Whatever our strengths, we'd had a key weakness and it had been exploited. Our Council hadn't upheld the principles that should have guided them. Honor was not an entitlement, but a reflection of our values. The leaders of our society, supposedly a society built on honor, had furthered their own causes while those without a voice suffered. The supercilious voices of entitled Councilors played around my head, whining, scheming, plotting, all the while holding themselves out as all that was right and good in the world.

"We're still missing the trigger," I said, to shift attention from my uncomfortable thoughts. "No matter what's been happening over time out there, something must have changed. People don't resort to violence as their first step." I wished again we had survivors from the first attack to question. "Was there any indication in the Council records that something had changed recently?" If Etan and Caslav had been alive when the siege started, would we know more?

"No," Tain said, rubbing his forehead. "I searched through meeting records for the last half year or so. There's nothing specific. But *something* must have happened. And those leeches out there aren't telling us anything." He glared at the nearest chair as if contemplating kicking it.

Letting him stalk around the room, I sat still, thinking. If Caslav or Etan had known things were at boiling point on the estates, why had they not told us? Had we truly been so removed from their affairs? Or had things only come to a head in the last weeks before their deaths? I cursed my absence over the summer. Tain rarely attended Council meetings; the Heir's seat was often treated as little more than an occasional tiebreaker available to the Chancellor. But I had to believe that Etan would never have been party to deliberate wrongdoing, and would have told me if he'd seen signs of it. I had to.

"What I can't understand is how they supported this." Tain flung the paperweight into a corner, the dull clunk muffling the curse he sent after it. I heard the same defensiveness and guilt that warred within me, and I didn't need him to elaborate on who "they" were. The thought of Etan being oblivious or uncaring about anyone, let alone tens of thousands of people, seemed too alien to be real. I couldn't reconcile it with all I knew of him: his compassion, his empathy.

But the more we found out about how our world worked, the more apparent it was that we'd been woefully, willfully blind. And neither of us had truly known our Tashien.

Bitterseed

DESCRIPTION: Poison derived from the inside of certain nuts, the seeds of some fruits, and the stalks of some grasses, deadly when combined with water. Poisoning can be by ingestion or by transfer through the skin.

SYMPTOMS: At low levels include weakness, confusion, shortness of breath, headache, dizziness, and seizure. In acute ingestions they are immediate and dramatic, usually involving convulsions, collapse, and death.

PROOFING CUES: Burns the tongue, acrid and bitter, detectable and difficult to mask in fatal doses. Smell is nutty and distinctive.

8

Kalina

I slipped out of our home into the rainy afternoon, hoping the combination of grim weather and a hooded waxed raincoat would discourage anyone from approaching me. My limbs and joints ached and I was still overtired from the previous day's exertions, but the empty homes in the poor neighborhood had given me an idea. The sewers were a dark and dangerous way out. We had temporarily dammed the main pipe to let our runners out that first night, but now the flow would be treacherous, perhaps impossible, to navigate. Still, for a traitor who did not need to fear being shot at the far end as our messengers must have been, it might be a risk worth taking.

The weather had eased to a light sprinkle when I set off to the north side of the city, where the lake turned wide and marshy and the minor sewer tunnels joined the main waste conduit from the city out into the northern landscape. Not a well-trafficked area of the city, for obvious reasons. My hooded cloak bore the added weight and chill of the drizzle and my chest wheezed and squeaked, unable to fill properly.

Shallow breathing was something of a necessity anyway once the smell hit, pungent and forceful. I wished I'd thought to bring some of whatever Thendra had given us to mask the smell of decay. The grate was guarded by a solitary woman, bored and miserable as she loitered under the eaves of the closest building, carefully arranged between fat drips from the edge. "Empty your bucket and move along, lady," she barked, when I'd stood there more than a few moments.

Instead, I joined her under the eaves, pushing back my cloak to show her my tattoos.

"Apologies, Credola," she said, smartening up.

I waved it away. "How long's your shift? This must be dull."

"It's the worst," she agreed, without rancor. "You get used to the smell after a while, but you never really warm to watching people dump their shit all day."

I laughed. "Fair point."

As if summoned, a figure trudged up with a bucket and dumped it over the grate. The guard offered me a scented rag and I breathed it in thankfully.

"Begging your pardon, Credola, but this is no place for a lady like yourself."

I shrugged. "A siege is no place for ladies such as either of us, but here we are."

This time she laughed. "Now there's a fair point if I ever heard one." Another few citizens came by, laden with foul buckets and sodden demeanors. She watched them, stoic, with barely a nose wrinkle. "Can I help in some way?"

"The Council's focused on deserters," I told her. "The sewer tunnel is an obvious way to try to leave the city."

She followed my thought easily enough. "Checking if anyone's tried coming through? Well the grate's locked tight, Credola, and there's one of us rostered here all the time." She looked me over. "'Course we were told that was to keep an eye out for the enemy trying to get *in* through the sewers."

I shrugged. "The longer we're in here, the greater the appeal will be to escape."

"I suppose. Drowning in other people's shit isn't the way I'd like to go, but each to their own."

"Anyone asking too many questions? Sounding out bribes?"

"Not to me. I can ask the others—there's four of us rotate here."

I paused to wait for another citizen to empty their bucket. This one didn't smell foul; perhaps my nose was adjusting. "Thank you," I said. "Please, if anyone does approach you, don't confront them. Come to me or my brother, Credo Jovan, or the Chancellor, instead." I handed her a small stone marked with the Oromani symbol. "You can bring that to Jovan or to the entrance of the Manor. Whatever you or your comrades are offered, my family will pay triple if you come to us instead."

"What good's money in this city now?" she said with a snort. "Three times useless is still useless. If you don't mind me saying, Credola."

I hesitated. What value had money in a besieged city when you couldn't use it to buy food or to keep yourself safe?

"Just a joke, Credola," she said, grinning. "Of course we would obey the will of the Council. Besides, you can still buy kori."

"Well, we aren't barbarians." I started to say more, but out of the corner of my eye saw that the last man to empty a bucket remained, lurking about between two buildings up the street. A small wiggle helped my hood farther forward over my face. His bucket hadn't smelled like household waste. And now he lingered in the rain. My brother wasn't the only one who could be paranoid.

I thanked the guard again and left her to her unenviable duty via one of the side alleys. Thankful for the rain now, I padded around the narrow street behind, head down, just one more faceless drudge on my own business, until I circled back to the sewer street. Our overly interested friend hung about still, playing a little skill game balancing and tossing stones on the backs of his hands. I didn't believe his false idleness for a moment.

When he spun about and stalked up the street, leaving his bucket behind, I'd enough time to slip back into the shadows of the alley, the heavy splatter from a broken eave providing further cover. He didn't even glance at me as he passed. I barely glimpsed his profile, hidden under a brimmed hat, and from behind nothing about his gait or physique seemed remarkable. He was thin, with dark hair worn long and braided over his shoulders, and his coat was plain and cheap.

Etan had taught me to observe, so observe I would. I tracked behind the stranger through a winding series of small lanes until he reached his ap-

parent destination: a kori bar called Branno's that had remained open, albeit to greatly reduced custom, during the siege. It had low, wide windows
with broad sills, and stone benches inside and out. In good weather and
better times, customers had probably sat at the front of the kori bar and
enjoyed their drinks outside amidst fat little citrus plants in glazed pots.
Today the outside was bare, the citrus plants stripped of fruit and the
benches cold and empty, pooling with little rain puddles. I loitered near a
table by the window with a good view of the inside of the building and
watched the man as he made his way to the bar. Without his coat it was
easy to mark him as a Doranite: olive-skinned and long-nosed, though his
garb was Silastian.

He said something to the barkeep and the ancient fellow closed his lips
over bulging teeth and shook his head. The man raised one hand then let it
drop, shrugged, and turned away. Refusing to serve him? A reminder that
the distrust within the city went beyond the Darfri; any outsiders were
finding things hard in the increasingly tense conditions.

I almost left then, until I saw who was sitting at the table he approached, and my heart started skidding around like a live thing in my
tight chest.

Varina the Theater-Guilder sat in a dark corner with Hasan, a prominent musician in her Performers' Guild and, I remembered, the same man
who had performed at Lazar's lunch on the day of the poisoning. She must
have come straight here after the Council meeting. Nothing prevented a
Councilor having a break and a cup of kori, but this bar was nowhere near
her Guildhall, her sector, or her apartments.

I lurked at the edge of the window, keeping the Doranite man in my
view but staying outside Varina's line of sight. The three spoke briefly and
then exchanged something, though a lamp and several cups obscured my
view, so perhaps they had merely moved their hands at the same time.

The Doranite man stood and strode toward the door. I stepped away
from the window and pretended to be reading the sign, but needn't have
bothered; he went past me without a glance, cramming his hat back on, his
pace quick. Before I could move away from the doorway to follow him,
Varina was upon me, too, Hasan right behind her, a pile of coins on the
table for the abandoned drinks. Her already tense face tightened at the
sight of me. I suppressed my frustration at being spotted and sauntered up,

casual, smiling, remembering how she had reacted the last time she'd been challenged. It gave me confidence.

"Theater-Guilder! I was passing and I saw you through the window." I gestured to the kori cups. "I was just on an errand—what brings you all the way over here?"

Varina swallowed. She smoothed a hand over her hair and glanced at her companion. "I've had a busy day with Council business, dear," she murmured. "And I met a friend for a drink. Even in these times, friendships are important, as you doubtless know, with your relationship with our Honored Chancellor."

The musician Hasan put a hand on her waist, one eyebrow raised and the hint of a smug smile on his lips. Varina wouldn't be the only one to assume my friendship with the Chancellor was something more. I suspected Tain let people assume that, for convenience, and though I didn't want to be bothered, it still had the power to wound me even after all these years. I couldn't tell whether Varina meant to insult, provoke a reaction, or simply fish for information. I smiled more broadly.

"Actually, I almost ran into your friend just now, coming in. I saw him sitting with you." Impulse and sudden wild speculation took me, and it was my turn to fish. "He's one of Credo Lazar's servants, isn't he? What was his name—Batbayer?"

The forced smiles dropped off their faces. Varina's gaze darted away to the side and Hasan's fat lips twisted into almost a snarl. I kept my face smooth as they shifted from foot to foot, sweating, trying to decide what I knew and what I didn't. Etan had taught me the value of silence.

Varina tried for a laugh, but managed only a husky "ha." "Not a friend, as such. Just a Guild member." For the head of the Performers' Guild, her acting was poor.

"Wonderful. Tain's been trying to speak to Lazar's servants since the day our uncle died, but it's been hard to find them. Now I know he's one of your Guild members, you'll be able to help us talk to him."

She didn't meet my gaze. "I don't know who he works for, Credola Kalina. And we don't keep address details for our members."

"That's funny," I said, my tone still light. "I've been looking over the Guild rolls, and they definitely listed members' addresses. Now that you say that, I didn't see his name, either."

Hasan folded his arms, glaring at me, his thick eyebrows drawn together. "Why were you looking at our Guild rolls, then?" He took a step closer, and fear surged inside me. I glanced around, but the bartender was the only other person inside, and he was hunched over with his back turned at the other side of the room.

Her companion's aggression seeming to restore her confidence, Varina put her hands on her hips and tossed her hair. "You're speaking with a Councilor, Credola. Kindly remember your manners."

"My apologies, Theater-Guilder," I said, all meekness. "I know you're terribly busy. I've got the rolls. I'll find the address myself, shall I?"

I wanted to laugh as they pushed past me; the sensation of controlling the situation was so foreign and so welcome. If they were our enemies, whether connected to the poisoning or the siege or both, at least direct attack was obviously beyond them.

Our apartments reeked almost as badly as the sewers, though in a different way. "Jov? What's going on?" I slipped the wet cloak off.

He was in the proofing room, wearing spectacles and a cloth over his nose and mouth, and he gestured at me to stay back as he closed the lid of a chest on the bench. I watched, wary, and jumped when a shattering *pop* came from within. He checked my position then cautiously opened the chest.

A puff of fine gray sprang out, and we both skidded backward. Jov waved me out and shut the door behind him. He pushed down his mask and gave me a satisfied grin; I'd never seen him look more like Etan, and I had to turn away to hide the flood of sudden, unexpected grief that struck me.

"What was that?" I asked eventually, masking the emotion with sharpness.

"You gave me the idea," he said, setting down the spectacles and mask. "I've been thinking of things I should carry in the pouches you made. Then I thought, what if we could use some of these during the next attack? When I used them down there, the rebels were terrified. Half our city seems to be convinced they're going to use some kind of spirit magic on us. So why not turn that fear around on them?" He showed me a list of notes, boyish excitement making him speak faster than usual. "Look, here's what I was thinking. If we put stingbark powder in water and tipped it over the attackers, it'd make their skin itch and burn; and if we mixed it with something viscous, it'd stick to their skin. Malek's acid will dissolve wood in a breeze, and metal, too, if you give it a bit of time; if we could get the engineers to make some—Etan knew how, he's got all the instructions here—we could use it to try to disable a ram or even a range weapon, if we could fire a container of it accurately."

I looked over the list, leery. Etan had loved to experiment with various chemicals, but I recalled more mistakes than successes. "And whatever you just burst in there was . . . ?"

"Oh. Art's tonic." He carefully didn't look at me. I was all too familiar with that heavy sedative. Etan had used it during my bad episodes, dissolving the powder in a solution, then boiling it so I could breathe in the steam. "If you breathe in the powder directly that works, too. Better, actually, though it's a lot less comfortable. I was just seeing if I could make it pop and spread broadly if I sealed it in a container and then added something that would react together to make a gas. That was pica paste with vinegar in a jar."

I couldn't remember what pica paste was, but it hardly mattered. "That's really clever, Jov." I paused. "And nothing that will kill."

He looked at his hands. "I *would* kill if I had to," he said, almost fiercely. "To protect you or Tain, of course I would. I did, on the walls, in the battle. But . . ."

But he didn't want to. Protectiveness was built into him; it was impossible to separate his duty to his family and Tain's from his identity, but I knew too well how fixated he was on the consequences of even his minor actions and inactions, playing out blame and judgment in a hundred different ways. He did not want extra burdens. "I understand."

He didn't respond, but some of the tension left his shoulders. "Anyway, where have you been?" He opened the secret door to check if the cloud had dissipated. "I thought you'd be back here."

I hesitated. Already his distraction was fading and his sharp eyes were taking in the damp ends of my hair and bottom of my dress. I'd been sure he'd be pleased. Suddenly that seemed shortsighted. As I recounted it my words faltered at his increasing frown.

"You what?"

"I followed him," I said. "He didn't see me."

"Lini." He rubbed his forehead, pained. "He could have, though."

"He didn't," I repeated. "Jov, he was a Doranite." I seized on his renewed interest and finished the story, avoiding eye contact as I mumbled through my confrontation with Varina and Hasan. My satisfaction with my discoveries had drained out along with my energy.

"What made you think it was Batbayer?"

I shrugged. "I had his name on a list of people to watch out for in any of the rosters. And when I saw them together I just made a guess. I didn't really expect to be right."

"You shouldn't have baited them," he admonished. He started to pace, but broke disjointedly to look me up and down, as if searching for undisclosed injuries. "I don't like any part of this. What were they exchanging? Something for Batbayer to smuggle out of the city? Information? We need to let Tain know."

My throat burned with things unsaid. Hating my silence but lacking the energy to quarrel, I followed him into the Manor. We met Tain, returning from the training grounds, outside the Manor gate. He dismissed his servant guards as we came inside.

When we passed Argo in the Manor entryway, I smiled at him, and fancied I saw a flicker of a response on the old man's face. Tain stopped. "Argo, you've been here all day, every day for weeks," he said. "Let me get some assistance for you to manage the entrance."

Argo shrugged, not making eye contact. His heavily lined face twitched a little as he replied. "I don't have any family, Honored Chancellor. I'm too old to help the defense on the walls. If I stay here, no one comes into the Manor without *my* say so, and there aren't any surprises for you."

Tain clasped the little man's shoulders. "Thank you," he said. "You've served my family so well. I want you to know I appreciate it."

Argo blinked, his pursed mouth working silently. I turned away to hide a smile. Tain had the charm his uncle had sometimes lacked. If we lived through this siege for him to rule properly, perhaps he'd be a leader to be reckoned with.

We filled Tain in on his way to his rooms, waiting while he cleaned and changed.

"And you're sure it was Lazar's servant, Lini? They admitted it?" Tain appeared, looking more presentable in a clean paluma.

"No," I said. "But there wasn't any doubt. It was like I'd slapped her."

"Then we need to find this man," he said. He fished around in his satchel and brought out a dark fold of bread, which he raised to his mouth. Jov sprang to his feet.

"Where did you get that?" He snatched the bread. "I haven't proofed it."

"I picked it up at the ration station when I was done with training," Tain said, his tone defensive. "No one knew I was going there, so it can't have been tampered with."

Jov sniffed the bread and opened the fold. "There's oku meat on this, which means it's not part of the normal rations. Who made it? What ration station?"

"The one in Bradomir's sector, up near the tournament grounds," he said, eyes on the food longingly. "I don't know who made it—whoever was manning the station, I guess. There was a woman there who helped me. Jov, I haven't eaten in forever. I want that. I'm not waiting for hours."

"You can have it once I've proofed it and we've waited. Were you even listening to Lini? A member of your Council meeting secretly with a servant who was there when our uncles were poisoned, and you think today's the day to start being a fool?" He broke off a small piece of the bread and sniffed, examining it with fingers, eyes and nose, then tongue. To me, of course, it looked like regular flat black bread. But like Jov had said, meat was not part of the rations being divvied out in the stations. Either someone had specifically prepared that meal for Tain, or ration stations were reserving superior food for certain classes of people. I hoped it was the latter—a problem, but one that could be fixed.

Behind us, Tain paced about, scowling. Hunger made him irritable. But my eyes were only for my brother. Even though I'd seen this a hundred times, my heart raced still. Always, always, at the forefront of my mind was that if Etan hadn't detected the poison that killed him, Jov wouldn't either.

"I've safe food at my apartments," Jov said. "We can—" He broke off, looking at his hand. I drew closer as he rubbed grease between his fingers, smelled it, then licked it gingerly. He took a bite of the meat and chewed. Tain was looking between Jov and the food and back again. He started to say something but even as he opened his mouth Jov spat the meat into his hand.

"Slumberweed," he said, stricken. "Honor-down, Tain, it's poisoned."

Praconis/
slumberweed

DESCRIPTION: Long-living and hardy ground cover favoring exposed, dry conditions, used by physics as a sedative for centuries. Grows small thorny fruit containing hundreds of lightweight seeds. Green parts and seeds are toxic.

SYMPTOMS: Consumption of leaves will induce drowsiness, peaceful sleep, eventually coma, depending on quantity. Seeds are far more dangerous and cause slow reduction of motor control, lack of energy, heart irregularities, and eventual sudden heart failure.

PROOFING CUES: Taste of the leaves is bitter, astringent; smell is refreshing, reminiscent of rain. Seeds are distinctively oily and have a burn similar to pepper.

9

Jovan

I rinsed the oily taste of the slumberweed seeds from my mouth. I hadn't swallowed any of the meat, and had an antidote on hand, but still my pulse pounded as I rinsed and spat a dozen times in the basin. Closing the secret cupboard containing antidotes and other supplies my Tashi had kept in Chancellor Caslav's rooms, my hands shook. I had taken the seeds in small doses before, with Etan, but finding them in Tain's food was different. Had he consumed the quantity in that portion of oku, his heart would have failed within the week.

Tain hadn't said a word since we'd arrived at Caslav's rooms—just helped me to the cupboard, handed me things, and refilled my cup after each rinse. His silence was unnerving and my nerves were frayed enough as it was. I wasn't enjoying being proved right about his being in danger. Kalina went back to our apartments to fetch him some proofed food and Tain dropped bonelessly into a cushion, burying his hands in his armpits, hugging his chest. I helped myself to Caslav's collection of kori, knowing it was probably a mistake—alcohol dulled the senses. I passed a cup to my friend and he accepted it in silence.

We put away the best part of a bottle together, more than I'd drunk in years, but finally setting my empty cup down, I had never felt more sober.

Tain looked up at me, haggard, his eyes years older than they'd been an hour ago. I didn't want to have the conversation lurking there.

"We need to know who made that," I said, blocking the topic before he could raise it. I knew the moment would come. I'd known since Caslav died, and probably before that, if I was honest, that Tain had reservations about my role. "We'll need to go back to the ration station. We'll need to know who was there, who had access to the food. . . ." I rubbed my fore- head, conscious again of the headache the poison had temporarily made me forget. Our enemy was still here, targeting Tain, and he or she wasn't familiar with only one poison.

"Jov, I'm sorry," Tain said, voice croaky. "I should have listened to you. I just . . ." He trailed off.

"I know," I said, heaving myself out of the chair, my stiff body and the alcohol making me awkward. "You stay here. I want to see where you got this."

It was a mark of how shaken Tain was that he didn't argue. I'd never seen him so unsettled, not even the day our Tashien had died. I left him sitting alone by the door, head in his hands.

Next I traced Tain's steps to the lower city, wishing I'd not drunk so much. In a way, though, the queasiness distracted me from the throbbing headache, the bruised ribs, and the compulsions threatening to overcome me. The miserable on-and-off drizzle was a welcome sensation on my hot skin. I wanted to first investigate the station alone; bringing an Order Guard would just announce to the poisoner that we had caught the poison and were actively looking for our enemy.

Every season since childhood I'd sat at the tournament grounds with Tain and Kalina, cheering and betting on my favorite athletes. Now it was barely recognizable. Where once the mighty stands had enclosed obstacle courses, marked fields for games and running tracks, the soggy grass was now peppered with groups of men and women under the direction of a few uniformed instructors. One sodden group fired arrows into straw targets while another hacked at one another with cane swords and axes. Marco, directing the archery group, spotted me and waved.

I joined his group. "It's been years since I've taken a martial class. Think I can still shoot a bow?"

He handed me one with a smile. "This shift is almost done, but join the line, Credo Jovan. I will soon have you in shape. Even in this weather."

There were a variety of men and women in the line, their tattoos showing a mix of Guild membership and even the occasional Family sigil. The arrows were cane ends blunted with fat little sacks. The arrow that had protruded from the man's neck on the wall had been bone. I made a note to ask Kalina if she could find out which countries used bone arrows.

My brain recalled the steps but my body fumbled through the old form: left foot in front, left index finger pointing toward the target, three fingers on my right hand drawing the string, arrow between them. It was harder to draw than I expected. The alcohol didn't help my focus, either. My arrow sailed pitifully past the straw dummy; Marco's face was a study in politeness. "Try again, Credo. No need to rush."

By the tenth round my arm burned and my fingers ached, but I was hitting the target. Marco's smile looked genuine as he passed by me. A shout came from the group working with cane swords farther along, and the Warrior-Guilder excused himself to deal with the scuffle that followed. I took the opportunity to fall away from the archers to look about.

Ectar and his servants were dotted around the field, obvious with their elegant movements and their pale skin exposed by training tunics. Marco had enlisted all of them to help teach. Squinting, I eventually identified Credo Pedrag, the Craft-Guilder, all but unrecognizable as he hacked away with a cane sword at a dummy, long hair tied back and plump form surprisingly powerful.

To have arrived at the ration station at which he'd been poisoned, Tain must have left the field there, through the gate, then gone left down the nearest street. Anyone at the grounds or watching them could have seen and followed him; no one was taking rolls and in the confusion of the different training groups it would have been easy to slip out unseen.

It took only a few minutes to reach the ration station, a converted dressmaker's shop. A woman and a girl, official city sashes swung across their shoulders, sat half-hidden behind vats and baskets at the table in the store. Colored cloth fabric rolls stood like bright soldiers at attention in the corners.

Again, Kalina's secret purse found a use. In an alley I bit into a lavabulb, then spat out the seeds, and my face beaded as the burn took over my mouth. I wiped sweat into my hair and rumpled my clothes, then trudged out of the alley and to the station. "Can I help, Credo?" the woman asked, her tone deferential as her eyes traveled over my tattoos. "Have you come for rations?"

It wasn't an official distribution time, and nor would it have been when Tain had been here, but no one would have refused the Chancellor food. "Is that all right?" I asked her, exaggerating my stiff gait and approaching the table. "I've just been training—I know it's too early for the next rations."

"Yes, Credo, of course," she said, opening the closest basket. "We haven't received our next shift delivery yet, but there is bread and dried fruit here." She pushed it toward me and I noticed the smallest two fingers missing from one hand. Inside the basket simple rounds of flat black bread nestled in piles between dark goa berries and peach slices. Where was the poisoned oku? I took a round of bread, sniffing and letting a hint of disappointment show through my smile. "Thank you. Much appreciate this—I'm starving." The girl touched her companion's arm, whispering. Both looked at my tattoos again, then the first gave me a wink. "We have some oku out the back," she said. "If you want something a bit more substantial than fruit. . . ."

I nodded eagerly.

"Wait here, Credo."

As she ducked behind the heavy curtain separating the front of the store from the back, I gave the baskets, table, and room behind a surreptitious examination. Nothing registered as suspicious. Other than bolts of cloth, the space was empty—no room for someone to hide. The bread was cool and hardening, but the smell made my stomach grumble just the same. Other than Tain's tainted food, I hadn't eaten anything since last night, and the kori sloshed about in my empty stomach.

"How long've you been here?" I asked the girl, trying to sound casual and sympathetic.

"All day, Credo."

"I guess it's pretty busy. And then people like me come in and make it even harder for you, right?"

A flicker of a smile. "The new Chancellor came in before," she said proudly. "He's nice."

"I bet he brought a whole lot of extra people for you to feed."

Another smile, this one wider. She looked up through her lashes. "He was by himself," she said. "And he said thank you and he was sorry to put us out. It was no trouble. We usually get all kinds of people asking to be fed outside distribution times, but today it was just him."

So no one else tracked in with him and poisoned the meal on the spot. "And at least you get to miss school and spend time with your mother, huh?"

Mischief dimpled her plump cheeks. "It's better than school," she agreed. Then her grin dropped off. "Uncle went off to the walls. I like seeing Mother, but I'd rather my Tashi be home." I saw the accusation in her dark eyes, and couldn't think of a thing to say to make it better. Unless things changed, many children would be left without their Tashien and mothers forever.

"Is this your family's shop?" I asked. She nodded and I looked at the curtain separating the front of the shop from the back. Like most on this street, it was multistory; the family who ran the business probably lived upstairs, with one or more other families. Which meant it certainly had a back entrance for the occupants.

The girl's mother pushed back through the curtain, wringing her hands. "Credo, I am so sorry. We had a little oku out back before, but it's gone." Her sweaty forehead and fidgety posture spoke of nerves, but from embarrassment or dishonesty?

"Credo Bradomir always says to keep a little extra aside for the Credolen," she continued. "I haven't been serving it to regular folk, I promise. The whole tray is just gone." Her hands wrung together with apparent sincerity and she shook her head. "My deepest apologies, Credo."

"It's not your fault," I said. "The bread is fine. You've got a back entrance, right?" She nodded, hesitant. "Keep it locked from now on. There are bound to be thieves as rations run shorter."

Frustration boiled inside me as I left. I circled surreptitiously around the store; it opened into a back alley with no facing windows. Tain's visit had been unplanned and our enemy couldn't control every ration station. No one had come in before or after him via the front of the store. But a careful person, who knew stations were holding back particular food for Credolen, could have followed Tain and added the slumberweed oil to the reserved stocks. Tain's heart would have failed and he'd have died, probably on the training fields or while otherwise exerting himself, without suspicion. We had come so close to disaster, it made me shiver.

I didn't want to return to the Manor yet. Kalina would be there with Tain; she could look after him. Head churning, I thought instead of what my sister had learned. We could set others to combing the city for Batbayer, but that might alert him. Though I hated that she had taken such risks, Kalina's strategy had been sound. If we carefully monitored the sewer site, we might catch the Doranite trying to make an exit.

I headed that way now, using the long walk north to think. The rain had stopped again, and my muscles enjoyed the calm repetition of walking. Deliberately, I went through poorer neighborhoods, often observing the silence and abandoned feeling Kalina had described. I walked quickly and kept to the sides of the roads. I felt like a target, walking alone, though I could not have articulated the danger.

At the sewer entrance I didn't speak to the guard, just observed from the shadows at a distance. I also traced back along the minor sewer lines; their underground passage was marked by brighter grass poking out between the stones of the walkways. There were other small access points along the way, but only a child could have fit along those narrow routes.

Eventually I came to the north edge of the city. The wall rose above me on one side of the street, gray and marbled with lichen and insect trails. Though the air carried distant sounds of industry, no noise came from any of the nearby homes; perhaps they too were deserted, or all their occupants were on duty. A few birds chirped from a perch on the iron railing of someone's balcony, and a muddy rain puddle by the wall rippled rhythmically. There was something almost hypnotic about it, the ebb and flow of the water, the reflection of the sky above it distorted into shards each time the water flexed.

I shook my head, forcing myself to move—I couldn't avoid Tain forever.

Heading back to the Manor, I had walked perhaps six paces before the oddity sank in. Rainwater rippling in a puddle. Except it wasn't raining anymore, and hadn't been for a while. *So what's causing the rippling?*

As I crouched beside the puddle, concentric circles sped across it, small but clear. I pressed my hand into the mud below it.

Vibrations. I drew my hand back. The cold from the mud seemed to penetrate my whole body as I sat back on my heels, head reeling. The vibrations were too faint to feel through my shoes, but they weren't imagined. Something was happening beneath the surface. I looked across the street. If any of those houses had basements or cellars under the buildings, getting below the surface to take a look would give us a much better idea of what was going on. I tapped on the nearest door.

No answer. A few weeks ago it would have horrified me to even contemplate, but now it seemed almost natural to glance around and then test the lock. I didn't have much of a knack for fine motor tasks like lock-picking, but I *did* have a phial of Malek's acid in my purse, a few squirts of which dissolved the lock with a faint hiss. The door opened without protest and I slipped inside.

The room was cold and empty, stillness lying over furniture in disarray. Thatched reed matting covered the floor. There was a place in the corner where the edges of two intersecting mats looked tattier, and prying them up revealed a trapdoor. It covered a ladder, crudely made, leading down into the darkness. My quick search of the house failed to turn up a lamp, but I made a serviceable torch from the flare oil and igniter in my purse and a pilfered bowl. After a moment's hesitation, I climbed down.

The air temperature dropped as I descended, and the faint light from the hatch above me barely penetrated the darkness of the shaft, let alone the room below. My injured shoulder made my one-armed progress jerky and painful. It took only a minute or so to walk the entire footprint of the cellar, bumping into barrels and shelves, stubbing my toes and bashing my shins a dozen times even with my little light. I found a bare section of wall and pressed my ear up against it.

The sound was clearer here than above, loud enough that I fancied I could still hear the *chick-chick* even as I took my ear from the wall. My heart beat faster.

Digging.

Someone was digging underground. While we'd been covering the walls and worrying about siege weapons, the rebels had somehow gotten a team of diggers close enough to the wall without being detected, and had made enough progress on their tunnel that I could feel and hear them from here. How close we were to disaster made me shiver.

Turning back to the ladder and stepping in what I hoped was the right direction, I cracked my knee on the corner of something hard. I swore, hopping back, and crashed into a set of shelves. Flimsy as it was, the whole thing tottered away from the wall and fell to the ground with a shuddering crash of metal, glass, and the fortunes knew what else. I swore again and tripped, arms reaching out to steady myself on the wall . . . which wasn't there.

My mishap had revealed a hole in the wall, taller and wider than me, which had been concealed by the shelves. *A hidden passage?* I chewed my lip, my hand lingering on the edge of the bricked section where it turned to earth, trying to decide whether to go for assistance or investigate further.

Curiosity won. The oil had nearly burned up, but the remaining flames would be enough to heat the strip of ardorol tucked into my pouch, and adding dried ek leaves would slow the burn. The resulting white flare momentarily blinded me, then settled quickly into a warm glow.

Fifteen paces in, the tunnel opened up, and I found myself in a round space connecting what looked to be another tunnel and metal ladder, leading down. This one felt rough and rusty under my fingers, ancient. I paused. The logical step was to turn around and return to the surface, but the urge to continue and find out where these strange passages led compelled me. Just a little farther.

From the bottom of the ladder it became obvious this was a different kind of underground area. The ground was hard-packed and smooth, worn from passage over time, and the ladder affixed to a carved rock wall. The air smelled different, too, wetter and older. This was no man-made cellar, but a proper underground cavern system. I suspected it must be at least partially natural, given the scale of work to construct an entire artificial system would have required a huge endeavor by the Builders' Guild and would have been hard to keep a secret. I passed not just one, but four or five entryways into other caverns or tunnels.

With one last glance at the ladder, I took the passage to its right, which led me into a smaller chamber. I took another right and found another chamber, then did the same again. Each space was still, silent and empty. The sound of my breathing and the stream of thoughts in my head sounded unnaturally loud. Stopping in another little round chamber, the initial buzz of my reckless decision fading, I gave it a cursory sweep with the shallow halo of my light. There was nothing down here, or at least nothing worth immediate concern. Somewhere on the other side of the wall—or even maybe on our side—our enemies were digging into our city. It had been stupid to waste time here when others needed that information.

Turning to retrace my steps, I glimpsed something at the edge of my pocket of light. This chamber wasn't empty after all. A rough pallet sprawled against the farthest wall, made from gritty, unbleached fabric and stuffed with straw. I crouched beside it, feeling the impression down its middle. There was a sack, knotted and grimy, at the base of the bed. Inside were clothes: several colored shirts in the country style; cotton trousers; poorly made leather sandals. A bone comb was wrapped in a red scarf, its carved inscription too worn to make out. A sudden sound startled me from somewhere in the distance. Grabbing my light, I slipped back out of the chamber, listening.

Someone was moving through the caverns, approaching from the direction I'd come. The focused beam of a proper oil lantern swept in big arcs. Though the holder lay in shadow behind the light, his steps were confident as he moved through the chamber. I backed away. Impulsive I might have been today, but I had my limits. We could return later, or send someone down here to investigate after we dealt with the tunneling from the other side of the wall. I slipped into a corner, hoping the man would go in a different direction.

Only moments later, the beam of his light appeared from the opening I'd just come through. I slipped through the opening to my left, hoping to be well out of his sight. It was a slight risk to take a different tunnel, but one I was happy to take to stay out of his way. The rocky walls of the tunnel were suddenly illuminated, and my breath caught in my throat. Then, just as suddenly, the walls were dark again as his lamp moved on. Tension drained from me. *No reason to be frightened.*

Except, my brain chimed in, as the light returned to my tunnel, indicating his return toward me, *except, he seems to know I'm here.* My heart beat too fast and sweat ran into my eyes and down the back of my neck as I found another entranceway and ducked through it, barely taking two steps before the probing light swept around the previous chamber. This tunnel wound round to the right, and sloped sharply downward. I glanced back as he rotated the lamp, and it briefly lit up his own hands.

My chest turned to ice.

In his free hand, my pursuer carried a knife; a wicked curved blade as long as my forearm.

The passage continued down, going lower and lower. His search was thorough and methodical rather than hurried; it wasn't clear whether he knew the trail he followed was only moments old. I recalled the unhurried pace of the "Speaker" down on the battleground at the foot of the ladder, the way she had followed me, and the fear from that weird experience, which I had been suppressing in the time since, returned doubled in force. The memory of the gritty hand around my ankle that had seemingly fallen away when the woman had. I didn't believe in Darfri superstitions or spirits. I didn't believe. And yet.

As I emerged from the tunnel into yet another chamber, the air felt different: colder and cleaner, almost wet. The angle and length of unbroken wall beneath my scrambling fingers suggested a much larger space. Still the bobbing beam of light followed behind me. I moved along the wall, found another gap, and flung myself through it.

I hit solid wall, cracking my head; the impact knocked me onto my back and my glowing bowl upended. I'd run into not another tunnel but an irregularity in the wall, an alcove of some kind. I felt blood run down my forehead and nose as I found my feet. My pursuer entered the room, his light falling short of where I cowered against the wall. My rib cage blew in and out like a set of bellows straining under my skin, my breathing too loud.

I scurried to what looked like the blackest space in a sea of darkness, and this time no solid wall greeted me. I flung myself into the dark passageway and ran, hands outstretched on either side of me to feel the route, beyond caring that my steps might be audible. I felt the path rise beneath my feet, the upward gradient giving me an intoxicating taste of hope. I staggered out of the passage and into a chamber so small there was barely time to stop myself from hitting the far side of it. Behind me, rising out of the stillness, came the unrelenting *tap tap tap* of footsteps, like the beat of a song, signaling my end. Trapped. There was only one way in and one way out of what seemed likely to become my tomb.

My little cage lightened from black nothingness to gray shadows as he ascended, still with that disturbing lack of haste. I crouched, waiting. My fingers were unable to distinguish between the contents of my purse and the space was too small to safely throw powders, but I would risk poisoning us both if it came to that.

As the lamplight crescent crept over the threshold like some sinister moon, I glanced at the other side of the chamber, and there it was. My salvation.

A ladder.

I dove for it and hurled myself up with all the remaining strength in my good arm. My hand hit something solid—a metal hatch above me. Pressing my body tight against the rungs I shoved it open and scrambled up through heavy blankets into a paved room, panting. Relief flooded me as the dim light revealed furniture, baskets: the ordinary contents of a cellar. I hurried up the stairs and out of the house into the same residential district I'd begun from. Staggering across the street, I took cover in the narrow space between two houses, waiting for my pursuer to emerge.

He never did. I waited until the sweat soaking my face and neck turned icy in the breeze and I could no longer ignore the fiery wetness spreading across my shoulder. Whoever had chased me would not come above ground, it seemed. And this time, nothing in the world could have convinced me to do anything other than the sensible, logical thing. So I limped off, bleeding and dizzy, to find Tain.

Rabutin

DESCRIPTION: Woody shrub producing clumps of yellow flowers. Green parts of plant, flowers, twigs, sap, and pollen are all toxic if ingested or smoke from burned branches is inhaled. Handling of leaves and sap causes skin irritation.

SYMPTOMS: Include excessive swallowing and salivation, frequent defecation, eye watering or blurred vision, cardiac distress, seizures, death.

PROOFING CUES: Strong, astringent, woody taste, earthy smell in the fumes.

10

Kalina

All signs of the rain had gone. We worked in silence, or close to it; too much activity above the tunnelers and they might realize we had detected them. Eliska and a group of her engineers stood a short distance away. They pored over drawings and calculations, talking and gesturing as they tried to refine their estimations of the path of the tunnel and its likely exit point. Tain and Marco strategized about the best way to handle the situation—collapse the tunnel, wait to see what the rebels used it for, try to capture the tunnelers to question them . . . and beside me, Jov sat, clearly only half-listening.

My brother seemed far more shaken than his discovery warranted; I could see he had left something out of his hurriedly relayed story. There had been no chance to speak privately, and whatever had happened, Jov obviously didn't want to disclose it in front of other Councilors.

"It all depends what they're planning to do with it," Tain was saying. "What do you think, Jov? You've been quiet."

The Chancellor—strange, how easy it was now to think of him that way—laid a hand on Jov's good shoulder and peered at him, concern wrinkling his brow. "Shit, I'm sorry," he said, and suddenly he was our friend again. "You should get some rest."

Jov shook his head, stubborn.

"At least sit," I urged, and that much he was willing to comply with. I sat cross-legged with him next to the rough diagram Marco had drawn in the dirt, while the Warrior-Guilder indicated various points in the wall with a long stick.

"Here, and here," Marco said, pointing to long sections of the old city walls. "Strip our defenses right back on these less vulnerable sections. We can use Credo Jovan's cloth sentries to keep up appearances. If we keep normal movement on these sections"—here he traced along the northwest wall, where the army was most concentrated—"they should not be aware that we have detected their tunnel.

"We position a force inside the caverns, as near as possible to where the Stone-Guilder's engineers predict the tunnel will reach. If the rebels attempt to use the tunnel for a nighttime attack, we will be ready to box them in, or collapse the tunnel on top of them."

"I don't think that'll be possible," Eliska interjected. "Not unless we have far more time to prepare. We know where they're digging right now, but it will take much more investigation to determine the layout of the existing tunnel."

"Can we send scouts out to figure out where the tunnel begins?" one of the engineers asked.

A pause. We still hadn't let the public know what had happened to our last messengers, both because of the gruesome nature of their deaths and because we wanted there to remain hope that the army would soon come to rescue us. Jov's hand found mine in the shadows, and I knew we were sharing that terrible memory. Though I had only seen the six heads carefully and respectfully wrapped at the private burial, somehow those cloth-bound shapes were as dreadful as the bloody images I invented in my dreams.

"No. Too risky for the scout," Tain said. The jut of his chin and the defensive look exchanged with Marco and Jov told me they had again been arguing about attempting to send out new messengers; despite the others' urging, Tain had refused to risk anyone else being slaughtered so brutally.

"It'll be some hummock or patch of rocks hiding the entrance, and they're shifting men and dirt overnight when we can't see." He studied the crude dirt map for a moment, then looked up at the distant wall, chewing his lip. "It'd take too long to build anything big enough to get a sizeable force through into the city without detection. If I were them, I'd use it to sneak small groups in, infiltrate our defenses, then open one of the gates at an agreed-upon time."

Marco nodded. "That is what I would do, also. We would have no way of distinguishing between the rebels and our own people."

"If they know about the caves, they might also try to move a force inside the caverns and hide them there," I said. "Then they could attack from both fronts." It would be impossible to defend against the army pouring in through a gate and rising from below our feet.

"Or the tunnel could be designed to be destroyed," Eliska said. "They might be digging with the intention of collapsing the tunnel below a section of the wall. If the ground beneath a section were destabilized, the wall above could crumple."

"So what do we do?" Tain asked.

The Warrior-Guilder rubbed his head, frowning. "Intercept the diggers, collapse the tunnel outside the wall. That would stop the rebels from using it to gain access to the city or weakening the wall. Then be vigilant about monitoring for other tunnels, in case they try again."

Jov's keen observation of the rippling puddle gave me an idea. "What if we put big containers of water at intervals around the wall as a warning system? It'd be easier to detect digging if we can *see* it."

Marco nodded, his usually solemn face granting me an approving smile. "Excellent idea, Credola. I will ensure this is done and monitored in every sector."

"But if we intercept them now, we lose any chance of using this against them." Tain paced around the diagram. "There must be some way of using this information, giving ourselves the advantage for once."

Everyone fell silent. Jov and I had been raised to expect and prevent attacks on the Chancellor's family, but we had never prepared for a disaster like this. Our expertise was defending attacks from the shadows. Open warfare had never featured as a scenario in our training.

"I mean no disrespect, Marco, but honor-down, I wish Aven were here," Tain said, shaking his head in frustration. Though the longing in his tone still rankled, I couldn't help but agree for once. She might be crude and unsubtle, but the Warrior-Guilder's military mind would be invaluable, not to mention the thousand-strong army she commanded. And after dealing for weeks with polite evasiveness and condescension disguised as assistance from most of our peers, I better appreciated the appeal of her directness.

Marco appeared to take no offense. "I am a poor substitute," he said. "I too wish for our commander. She would know what to do."

Eliska cleared her throat. "For now, let's try to get a clearer idea of where that tunnel might end up. Once we know, we can at least prepare for any-one who comes through, whether that means engaging or tracking them if they attempt to hide in the city. With Credo Jovan's assistance, I'd like to take some of my engineers into these underground caverns to identify the best interception point."

Jov stiffened beside me and I again wondered what he wasn't telling us. This wasn't the first time he had withheld information from me, but it was rarely so obvious. "We don't know who or what is down there. Marco, perhaps you'd come with us?" We took several lamps between us, and I took Jov's when it became obvious his injured shoulder couldn't cope with its weight. Worried, I hovered close behind him as we moved through the secret passage and into the little opening space. Jovan led us through to an old ladder, where he had descended to the caverns, but Eliska paused, con-sulting her engineers and a compass.

"Not down," Eliska said. "They'd hit rock if they tried to dig that deep." She indicated the other passage. "This way."

Some of the tension left my brother. Ahead, the engineers murmured to one another, touching walls and consulting their diagrams, explaining their observations to Tain and Marco. "How big is the system below?" I asked Jov.

"Huge."

"Big enough to hide in. . . ." I mused. I looked back toward the cellar we'd come down through. "That house above us isn't the only deserted one."

He nodded. "There were signs that people might be living down there."

"Do we need to tell the Council?"

He hesitated. "I guess? But I think it's probably too big for us to properly monitor; if it connects to this cellar who knows how many others?"

I nodded. If the army outside could access the cave system already they'd have infiltrated the city, and most likely the siege would be over. The best thing to do was to concentrate on their tunneling activities and hope the people underground were not planning anything. "But there's something else."

"Yes." He paused. "Someone was down there, someone who knew his way around. I couldn't see him. But he had a knife, and he was following me. I don't think he meant me well."

"We've found it," Eliska called back to us. Lit from below by the lamp, her face looked gaunt, her scraped-back hair exposing the shape of her skull and her sunken eyes lost in shadow. "Up ahead. Be silent."

We followed her up the passage, mimicking her stealth. "Here," she whispered, indicating a portion of the wall. "As best as we can tell, their tunnel will break through here. Listen."

The *chip chip* sound crunched through the air here, much louder than before. "They're right there," I breathed, stepping away from the wall. Eliska nodded, then beckoned, and we followed her back down the passage.

We were back in the cellar before anyone spoke.

"They're probably digging during the day, when the noise from the city would mask the sound, and taking the dirt out at night," Eliska said. "They've dug well past the wall, so I'd guess they're looking to get access, not to sabotage the structural integrity of the wall. Whether they intend to or not, they're going to break into these tunnels soon—perhaps as early as tomorrow."

"So no time for us to intercept," Tain said. He looked at us, his indecision apparent. But we were going to have to decide, and soon.

Dark violet shadows spread across the street as we emerged from the empty house. We had waited there for what had felt like an age while Marco went off to the nearest sector to send us an Order Guard and several messengers to wait in the tunnel below to listen for further digging. Though Eliska had predicted work would cease overnight, the Guard had instructions to send the messenger immediately if there were any changes. The other messengers had been sent to alert the rest of the Council to an urgent meeting at first light.

Now we made our way through the streets, heading for the bridge. I was grateful for Eliska; the Stone-Guilder led the way with ease, where I would have struggled to find the right route. These homogenous residential areas were even harder to distinguish at night and the streets meandered and crisscrossed in a way that was totally confusing to most.

But not, apparently, to Eliska. Her straight, dark tail of hair swung against her strong back as she led us with confident steps. We walked through a residential area, out of the way of any of the main thoroughfares, far from the Builders' Guildhall and the industry warehouses, in the dark. Yet Eliska led us back to the lake like she'd walked this route a hundred times. She wasn't a Credola—I wondered suddenly if she'd grown up in a place more like this than the upper city. Yet of all the Guilders she seemed the least sympathetic to the rebellion, her attitude more like the Families'. Perhaps she believed that if she had built a successful lifestyle for herself despite starting with little, anyone could do so? Sometimes the least sympathetic to a plight was one who'd escaped it.

A cry sounded. Then laughter, but harsh rather than merry, came from an alley to our left. The four of us looked at each other and without speaking followed the sound, our pace quickening as a loud sob cut through the continuing jeering laughter. Jov glanced back at me, anxious, but I avoided eye contact. As we approached the alley, a dull grunting interspersed the laughs.

The sight that met us made me gasp. The grunts and cries came from a boy, perhaps in his late teens at most, with coltish long limbs and dark brown hair flopping over his face. Four men taunted him, pushing and kicking at him as they circled, predatory, driving him back toward the canal. One landed a heavy fist to the boy's stomach; his whole body curled in on itself as he stumbled to the side, almost falling into the water.

I froze, but Tain sprang to action. "Hey!" he yelled. All four turned as he and Eliska charged toward them, Jov struggling behind awkwardly.

Radiating fury, Tain hit the nearest with a short, brutal punch to the face, spinning in time to avoid a blow from another. Eliska, with surprising viciousness, kicked that one in the knee and I winced at his scream of pain as he dropped next to his fallen companion. The last two were too quick for Jov, scurrying out of his reach, their eyes wide as they stared at Tain. They hadn't yet noticed his tattoos, and they saw not our honored leader, but the protective, impulsive young man I had always known. Tain would never suffer a bully. All those times in our youth, when Jov had been the source of mockery and ridicule, Tain had stood up for him.

The two men left standing eyed us dubiously. It had only taken moments, but the odds were in our favor now, even if Jov was injured and I was useless, standing well back. One of the men on the ground staggered to his feet, clutching his cheek, moaning. "This isn't your business."

"Oh, I think it is," Tain said. He advanced again, but the young man they'd attacked let out a gurgling sob, and Tain instead dropped to a knee beside him. "Are you all right?" he asked.

The three men took their chance and fled. Eliska half-started after them, then obviously thought better of it. My paralysis lifting, I joined Tain on the edge of the canal to help the boy sit up.

The fortunes knew how long the men's amusement had carried on before we arrived. Swelling distorted the boy's face, and a deep cut, perhaps only as long as a finger joint, spewed a waterfall of blood down his forehead. The bloody lines spread like a red spiderweb over his face. I asked his name, as gently as I could. He didn't respond, but one eye, the white part shockingly bright in the mass of discolored flesh, tracked us in terrified jolts.

"We're going to take you to the hospital, all right?" The boy slumped against Tain's shoulder as we lifted him to his feet. His head lolled forward and his feet dragged as if he were a half-filled moppet.

"What about him?" Eliska asked, her tone harsh as she regarded the remaining man, who lay on the ground in a fetal position, sobbing and clutching his knee.

Tain looked down at him. "What was this all about?" he asked the man. "Talk quickly."

At some point Tain's tattoos and face must have registered because when the man spoke his tone was as deferential as it was possible to be between hiccoughs and sobs. "Honored . . . Chancellor . . . I . . . he was one of *them*, sir. . . ." He pointed a shaky hand to what looked like a broken pile of sticks on the ground. I scooped it up. Hard to see now that it was in pieces, but I thought perhaps it had been bunches of twigs shaped like a figure, and tied together with string. "He was going to do magic with it. Put a curse on us. Filthy earther, we caught him bringing it to the canal, probably to poison us all."

"He's a Silastian citizen," Tain said. "And half your age. Here, look, see what you did? Look at his face. Four grown men beating on a *boy*. You disgusting cowards." He looked up, dismissing the man on the ground. "Let's get him to the hospital. Tomorrow I have some things to discuss with the Council." His jaw was set. He was angry, angrier than I'd seen him in years.

Tears and snot ran down the man's face. "Please, Honored Chancellor," he cried out after us as we left. "I need the hospital, too!"

Tain looked down him, his face bereft of pity. "Then start crawling."

The man's sobs followed us around the corner.

A few moments later Tain stopped a woman heading to her shift on the wall, carrying a piece of laminar armor and a dented conical helmet. She stared at our burden, eyes so wide her eyebrows disappeared into her hair, and nodded as Tain instructed her.

"I'll need the man with the knee injury escorted to the hospital by someone armed, then taken to jail once he's been tended to," he finished. "Tell the Order Guards if he gives them the names of his friends who were with him, I'll want them tracked down and arrested as well."

"One might show up to the hospital with bruising or swelling to the face," Jov put in.

Tain nodded. "We can ask the physics to keep an eye out."

She scurried off and we continued to the hospital, where we gave the boy to the care of a bearded physic in stained robes. "Here, lad, let's get you down here," he said, lifting him with practiced ease onto a pallet. The physic's face was lined and weary as he checked over his patient and glanced up at us. "Fourth one this week," he said. "I don't suppose you caught anyone this time?"

"What do you mean, the fourth one?" Tain asked, brow tightening.

The physic felt along the boy's arm, probing with competent fingers. "It's all right," he said when the boy jumped. "We'll get that sorted." He cleared his throat. "The fourth Darfri patient beaten half to death," he said, meeting Tain's gaze, chin high. "And I'm not the only one treating them. There must have been at least a dozen more in here this week. So, since I reported to one of your Order Guards that this was happening three days ago, I assume you are doing everything you can to track down those responsible. Honored Chancellor." The last he tacked on as an afterthought.

Tain's face was very still. "To be clear—other Silastian residents have come to the hospital, or been brought, after having been beaten. And those patients have all been Darfri. Do they tell you that?"

The physic scoffed. "No, Honored Chancellor. They won't tell us a thing. The first one or two, we thought were drunken fights. The third was a woman and she was conscious enough to say a group of men attacked her on her way home from her shift at the wall. Didn't seem likely she'd been in a fight at a bar. Nice lass, well spoken." He turned back to the boy on the pallet, continuing his examination. "Then we got more, and more. They stopped talking to us. Started hiding their necklaces, if they were wearing them. Look at this." He indicated a thin red line of abrasion at the back of the boy's neck. "Oftentimes the attackers tear it off."

"How is it I don't know about this?" Tain's question seemed aimed as much at the rest of us as the physic.

"Like I said, I went to the nearest guard tower on my way home earlier this week and reported the whole thing to the Order Guard there. But no one ever came to ask us about it."

Right under our noses, our own citizens were being attacked, and no one had told the Chancellor about it. Servants failing to turn up to their posts, all my troubles finding any Darfri to talk to . . . perhaps even missing street people. We'd guessed they'd been frightened to admit their beliefs, but perhaps they were hiding from a much more immediate danger. I remembered the moppet I'd found, with its frayed little skirts and shawl, its face worn off. Lying alone in an abandoned house. Had the family fled, or been forced from their home?

Tain's face had darkened, his jaw ticking with a tiny vein. "No one brought this to me," he said, his voice taut as a drawn bowstring.

The physic looked him over, heedless of his casual discourtesy as only physics seemed capable. "I suppose they didn't," he agreed. "Perhaps there has been a gap in your reporting system, Honored Chancellor?"

Tain nodded, stiff. "Perhaps. Something I'll be remedying. If you'll excuse us, we'll leave him in your care."

The physic nodded, turning back to his patient. Before we left, I looked back down at the injured boy. I could smell his blood and sweat—or perhaps it was the smell of the hospital in general. *What is going on in our city?* I knew Tain well enough to leave him to his own thoughts, but watched him as we walked, storm brewing.

That storm erupted in the Council meeting in the morning.

"Do you know what the physic treating him told me?" Tain asked the assembled room of Councilors—some more disheveled than usual. He had relayed the story with a deceptively calm tone, but the faces of the Councilors below me suggested most detected the emotion simmering under that facade. Tain had always wanted to be liked more than he wanted to be respected. Perhaps only Jov and I truly knew what he was like when he stopped caring about making people happy. "He said this was the *fourth* victim of a beating he'd treated, and there had been at least a dozen similar incidents this week."

I scanned the room, stiffening. Too many signs flashed before me. Lazar, to Jov's right, squirmed in his seat. A weak man, buckling under the pressure, unable to even look up from the table. Pedrag's fingers paled around his rings as he clenched his hands together, and Bradomir smoothed his moustache with more vigor than usual. Marjeta and Budua looked neither nervous nor surprised; both regarded Tain with calm scrutiny. Javesto leaned forward, mouth tight as though straining to hold his desired words in. Varina scowled, though of course that wasn't unusual, her eyes bloodshot and nose red. I wondered if she was ill. Eliska, though she had acted quickly enough to help the boy yesterday, was pressed back in her seat and hunched as small as possible, as if hoping to be overlooked.

"And the most interesting part was that the physics reported these incidents," Tain continued. One of his hands made a fist. "They reported it to the Order Guards. Now, what I'd like to know is, are the Order Guards for some reason not reporting properly to each of you in your sectors? Or"— and here he paused, his gaze sweeping the table like two hot coals burning a path around the room—"did someone receive this report but not see fit to bring it to the Council?"

I could have told him, then and there, from the body language around the table—it wasn't some*one*. It was most of the Council.

"Well?" Tain demanded. His tone was no longer level, and the tic in his neck had returned. "Who's going to say what's going on? I haven't had time to talk to the Order Guards yet, but presumably they're going to tell me who they passed it on to, so you might as well talk right now."

The room stayed silent and brittle. Javesto, never one to control his tongue, was the first to break. "I didn't get the report," he said, "but I've heard rumors that Darfri in the city were being terrorized. Threatened, beaten, scared half to death. Why do you think they all scarpered?" Javesto pointed a finger around the room. "I'm not the only one who's noticed, am I though?"

"What are you accusing us of, Credo Javesto?" Bradomir asked. "No one made any report of beatings to me."

"Nor me," Pedrag agreed, wringing his hands.

"But you knew something was going on, didn't you?"

The room descended into bickering and accusations, the volume rising all the while.

"And why didn't *any* of you say something?" Tain shouted. He pushed back from the table and stood. "We've sat in this room every few days, sometimes even more regularly, for almost two weeks. You've got information about our citizens being targeted and attacked and you say *nothing*? Why?"

"Well, I tried," Javesto said, his face dark. "But I wasn't exactly popular when I dared say something about Darfri that wasn't a call to arms, so do you blame me for not bringing it to the Council?"

"What about the rest of you?" Jov asked, diverting that confrontation. "Who got the report?"

Credola Nara sat back and folded her arms. "I did." The old spider curled her lip, chin thrust out, as she surveyed the room. "So what? These earthers are outside trying to kill us all, in case you hadn't noticed."

"*Darfri*," Tain corrected. "Don't use that word again, please."

"You can understand, Honored Chancellor, that tempers and fears are running high within the city," Bradomir said. He spread his hands. "We are under siege by an army chanting curses at us. People are terrified. Of course it's silliness, but not a day goes past without someone reporting some supernatural nonsense or another. Faces in the side of the mountain, or plants reaching for them as they walk home at night. Ghostly figures in the canals and invisible hands on their backs. You can see why the sight of some boy praying to the spirits they think are trying to destroy us would enflame that. It's not to be *encouraged*, of course—violence is always unsavory. But surely you can see how our citizens might feel—"

"It was 'our citizens' being brutalized," Tain snapped. "Inside our walls. By all the fortunes, what is wrong with you all? We're fighting a war here, trying to defend our city, and our own people are turning on one another?"

He thumped both fists on the table, causing a few people to jump. "Well, I have at least one of these thugs locked up by now, and I've a mind to send a message to the rest of them out there. You know what I call it when people are attacking our own citizens instead of our enemy? I call it without honor, and I call it *treason*."

The room hushed. Even I suppressed a gasp at Tain's choice of word. While I understood his frustrations, if he wasn't careful he'd make enemies out of everyone around this table.

"Honored Chancellor, you cannot—" Bradomir began, but Tain ignored him, turning instead to Marco.

"Warrior-Guilder, how do we treat treason in a time of war?" he asked, his tone dropping back to normal speaking volume.

Marco cleared his throat. "Treason is generally punishable by death, Honored Chancellor."

No one spoke. The entire Council stared at Tain, mouths open, eyes wide. Even the ever-composed Bradomir seemed at a complete loss. Only Marco, though clearly uncomfortable, didn't look shocked—in Perest-Avana, I supposed it was quite normal to talk of executing people. But in Silasta, that sort of barbarity didn't happen. *Tain, what are you doing?* The Chancellor leaned over the table, his face hard as he surveyed the room. The Councilors stared back as though looking at a stranger.

Lazar was the first to break the silence. His fat lips quivered. "But . . . Honored Chancellor, surely we wouldn't consider . . . I mean, we're not savages!"

Marco raised his eyebrows, and I admired again his ability to ignore insults. "There is no greater discouragement for such violence than a punishment so severe none dare risk it," he said. "The Honored Chancellor makes sense."

"Well, the Honored Chancellor isn't a dictator, or an emperor," Nara said. "This is a Council of equals. And I will *not* be party to executing Silastians for succumbing to frustration and desperation in a time like this!"

"Nor will I," Varina said, sniffing angrily. "This is absurd."

"Absurd would be letting our people destroy themselves before the army out there can do it!" Tain pointed across the table. "Well? What do the rest of you say? As my colleague has pointed out, this is a Council. So let's hear it. Budua, your Guild is responsible for justice. What say you?"

The Scribe-Guilder pursed her lips, pearl-black gaze calmly meeting Tain's. "I agree any culprits found guilty should be punished," she said. "This is a new kind of crime, one for which we have no precedent. But our founders built Silasta with the intention that our government not succumb to the military rule of their ancestors. I consider a severe punishment is warranted, but not execution. Not for assault and intimidation."

Tain raised an eyebrow. "And if this continues to escalate, and we end up with murders?"

She shrugged. "There is an argument that, in a time of war, such actions must be punished as strictly as the law permits."

Bradomir shook his head. "I think it hasty to talk of such things. This is a civilized city. Certainly we are under siege, but our citizens are not in the Warrior Guild, and should not be treated as if they were. It is regrettable, but understandable, that some people may have made mistakes in the heat of the moment."

"I agree," Varina said. "We can save our killing for the people outside the city."

"I agree with the Chancellor," Pedrag said, puffing out his chest. "If we are seen to take a strong stance we can stamp this out right now."

Around the room, everyone gave their opinion. Marjeta, Lazar, and Eliska favored imprisonment and financial reparation; Varina, Bradomir, and Nara urged leniency. Marco, Pedrag, and Javesto endorsed execution. It had come to Jovan's turn to speak. Instead, though, he was staring around the room in his usual fashion as observer. The room quieted again and people began staring back at him; he visibly started.

He looked at Tain, his face troubled. My heart pounded. *Jovan,* I entreated silently. When he spoke, his voice sounded croaky, as though it had rusted through lack of use. "I . . ." He shook his head, mouth dry, and looked away from his friend. "I'm sorry, Honored Chancellor. But I can't support execution."

I closed my eyes for a moment, relieved. Tain crossed his arms and settled back in his chair. "Very well," he said. "The Council has spoken. No execution. But I *will* be tossing these bastards in our jail until after the siege, and authorizing the Order Guards to use whatever force necessary to stop anyone caught terrorizing Darfri."

Tension was palpable the rest of the meeting. Tain barely looked at Jovan for the remainder of the discussion, and I could feel his distress from my hiding place. Jovan's hands flexed in rhythm and the furrow in his brow suggested he was counting internally, trying to manage the tic.

I felt strange inside, anxious but something else, too. By the end of the meeting I realized what it was. I had just watched Tain stop trying to please the Council and stand up for something more important. And suddenly I knew it was time to stop hiding myself from my brother in order not to worry him. Yesterday had been a day of revelations; he might as well get used to another one. The feeling in my chest was release. Even elation.

Though I was exhausted and slow, I still caught up with him; he was trailing a circuitous route through the Manor, presumably to avoid the rest of the Councilors, or even Tain.

"What are you doing?" His tone was weary.

"I was watching the Council meeting," I said, my confidence from a moment ago shaken.

"Yes, I know," he said, somehow sounding both disappointed and amused. He kept walking, but crinkles formed around the corners of his eyes. "I'm surprised you don't get a cramp up there."

"You knew?"

"Of course. I didn't think you were doing any harm. You're very quiet."

It didn't matter, and it was easier than explaining it, so I should have been relieved. Instead, the condescension in his manner rubbed the small, irritated core inside me. Honor-down, why did he have to diminish this? "Well, if you—"

Tain stepped out of a doorway, sending the hanging beads swinging into me and cutting off my rising voice.

"Sorry," he said. "Oh! Lini. Jov. I was looking for you." He called back over his shoulder, "Guards? I'll be in the meeting room. Can you stay in the hall, please?" There was a murmur of ascent, then we were alone.

We stared at each other a moment. The feverish anger had burned away from his face, leaving him wan and drained, but he smiled at us as though the awkwardness wasn't there, and, just like that, it wasn't. My anger drained away as quickly as his.

"I'm sorry about before," he said, clasping Jov's forearm. "I was . . . angry."

"You hid it perfectly," Jov said.

A beat, then we all laughed. The fortunes knew there'd been little enough to laugh about today. Tain steered us back down the hall toward his favorite sitting room, his smile fading.

"I assume Jov filled you in, Lini? I've no intention of executing anyone," he said earnestly. "But I figured if I pushed the treason point, no one would suggest letting them all off with just a warning. I can't believe this has been going on."

"It makes sense, though, doesn't it," Jov said, following him in and sitting. I slumped into a corner and rested my head on one hand. Though I had slept deeply last night, my body still hadn't forgiven me for yesterday. "They've been driven from their homes, or they've fled. Their shrines are being destroyed so they can't even observe rituals that comfort them. It's apparently not safe for them to walk around the streets. No wonder they're hiding in the caves."

"And from what we've found in all the records, the countryfolk have no reason to think the Council would treat them fairly. They aren't to know you're not like your uncle."

"Except you are."

We all startled. The hanging beads jangled as someone stepped through the doorway, and we rose, turning, as a diminutive figure stepped into the room.

"Marjeta?" Tain's eyebrows rose as the Artist-Guilder approached us. Her birdlike frame reached no taller than his shoulders, but she could have been a giant for the presence she commanded at that moment.

"I'm sorry," she said, perching on the edge of a footstool so she shrank down even smaller. "I didn't mean to eavesdrop." She had a peculiar way of talking, with a slight lisp and a light, girlish voice belying her years. "But I said, you *are* like your uncle, Honored Chancellor; you probably don't know how much. I didn't think you were, not in the way that counts . . . not until today, at least." She met Tain's gaze with quiet confidence. "I saw how angry you were that your people were being victimized, and I saw you thought they were your people, worth as much as anyone else. That's how Caslav thought of it, too." She glanced at Jov and then me. "And Etan as well, though he hid it, just like he hid their true relationship."

I'd always liked Marjeta. She was a brilliant painter and a kindly Guilder, with never a harsh word for anyone. I stared at her now, feeling as though I didn't know her at all.

Tain's face twitched between caution and hope. "What relationship?" he asked her, tentative.

She smiled. "They were friends, of course, as you two are, but they were so much more. They were bound together by honor and tradition, and by all the times Etan must have saved Caslav's life."

Jov's skin seemed to gray. My stomach rose to my throat. I opened my mouth, but nothing came out; Tain was equally mute, staring back at the Artist-Guilder. Marjeta regarded us calmly. She spread her lovely, long-fingered hands. "I didn't come here to shock you," she said. "But you should know I'm not the only one who knows who you are, Jovan, because I wasn't the only one who knew who your Tashi was."

"Who else?"

She shrugged. "Budua and I have known for years. And there will be others. Oh, Etan was good, but Caslav was always that bit too cautious whenever food or drink was involved, and once you'd seen that he didn't ever take something directly from you, you started to notice how Etan was always there near him, so quick to try anything." She reached out and touched Tain's hand. "Honored Chancellor, I would have kept that secret forever. I have no interest in the intrigues of the Families, but I understand the dangers and the power shuffles, and I wouldn't begrudge you this protection. But things are different now. There are people on the Council you shouldn't trust."

"Who?" I asked, at the same time as Tain said, "Why now?"

"Your uncle was working on something," she said, addressing Tain. "Some of us supported him, but most didn't. He wanted things to change—he wanted Sjona to change. Things out on the estates have fallen behind the cities. The Families have been taking advantages, too many— and we Guilders were letting it happen, too. Caslav was trying to change things, build relationships. But then he died. And you . . . well, forgive me, Honored Chancellor, but I didn't know you well. You never seemed much interested in the ancient responsibilities of the chancellery, only its benefits. And almost immediately you started taking private meetings with Caslav's biggest opposition." I realized then that she'd answered both our questions after all.

"Bradomir," Jov murmured. "Lazar . . ."

She nodded. "Along with others—Nara, Varina—they opposed the measures Caslav wanted to introduce. He and Etan were working in secret to build support. The common people have no reason to trust us, you know. But he was trying. Before he died he was supposed to meet with a large party of respected elders from the estates. But the meeting never happened, and I have speculated that someone was undermining his attempts. Prob-ably the people with the most to lose. The richest Families, with the biggest estates."

My chest felt heavy. I had searched for connections between Councilors and the rebels and too quickly dismissed the possibility of the poisoner operating for different reasons than the rebel cause.

Marjeta sat, looking between us. Her voice shook. "Budua and I hid the records. When you were asking about them before, we removed Council minutes and discussions. We weren't sure who killed Caslav, and we thought . . ." She dropped her gaze to her hands on her lap.

"You thought I might have been involved," Tain finished, sounding hol-low. "That I might have . . ."

She nodded. "Whoever did this knew enough to get through Etan, which meant they knew what they were doing. You two turned up mysteri-ously and unexpectedly on the day the Chancellor died, and though you must have known it was poison you seemed unconcerned about your own safety. And everyone knew you and Caslav disagreed about a lot of things. He loved you, but he said you had a lot of your mother in you. Some-times . . ."

"He despaired of me," Tain finished again, a half-smile touching his lips. "He used to say that all the time."

"He wouldn't have been the first person to misplace their affection."

"Well, he didn't," Tain said, the smile gone. "I loved my Tashi. And we never disagreed about the important things."

"The Families have a lot to lose if the working people start having a voice on the Council, or even in the city," Marjeta said. "The spice and gemstone mines make them rich, and Caslav was looking into their working conditions, and making noises. . . ." She pinched her nose. "At the time, of course we didn't think anyone would do something like that. We thought there would be pressure and politics, not murder."

"Etan must have thought the same, or he'd have told me," Jov said. He still looked stricken. My own thoughts spun. Had Etan been ashamed of his own ignorance, too embarrassed to confess to us what was happening without first having taken steps to remedy it? Like Jovan, he had been a proud man, and one who viewed any failure of his duties harshly.

"And the army outside?" I asked. "What has that got to do with it? If Caslav was making changes, why would they attack us? That wasn't a sudden decision after he died; this is an organized rebellion."

"If I knew that, I'd have come forward sooner, suspicions or no," Marjeta said. "We're all in this together, aren't we?"

"Maybe," Jov said, and I knew he was thinking of the tunnels, and his dark pursuer.

Tain sighed. "At least tell us more about what was happening on the estates. I still don't really understand how this relates to the Darfri. Kalina studied the records and we know the city lost control of the schools and lawkeeping out there decades ago. But what does it have to do with religion?"

"It's all tied together," Marjeta said. She ducked her head. "And I have shared in it as much as anyone. Disrespect of the way of life we once all shared. The contempt the cities hold for the Darfri—'earthers,' we call them, and treat them like they're foolish, or diseased. They had complaints about the use of land, and the sites they consider sacred spirit places."

One of Tain's guards called in. "Messenger, Honored Chancellor."

We turned to the doorway and a girl in a messenger's sash came through.

"Honored . . . Chancellor," she gasped, panting. "You . . . you said to come . . ."

It took me a moment to recognize the long, chinless face and big eyes: the messenger we'd left in the tunnel.

"They're coming, Honored Councilor—the rebels are breaking through."

Art's plainsrose

DESCRIPTION: Woody shrub found along dry creek beds, watercourses, gorges, and rocky slopes. Flowers range from pale pink to mauve and round leaves are strongly scented when crushed. Dried, powdered leaves form the main ingredient in Art's tonic, a sedative used extensively in medical care.

SYMPTOMS: Pain relief and drowsiness, unconsciousness.

PROOFING CUES: Distinctive smell when dissolved in fluid.

11

Jovan

We returned briskly along the increasingly familiar route back to the tunnel entrance, my feet slipping in my sandals and my heart and head racing at equal pace. Anxiety strangled the logical part of my brain as I tried to balance the conflicting information we had gathered. I needed time, space, and good health to sort through it, and I had none of those things.

But despite that, through the various complaints my body threw at me as I ran, and all my doubts and fears, a tiny knot inside me had loosened. The possibility that Etan had willfully contributed to the oppression of our countryfolk had chipped away at my regard for him, tainting my memories. But now I knew he had become aware of his damaging ignorance and had tried to change things rather than cover them up, and that reenergized me. I saw the same thing in Tain, a brightness to his eyes that had been missing. Not even the grim purpose of our return to the lower city could take the new information from us, or stifle the hope it ignited within.

"What are we going to do when they break through?"

"Capture the miners," Tain said. "We have the advantage, knowing they're coming. We need to talk to the army, and this is the best way I can think of to force someone to listen. We can finally find out what started this, who's controlling it. We can talk and hopefully have them listen and then send them back out to talk to their leaders."

A trumpet sounded.

We looked at each other, confused, as it sounded out, mournful and carrying, blaring out from somewhere up ahead, but unaccompanied by the warning bells from the towers to give us a better sense of the direction of the attack. The trumpet sounded again as we picked up our pace.

"It has to be the tunnels," Tain said. "They must have broken through early. . . ."

"So much for surprising them," I muttered, though with a pang of relief that Kalina had not attempted to come with us.

As we entered the district we ran into a line of men and women moving in rough formation toward the sound of the trumpet, clutching swords and spears and led by a shouting Order Guard. We fell in with them. Anxiety twisted inside me. Had the rebels shifted a force in through the tunnel and attacked already? It should have been a small mining team, easy to capture, and we should have been able to do it quickly and quietly.

We made our way up to the Order Guard. "What's going on?" Tain asked.

"Some sort of attack within the city," she reported, checking the column of people over her shoulder as she answered. "I don't know anything else, Honored Chancellor. I heard the summoning horn and came at once."

Tain pushed ahead and I followed, wincing at the effort the dodging and twisting cost my battered body. My insides felt cold and tight. *This isn't right.*

We reached the house containing the tunnel entrance, and found a boy standing at its entrance, shifting the horn between his hands, back and forth. When he saw us he almost dropped the great thing.

"Honored Chancellor," he stammered. "Quickly, below. They sent me up, but they're fighting down there."

We raced inside the house, already hearing the muffled sounds of conflict below.

"I didn't want this," Tain said to me, his voice tight.

Someone had left a lamp in the cellar, but as we scrambled down into the tunnel we didn't need it. Lights surged ahead of us, flickering and bouncing, shadows rushing between them like live things. Metallic clashes and human cries and grunts echoed around. We burst into a thicket of it, finding our own men, packed in too close in the narrow space. The inconsistent light made it impossible to see clearly and no one seemed to recognize Tain as we pushed through, trying to get to the front of the line. I took a rough count: a dozen, twenty . . .

"Space yourselves out," Tain told them as we passed. "You're too close, get some space around you."

But they only shuffled back and forth, wide-eyed in the flickering light of primitive open torches.

We found the battle itself, such as it was, near where we'd left the Order Guard and messenger. The wall had crumpled away, forming a ragged hole like a monster's mouth, and through it shadowy figures, tall and broad, held the entrance. Metal rang on metal, and when one figure raised his arms to block a downward strike from one of our men, I saw they defended themselves with shovels, not weapons. In a flash of torchlight their faces showed: grim, dirty, and terrified, holding together, trapped in the space. Not part of the army moving in as a surprise attack, just the miners we had wanted to capture.

"They're miners," I said to Tain, having to yell to make myself heard. "Tain, they're just the miners!"

"Fall back!" Tain shouted, pushing our men back away from us with rough shoves to their shoulders as he moved. "Fall back, stop fighting!" But the weapons kept swinging, and we were jostled around in the half light. Ahead, I saw the Order Guard's head, clad in a decent metal helmet, sitting higher than the others around him, and his sword chopping down. The space reeked of dirt and sweat and fear. With a scream like a dying animal, one of the miners dropped; I couldn't see what had felled him, but at the sudden break in their tightly packed defense our attack surged, the crush of men pouring forward into the tunnel entrance.

"Stop!" I yelled, adding my cries to Tain's, but even as the surrounding men recognized us and fell back, the faces of the miners ahead dropped out of sight. More screams and cries pierced the air as the last miners fell.

By the time we reached the front row of the swarm, the miners lay crumpled in the piles of dirt, their shovels fallen around them like careless litter. Tain snatched one of the torches and swung it about, spitting out an impressive string of profanities.

"Get back," he warned the Order Guard, his face twisted into a snarl, brandishing the torch like a weapon. "All of you, get back." He knelt next to the closest miner's body and I dropped down beside him, checking for signs of life.

"Someone get a physic down here, *now*," Tain said. "Now!"

I was grateful for the darkness as still-warm blood slipped over my hands and arms while I checked for pulses and breathing. Tain swore, a steady stream under his breath, which grew louder and angrier as he moved from man to man, finding the same as me: dead and dying.

"Hold on," I heard him tell one man, but when I looked over, hopeful, a horrible dark mass glinted in the torchlight where the man's stomach should have been, and I looked away again.

"Hey!" someone cried, and behind the clumsy pile of fallen men, a shadow detached itself from the ground in the corner: one of the miners, darting away down the tunnel. I was the closest; I scrambled to my feet and chased after him. Although he'd had a head start, he ran half doubled over, staggering in a zigzag as he ran. I caught him with a wild tackle and he crumpled under my weight, dropping us both in a tangle. He struggled feebly as I wrapped him up from the back, pinning him to the ground with one forearm around his neck.

"Hold still! I'm not trying to hurt you," I told him, but he twisted his head around to glare at me from the corner of his eye, and spat at me. Tain and the Order Guard skidded to a halt beside us. They helped us stand, me still holding my captive from behind. "We're going to let you walk on your own," Tain said. "But please don't try to run or attack anyone."

The man stared at Tain. Finally he nodded and I released him at Tain's signal. Tain addressed the Order Guard as we returned up the passage. "What happened?" he demanded. "Why didn't you send for us? This is exactly what I ordered you *not* to do. I wanted to talk to them, not kill them."

The Order Guard avoided looking anywhere near Tain. He took off his helmet and cradled it in front of his stomach. He spoke down into it. "I called for reinforcements when they started up again, and by the time the backup got here they'd broken through." The Guard glanced at our prisoner, his tone accusing. "They had weapons, and they attacked us when they saw us waiting on the other side."

I felt my prisoner stiffen, but he stayed silent.

Tain reached down beside one of the bodies. "They had *shovels*," he said bitterly, straightening and brandishing one.

The Guard ducked his head further. "Shovels can kill you as easily as swords, Honored Chancellor," he mumbled.

I supposed that was true enough, but there were no serious injuries on our side. Only the sad cluster of grubby, stained corpses in their rough tunnel, piled like the dirt in the barrows behind them. "Was there a scout?" I asked, holding a torch up to examine the space. "Did they have any way of sending word back down the tunnel?"

He gave a little half-shrug. "I don't know, Credo. I suppose they might have."

We had to assume they had. Which meant they knew already that the tunnel was compromised. I brought the torch back closer to me, turning to face our prisoner, searching his expression for a clue, but he gave nothing away. No flicker of a response.

But as it turned out, we didn't need one.

A rumbling sound was our only warning, then a sudden shower of dirt rained on us as the entire structure seemed to shake.

"Everyone out," Tain said. "Quick!"

The entrance back into our tunnel system was narrow and half of our soldiers had milled through, so there was another moment of confusing crush as everyone tried to get out again in a hurry. The four of us were the last ones through, and I felt a whoosh of air against my back as I leaped into the reinforced tunnel.

"Collapsed." Tain glanced back over his shoulder. "How did they do it so quickly?"

"They must have prepared it to go if they needed it to," I said, shaking the coating of gritty dirt out of my hair and trying to ignore the itchy trickle down my back. "Guess that answers the question about the scout."

Our prisoner looked at me then, a little sidelong glance, and though his expression never changed, I still read the satisfaction in his eyes.

Eliska crawled about on her hands and knees at the foot of the wall, rubbing one grimy hand across her forehead.

"I don't like it. Do you see these cracks: here, and here?" She gestured. "These walls are old, and strong, but they take strength from how the stones fit together. The collapse disrupted the pattern and weakened this section. It's susceptible to attack now."

"Did they know that? Do you think that's why they collapsed the tunnel?" Tain asked.

"Impossible to say, Honored Chancellor," Marco said. "The value to them in the tunnel was secrecy. Their numbers are neutralized in a tight space so it is no use as a direct line of attack. They may have merely prepared to collapse the tunnel if discovered, rather than giving us any kind of possible exit."

"If they just intended to use it to collapse the wall, they could have stopped well short of here," Eliska said. "But in any case, we'll know soon enough. If they target this spot with their siege weapons . . ."

Marco helped Eliska to her feet, and the two of them regarded Tain, their frames—so different in size—sharing the same wariness as they watched the Chancellor's reaction. "I think we need to think about options for falling back."

"You mean abandoning the lower city and retreating to the old city." He looked over his shoulder, his eyes searching the thin gaps between buildings through which glimpses of the old city could be seen, rising up from the east bank of the lake. "That's a last resort."

"Be that as it may, Honored Chancellor," Marco said. "The worst may come about. We are holding the city only because of the strength of the walls. If they break through, we will not be able to defend ourselves. They outnumber us ten to one."

He was right, of course, and Tain knew that as well as I did. But by the fortunes, the idea of having to abandon half the city . . . it was hard to even think about.

"What would happen if we did?" I wondered aloud. "Would the old city hold?"

The Bright Lake separated the two halves of the city, but the original wall on the west bank had been dismantled after the completion of the lower city. Only the structure around the Finger remained of the fortifications around Trickster's, and none at all around Bell's. If the rebels held the lower city, what would stop them from storming the bridges and taking the old city as well? Their sheer numbers would overwhelm us.

Marco spread the city map out on a rock. "If they cross the lake, we have no way to fortify the city. We could use the buildings of the old city, and what is left of the walls, to lay many traps and ambushes for them. But that would be to hurt them as badly as possible. Not to win." Marco looked up at Tain, somber. "You understand, Honored Chancellor?"

Tain nodded.

The Warrior-Guilder traced across the map, thick fingers lingering as he drew them across the two bridges—Trickster's on the north, Bell's on the south. "Our best chance is to destroy the bridges."

Eliska looked torn; I could see the engineer in her rebelling at such a suggestion. "It's a terrible step to have to take. It took decades to build them."

"How would we even do it?" Tain stared down at the map. Such small marks to represent such mammoth feats of engineering.

"I do not know," Marco said. "Where I grew up, our bridges were wood, not stone. We would have to smash the support pillars, I suppose?"

Eliska sighed. "Bell's, perhaps we could do. Great force applied to the supporting pillars, yes, perhaps. But Trickster's?"

The main bridge across the lake, and an integral part of the famous and enviable vista of our city, Trickster's was a massive single arch towering over the north side of the lake between huge supporting buildings. I had no concept of how it had even been built, let alone how that could be undone.

"We'd have to knock down the entire supporting structure," she continued. "And even if we could . . . please, understand, we would be safer with no bridges, but we would be condemning ourselves to years of rebuilding, maybe even decades. The bridges are the lifeblood of our city."

Tain stared at me, beseeching, but I had no counsel to offer. It was a terrible decision to have to make. "You said the tunnel neutralized their numbers, Marco," he said eventually. "Wouldn't the same be true of the bridge? Couldn't we hold them back from the Finger if it came to that?"

"For a while, perhaps. But we would be left with no further retreat, Honored Chancellor."

They continued discussing options, but I lost track as I stared at the map. On the map, the city was a mere collection of pen markings: geometric shapes and neat lines. But in my head, I saw those markings as they were in reality—a living city, people's homes and work and studies, a beacon of peaceful and secure trade for people all over the world. The lower city was far bigger than the upper; all those neat diagrams showing Guilds, marketplaces, and residential districts. . . . I tried to imagine how we could function without access to its facilities. Not to mention that the lower city housed the vast majority of the city's population. I pictured the bustling lower city burning, the upper filled with desperate crowds, and the thought made me sick and sad.

"How long do you think we have?" I asked Eliska. "How long would the wall hold out if it was struck with catapults in a full attack?"

She sighed again and stretched. I heard cracks and pops as her joints protested. "They'll focus on the weakened part of the wall. Under sustained force from projectiles and rams, it might only be a matter of days to knock a hole in it or bring that part down."

"It will be critical to target their siege weapons," Marco said. "That means we must have catapults of our own that are accurate enough to destroy theirs, and we must be ready to stop a ram." He looked us all over, his face grim. "As we did when they attacked the gate, we must be ready to pour demons down upon them, so they are too frightened to approach. More oil, more stone and metal . . . these things we need."

Tain nodded, rubbing his forehead. "All right. Listen. I don't want them killed any more than I want city residents killed. Our goal here is still peaceful resolution. I want peace flags hanging from every available space on the walls, and I'm going to talk to our prisoner and make him understand we want to negotiate, not fight. I've sent a physic to look after him for now; hopefully after a day of being cared for decently he might be inclined to listen.

"In the meantime, Eliska, can your Guild make a plan for destroying the bridges—just work out if it can be done, and how? Jov, we need people on the spyglasses every hour of the day, watching for signs that the rebels' weapons are ready. Marco, we need a plan for defending the weak spot—give us as much time as you can, and a strategy for falling back if we need to."

The two Guilders left us and I shut my eyes, trying to silence the clamor of disjointed thoughts and images in my head. Every part of me hurt, from the inside of my brain to the ends of my toes. *I'm drowning,* I thought, *drowning in my own head.*

But self-indulgence wasn't going to get us through the day, let alone the siege.

Tain stood beside me, fingering the map Marco had left, his eyes unfocused. "We could lose half the city in a few days—more than half. Hundreds of years of buildings, industries, markets, and lives. I can't believe this is happening."

"Well, it is," I said bluntly. "And things are only going to get worse. We need to start thinking about keeping you out of the front line. It was stupid going down into the mines today. Your guards can't protect you in close quarters fighting and neither can I. You're not just the Heir of a peaceful city anymore. You can't act like it."

"I know you're worried, but there are more important things—"

"Tain." I cut him off, dropping my voice so the guard servants couldn't hear. "Tain, for fuck's sake. Someone tried to kill you *yesterday.* There's no more important thing."

He clenched his jaw, but I pressed on, having to work to keep my voice level. I couldn't fail at this. Not this. I was all that was holding up our family's ancient duty.

"Defending the city is everyone's duty, but mine is you—just you. And someone watched you at training yesterday, followed you, and poisoned your food. They're careful, they're biding their time, and they will try again. The only thing protecting you so far is that whoever the enemy is seems to want your death to look like an accident. If that changes . . ."

Tain looked down, lips tight. His generosity of spirit, the good-naturedness I had always admired about him, suddenly seemed like dangerous naivety. "Fine," he said eventually. "Fine. I'll be more careful, all right? I won't go rushing in. But Jov, you've thought we had a traitor the whole time but you don't know who it is. I can't avoid everyone on the Council."

I thought back to Kalina's list of names, the people who were in the Manor to have poisoned the leksot in the garden: Javesto, Varina, Marco, Eliska, Bradomir, Budua. Before, I'd thought those least sympathetic to the rebels were the safest. Perhaps Javesto was helping the city Darfri, and perhaps Budua was evasive with Council records, but now that made them seem less likely, not more, to have wanted to harm Caslav. Marco and Eliska, too, it was hard not to trust given I doubted we'd have held off the siege for even a few days without the guidance of those two Guilders. And Marco, at least, had risked his own life to help save mine while I climbed that ladder. Yet still, I couldn't rule anyone out.

"I just need to know you aren't going to do something stupid again. Don't put yourself in a vulnerable position. I have to be able to trust *you*, at least."

"You can, I promise," he said. But I couldn't be sure, and worry and anger and frustration gnawed at me.

It took longer than I'd hoped to check over our sector and update Chen with the new instructions. We were leaning too heavily on the Order Guard to manage things, but she was competent and Kalina and I were already being pulled in too many directions with competing priorities. By the time I was able to return to my apartments, it was afternoon. Outside our property I crossed paths with Lord Ectar and two of his silent, expressionless servants. Irritation and worry sprang up inside me. Kalina was in there, resting; she'd pushed herself too hard the last few days. What was Ectar doing, bothering her? "What can I do for you, Lord Ectar?"

Apparently he shared my irritation, because his usual careful manner seemed ruffled. "Nothing, Credo Jovan. I have been turned away from seeing your lady sister."

"She's unwell." Grateful I'd sent a messenger to wait outside our apartments in case Kalina needed me, I made to step past him. He made a kind of huffing sound, so put upon that it rankled me. "My sister's ill health bothers you, Lord Ectar?"

"What is wrong with her?" he demanded. "She seemed fine when I saw her."

For most of my life I'd had to hear the same sentiment—sometimes asked in confidence, sometimes with brashness or suspicion or disbelief. They couldn't see what was wrong so they assumed it was not real. "She's been doing too much," I snapped. "She is *always* unwell, she's just very good at hiding it."

He raised an eyebrow, the expression of polite skepticism recognizable and familiar even on his pale, painted face. I pushed past him without bothering with any more false pleasantries; he could take his nosiness and ignorance elsewhere. I'd never have dared to do it a month before, for fear of someone noticing the rudeness. How foolish our social rules seemed now.

My sister was awake—thanks, no doubt, to the unwelcome visitor—her eyes bruised and sunken, skin dull. I made her tea and a portion of rations; she argued, but feebly, and eventually ate a small amount. I held her hand as we talked over the day. She refused my offer of a numbing agent but didn't comment on the low-level sedative in her tea, though I suspected she had noticed. Without sleep, things could get worse rapidly, and we lacked our usual luxury of a physic on demand.

While she drank I unfolded the clothes I'd picked up earlier from the Manor, and turned them inside out. I took out the naftate powder, one of the few substances that didn't need to be hidden away, and began dusting the insides of Tain's clothes.

"What are you doing?" Kalina asked. She would know naftate powder as the drying agent that absorbed geraslin ink, allowing papers to be reused after the text had been removed—or, as in our old games, brought back to life under heat in a "secret" message. It had another use to a proofer.

"Naftate powder will highlight certain toxins. A Chancellor a hundred years ago nearly died because the servant who dressed him every morning rubbed manita fungus on the insides of his clothes and his skin gradually absorbed it."

She watched as I worked. "What happens if the fungus is there?"

"It'll dry up and leave a faint blue residue." Nothing appeared as we sat there, watching, but I fully intended to do it to every item of clothing he wore from now on. Just in case.

"I want to go to the Builders' Guildhall," I told Kalina after she had finished her tea, and her eyelids drooped. "Some of Etan's work might be useful for the engineers working on the bridge options, but I'd rather the information came through Eliska's Guild than straight to her from me. Etan knows—knew"—I remembered, breath catching in my chest for a moment—"a few people there who liked to dabble in chemical reactions."

"What about the rebel prisoner?" she asked. "Has anyone spoken to him?"

"He was pretty hostile," I said. "They had to take him to the jail because he attacked one of the physics at the hospital when they were trying to treat him. There's a Guard supervising now. Tain wants to give him some time to be treated fairly so he might be more amenable to talking."

"I want to try talking to him," she said, voice slurring.

I squeezed her hand. "You sleep some more, for now, all right? You'll feel better after a proper rest." I tried to sound confident rather than hopeful. She only ever had so much energy to spend, and it was all being sucked up by this mess we were in.

I was half-afraid she'd ignore my advice, but by the time I'd gathered up some of Etan's papers—carefully curated first, of course—and our supply of dung crystals, her breath had deepened into sleep.

The Builders' Guildhall was abuzz with activity. Eliska must have had every engineer and master builder in the city at work on the bridge plan. On one wall of the entrance hall a great diagram of Bell's had been drawn and three engineers were arguing about how much force would be required to pull the support pillars out. "A team of oku," one began, and one of his colleagues laughed.

"Oku from where? How many oku do you think we have in the city now?"

"Someone find that out," the third muttered. "We haven't eaten them all, have we? We're still using them for milk and pulling carts."

I wandered through the back laboratories, searching. At last I found the scientist I sought: Baina, clever and ambitious and discreet. She was bent over a bench, her bulk spread over enough space for three people, writing notes with one hand while stirring some unidentified substance in a massive ceramic bowl with the other.

"Good morning, Credo Jovan," she said.

I smiled. "It's well into the afternoon now."

"Oh." Baina went on stirring. "Well. I've been here awhile. I'm trying to work out what will best dissolve mortar. That lot out there"—she waved scornfully in the direction I'd come—"are mad if they think the supports will come down without internal weakening first."

"That's why I came, actually. It occurred to me that Etan might have some notes about chemicals that could help—you know how he was always tinkering."

She paused, eyes narrowed in interest. "He was clever, your uncle."

"He was." To mask the shake in my voice, I pressed on. "I remembered him telling us about a few things you might find useful." I handed her my collection of papers and the box of crystals, along with my most baffled expression. "I don't understand it myself. But I remember him making something burst in a stone bowl with these crystals he'd gotten hold of and it completely smashed up the bowl and made such a mess in our kitchen I wondered if, on a larger scale . . ."

"It might damage a stone support?" She shoved aside her own notes and pawed eagerly at Etan's. "No one has any real ideas about Trickster's, but if we could find some way of applying a burst of force to particular spots, we might have something."

"Is there anything you need that you don't have?" Reading upside down from her discarded scribblings, I recognized a few acids I knew from my own work. "Do you need me to get the Stone-Guilder to assign more people to help you?"

Baina grinned, looking me over. "No, thank you. Some of what I do is not . . . Guild-endorsed. I've already arranged some supplies from people who aren't exactly on the books."

"At this point, anything that's for the defense of the city is on the books," I said. "You can use my authority for anything you like."

She suddenly looked off to the side, a sly twist to her lips. "You know, this material is very rough, Credo Jovan. I'll need to be doing my own experiments, figuring things out. . . . I don't know how much use your uncle's work will really be. . . ."

I'd read her right, in our brief contact. She'd never mention my name or where the information came from. It would be *her* innovation, exactly as I'd hoped. "Of course," I assured her. "The other Credolen thought my uncle was odd for his interest in experimentation anyway. I'd rather not give them anything to gossip about." Our gazes met; we understood each other.

But of course, we didn't trust each other, not quite. An abandoned barrel across the street from the Guildhall provided me with sufficient cover to hunker down to wait. I was curious about her contacts; they likely moved in circles beyond Council access.

I didn't have to wait too long. Baina's massive form was easy to spot coming out of the Guild with a crowd of others at the end of a shift change, and her pace slow enough to track even in the fading light. North she went through the streets while I followed, keeping my footfalls light. She spoke to no one and kept her head down; as we headed into increasingly poorer neighborhoods, my confidence that she was meeting her contacts and not merely returning home grew. When she ducked into a building I slipped closer, excited, until I saw it was a kori bar. It was still doing good business, despite what must be dwindling supplies and useless currency in return, though if the city survived the siege, half of it would probably belong to these bar owners. Perhaps Baina wasn't quite as single-minded as I'd counted on.

Then I saw the sign above the door: Branno's.

Frowning, I moved closer, the coincidence tingling in my head. A dingy area of town, a crowded, dank bar . . . not such a bad meeting place. Inside, Baina had moved to a table in a corner. Oil rations meant that the place was lit poorly with candles, and she was only recognizable by her size. I wished I'd thought to bring something to wear over my paluma; my tattoos would stand out too easily in a place like this. It might be better to watch from outside. I turned, and froze.

Three treads away stood a Doranite man in nondescript clothing; I had only seen Batbayer briefly at Lazar's, but his face was seared into my head. He was staring straight at me. His eyes dropped to my arms, then back to my face.

He ran.

It took me by surprise and I lost critical moments in the shock of recognition; by the time I found my senses and sprinted after him, he'd already disappeared down an alley. I followed, pelting into the shadowy passage. Whatever his role, whoever he really was, he knew me and feared me. That was enough.

I quickly lost sight of him between buildings, but the sound of his footfalls guided me in my pursuit. My heart pulsed through my chest as I skidded to a stop at a junction. Half-sized stone walls and iron gates enclosed two small yards on the other side of the pathway. Trusting my ears, I crossed quickly and vaulted over the opposite wall, stifling a curse as my ankle turned on the soft, earthy landing. *Teach me to try acrobatics.*

Across the yard, over another wall. My ankle rewarded me with a jolt of pain. I listened, but this time I couldn't hear anything. The ground was too soft. I was in a maze of residential buildings, yards, and narrow passages, and I'd lost him.

I cursed. My one chance to figure out his connection to all of this, and I'd ruined it. What would he do now?

"Do you think Baina is connected?" Tain paced the room like a hungry graspad, padding back and forth. Earlier I'd been concerned he wasn't taking the threat seriously enough; now I worried about the opposite. His erratic temper was on the rise, just when we needed care and caution.

"Not really," I said. "We should talk to her, and I'm sure we'll confirm he was there to meet her, but I don't think she's involved in any kind of conspiracy. She's just an unconventional scientist. She knew unsavory types, un-Guilded traders and such. We were assuming because he was a Doranite that he was working for his own country, and maybe that's true, but given Baina was seeing him about acids and other restricted supplies, I'm more concerned that he might have supplied Varina with poison."

Tain stabbed a finger down on the Theater-Guild sigil on the map on the table, pinning Varina's name like skewered meat. "I've had enough," he said. "This ends now. We can't keep functioning like this, not being able to trust anyone. I'm going to find out what's going on. Today." He stood, his jaw set and a little vein pulsing in his neck. "Are you coming?"

I nodded, not entirely sure what he planned. "Where are we going?"

"We're going to talk to Varina," he said, and his smile held nothing but icy anger.

Varina looked even worse than before, her nose raw, the skin cracked and almost bleeding around the nostrils, her eyes bloodshot and her usually immaculate hair and clothes in disarray. It had taken some time to find her, in the home of Hasan, her Guild favorite. He sat on the floor, naked, staring up at us with wide, wild eyes and an open mouth. The Order Guards we'd brought with us pulled up short, obviously unsure how to deal with the sight greeting us.

Tain seemed unfazed. "You've been keeping things from us," he said, contempt dripping from him as he glanced around the apartment. "Start sharing."

Varina sniffed, trying and failing for haughtiness as she hoisted the slipping fabric around her bare shoulders. "This is unacceptable."

Tain nodded to the nearest Order Guard. "Can you assist this man to his feet, and into some clothes?"

Hasan stared, slack-jawed, as the Guard seized an arm and pulled him to his feet.

"Stop this immediately!" Varina's voice raised an octave as the other Order Guard stepped closer. "You have no right to come here and manhandle us!"

"No one's manhandling anyone," Tain said, impassive. "But we have some questions about your relationship with a man named Batbayer."

Her face tightened and her gaze snapped to her companion. He swallowed, trembling as he dressed in his discarded paluma. Tain picked up a silvery cord draped over a chair and handed it to Varina as calmly as if handing her a drink. She raised her chin and wound it around her torso and hips, watching the Order Guard with narrow eyes.

"You gave something to Batbayer," I said to her. "Or took something from him. What was is it?"

Varina would never have fallen for something so obvious if she had been her normal self, but she couldn't have been further from it, and I was ready. "I've no idea what you're talking about," she said, but her gaze flicked to the carved bone chest by the window. "Don't you *dare* touch that!" she shrieked, following my gaze, trying to put herself between me and the chest. Her balance was in the same state as the rest of her, and she stumbled and fell hard against a chair. I grabbed the chest, opening it to reveal a polished horn box, long and shallow.

Varina staggered to her feet, outrage draining to fear. Her full lips quivered. Hasan's throat worked up and down, frantic, as if he were trying to swallow a rock.

A fine gray powder rose up in a cloud from the opening of the lid. I held it away, blocking my lips and nose instinctively, then closed the lid on what could well have been the poison that killed Etan and Caslav.

I headed toward a table around the corner, spread with a variety of implements useful to both proofer and poisoner. Varina struggled, wild-eyed and desperate, in the arms of the Order Guard.

A wide, flat knife on a marble board, a glass phial in a stand, a small brazier and a series of small jars containing powders, liquids, and crushed greenery. I looked them over numbly. I picked up a jar and swirled the liquid inside, watching it cling to the sides and make little thinning legs down the glass. I'd need time to work out what everything was. Already I began cataloguing, planning how I would analyze it all back in my own workspace.

"Do you want to say anything? Explain?" Tain asked Varina. She stared, stricken and silent, which seemed to increase Tain's resolve. "You're a Councilor. And a Credola! Why would you betray us all?" She shrank back from his disgust and disbelief, but offered no defense. I wasn't strictly sure she could, given her unsteadiness.

"Please take them to the jail," Tain directed the Guards. "Maybe you'll be more inclined to talk once you've sobered up in a cell."

We searched Hasan's apartment and found more tools and some chemicals I recognized, but nothing else of significance. Tain joined me by the table. He ran his fingers over the implements. "So this is it, then?" he asked, voice dull. "This is what killed our uncles?"

I pushed a portion of the powder about carefully with the back of a knife, watching the fine particles rise again. "I'll need to examine it," I said. "At the moment all I know is they've been distilling it into liquid form, whatever it is."

"They didn't exactly leap to deny it, did they?" he agreed, glum. "I thought . . ."

"That you'd be glad it's over? That we know who the traitors are?"

"Yeah. Only I'm not."

"Me neither." In fact, gathering up the tools and substances spread out over the table, I felt rather hollow. "Varina wasn't my favorite person, but I never picked her as a murderer."

"I guess at least we'll learn more about why this happened after she's stewed in the cells overnight."

I nodded. "Varina's from the wealthiest family in the city. She's probably never been uncomfortable in her life. A night in jail might make her think about what happens if she doesn't try to help us now." I needed her answers to a lot of questions, mostly about whether she had conspired with Doran or had been acting alone against the Chancellor to protect her interests and lifestyle.

"What do we tell the rest of the Council?" I closed the box of powder and placed it in my satchel.

Tain sighed. "Nothing, I think. Marco and the Guards know, obviously, but they won't say anything to anyone until we tell them to. I don't want every other Councilor busting down our doors asking questions or arguing about whether we can put a Councilor in jail."

Despite the grim situation, I almost smiled at the thought of Bradomir's face when he heard we'd arrested his cousin.

Esto's revenge

DESCRIPTION: Complex compound derived from the crushed shell of a glintbeetle and alternately combined with salt and sugar over repeated heatings and coolings.

SYMPTOMS: Immediate blurred vision, headaches, dizziness, intense pain in the ears and sometimes upper sinuses, seizures, heart failure.

PROOFING CUES: Virtually undetectable; faint sweet smell and taste only in purest form; essentially odorless and tasteless in food and liquid.

12

Kalina

A noise broke the tense silence: a scraping outside the door. I struggled to my feet. Jov had been testing portions of the powder they'd found at Varina's in a range of solutions and under a range of temperatures since the early hours of the morning. Once he descended into that level of concentration, I might as well not have been there.

I padded across the tiles and paused at the doorway, but no solid knock followed. Maybe I'd imagined it?

Outside was nothing but a glary, overcast morning. Further down the street, a group of armed men and women traipsed off toward the wall for shift change, and a stiff wind lifted the vines that hung from the windows of the residence opposite ours and kicked debris and a few loose grasses down the road. I squinted against the bright sky, shielding my eyes with one hand. There, was that something? A flash of red or purple, something that didn't belong among the white stone and greenery. It almost looked like a face, there, in the shadow, a face in a red scarf, but I couldn't be sure. I took another step, and slipped on something underfoot.

A necklace, made of fine braided leather, and carrying three small carved charms. I picked it up slowly. I recognized two out of the three charms: one for the spirit of Solemn Peak, one for the spirit of Bright Lake, just as Tain's servant had shown us. The middle charm bore a symbol that looked familiar but I couldn't immediately place it: a set of interlocking circles bisected by straight diagonal lines.

"Jov?" I backed inside, fingering the Darfri necklace. My brother didn't respond. I went into his laboratory behind the kitchen. He was bent over a flame, his lips moving and his eyes narrow, oblivious as I approached. "Jov? Take a look at this."

He snapped his head up, face caught in a frown. "What? This isn't . . . I don't know what this is." He removed the small ceramic bowl from the heat and set it down carefully. "I wanted to know exactly what we were dealing with before we . . . what is that?" He finally registered that I was showing him something.

"It was outside the door," I said. "Someone left it out there."

He turned it over in his hands and traced the rough symbol with one finger, his face lost in its familiar mask of concentration. "Darfri," he murmured.

"I want to talk to the prisoner," I said, plucking the necklace from him and avoiding his gaze.

He frowned. "Don't be ridiculous, Lini. You're barely out of bed. You aren't going anywhere near the prisoner."

Irritation flared. "He's in *jail*, Jov. He can't hurt me."

"He—" Jov began.

"I'm good with people," I persisted. "Better than you, at reading them and talking to them. You know that. You're not the only Oromani with skills."

"I'm only worried about your health, Lini."

I tightened my arms. *I'm twenty-two years old,* I wanted to say. *And you're my little brother, not my Tashi.* But I squashed down that cruelty and instead pulled on a pair of sandals.

He stared at me. "All right," he said at last. "Come on."

I followed, necklace in hand, hiding a smile.

The jail was one of the oldest buildings in the city, the entrance built into the side of Solemn Peak and the majority of the building underground in the mountain itself and beneath the Manor. We met Tain at the entrance, where he left his guards. We spoke in hushed voices as we descended the stairwell entrance.

"I spoke to Baina this morning," Tain said. "You were right, I don't think she knows anything. She says she doesn't even know Batbayer. She left a message for a contact of hers who said he'd send someone who could get her a supply of some metal she needed. She was just meant to meet them at the kori bar."

"And you believed her?"

He shrugged. "I don't know if I'm the best judge, but I did, yes."

Jov nodded. "She might be a bit unscrupulous, but I think it's only driven by ambition and curiosity."

Truth be told, we couldn't really afford to disbelieve Baina; we needed our smartest people working on the defense of the city. "What about her contact?" I asked.

"She gave me his name and how she contacts him. I sent one of my household guards to go find him. Hopefully he'll help us find Batbayer." We were almost at the foot of the stairs; Tain gestured ahead. "But if not, Varina looked about ready to crumble yesterday. After a night in the cells, she might be ready to tell us everything we need to know."

"I want to talk to our prisoner first," Jov said. "If he's willing to tell us anything, we might be able to use it to check whatever Varina says. We'll need to know if she's being straight with us about whether Doran is involved."

Tain nodded. "Hopefully we can make him understand we're trying to stop the war and we're willing to listen. There's so much more to this than we knew—maybe there's more to it than he knew, too."

"And I want to ask him about this," I added, showing Tain the necklace. It had left dents in my palm where I'd crushed the charms as we walked. "I think someone might have been trying to give us a message. They left this outside our door."

Tain looked closely. "What do you think it means? Does someone want to talk?"

"We didn't see who left it, but that's what I'm hoping."

The prison guard, a stocky woman with short hair and a dour expression, directed us to a cell. I shivered, wrapping my arms tightly around my body.

"If it isn't the gracious Chancellor, sharing his exalted presence," a gravelly voice said from the darkness, making me jump. I drew closer to the barred cell on the left. The light from the hall was set too high in the ceiling to penetrate much of the gloom of the cell, but squinting revealed a figure cross-legged on the ground. He was dressed country style, in baggy trousers and a shirt and vest. Despite the chill, the prisoner spurned the supplied blanket folded on the pallet.

"Good morning," Tain said.

"Morning, is it?" the man asked. He looked about with exaggerated confusion. "If your Excellence says so, I will defer to you."

"You'd be in the hospital in a nicely lit room if you hadn't attacked the physic," Jov said sharply, but Tain shot him a look.

"We're not enemies," the Chancellor said, stepping up close to the bars. "I want you to know that. We want to stop this war. Help us."

"I think your Worship has been helped by our people for quite long enough."

"We're all Sjon," Tain said. "City or country."

"Yes? You treat your country people in an interesting fashion, then."

Tain crouched by the bars so their heads were of a height. "May I have your name?" he asked. "I'm Tain Iliri, but I'm sure you know that."

Jov detached a lamp from the wall and passed it down to light the cell. The light cast a wedge onto the man's face, illuminating a narrow bright brown eye, sharp jawline, and below that, a charm necklace much like the one in my hand. The prisoner said nothing as his gaze raked over Jov and me, then dropped away, finding us insignificant.

Tain had seen it, too. "Il-ya, then," he said, using the formal old-style Darfri address for an adult man.

"Highness," the man said, deadpan.

Tain winced. "I'm not looking for deference here. I know this city has made a lot of mistakes. Please, I just want us to work together so lives can be saved." His tone rang with sincerity, and I felt a rush of affection for him. Tain had his flaws; he could be unreliable, irresponsible, certainly oblivious at times. Yet he had the best heart of anyone I knew, and I only hoped the prisoner could see how genuine he was. But the Darfri man didn't even stir from his position, merely watched with cold eyes.

"We know your people were provoked," Jov said. "Cut off from the privileges we enjoy in the cities. And people like us have been the biggest culprits, profiting from your work while being blind to what was going on.

We know. We want to fix it." He squatted down close to the bars, beside Tain. "I think we've all been tricked into a civil war that doesn't benefit either side. What do the country estates gain if the Bright City is sacked? Destruction, sure, but even though you've cut off our messengers you must know our army will come back sooner or later. And the city gains nothing if half the people outside the walls are killed. We can't feed any of the cities without the people and lands that support them." He twisted his hands together. "We had traitors in our midst. Traitors who murdered the Chancellor when he was working to address some of the injustices you face."

The prisoner did react then—the tiniest twitch, a thinning of his lips. Jov pressed on. "We have those traitors here, up the hall from you right now. There won't be any more sabotage. We can negotiate, in good faith, to end this siege."

"We just need to know what you want," Tain added.

The prisoner smiled, a broad, slow smile of pure delight. "We want you brought down," he said. "There is nothing to negotiate. We will not stop, we will not be tricked into your false peace. Your city will fall."

Jov and Tain took turns trying to engage with the prisoner, but when the man spoke at all it was only to mock them. I had never seen anyone pay so little respect and courtesy to any Credolen, let alone the Chancellor himself. My initial irritation turned to reluctant admiration. Whatever motivated him, it was no petty issue, and it was not someone else's cause. He believed in what he was doing.

Eventually, a break in Jov and Tain's questioning came about. I stepped up to the bars. The prisoner cocked his head the other way, brows rising. "I thought you were just decorative."

I ignored the jibe. "What is this?" I held out the necklace.

The prisoner snapped his head down, reaching for it with an involuntary twitch, like a suppressed lunge. "Where did you get that?" he asked, and I had to force myself not to step back from his sudden intensity. I shrugged, tossing it between my hands with feigned indifference. Behind me, Jov and Tain melted away without words, and a rush of gratitude washed over me at their show of confidence.

"Where did you get it?" the prisoner repeated. "Did you take that off someone? You have *no right* to touch our sacred things." He stood and clenched the bars, his composure shredded into anger and confusion.

"Someone left it for us."

"Who?"

I shrugged again. "Someone who wants peace between us, I suppose."

His lips thinned, pulling back over his teeth like an animal. Through his open collar the hollow at the base of his throat sucked in and out with his breath. If I could only stay calm, we might learn something critical.

"No one should have given that away, not to a heathen," he said, spitting the words out as though each caused him physical pain. "Is there no end to what you will do to us? It's not enough, what you have already done? Whoever gave you that is a *traitor*. There will be no peace, do you understand me? No peace. Anything they tell you is a lie. They cannot speak for us."

"Well, you're not doing much speaking," I pointed out. My voice was higher than usual, tight with nerves, but I hoped the man wouldn't notice. "So if someone else wants to deal with us . . ."

The prisoner spat and swore, pacing back and forth in the cell, and gave me no further responses. He seemed lost in his fury and frustration. Eventually, Tain steered me by the shoulder back out of the cell corridor.

"He's not going to say anything else for now, I don't think," he said. "I can't believe the reaction you got, Lini. We're obviously still missing something big about the Darfri. You're sure you didn't see who left it?"

"No." I remembered the flash of red in the shadows and blew out my breath. "Well, maybe for a moment. I think someone hid across the street and watched me pick it up. But I couldn't even be sure it was a person, at the time."

"But they must want to talk," Jov said. "So that means they'll be in contact again." He crossed his arms, his expression thoughtful. "Do you think it's the Darfri in the caverns?"

"Anyone being willing to talk is better than no one." Tain sighed. "Speaking of which, are we ready to go talk to our other prisoners?" Jov nodded, and Tain raised his voice to address the guard at the opposite side of the room. "We're going back to see the Councilor."

But as we started back down the corridor, a breathless cry followed us from the outer room. "Honored Chancellor!" Erel, Tain's messenger, came running through and skidded to a stop in front of us. I smiled at the sight; he never seemed to move at any pace but a run. He flattened his hair nervously. "Honored Chancellor, I'm sorry to disturb you. But she came to the

Manor and she said she needed to speak to you, and that it was important. She said she'd tried the Oromani residence but there was no one there."

"Who?" Tain asked, and for a moment I thought our Darfri messenger must have returned, but then I caught sight of the stone marker he held, bearing our Family sigil.

"The sewer guard." I took the stone. "I told her to bring this to us or to the Manor if she learned anything about someone trying to use the sewer to exit the city. Did she leave a message?"

"She asked for someone to come and see her straightaway," Erel said. "She said it was important, that she had information about a foreigner? She wouldn't say more."

"Batbayer," Tain said, squeezing my shoulder and smiling; the most genuine smile he'd given me in weeks. It felt like the sun on my face. "He's panicking, maybe trying to get out. Well done, Lini."

Jov, too, looked delighted. "I thought he'd go underground—maybe literally—and we'd have no shot at finding him. We should go straightaway, before we lose the chance. And take help this time. I'm not letting him get away again."

"What about Varina and Hassan?"

Tain shrugged. "They're not going anywhere, and they can't do any harm back there. They can wait a little longer."

"Maybe you should stay here and wait for us," Jov began, and anger closed my throat for a moment so that I couldn't even respond. Thankfully, Tain scoffed at my brother on my behalf.

"Don't be ridiculous. She's the one the guard spoke to in the first place. You're all right, aren't you, Lini?"

I nodded, but my gratitude to him for standing up for me was tinged with inescapable sadness. The one person who really saw me properly, not as a weak thing to be protected. Familiar loneliness made my heart hurt. "Of course."

"Then let's go."

The sewer guard met us in the Manor entrance hall. "Honored Chancellor, Credola, Credo," she said, respectfully enough, but her chin jutted out as she quickly added, "You told me to come to you if I got a bribe."

"I told you I'd triple it, and I meant it," I told her. "Tell us what happened."

The foreign man had approached her near her home that morning, with a murky story about escaping persecution in the city and returning home. He'd given her what amounted to half a year's earnings on her regular job—repairing pots and other household items—to help him escape that night. "I told him if he wanted to go shit-swimmin' I was happy to help," she said. "He's supposed to show up partway into my shift tonight."

Jov paced behind me, visibly excited. Tain, calmer, squeezed the woman's shoulders. "Tonight, I want you to do everything you would have done if you were really helping someone get out of there. Unlock the grate, lower the sewer dam, whatever. We'll be there, too, ready to take him in."

She shrugged. "I'd lower the sewer dam partway," she said. "Drop the flow without too much risk of it all backing up."

"You've earned much honor for this," Jov said. "This might make a real difference to the defense of the city. Who knows what he can tell us?"

Relief filled me with renewed energy. We had the crooked Councilor—now we could take the poisoner, too, and perhaps learn how and why Doran had mobilized against us.

And now we could finally use our own resources without fear they'd betray us.

The afternoon was spent with Marco, several of our precious Order Guards temporarily borrowed from the sectors, and a sanitation worker from Eliska's Guild. Batbayer had been elusive before; this was our one chance to catch him. We gathered information carefully and subtly, using diagrams, maps, and intelligence from recruited former servants from the Manor—we wouldn't risk anyone prominent or identifiable near the site in case Batbayer was watching.

The plan was simple: station ourselves in the surrounding buildings, both upper stories and ground level. Watchers would form a perimeter to alert us when he approached. Order Guards lay ready to block every exit. Once he attempted to enter the sewer, our men would close in, but use no blades or arrows or anything else that could risk harming him. We needed his knowledge, and we needed him alive and available to play off against Varina, if it came to it.

I helped tie weights to the edges of fishing nets and Marco brought in some civilians who were competent hunters, capable of using a hunting tool consisting of rocks on the end of a short length of rope with surprising effectiveness. "You can take down a wild bindie in midflight, if you've a good eye," one of them told me. "Feed a whole family hunting in the shallows around Green Bend." Another bragged he could snag a kitsa on the prowl. When I tried, just for fun, the rope somehow came back at me and hit my *own* leg, causing great amusement among the hunters.

I had been expecting an argument with Jov about my role, but fortunately Marco headed that off before it could start.

"Credo Jovan, this man already knows you are looking for him. You are too well known in the city; he could easily have someone watching for your whereabouts to make sure this is not a trap." When Jovan started to speak, Marco held up a hand. "I think you and the Chancellor should do something, visibly, at the other side of town tonight. Perhaps pay a public visit to inspect the sectors; visit the workers, boost morale?"

Tain nodded. "You're probably right," he said reluctantly. "We don't need to be there, Jov, and it could put the plan into jeopardy. We can't lose this chance."

Then, even more unexpectedly, Marco turned to me. "Credola Kalina, would you be willing to come? I would keep you well away from any danger, but you have seen this man before, and your face is not so well known. I would value your presence if you are willing."

"Of course," I said before my brother could speak.

And so it was that I found myself wrapped in borrowed clothes, tattoos covered, in the attic space of a building near the sewer entrance. Marco removed a tile and propped the spyglass into the space, then showed me the points at which our watchers would flash a lamp if they saw someone approaching who looked like he could be our man. Oil rationing had meant giving up most of the street lamps, so the square below was dim, but the pool of light showed the grate and the guard standing watch to the side.

"It could be a while, Credola," Marco said. "Will you be comfortable enough?"

I nodded. I was well practiced at holing up in strange places, observing from above. It felt strange, though, sitting there in the dark. To break the silence, I asked, "How did he expect to make it out of the tunnel at the other end, do you think? What if the rebels just killed him on sight? They killed our first runners through the same place." I remembered again the cloth-bound heads and suppressed a shudder, sorry I had brought it up.

"He may have some way of signaling who he is at the other side." Marco scratched his beard with a sigh. "Though I do not think this was a pre-planned exit, so perhaps he is merely taking his chances."

I peered through the glass again. Nothing. "You've fought Doranite tribes before," I said. "Why do you think they'd do this? It can't be all about a couple of mines."

He sighed again. "I do not know, Credola. Sjona has been largely a stabilizing force for good, and though it has profited from the trade route, so have its neighbors in both wealth and peace. Doran is more prosperous than it has ever been before. I suppose this has led to an increase in centralized power and organization—we thought that was a good thing, but perhaps they grew greedy."

Outside, a tiny light flashed in an upstairs window. Marco made room for me with the spyglass and I watched, breath held, waiting for the approaching figure to reach the light.

Then I put down the spyglass and shook my head. "No," I said, disappointed. The figure had not paused or even glanced toward the grate as they passed down the street.

Marco patted my shoulder. "Patience, Credola," he said, and I could hear the smile in his voice. "He will come soon enough. We are ready."

We sat there a while longer. I wondered about the big silent man beside me. While tensions ran high between locals and foreigners, he occupied a strange position, being both a trusted leader and yet obviously not a native Sjon. "Why did you leave Perest-Avana?" I asked him, curiosity getting the better of me. There was a long pause. Below, a chattering group walked past. One spat in the gutter, and I heard the faint sound of the guard giving him a warning to "move along."

Then Marco chuckled; it might have been the first time I'd heard him laugh. He immediately seemed smaller, less remote. "I followed a boy," he said. "He wanted to go to the 'center of civilization.' Unfortunately, there were more exciting things in civilization than the unsophisticated soldier he brought with him to Silasta. His interest in me waned shortly after he discovered the curtained sections of the bathhouses."

"Oh. I'm sorry."

He chuckled again. "It was a long time ago and I do not regret it. I was quite young, and he was quite beautiful."

"So you stayed?"

"Oh, no. I went home, but I was never happy there again. Eventually I left the army and became a private guard for a merchant. We traveled all over the world. When I came here again, I found the city did not have so many bad memories after all."

"I'd like to travel the world," I admitted. "I—" A blink of light from the west flickered on the outside of my field of vision. I grabbed the spyglass and peered down. The west entrance was through one of two alleyways, both dark; my magnified gaze switched between them swiftly, searching for movement. "There," I whispered, making room for Marco.

"Is it him?"

I bit my lip. He moved slowly, quietly, and his head was covered. "Can't tell."

Marco made a whistle that sounded like a gull, the signal for everyone to be ready to move. I shifted position, trying to get a glimpse of the figure's face. He paused on the other side of the road to the guard, placing something on the ground. *The payment?*

"Is it him, Credola?" Urgency in his tone. We didn't want to spring the trap on the wrong person, but we couldn't let him enter the sewer, either. But still my vision was obscured by the light and his clothing and our angle.

Helpless, I shook my head. "I don't know."

The man sauntered close to the grate and paused. I caught a glimpse of his face as he pivoted, checking around him with exaggerated casualness; still not enough, just a pale reflection of the lamplight. Then his foot edged out and stuck into the grate, tucking under a bar. Testing it.

"Good enough," Marco said, and blew the whistle again. This time there was immediate action; suddenly the yard below was full of sounds, and Marco had leaped up and was barreling down from the attic to assist. The man at the grate sprang away toward the nearest alley but someone from above dropped one of our weighted nets and it caught his head and one shoulder. Instead of slowing him, it seemed to spur him on; a bladed weapon appeared in his free hand and he charged fast at the exit, slashing out at whoever blocked his path there. It was all frantic moving shadows and shouts to me. Balls and ropes flying through the air. A flurry of bodies across the cobbles. Shouts and groans. I gripped the edge of the roof opening, throat tight.

Then a loud curse. Marco? I squinted down; someone had lit a small lamp and the huddle of bodies was illuminated. "We need a physic!" someone cried, and another voice said, "No good."

Enough was enough; I abandoned my perch and scrambled down from the attic, the horrible tightness in my throat expanding through my chest and stomach as I skidded out, dreading what I would find.

The worst outcome. "It's too late," someone said, and to the side the bribed guard stood, shaking, a bloody shortsword in her hand.

"He ran at me," she mumbled, looking dazed. "I'm so sorry. I didn't mean . . . I'm so sorry."

No, I thought, *no, we needed him alive.* I slipped through the confused clutter of Order Guards and hunters to where Marco knelt beside the man, his hand searching for a pulse. He rocked back on his heels, shaking his head, even as I reeled back in horror.

The lamp illuminated the man's pale-skinned face.

I had just enough time to spin around so that my sudden bitter vomit didn't spill over the body. It wasn't Batbayer. It was one of Ectar's servants. We had the wrong man, and we'd killed him.

Manita fungus

DESCRIPTION: Fungus growing in damp, shaded, rocky areas with orote deposits, growing from a white fuzz to a series of slender, hollow-stemmed mushrooms at maturity. Poisonous if ingested or skin exposed to dried mushroom powder.

SYMPTOMS: Weakness in limbs, intense abdominal discomfort, constipation, kidney and liver damage, confusion, restless sleep; large doses can cause collapse and heart failure.

PROOFING CUES: Smell and taste of fresh or cooked mushrooms is mealy, earthy, and difficult to disguise. Dried powder becomes odorless but retains strong taste. Powder form reacts with naftate powder to reveal a blue residue.

13

Jovan

In the course of only a few hours, everything had unraveled. We were supposed to have the connection to Doran as well as the chief conspirators behind bars, ready to turn on one another and give us the information we needed. Instead, we had a dead man from an entirely different country, with no idea how or if he fit into the broader plot, and no leverage over the imprisoned Councilor.

Bradomir was around town rattling doors, trying to locate his missing cousin, and meeting only obstruction and misdirection. We had no idea what to do with him. Or with Ectar. And we now had a bunch of Order Guards and civilians we'd had to swear to secrecy without properly explaining ourselves.

All in all, today had turned into a heap of shit, as Tain had put it.

We'd left Varina and Hasan long enough. "We haven't caught Batbayer, but nothing else has changed," I tried to reassure my friend. "He might not have been trying to escape the city, but that just means he's gone to ground here. He was still working with Varina, he was still at the lunch, and they were still making poison." *Even if I hadn't managed to identify it yet.*

We passed by the guard at the entrance and descended the stairs to the cells below. The jail felt still and cold and empty. All but one warden had been pulled from guard duty after the Council released all the petty criminals to help defend the city. With the few remaining prisoners locked in their cells, there was no real reason for my apprehension as we passed through the dim corridor that held our Darfri prisoner—silent and still, again—and, at the end, Hasan.

We planned to speak to the musician Hasan first. He was a weak character; after a day and a night in a jail cell he ought to be suffering, afraid, and ready to talk.

His singing greeted us before we could see his thin hands gripping the bars. A pitiful lament in his high, smooth voice, broken with tiny hitches that might have been sobs. The melodrama almost made me smile, before the seriousness of the situation hit me again. This was a man who might well have poisoned our uncles and perhaps been involved in inciting a war. No matter how pathetic he sounded, we couldn't forget that.

His song broke off when he heard our footsteps, and the pale-nailed fingers on the bars withdrew for a moment. Then, as we came up in line with the door, Hasan threw himself at the bars, pressing his face into them as if he hoped he might somehow force his head through the iron. "Honored Chancellor," he croaked, blinking at us with eyes feverish and bloodshot. "Credo Jovan. I beg you. The *indignity*."

Tain took a step back, looking Hasan over with cool contempt. Uncorded, the tunic we'd put him in looked like a grimy sack. His skin dripped with sickly-smelling sweat. His long hair, usually intricately beaded and impeccable, hung about his cheeks and neck like sodden rope strands. He looked as if he'd been languishing down here for months.

"We found poison in your rooms," Tain said, and I watched for the man's reaction. He winced, swallowed, opened his mouth as if to protest, then shook his head, pressing his lips back together. "Do you deny it?" Tain asked.

"Yes, of course!" The words burst out, and Hasan let go his death grip on the bars for a moment to clutch at his face. "I mean, I know some people call it that. But it's not . . . it's not meant to hurt anyone."

Tain struggled to conceal his anger. "What's that supposed to mean?"

"It . . . we don't use it often, and it's not for the compositions, I swear," Hasan said. "Please, Honored Chancellor. We didn't mean . . . Please don't let anyone know about this. It just got out of control."

Tain stared at him, baffled, but my face grew hot as things fell together in my head. The powder in his room. Varina and Hassan's apparently drunken demeanors. Varina in Council, wan, constantly sniffing, red-eyed. . . . I'd assumed it had been tiredness and stress. Just as we had assumed the foreigner bribing the sewer guard had been Batbayer. How many more false assumptions had we made?

"Honor-down, Hasan," I said, any remaining energy dropping from me. "What were you using?"

He licked his lips, gaze darting between us. "It was a new cut," he said. "Our supplier calls it mist. We had . . . stronger . . . stuff we were trying, but we were mixing it to make it milder."

Tain blew out his breath, catching up. "You were mixing *hallucinogens?*" He swore. "And your supplier?"

"Batbayer," Hasan said. He frowned. "You said you knew that. . . . Credo Jovan—and his sister—they saw us. The lunch. And Branno's."

I rubbed my forehead, fighting the urge to pace, and shifted my weight between my feet, left and right, sets of eight. "The powder we took from Varina's chest. It was the drug?"

"Of course. Listen, please—"

"For the love of . . . why, *why* did you not say something when we arrested you?" Tain kicked the wall, shouting. "We thought you were bloody poisoners! If you were only using drugs, why would you think we'd haul you to jail?"

Hasan pulled at his hair. "For the selling. I thought you knew we were selling, it's—"

"It's a crime." It was, just not a common one. Decades ago, as trade was exploding in the city but the Guilds were not yet properly equipped to police imports, Silasta had been inundated by a range of narcotic substances from around the world: hallucinogenic smoke, powders, creams made from certain insect shells, even atrapis tinctures, which were medicinal in certain circumstances but toxic in large quantities. The medical and criminal consequences had been significant, and the Council had outlawed recreational drugs in an attempt to stop the problem. It had worked; in our lifetime, drugs had never been common in Silasta. I'd certainly never heard of anyone arrested for selling them, and I'd had no idea a new one had found its way to Silasta. "But Varina's a Councilor. And a Credola. Did you not think it strange that we'd come storming in like that? Why didn't you object?"

"It's not just that it's a crime," Tain said suddenly. "It's your Guild, isn't it?"

Hasan nodded. "If word got out we'd been using, our music, our performances, my reputation, it would all be discredited. You can't let people know, Honored Chancellor. Please. I never composed using it. It was just for fun. And then it got harder and harder to resist . . . and people want something to take their minds off things these days."

The stupidity of it almost made me laugh. All these two idiots had been worried about were their precious reputations in the Guild. They'd been frightened and incoherent when we arrested them and none of us had realized we were at cross-purposes. A new cut of some experimental hallucinogen; no wonder I hadn't been able to identify the damn powder.

Varina gave us the same story. Though less pathetic than her companion, she confessed to using the substance—though not to selling it—and admitted she'd been afraid it would affect her reputation and position. Even sniffling and red-eyed, her skin damp and face drawn, she retained her imperious air.

"If I had not been affected by the mist—in a private home, no less—I would never have allowed you to treat me this way," the Theater-Guilder said, chin high and voice hoarse but chilly. "I am a Councilor. You cannot throw us in these mangy holes and expect no repercussions."

Tain gave a humorless bark of a laugh. "The Chancellor was poisoned, Varina," he said. "And we were attacked while our army is skirmishing with Doran. And here you were, cozying up to a Doranite man, accepting strange powders from him in dark corners. We confronted you, said you'd betrayed Silasta, and you didn't disagree. What did you expect us to do? You're lucky Marco or, fortune favor you, Aven, wasn't there—you've heard what they think about crimes in time of war, and you'd have been lucky to get out of your room with your head."

"A meaningless threat, since justice in this country isn't run by the military," she retorted. "Much as their pathetic Guild might wish it were."

"Well, maybe if it was we wouldn't be in the middle of a damn siege," he snapped back.

"I wouldn't say that near dear Credola Aven," Varina said, "or you'll be giving up your chancellery before you know it. Violent, power-hungry creatures they are, I—"

I couldn't even participate in the conversation. It was all I could do to keep any of my attention focused on them; while my brain whirled with the new information and tried to sort and reconcile it, my feet carried me back and forth, back and forth, and the insistent rhythm played out in my head. The longer this situation went on, the more the compulsions built up, so by the time Tain was satisfied with his questioning, there were five different patterns: pacing, hands squeezing, toes scrunching, thighs tensing, and teeth clicking. Counting sets of eight for each muscle group took all my concentration. If I didn't get a handle on it soon I'd end up stuck down here all day, trapped by my escalating madness. I hated myself for my lack of control, but I could no sooner stop the patterns now than grow wings and fly out of there.

"Jov," Tain said, touching both his hands to my shoulders in a firm, gentle grip. "Jov, come on."

He led me back down the corridor toward the main chamber. Walking, I concentrated hard on four of the patterns until my jaw could relax, then three, until my thighs went the same way, then two, until my poor crushed toes were able spread out in my shoes again. By the time we entered the main chamber, I was down to counting steps and hand squeezes, a manageable level.

Used to my limitations, Tain waited, patient, as I circled the room. Getting frustrated didn't help, but the compulsions had never before been so desperately inconvenient.

Eventually the pacing urge abated. Without judgment, Tain spoke as if no time had passed. "I'll get the guard to release those two," he said. "Honordown, we're barely holding off the rebels. What are we going to *do*?"

We headed up the long staircase, and the count in my head with each step lacked the frenzy from below. "I wonder," I began, then stopped.

The sight before us registered like a punch in the stomach.

The guard's body filled the staircase. Blood pooled beneath her and crept over the edge of the stairs. She lay backward as she'd fallen, her head hanging over the edge of one step, eyes staring wide and sightless like a grotesque doll. Tain sprang toward her, but I caught him.

"Wait," I whispered, my heart rate accelerating. "Look how she died." I crouched, trying to source the blood. "Stabbed or struck from behind." My voice sounded thin, squeezed past the tightness in my throat.

"From downstairs," Tain said, eyes wide. Whoever did this came from *inside* the jail, not outside. As one, we turned and raced down the stairs and back into the corridor. We'd passed by the Darfri prisoner's cell on the way in and out without noticing anything. *Surely he couldn't have escaped. He had nothing in there to break out with.* But dread gripped my chest.

We reached the cell and stopped short. He hadn't escaped. In fact, he'd never be leaving that cell, at least not the way he came in.

He lay facedown in front of the pallet, as though he'd risen to meet whoever had opened the door. A lake of blood soaked the floor under his head, dark and glimmering. I felt numb as Tain pushed open the unlocked door. We picked our way over to the sprawling corpse and Tain crouched to check for signs of life. He tentatively moved the man's head, exposing the massive, ugly wound across his throat. I turned away, my stomach roiling. His killer had nearly sliced his head off. Death had become a commonplace sight in the last few weeks, but somehow the savagery of this one, this murder of a nameless, unarmed prisoner, unsettled me more than all the rest.

Tain dropped the man's head back down and stood, fists clenching. By unspoken consent, we left the cell and moved out of sight of that horror, back to the main chamber. The empty desk and chair, which should have been filled by a warden, mocked us. It had seemed like such an obvious idea to pull the jail staff onto more important duties. That decision might have cost us critical information, and two people's lives.

We found the keys to the cells abandoned on the guard's body on the stairs. Her killer must have dropped them there as they fled. The jail logbook she'd carried was gone—I'd expected nothing else, of course. Our enemy didn't make mistakes. Indeed, our enemy could do whatever he or she wanted, without fear of us bumbling into their path. They had come in, stolen the keys, waited until we had gone to speak to Varina, then killed a prisoner and the guard on the way out, all without us hearing a thing.

I sat in the empty warden's chair, feeling more pathetic, more incompetent, than ever before.

Anger and frustration drove me as I headed to our apartment. We'd released Varina and Hasan—there hardly seemed any need to keep them locked up, and their fear of being exposed to their Guild had made them practically volunteer to keep the whole matter silent. A certain stiffness and pride had been missing when they had left the jail through the Manor exit.

I rounded the last corner and saw a silhouette outlined against the light from our side window; just a glimpse as the figure slipped through our gardens. Heart thumping, I flattened myself around a corner and watched as the figure crossed the road and disappeared into the far side of the Ashes' garden.

As I'd hoped, he'd used the garden as a route back to the smaller lane that ran parallel to the road, lower down the hill. Having cut through there many times myself, even in the gray moonlight, I knew the best place to climb the wall and slide down the other side, and I was closer to that point than my quarry. I ducked behind the fair lady bush by the wall and waited.

Beyond the fat, silvery leaves he flitted wraithlike across the overgrown lawn, a hooded shadow. I waited until he had two hands and one knee on top of the wall, then slipped out from behind the fair lady, grabbed his free leg, and pulled.

With a grunt he fell backward, landing hard on his backside. I might have been stiff and exhausted but it took little energy to drop my knee down onto the base of his sternum, then twist an arm around behind him, forcing him to his side as I sat on his hips.

He bucked and wriggled, but my knee had winded him and he wheezed feebly.

"What were you doing at my house?" I used my free hand to pull the hood off his head, and was completely unprepared for what greeted me.

"He" was a "she"—tall and wiry, with unruly hair half-obscuring a face twisted in a combination of scowl and pant.

She gasped in pain, then abruptly stopped struggling. Between sucking breaths she spat her hair out of her mouth and glared up at me, still but for the unsteady rise and fall of her chest.

"Who are you, and what were you doing at my house?"

She muttered a curse.

"Let's try again," I said. "I think you know my name. What's yours?"

"None of your concern," she spat.

I gave her arm a fresh twist and she arched her back, hissing in pain. This time I clearly understood the word she called me. "It rather seems like it is," I told her. "Why were you at my house?"

After a moment of meeting her scowl with silence, she unclenched her jaw and spoke, more civilly, but with apparent distaste. "I was delivering a message." The long vowels and lilting cadence of her voice were similar to the Darfri prisoner's.

"You're from the estates," I guessed aloud, and relaxed my grip, a little. "You left your necklace at my house." I looked at her more closely. "And I've seen you before. You've been watching me."

"So he is not as thick as he looks," she replied, contemptuous. Her eyes raked over me. They were faintly green in the moonlight. "It would not be hard, I suppose."

"This isn't the best time for insults, given your situation."

"Ha!" She blew another chunk of errant hair out of her mouth. "You think I do not know you need us? We have seen you floundering about trying to talk to Darfri in the city. I even followed your clumsy tracks through our catacombs." She twisted to see my reaction, and laughed at my shock.

"You? You were following me in the caves?" I thought back. The figure behind me had always been hidden by shadow. I had glimpsed the knife, but only my assumption had painted my assailant as male. "You tried to kill me?"

"Kill you?" If possible, her contempt intensified. "I strolled after your lame-bird tracks to see where you went. Why would I try to kill you?"

I stared at her, confusion rising. "You had a knife."

She raised an eyebrow. "I always have a knife. You would too if you were Darfri living in *this* city." She smirked. "I did not realize how close behind you I was. You saw me and feared me, then? Good. Perhaps it felt like our people feel when they are hunted down through the streets of their own city like vermin."

There was satisfaction but no deception in her expression. Remembering my abject terror during that dark chase, humiliation flooded me. It had all been in my mind, fueled by my own fears and projections. "Suppose I believe you. What's the message? You're here, I'm here. Why don't you deliver it?"

"Let me up first."

I hesitated. But, honor-down, she wasn't wrong—we *did* need the Darfri. Now more than ever, since we had been so wrong about Batbayer and Varina. Releasing her arm, I stepped back, wary. She rolled to a sitting position and rubbed her upper arm and shoulder. Now that I could see her properly, I wondered how I could have mistaken her for a man. She was as tall as me, or taller, and her shoulders were broad, but her scowling face, painted with shadows and swathes of dark hair, was undeniably feminine. The gray cloak had fallen open, revealing a red cotton blouse, stitched with bright contrasting colors.

"You're welcome," I offered to her silence.

Her mouth twitched, but whether she suppressed a smile or a further insult, I couldn't tell. She raised her chin and crossed her legs, spine straight, watching me without apprehension.

"Your message?" I tried again.

"It is not *mine*," she said, not hiding her resentment. "My mother's. She was too afraid to come out, but she would not be talked out of this madness."

My heart beat faster, pumping in my ears like a drum. "What's your mother's message, then?"

"She wants to meet with you," she said, the set of her jaw making it clear how she felt about this idea. "She thinks you and the Chancellor might listen to her about why our people have risen against this broken city of lies."

"And you disagree."

"Yes!" Her eyes flashed. "The Council betrayed us. You all did. And now you are getting what you deserve. *Ruin*."

"So why deliver the message?"

She shrugged. "I love my mother. Would you disrespect yours so?"

My throat tightened. "I don't even know if my mother's still alive," I told her. "We're in a bloody siege, and she's out there somewhere. And someone in here killed my Tashi, so frankly I don't have that many people left to disrespect."

At that she did drop her gaze. "Spirits protect them."

We both fell silent, the momentary drop in hostility making it suddenly, intensely, uncomfortable. I took a step backward, gesturing for her to stand. She rose in a single, graceful movement, and covered her hair and clothes again. "I will take you to her," she said.

"I don't think so." Perhaps she didn't intend to attack me herself, but I would not be so foolish as to put myself at the mercy of a people who viewed us as responsible for some great ill. "We can meet at my apartments."

"Ha! Do you know what would happen to my family if it was discovered we talked to you?" She folded her arms and looked me over, her superior height allowing her an imperious air. "It was enough risk for me to leave you a message."

I nodded slowly. "We showed . . . Someone saw it, and they said whoever left it was a traitor."

"Many would regard us as traitors for seeking a peaceful meeting with you." She tightened her arms across her chest. "Who did you show? That was a private message for you alone. Can we not even trust you not to—"

"Well it wasn't a terribly *clear* message, was it?" I snapped back. "You could have left a note."

She scoffed. "And what would I have put in it? My handprint?" She shook her head at my slow understanding. "You assume everyone has the luxuries you enjoy, or do you just not care to think about it?"

My face grew hot. We knew the capital had ceased to oversee the regional schools, but honor-down, *were* there even schools anymore? Surely things couldn't have gotten so bad that country children weren't being taught to read and write?

"You must have been here for weeks," I said, suddenly wary. "And you've been watching me. Why haven't you come forward before now?"

"We came to see the Chancellor, not you." She looked away. "My mother had met him, some time ago, and for some reason believed he could be trusted. She is very trusting, my mother. And we have my young brother to think of." She gave me a fierce look, and I felt a sudden strange kinship with her. I knew too well what it was like to protect a person like that. "You and your friend are the men who seized power after he died so mysteriously. I did not want my mother approaching you until I had a sense of who you were. Now. Will you meet with her, or not?"

I searched her defiant face, and found some comfort in her open hostility. "Not my house, then. But not the caves, either. If your people think your family are traitors for speaking to me, I'm not going in any dark spaces with them lurking about. We'll meet somewhere we're all safe."

"I don't think they're coming." My compulsions grew the longer we waited. I had let myself get too invested, too excited at the prospect of uncovering the missing parts of the puzzle. But now, here we were, waiting before dawn in a deserted old gazebo in a garden we'd once favored for games of Muse, running out of time and hope that this Darfri family would turn up, while also fearing we were being deceived yet again. Imaginative disastrous scenarios swam around my brain, over and over, until my head felt as if it would burst from the effort of keeping my thoughts straight.

Tain sat, composed, on the spindly old iron seat running the circumference of the gazebo, seemingly unfazed by the lateness. I wished I shared his optimism. Risking him on a meeting that could be a trap was stupid, but once I'd told him about it there was no talking him out of it. We had snuck out without his guards, telling only Argo that we were leaving. Kalina, hidden away in an abandoned shop across the street from the entrance to the garden, would provide our only warning of impending trouble. She had expanded my hidden pouch with new slots and flaps, and now it comprised a miniature arsenal of chemicals and poisons.

"They'll come," he said. "They have to." He knew better than to tell me to calm down, or sit. We each dealt with the wait in our own way.

They appeared so quietly that they nearly reached the gazebo before we spotted them. My messenger from earlier led the way, garbed in her dull cloak, pushing past hanging lacy vines and graying tendrils, scattering silver clouds of insects. She entered the gazebo with a glance at me that, while not quite a glare, was by no means friendly. Behind her glided an older woman who smiled at the sight of us—tentative, but warm. Clutching her hand, a boy of perhaps three or four stared up at me with eyes like little lamps beneath brown curls like his mother's.

"Thank you for coming," Tain was already saying. "My name is Tain Caslavtash Iliri. I hope you don't mind Jovan bringing me, but I wanted desperately to meet with you."

I watched their reactions, hoping Tain's sincerity reached them. So much rode on this meeting. The mother lowered her head while the boy pressed against her leg, silent. My messenger tilted her head with enough respect to avoid outright rudeness, but cynicism radiated off her like an unsubtle perfume.

"My name is An-Salvea esLosi," the mother said, the syllables dripping like honey in her low, melodic voice. "It is a great honor to meet you, Honored Chancellor, Credo Jovan." She gestured to the boy at her feet. "This is my son, Il-Davior, and my daughter, An-Hadrea, whom I understand Credo Jovan has already met." Like her daughter, she spoke slowly and with great formality and pride.

"A pleasure to see you again," I said to An-Hadrea, noting the furtive glance she gave her mother, which told me she'd not described the nature of our meeting. I handed the necklace she had left at the door to her, and she snatched it from my hand, quick as a snake striking. "And a pleasure to meet you, An-Salvea, Il-Davior. Your family is from the Losi valley?"

An-Salvea nodded, her smile showing surprise. I only knew the country surname convention because my mother had introduced an assistant who accompanied her to Silasta years ago, and had explained it. "Please, you must call me Salvea." She ducked her head to Tain. "May I sit?"

"Of course! It's not the most comfortable chair, I'm afraid."

She shrugged her cloak off and spread it on the rusted seat and settled herself among her layers of embroidered clothing, elegant and poised. "It is quiet here. That is prudent."

"Will you sit, An-Hadrea, Il-Davior?" Tain joined Salvea on the bench and turned his warmest smile on her children. The boy sprang up beside his mother with his feet tucked up on the seat. An-Hadrea glanced at her mother and then nodded stiffly. She sat as far from us as possible, back pressed against the twisted old iron, her eyes constantly searching around the garden, suspicious and alert.

"I was born in Losi," Salvea told me. "On the Ash estates. We served there for most of my life. My family tend the kori crops, and distill the spirits."

"Mother," An-Hadrea said, "we do *not* have time for a family history."

Salvea sighed. "There is always time for manners, Daughter," she said. "And our history is not irrelevant to this discussion."

"We're so grateful you've come," Tain said. "Terrible mistakes have been made, and I want to put them right."

"*Mistakes?*"

"Daughter," Salvea said, her tone a bit harder. "Please."

"Please, let her speak," Tain said. "We've wanted to hear this. But no one will talk to us, and there are people trying to stop us learning the truth."

"You are the Chancellor," An-Hadrea said. I could almost hear the omitted *supposed to be.* "How is it that you say you do not know what has happened?"

"Please," Tain said again. He sounded old and tired. "Please, can you start from the beginning. Assume I know nothing. Assume I have been a thought-less boy, concentrating on my own affairs without looking outward. You wouldn't be wrong. Please tell me what's happened."

And so they did. Salvea with sadness, An-Hadrea with tightly contained fury. And the tale they told . . .

Part we now knew. The beginning, decades ago. Deaths at the mines, and help and attention from the city slowing and fading. On the estates, life growing worse. Salvea told us how conditions on Credola Nara's Losi valley holdings, where her family had lived and worked for generations, had become harder. "Once, before my time, they say others envied the es-Losi," she said, shaking her head. "The estates were prosperous. We worked hard for decent wages, and we had great *tah* with the land."

"*Tah?*"

Salvea looked flustered, fluttering her hands, searching for words, and looked to her daughter. An-Hadrea rolled her eyes dramatically.

"*Tah.* Connection to the secondworld, to the spirits of the land. We no longer have your letters, out where we live, but you have forgotten more important things." She pulled the middle charm from the necklace I'd re-turned, and held it aloft, as if the symbols should have been clear as text. She indicated the two interlocking circles, one at a time. "*Tah* and honor. Re-spect for the land and the spirits, respect for humankind. If you have good *tah*, you are in harmony with the spirits of the land. If you have good honor, you are in harmony with the people around you." Scorn tinged her words. "This is your history, not just mine. Your vain and greedy cities have forgot-ten half the code they once lived by, and twisted the other half to something your ancestors would not recognize."

"Daughter," Salvea admonished, and An-Hadrea frowned and fell silent. Her fingers still twisted the necklace aggressively in her lap.

"Over time, things changed," Salvea continued. "Families spent less time on their properties, no longer sent their heirs there to learn the estates. Stewards became distant relatives or simply employees, sometimes kind, sometimes not. But the orders kept coming from the cities. We must work longer on the land each day. We are told we must produce more in less time. Lay crops in fields that need fallow time. Things the estates once did for us, they no longer do. And so we are pushed from one side, and pulled from the other, and there is always more work.

"My grandmother told me stories of when she was a girl. Then, there was a little school in the village, which she attended. Her mother was very clever, and was even sent off to a city for school. But I have never known this. There is no longer any time to send children to school, to memorize all those little symbols. What use do the greedy stewards and Families have now for their workers' learning? We cannot read, so we do not need books, or art, or science. Instead of sending our children to learn from a Guilded carpenter or shipwright or mathematician, the Families send city-folk in to perform high skilled jobs, then send them away again. Our live-lihoods are diminished. The Families dispense what orders they wish, and we have no recourse to complain."

Salvea paused, jaw quivering, then gave us a sad smile. "All this is the way of the world, is it not? The powerful Families divided up the lands all those years ago, and they have grown wealthy off them ever since. We are not starved, on the estates, nor physically endangered. Perhaps if we did not remember what we had lost . . . but our grandmothers and our aunties and our Tashien whisper the stories of the past to us as we sleep, and we know that this was not how it was meant to be."

"No," Tain said. "This is *not* how it was meant to be." He sounded queasy and looked ashen.

"And what about your religion?" What Salvea said confirmed the worst of our fears about the growing chasm between the city and country, but there was still more. The fury in those men's faces, the strange magnetism of the Speaker woman, the cruel murder of our messengers. Spirit killers, they'd called us, and they had meant something by it, something more than schools and language and lost chances.

"You have *forgotten*," An-Hadrea said again, with even more venom. "*Your* religion, you say? This is not religion. This is the essence of the very land we stand on. Your ancestors on the first Council signed a compact, a promise of a country built on both *tah* and honor. And then they built your cities and they forgot that what they take from the land is a bargain, not a right."

"We warned them," Salvea said softly. "Just as the Speakers all over the country warned us."

"Speakers?" I had not told Tain—or anyone else—about my experience, and I tried to keep my tone interested but not over-intense.

Salvea answered quickly this time, before her daughter could interject. "A Speaker is one with a very strong connection to the secondworld. They are a conduit for the spirits, to communicate or act in our world."

"We do not have many left," Hadrea put in bitterly. "None at all in Losi anymore. When I was young a traveling Speaker told me I had great potential for *fresken*. But there are no teachers, anymore, and what use is ancient power and heritage when I could be making drinks for spoiled—" She cut herself off this time without comment from her mother, as if her brittle fury had simply snapped.

I wanted to ask more, but Tain was already prompting Salvea. "What did the Speakers warn you about?"

"That the spirits were growing angry at the lack of heed and respect the people are paying. We took too much from the mountains, and the earth, and the rivers, with no offerings in return to strengthen them. We drew on the special places at the core of them, the sacred places that should not be depleted." She shook her head. "In truth, though, we did not need the Speakers to tell us that. The land told us itself."

"Yet even this you ignored!" An-Hadrea said. "It was more important to keep taking stone and spices than to listen, and so when the spirits acted out, people died."

"The earthquake," Tain said, frowning as he looked between them. "You mean the earthquake at Sabir Quarry?"

"That is only the most recent. Earthquakes, floods, collapses, rains that never come where they are needed, fields that will no longer grow anything but scatterburr. The Maiso grows fiercer each year, and drier, but no matter how he howls a warning with his breath, he is not heeded. Each year it grows worse. The Families closed their ears. They did not care. They treated our warnings as the foolish squalls of children, for that is how they see us now."

I avoided eye contact with Tain. An-Hadrea watched me with unblinking scrutiny, waiting for a chance to attack, and I had no wish to appear skeptical of the claims. Whether the cause of the natural disasters was supernatural or not—and the strangeness of my encounter with the Speaker aside, I doubted any such thing existed—it hardly mattered; the land could be abused by overuse either way.

"I know this is a lot to understand, all at once, if you have never heard it before," Salvea said gently, as if reading my mind. "But *tah* and honor are the backbone of our very culture. Without respect for our culture, it became harder to live a balanced life. We are told we may not have public shrines, because visiting Credolen see them as rubbish marring the landscape. Some of our most important rituals we are no longer allowed to perform out in the natural world where they belong, because it is said they make people who are not Darfri uncomfortable. We are given no chances to connect to the secondworld. My daughter, who might have been a very strong Speaker in my great-grandmother's time, has been denied that connection. Do you see? Our children are being denied their very birthright as people of this land."

"I can see." Tain crossed his arms over his chest, hands tucked under his armpits and head sagging, like an embarrassed child receiving a deserved lecture. And we did deserve it. Only a few weeks ago we had sailed past lands and raised a lazy hand to people working in the fields. They had looked healthy enough, and had waved back, so nothing had challenged my basic assumption that an oppressed people would look thin and cowed and starving.

"I've kno—well, I've been told that my uncle was trying to do something about this. That he was meeting with elders and pressuring the other Families."

She sighed. "It is true. In fact I met the Chancellor, weeks ago, and his sincerity struck me. He did not deflect or defend, but listened. It is why I am here. I had hoped to prevent all this."

"Was he just too late? After all these years, how did it turn into a rebellion?"

"Ah. Well. There has been quiet talk for years. Many grandmothers whispering tales into headstrong young folks' ears, about what we lost, and who was to blame. But it is a big country, and we are scattered. I do not think anyone truly imagined all the estates coming together like *that*. But then there were some things that changed it all. First, the travelers."

I leaned forward, blood pounding in my ears. We had always been sure the rebellion was aided by someone external. Were we at last to know who? The Doranites? A western allegiance?

"They came in wagons but traveled off the main roads, avoiding the main estates, coming into the villages. They had peddlers, healers, and priests. And they took our hospitality, and returned it with kindness and good trading. They were so charming, you understand. They listened to our stories."

"Who were they?" Tain asked, a hint of intensity in his voice. "Where were they from?"

"All sorts of places," Salvea said. Il-Davior, visibly bored, climbed down off her lap and started drawing patterns in the dust and dirt scattered on the tiles. She stroked his curls absently with one hand. "All colors and shapes, they were. Many from other lands, though some claimed to be Sjon who had abandoned a life of excess in the cities, or quit the army." She shrugged one shoulder eloquently. "They said we were not alone, that they had heard the same tales all over the country. That the hardworking people of this country were being left behind, kept fat and compliant on the slops of the cities like animals. People listened." She smoothed her hair back from her brow and I was struck by her poise and calm.

"In truth, they merely said aloud what many had been thinking. It gave us kinship with people on the other side of the country, to know the same things happened there. And it gave strength and courage to those who had already whispered romantic fantasies of taking the cities back from the oppressors. Once those ideas were planted, they were easily fertilized.

"And all the while, the damage to the secondworld grew even worse. Some spirits, the stronger ones, were angry, yes, and lashed out. A sudden flood, a blight that destroyed six fields of crops overnight, a cave collapse. These spirits are strong enough to punish us. But the younger spirits and the ones in quieter, lonelier places, they did not have the strength to reach out to us in that way. Without offerings, and without balance, they have . . ." Salvea broke off, for the first time seemingly too emotional to continue.

"They're dead," An-Hadrea supplied, and the comforting hand on her mother's shoulder quivered with rage. "You are murdering the very spirits of the land. There could be no greater betrayal of the Compact. Ask yourselves why the people should *not* tear down this shining place you have built on the shoulders of suffering. You spit on the traditions that formed this country, you kill our souls and then eat and laugh and dance and gamble all the way to hell. You—"

"Please calm yourself, Hadrea," Salvea said. She took her daughter's shaking hand and squeezed it. "You are upsetting Davi."

The small boy was in fact staring up at his sister, wide-eyed, though to my eye he looked more interested than upset, channeling a child's uncanny ability to blissfully ignore adult conversation unless and until you wished them to. Still, An-Hadrea took a breath and smiled down at Il-Davior. "Are you all right, poppet?" she asked him.

"Ye-es," he said with an indignant huff, then went back to his game. The brief interlude had given Salvea a moment to regain her composure, but it did nothing to improve mine; a dark and hollow feeling inside me had taken root and was spreading through my whole body. If the country people of our land believed our abuse had literally killed their spirits, how could we possibly get them to ever negotiate with us at all? How could we overcome anger that must run to their very hearts and souls? I didn't have to believe spirits existed to understand how people who did would feel about their apparent demise.

"Even after this, when plans for an uprising were murmured in the shadows, some of us tried to raise our complaints peacefully. Please understand that, Honored Chancellor. We were heartbroken, but we still believed that the right thing to do was to bring a case against the Families. From Losi we sent representatives to Moncasta to bring a case to the determination council there. But they demanded forms and papers that we did not have and could not complete, and they told us our relationship with the Families was outside their business. Private affairs, they said. We paid for a scribe in the city to send a message to the Chancellor but heard nothing back."

"But my uncle found out eventually," Tain said.

"Yes. When we had no success in the other cities, several men from Losi traveled here to Silasta. They had no luck reaching the Chancellor in the normal petitions, but they were . . . well, resourceful, I suppose you would say, and they managed to intercept him and speak to him alone."

"In his private bathhouse," An-Hadrea noted with the faintest of smirks.

"He listened, and our men believed him when he told them that he would investigate. And truly, only a few weeks later he came to Losi. Just he and Credo Etan, and a handful of servants. I met them, Honored Chancellor, and I know they genuinely wanted to help. I believed he had not known what the Families had let happen."

"That is no excuse," said An-Hadrea, her chin high as she looked both of us in the eye, daring us to disagree. "He was the Chancellor. What good is a government if it does not know its own people, if it does not care what happens unless it is two treads from its door?"

"Hadrea."

"It's true! And he did not believe us about the spirits, either."

"He was respectful of our beliefs, even if he did not share them himself," Salvea corrected gently. "As was your uncle, Credo Jovan. Though he spoke little, I could see how disturbed he was. Not just disturbed. Ashamed. I believe they were both good men who blamed themselves for their ignorance."

I had lain awake last night, unable to go to sleep for the questions playing over and over in my head: Why had Etan kept this from us? Especially, why had he not thought to give us this information as he lay dying? But now I remembered his last attempts at speaking. *Go home,* he had whispered, with a mouth thick with suffering. Not an expression of his own desire, but a final instruction. *You go home.* Faced with the realization there would be no more time for him, he had tried with his last energy to turn our attention to our own family holdings. Why had he not spoken sooner? I could make a guess. As our Tashi he had been our moral guide. He had been ashamed. Ashamed and proud and so afraid of failing in his duties to the Chancellor and to us.

"You're right, though, An-Hadrea. It's no excuse that we didn't personally know." Tain's usual exuberance was dimmed; he seemed diminished. "So many things I believed were just fantasies. I should have known that."

If anything, Tain's humility seemed only to spur An-Hadrea to greater anger. She had wanted a fight, an outlet for the whirlpool of frustration and injustice that must have been bursting to escape her, and he was denying her that.

On the ground, as if sensing his sister's rage, little Il-Davior tugged at her skirt. "Too much *talking*, Haddy," he moaned. "I am bo-red."

Her anger visibly fizzled as she crouched down beside her brother. "They like nothing more than to talk, in the city," she agreed, with a tiny sidelong glance up at me. A bit rich, I thought, considering I had done nothing but patiently listen this entire time. But as she helped Il-Davior build a small tower out of pebbles I appreciated the distraction all the same. We deserved to be shouted at, but it wouldn't help us end this siege.

"So. The last thing." Salvea's voice slowed even further, and I tried not to be impatient at her long pauses and carefully considered words. "The Chancellor left word among all the estates, quietly, that he wished to meet with our elders, and confront the Council with our matter. Our wisest elders and Speakers left to meet with him in Silasta."

I frowned. Marjeta had mentioned a contingent that had been supposed to come, but had never arrived. "My Tashi planned to meet your elders," Tain said, confused. "But we were told they never showed up."

My heart sank as An-Hadrea's thin-lipped face supplied the other half of the story. "They never came back, did they?" The dull pounding of blood in my head was so loud I could barely hear my own words. No wonder the rebels wouldn't respect our peace flags or trust our messengers. They'd tried that, and we had betrayed them. We were the ones without honor.

After that, Salvea told us, things had moved swiftly. There was no more room to protest the uprising after the elders had never returned; it was assumed that they had been imprisoned, at best. Her face held such hope as she said that, and Tain looked like a broken man as he shook his head; something much worse had befallen that group. Someone had prevented that meeting from happening, and when that hadn't been enough to deter Caslav . . . The roaring was so bad I couldn't open my eyes, or focus on anything but my own wild heartbeat in my ears. Someone—or more than one someone—had not wanted any disruption to the arrangement making them so rich, and had been willing to murder anyone who put their luxurious lifestyles at risk. And potentially our own relatives had participated in this. Easy enough to believe Nara complicit in such evil, or Bradomir, but Mother? Our cousins?

Not wishing to be caught up in the rebellion, and still hoping to be able to present their case to Chancellor Caslav, Salvea and her children had fled Losi, seeking refuge in the city. Upon arrival they had found it difficult to get into the city without documentation from the Ash estates. "We snuck in," An-Hadrea said, chin high, cool eyes daring us to criticize. "A merchant from the southern mountains let us hide in her wares."

"We smell like potatoes," Il-Davior put in brightly.

I grinned at him, and out of the corner of my eye noticed An-Hadrea doing the same, her face transformed. She caught me staring, and the warmth of an indulgent sister snapped off faster than I could blink.

"We tried to make an appointment to see the Honored Chancellor Caslav," Salvea said. "But it was too late. He died before we could see him."

"On the day *you* came back," An-Hadrea muttered, and again focused her glare on me rather than Tain. This wasn't the first time someone had relayed that fact in an accusatory fashion, and it rankled me. Tain, without looking, put a conciliatory hand on my shoulder. Of course Salvea and her family had good reason to distrust us, but that didn't make it feel any better to be thought of as the kind of person who would murder their own Tashi.

"Do you . . . Do you know who killed him?" Tain asked, his words a tight spring of ungrieved pain and hope. And though expected, Salvea's regretful negative cut deep.

"I'm sorry," she said. "My feelings about violence were too well known, so I was never privy to any planning. I could not tell you who the rebels were working with in the city, or even whether this action was at their hands, or the hands of whoever stopped our messengers from reaching the Chancellor.

"Our story ends there. But of course our people's does not. I deeply regret that it has come to this, Honored Chancellor. I thought we would have time to stop this, but it was too late."

I doubted her reaching Caslav before his death would have achieved much; the seeds of the rebellion had been germinating for so long under our oblivious and selfish noses. Greed and corruption and secrets in our own estates and probably in our own Council had fed the uprising, and once the travelers had arrived to give it teeth, the uprising had been inevitable. Another question still remained: Who were those travelers? If indeed they had been made up of people from all different backgrounds, including some of our own disgruntled Sjon soldiers, it was likely they were mercenaries. Which led us no closer to knowing who had hired them, but it was a start.

"We have spent too long here. You have the information we came to give you. Now we must go." An-Hadrea looked back through the garden again. "Someone might come looking for you, Honored Chancellor."

Tain offered his arm to help Salvea, and she stood gracefully. "It's inadequate to say, but I'm so sorry," he said. "It is the Council's fault, and the Families' fault, and our fault. I won't beg you to forgive me for my ignorance, because I wouldn't deserve it. But I'm not too proud to beg you to help me find a way to stop this siege. I don't want anyone else to die. If we can stop the siege and talk, we can change things. Together, on my honor I swear, we can change things. Thanks to you, I know where to start." He squeezed her hands. "There's one more thing I need to ask of you, Salvea."

"Of course."

"Can you let the Darfri people hiding in the caverns know that I will protect them? We only just found out what's been happening in the streets, but I know they've been victimized for a while. We've put three men in jail so far and I plan to find more of them. Everyone in this city is under my protection and anyone who threatens that will find out what sort of Chancellor I plan to be. Please, I just want them to know they can come to me and I'll keep them safe."

"No," An-Hadrea said, before her mother could speak. She crossed her arms across her chest and took a step closer to Il-Davior. "No, Honored Chancellor. We will not let them know that we have seen you. It is not safe."

"You keep saying that," I said. "Are they just cityfolk scared of being targeted, or are they rebels down there?" The rebellion had been organized over time. There must be agents in the city as well, and where better to find them than among the Darfri hiding away from the fighting?

"Why shouldn't they be? Why would we side with you, when those outside would welcome us instead of attacking us in the dark like cowards?" She looked at me, anger simmering in the cold depths of her eyes. They were an earthy brown, mottled with green like interwoven leaves. I found myself unable to break the contact.

"The people in the catacombs are not rebels," Salvea said. "They are scared, and they are angry, and many have family outside the walls. They likely sympathize with the uprising because many of them came from the estates and understand the struggles we have faced. They do not want to take arms against their brethren outside. But they do not want the city destroyed—it is their home, too."

"Then why do you fear them?" I asked. "You went to such trouble to contact us secretly, An-Hadrea, and you're still checking no one can see you now. If you believe the Darfri in the city are loyal to the Chancellor, why are you worried about them seeing you talking to him?"

She scowled. "Like my mother, I have heard no treason. That does not mean I trust that everyone down there means the Chancellor well. No one openly speaks of working for the rebellion, but there are whispers, and rumors of what the Council has done to the secondworld. Many may hope that the Council falls for these crimes. I am certain some would regard our family as traitors for coming to speak with you."

"Will you be safe going back there, then?" Tain asked, looking down at Il-Davior, who was peeking out at Tain from behind his mother's skirts. "You don't have to. All of you could stay in the Manor; you'd be safe there."

I shot him a look. We had just met this family, and critical as Salvea's information was, and genuine as her desire to help seemed, trusting them in our space was absurd. And as An-Hadrea had already made clear, they had little cause to trust us.

"Mother," An-Hadrea said, her voice tight.

Salvea looked at her daughter, brows drawn, but did not speak. I glared at Tain.

"*I* want to go to the Mander," Il-Davior announced into the silence.

It broke the tension. Even An-Hadrea smiled, though it slipped quickly away as she looked at her mother again.

Salvea sighed. "It is kind, Honored Chancellor," she said. "But I think it safest if we remain in the Darfri community and do not attract notice. We will meet you here, to talk more, whenever you like."

Before Tain could protest, I said, "We'll leave a stone on the sundial here, marking the hour we should meet."

"I will send Hadrea to check daily," Salvea said, avoiding looking at her daughter. "And we will help in any way we can."

As Tain helped Salvea back into her cloak, An-Hadrea shrugged hers on as well, brushing close to me as she did. She gave me a scowl while the others were occupied.

"I'm sorry," I muttered. And I was. For everything.

But no mere apology would ever fix what had been done, and we all knew it.

Eel brain

DESCRIPTION: Brain of common river eel, ordinarily removed during cooking (although toxicity greatly reduced after exposure to heat).

SYMPTOMS: Vomiting, diarrhea, excessive salivation and perspiration, dehydration, loss of appetite, death.

PROOFING CUES: Taste in toxic raw form is mild but has an intense, greasy mouthfeel and thickens liquids noticeably.

14

Kalina

The first pink rays of sunlight warmed the pale stone beneath my fingers. I stretched out my stiff back, moving my aching joints through a greater range of motion, and squinted out at the army, which was stirring to life like some great beast coming out of hibernation.

For the first time in my life, I understood my brother's desire for routine and repetition. Everything had fallen to pieces, but there was some semblance of comfort in a routine; get up, go to our sector, walk the length of the wall, meet with Chen and our other leaders for an update.

Armored poppets stood at intervals around our stretch of the wall with only a skeleton crew of real people patrolling. The rest of the Oromani section was assisting with moving key supplies from the other side of the lake. We prepared for evacuation in earnest now. Daily our watchers in the towers reported additional functional-looking contraptions rising from the army outside. The rebels had been working on some kind of tower, adding height each day—my eyes found it now, rising in the midst of their forces, menacing and silent. Eliska speculated when finished it would be the height of our walls, and would be wheeled over to allow them to cross without the vulnerability of ladders.

Chen drew my attention now to the configuration forming. "Do you see the machines there, and there? They're moving them together. They'll be aiming at the damaged wall."

One of the engineers had tried to explain to me how they expected the weapons to work. I hadn't been able to feign understanding of the mechanics of it. The tower would assist the rebels to reach the top of the wall, and the engineers suspected it would also house other weaponry at the lower levels; perhaps a suspended ram. There could be other surprises out there, waiting. But we wouldn't be waiting much longer.

I left Chen after the report and returned to the main streets, which teemed with traffic. People carried litters or pulled small carts full of supplies, transported from the lower city. We were attempting to move not just people and possessions but also our industry facilities; all our metalworking, leather, cane, and textile works were currently in the lower city, and we needed to retain the ability to make weapons and armor if we were forced to defend from the upper city. People were being forced to work long hours in physical jobs to which they were not accustomed. Everywhere the darkened mood of the city showed itself in scowls and bickering and microaggressions.

Discontent wasn't confined to the common man, either. Last night I'd heard Credola Nara arguing with her nephew Pedrag, the Craft-Guilder, outside their apartments; a rare sight for family members to allow such a display in public. Tain had insisted that Councilors, like everyone else who had housing in the upper city, billet residents from the lower city after the evacuation, and it was causing tantrums. Jov was moving all his essential proofing supplies and research materials out of our apartments and into the Manor. Bank staff had been released from city duty for the present to deal with all of the requests to store valuables; none of the wealthy upper-city families wanted to share their homes, let alone their portable wealth, with strangers.

Down toward the lake I passed a ration station, where several arguments had broken out in the line.

"This is half the size it was a week ago," someone complained, causing a ripple of anger in the still-waiting crowd.

"Reduced *again?*"

"I heard more food's gone missing," a woman near the back muttered, and I ducked my head and moved swiftly, hoping to go by unnoticed. We had exhausted all the vegetables; rations had become blander and less satisfying. I couldn't be the only one sick of thin fish broth and millet porridge. Things would only escalate as our supplies of the last essentials dwindled.

If the streets were teeming, the bridges were worse. People had been assigned to direct traffic on Trickster's to cope with the congestion. Strange shapes hung from the sides of the Finger and below the bridge; drawing closer they became people, suspended in slings on great ropes. Engineers, examining the structure for potential weaknesses that could be exploited. There were no series of smaller supports that could be attacked as with the much smaller Bell's, which had been built only for lighter pedestrian weight. Looking up at the beautiful, immense white stone joining the two halves of the city, it seemed both an impossible task and a criminal one.

I checked in with Eliska, who directed an orchestra of papers and babbling Guild members outside the foot of the Finger. She took me through the day's progress on the new fortifications. "If we run out of time, or we can't take the bridge down, or if"—she glanced over her shoulder, dropping her voice—"if the Council were to change its mind about destroying it, we could hold the bridge from the Finger, at least for a while."

Like spirits rising from the dead, the remnants of the old fortifications were being rebuilt. The two wedge-shaped walls, which spread from either side of the tower like stone wings, had been reinforced and freshly equipped with ledges and crenellations for archers. The old murder holes in the Finger itself had been cleaned out. The layout of the west side of the lake and the buildings on the opposite side left limited space for the rebels to set up catapults. They would have to set them within the range of the Finger's archers. All our ships, even small fishing boats, were anchored or moored on the eastern shore, clumped together.

"This place was built for defense," Eliska said, almost grudgingly. "The bridge is beautiful, but you can see how it used to form a formidable barrier. See there, how the wall would have stretched along?"

I nodded. Our ancestors must have feared something, that they had built this city under no apparent threat to withstand an attack that had never come.

And now it had finally come, centuries later.

I left Eliska to her work. She didn't seem too optimistic about, or committed to, taking the Finger down. Some part of me hoped it would not come to surrendering half the city. Perhaps word had reached Aven from some source. Tain would not attempt any other messengers; the gruesome slaying of the originals had scarred him. It was a continuing source of tension between my brother and him, and the cause of several arguments in Council, where he still pretended we did not know what had happened to the messengers—if word got out about the runners' desecration, there would be no persuading the city residents that the rebels had a just cause. But perhaps help might still arrive from one of our allies, assuming we had any.

We were back to not knowing who to trust. Tain had wanted to confront the rest of the Council. But we had no time to properly investigate who had known what, and our city's defense couldn't tolerate half its leadership suddenly vanishing. I saw what it cost Tain to leash his immense fury, and I knew like mine it was fueled as much by guilt as by judgment of others. No matter what, the priority had to be to find a way to avoid direct fighting with the rebels. Still, he was making no secret of his views that the countryfolk might have had good reason for rebellion, and tensions ran high within the Council. After all, though our own behavior had caused this, hanging over us was the near certainty that the first act of the rebellion had been to take control of the estates, and possibly the other cities. We were asking people to put aside the possible slaughter of members of their family.

It was a conflict I felt, too. Mother, Alozia, all our other cousins . . . Jovan might be good at burying the parts of himself that hurt too much, but I was not so practiced. I could forget, most of the time, distracted by our own danger, but then everyday occurrences reminded me of Mother without warning: a teapot, a familiar smell, an item of clothing. Our relationship had been difficult, but at least before there had been a hope things might one day be different. The memory of her last message, asking me to visit her on the estate, kept me up at night wondering—what if I had gone?

I walked the length of the shore, trying to clear my head. At the south end, things were further progressed. Every remaining oku in the city seemed to be herded on the grass there, a placid, shaggy little army of beasts, chewing grass and conversing comfortably with their distinctive low hoots. There were even some graspads there, picketed farther up on the shore, though I'd no idea how they were expected to help. Smaller than oku, with paws rather than hooves and long, slender necks, they were less tractable, almost inedible, unable or unwilling to pull carts: less useful than oku in every way. Farmers kept them because the omnivorous creatures ate crop-destroying madges and scatterburr, a particularly virulent species of weed toxic to other animals. You could ride them, if you weren't too heavy or traveling too far, but I'd never seen one harnessed to pull a load.

A round man carrying a box of bottles almost bumped into me on the path. He swore, clutching at his wobbling load, and I helped him steady it. "Thank you," he mumbled. "If these bottles cracked . . ." I looked closer and recognized the style of bottle Jov and Etan frequently used: glass with a wax-lined interior, for storing acids.

"For the mortar?"

He nodded. "We're going to attempt it today. But this stuff is hard to make, and they'd have my hide if I dropped it."

"If you'd dropped it on us, that'd be the least of our worries." Etan had once spilled two heavily diluted drops on his leg and left holes scarred in his flesh. "When are you planning on starting?"

He shrugged. "Later this morning, Credola, that's all I know."

I checked the sky. If I left now to meet Tain and Jov, there would be time to return to see the attempt. It was something that ought to be witnessed.

"Credola Kalina!"

Suppressing my instinctive flinch, I forced a smile. "Oh! Lord Ectar, you gave me quite a shock." I kept walking, slowly enough for him to join me and for me to satisfy politeness, but hopefully conveying an air of urgency.

"I have left messages, Credola," he said, tone heavy with reproach. "It has been days. I have sought audience with the Chancellor but am told, over and over, he is too busy."

"Our sincerest apologies, Lord Ectar. With the evacuation, I'm afraid there aren't enough hours. The Chancellor is overseeing so much. As are we all, I fear; there is so much to do."

"My man Geog is missing still," he carried on. "It has been three days, Credola. I am concerned. I inform your Order Guards, but they give me nothing."

Ectar was a problem we didn't know how to solve; his servant's actions notwithstanding, we still had no proof of his involvement in a grander plot, so we avoided and spied on him in equal measure. If Ectar meant us no ill, admitting to him that we had killed his servant would not help our relations with the Empire. So we played out this strange game, each wondering what the other knew. If Geog had acted on his orders, had Ectar guessed we had foiled the plan, or did he believe Geog had safely left the city, and his concern was all a ruse?

"That is concerning," I agreed. "But be patient, I beg you. The city is in a state of great turmoil. It's hard to find anyone at the moment. He wouldn't be the first servant to abandon his master in a foreign city."

Ectar bristled. "He was a deeply loyal servant. He would not have run away."

"Then I am certain he will turn up soon, Lord Ectar."

"I tell you . . ." he began, grabbing my arm with some violence; I recoiled and he dropped it like a burning coal, recognizing his mistake.

"I'm late for an appointment," I told him coldly. He mumbled a response and I swept away, grateful to have been given an excuse to feign insult. My path eddied along with the flow of people moving up Red Fern Avenue and into the upper city.

"There are rumors about that one," someone said in my ear.

I jumped but kept walking without glancing around. An-Hadrea's voice was distinctive, though we'd only spoken briefly. Jov had told me she had followed him for some time before approaching him; had she been following me, too? "Which one?"

A glimpse of An-Hadrea's profile beside me, her voice soft and low. "The pale man. Ectar. People are talking. They say he tried to flee the city."

I stiffened. Her family was helping us, but perhaps some of Jov's suspicion had rubbed off on me. A contrast to her sweet-tempered mother, An-Hadrea appeared to hold us in contempt. And yet, this was at least the second time in the last few days that she had approached one of us with information.

Perhaps she was just showing off how easily she could follow us undetected. Jov had told me, with some frustration, that she had dropped into his path like a shadow from nowhere a dozen times already. He seemed incapable of detecting her. "How could anyone flee the city? We'd have tried that if it was an option."

Ahead, a cart full of some kind of assorted metal objects had spilled, and people jostled to get around with loud complaints. A few weeks before I'd seen something similar; then, passersby had immediately stopped to help. The difference made my heart hurt.

An-Hadrea swerved to avoid the spill and the ensuing scuffle. Reluctantly, I followed as she peeled off to the side, down a lane. She leaned against a wall and regarded me frankly. "The rumor is that someone saw the body of one of his servants at the hospital. But he is all around town asking people about him."

It wouldn't take long for the rumor to reach Ectar's ears if people were already talking about it. "What else?" I asked.

"People are saying he infected the Chancellor with a fatal disease. Or poisoned him." She looked at me with her peculiar directness. "Is this so?"

Glad to be able to give an honest answer, I shook my head. "We don't think so."

"Hmm. Well, you should know, your people will turn on your Talafan neighbors as easily as they turned on us believers, you will see. Already they mark out differences. Who is to blame. Who is like me, who is worth protecting."

"Everyone in our city is worth protecting."

She scoffed. "Listen to what is being said, if you are so foolish to think that. It is not just *my* people they will blame, if you let them have a target. There are not enough of us to satisfy them. Your Chancellor says pretty things, but even if I believed him and believed you, you do not control your city. You are just a few people." Then she suddenly patted my shoulder, her manner shifting to something almost maternal. "I just say, you should protect him, if you do not wish to start another war. You need all the allies you can get."

Perhaps so. So far, having Darfri allies had not proved any great advantage. Salvea was a fascinating source of information about their customs and etiquette, but while she could doubtless have spoken persuasively to any individual in the army, she had no more capacity than us to make herself heard. Her daughter offered intelligence about what the city Darfri were doing down in the catacombs, just not without some biting criticism alongside it.

I'd never met anyone quite like An-Hadrea, with her strange, blunt manner of speaking, and the way she smiled at the end of an insult and somehow took the sting from her words. One moment I thought she wanted to murder us all, and the next she would offer a random kindness.

"I've got to go to the Manor," I told her, sensing in the glint of her eye that another tirade might be waiting. "But thank you. We're watching Lord Ectar."

She nodded and ducked around the corner; by the time I'd returned to the street, there was no sign of her. I thought I knew how to be unobtrusive and unnoticed, but she had a superior game.

I could guess what I'd missed at the Council meeting by the conversations of exiting Councilors: more arguments about billeting, a few protests about the destruction of the bridges—did Lazar really think that we could hold both bridges, or did he just not truly understand that the lower city could fall soon?—some secretive whispering. Varina trailed well behind Bradomir, speaking to no one. Only Marjeta, Budua, and Javesto acknowledged me as we passed.

"They're all angry," Jov told me, inside. "Angry and frightened."

"Aren't we all," I murmured. "I saw An-Hadrea. She says that people are starting to target other foreigners now that they can't find anyone openly Darfri. We'll need to be careful when we evacuate that we don't make things worse."

"Maybe we should billet the Darfri—those who aren't in hiding, anyway—and anyone else who needs protecting in a separate section of the city," Tain suggested. He pulled out a city map and circled a section to the south. "We could use these buildings here—we could fit hundreds of pallets in that hall, there—and we could allocate Guards to protect the area. Just in case."

"We'll need to tell Marco's watchers to keep an eye out for hostility against Lord Ectar, too," I added. "Someone saw the servant's body at the hospital and rumors are spreading fast. People are saying the Chancellor was murdered. And I don't know who's been talking, but An-Hadrea already knew there was an escape attempt."

Tain frowned. "There were too many people involved the other night. We should have known they wouldn't all be quiet about it."

"An-Hadrea's right, though," Jov said. "The mood of the people isn't good. They're angry and they're hungry. If they were beating up Darfri a week ago, what will they do if they think Talafar is behind all this?" He took a sip of water and pushed the cup across the table toward Tain like a challenge.

Tain stared at it. The silence stretched between them.

Every meal had become a battleground. While Tain focused on the grander scheme of problems—how to feed our citizens, defend the upper city, find a way to negotiate with the rebels—Jov retreated into the part of his life he still felt he had control over: his duty to the Chancellor. He obsessed over the potential threat to Tain, as if protecting him could redeem the broader failures of our family. Tain, on the other hand, seemed to process his own guilt as a repudiation of the trappings of the Chancellery; with every meal, his discomfort at his friend's role grew more obvious, as did his impatience with the restrictions on eating and drinking while he tried to scramble to save the city. Their friendship grew more brittle every day. Tain hadn't yet defied Jovan, but inevitably Jov's prickly honor and Tain's unease would clash at some point.

I rubbed my eyes. My face felt too small for my skull. Honor-down, I hoped it wasn't today. I was exhausted, physically and mentally, and we had so little time to be alone together now.

Tain took a slow sip of the water, and I let my breath out in relief. Deferred for another day. I was about to comment on what I'd seen of the siege tower this morning when Jov spoke suddenly.

"This is getting ridiculous."

"I agree," Tain said, relief pouring from his voice in a rush. "Honor-down, Jov, I've been—"

"Half of them know anyway. Probably more than half, truth be told. It's a waste of our time and attention, playing these games."

"What?" Tain set the cup down. "What are you—"

"I say we stop hiding," my brother plowed on. Some part of me took a tiny bit of amusement in seeing Tain so flummoxed; he had probably never been interrupted so much in his life. "You've got to be able to eat. No one will accuse you of dishonor, not now that everyone seems to know Caslav was poisoned."

Tain shook his head. "You're talking about proofing in front of people? I thought we were talking about us moving on from this. Putting yourself in the poisoner's path, it's not right. I'm not all right with it."

Jovan looked at Tain as if he'd slapped him. I shrank back into my chair, wishing to disappear.

"You know how much I value you," Tain said. "Your family's always protected mine. But now . . . there's no good in you constantly risking your life for me."

"No good? That's what I'm *for*."

I understood, honor-down I understood how much our family duty meant to him, but it broke my heart a tiny bit to hear my brother express it like that. "Jov . . ." He sprang to his feet, ignoring me, and paced with one hand to his head as if to contain whatever swirled around in there.

"That's our family's honor you're talking about. That's everything we *are*. We protect you, we advise you. We're your shield. You need us more than ever."

"Don't be ridiculous," Tain said, his temper flaring. "Since when is dying so honorable? Haven't we had enough bloody dying around here?"

All three of us startled at a rattle outside the room. One of Tain's servant guards stepped in.

"Sorry to interrupt, Honored Chancellor," she said, ducking her head. "You asked me to let you know when you were due at the bridge?"

"Yes, of course." Tain closed his eyes a moment, visibly containing his emotions, then smiled at the guard and stood.

The argument was over for now. But we could never go back to the way things had been before.

Quite a crowd had gathered to watch the grim spectacle. The wind had picked up, its distant howl a constant buzz in the background. The whole Council was gathered on the steps up to Bell's Bridge; Tain had forced them all to attend. "If I'm going to be remembered as the Chancellor who destroyed some of the best architecture in the world, they can at least stand with me as the Council that endorsed it," he'd said. There were some sulky and resentful expressions during his short speech, reminding everyone of the necessity of protecting ourselves but also the surety that we would rebuild Bell's in time. As soon as he had finished, the majority of the Council dispersed. Eliska had promised destroying the support pillars for the bridge itself would not destabilize the stairs, but most Councilors either didn't care to risk it or wanted to distance themselves as much as possible from the decision.

The engineer Baina was up on the top of the steps, yelling instructions at the men and women doing the last checks on the acid damage in her heavy, brash voice. Eliska and Marco stood between Jov and Tain, pointing and explaining something to them while Tain nodded, his face grim. Dozens of other workers and engineers went up and down the stairs, making last-minute adjustments and reports. Ectar, unaccompanied by servants, made his way up there, too, possibly in an attempt to gain an unscheduled audience with Tain. His persistence was indisputable. He looked down and found me in the crowd, the eye contact registering even from back here. I half-raised an awkward hand in a wave.

The herd of animals, all connected with a complex harness-and-pulley system to the closest, partially submerged, support pillars, would be heading away from us to make sure there was no risk of flying debris in our direction. Eliska called out for everyone to take safe positions, and the movement of people between the stairs and the crowd petered out, then stopped altogether.

"Bloody shame this is," an old man beside me muttered.

As if protesting its fate, the great bell hanging beneath the bridge made a tinny little whine in the wind.

I caught a glimpse of a familiar person, just a shape in the crowd heading up to the platform. Too quick to process. My attention caught. Something about her registered as wrong even as I struggled to catch another look. There, moving up the stairs.

"Everyone back!" Eliska shouted into her speaking trumpet. The last of the engineers clambered up onto the bridge and back to the platform.

The sewer guard, the one who helped us set the trap. Last I'd seen her, she'd been led away by an Order Guard who was comforting her after she'd accidentally killed Ectar's servant. She wasn't in the Builders' Guild or assigned to guard duty for any of the Councilors. What was she doing there?

"Positions!"

I looked up at Ectar again. He had managed to move close to Tain, almost behind him, and hovered there waiting. He glanced down at me again, this time with a smile.

I took a step out from the crowd. "Get back!" someone called, but my legs moved forward on their own. Was the guard the person Marco had assigned to watch Ectar? Was she following him? The sense of wrongness intensified. There had been nothing subtle about that guard, and she had taken the bribe from Ectar's servant; he might well have been able to identify her. And she had apparently been traumatized by her involvement. There was no way Marco or any of the Guards would have set her on such a task. My breath caught in my chest. Honor-down, what was she doing up there?

"Jov!" I called out with sudden urgency. But my cry was lost in Eliska's, and the cries from the animal handlers as they started the herd off on its pull, then the screech of stone as the harness tightened around the acid-weakened pillars. I caught another glimpse of the woman, closer this time, coming behind Ectar, her face a stone mask—or was that just the distance?

A great jolt shook the bridge as the supports buckled under the strain. Some of the crowd behind me cheered as it groaned; others merely cried out with wordless grief as the stone cracked and shuddered. The woman came closer still, just behind Ectar.

"Ectar!" I yelled—it came out as a desperate screech, and his head whipped around to find me below. "Behind you!"

He pivoted just as she lunged forward, and they came together in a confused scuffle just before the great stone pillar gave way in an explosion of rock and a drenching spray of water. The great stone pillar gave way in a sudden explosion of rock and a huge spray of water. I must have been the only one looking up instead of down, and saw Ectar wrestling frantically with the woman, their bodies tugging to and fro as onlookers scuttled away.

Then with a final pivot they fell against the wall and the woman's body bounced over the barrier in one horrible jerky motion. I covered my face, but not fast enough to miss the sight of her plummeting like a rock to the lake below.

Amidst the shouts and screams and roars of the animals and the cracking of the bridge, I looked up again to see Ectar leaning against the edge, hand on his heart, staring down at me with eyes huge in his pale, stricken face.

Feverhead

DESCRIPTION: Common water weed with bulbous roots and serrated, fleshy leaves. All parts of the plant but particularly the leaves are toxic on ingestion or inhalation of fumes from heating.

SYMPTOMS: Short-term overstimulation of the brain and heart, increasing heart rate and causing intense hallucinations. Longer term with repeated doses, interferes with bodily functions including absorption of food, and kidney and lung function. Causes weakness, listlessness, weight loss, shortness of breath, starvation or suffocation, heart failure.

PROOFING CUES: Peppery, hot taste with a metallic aftertaste.

15

Jovan

No one seemed to know what had happened. Shouts clashed around me and the platform was suddenly a press of panicking bodies: some hanging off the edge, trying to see below, some fleeing from unspecified danger. Several figures in physics' blue sashes splashed into the water, trying to pull out the body. Oku and graspads had broken free of the harness and trampled about, hooting in panic and confusion from the noise.

But my sister stood alone, ten treads clear of the crowd, staring up at us, and I'd heard her voice in the moments before. She'd warned Ectar of something behind him. Which meant Ectar hadn't initiated whatever had happened here.

I pushed through to where Marco was holding the Talafan noble's shoulder. "Marco, please," I said, and the Warrior-Guilder obliged, releasing his heavy grip as he regarded me quizzically. "I saw what happened," I lied. "Lord Ectar was attacked."

"We'll take care of him," Tain agreed. "I need you down there to keep that crowd back. See if Lord Ectar's attacker survived the fall?"

Tain's gaze flicked down to Kalina; he must have heard her, too. Marco nodded. His big form sprang away down the steps, nimble as a child's, and moments later his voice boomed out, pushing back the approaching gawkers.

"Everyone move off the platform now," Eliska shouted, trying to herd her Guild members away from us. "Down the stairs, please, and wait with the Warrior-Guilder down there." She leaned over the opposite side. "Someone get those damn animals under control!"

Finally, a moment of space around us. I kept my voice low. "Lord Ectar, what happened?"

"That woman . . ." His face blanched. "She pushed into me. Your sister, Credola Kalina, called out a warning. I did not . . ." He trailed off, looking again over the wall behind him. "I did not mean . . ."

"Did you recognize her?" Tain asked the question of me as much as Ectar, but we both shook our heads. I had been on the wrong side of the platform and hadn't seen anything through the press of bodies.

"She came up behind me," Ectar said. "I do not understand. Was she trying to push me over the edge?"

Kalina, puffing and shaking, stepped onto the platform. "No. She was trying to push you into the Chancellor." I caught her under the shoulders as she slumped a little. My heart pounded with worry as much as confusion. But she shook me off and moved to the edge of the platform. She pushed at the stones experimentally, and checked the ground. "Here."

I crouched beside her. "It's greasy." I touched the slick substance to my tongue out of habit. "Gadfish oil." The kind of thing that *might* have been accidentally spilled on a bridge near a major fishing spot.

"You were standing right behind the Chancellor, on slippery ground. If you'd shoved into him, he could have gone over."

"And you'd have taken the blame," Tain murmured. He squeezed Kalina's hand. "How did you know to warn him?"

She glanced around. We were temporarily alone, above the chaos below. "It was the sewer guard. I saw her following Lord Ectar. I don't know. I don't like coincidences." We exchanged glances deep with shared memory and pain. *Oh, Etan.* What I wouldn't have given for his steady presence and years of experience here.

Ectar mumbled a string of Talafan, shaking his head. "I do not understand," he said again. "What is a sewer guard? Who was this woman?"

"She probably started the rumors herself," I said, and Kalina nodded. We should have realized Thendra never would have been so careless as to let someone else see the body in the hospital. I looked Ectar over, weary. He had never looked so young. I doubted he had known much of anything. "Your servant Geog tried to bribe that woman into helping him get out of the city via the sewers." He took a stumbling step back in apparent shock. "He was killed in the attempt." *And almost certainly not by accident.*

"I am sorry for not telling you," Tain said. Someone below called up to us, and he went on quickly, his voice low. "But we didn't know if you were working with someone outside."

"We were meant to think that," Kalina said. "I suspect your man was just trying to get help from your family. You said he was loyal. I wouldn't be surprised if the guard initiated the so-called bribe herself. Imagine what would have happened if half the city had seen you knock the Chancellor off the platform."

"They'd have torn him apart." A chill came over me at the thought of how close we had come.

Another insistent shout from below. "We have to go down," Tain said. "Lord Ectar, I don't know who that woman was working for, but I'm sure she wasn't acting alone. Whoever tried to kill me wanted you to take the blame—and the blame for my uncle's death, too. I want you to move into safe custody at the Manor. No more training, no more duty on the wall."

"I'll take him back to the Manor," I said. "Stick with the story that I saw the whole thing. No one is to blame Lord Ectar. In fact, he's the hero who saved your life."

Tain nodded. "Yes. Yes, you *were* heroic, Lord Ectar. The city—and I— offer our sincerest thanks."

The nobleman didn't seem to know what to say. He looked between us, lips moving silently.

"Come on," I said. "You can get a medal later. For now, let's get you to safety."

Ectar's assailant was dead, her neck broken in the fall. "And half the bones in her body," Thendra told me, as disapproving as if I had thrown the woman over myself. We had set the shaken Ectar up at the Manor, with one of Tain's servants assigned to guard him. No one from Credo Pedrag's sector, to which the sewer guard had belonged, offered any useful insight about her. She had lived with an elderly cousin until his death the year before, and while she socialized casually with others in the sector, none could speculate on why she had tried to attack the Chancellor.

Over the course of the rest of the day, this time without fanfare, more supports came down at Bell's, and finally the surface of the walkway itself. By the time we finally reached our beds, the bridge was impassable. I took some uneasy hours of rest, with the looming threat of the war machines competing with our faceless enemies within the city to cause me the most anxiety. My dreams were filled with disturbing images: Kalina tumbling over the wall in place of the mysterious assailant, disintegrating stone hands pulling me down into a pit while a Speaker chanted in the background, Tain being knifed in the back, and over and over the decapitated head in the bag that had been the first real brutality of this war.

In the morning, feeling as if I had not slept at all, I visited Trickster's, which now had the attention of the majority of the Builders' Guild. Despite the early hour the bridge was covered in people. On my request, Baina showed me the devices fastened around the arch point. "I don't think it'll be enough," she told me, frankly. "We're all assuming we're going to have to hold the position. But no one's got any better ideas, and I'll be the bloody hero of the day if it works."

Though the destruction of Trickster's was partly my handiwork, I couldn't bring myself to be hopeful. Honor-down, I could only hope it didn't come to that.

Tain was already by the short side of the wall at the Finger, gesturing as he spoke to a group of engineers. A short distance away, workers bustled back and forth with armfuls of tools and weapons to stock the tower. The lake looked deceptively peaceful, the water moving in lazy ripples like a silvery green cloth and the tower wall smothering most of the noise of the people hurrying across the bridge. We'd walked its length so many times in our lives; it was hard to imagine this being the last frontier of our city.

Eventually the engineers moved on, and Tain said, "You know, you missed my very stirring speech about Ectar's bravery yesterday. Lini helped me write it. We're hoping it'll go some way to stop people thinking anyone not born here's our enemy." He sighed. "Do you think Lini's right? Was that guard really trying to kill me? She targeted two Talafan, couldn't she just have had a grudge against them?" I raised an eyebrow and he gave a half snort. "All right, all right. I could hope." His eyes were distant as he stared beyond the bridge. "Do you think they'll destroy it? The city, I mean. Assuming we can knock the bridge down, or hold it. When the rebels break through, will they wreck the lower city?"

I shrugged. "They might have to take time to regroup and restrategize. Ten thousand bored, angry rebels with a grudge against the city. . . . I'd guess they'd give it a go."

"So, even if we survive, I'll be remembered as the Chancellor who let half our city be destroyed."

I put a hand on his shoulder. "Don't worry. You'll also be remembered for having the biggest ears."

He grinned. "Small mercies."

"Sure, the losing-the-city thing will probably get written down in a few books. But it'll be the ears everyone remembers." I squeezed his shoulder. "Even if they try, how much can they do? They could set fire to the gardens and things, but the buildings are stone. It'd take a long time to do any serious damage. Whatever happens, we can rebuild." *If we survive.*

He nodded, but the lines on his forehead remained. "Everyone knows the evacuation signal, right?"

"Kalina visited every sector yesterday and spoke to every squad leader personally," I said. "They all know it. If—when—it sounds, everyone knows to fall back."

"And the evacuation plan? What about the routes? We can't have anyone cut off from the retreat."

"Tain, it's all done," I told him. "There's not much more you can do. Except, of course . . ."

"I know," he said heavily. The lines between his eyes grew deeper. "We have to decide now, while we still have time."

The cavern system, what An-Hadrea called the catacombs, was on the west side of the lake. If the Darfri hidden there didn't evacuate to the upper city with us, they'd be trapped beneath the invading army. Which either meant loyal citizens would be put in danger, or we would be handing sympathetic people who knew the layout of the city and the state of our resources to the enemy. Or, more likely, both.

But it was a maze down there, and we'd no idea who was hostile to us.

"We could go down there and round people up," I said, but guessed his reaction even while suggesting it.

"And what if some of them resist? They're terrified down there. The city already turned against them, for all they know, without us even trying to defend them. If we show up with armed guards to round them up, some might fight back. And I'm not going to be responsible for any more of our own people getting hurt."

I squeezed the fingers of my right hand against my palm, then my left, keeping the pace even. We were going in circles again, and I had no fresh answers, just the same old tired arguments. "We could leave them there," I said. "You're the Chancellor and *you* didn't know there were caves down there. The army likely wouldn't find them. And even if they were found, they're Darfri. The rebels probably wouldn't hurt them even if they found them."

"It isn't right," Tain said. I went back to counting in my head as we fell into silence. There was no easy answer.

"I will go."

We both spun around.

"An-Hadrea," Tain said. "What are you doing here? I thought you were staying out of sight?"

For days I had suffered through her glowering presence in our meetings with Salvea—too obedient to disrespect her mother openly, she displayed her hostility and resentment through sheer presence—and contended with her melting from the shadows to throw barbs at me at all hours of the day. Her tendency to follow me was annoying, especially as I rarely noticed her until she wanted me to.

The trouble was, no matter how hostile she was to me, and no matter how she used that distance between us like a shield—never offering to let me drop the "An" from her name, as would befit a friend—I was starting to enjoy her company. Her wit was sharp and unexpected, and her passion for the country way of life infectious. Watching her with her little brother—Davi, she called him—she radiated affection, balancing out the harshness with which she regarded Silastians. And I had begun to suspect she liked being around me, too. It was as though she found my inability to respond to her taunts to be some kind of amusing challenge. She hadn't called me a heathen in days, and I occasionally found hints of warmth in her glances, or a twitch of her lips or creases at her eyes suggesting a suppressed smile.

I hadn't told Tain she'd been following me around the city. He knew me too well, and he'd have seen the mixed emotions her continual presence generated in me. She glanced at me, a quick, sidelong flash of calculation.

"Honored Chancellor," she said, tilting her head. "You do not know how to talk to our people. I will speak to them for you."

"Why?"

"Jov!" Tain glared at me, but he'd not been subjected to her commentary about our self-indulgence and ignorance and lack of *tah* for days, peppering his every movement, so her sudden offer of help probably didn't sound so incongruous to him.

"Why would you help?" I asked. "You told us you wouldn't admit to speaking with us. And you tell me at least once a day that the city deserves to fall, that we brought this all on ourselves."

"You care so much about these petty matters, Credo Jovan," she said to me, her voice cool but her eyes sparkling. "You should not pay so much mind to the things people say."

"Should I stop listening when you talk?" I muttered, and this time I definitely caught a twitch of her lips.

"This is not about me," she said, returning her attention to Tain. "This is about helping my people. They will hide if you go into the catacombs, but I could spread word that the lower city is being evacuated. Then those who want to come into the upper city can do so."

"We'll protect them," Tain told her, hope burgeoning in his voice. "I've made it clear what will happen to anyone who attacks another one of our residents. And we can provide safe accommodation." We had already planned for a whole section of the city for the Darfri and anyone else who could be, or felt, at risk from other residents. It wouldn't be glamorous, but it would be clean and safe. *And a damn sight better than living in a cave.*

But I frowned. "You were worried about being branded a traitor just for talking to us. How could you pass on a message from us without putting yourself in danger?"

She pushed fabric back from one hip, revealing a long, curved dagger hanging from her woven belt. "You will see that my mother and brother will be protected, yes? You move them to your Manor. I can care for myself."

"Are you sure?" Tain asked her. "You don't have to do this. Your family's already risked so much."

"Forgive me, Honored Chancellor, but I do not offer for you. I offer for the sake of my people."

"I respect that," he said. "If I had any other viable options, I want you to know I wouldn't allow you to bear this risk, but the truth is, we couldn't think of a way to do this."

"I know," she said, with no trace of embarrassment. "I was listening to you talk. You two, you talk, talk, all the time. Like old folk around the fire."

Tain laughed. "I guess we do. Let's hope we're good enough at it to convince everyone to stop fighting." He stood up straight, stretching his back and shoulders. "Tell them to listen for the gongs, for the retreat signal. Three quick strikes in a row, pause, three more. It'll keep ringing as long as we can manage it. At that signal, they should retreat over the bridge and head for Potbelly Square. There'll be people there to help everyone find their way."

"Three gongs, repeating, and go to Potbelly Square," she said.

"Try to convince people to come now, if you can. Especially families. I'd prefer it if we didn't have any panicking children running about if we have to call a retreat."

An-Hadrea shrugged. "I will try."

"Thank you," Tain said. "Do you want me to send a guard with you?"

"Credo Jovan will walk with me to the catacombs," she said, her inflection suggesting it was not a question. She looked at me, straight-faced. "But it will be best if I go alone from there."

My mouth dried up as I struggled to think what to say. She rendered the issue moot, in any case, starting down the stairs without another word. I shrugged at my friend and then sprang after her, struggling to keep up as she slipped down the stairs and into the growing crowd at the base of the tower. We made our way across Trickster's Bridge, dodging dozens of carts dragging equipment and supplies to the old city, the press of people and oku and carts creating a blanket of smells and sounds. The buzz of their endeavors almost made it feel like a busy day at the wharf or markets; though the suffocating closeness of the crowd made me as anxious as always, it was balanced by a feeling of familiarity. Strange how I could feel both at peace and on edge at the same time.

"I have not eaten this morning," An-Hadrea said, stopping after we stepped off the far side of the bridge. "I will visit the ration station before I go below. You will eat with me?"

I searched her expressionless face, frustrated by my inability to read her intent. "I suppose." Truth be told, I was starving. I'd proofed Tain's meal last night but been too tired to seek my own, so hadn't eaten anything since early yesterday but a few mouthfuls of Tain's millet porridge and some lukewarm tea.

"Do you have special access to the food? Or do you wait in the line with the rest of us?"

"I line up," I said, terse. When I visited a ration station, I did. Usually I ate from the Chancellor's kitchen, one of the few private kitchens not commandeered for communal food preparation. But I wasn't going to tell her that.

"Then let us line up," she said, unruffled.

A passing group of men and women, approaching from the direction in which we headed, brushed too close for my liking, and one or two of them stared at the two of us walking together. We'd had no further reports of violence toward Darfri, but the air of ill feeling toward them was worse than ever. Given that the last Darfri to whom I had spoken had been murdered, I feared what our enemies within the city might do.

"Maybe you should think about dressing like a Silastian," I told her, conscious that the wide gray scarf that covered her head and torso, while useful for blending into shadows, stood out among the crowds of white cloth and bare dark heads. She had not hidden her charm necklace.

She snorted. "I am proud to be Darfri. You have made us hide for your convenience for long enough."

We were too early for a line at the station. "Porridge is just done, Credo," the boy there told us. The ration station was a reconfigured school class-room with tables stacked with crude bowls and pots cluttering the floor.

"Mind if we take a few bowls?" As he scurried off, I said to her, "We've hardly time to wait to create a line to satisfy you, have we?"

She didn't reply, but when the boy returned with two steaming bowls, she thanked him in her soft, lilting voice, and the lad looked at his feet, embarrassed.

I began the bland fare. Salt and spices had been the first things to be thinned from the rationing after fresh food. I didn't need proofing skills to tell me this was millet and hot water, nothing more. Habit made me breathe in the scent of each mouthful first, and to work the food around my mouth as I ate, feeling for reactions.

My companion, on the other hand, dove into her food with apparent relish, using two spoons as she ate, the bowl nestled in her lap between her crossed legs. She looked up at me, midscoop, and laughed.

"What?" I stopped, self-conscious.

"Do you not know how to eat?" She dropped a spoon and mimicked a careful mouthful, exaggerating the chew with a grim expression. Then she laughed again. "Food is not so clinical. It is an experience. A pleasure. For all the indulgences of this city, have you forgotten this?"

I dropped my own spoon and frowned. "It's just porridge."

An-Hadrea shook her head. "No. It is nourishment. It is a gift of warmth and of satisfaction."

I shrugged, defensive. Food was my job, my duty. It was difficult to take pleasure in something that from an early age had been analyzed for taste, texture, and smell to prevent sickness or death.

"You are an odd person, Credo Jovan."

I changed the subject. "What are you going to tell the others in the catacombs? Will they help defend the old city once they come over the bridge?"

An-Hadrea shrugged. "I do not know. They have chosen to live here in the city. Perhaps they will defend it as their home. But then, they are Darfri. From what I have heard, even before this siege their beliefs were mocked and belittled. Their neighbors use what parts of our culture they find useful or charming, then discard them like a fashion. At best Darfri have been regarded with condescension and derision. What have they truly in common with the rest of you?"

There was nothing to add to that, really. After all we had learned, I didn't want to fight the rebellion, either. The best we could hope for was that we found some way of stopping the army before open battle. But the people of this city did not deserve to be murdered for the crimes of their government, and if the rebels wouldn't listen to reason or negotiation I wasn't prepared to lie down and let us be trampled, sympathetic to their motivations or not.

"Not everyone will come to your old city," she added. She blew on her porridge to cool it. "What will you do about those who will not follow?"

"Well," I said, "it's absurd to leave people in the old city to join the invading army, especially as they know the city like the mercenaries and the countryfolk don't."

Silence.

"But, nothing," I said, sighing. "Tain won't force anyone to come over. So if your people want to join the army, we won't stop them."

She took another spoonful, regarding me with a tilted head. "And what about people who are too scared to come across? Who do not want to join the army, but fear beatings or worse from your citizens?"

"I hope you'll convince them Tain will protect them, and punish anyone who threatens them. His honor is everything to him. You must have seen what kind of man he is, by now."

She pressed her lips together; agreeing, but reluctantly.

"So trust him. And let them see you do."

"The Chancellor wants to do the right thing, I believe that," she said after a pause. "But I have spoken to him in person and seen his generosity of spirit. The people below only know what this city and its people have been to them. Some will not come, you must know this."

"I do," I admitted. "You heard us before. We just don't know what to do about it. We can't drag them out by force. We can only hope they listen to you, especially families with children."

"And if you leave them there, hiding from the army and from you, what are they to do for food?"

We looked at each other for a long moment. Then I looked back down to my porridge. "I think we both know they have supplies down there," I said quietly.

It hadn't taken me too long to piece it together. The missing supplies, the Darfri man who had knocked me out . . . Hundreds of people could hardly hide under our feet without food stores. With the stolen food they could continue to hide down there even if the city above them were occupied.

An-Hadrea stirred her spoon around her bowl. I saw a softening around her mouth and eyes: the hint of a smile, free of mockery. "You are not so bad," she said, just as quietly.

We finished our meal in silence, but it was almost companionable.

I left An-Hadrea near the entry to the tunnels. Or, rather, she left me; one moment we were walking, the next she told me, "I will go now," and I was alone in the ghostly street. Walking back, I stared at the ground, wondering what transpired beneath. An-Hadrea had not told me what she planned to say, or even how she planned to deliver the message. We would have to trust her.

I wondered what Salvea would say when Tain told her where her daughter had gone. An-Hadrea might be confident with that wicked belt knife of hers, and she had bragged that country children all brawled for sport and fun on the estates, but her mother wasn't quite so casual about the potential danger. As I made my way back to the east side of the lake and headed for the wall, I catalogued the things that needed doing today.

"Ho!" Pedrag waved to me from the battlements as I ascended the stairs. "Credo Jovan!"

I joined the Craft-Guilder, clasping his age-spotted forearms as I stepped onto the stone walkway. "Good morning," I said. "How does it look out there?"

His jaw trembled as he turned back to the view. "I think they're coming for us," he said.

I followed his gesture, out to where the rebels appeared to be massing into organized lines. A figure in red, mounted on a graspad, moved up and down the assembling lines, waving some sort of banner—the wind whipped it around and I couldn't make out the symbol, if any—and as he passed, the army cheered and roared, stamping their feet and bashing their weapons and shields. Behind their front lines their war machines loomed: half a dozen catapults and the great siege tower, standing the full height of the walls. I felt cold. This was no tentative foray. They meant to enter the city today.

"Have you sent word?"

Pedrag started to answer, but the attack bell rang out from the nearest tower, and within moments the sound was echoed by the other towers around the city. His gnarled fingers clutched my forearm and we both stared, transfixed, over the ramparts as the army moved forward. Though I'd spent a lot of last night lying awake, picturing this event, it still didn't seem real to see the catapults being wheeled out like great, silent soldiers, and to hear the baying from the army, like wild animals surrounding their prey.

Our own catapults, designed and built by people who had never done anything of the sort, were in position: one on each of the north and west tower gates and one that was set back on the road and intended to throw over the wall, essentially blind. Their accuracy was untested.

The first of their catapults went off without warning. The great rock sailed through the sky from somewhere to my left, oddly graceful and silent as it flew over the heads of the approaching army. The ugly chunk of boulder hit the wall not far east of where Pedrag and I stood, and the *crack* made the very stone beneath our feet vibrate. A cheer spread across the army at this first strike.

"Look sharp, Credo," Pedrag said, and his grip on my arm became an encouraging pat. "Now's not the time for gawking."

I blinked. Sounds returned to full force, slapping me into action. Pedrag was right; there was no time left for watching and wondering.

By the time we reached the section of wall being attacked they had struck it again. A confused scramble of disorganization met us as our people filled the battlements and massed around the area in response to the still-pealing alert bells. Marco was up on the wall and Order Guards attempted to direct the hordes below. The first of our catapults retaliated at last, sending a hunk of white rock that might once have belonged to Bell's Bridge flying over our heads. The visible deflation of our people on the wall moments later told me it must have fallen well short of the line.

Through the cluster of people streaming in I finally identified the small group I'd recruited to help make non-lethal weapons, struggling to haul in a barrow loaded with supplies. Relieved, I ran to join them, surprised to find Pedrag beside me. A mix of cooks, chemists, physics' assistants, and artists who worked with chemicals to make dyes and paints, they had taken to the task with enthusiasm and ingenuity, improving on my rough ideas.

"Credo Jovan!" one man puffed. "This is all we've had time to make."

"Let's get them up there," I said.

The steps were choking but we forced through, up the north river gate tower, past weapons stockpiles and a readied firepit, and unloaded our collection. The wind was blowing hot and fast, and the approaching army drew closer, unhurried but menacing. My team had produced three kinds of defense: one to form a smoky, burning barrier around the most vulnerable part of the wall, to make it harder for the rebels to identify weaknesses; one a flammable liquid to be poured on any close-range siege structures; and finally a collection of miniature sedative pouches that would release Art's tonic in gas or powder form to cause unconsciousness. The goal was to protect the city while harming as few people as possible.

First, barrels of ash. "Mixed with the last of the hot spices," one of the cooks said. "The Chancellor gave us permission." I had wondered about the abrupt absence of spices from the ration stations. Bland food seemed a fair exchange.

We staggered ourselves, three to a barrel, along the wall. The ash mix would form a kind of border across the most vulnerable section of wall. "Make way for the barrels!" I yelled, and Chen's familiar voice farther down the line echoed my shout. I helped haul one to the edge, then together we upended the mess below.

"Now the oil mix!" One of the engineers had rigged up a kind of tube operated by a bellowlike contraption that pumped oil down into the piles of ash. The marching troops were almost within arrow range. Marco's voice, elevated by a speaking trumpet, boomed an alert to the archers to get into position. The smell of smoke from the firepit in the tower carried in the air. People ran along the battlements, setting up or restocking containers of broken pottery, cutlery, metal scraps, rocks, and other shrapnel. Others delivered buckets of hot sand to the murder holes. The cacophony created a kind of disjointed song in my head: the beat of the approaching feet, horns, shouts, my own breath in my ears.

A woman no taller than my shoulder held a lit torch in one hand and shuffled her feet nervously as she waited for the call, and a thickset man with a copper helmet and an open mouth scurried through, barking orders in a reedy, nervous voice.

"And . . . loose!" The archers drew back, and the high whine of flying arrows filled the air. "Back! You, there! Keep a clear path! We must be able to move!" He spotted us and wiped his forehead. "Credolen. What do you need? I'm in charge of this stretch here."

"A bow, if you've one handy," Pedrag said. I glanced over, surprised by his vigor. He smiled, his eyes disappearing into the heavy creases of his face. "I'm not a bad hand with one." He slipped into a gap between archers in time to loose with the next cry.

"The tower is on the move," someone shouted, and I peered out through the crenellations to see, only to be faced instead with the sight of another huge chunk of rock from a catapult hurtling toward us. "Brace!"

The crack it made as it connected with the wall was louder than before.

The physic's assistant beside me scrambled to her feet and squirted the last of the oil below. I checked the flag on the tower; it whipped off to the east, same as the last few days, still favoring neither side. If only the wind would turn more southerly and blow back against them. Already the ash swirled about, masking the wall, but it would disadvantage us as much as them if the wind turned against us.

"Archers ready!"

My companions unloaded another set of tricks—this time a viscous, treacly liquid in thin jars that we could light and hurl at the siege tower. I coughed, assaulted by the putrid stench. "What's making it smell like *that*?"

The man looked confused, shaking the bottle slightly. "It shouldn't be—" Then he gestured behind me, where someone tottered past carrying buckets of what appeared to be human waste in each hand.

I glanced at my companion, grinning despite myself. "Can something be both a horrible idea and an excellent one?"

"Well we certainly aren't short of shit," he said with a snort of laughter. "We'll all need to take a squat for the city if it comes to that."

The woman next to him gave us a hard look. Chagrined, I started to apologize, but calm as anything, she spun and yanked up her tunic to expose her bare backside to the parapet. "Shitting for the honor of my city!" she bellowed, and the group of us around laughed so hard at the unexpectedness of it that I barely felt the next crack of stone against the wall.

Credo Pedrag, between shots, wagged a finger. "Discipline in the armed ranks clearly isn't what they say it is," he said. His eyes crinkled into a grin under his helmet. "Why, in *my* day, we knew how to *really* expose an ar—"

The arrow struck the side of his helmet and he fell so fast that it took a moment to even register what had happened.

"'Ware!" someone shrieked, and everyone scampered against the parapet as the clattering of wood on stone signaled that the army's arrows had found their range. "We need shields!"

"Pedrag!" I yelled, but the old man lay motionless on the walkway. I scurried over, cowering at every sound, and tugged the Credo's closest leg, pulling him back closer to the wall edge. "Physic!"

But they were already calling the next volley, and my shouts were lost in the crush of noise. I dared a glance between crenellations and saw the great tower tottering closer and closer; built something like one of our own wall towers, but wooden and on wheels, narrower at the top but not substantially. I couldn't tell what was propelling it toward us. I dropped back down and checked Pedrag's pulse. For a few agonizing moments, nothing. Then, there it was. The arrow had punched down above his ear, denting the helmet but not penetrating it. One small blessing, at least.

"Light arrows!"

"Hit the tower! Aim for the tower!"

Someone came racing by, handing out arrows with oil-soaked rags tied around the heads, followed by the torch carrier. People on either side of me drew back now-flaming arrows. As we settled into the attack the panic was subsiding and Marco's careful defense plans were starting—slowly—to come together.

My companions were readying the bottles. When I dared another check the tower was creaking closer and closer. My group gathered our supplies and moved farther along the wall just as two men in physics' blue sashes ran by with a litter to take Pedrag to safety.

We moved west along the wall until we were almost right above the weakened part. We had arrived in a temporary lull, perhaps as the rebels adjusted their weapons. The seige tower approached, its trajectory as far as possible from our towers to the south and west but close enough to take advantage of the weakening wall. A sealed cask of unknown evil, it could hold a hundred soldiers at least. Just as Eliska had speculated, a lower level of the tower was hinged and strapped up, likely containing a swing-ing ram.

Our catapult operators must have either found their rhythm or a way to load more efficiently, because the intervals between our staggered shots decreased. As we readied the bottles, cheers rose around us as one of the city rocks struck close to a rebel machine. Up on the north tower, there was a flurry of movement from the roof as the engineers moved to make slight adjustments.

Then the pounding of drums started up far below, and a sudden coordi-nated chanting, spookily loud, in words or sounds that made no sense to me. "What are they *doing*?" someone demanded, and uncertainty rippled up and down our lines. My heart sank as I spotted unarmed, half-clothed women approaching in a slow procession well behind the front lines. Smaller people, possibly children, were scattered among them with drums strapped to their torsos. I tried to push down the fear clutching inside my chest. *Superstitious foolishness,* I told myself. *Intimidation and trickery, nothing more.* I shook my head and went back to where the archers were shooting at the approaching tower with flaming arrows.

Then the wind changed.

East to north, it changed without warning, one moment streaming off to the side and the next in our faces. The chanting below switched pitch, seemingly growing triumphant, and all the while the ominous *pound pound pound* of the drums punctuated their voices. "It's them, they're doing it," someone moaned, and similar fearful cries spread from our ranks.

"Keep going, keep going, it's just the wind!" an Order Guard shouted as she sprinted past us. But then it wasn't just wind; it carried grit and dirt in a stinging cloud blown into our faces, as if it really were being controlled by the women below. I spat and shielded my eyes with everyone else, and couldn't pretend I didn't share their increasing panic. Anxiety choked me as effectively as the grit in the air.

"The flames aren't catching, Credo!"

I dared a quick check and indeed, though some arrows struck the men-acing structure, many others dropped off, diverted by unpredictable bursts of heavy wind. Even when they did reach their target their flaming heads did not catch; whether due to poor landings or the wood being treated with something nonflammable, I couldn't tell.

Distracting myself from the fear building from my stomach through my chest, I gave the bottle a swish; the dark liquid within wobbled lazily in response. "What did you add to thicken it like this?"

"Resin," a tattooer said. "Same one we use for the inks we have to extract in water. It's hellish sticky."

Archers were shooting frantically and orders were barked down from the line: "'Ware the tower! Hand-to-hand fighters, move in!" From both sides the battlements filled with approaching men and women, armored and bearing swords, cudgels, and other close-range weapons, coughing and spluttering in the dirty wind. As if controlled by giant bellows, the wind rose and died in sudden bursts and spurts like at the crossing of the Maiso. The fear spreading among us was palpable. "I can see things in the air," a man said to the woman beside him as they passed me. "Do you see that? It's like there are *hands* in there."

I shuddered. *Trickery,* I told myself again. We were frightened and the ritualistic Darfri chants were creepy and intimidating; panic was simply making us see things. But the flag on the tower in the distance caught my eye, and my overwhelmed brain registered its stiff, jerky motion parallel to the walls. A shiver ran over my skin. The wind was only blowing at us, at our section of the wall above the breach. How was that possible? How were they *doing* that? They couldn't be; it must be a trick of the angles that made the flag act that way. The rebels could not control the very wind.

"Archers, prepare to retreat!"

I could hear the tower shuddering toward us into range, and soon its shadowy shape was visible through the clouds. This was our moment. I squeezed the shoulder of the man beside me and together we replaced the nearest archer against the wall. My companion threw hard and accurately and though the burst of dark goo was not properly visible, the sound of smashing glass told us it had landed. But would it be enough? Somehow, even logically knowing the size of the great machine, faced with it now I struggled to process its immensity. Our quantities were so limited, we'd never be able to generate the kind of destructive heat we had hoped. Trying to quiet the roar in my head, I took my turn, hurling my bottle against the tower.

Someone behind me was coughing and the cough grew increasingly frantic; I turned just in time to see him fall to his knees, clutching at his neck and wheezing. "Choking," he gasped, blinking at me with wide wet eyes. "Someone's . . . choking me."

"It's just the dirt in the air," I told him as I helped raise his arms up behind his head, but the sudden memory of a strange hand gripping me on the ladder was so vivid that I almost clutched at my ankle. "Try to slow down your breathing."

"*Hands,*" he whispered, and collapsed in a slump.

"Physic!" I yelled. Someone pulled on my arm and dragged me back to the tower, which wobbled closer, ever closer, as bottle after bottle hit it.

The resin base seemed to be working; dark stains spread slowly on the wood, dripping down the sides and covering more and more surface. A great screech and thud sounded as the drawbridgelike lower panel dropped open, exposing the metal head of a great ram, suspended by internal chains.

"Light it! Light it!" The cry went through the archers farther down on either side of us and they leaned out and shot with increased vigor. We all watched for a few breaths, temporarily protected by the siege tower, as the arrows peppered the sides, some digging in and some bouncing off uselessly. But the flames caught this time, rippling across our black smears with enthusiasm, even seemingly jumping between patches like a live thing. What started as a few patches soon spread to a waterfall.

Too late, I realized our mistake. "The top!" I yelled. "We need to get the top burning!" We had aimed for surer targets instead of lobbing some onto the top platform, and as I watched with a stifling sense of dread, that top panel burst open, spewing forth soldiers like a volcano. Lower panels burst open too and there were soldiers everywhere, bearing great ropes and hooks—did they mean to climb?—and the first swing of the ram crashed into the cracking wall below just as the wave of rebels poured over the parapet and fell upon us.

Our fledgling organization erupted into chaos again. The visceral memory of my last battlement fighting experience filled me with pure, gut-melting terror: being surrounded and alone and injured, and falling. I fought down panic. I wasn't armed for close combat and neither were the rest of my eccentric little team. Unable to make myself heard through the roar, I grabbed arms and pulled my comrades away from the fighting and up toward the east tower. "We have to light the ash now!" Fortunately other members of my group had the same idea and were already dropping torches onto the ash bed below. The oil caught and a whip of red flame leaped from the ashes and shot down the line to smoke and burn under the siege tower itself.

A cheer broke out among our people and it took a moment to realize why: one of our catapults had finally hit the rebels' catapults. This small victory gave everyone heart; people raced past me with manic grins and increased vigor.

To my left, someone released a huge metal ball on a chain, fastened in place with a cunning hook in the parapet, and it swung like a colossal pendulum across the front of the wall and punched into the side of the now-flaming tower. A man with arms as thick as my thighs was already winding the reel to recover it.

Below, behind swirling clouds of black stinging ash and fire, much of which was now being blown up at us as well, rebels on the ground persisted with their great hooks. Now I understood their purpose as the metal teeth bit into mortar and cracks in the wall and with coordinated effort the troops hauled on the rope, pulling out hunks of stone each time. Screams and cries sounded regularly as arrows found marks. The wall shook with the regular droning pound of the ram. Smoke from the flaming tower and ash carried up from our own trap below stung my eyes. And the brutal clash of fighting on the battlements continued.

We had one set of tricks left: the sedative pouches. Some were sewn and some twisted closed; the former would react with vinegar to release gas and the latter would simply burst on impact and spread powder. However, if we released them into the fray, our own people would be affected as well.

"The top platform," someone suggested, and I nodded; if we could hit the rebels still emerging from the structure we could stem the tide of attackers over the wall and buy ourselves more time to destroy the tower. But there was no clear line of sight between us and the platform. We'd never make it through the fighting to get close enough to throw.

The smallest of our team, a young woman with beautiful decorative tattoos across her shoulders and hands, shoved the pouches into her satchel and slung it on. "Wish me luck," she said, then clenched the neck of a vinegar bottle in her teeth and leaped up onto the parapet.

The rest of us were too shocked to protest. As we watched, terrified for her, she scramble-climbed and leaped her way along the stone, bypassing the clashing troops on the walkway. Surely, any moment she'd be shot down.

But the rebels weren't firing at this section of the wall, presumably to protect their own people. Still, any moment someone on the battlements could spot her and knock her off.

"By the fortunes, the kid's brave," someone said.

She was. Fearless, she scampered like an animal into range of the tower. As we watched, she doused the cloth bags in vinegar and threw them in quick succession onto the platform. Then the paper ones followed, sending a temporary cloud of pale gray rising into the air. She gave us a quick wave of triumph, then just as suddenly she was gone, out of our sight, dropping into the crowd fighting below.

"What happened? Did she fall?" The chemist beside me clutched my forearm. "Did she . . . Was she . . . ?"

I shrugged, helpless, unable to answer. It was impossible to see through the thicket of bodies. But my heart felt like stone in my chest. She hadn't been armored. I wasn't sure she'd had any kind of weapon. Then the hand on my forearm became a claw and my companion pointed wordlessly at the sky.

The rebels' catapults were firing again, and this time they aimed higher; as we watched in horror a huge, boulderlike stone powered into the north watchtower with an enormous crash. Fragments of rock spread almost as far as us, and as the debris cloud cleared it exposed the missing corner of the tower.

"Time to get off the walls," I told my remaining companions. "We're out of ways to help for now." The roar in my head drowned out my own words, and it was hard to take my own advice. As I urged my team toward the stairs in the distance, somewhere in the orchestra I recognized animal screams. It took a long moment to figure out from where. I leaned through the battlements to see the siege tower, aflame and steaming with gaseous clouds, jiggling like a boiling pot on a stove. The tower must have been propelled by oku or some other beasts harnessed in the base, and the poor desperate beasts were trapped and cooking in fire and stinging ash. Though the stream of people through the top had stopped, the ram kept pounding at the walls with its menacing, repetitive swing. Our pendulum had punched a widening hole in the side, exposing one of the support beams, and the persistent flame from resin-assisted oil spread inside the tower. Arrows streamed past me with a gut-churning whistle, but I was fixated on the sight as the siege tower shook and burned.

Then two things happened at once: another shot from the rebel catapults struck the north tower, this time blistering through the parapet and into our own machine. And the top half of the seige tower, engulfed now in foul black smoke, collapsed from one corner and with two or three shuddering crashes, crumpled like a collapsible fan.

Someone grabbed my arm and pulled me along, and I tried my best not to throw up on my shoes as I ran, blinded by smoke and a choking mix of fear, relief, and sadness.

Stingbark

DESCRIPTION: Swamp tree with loose bark covered in fine "hair" resulting in a painful sting when touched. Stinging exacerbated by touch and cold temperatures.

SYMPTOMS: Localized pain at exposure site; if left untreated will build into high fever resistant to cooling, hallucinations.

PROOFING CUES: Currently no evidence of toxicity in a disguised form.

16

Kalina

The shroud of smoky haze and the distant sounds of conflict were detectable even from the upper city, where I had spent an anxious morning assisting with the evacuation of children and the elderly. On Marco's heavily worded advice, Tain had refrained from participating in the fighting at the wall; perhaps finally, after two attempts on his life, he was making smarter decisions.

I felt his frustration, though. Evacuating the city was as important as repelling the attackers; the damage to the wall made it only a matter of hours before it was breached. And I was no use as a fighter. Still, the helplessness of being far from that last desperate defense, not knowing what was happening, was a constant low ache in my bones.

An-Hadrea had appeared at Trickster's Bridge earlier with a procession of children and their caregivers from the caverns. They milled behind her in groups, linked at the elbows, like rattling beads, bright and brittle, looking around with suspicion and anxiety.

"Thank the fortunes," I told her. "And thank you."

"They will be safe, you have promised," she had said to me fiercely, and I surprised her for once by embracing her as I reiterated my promise. She took it stiffly and stepped quickly away from me afterward, but I took no offense; I'd observed that she and her mother were used to a greater space around them than Silastians.

I would have preferred to take guards to lead them, but everyone was at the wall, and in the end perhaps they found a lone woman less intimidating. "I know it's far from glamorous," I said to An-Hadrea when we arrived at the first of the halls that had been set up with supplies and sleeping pallets. "But it's safe."

"We will take safety," she said. Then she smiled at me without warning, a warm beam that transformed her face. "You can help with the glamour later, Kalina. You have some very fine jewelry."

I laughed.

Tain arrived soon after, and took the time to move around the quarters, meeting people and reassuring them. His natural self-deprecating charm, coupled with genuine relief that they had come, made the young Chancellor a success among this group, at least. Perhaps things would change if or when the rest of the adult Darfri from the caverns arrived, as most of the potential danger of treachery came from that group. Still, it boded well for the future if we could find peace with the army outside. Tain could bridge the gap between the city and the country if anyone could.

He was still there when the messenger arrived to tell us that we had lost our north tower catapult but destroyed one of theirs and half of the siege tower. "They had to abandon it in the end," Erel said breathlessly. "It wouldn't stop burning. But they're still going with the hooks and smaller rams, and the Stone-Guilder said to tell you the wall won't hold much longer. Warrior-Guilder Marco says we need to start full evacuation."

My stomach plunged and I shared a look with Tain. Jov had insisted he must help his little team in the hopes of holding the rebels back with minimal casualties. He had promised us he would stay out of real danger, but who could trust that nothing had gone awry up there? But then Erel smiled up at me. "Credola Kalina, Credo Jovan asked me to tell you he will be at the Finger helping with the retreat there."

I let my breath out and Tain squeezed my shoulder, sharing the relief.

An-Hadrea accompanied us back to the lower city, saying she would assist any additional Darfri in the caverns who wanted to come to the upper city. I had caught her keen interest in Erel's message and seen tension drop from her shoulders just as mine had, and wondered.

Jov was on the bridge with Baina, dangling in a harness over the edge to examine their work. I had to blink away tears at the sight of him whole and well, and hugged him hard when he was hoisted up.

"We've had no time and not enough supplies to get any real measure of force, Honored Chancellor," Baina reported. "I can't say this'll work."

"The fortunes have to be with us sometime." Tain slapped her broad shoulders with false cheer. Jov looked unconvinced. But either way, we needed to get everyone possible out of the lower city and into safety.

"How much time do we have?" Baina asked, arms crossed over her chest and gaze darting about.

Less than we'd expected, as it turned out. Before we could even make it down closer to the breach spot, a messenger from Marco intercepted us to report the wall was showing catastrophic damage, and indeed, by the time we were within view, huge fissures had spread through the base of the stone and extended into the earth beneath the sagging section. We met Marco at the command point. "They can smell victory, Honored Chancellor," he said, grim. "We need to hold this spot while we get everyone else over the bridge." Eliska and her engineers marched past with a team of oku pulling the remaining catapult off the road and across the bridge. "We cannot risk people engaging in hand-to-hand combat within the city. Once we are unable to hold the breach, we must have a retreat that gives us time."

Here, at least, I could help.

When the frantic bell announced at last that the wall had given out and the rebels were at the breach, we had done our best to prepare.

A force of our mismatched troops gathered around the damaged wall, meeting the army at the breach, and scattered around the retreat route more people were poised, waiting; in windows, clinging to the tops of archways, even roofs, and lining the streets. The breach itself was a great, V-shaped tear in the pale stone, bleeding rubble and mortar dust. Chunks of rock spread across the ground like a rough bridge from the hole down to the ground.

Fear, anticipation, and bravado buzzed in the air. Some made coarse jokes, some swore, some cried, but all stood their ground. Even with the roar and pounding of the army at our door, even with the frantic pump of my heart and the icy river of fear-sweat down my spine, I felt a sense of connection with those around me. For the first time, I understood a little of what Tain admired so about the Warrior-Guilder, and the pleasure he had found training in her Guild. There was a camaraderie here that was almost exhilarating; an intoxicating feeling of strength and togetherness in the face of danger, tinged with a lonely reminder of how different I was from the strong and brave.

My brother seized my elbow. "Move, Lini," he said. "You shouldn't even be here." For once, he was right. I was more scared than I could ever remember being.

We had the advantage of position; the breach was still only the width of a few men, and from the wall above shrapnel, sewage, and hot sand and liquids fell in a deadly waterfall. But the sheer force of their numbers was already apparent as Jov and I followed the retreat path. We wouldn't hold it for long.

Attempts at an orderly retreat had been fruitless. Those not locked in behind comrades broke ranks and fled, then we were all jostled as people panicked and tried to run. I glimpsed over my shoulder the last efforts of our defenders on the walls, trying to buy us time to escape, hurling everything they had left over the edges. Swept along with the retreating forces, I hoped desperately that the rebels would follow us through the city and be caught up in the traps we had laid, or at least that triumph would distract them and temporarily destroy their discipline. If they instead followed the line of the walls and blocked off the stairs on the west side of the lake, our people on the battlements would be stranded without a way down to safety.

The traps were crude and simple. Along the main thoroughfare between the breach and the bridge, our people lay in wait in houses and shops by the roadside, ready to spring. Part of my night had been spent in the temporary new Craft Guildhall sewing sharp things—metal, broken glass and crockery—into fishing nets, which could be thrown out quickly over the road to slow down our pursuers. Over alternative routes to the bridge we had spread oil on the roads and strung wires between buildings and plants, all to delay them and give us more time to get everyone over the bridge safely.

Trickster's was in sight when all of a sudden I couldn't get a breath. My slowing pace saw me bumped to the outside of the current, losing my brother in the process. Stumbling against an old archway with great chips of crumbling rock, I leaned on it to stop my head spinning. One side was broken enough to form a kind of stair, and my shaking limbs hauled me up a few steps until I was able to relax my chest and expel the stale air. I craned in both directions, looking for Jovan.

My position gave me a good view of the pursuit down the slope toward the lake. The chasing rebel horde was not the immense force I had imagined; at least some of their soldiers must have been caught in our traps or split in different directions upon entering the city. Two women sprang out from houses on either side of the road and hurled some of my nets across the path. The approaching rebels saw the trap too late and their intimidating roars turned quickly to howls of pain. Glancing back the other way, heart thumping between my chest and the cool stone, I saw Jov at last, just as he saw me. He diverted out of the crowd and I fell against his broad shoulders, grateful and shaking. He helped me stumble-run the last distance, flooding with everyone else over Trickster's Bridge. Perhaps for the last time.

"Jov! Lini!" Tain saw us from inside the Finger and was already halfway down the stairs to help us by the time we reached its base. "Honor-down, what were you doing there so long? I was tearing my hair out." His hug was ferocious. We pressed together in the middle level of the Finger, where we could see through the slit windows the nearer side of the great arch.

Although everyone had been instructed to gather in the biggest square in the old city, to regroup, most people had lingered instead on the shores of the lake to see what would happen. A hush lay over the crowd, as if the fear, excitement, and desperation of the morning's events had snuffed our voices. Beside me, watching the stream of people continuing over the bridge, Jov breathed raggedly, and I felt his muscles contracting frantically: making fists, clenching his jaw, shifting his weight back and forth, over and over. He registered the reactions of those around us: raised eyebrows and a careful lack of eye contact, a gradual backing away. My heart ached for him as his complexion darkened with humiliation. I put a hand on each shoulder, careful to use equal pressure.

In time his muscles stopped their rhythmic spasm and his relieved breath signaled his return to calm. The bulk of us had made it to safety now, but stragglers continued to appear in view, frantic as they pounded the last treads to the safety of the Finger. Probably those who had been involved in laying our delays and traps.

"Now!" Marco's voice boomed down from the roof of the tower above, and the men and women waiting for that command swung down with torches to light Baina's series of devices.

"But there're still people coming," I said to Tain, and he shot me an agonized look.

"Marco has command," he said. "It needs to blow before the rebels reach the tower."

But he gripped my hand as we saw three more of our people emerge over the high peak in the middle of the bridge. Then their pursuers plummeted into sight, too, thick and fast toward us.

I couldn't even breathe, hoping the collective will of those of us watching could somehow spur the last of our people across to safety.

But the last few runners were finally outpaced by their pursuers. I felt the strikes at their backs as if I'd been struck myself. A woman beside me screamed, and the smell and sound of vomit assaulted us as the sight proved too much for a man a few paces over. Even after all we had seen over the past few weeks, this was somehow worse.

And still, the bridge stood. "Is it going to blow?" I asked my brother in a whisper.

The gate clanged shut behind the engineers as they scrambled inside. "I don't—" he started, but broke off as a massive crack split the air, then two, three, five in succession, a hollow boom. Black smoke and rubble blasted through our vision, and in the background howls rose like a siren. Tain's grip on my fingers turned to a vise.

"Did they—are they—?"

It took forever for the smoke to clear, and all the while the ringing in my ears lingered as we peered desperately through the mess.

"It didn't work," Jov said in horror. "Tain, it didn't *work*."

The bridge path remained; whatever the devices had done, it had not been enough. The rebels realized it, too, and charged again, but Marco was prepared. "Full might!" he shouted, and the archers on the roof and behind the wing walls responded with gusto: a forest of arrows flew at the bridge. The rebels were unprepared; this annex of their army had perhaps become caught up in the pursuit and had not contemplated the fortifications of the Finger.

They pulled back out of range in a hurry, fleeing in a disorganized rabble back across Trickster's. "They're in full retreat!" Marco called out, and people around us let out a halfhearted cheer. One or two people simply sobbed.

Ultimately, though, it was the rebels who had the victory. Their force, growing by the moment as more of their army emerged from the city, spread out across the opposite bank, a crude mirror of ourselves. Cheers and jeers echoed across the water.

I turned away, bitterness rising in my throat. They were right to cheer. Whatever happened from here, they had taken half our city, and we were penned in, missing most of the facilities we needed to properly defend ourselves. If we didn't find some way to negotiate with them, the city was lost and us with it.

Lockwort

DESCRIPTION: Attractive climbing plant with small red leaves and dark, indigo flowers, growing primarily in extremely moist conditions. Flowers are toxic if consumed over time.

SYMPTOMS: Over time, mood alteration and depression, tiredness, weight loss, and muscle wasting, visible broken capillaries on the skin above waist level, liver damage.

PROOFING CUES: Fresh flowers smell sweet but are very bitter to taste. Lose taste when dried but retain pleasant aroma.

17

Jovan

The hospital was my first stop after it became clear that the rebels would wait to regroup and strategize. It teemed with people: confused, grieving, terrified, displaced. Only the physics in their blue sashes were easily identifiable, darting from pallet to pallet and in and out of the surgery rooms.

Our injured numbered easily in the hundreds, and that was only those who had been lucky enough to make the evacuation. The fortunes only knew what had happened to those left injured at the breach or on the wall—would the rebels care for them, or leave them there to suffer and die? Or worse, mutilate and desecrate their bodies as they had done with our messengers? As I moved through the hall, assisting where able, searching for familiar faces, a thickset man with tear-reddened eyes jostled past, muttering under his breath. Something about "bloody traitors." I followed his trajectory and moved to block his path.

"Here, take this to the cleaning station, please," I barked in my best physic tone, and shoved a bucket of blood-soaked rags into his fists. While he was distracted I made haste to the physic tending a bleeding woman whose simple armor over country-style pants and shirt easily identified her as a rebel. "This is going to get ugly," I told the physic. "We need to get the rebel wounded into a different part of the hospital. There are grieving people in here spoiling for a fight."

She gave me a cool look. "And compromise their care and our efficiency? It is part of the honorable code of physics that we treat *all* persons who need it. Should that not be a matter of everyone's honor, not just the physics'?"

"I agree," I said. "But you can't watch everyone in this room *and* care for your patients, and someone is going to get hurt if we don't do something." I followed her pointed glance down at the stomach wound she was compressing. "More hurt."

Her mouth twisted, but she nodded. "I'll arrange it."

I found Pedrag eventually—he still hadn't regained consciousness, and a young relative of his told me tearfully that the physics weren't hopeful. I hadn't known the old man well but had grown to like him these past few weeks, for what that was worth. "May the fortunes be with him," I said, and meant it. "He was brave. And surprising. He'd a good sense of humor." Not to mention, he was the only Councilor injured, and the only one who had fought with our men and women on the front line. But the dead and injured weren't confined to the lower born. I imagined that none of the Families had come through this unscathed.

Several days passed in a rush of reorganization as we set new priorities. Battle lines were redrawn since the rebels had only one narrow approach path now, and both sides were hastily reworking their respective attack and defense plans. We focused on increasing the fortifications on the Finger and developing ways to make the long descent from the peak of the bridge deadlier for the rebels to attempt. The fortunes only knew what was being cooked up across the lake. Most of their force had moved into Silasta to occupy the lower city, though a contingent remained outside the external perimeter to the north and south, still guarding against any attempts to send messengers out from the upper city.

We had earned a short reprieve, but things were worse than ever, with too many people crammed in too little space, and internal tensions rising. It seemed certain something would break.

Evening on the second day after the lower city fell, I found myself daw-
dling on my way to the Manor to join Tain and Marco for a pre-Council
strategy meeting. I had a new portion of safe food for Tain, but the truth was
they didn't need me to plan logistics of our defense. It wasn't my strength.
And what is your strength, then? My mocking inner voice asked me. *You can't
even get the proofing right. You're a failure at the only thing you need to be good
at.* I shook my head, trying to clear the thoughts before the loop of obses-
sive self-judgment and speculation could start again.

"Why do you do this thing?" a now-familiar voice said, and I only jumped
a little as An-Hadrea dropped from the stone wall beside me. I was getting
better at reacting when she did this to me, this time trying to turn the shock
into a shrug, though her smile suggested she wasn't fooled.

"Do what, An-Hadrea?" I asked, keeping my tone courteous.

"This thing. Where you eat the Chancellor's food, and check it for poison." She met my surprised gaze, guileless, as I blinked, searching for
words.

"I . . . what do you . . . I don't know what you mean."

She blew out her lips in scorn. "Do you think I am stupid? You think I
have no eyes?"

"Oh, I know you have eyes," I murmured. They seemed capable of spying on me at will.

"Well, then. Why do you do this thing?" She fell in beside me, patient,
confident of receiving an answer.

"It's something my family's always done," I said at last. "We protect the
Chancellor."

"By eating poison."

"By proofing," I corrected, prickling. "Testing for poison. I know the
flavors, the smells, the textures, to make sure it's safe."

"You protect him by dying in his place? But why would someone highborn do this? Is it not a job for an animal or a servant?"

"No," I said, annoyed. "You don't understand. We don't just die, like
some replaceable animal. It takes a lifetime of training. We know poisons—
all the poisons." I forgot that was wrong until it came out. Not *all* the poisons,
obviously. "We have immunities and antidotes. We know how to protect
ourselves, and protect them. And this is *everything* to us. It's our family's
honor."

"Honor," An-Hadrea said. "How is it you are all so obsessed with one half of our creed and you apply it so strangely? You have twisted it into yet another system of rank, a way of measuring who is more valuable than whom. Honor is not a score in a game, Jovan. Honor is about your connection to other people. It is how you show yourself to other people and the regard in which you hold them, which in turn feeds the regard in which they hold you. And honor is only one half of the whole. You have forgotten *tah*. You understand nothing of the *fresken* of the land, and you know nothing of the secondworld. But you cannot stop talking about honor. What is honor if you are dead? Or your friends or family are dead?"

It was difficult to explain the notion. "Honor lives on after you die. It's the mark we carve on the world. It's living fairly and respectfully. If you don't live with honor, what's the point?"

"Fairly? Respectfully? Perhaps I understand these words differently. Where is the honor in how my people are treated?"

I sighed. "You're right, it is dishonorable. I don't deny that. But I didn't know." It sounded weak because it was, but she had me flustered.

"But you did not spare thought for the people who feed you, here in your shining white city."

No words came to my defense. I never *had* thought about the people in the country much. They were just . . . there, like the landscape—an important part of the infrastructure, but not something to which I'd ever turned my attention. That thought shamed me now. "I didn't. Honor-down, I wish I had." I caught her arm, compelled to make her understand. "You always saw this city as greedy and indulgent, so nothing's changed for you. But I grew up here, An-Hadrea, I grew up here thinking we were the most civilized city in the world, that we were better than all our barbarous neighbors. And then I found out we're not better, we're worse, because our foundations are rotten. Don't you see? My whole city . . . my whole world, it's all been built on lies."

She stared at me, calm as the eye of a storm. "You are right. You poor thing, having to learn what monsters live inside you. You are as much a victim as the people who have been treated no better than valued livestock."

"I didn't mean—"

"No, no," she continued, savage. "Let me comfort *you,* for it is you who are suffering. Confronting your role in destroying our way of life is truly just as painful as having that life destroyed is for us. Your feelings must be *so* hurt. Let us focus on *those* feelings. They are the most important thing, just like everything in the cities is more important than in the estates. Forget that you are murdering the spirits of the land, that you have taken everything from us."

I dropped her arm, angry and defensive. "Let's not pretend one side is all to blame here. Is everyone in this city to blame for what their government's done? Are innocent children supposed to die a violent death for the crime of being born here? Did a peace negotiator sent out to talk in good faith deserve to be murdered for trying to talk and listen? Tearing the very heads off the bodies of our messengers—not even soldiers, just people who could *run fast,* and dumping them at our gates like refuse? One side doesn't have the monopoly on honor."

She looked discomforted but not stunned; clearly the rumors had already reached her about the messengers' fates. But her tone, if anything, increased in ferocity. "Did I ever say such brutal acts were honorable? No Darfri would do such a thing to their most despised enemy. But there are lesser people within the rebellion, people who would use us for their own ends. Do you not remember my family came here at great risk and cost to help you, because my mother believes that such violence is unjustified no matter what you have done to us? I suppose you have forgotten that?"

I met her furious brown gaze and hated the guilt she was making me feel, hated myself for being angry about it, hated the explosion of feelings like a physical swarm eating me from the inside. But she was right. I couldn't stop feeling those things—honor-down, there was nothing in the world I was worse at than stopping myself thinking the wrong things—but I could stop blurting them at her and expecting her sympathy.

"I'm sorry," I said, a little stiffly. "It isn't your fault or your concern how I deal with my part in all this, An-Hadrea. I know that." I wanted to say more, but it would just be further justification, and I hadn't earned the right to expect her to care about it.

We sat in silence for a while. Despite my deserved dressing down, I didn't want her to go. I strove to think of something conciliatory. "Will you tell me more about *tah*?" I asked.

She considered me for a moment, and something softer glimmered in her expression. "Come," she said. Then she sprang away, leading us in the opposite direction, back down the hill toward the lake. It took all my efforts to keep up with her in the dark. Once or twice I thought I'd lost her. Then we almost collided in the grassy space leading down to the shore, and she chuckled, catching my shoulders as she spun around.

"Easy," she said. "Here, sit."

Tongue-tied with the usual confusion her sudden changes of mood inspired, I sat beside her on the cool grass, a respectful distance in accordance with her country preferences and my own. She leaned back on her elbows, her gleaming hair half-masking a still profile. Across the dark silky expanse of water, life flickered in the buildings of the lower city. For this quiet moment, it seemed almost as though there was no war, just the shores of the Bright Lake on a warm evening. Sometimes it surprised me how much some parts of the city had *not* changed.

"So. *Tah*." She paused, thoughtful. "*Tah* is about your place in the natural world around you. Like honor, it is about connection between things. I am respectful to the earth and the spirits dwelling in the secondworld because I know myself to be part of a greater whole. Here, at the Bright Lake, do you feel nothing? No connection?"

I shrugged, feeling awkward, but answered honestly. "I don't think I even know what that kind of connection would feel like."

She gestured to the still water before us. "This was once the most sacred place in all Sjona. The Bright Lake was much different back then, but it was the place where all our tribes used to gather for the karodee."

We still held karodee in Silasta as our biggest annual celebration—a week of sporting competitions, games, and parties—and even I knew it had its origins in the old annual spring festival of dance, song, and trade between tribes. But I knew little about ancient karodee and its significance to the Darfri.

"The karodee was our most important event. We traded fairly and we bonded joyfully with the other tribes, which brought us all honor. And we gave offerings of these great emotions to the mighty spirits of the Bright Lake and Solemn Peak, who dwell here together so close."

"I'm not sure I understand," I admitted. "What do you mean by offerings of emotions?" I recalled the little things I'd seen left at Darfri shrines around the city—flowers, hair cuttings, figures of sticks.

An-Hadrea shook her head, astounded at my ignorance. "The spirits of the secondworld take strength from our offerings." She looked all over my face like I was a puzzle she couldn't solve. "We give them our hearts. What we feel. Joy. Grief. Admiration. Love. Passion. Hope. These make the spirits strong. Karodee was a time of great excitement, and so the spirits drank up all of that joy and connection and were renewed for the year. And they were grateful for our offerings, and gave us back a bountiful year and blessings on the bargains made and relationships forged at the karodee. It is said babies born or conceived during karodee would grow to be the strongest and wisest of all our people, blessed as they were by such great power.

"This is the same reason mothers take their babies outside to the sacred places close by, and exchange their love and fear and satisfaction and gratitude for blessings for the child. My mother brought me all the way here, to this very lake, when I was just a baby, to have the lake spirit Os-Woorin know me. That is not so common now. But it is why when you take a lover you consummate that in a sacred place, if you can, to feed the spirit there with your passion. Or—this you should understand, at least—why you all gather together to lower your Chancellor into the Bright Lake and feed the spirit with all your grief and loss and sadness and love."

Was it really only a few weeks ago that we had gathered here for the funeral? I had never thought much about its origins. "It's a tradition. I never thought about it as relating to a spirit of the lake, though."

"You lower him into the lake so that his wisdom and knowledge may be absorbed by the great water spirit Os-Woorin. And Os-Woorin guides him safely to the afterlife." She sighed. "I do not understand Silastians, Jovan. These are the simple things that are told to a child. I have seen all the libraries, the books. Your sister might be a page in one, so often is she squashed between them. What do your books say, if they do not tell you the stories of your past?"

Again, she left me unable to think of an answer. I supposed that as residents of the city grew further from religion over time, they had stopped valuing the Darfri stories of their past, and ceased recording the spiritual significance of things. Etan had always said that language was not neutral. There were consequences and value judgments in the manner in which we chose to record things. History recorded in the written language of the

Credians' past had no words for these Darfri concepts. So while the Darfri
in the estates had continued their verbal storytelling tradition even after
we had robbed them of the right to read and write, we had forgotten.

An-Hadrea seemed unbothered by my silence, and showed no sign of
wanting to leave. She breathed the night air in deeply and looked up at the
stars. The moonlight gave her profile an otherworldly sheen. How could
she be so righteously furious at me, with just cause, but then such a short
time later relax in my presence as if it were the company of a trusted friend?

"Will you tell me a story of our past?" I asked at last.

She smiled. "Yes. Shall I tell you about how your city came to be?"

"Please."

"Before the refugees came here from across the Howling Plains, our
tribes were not so settled in a single place. We moved around the lands,
following the seasons. You know this?" I murmured agreement. The mechanics of history were taught to every Silastian child. The arrival of the
refugees from Crede, their integration with the local tribes, and the sharing
of their superior technology and engineering skills, which made it possible
to build safe and manageable trade routes out of the resource-rich but geo-
graphically isolated Sjona. Our eventual government formed by the emerging leaders of the regions around new Sjona—some of original Credian
descent, some local. This I knew. And objectively I knew that Darfri had
been the dominant belief, part of the accepted main culture, but there was
little mentioned in the texts about what that belief had meant.

"Over time, the idea of one country with central leadership grew more
appealing, and with it the dream of a central city. *Silasta*, the word, meant
meeting place, did you know? The first Councils met here, still really just a
group of leaders and allies from around the land more than a true government. There were settlements here for many years but there was debate
about the building of a permanent stone city. It held the promise of many
things; prosperity, security, learning. But it involved taking much from the
spirits here. Dredging channels in the marshlands, carving out much of
Solemn Peak to use its rock, reshaping the Bright Lake and the path of the
great river. Some Speakers argued that the spirits would not support such
infrastructure."

"What changed their minds?"

"The first Chancellor, Telasa. She was a woman of great charisma and vision, and also great understanding of the *fresken* of the land, though she was not a Speaker."

"And a Speaker is someone who can communicate with the spirits." That one I knew. "What is *fresken*?"

She looked at me, a half-smile softening her exasperation. "How is it that you can live here and not understand the land on which your city stands? It is like you walk around with one eye shut."

"I wouldn't like that," I murmured, and she laughed.

"I have seen that about you," she agreed. "You do not like being unbalanced, yes? I told you before, *tah* is all about balance. Understanding that the country is more than dirt and grass and wind and stone. There is power in the land. Great spirits, long memories. This power is what we call *fresken*."

She gestured at the lake. "The stories say the Chancellor understood the *fresken* like our greatest elders. And she called upon the great spirit of the lake, Os-Woorin, and it blessed this place as the site for a great city. Water spirits are very powerful, and Os-Woorin the most powerful of them all. Its blessing held much sway."

I chose my words carefully, not wanting to disrupt this fragile warmth she offered, though I didn't quite want to articulate why. "How did the spirit show itself?"

She shrugged. "The stories vary. Some say the spirits spoke inside our heads and gave us a message. Others say Os-Woorin itself rose from the lake, a glistening and magnificent being, and spoke in a great, booming voice that all could hear. But no one has seen such a thing in so long, we do not know for sure."

"And if your lake spirit spoke now, and told the army to stop attacking? Tain needs to be able to speak to the rebels if there is going to be any chance at stopping this. Could your lake spirit give him that chance?" I smiled, but was only half-joking. The things I'd seen and felt, first at the base of the walls and then again at the fall of the lower city, couldn't quite be explained. It was unlikely there were powerful beings hidden in the water, but the idea didn't seem as impossible as it would have a month ago.

She regarded me seriously. "I suppose it could, if it so wished. But I am . . . I am not trained in the handling of *fresken*, though once I was told I would have the aptitude for it." She dropped her gaze to the side, giving me the sudden sense that she was hiding something, though perhaps it was just suppressed anger at having been denied the learning she had clearly wanted. Her voice sounded fainter when she finally added, "Handling *fresken* without the instruction of a Speaker is forbidden. Without training, how could I know how to persuade a small spirit, let alone a great water spirit?"

"I think you could persuade anyone of anything," I said, and she returned my smile. We sat there in silence awhile and I shut my eyes, enjoying the new peace humming between us.

Eventually I found myself saying, "Proofing, it's called. What I do. And it's not only because it's tied to my family's honor. I do it because Tain's my Chancellor and my friend, and he's in danger. Whoever killed our uncles is trying to kill him, too."

"But he does not want you to continue?"

Apparently any conversation I had could be prey to An-Hadrea's excellent hearing and her ability to hide her tall form in unlikely spaces. "No."

"He says this because he loves you, yes? And he does not want to put your life before his."

"Yes. He means well. He's a good man—better, I think, than any of the Council knew when he took over. Maybe better than his uncle knew, too. But he's thinking as a good man and a good friend, and not as a Chancellor. Some or all of the most powerful people in the Council are the ones responsible for what's happened out on their estates. If Tain died, even if we somehow broke the siege without killing one another, there would be no one to hold them accountable, no reparations for you, no conciliation. Without him, we have no hope."

She bit her lip, her head cocked to one side. "I suppose he thinks he would not be the Chancellor that you need, if he did not care about his friend's life."

"I don't mind him caring," I said. "Our families have always cared about each other. I don't expect him to view my life cheaply. But he's seeing only half the picture, thinking only about how he'd feel if I died."

"But you, too, are looking from the other half. You are thinking only about how you would feel if he did."

The truth of it hit me like a barb in my chest. If the poisoner reached Tain without me stopping them, I would have failed in my duty, and the city would be doomed. But, honor aside, the true pain, the true fear, was the thought of losing my best and only real friend, the only person outside my family who truly knew me, who understood how I worked inside and didn't judge me poorly for it. Who would I be, without his friendship? What would I do, without my role at his side?

"I suppose you're right, An-Hadrea." I stared back at the water, no longer able to meet her shadowy gaze.

The small puff of her breath against my cheek alerted me that she had rolled close, and I turned with a start. She lay propped on her side, her face close to mine, and silvery moonlight illuminated the dusting of freckles across her nose and cheeks. "Hadrea," she said, and for the first time, her eyes held a trace of vulnerability. "You may call me Hadrea, Jovan."

"Hadrea," I tried, frozen on the spot. Her skin smelled like oranges.

She smiled. "I like the way you say it," she said.

And then she kissed me.

After a night filled with dreams of boons asked of and granted by strange watery men, I woke early and picked my way through my crowded apartments, trying not to disturb any of the sleeping people. Only after stepping outside did my heavy cloak of anxiousness lighten. So absorbed was my mind with thinking about Hadrea that it hadn't had the space to think about the encroachment or the change to my careful routine.

I checked on the new food production hubs first, and found them running smoothly. We still had stores of millet, dry scarlet beans, rice, and some salt, but everything else had been run down to the dregs. The sealed cases in cool storage still held some cheese and a small, mismatched collection of bindie eggs, and our lutra and oku still produced milk. Tain had warned the Council yesterday we would be searching everyone's homes, so today we welcomed "anonymous donations" at the collection points, hoping to shake out some hoarded supplies. One of the cooks told me he'd already had parcels left by the door early this morning.

That finished, I headed to the Manor, feeling strangely lighthearted and wondering whether Hadrea would appear. She'd vanished so quickly after the kiss last night, I didn't know what to expect on seeing her again. I passed Marco on my way to report to Tain, on the front steps of the Manor, and greeted him. "Is the training going well?" Most of the Warrior-Guilder's time since the retreat had been spent drilling civilian groups in the use of hand-to-hand weapons.

He shrugged. "I don't know about that, Credo. Some are improving. Some resent being present, and are sullen and disrespectful. Some are trying, but they are barely strong enough to hold daggers, let alone anything bigger. Their lives have been soft, without physical labor."

Athletes and certain tradespersons had the musculature and coordination to respond to the training, but so many Silastians lacked those physical skills. They weren't the kind of thing you could learn in a few months, let alone a few weeks. "I know it must be frustrating, working with people like us."

Marco patted my shoulder with a smile. "I am a teacher. If I grew frustrated teaching, I would not be much of one. In any case, in these times, what satisfaction is there better than the satisfaction of a job done well? They'll do the best they can."

"That's all we can ask," I said, but we both knew it wasn't enough.

Inside the Manor, Argo directed me to the Council room, where a bleary-eyed Tain and Eliska pored over a model of the bridge tower fortifications set up on the great table. As I sat down to join them, Eliska offered me a dried fig from a small jar.

"Part of the food 'donations' Argo found this morning," she said, taking one for herself. "Along with a few bottles of spices—cinnamon and barbanut, I think. I suppose one of the Families had them hidden."

"I wonder what we'll find in the search," Tain said grimly.

Eliska chewed with impolite delight. "Honor-down, I haven't had anything sweet in weeks."

I took one, only then noticing Tain had a piece beside him. I glared at it, then him, and he glared back.

"By all the fortunes, Jov," he said, weary. "We took them out of a sealed jar. Marco had two already."

Glancing at Eliska, who was studiously concentrating on the model bridge and pretending she couldn't see us, I sighed. *It was only a matter of time anyway.* "I don't care." I meant it in two ways. "You think poison can't be sealed in a jar?" I examined the dark brown and purple shades and took a deliberate and careful bite. They had been preserved with sugar and citrus, and caused a normal drying sensation on my tongue.

Eliska stopped chewing as I ate. She looked panicked, as if torn between spitting out the fig and risking poison to avoid the rudeness. Tain,
on the other hand, set his jaw and met my gaze.

"You can't be here all the time, Jov," he said. "And we have more pressing things to worry about. Now, enjoy your fig, and tell us about the food
stores." He took a bite of the fruit and chewed deliberately. My heart beat
faster, fury rising within me. I pressed my hands hard on the table to fight
the urge to gouge it out of his mouth. Poor Eliska sat there, staring at the
model with her mouth half open, her skin darkening with embarrassment.

I was saved from making things even worse by a knock at the chamber
door. Credo Javesto came in, hands woven together and brow a mass of tight
lines. "Honored Chancellor," he said. "I'm sorry to interrupt. Fighting's
broken out in the south block food station, between some of the city Darfri
and some Credolen. You'd better come."

We all stood and followed, but as we did, Tain gave me a sidelong glance
and dropped the remaining fig on his papers on the table like a tiny apology. I nodded stiffly, trying to swallow both my instinctual anger and the
sting of guilt, and couldn't help but remember what Hadrea had said last
night.

"Please take a break, Credola," the fletcher told my sister when I stuck my
head in the door. Kalina looked up from her perch, balanced on the end of
a stone bench with a bucket of feathers, down stuck to her hair like a little
wonky crown. I smiled at the sight.

She unwound herself and left her half-sorted work with the fletcher and
came with me out into the open. "Did you hear about the riot?"

"I *heard* it," she said. "Budua was here and she shut the doors and told
everyone to stay put. It was frustrating not knowing what was happening
but it was probably for the best."

With the city as tense as a badly strung instrument, allowing onlookers
to gawk at a riot would only encourage the violence to spread. "We're still
trying to sort out how it started, but we think some Credolen went into the
protected area and started causing trouble. They're claiming the Darfri cast
curses on them and made water spirits rise from the canals to drown their
children. Or some such nonsense." I couldn't be sure the idea of water spirits

was entirely nonsense, not after some of the strangeness witnessed recently, but I was confident there weren't people conjuring up attacks on children out of spite.

We'd contained this one to a few dozen people, fortunately, thanks to Ectar and Javesto's quick actions. Ectar was living in the protected sector with the Darfri and foreigners, including Talafan, Doranites, and wet-landers, and had become something of a guard and community leader there. Javesto, too, was proving helpful dealing with the segregated sec-tion. Tain's support of the city Darfri had made a useful ally of him, and we hoped having some openly sympathetic Councilors, one of them the Chancellor, would discourage violence and reassure the people in the sec-tor. They needed to know we were going to change if we got through this. If we couldn't convince a captive audience under our protection, how could we expect to convince a hostile force who had already been betrayed before?

"What did you need me for?" Kalina asked, once she'd listened to my recounting of the scuffle (some bruises and scrapes, some minor damage to a few buildings, and twenty-eight people feeling sorry for themselves in the jail cells; all in all, much better than it could have been).

"Tain, actually," I said.

"Has he rethought my idea about the river?" Her pace increased a fraction as she started, with enthusiasm, "If they went at night, they could make it. The rebels have people watching from the wall on the west side, but there's no lights on the water itself—"

"No," I stopped her. "You know he won't send anyone, not after what happened last time." She deflated, and I hastened on. "He's planning what to say if he can somehow force the people across the lake to listen. He's going to have another go with the speaking trumpet—now that they're closer it'll be harder for them to ignore him. Only, speech writing isn't his strength."

A faint smile passed over her face. "He wants me to write it?"

"Well, to help." Tain could be a persuasive speaker, but something this important couldn't be left to instinct. Planned words were never something he'd enjoyed. My sister, on the other hand, had excelled at written argument at school and in her work.

"Of course I'll help," she said. "I've been jotting down ideas for days, actually. We're not going to fix what's happened with a few pretty words, but we need to say enough to convince them that we will listen. That has to be a start, at least."

"Do you think you could work with Salvea and Hadrea? I'm hoping they'll have some ideas about ways we could convey trustworthiness, especially to the Darfri. Some gesture that shows we will respect their beliefs."

Her brown eyes widened at my slipup. "Hadrea?" she asked, mildly.

I tried to keep my face smooth and my voice relaxed. "Yes, apparently I'm no longer so repellent."

She smiled, the first real smile I'd seen on her in weeks. "Oh, quite," she said. She didn't add anything, but I knew immediately it wasn't going to be possible to keep my relationship, whatever it was, with Hadrea secret from my sister.

As though I'd conjured her with my thoughts, Hadrea slipped out from between two fair lady bushes in front of us. I blinked at the sight of her. Instead of the increasingly raggedy layered skirts and embroidered blouse she had always worn, Hadrea was dressed in Silastian style, in sandals and a one-shouldered white dress gathered with red cording. Only the bright scarf over her hair remained. Arms folded across her ribs, she regarded us with a mix of embarrassment and defiant bravado as we both stared.

"I tried to find catacombs on this side of the lake," she said, chin high, her gaze fixed somewhere between us. "I slipped. I had no other clothes, so Argo's sister lent me this thing."

"You look lovely, An-Hadrea," Kalina said, studiously not looking at me. "I know it must feel odd, but I'm sure we can get your clothes clean quickly if you'd like."

I stole a glance at the brush of her warm brown hair over the line of her bare shoulder, and suppressed an urge to correct my sister to say there was no spare water for washing clothes.

Hadrea smiled at Kalina, her gaze avoiding me with precision. "Thank you. You may call me Hadrea, if you would like," she added, glancing at me for the smallest moment.

Kalina, to her credit, carried on as if oblivious. "I'd be honored."

"I'll take you both to Tain," I said, trying to sound casual.

I listened to them talk as we walked, surprised by the ease with which

Hadrea drew my shy sister into conversation and made her laugh. Hadrea pointed to buildings and gardens and even little statues set in walls, peppering Kalina with questions and commentary about the city.

"Why do you wear so little color?" Hadrea asked. "It is all white, white, like you do not know any others."

Kalina smoothed down her own dress. "I don't know. All the nicest fabrics are white. I suppose it shows off the other things—your cording, or jewelry. Like colored mosaic tiles on a white building."

Hadrea plucked at the red cording over her bust. "It is like being a giant parcel, wrapped with string."

Kalina smiled. "Do you get hot in all your layers?" she asked. "The embroidery is beautiful but your skirts look so heavy."

"No, it is not hot. The wind, out on the lands, it keeps things cool." She laughed. "It would be too cool to wear your little dresses and tunics. The men would not enjoy the Maiso without pants."

As Kalina joined in the laughter, Hadrea pulled the scarf from her hair and ran her fingers over the embroidery. "Our mothers teach us needlework early." She smiled. "We practice on our ordinary clothes and scarves to perfect our skills—this is not the best I could manage. I could show you my festival clothes, back home!" She passed the scarf to Kalina, who smoothed the bright threads between her hands. "You can have that, if you like it."

We reached the Manor, and as I opened the door for them, both gave me a half-startled look, as though they'd completely forgotten my presence. *Flattering.* Evidently Hadrea wasn't wasting as much of her thoughts on me as I was on her. I'd been captivated by but unable to participate in their conversation about clothing and public bathing and tile glazing, chiefly because everything that came out in her slow, lilting voice seemed to mesmerize me.

We had barely stepped inside when Tain met us, alone.

"Jov," he said faintly. My breath suddenly thunderous in my ears, I crossed the room, taking in all the signs parading in front of me like a list. Slick skin, when the temperature within the Manor was mild and pleasant. Voice strained, weak. Hands pressed under armpits.

"I thought it was just exhaustion," he mumbled as I looked him over, numb. "But I'm sorry, Jov, I don't think it's that."

No. My ears hurt, like my brain was swelling inside my skull. *Can't be happening. Not now, not after everything.* Kalina gave a strangled cry. When my voice came out, it sounded so cold, so dispassionate, I almost couldn't believe it was mine.

"When did you start feeling unwell?"

"I'll send for the physics," Argo said, voice trembling.

"No," I snapped, startling the old man. Even Tain looked shocked at my tone.

"If the Chancellor is sick . . ." Hadrea began.

"No," I repeated, trying to soften my words. "They don't know how to help," I said, part explanation, part plea, meeting Tain's eyes. "They couldn't help Etan or Caslav. They can't help you, if that's what this is."

He looked at me, confusion and fear stripping years from his face. Kalina grabbed my arm. "Jov, we have to *try.*"

Tain shook his head. "He's right, Lini," he said. "Argo, An-Hadrea. Please don't."

The elderly doorkeep froze by the edge of his desk, staring, as if searching for some sign I was coercing Tain.

"We can't tell them," Tain said. He sounded strong, like a leader. Perhaps only I knew him well enough to detect the hint of desperation in his eyes. "We can't tell them, because if we've lost a single leader's voice, we've lost this war. And once they know I've been . . ." He stumbled for words, then shook his head again. "We can't tell anyone yet."

"Argo, no one is to come in the Manor. *No one.* Tell anyone who comes that the Chancellor and I are out inspecting the north wall." Kalina let go of my arm; her fingers left marks on my skin. "Lini, you and Hadrea take Tain to his rooms. I have to go check something. I'll be with you soon." I squeezed Tain's shoulder and tried to sound comforting instead of stiff.

I left them there and ran.

The Council chambers seemed eerie and cold, even with the sun pouring in through the dome and spilling over the table, where the little model walls and bridges sat abandoned and pitiful. Where the fat pot of dried fruit had sat, there remained only the faintest sticky circle. And where Tain had left the partial fig by his papers, nothing. I used a paper to take a sample of the sticky residue and checked under the table and chairs, inside the model, all over the room, conscious of the futility of it. Frustration tasted bitter as bile in my throat. I knew now, as close to certain as could be, that the poison had been on Tain's fig. And I had lost the chance to study a trace of that poison to develop an antidote. I thought I might choke on my own anger.

Without even realizing I'd begun, I found myself halfway around a loop of the table, pacing anxious rounds under the sullen and watchful eyes of the Councilors in the paintings above each chair. Unable to look at Pedrag, or Etan or Caslav, I circled, feeling the painted eyes of our diminished Council above me, judging. I tried to shut down the doomsaying part of my brain. *You've failed. It's all over,* it told me, and despite my best efforts it showed me Tain's death, how he would look as he got sicker and sicker.

Anxiety rose within me, a choking intruder in my chest, making my ears ring and my lungs and throat contract. In sudden need of air, I stumbled out of the Council chamber and took two steps toward the exit before realizing the stupidity of leaving the Manor and risking observation. Backtracking, I hurried to the glass-walled garden where Kalina had found the dead leksot what felt like years ago. I knelt on the grass there, sucking in breaths of earthy cool air, my quivering hands pressed into the soft layer of decomposing leaves.

As I breathed, the panic subsided. Between my toes, I felt the prickly edge of a feverhead springing from the grass. Left unchecked for weeks without a gardener, the toxic weed had probably spread throughout the entire garden. Even though it was pointless, I tugged at the base until the bulbous roots came out. I pulled out another weed, and another, and scraped the just-rotten leaves from around me, gathering the cold, dead remnants into a moist pile. The repetitive, soothing actions gave me slow comfort.

Eventually, I stretched out, joints cracking. The cool water in the pond stung the raw scrapes on my skin as I cleaned the dirt and sticky plant residue from my hands and fingernails. I felt calm now, dispassionate. I'd learned distrust and calculation at the feet of my Tashi, learned to analyze and to act without emotion. It was that Jovan who left the garden. I had, at best, one night to find an antidote to the poison, or Tain would die. There was no Heir. Our Council was corrupt and dangerous, and our city was on the brink of falling. If I couldn't save Tain, it spelled the end for Silasta.

Gardening had given me time to breathe. We'd not found a cure last time even with my uncle's brilliant mind and a dozen physics working alongside me, but a more stubborn, visceral part of me still searched for a solution.

With Etan and Caslav we had tried all of the standard antidotes, and that had taken time. Now I knew what wouldn't work. Where *not* to focus my attention. And perhaps that—coupled with even greater desperation—gave me a new advantage.

The front section of Tain's rooms was empty but voices came from his bedroom, and Kalina came out of the doorway, her face streaked and blotchy. She threw herself at me, body quivering with sobs, and I held her for a moment, trying to think of comforting words. Of course, there were none. My tongue felt like a dry block of cheese as I patted her shoulders awkwardly.

"It's like with Etan," she mumbled into my chest. "He's being brave, Jov, but it's just the same."

I took her hand and led her back into Tain's room.

He sat up in bed, and for a moment another image transposed itself: my uncle, looking at me from his bed with much the same pallor and demeanor. A wan smile with swollen lips, skin slick with sweat. "Is there any point in me being in bed?"

I took his pulse. "You'll be exhausted soon enough." For the first time I noticed Hadrea in the corner. His pulse, given Tain knew what was coming, was faster than a normal resting rate, but, unlike Etan, his own nerves might be speeding his heart. I glanced at her and a stab of worry pierced my calm. Now she'd see me in the same way everyone did, eventually. Bound by my compulsions, unable to react like a normal person. Cold. I realized then the depths of my longing for her to see me differently.

But there was no time for that worry. I counted backward in my head. Tain had eaten the fig reasonably early this morning. It was late afternoon now. His symptoms had progressed at roughly half the pace that Etan's had. Maybe less. Did that mean he had ingested less poison than his uncle, or simply had better resistance to it? Caslav had sickened slower than Etan, also, despite likely having a greater dose.

"How many figs did you eat? Was it just the one?"

His jaw tightened with guilt. "Not even a whole one."

Almost certainly a smaller dose than Caslav, then. I tried to suppress the flare of optimism—*if we have more time, if the dose was less, perhaps it won't be lethal*—no point relying on that.

"Are you sure it was the fig?" Tain asked. "You ate one, too, remember.

And Eliska. And Marco." I heard the plea in his words. How much we both wished he had not chosen this morning to rebel against our traditional roles.

I nodded. "I made your broth after the riot. Unless you ate something else today, it was the fig. And the jar is gone from the Council room." I hadn't been poisoned, but had chosen a fig at random from the jar. How had the poisoner known which one Tain would take? I looked up at my sister. "Kalina, can you find Eliska and Marco? Don't warn them, just let me know if either looks ill. We all ate from that jar." If our enemy had poisoned a selection of the fruit, chances were Tain wouldn't have been the only one to take a poisoned fig. If somehow they had been able to poison the actual fruit Tain had taken, then only those two people had been in the room with him at the time. Though a chill spread through me at the thought, I set it aside. Finding the poisoner had ceased to be my first priority. Now that the worst had happened, saving Tain's life was what mattered.

We needed to find something to counteract whatever was in his system. Last time we had gone through every book, every page of Etan's notes on remedies, and had come up empty. But there was one area my training had neglected, and my ignorance on the subject had already had consequences. I glanced over at Hadrea. "I need you to do something for me, too," I said. "I need you to find me a Doranite man called Batbayer."

Salgar
(red death)

DESCRIPTION: Naturally occurring mineral, reddish, soft and crumbly; often coexists with gold, orote, and opal. Often used in dye-making, cosmetics, illustrations, and other artworks.

SYMPTOMS: Tightness in the throat, vomiting of a brown mucous character mixed with blood, fainting, excessive thirst, abdominal pain, shivering, stools dark and offensive, pulse weak and rapid, great nervous prostration, and delirium.

PROOFING CUES: Strong metallic taste difficult to disguise in food, sharp smell.

18

Kalina

I lit the last of the wall lamps and returned to my seat by the bed. On Jov's request I had observed that Marco and Eliska both remained in apparent good health; it hurt knowing one of those most trusted Councilors was likely the poisoner. Hadrea had left in search of the drug seller Batbayer, who, she guessed, might be hiding in the protected quarter, while my brother intended to pressure Baina and all of his other contacts. His desperate, unrealistic hope was that something used in the production of new recreational drugs, ones he had not heard of, would be the source of the poison. As I rested my head against the back of the chair, watching Tain through half-lidded eyes sore from tears, no part of me felt Jovan's optimism.

At first Tain and I had pretended together. He'd made jokes. I'd read from my notes about the Darfri, as if he might still have a chance to deliver the speech I'd planned. But brave as he might be, Tain couldn't stop the fear showing through in the end. Eventually, instead of jokes he spoke of his frustrations, the things he felt now he would never do. I had listened and held his hand, as he admitted his stupidity and rashness in taking food against Jovan's wishes. How he had been wrong in whom he trusted. How he wished he had done so many things differently: respected his responsibilities as my family had, learned sooner about the city and the estates and especially the Darfri. Listened to his uncle.

He spoke as a man who knew he would see no more tomorrows.

There was little to say to comfort him. I found, in any case, that when I tried to say anything, a vise clamped around my throat, and my eyes ran with tears that soothed and then stung as they dried. He loved me, in the purest way our culture valued the most, but my feelings for him were a thorned flower, painful and beautiful and scarring. No lovers I took knew me as he did, saw me as completely. I was a sister and not, beloved but alone. It had never hurt so much as now.

Tain lay silent, blank eyes staring at the wall. His comfortable chamber felt stifling. The parcel at my feet that I had brought here from our apartments seemed to pulse with magnetic life, to the pounding rhythm of my heart. I forced myself not to look at it. I would stay here for Tain as long as he was awake. Outside, dusk had turned to darkness, and the exhaustion of his body fighting the poison had drained him. He would sleep soon.

When he spoke again, his words were slurred. "I . . . didn't do the right things," he murmured, his eyes fixed on the wall at the other side of the room. I leaned in closer, bringing my hand to his hot forehead, unsure he was fully conscious.

"Maybe none of us did," I managed to say, my voice squeaky and tight. "But you saw me for me, and I *always* loved you for that." My stupid eyes welled up again; my free hand swiped them away. Tain needed strength and comfort, not weakness.

I sat there with him until he was asleep. Then I extracted my hand gently and stroked his cheek. I tried to say goodbye, but nothing came out.

Everything felt a bit colder as I bent and picked up the parcel. I'd written a short message to Jov on the back of my notes for the speech; those I left on the chair. When Jov came back and read it, it would be too late to stop me. If anyone else found it first, Etan's code would look like nothing but a series of lines and dots.

No one paid me any heed on my way through the dark streets, down the hill toward the lake. The shores were deserted and unlit, and the overgrown grass tickled my bare legs like little wet fingers clutching at me. I stopped within sight of the south river gate tower, hovering by the ruins of the destroyed bridge.

The river flowed into Bright Lake from the south and then out through the marshlands to the north. River gates controlled the waterway. With the army patrolling the entire perimeter of the city, an exit through that gate had been as unfeasible as any other, but now that most of the rebels were inside the lower city, only the eastern shore of the river was patrolled. If someone could leave via the river itself, they could perhaps make it to the west shore and out of range of the army unseen. At least that was my hope.

My hands quivered as they extracted a rolled-up paper from the cording of my dress and nerves made my stomach clench. There hadn't been enough time to plan this first part fully. Still, it was too late to back out now. Soon Jov would come back and find the note on the chair. The thought of my brother's expression when he read it . . . I swallowed, placed the parcel between two rocks, and strode toward the tower with my chin high.

The Order Guard Mago let me in. "What can we do for you, Credola?" he asked.

I wiped my hair from my face, taking that moment to scan the room. Three guards, one near the gate wheel. Heart beating faster, I handed the paper to Mago, nonchalant. "New rosters."

Mago frowned, unrolling it. "I thought the roster was settled."

I shrugged, edging back around the curve of the wall, toward the gate wheel. "The Warrior-Guilder was handing them out earlier. I was coming this way so he asked me to pass it on."

He glanced up at me, eyebrows raised. But as he started reading, his confusion gave way to an angry frown. "What is this?" he muttered. "I can't do dayshift. My cousin's on days and someone's got to look after my little Tash." He shook the paper at me; I shrugged again, trying to look confused and innocent.

As I'd hoped, the other two guards joined Mago in examining the roster. Soon all three were exclaiming in annoyance, pointing at parts of the document and swearing. I backed away, eased my hands behind me, and got a grip on the wheel. Eyes on the three guards, I pulled.

Nothing.

My stomach turned over. *The lock, idiot.* I took a step to the right and fumbled for the lock lever.

"This is *ridiculous*," the female guard said, rounding on me. "Whoever wrote this must've been drunk. We can't do these shifts."

My hands froze behind my back. "I didn't write it, sorry."

"Honor-down," Mago said. "Look, there're people rostered back-to-back here. What was wrong with the old roster?"

The three of them bent over the paper again, and I tugged behind me. The lever moved with little protest. Biting my lip, I stepped back to my left and took the wheel again. Just a little, now, turning gently, one hand over the other. . . . *Don't make a noise.* . . .

That would have to do. I stepped back to the lever again and relocked the gate mechanism. It made a slight click as the lever fixed back in place and I froze as Mago looked over. "Credola, are you certain this is the current roster? It's nonsense."

Breathing easier, I walked back over to the door, spreading my hands out. "I took it from a pile on the table," I said, pitching my voice a bit higher, making myself sound a fraction younger, less certain. "The Warrior-Guilder pointed them out and said they were the rosters for the south wall." I frowned. "There were lots of papers there. . . . Maybe I got it mixed up with an old one?"

Mago blew out his cheeks. "I hope that's the case, Credola. Pardon the slur, but the Warrior-Guilder's gone mad if he thinks we'll take this nonsense."

"I'll take it back and check," I volunteered. "Maybe it was my mistake."

I took the paper and bid them a hasty farewell.

My breath came too fast as I slunk behind the ruins of the bridge again. Now, when it was too late to turn back, this seemed like a terrible idea. Tain hadn't wanted to hear it when I'd suggested it, unwilling to risk another messenger. Heart hammering, I untied my dress cording and wound it around my hands, making neat coils even Jovan would be proud of, and laid the loops on the ground. I took off my dress and bound the oiled parcel against my back with the loops of cording. There, arms wrapped around my shivering body, paralyzed by fear, I paused. In the end, I *wasn't* brave, no matter how much I wished to be.

But Tain was as good as dead, and Jovan wouldn't be far behind if the city fell. We needed dramatic action and this was the only idea that might work. My whole life I had wanted not just to contribute to something

greater but—perhaps selfishly—to be *seen* to contribute. Not to be immediately forgotten by the people I met, or only to be thought of by reference
to my limitations. I might never have done anything special or courageous
in my life, but this could be the city's only chance.

I dropped down onto my belly, the soggy soil chilly through my thin
undergarments, and watched across the lake for any sign I had been seen.
There was at least one watcher on the wall on the west side, but their light
was being used to monitor the top of the gate, not the water below. Hugging the shoreline, I crawled through the sand and mud toward the tower,
low and slow.

The water felt shockingly cold, tightening my lungs. My feet crept along
the slimy bottom, silent and slow to minimize ripples, water lapping up to
just below my nose. Close to the gate now, one of the most dangerous points
because of all the guards on our side of the water. The water grew deeper as
the tower rose out of its bank until my toes lost touch with the mud. *Just
like you practiced.* I let my face drop lower underwater, swimming with just
my eyes and the top of my head above the water, turning my face for breaths.
The tower loomed up ahead, lit windows illuminating the lake with patches
of dark green and silver, then beyond that, the great river gate. It became
harder to move through the water with the turbulence underneath; though
the surface looked sluggish, the water below rushed through, cold and strong,
carrying the power of the river from beyond the walls. I had underestimated
the strength of the current on this side of the gate. From a boat, or from
the shore, the river seemed barely to move as it trailed into the city.

The hum of guards' voices inside the tower, possibly still complaining
about the false roster, reached me. But no one came to the window, and
there was no movement from the guard on the other side of the water. I
reached the gate and clenched cold fingers around the wide metal bars and
chain links. The current buffeted me backward, flattening me out and bubbling around my face.

Steeling myself, calming my breathing, I filled my lungs, tucked my head
down, and dove. I kicked hard, fighting against the current to claw down
the gate like an upside-down ladder. Even with my eyes open it was too
dark to see anything. My lungs burned and my arms weakened quickly. I
struggled, flailing. I was going to have to give up; I'd never make it below.
I hadn't raised the gate enough. I'd failed.

Just as my shaking right arm lost the last of its strength, my scrambling fingers wrapped around a different type of bar: a solid, long one. A spike. Hope triggered a new burst of energy and I thrust myself under the bottom of the gate. For a moment I floundered, stuck halfway, tightness spreading from my chest to my throat and face until it felt like my head was going to explode. Then with one last frantic wriggle, I passed under. Now, instead of pulling me away, the water buffeted me against the grate. I scrambled hard, head spinning. The dark water seemed to stretch on forever.

Finally my head broke the surface, and I sucked in burning air that hurt going in almost as much as *not* breathing. Gulping, forehead pressed against the bars, water slurping in and out of my open mouth, I hung there, steadying myself with desperate, grateful breaths.

The river slapped and bubbled through the gate, ferociously loud. Light from the top of the tower spilled over the ramparts and lit part of the wall, but left the river inky dark. Lights flickered from afar on the east shore: a small encampment of rebels, guarding the south wall of the upper city. The opposite shore was an endless field of black. I eased my way west, toward the lower city, with numb hands and a thumping heart, watching the lights. If anyone saw me now, friend or foe, they would shoot to kill.

The moon was still shielded by clouds. With another deep breath, I pushed off the grate, half swimming, half scrambling against the slick wall until the water turned thicker. My toes brushed mud. A surge of relief propelled me out of the last of the current and up to my ankles in the gooey riverbed. I scanned the shores again, searching for movement. Though my impulse was to get out of the water and onto dry land, I stood the least chance of being seen while in the water, for the moment, at least.

The current still worked against me, but in these shallower parts of the river it was possible to walk against it. Moving along the bank at a crouch, progress seemed glacial, but speed could wait until I was safer. So I swam-crawled, counting steps like my brother to avoid obsessing about what came next. Once, something cold brushed against my thigh, causing an involuntary gasp and a mouthful of water. Another time, the clouds masking the moon shifted and everything around me was so clearly illuminated that it was necessary to submerge completely and trawl under the water, surfacing only to breathe, until the clouds moved again and the light dimmed.

Eventually, at a decent distance from the lower city walls, I pulled up on the rocky embankment and slipped out. The air on my soaked, exhausted limbs felt icy, though it wasn't a cold night. I moved silently through the medley of plants and rocks on the bank until I found a suitable pile of boulders and slipped in between them. Panting, I rested my back on the stone to recover my breath.

I fumbled open the packet on my back and found with a warm rush of relief that the greased leather had done its job. Though the towel was a little damp, everything underneath seemed dry. I could have wept as I rubbed my limbs free of the last of the river water and donned the dry traveling clothes. My feet felt swollen and puffy in my shoes, and the clothes, pilfered from Salvea, didn't fit properly, but for those few moments, leaning against the rock with my eyes shut and my body feeling warmer at last, I had never felt so comfortable.

Okubane

DESCRIPTION: Fleshy shrub common in agricultural areas, with silvery green leaves. Leaves are toxic to oku, lutra, and other ranging beasts and humans in large doses.

SYMPTOMS: Twitching, itching skin, restless sleep from which it is difficult to wake.

PROOFING CUES: Tingling in mouth and tongue, mild bitterness. No discernible smell.

19

Jovan

Shit.

When Hadrea came back to me a few hours later, I'd assumed she had managed to find some information about Batbayer's whereabouts. I certainly hadn't anticipated the scene that greeted me.

The Doranite was tied to a chair, his mouth gagged with a colored cloth that looked suspiciously like one of Hadrea's scarves. Her stride was broad and relaxed as she approached him and lifted the wicked knife swinging from her hip, half-masked by the folds of her Silastian-style dress. She felt its weight in her hand, her expression measuring, and looked between Batbayer and me.

"Credo Jovan would like to speak to you," she said to him, gesturing casually with the knife.

I stared at her, torn between admiration that she had managed to do in hours what we had not managed in days, and frustration that she had forced us into an adversarial position with the man. I cleared my throat.

"You sell narcotics," I said, pulling up a chair in front of him. Hadrea jerked her head to the side; I took the message and set the chair behind him instead. He tried to crane his head around to follow me, but Hadrea was there, pushing his face back straight again.

"You had best keep eyes on *me*," she told him, her tone somehow all the more menacing for her lilting, seductive voice. His frame stiffened, then he nodded. *Honor-down, how much has she already scared him?* This was the Hadrea I'd seen first, the easy predator. She was a farmer. Where, and why, had she learned this side of her?

I repeated my statement. "You sell narcotics."

"Mmph."

Hadrea leaned in close to Batbayer's face, slid the knife under the scarf, against his cheek, then turned the edge into the cloth and sawed through. He spat out the rest of the scarf as she stepped back with a cold smile. Batbayer panted, craning around to look for me again. "Crazy bitch," he said, but a tremor belied his apparent rebellion.

"Credo Jovan is speaking," she told him, as though she'd not even noticed his insult.

"I don't have to say a thing," Batbayer said. His accent was faint; I guessed he'd spent most of his life in Sjon. "You untie me, do you hear? Untie me, you fucking—"

Before he finished that sentence, she drove her elbow into the center of his body. He gasped as most of the air in his lungs was forced elsewhere. I winced, half-stood, then dropped again at the look she shot me. Batbayer wheezed pitifully. The memory of Tain lying in his bed, my sister hovering by his side, drained Batbayer's spluttering of potency. I'd do what it took to get the answers to save the people I cared about, even if it meant resorting to unsavory techniques.

Hadrea smiled again. "We are short of time, Doranite. We will need some more civilized words from you."

I cleared my throat again. "You do sell narcotics, because we've got some of them, Varina and Hasan admitted you sold to them. That's against the law in this city."

He said nothing.

"Here's the thing. Keeping someone in jail at the moment is impractical. But we have excellent jobs for criminals. Clearing out the sewage system— it's not just disgusting, but dangerous, because the tunnel entrances are exposed to the outside of the walls. Wall repairs—we dangle you down on a harness and you patch weak spots in the wall. You're a target, but it's a noble job. Keeping watch on Trickster's Bridge to see if the rebels move within arrow range. . . ."

Batbayer remained silent, but his shoulders rose and the muscles in his neck tightened. I'd gambled that he led a soft life, and the more dangerous and disgusting the task he was forced into, the more it would pressure him to cooperate. I plowed on.

"But I don't *need* to have you arrested, because lucky for you, I want something you have."

"For someone who's so scornful of narcotics, you're willing to bargain to get some?" His cold trill of a laugh broke off when Hadrea stepped closer again, knife raised.

"I don't want your *product*," I said. "I want your *knowledge*."

Batbayer tightened his arms against the bonds, but she'd done an excellent job on the knots.

"I don't know how you make the narcotics. It's possible the Chancellor could have been poisoned by an ingredient we've never heard of."

That surprised him. "The Chancellor? The Chancellor was a user?"

"No," I said, stepping around to face him. "Someone poisoned him, Batbayer. And it wasn't a poison that's in any of our records. But you use chemicals I'm not familiar with, and something you use—or have come across—could have caused what happened to him."

He licked his lips, glancing between me and Hadrea. "All right," he said. "But you untie me, and you give me your word, on your honor, that no one else will find out about my . . . occupation."

"Yes," I said.

The twist of her lips showing her disappointment, Hadrea sliced the cording with a deft flick of her knife and stepped back as he stood, rubbing his wrists and glaring at her.

"Now," I said to the Doranite. "Start teaching me about drugs."

It was full dark when I left Batbayer, my eyes and hands aching from hours of note taking. I slipped back into Tain's rooms, hoping not to disturb him, the new knowledge burning in my head. Whole lists of ingredients and compounds and combinations of which Etan had known nothing, or at least nothing he had deemed worthy of teaching. Batbayer had taken me through the basics of how his merchandise was made, but there remained much more to learn. Many ingredients, he thought, were toxic. It baffled me to think about intelligent, learned people effectively paying to ingest poison for fun.

I took a seat by the bed, fumbling in the dark, accidentally knocking something down—some papers, perhaps—but Tain slept on. Kalina must have left for bed. The lamp had run low on oil and flickered unhappily, casting alternate shadows and patches of yellowish glow on Tain's puffy, sweating cheeks. He breathed easily still. I didn't trust the swell of relief I felt at that. He might sicken slower than Etan and Caslav, but unless I found the answer, his end would likely be the same.

Watching my friend sleep, suspicions clawed at the corners of my thoughts. Kalina had found Marco and Eliska in seemingly perfect health. The whole jar of figs could not have been poisoned; the poisoner *must* have been there.

Marco was from Perest-Avana, far to the west. We shared no borders and had no quarrel with that distant country. We'd never identified an interest it could have in this conflict. And Marco had lived here close to two decades; had he been an agent of another power all along? Hard to reconcile with a man who had worked so tirelessly to help defend the city.

And Eliska had no connection to any other country that we knew of. She was born in the city. Though she had seemed broadly unsympathetic to the motives of the rebels, she had no real stakes in the estate business. No reason to hate us, no quarrel with Caslav.

Even all that aside, I had always trusted my instincts when it came to judging people, and neither the Warrior-Guilder nor the Stone-Guilder seemed dishonest or secretive.

Which only told me how flawed my instincts must be.

I shook my head and pulled out the new notes. Half of the compounds listed there I'd never heard of. Apparently a lot of wealthy Silastians now indulged in "black pot," the steam from a combination of imported dried herbs heated in an iron kettle like tea and inhaled, which Batbayer said was wildly popular in Perest-Avana. "Mist," the powder we'd caught Varina with, was derived using a combination of complex chemical reactions and then snorted up the nose, which could not sound more revolting. And there were three other ingestible products Batbayer sold that were made from mildly toxic plants and minerals. I made notes on top of notes in the flickering light, marking where further research or duplicating a test or production was required. My head drooped and my concentration lagged. But sleep was an indulgence for which there was no time.

Eventually I snuffed the lamp and moved to Tain's outer chambers. If he woke or became distressed the sound would reach me, and it had superior light for my work. I'd moved most of our books and supplies to the Manor after we'd taken billets in, unwilling to trust their safety to strangers. Everything we'd saved from the library at the school was piled up in a room down the hall. It didn't take me long to track down some relevant references, and settling myself down close to the entryway to Tain's bedroom, surrounded by books and notes, I felt almost calm. This was what I had been born to do.

I worked for hours, through almost all the oil in the lamp, searching for anything that might have been our poison. Though there were plenty of gaps to be filled in with my own experiments, I could look up quite a few ingredients on their own. At some point I considered finding Kalina to help with the research, but quashed the selfish thought. If my sister had managed to find enough peace to get some sleep, I shouldn't interfere. We'd need all our strength in the coming days.

Turning the next page with a sigh, I leaned back over my notes.

In the harsh light of morning, my last desperate plan seemed foolish. The chances of finding the poison among narcotics ingredients were beyond remote. I blinked, bleary-eyed, at the pages in front of me. The poison wasn't here. There were still ingredients to combine and experiments to conduct, but the optimism that had driven me yesterday had seeped out through the night, along with my energy.

And yet I persevered, because what else was there to do?

I startled at a soft cough. Hadrea hovered behind me. She wore yesterday's dress, though it had slumped and crinkled between the ties; she must have slept in it. Her skin looked brittle and the smattering of freckles stood out across her cheeks and nose.

Still, she was utterly lovely.

"Did you sleep?" she asked.

I shrugged. "No time."

"Did you find anything?"

I swallowed my disappointment and shame and gestured to the books. "No. There are some poisons here, but nothing like what's happening to Tain. The things people do voluntarily! This stuff they breathe the smoke of—black pot—even has feverhead in it. It'll kill them if they keep smoking it."

"What is feverhead?"

"It's a toxic water weed." It resembled a safe cousin often used to wrap fish cakes and ground nut paste, so the city had attempted to eradicate feverhead years ago to prevent accidental poisonings—though, as I knew from my visit to the Manor garden, it still crept up here and there. Batbayer had used a different name for it than the common name by which it was known here, but I'd matched his description. "It's not the poison, though. The symptoms are totally different, and it's only fatal through repeated use."

"What does it do?"

"It causes hallucinations, and it sort of coats your insides, stops you from absorbing the nutrients from food and air. People used to chew it for 'visions' and then basically starve."

Frowning, she pulled one of my open books toward her. "This is it?"

The illustration, in excellent penwork and glossy colored ink, showed the fleshy little plant with its broad leaves.

"I know this," she said with a nod. "We call it *babacash*. Some of the elders use it, especially out in the west. It is said to aid in the use of *fresken*. They use it to connect to the spirits in the land."

"But it's definitely not the poison. It almost does the opposite. . . ."

I trailed off, staring down at the picture. Something nagged at me, a thought caught on a rusty nail.

"What is it?" Hadrea asked, but I barely heard her.

The poison was damaging Tain's internal organs, corroding his body from the inside. Feverhead *slowed* absorption. It would overstimulate Tain's mind, and possibly cause him long-term problems, but would it also slow down and interfere with the absorption of the poison, allowing his body the time he needed to fight it off gradually?

My mouth went dry.

I'd been looking for the poison in these drugs and ingredients. What I might have found was a treatment.

"Shit. *Shit.*" I scrambled to my feet.

"What is it?" Hadrea asked again, touching my arm.

"The garden."

I hurtled through the corridors of the Manor, my mind racing. Feverhead growing in the Manor garden—a toxic weed? In an enclosed, glass-walled garden, protected from winds that might carry foreign seeds inside? How had it gotten there?

What if it was there because the poisoner had needed an antidote readily available—or a preventative? Something that blocked absorption could possibly guard against the effects of the poison—and wanted it accessible somewhere that couldn't be traced back to them? They'd need an antidote if, for example, they had to handle the poison while eating with the Chancellor and might risk getting some in their own food. . . .

The garden lay dark and quiet behind its glass walls, the morning sun not yet lightening the sky enough to illuminate the garden and the lamps cold and cobwebbed. But I had been here only yesterday—Was it yesterday? The days seemed to blur together—and I knew exactly where the feverhead lay piled with the other weeds I'd removed. I only hoped the plant didn't need to be fresh to have proper effect.

Feverhead had distinctive, plump leaves I identified by feel. My hands shook as I gathered up as many of the plants as possible. I turned to go, then another thought struck me, and I scooped a few handfuls of rich dirt from a nearby patch and cradled it using the folds of my clothes. If this worked, Tain might need a decent supply of the stuff, and the plants might recover if planted again.

I must have looked an odd sight, running through the Manor with dirt and weeds held in my tunic like a swaddled baby. Optimism surged through me even as the cynical part of my brain catalogued the ways my theory could be wrong. I could just be adding to Tain's discomfort in his last hours or, worse, sabotaging his body's ability to fight the poison. Or I could be right, but too slow; perhaps the poison had already done too much damage.

Hadrea looked up as I came into the bedroom. "He breathes still," she said. "But he has not woken."

I stuck a few of the plants in the cup of water by the edge of the bed and tipped the dirt and remaining plants in a pile on the dresser. I felt my friend's forehead. "Tain?" I said. "Tain, you need to wake up now."

No response.

I shook his shoulder, gently at first and then more insistently as his head lolled around but his eyes remained closed. Panic rose inside me. "Tain, come on!" I couldn't force an unconscious person to swallow. "Tain!"

His eyelids fluttered, then opened. I squeezed his hand, trying to convey confidence. "There's something you need to try, all right?"

He stared at me, eyes unfocused. His lips worked, but nothing came out.

I broke a wilted leaf off one of the plants. "You need to chew this," I told him. "Do you understand?"

He blinked, and my breath caught in my throat. Was he still there? Then, slowly, he opened his mouth. I pushed the leaf in, crouching beside the bed as he chewed. His jaw worked while we watched. Each movement seemed to take an eternity. "Swallow when you can."

Once he had swallowed the first leaf, I gave him another. Then another. We repeated it with five leaves, until his chewing grew too weak and he fell back asleep—or unconscious. I let him have the break.

The burst of energy that had come over me drained away, and I once again felt like . . . well, like a man who hadn't slept. A warm hand slipped into mine. Hadrea, perched on the stool, smiled down at me. Confused but pleased by the sudden gesture, I wound her fingers through mine and rested my head against her hip.

We waited.

Sitting in silence, I thought of my first poisoning. The fears of a seven-year-old boy played over me. Not knowing what was happening, not knowing when, or if, things would ever improve. Hadrea stayed with me, quiet and oddly calming.

The first sign of change was a cough. The sudden spasm of Tain's chest made Hadrea and me jump. He spat out some yellowish gunk, then flopped back onto the bed. I wiped up the gunk and checked his pulse. "A little faster than earlier." I noted it in my book. His breathing hadn't changed over the course of the morning. It was hard to tell whether the feverhead was having any effect, but at least he hadn't deteriorated.

I checked his temperature. "Tain?" No response. But increasing movement was apparent behind his eyelids. Etan and Caslav hadn't appeared to dream during their periods of unconsciousness. I felt his forehead again. Was it my imagination, or did his skin feel a touch cooler? *Don't get your hopes up.*

But over the course of the next few hours, they rose all the same. Tain wasn't getting worse. His color looked fractionally better, and his breathing seemed strong. He didn't wake, but his eyes raced around behind the lids, and sometimes his body twitched or his lips moved as he dreamed.

When the morning sun had reached the foot of Tain's bed, Hadrea startled me, breaking our vigil. "If he gets better, what happens now?"

"What do you mean?"

She gestured at Tain. "Last night, every breath seemed shallower than the last. Now he is almost relaxed. Your feverhead seems to have at least stopped the effects of the poison. Would he not be dead by now, otherwise? Or close to?"

I hadn't wanted to give voice to my hope, but found myself nodding, a smile creeping over my face. "I think so. There may still be too much damage for him to recover. But the poison seems to have stopped attacking him."

"Well, then. Someone poisoned him, yes? Do you know who?"

My hope froze over with that grim reminder. Knowing about the antidote, it no longer seemed reckless for the traitor to have so boldly risked poisoning food in front of us. Either Marco or Eliska—or even both—had to be our enemy. I felt sick. Both presented loyal faces, and both had been trusted with the city's safety in their own way. But one of their faces was nothing more than the mask of our enemy.

"Eliska or Marco." It burned to say it aloud.

"Will you accuse them directly?"

We *could* arrest both, then sort out later who the traitor was. They couldn't do any damage from a cell. But could we learn something by letting them continue to think we trusted them? They hadn't resorted to outright attack on Tain, so they must still believe there was a benefit in poison over something more direct. They must still believe us ignorant of Caslav's true fate.

"They think Tain's poisoned." I glanced over at his prone, twitching form. Was there an advantage we could gain here? If nothing else, could we learn what the traitor had planned to do once Tain was dead? "If days pass and no one sees him, the traitor will think he's dead and we're covering it up. Let them believe that."

A sudden thought sprang up. "Where's Kalina?" It was past midmorning. I'd have expected my sister here as soon as she woke, but I had been too distracted to wonder at her absence.

"Perhaps she overslept? She was exhausted."

"Perhaps." More likely she was staying away, fearing what she'd find when she returned. "I might go find her. Can you stay with Tain?"

I searched the closest rooms, thinking to find her sleeping close by. When that proved fruitless, I stopped by Argo, who told me my sister had left the Manor late yesterday evening.

"How is the Chancellor?" he asked, his words spaced too far apart, like he didn't want to ask the question.

I gave him a wan smile. "Hanging on." Best not to impart my possibly false hope on anyone else for now. "We can only hope the fortunes favor us."

The doorkeep nodded, solemn, and I headed out of the grounds and down to our apartments.

But my sister wasn't there, either. The bed coverings were cool and the pallet flat. If she'd slept there last night, she'd been up for a while. If she'd decided not to come to the Manor, it was because she had needed the space to come to terms with what she must have thought would be Tain's death. As her brother it was my responsibility to protect her, but she needed to choose her own way of dealing with things sometimes.

I left a short note on her bed, in case she came back there in the meantime. When she felt strong enough, hopefully she would return to good news.

My own footsteps slowed, though, as I returned. Optimism and realism battled inside my head—one part of my brain constructing images of Tain healthy, the other seeing his lifeless form. No matter how I counted my steps or the clenches of my fists, the overlapping images and ideas swamped me. Pushing down the nausea and trying to suppress my imagination, I nodded to Argo and returned to my friend's rooms.

"Jov?"

Relief drenched me as I stepped inside. Hadrea beamed at me from the stool by the bed, one hand gently wiping Tain's forehead. Tain was propped up on pillows, eyes open, looking at me.

"You're awake!" I raced over, scanning his pallor and the puffiness of his lips.

"Why're you here?" he asked me, eyes wide. "I thought you were in the mountains."

I turned, confused, as his dark gaze fixed on a spot behind my left shoulder. Nothing there.

"Tain, there's . . ." I caught Hadrea's glance, and she touched her temple, eyes flicking over to Tain. *The hallucinations.* "There's no need to worry," I said instead. "You need to eat some more of this. It's helping."

Hadrea had planted the remaining feverhead plants in a ceramic cup, and Tain let me put another wilted leaf in his mouth, but a few passive chews in he started thrashing about and spat out the leaf. "Get away!" he yelled. "Get them off me!" He swatted at his own body, face twisted in terror, but his own weakness defeated him, and he panted and flailed helplessly. We had to restrain him while he sobbed and rolled. When he finally settled, only half-conscious, Hadrea squeezed my hand.

We coaxed him into eating another few leaves, and waited.

The hallucinations presented us with challenges over the next few hours; it was in parts heartbreaking trying to calm his distress and absurd to see him giggle childishly at things that were not there. But even as I worried how the feverhead was affecting his brain, hope built inside me about his body's recovery. His temperature continued to cool and steady, and though he coughed up phlegm from his lungs, I grew surer that the feverhead had stopped the effects of the poison from spreading.

"I think it's up to his body now," I told Hadrea after he had slumped back into sleep following another bout of babbling and thrashing. "There was only limited poison in his system and it's stopped attacking him. It'll just depend on if he's strong enough to recover from the damage already done."

Hadrea brushed her hand over the leftover stems of feverhead in the cup. "Is this all of it?" There was a strange intensity about her gaze on the wilted plants.

"We shouldn't need any more. He'll either make it or . . ."

She slipped her arm across my shoulder. "He is strong. Young and healthy. He will defeat this."

I leaned into the warmth of her. "I think you're right." I slipped my fingers through Hadrea's, grinning up at her, and found my own happiness reflected in her face. Though drawn with tiredness and strain, she had never seemed more beautiful.

Seized by the moment, I stretched up and kissed her.

It started out almost platonic, a shared moment of joy. It didn't stay that way for long.

Hadrea responded with a hunger that surprised me. She returned the kiss, winding her fingers in the back of my hair. In a haze of dizzying warmth I staggered to my feet, pulling her close against me. I couldn't think. Sensations flooded me: the faint saltiness of her skin, the spring of her hair against my cheek, her smooth, strong back beneath my palms, the soft pressure of her breasts against my chest.

"Wait," I said, breaking the kiss and holding her by the hips, a safer distance from me. "Tain . . ."

Her eyes were almost black as she took my hands in hers. Looking at her made me hurt, like there was too much air in my lungs and too much blood in the skin of my face. "He is sleeping," she said. "Let him rest for a while."

Then she moved my hands around to the curve of her backside and stepped back into my arms.

Driven by desire and relief and fortunes knew what else, we stumbled backward out of Tain's bedchamber and into the sitting room, our steps clumsy as we worked our way over to the window seat. She pushed me against it, coming down on top of me. We got half-caught in the drapery, and she laughed. The feel of her smile through her kisses was intoxicating. Her bare legs straddled me and it felt like the most natural thing in the world, even as part of me recognized the strangeness of this moment. But perhaps for the first time ever, I shut off my brain and gave in to the feeling of her.

She lay in my arms for a time afterward, her long, beautiful body tangled limb around limb, her hair spread over my chest and her head resting in the curve of my shoulder. I stared up at the ceiling. One part of me reveled in what we had just shared; another stirred yet with desire. But guilt twisted inside me as well, a cold coil of doubt for abandoning my post at Tain's side, for indulging in something purely selfish when my friend battled for his life.

Her breath tickled my chest as she sighed, and when she tilted her chin and looked up at me through her lashes, I saw no conflict in her face. She stretched, grunted, and pushed away from me, shifting awkwardly.

"You wonder why I make fun of your clothing," she told me, her voice a touch throatier than usual, laced with a purr of satisfaction. "These knots, they are not meant for lying on."

We had come together in such a flurry, the limit of our undressing had been to crumple her dress and my tunic up around our waists. Now that she mentioned it, I, too, felt the uncomfortable pressure of the knot of my cording against my back. I helped her sit up, though part of me was disappointed at the loss of the sensation of her body against mine. That disappointment surprised me. I had never before been able to sleep comfortably with another person, unable to properly rest with the asymmetrical body contact. Yet despite the awkward position we had lain in, I'd felt no compulsion to extract myself.

"Unwrapping of the cords is part of the experience," I said. "It can be romantic. You can make a dance of it."

She laughed. "Well, let us do this in reverse. Help me?"

She stood, graceful, and offered the knot in the small of her back to me. Trying not to be distracted by the sight of her long, naked legs and the half-visible curve of her backside, I untied the knot and unwound the red cord from around her waist and chest. The dress fell back down around her like a nightgown, but I could still see the shape of her through the soft fabric. I helped her rewrap and tie the cording, counting in my head to try to suppress my reaction to even the brushes of contact.

Hadrea appeared to suffer no such affliction. She stretched, ran her fingers through her hair, and looked me over with an indulgent smile. She tugged my tunic back into place and took my hand. "We should check on the Chancellor."

We found him still asleep, but restless again, mumbling and shaking. I checked and noted his signs again; his temperature felt almost normal. In our haste we had knocked over the chair by the bed, so I bent to pick it up, and noticed then something under the bed—a small stack of papers, partially concealed by the overhanging bedding.

"What is that?" Hadrea asked as I picked it up.

"Notes on some things to offer the rebels. Ideas for reparations, that sort of thing." I smiled; Kalina had worked on this, thinking it was futile—I couldn't wait to show her the truth. I set the papers down, then noticed markings on the reverse side of one page. It took my brain a few moments to register what I was looking at. Tiny lines and dots in rows, familiar yet unfamiliar; Etan's code.

"You know I cannot read," Hadrea said, peering over my shoulder. "But that does not look like your writing."

"It's not," I said, and my voice came out so cold and distant it was like it came from another person. "It's my sister's."

Bloodroot

DESCRIPTION: Root tuber with attractive bright green foliage similar to other edible tuber vegetables; the leaves and stems are mildly toxic and the enlarged tuber is dark reddish-brown and poisonous.

SYMPTOMS: Intense stomach pain, repeated vomiting, exhaustion.

PROOFING CUES: Will discolor other food products; unpleasant strong, mealy taste.

20

Kalina

Breath burning in my tight lungs, I stumbled off the edge of the road and into the shelter of another collection of rocks. I rested against the scratchy lichen, legs too weak to lower myself to the ground. Dawn cast a pale pink-gold sheen over the plains and glinted on the distant river, giving everything an ethereal glow. I couldn't appreciate a moment of it. The plains had become my enemy.

I had worked so hard over the past year to strengthen my lungs. Though my illnesses would always be part of me, I had swum and climbed and run the tournament courses, and improved my fitness and strength as much as was physically possible. But it counted for nothing. I couldn't run to the army. I couldn't even run for a single night. My pace had slowed to a jog and then a walk and eventually a stumble. My breath came in short gasps and my legs ached. The journey to the mining outpost in the southern mountains took three days by boat, upstream, in good conditions. By foot, even running the whole way, I couldn't imagine getting to the army in less than a week. Maybe too late to save the city.

I had found the south road in the dark, more by chance than design, and by that stage the uneven ground, dotted with rocks and twisted, tough bushes, had given me enough grief to bear the risk and take the road instead. I had seen no one on my desperate journey. But my risk of exposure rose with the sun. On the other hand, going cross-country made it easier to lose my way and lose more time, not to mention turn an ankle or trip. In any case, the Maiso limited any serious cover. I peered over the rocky outcrop, searching the distance for signs of movement. Nothing.

Or was there? Up ahead, just where the road twisted, there was movement— a tiny flutter. I ducked back behind the rock, heart thudding again.

The rocks provided no proper shelter. If someone approached from up the road, I would have to shift around to stay out of sight. With still-shaking legs and sweaty palms, I braved another look over the rocks, this time from a different position.

And then I almost laughed. From this angle the edge of a pole was visible; I'd been frightened by a road marker. The relief flooding my senses gave me new energy, and with a small sip of water from my flask, I continued up the road.

The flag blew away from me in the wind, so I was almost upon it before the symbol was apparent. Even then, gazing up, I furrowed my brow. A white flag struck in the center with a raggedy black mark, like a dark, gaping mouth. The symbol for plague, instantly recognizable anywhere in the world. Had the villages ahead been struck by plague?

It took my exhausted brain some time to understand. We'd wondered how our other cities had been cut off, how someone, anyone, had not seen the siege and sent word to the army, either out of loyalty, charity, or a hope of reward. Here was the answer. The rebels had marked out the roads and spread word of a plague in the city, to delay any potential travelers and prevent outsiders learning about the siege. No wonder there had been no help for the city from any front. Plague signs would keep any visitors far enough from the capital that they wouldn't see the besieging army; they might even deter our own army from returning. Honor-down, even if we somehow came through this thing, it would take months to convince the world the city was safe again. Our trade interests would be crippled. Perhaps our enemies had thought of that, too, as a secondary way of striking at the city if the siege failed.

Well, fail it would not, if I didn't get word to Aven. My legs might ache and my lungs might weaken, but what would that matter if my home and everything I loved was destroyed?

Green Bend, more a hamlet than a real village, sprang into sight around midmorning. Panting, I hobbled off the road and found a protected vantage point among the prickly glibflowers to survey the route ahead. By wagon, Green Bend took half a day. The pace encouraged me, although I'd never be able to sustain it.

It seemed there were only half a dozen people in the hamlet: a few children playing in the square with a woven cane ball, an elderly woman outside a hut, head bent over her sewing, and one or two people working the field at the far side. Many of the crofts appeared deserted. Presumably everyone able-bodied had joined the siege. Still, giving the place a wide berth should avoid detection.

But just as I was about to move on, something caught my attention. At the close end of the field, behind a thick hedge, was the wide back of an oku. The big animal grazed there untended, its thick neck bent low as it ate. There must have been something wrong with it; surely the army would have taken all the useful animals. Yet my protesting legs twinged, jabbing at me, and I bit my lip, watching as the animal moved about. Circling dangerously close to the hamlet, I came down the slope. My heart hammered as I approached the thorny hedge and the sensible part of my brain screamed a warning. I'd barely started the journey, and yet already risked detection. My legs moved as if by their own volition until I could peer over the dense, spiky bush to get a proper look.

The oku looked fine. It walked about as it ate, its powerful legs showing no signs of injury. But an animal, even a healthy, easy-to-handle one like an oku, was no good to me on its own. I shuffled along behind the hedge, keeping a look out for any of the villagers, moving toward the rough shelter at the east end of the field. Sweat ran down the back of my neck, under my clothes, like a slimy finger of dread. The gate was in plain sight of at least three buildings, any of which could be occupied. The faint cries and laughter of the children playing were audible. I dropped low and crept around to the east side of the hedge.

For the first few steps the back of a building blocked me from the rest of the village. But it meant crossing into the open to reach the gate—three or four steps of exposure. I took a breath and scurried across toward the gate, mouth dry.

I saw no one in the string of buildings as I fumbled for the latch on the gate. A surge of optimism sped my fingers and I slipped through the gate and around the hedge. Sharp twigs tickled my back as I waited, eyes screwed shut, expecting a cry of alarm, the sound of approach. . . .

Nothing.

I opened my eyes. At the other side of the field, the big, shaggy beast regarded me solemnly. A bird chirped from the hedge. Children still laughed and shrieked in the distance. No other sounds marred the warm morning. The blue of the sky set off the green hedges and the speckled, flowering fields in the distance. Could I be so lucky?

Perhaps the fortunes did favor me today, because the rough shelter in the corner of the field housed a light wagon—not a proper passenger vehicle, but a cane cart for transporting supplies around the farms. I knew enough about animals to know oku weren't suitable for riding, but they'd happily pull a cart. A leather harness hung at the back of the shelter. *Perfect.* I approached the oku and, conscious of my unfamiliarity with animals, held out one hand in a hopefully nonthreatening manner.

The animal glanced up, liquid eyes huge in its wide face, and to my relief it stood still and allowed me to place the harness over its shoulders and back with shaking hands. The oku followed me, placid, all the way to the edge of the field, and held still as I dragged the cart over. It clipped easily to the harness, and the oku shrugged and shifted until it settled into place. When it came to getting out of the field, though, my heart started hammering again and my fingers trembled on the harness. I opened the gate, wincing at the squeak even though it was barely audible over the wind, and then led the animal through, blood pounding in my head.

Still, my luck held. No cry of alarm sounded. I led the oku around the corner of the hedge, back to the unexposed side of the town, and let out my breath, sick with relief.

And then I saw him.

Standing at the far corner of the hedge, an elderly man was propped on a stick, staring directly at me. My hand fell from the oku and my insides clenched, but my feet somehow stuck in place. I couldn't breathe.

We stared at each other for a long moment—I couldn't have said how long, because it felt like a slow torture as the world closed in around me—before he slowly walked toward me. *Run,* I told myself. *Forget the oku.* But my stubborn, tired legs just stayed there as if someone else controlled them. I could outrun an old man, but he'd only have to send someone after me. *It's over either way.*

He stopped close enough that the patchwork of puffs and wrinkles covering his face and the slumps of skin on his neck were visible. His eyes glittered, wide and deep. He was all one color: skin, eyes, and hair the same tawny brown. Darfri charms, worn with age, dangled from the crinkles of his neck. I opened my mouth to say something. Anything, any lie, something to disguise my theft of the oku and my flight from the city.

The man's lips tightened as he looked me over. I must have been a sight, with ill-fitting clothes, snarled hair, and terror on my sweat-slicked face. The stick he held was not a walking stick but a scythe, with the blade facing down, hidden as he approached. He lifted it, and the morning sun caught the glint of wicked, curved metal. The flash sent a jab of terror inside me so strong it felt like he'd struck me with it.

For a few more heartbeats we regarded each other. Then, slowly, the man lowered the scythe. His gaze followed it to the ground. At last, I found my legs, backing away outside the reach of the tool. He looked up again and this time there was sadness and pity in his old face. Then, with deliberate gentleness, the man turned and walked in the opposite direction.

I hesitated, looking at his retreating back and then at the cart. Waves of relief drowned my thinking. Why was he letting me go? He wasn't raising the alarm, and he hadn't even taken the oku. I didn't understand. *You don't have to understand. Just go!*

I snatched up the oku's reins and clucked her along. "Come on," I whispered as it followed me. "Come on, girl. We need to get out of here." Still the old man walked, not even glancing back over his shoulder. The oku finally took my frantic cues and picked up its pace to a heavy trot; the cart jolted along behind us on the uneven ground as we headed up the southwest slope. As the gradient steepened the oku slowed, then stopped altogether when we reached the top. It dropped its head and seized a mouthful of a thick, fleshy plant. Little yellow flowers got caught on the beast's hairy lips as it munched, ignoring my pleas. I glanced back down the slope toward Green Bend.

The old man stood at the edge of the field, watching me, still as the hedge behind him. Not knowing quite what to think or do, I raised a hand, still shaking, in something of a wave. After a moment, the man inclined his head, then turned away, carrying his scythe, back to his work.

Geraslin ink

DESCRIPTION: Formerly popular ink made in part from charcoal and nuts of the hardy geras tree. Fumes released from ink reacting with air and light over time are toxic in poorly ventilated areas.

SYMPTOMS: Light-headedness, confusion, tiredness, loss of balance.

PROOFING CUES: Distinctive pleasant, musty smell indicates the gas is still active.

21

Jovan

Anger and fear swamped me. Making my way to the south river gate, all I could think about, all that played over and over in my head, were images of my sister meeting one of a dozen horrible fates. Drowned in the river—with her weak lungs, how could she have hoped to make it under the gate? Picked off by an arrow from the other side, or ours. Caught on foot and given the same treatment as our original runners. That was the worst image, the one that made my stomach rise up into my throat. Kalina's head in a sack, burying her wrapped in anonymous cloth like the remains of our messengers. Perhaps Hadrea's beliefs were rubbing off on me, because now the idea of my sister losing safe passage to the afterlife kept spinning through my head.

And through all my questioning of the guards there, my head rang with the worst emotion of all—crippling, bone-deep guilt. I had failed her. The one person I was always supposed to protect. My absorption with the poisoning had obscured the warning signs. She had been desperate with grief for Tain, whom she had loved since childhood, and instead of giving her comfort or even attention, all I had done was allocate her tasks like a servant and gone off to solve my problem, oblivious to her pain like the emotionless fool our peers had often accused me of being. I knew how important it was to her to feel visible, yet I had disregarded her, not valued her enough.

Now my sister was almost certainly dead, and I could never, ever forgive myself.

No one had seen Kalina; at least no one from our side had shot her in the water by accident. But even if she somehow hadn't drowned—and there flashed another terrible image of her caught skewered beneath the river gate, body flapping in the current, hair streaming out like a cloud—chances were she'd been spotted and killed or captured by the rebels on the shore.

She must have been so frightened. My fury at myself surged even higher. *Her head in a sack, and it's my fault.*

But another colder part of me whispered blame somewhere else, as well. Not just my fault, but Tain's, too. Marco and I had argued repeatedly that we should send more runners, especially after the lower city had fallen, but Tain, burned by our first attempt, had continued to refuse. He had disregarded Kalina's plan even though it would have been sound if a strong swimmer and runner had executed it. I'd thought him motivated by compassion and, though I had disagreed, had respected his principles. Now it just seemed like weakness, a desire to protect himself from the responsibility of terrible deaths. Hadn't he always tried to avoid responsibility? Wasn't that, too, the reason he was lying deathly injured, when listening to me would have prevented that?

The guilt and anger inside me twisted me tighter and tighter, until I felt like a walking trap, waiting to burst. The two people I most wanted to shake and rail at, I couldn't. One was lost to me, probably forever, and the other . . . well, I was reasonably sure honor did not permit an attack, even verbal, on an unconscious, deathly ill Chancellor.

I stopped outside Tain's room, hearing voices. Suspicion flooded me and I listened outside the doorway.

"What did you play?" Hadrea's voice.

"Um . . . I dunno." Davior's high voice. The suspicion drained away, leaving me feeling tired and old. Hadrea could hardly have kept this from her mother, and despite the risks, I trusted them. In any case, I would need the extra set of eyes Salvea could provide. I tried to suppress the painful thoughts of the utterly trustworthy set I had just lost.

"Was it a new game, that you had not played before?"

"*Mmm* . . . No. I was catched. And some baddies. I got the prize!"

I walked in. Davi sat on his sister's knee by Tain's bed, his little round head leaning back against her shoulder as he looked up at her. He smiled when he saw me and I smiled back, but it felt wooden. Salvea stood on the other side of Tain's bed, daubing his forehead with a cloth.

"My mother is good like this," Hadrea said to me, tone hesitant.

"We'll appreciate the help," I told her, trying to warm my tone. Like throwing a blanket on an icy lake, but it was the best I could do in the circumstances. "Could you stay with him awhile?"

"Of course." Salvea reached out a hand as if to touch me, then dropped it away. "He is a strong young man. The spirits will not have him yet."

I nodded, stiff.

Without asking, Hadrea set her brother down and followed me from Tain's room. I told her what had happened at the gate tower.

"Your sister is so brave," Hadrea said at the end, her tone admiring. I stared, unsure I'd heard correctly.

"No, she's not," I said. "You don't even know her. Kalina's not brave. And she's not strong. She would have been so frightened. She's probably dead, and she would have been so *frightened*." My voice caught in my throat and I turned away, blinking furiously.

She snorted, disbelieving. "How can you say she is not brave? Doing this thing . . . If she was not frightened, it would not have been brave to do it. You say she is not strong, but she was strong enough to risk her life for those she loved! That *is* courage."

Even as some part of me recognized she was right, the other, tightly wound part, the part that wanted to lash out, won the day. "She made a stupid, impulsive decision, and I wasn't there to stop her." My voice climbed. "I didn't watch out for her. And I was, *we were* . . . doing what we did this morning, while my sister was probably lying dead in the mud somewhere."

She reeled as if I'd slapped her. "I do not regret this morning," she told me, her voice dropping as much as mine had risen.

"Well, I do."

Without a word, she pivoted angrily and walked off in the direction in which we'd come. I opened my mouth to call her back, to explain, but no words came out. The truth was I *had* meant it. If I had thought of my family instead of myself, Kalina would never have made the attempt. I hadn't deserved the pleasure and contentment I'd found with Hadrea today, and would never be able to enjoy it again. It was for the best that she knew that.

Having wounded the one remaining person who mattered, I might as well turn my bitter attentions to someone who deserved them. Feeling hollow, I left the Manor in search of a poisoner.

I found Marco first, and had a few moments to observe him, unseen. He was in our new training hall—formerly a theater—directing an Order Guard and several others who had shown aptitude and had been designated as training supervisors. Hovering in the shadows of what had been the wings, I searched for signs of something, anything, to confirm or deny my suspicions.

He looked agitated. Although he spoke patiently and politely, his relentless pacing about on the stage reminded me of myself. *Anxious to know if his poison worked?*

I stepped out.

"Credo Jovan!" Unmistakable relief at the sight of me. "Bosco, Garaya, please carry on without me." He put a hand on my shoulder and steered me back into the wings. "I've been worried." I tried to relax the tension in my back and shoulders.

"Why were you worried?" I asked as we stopped in a back room of the theater. I propped myself against a set of crates, casually checking for exits. Being in a poorly lit, cramped space with him didn't seem wise.

He gave the room no such consideration, sitting on the crate next to me with a heavy sigh. "I've been trying to find you and the Chancellor since yesterday, Credo," he said. "I've left word with your messengers and went to the Manor a dozen times. Every time they said the Chancellor was out somewhere and they had not seen you. It was like you'd vanished after I saw you yesterday morning."

I shifted, uncomfortable. I'd forgotten about the messengers. I'd have to find some way of dealing with them. "We haven't vanished," I said. "I had a headache yesterday and stayed indoors. I must have forgotten to pass that on to a messenger."

He nodded, but his brow furrowed. "And the Chancellor? I met with him yesterday and we talked about how we might try again to destroy Trickster's Bridge. He was going to meet me by the lake at dusk, but he never came."

"I saw Tain this morning. He wasn't in high spirits." *That's true enough.* "He needed a break from the Council and meetings and everyone pulling him in every direction."

A pause. Marco leaned forward, staring at me. Then he shook his head. "I am sorry, Credo Jovan. But I do not believe that."

"What do you mean?" I readied my legs. I was closer to the door than him, but would need the element of surprise to outrun my much more athletic opponent. "You don't believe what?"

He sighed. "Chancellor Tain would not avoid his advisers and friends because he needed a break, Credo Jovan. He is honorable and bound by duty. He would not decide to avoid people on a whim. And a headache? You look more like a person to whom something terrible and grievous has happened. Please, tell me what is the matter with you both."

I rubbed my hands together, stalling. Innocent or guilty, he already knew something was going on. So I gambled. "I don't know how to tell you this. The Chancellor, he . . ." I buried my head in my hands.

"Credo? What is it?" It *sounded* like genuine alarm.

I took a shaky breath and looked him in the eye. "You must promise not to say anything. The city's a tinderbox. If they find out . . ."

"Find out what? Of course I promise. Please, Credo, you're frightening me. What's happened?"

"Tain's dead," I whispered.

Marco sucked in his breath. "What? Wh—what?"

"He fell suddenly ill yesterday, Marco. He died last night. I didn't know what to do. We thought it was some foreign disease that killed Chancellor Caslav and my Tashi, but now Tain, too? It *must* have been poison."

Marco stared at me, then at the floor. His big shoulders shook. A small noise escaped him, as though he had tried to say something and failed.

"I didn't know what to do," I said again. "If the city knows he's dead . . . I just kept thinking what it would do to morale. There are so many rumors around the city about what caused the uprising and the Council's role in it. The rest of us just aren't beloved like the Chancellor. He is—was—the only thing keeping spirits up."

"I can't believe it," Marco said at last, his voice hoarse. "I saw him in the morning. He was fine. I don't understand how this could have happened. Who would do this? What purpose does it serve? We might all be dead in days anyway."

"But do you see why we can't tell the city? If they know the Chancellor is gone they'll lose hope, and we still need to defend when the rebels attack the bridge."

Marco nodded slowly. "What about the Council?"

"I don't trust the Council. Whoever got to Tain was someone close to him. If one of them poisoned him, I don't want them to know they succeeded."

He frowned. "Credo Jovan, I understand that Council politics can be trying. And I can't pretend I haven't heard rumors, too. But surely no one on the Council would actively harm the Chancellor. This war is destroying our city. No one on the Council benefits from that. I truly believe there must be foreign agents at work in our city."

"I suppose," I said. "But all the same, I'm not willing to risk them knowing what's happened. At the very least, not all the Council would be happy to keep this secret."

"All right, then. But we will need a reason why they cannot see him when they ask." His mouth twisted in a half smile. "I am not subtle and I'm no real Councilor, Credo. I do not understand the games. If *I* was suspicious about the Chancellor avoiding me, others will be, too."

I studied Marco's face, with all its earnest openness. An honest man's face. Honor-down, he was convincing. He drew me in and made me want to trust him. The emotional part of my brain still insisted here sat a good man even if the cynic in me made an enemy out of everyone. "No more Council meetings," I said. "We'll run out of excuses. Argo at the Manor knows what happened and he can be trusted to pass on whatever messages we want to anyone who comes to the Manor. You and I can both vouch for having met with Tain."

He gripped one of my shoulders. "Thank you for trusting me with this, Credo. But is there no one else on the Council you trust?"

"Well, I thought we could trust Eliska but . . ."

"I trust her," he said. "And I think you should, Credo. The Stone-Guilder would never be involved in any plot against the Chancellor. She is an honorable woman, reliable to a fault. She has been invaluable in the defense of the city."

I shrugged. "She was alone with the Chancellor on the morning he died. I don't know how he was poisoned, but we can't discount that."

He shook his head, jaw set. "She was not the only one who saw the Chancellor that morning; not even the only Councilor. I did, too, and I hope you know I would never have harmed him. I can't believe it of Eliska, either. She must have been alone with the Chancellor dozens of times since the siege began, with any number of opportunities."

"I suppose," I said, trying to sound persuaded.

"The Scribe-Guilder, too, could surely not be involved," he added. "And the Artist-Guilder. What could Budua or Marjeta possibly gain from betraying a Council they've served on for sixty years?" He counted out on his fingers, "You, me, Eliska, Budua, Marjeta—if the five of us work together I am sure we could keep the illusion for at least a few days."

"All right." I clapped his shoulder. "Say nothing of this, and I'll talk to the others."

He nodded, his wide face earnest. "We will honor his memory, and hold the city, I swear it."

I wanted to believe that, but even if Tain recovered I didn't think we would save the city, not anymore. *But I'll catch you*, I told Marco silently. *If it's you, I'll catch you and I'll make you pay, before the end.*

If I had found Marco's performance convincing, Eliska's was equally stirring. It had taken until the evening to have a chance to get her alone to explain. Her eyes filled with tears at the news, and it took her a long time even to speak. When she did, her tone matched my heart for bleakness.

"We're lost," she said dully. "We can't hold out against that army. They're taking their time to regroup, but they know we're trapped in too little space with diminishing resources. Sooner or later they'll take the tower. We were all counting on Tain somehow getting through to them and convincing the rebels to negotiate instead of attack. Now we don't even have a leader, and there's no one from the Families we could elect who'd have the credibility to convince them anyway. No slight to your honor intended, Credo," she added hastily.

"None taken." I had neither the contacts nor the presence to be a leader, and my compulsions were too obvious and inhibiting to be under such pressure. My role had always been to support and protect. *You did a great job of that.*

Unlike Marco, Eliska seemed unconvinced by my plan to keep Tain's "death" a secret. "I don't see the point," she said, voice wooden. "But I'll go along with whatever you want."

"I need you to keep being the Stone-Guilder," I said. "You can't give up. We need your engineers and builders; if we can keep holding the rebels off we have more chance of negotiating peacefully with them."

"Fine," Eliska said. But she sounded the way I felt: empty. She volunteered no insight into whom we could trust on the Council. I had to prompt her.

"You have to be careful what you say around the other Councilors."

"Is that what it's come to?" She gave a harsh bark of a laugh. "Honordown. This city was lost before the siege even started, wasn't it?"

Sometimes I thought the exact same thing. "Maybe it was. We caused this. We created enemies of our own people through inertia and ignorance. If we'd treated our country citizens like equals instead of resources, if we hadn't treated the Darfri beliefs as unimportant superstitions, this would never have happened."

Eliska glanced at me out of the corner of her eye, and her tone changed, just a little, becoming higher and a fraction quicker. I wouldn't have noticed if I hadn't been listening for it. She rubbed the back of her neck. "Chancellor Tain was openly sympathetic to the rebels, and seeking peace. I don't see why any sympathizer would have murdered him when he'll likely be replaced by someone worse."

I nodded. "It's possible the siege and the poisoning aren't connected." I might have once regarded the Stone-Guilder as naive, but never stupid. "But where does that leave us? I still don't know who on the Council we can trust."

"If this was a political act, given who owns the estates you would be better trusting only the Guilders who aren't Credolen. Marjeta, Budua, and Marco. Although . . ."

"What?" I asked.

Her lips tightened. "I can't imagine a deceptive bone in that man's body," she said. "And I hate to even raise it. But I guess we can't ignore that he's a foreigner by birth, and a trained soldier. I suppose it's possible he might be less loyal to Sjona than he seems."

"Maybe." But we had no conflict with Perest-Avana that would seem to justify a twenty year espionage. And though I didn't say it, on a personal level I had seen the reverence with which Marco spoke about Warrior-Guilder Aven. His loyalty to her, and the debt he felt he owed her for giving him a home and a place here, seemed absolute. I would have said he loved Sjona more fiercely than many native to it. But, again, I could not trust my impressions of people's loyalties.

I left Eliska, turning over the facts in my head as I walked.

I wanted to watch both Marco and Eliska but realized, my feet turning leaden, that I would need help to follow them both. And I couldn't ask Hadrea to do me a favor, after this morning. I still didn't know which of Tain's servants were trustworthy, even if I were willing to endanger an innocent party by setting them to watch a murderer who now knew we were searching for them. Of course, some of them would at least need to believe he was dead and that we had to maintain the ruse of his health. That he was alive but incapacitated would have to be kept from them all.

I couldn't sleep at my own apartments and check regularly on Tain, nor did I relish the prospect of being there without my uncle and sister. The thought of facing Hadrea, being confronted by her anger and hurt and my own shame and guilt, tightened the ball of stress inside me even more.

But only Salvea waited in Tain's rooms, head bent over the restless sleeping Chancellor. She told me Hadrea had taken Davi to bed, her tone without rancor; clearly her daughter had not shared our altercation.

"The Chancellor's hallucinations are growing worse, but that may be because he is growing stronger," she told me as she stood and stretched. "His thrashing is more powerful and his voice louder."

I thanked her and took her seat. "Go and get some sleep," I said.

She kissed me on the forehead as she left, a Darfri gesture notable for its rare intimacy, and her kindness and affection only made me feel a fraud. *Just find the traitor,* I told myself, dragging some cushions in from the sitting room and constructing a rough pallet on the floor. *Then it won't matter anymore. Nothing will matter anymore.*

With that reassuring thought, I lay down to rest.

Though my body craved it, my mind avoided sleep. I forced my eyes shut while my brain chased itself in ever-painful circles. Images tumbled through my head, still the worst being Kalina's head in a bag, so real I could almost feel the texture of the material, the blood dripping through its base. I counted in sets, trying to use the patterns to disrupt the loop of bad thoughts. But it was no good; something about the images tickled my brain, as though it danced on the edge of a memory. Had I missed some clue, some part of the puzzle? I didn't know what could be found in a head in a bag except trauma and a reminder that both sides of this war were capable of atrocities. Maybe it was just another sign that I would lose my control and purpose without my family. After all, I reminded myself, poking at the wound like a fool, I was alone in the world now.

After a while it grew too much and I was forced to stand and pace, counting steps and squeezes of my hands and breaths to calm down. Eventually, my head quieted and my body won the war, first causing me to stumble and then to collapse on the pallet. I fell at an awkward angle but couldn't summon the energy to shift. At last, I slept.

Atrapis

DESCRIPTION: Dull green herb with small yellow flowers and fine black seeds, very common. All parts, especially seeds and flowers, are poisonous in large doses. Useful as a blood-borne antidote to poisons that slow heart rate (such as bluehood), and in surgery to decrease salivation. Formerly used as a recreational drug.

SYMPTOMS: Blurred vision, loss of balance, dilated pupils, reaction to light, dry mouth, and potentially extreme confusion, dissociative hallucinations, and excitation, especially among the elderly.

PROOFING CUES: Has biting, crisp taste and noticeably dries mouth. Smell is sharp and tart.

22

Kalina

The harsh cry of a firebird jolted me awake. I blinked up at the sky, catching a glimpse of the scarlet underwing of the big bird of prey as it wheeled overhead, suddenly conscious of the dozens of things that should have kept me awake and hadn't: the rickety, jolting passage of the cart in which I rode, my head lolling at an awkward angle, the brightness of the sky.

My left side prickled painfully as I straightened. It took a moment to orient myself and realize the oku had continued to plod on down the road as I'd slept. The cart had only been intended as a chance to rest my legs and lungs so I could continue on foot again, but apparently the stress of the night had beaten my resolve.

Ravenous, I fumbled in my pack for supplies and extracted some fish jerky. Not for the first time, I cursed myself for the meager quantities in my pack. My foraging attempts had made plain that while I had an excellent understanding of which plants not to eat, I had none concerning those that were safe, let alone pleasant. Jovan doubtless had memorized entire books on native plants and would probably be able to make a sumptuous meal from roots and moss. I almost smiled, but the thought of my brother was too painful. What had he thought when he'd found my letter? *He'd think I'm dead. His whole family and his best friend, all dead.*

Shaking my head, I distracted myself from melodramatic dwelling by trying to determine our location. The sun was low and the homogeneous scenery gave me no clue how far we'd traveled. I pulled up the beast and climbed out, leading it off the road. The wheels caught quickly in gnarled plants and, despite my tugging, it was soon apparent my new friend would be no good off-road.

Panting, resting my forearms on the placid animal, I looked back at the road and then at the difficult path over the wilds. The choice knotted my stomach. I'd make better time and could preserve my energy with the wagon, but it would mean trusting my safety to the road.

"I'm sorry, girl," I said to the oku. "You'll have to find your own way home." I patted the beast and then, breathing deeply, set off across the hills.

Dumbcane

DESCRIPTION: Species of giant grass with strong, supple canes suitable for drying for building material. Grows rows of fine, clear, needle-shaped crystals, which are poisonous on piercing the skin. Crushed crystals removed from cane in production are poisonous if ingested (not soluble).

SYMPTOMS: Intense burning irritation, immobility of the tongue, mouth, and throat; swelling can block breathing if severe enough.

PROOFING CUES: Tingling in tongue and lips, faint astringent smell reminiscent of urine, gritty texture in most foods.

23

Jovan

Vivid dreams stripped my sleep of restfulness. When I awoke to Tain's babbling and thrashing my skin dripped with sweat and my palms bore little crescent marks from my fingernails. My muscles felt tense, as if I'd run a race rather than slept for hours. This was my fourth night of sleeping here by Tain's bed. Four long, cold days, while the rebels had exercised their patience and in which I'd learned nothing new about Eliska or Marco, and exchanged nothing but awkward silence with Hadrea. I avoided her as diligently as she did me. I tried not to think about Kalina but it was hard when I'd never felt so lonely in my life.

I tried to rub the images from my dreams away from my eyes. Yet again, I'd been haunted by brown sacks and arrow-flecked corpses. The dreams left me sick and anxious, knowing I was missing something important, but unable to understand their significance.

I sat up when Tain did. He pressed against the wall, his head jerking around, eyes wide. "Jov?" he whispered, hoarse. "Jov, is that you?"

"Yes," I said, rubbing my eyes and finding a stool by his bed. "I'm here. You're all right."

His breath hitched as he reached a hand out, trembling. "Jov, what have they done to you?" His eyes scanned me, mouth working, as if he visually catalogued a score of wounds.

"I'm fine." I went to take his hand, but he snatched his back with a shriek.

"Your hand!" he cried. "Fortunes, Jov! What have they done?" He cried, heavy wracking sobs. "I'm sorry, I'm so sorry."

"I'm going to be all right. Just relax. It's over now, Tain."

He continued to sob, but when I touched his shoulders this time he didn't recoil. "I'm so sorry," he repeated. "Oh, Lini."

My head snapped up and my hands dropped from his shoulders as if pulled by invisible strings. My mouth went dry.

When he looked up this time, some of the wildness had left his eyes. "Lini," Tain said again. "She's gone, isn't she? She said she was going to go to the army and find help. She thought I was going to die, and she said good-bye." He squeezed his eyes shut as though even looking at me hurt. "It was like I was underwater. I could hear her but I couldn't say anything. And the next thing I remember, she was gone."

My lungs wouldn't fill properly. I tried to speak, but nothing came out.

"Tell me it isn't true," he begged, but all I could do was shake my head, mute.

He dropped his head back against the wall with a dull thud, face wet with tears. "Tell me."

My voice came out tight and high as I told him what I knew. I couldn't keep the anger and shame out of my voice but he seemed not to notice, barely looking at me as he digested it. Then he gave me a weak attempt at a smile. "She was right, though, the west bank's probably not patrolled. If she wasn't seen in the river . . ."

"She probably was, if she didn't drown first," I said harshly, his stupid hope like bellows on the flames of my rage. "But even if she wasn't, the rebels presumably control all the estates. Do you think a lone Silastian woman could get through all those villages without being seen? Maybe someone with the physical strength—" I had to tear my gaze away and stare at the wall, willing myself not to finish the accusation.

"Jov, I'm sorry," he said, reaching a hand toward me and letting it drop as it was ignored. "You know I'd never have let her go if I'd been able to do anything. This is the longest I can remember being awake since the poisoning. Honor-down, I don't even know how much time's passed."

My face felt stiff as I answered. "Five days." I almost hated him for crying, when I hadn't. Couldn't.

"And I'm going to live?" He stared down at his own hands and chest as if they belonged to someone else. "How? What happened?"

"You've been chewing feverhead," I said. "It stopped your body from absorbing the poison, and now it's just trying to repair. I don't know how much damage it did before we got to it, though." He likely had permanent digestive and breathing problems in his future even if he didn't succumb to an infection or some other secondary condition in the short term. It took effort not to elaborate, when a part of me wanted to.

"Feverhead? I guess that's why my hands look like spades?" He swiped them around in the air.

"There are side effects. You've been hallucinating for days. This is your first lucid conversation."

It felt odd describing our last five days, which had felt much longer. The elaborate games of distraction and misdirection exhausted me: bribing Tain's little messenger, Erel, and convincing increasingly irate Councilors that Tain was occupied elsewhere, keeping a handful of his servants and the few Councilors who believed Tain dead assisting us to hide this "truth" by pretending to have met with him. The climate of fear, suspicion, and hopelessness from which we'd hoped to protect the people of the city now ran rife through our own ranks.

"Do you remember anything about that jar of figs?" I asked. "Who touched it, who offered you one, how Marco and Eliska chose theirs? You were the only one poisoned, so I think it was done on the spot by sleight of hand."

Tain shook his head, his eyes drooping. "I walked in with both of them," he said. "I think we met in the gardens on the way to the front door. Argo told me he'd found a few things left by the door. I figured they were part of the food amnesty. I think . . . I *think* Eliska looked so excited by the figs that I took them with us. Or was it Marco?" He shook his head again. "I don't have your memory, Jov, I'm sorry."

"It's all right," I said, though inside my frustration boiled. These details were critical.

"When we were meeting, I don't know, I wasn't going to take one—I could picture your face—but Eliska and Marco had both taken a few, and I'd opened the jar myself, so it just seemed silly. . . ." He trailed off, face darkening. "Honor-down, Jov, I'm such a fool. They'd never have been able to get me if I hadn't been such an idiot."

"So you chose your own?" I asked, ignoring that last comment for fear of saying something I couldn't take back later.

He nodded. "I opened it, and offered it to both of them. I can't remember who chose first, but they both took several. The jar was there and open as we worked."

When I glanced back at Tain, his eyes had shut again. I stood and stretched. *Another day.* It was hard to even take heart in my friend's apparent recovery; too much of that was bound up and soured with my guilt and anger about Kalina. And still, any day the rebels could storm the bridge, and it could all come to a head.

"Any change?"

Salvea's gentle voice interrupted my bleak thoughts. She came into the room with Davior at her knees. Hadrea hovered behind, eyes firmly fixed on her mother. I'd barely seen her for days, and despite my best efforts, I found my gaze sweeping hungrily over her with a longing that alarmed me. Honor-down, I had missed her.

"He's been awake and lucid," I told Salvea, my voice squeaky as I dragged my gaze from her daughter. "But he's fallen asleep again."

"Did he eat anything?"

"I was so focused on talking to him, I didn't even think of that," I admitted. "There's some broth by the bed I proofed last night."

She settled herself by the bed, a mound of skirts and calm, and tasted the broth. "It is drinkable cold," she said. "If he wakes again I will have him attempt it." She glanced up at her daughter. "Hadrea, was there not something you wished to discuss with Credo Jovan?"

"Just Jovan." I'd corrected her countless times, but her formal country manners prevailed. I watched Hadrea, my heart rate increasing. If I had known what to say to her, I'd have said it before now. I had nothing to offer. But I wanted . . . honor-down, I wanted her not to hate me, all the same.

She cleared her throat and I forgot to avoid eye contact. Piercing judgment pinned me to the spot. "I have found something interesting you should see," she said. Her mouth twitched with cold amusement at the look of surprise that must have passed over my face.

"All right," I managed, standing.

"Not now. When it is darkest." She looked me over. "Wear shoes," she said. Embarrassment swept over me at my disheveled state, but I resisted the temptation to straighten anything.

"I'll meet you in the hall at midnight."

That seemed to satisfy Hadrea; she swept from the room without another word. When I turned to rescue some clean—or cleanish, anyway—clothes from the pile I'd brought in from my apartments, Salvea was watching me out of the corner of her eye, but she looked away so quickly I might have imagined it.

The armor I'd built with clean clothes, a washed face, and combed hair crumpled at the sight of Hadrea waiting for me in the hall outside Tain's rooms. Dressed country-style again, with tattered layered skirts, an embroidered blouse, and a scarf binding her hair, her composure remained intact as she nodded at me, cool.

"I followed your Stone-Guilder last night," she said, already walking so I had to trot to catch up. "She went somewhere interesting."

"You were following Eliska?" I asked. "Why?"

This time she did glance over, so I could fully appreciate the roll of her eyes. "Is she not perhaps your poisoner?"

"Yes. But I didn't realize you . . . I mean, I hadn't asked you to help. I thought—"

"You thought I would not care about catching the murderer, just because you had sex with me and then wished you had not? I am not so selfish. For all your 'honor,' you must have little regard for mine."

And I had thought I couldn't feel worse. "Hadrea," I said, catching her shoulder, and she didn't pull away but instead fixed me with her gaze, cold as a winter pool. "I don't think you're selfish. I knew you would be hurt by what I said." I searched for the right words. Tain would know what to say to turn this around, and so would Kalina. And then the memory of my sister froze over my mind again, and I dropped my hand away. I couldn't be trusted to look after those who cared about me.

"Then you may rest easy," she said, "for I am not." She turned away again, and this time I thought there was a crack in the facade. But she walked so fast it took all my effort just to keep pace. I'd spent the day dodging angry Councilors wanting to speak with Tain—Bradomir had been a particular pain in my rear—and helping dig trenches. I was mentally and physically drained. I followed her, silence brittle between us, all the way down to Red Fern Avenue, the street that ran parallel to the lake shore with the hospital at one end and the bank at the other. The plants that gave it its name sprouted out between the old buildings like wild tufts of bloody hair, fronds colorful even in the darkness.

A memory sprang up, of walking along this street with Lini and Tain on the way to the hospital to receive the autopsy report, weeks ago. Like poking at a wound, the images of them both alive and healthy hurt in a satisfying way. As clear as if it were happening right now, I remembered: a man, a petitioner, had been jostling through the crowd, trying to get Tain's attention. Thendra had met us and we'd gone with her, and I'd never thought of it again. But now, thanks to the vividness of my dreams over the past few nights, his face was an ordinary stranger's face no more. The man who had tried to speak to us that day was the man whose head had been in the sack, whose dead eyes and open mouth haunted my dreams. The spy from the southern border whose head had been returned to us with our runners'. My thoughts buzzed, trying to process that connection. *What does that mean?*

But Hadrea slowed suddenly and jerked me back to the present as she pulled me into a clump of ferns in a crouch. "I followed Eliska here. It was dark, but she looked about often as though suspicious of someone following." The closeness was distracting; even if I kept my gaze from the graceful curve of her neck, the tangy citrus smell of her skin and memories of the feel of her beneath my hands threatened to swamp me. I took a deep breath, squeezing my hands together and counting in silent sets with each exhalation. "I hid here to watch her, and saw her go into that building." She pointed across the street to a little tailor's shop, its commerce long abandoned, its sign crooked and window empty of wares.

"Not long after, someone followed her in," Hadrea continued. "A woman I did not recognize."

"Did you see them come out?"

She gave me a sidelong look, almost a smile. "Better." She glanced up and down the street. Empty. Then she sprang across to the other side so quickly I didn't even have time to stand. She'd already jimmied the door by the time I caught up.

It was a small shop, the wares long gone and even the leather dummies commandeered as poppets on our walls. The front section, for customers, was no more than a few treads deep, and separated from the back workshop by a shabby curtain, just cloth, no beading. "What were they doing in here?" I asked, pushing aside the dingy threads and following Hadrea into the workshop. It wasn't much bigger than the front space, and just as bare, all of the materials and tools taken by the Craft Guild. There was nothing here.

"I waited a few moments after the second woman went inside, then followed," Hadrea said. "I watched through the window. They went into the back, but did not come out, and I could not hear anything. So I risked the door."

Out the back, a good moon illuminated an enclosed courtyard with an old woven barrel in one corner and a grill leading down to the sewers in another. The barrel swarmed with fat black flies, crawling over the remnants of whatever refuse had been stored there. I looked around, confused. "There's not even a way out. What were they doing back here?"

"I wondered the same. Then I heard something below." Hadrea pointed down and I followed her gaze to the sewer grill. "The *sewers?*" The cold feeling increased in my chest. It was impossible to imagine an innocent scenario that might have led Eliska into the sewers at night with a mysterious woman. I bent to help Hadrea shift the grill. It should have been welded down but came up easily. *Eliska's the Stone-Guilder,* I reminded myself. *A bit of metalwork wouldn't slow her down.*

"You stopped here?"

She snorted. "I was quiet," she said. She dropped her feet into the exposed hole and lowered herself down. I heard a thump and a splash as she landed below. I crouched at the edge, hands clammy with trepidation. There was no ladder. How were we supposed to get back out?

"Come on," she called, her voice echoing in the tunnel. I took a breath and dropped down. Outside the small circle of light, the tunnel stretched away into blackness. Hadrea's hand found mine, her grip firm and easy. The intimacy of the gesture surprised me.

"Did you bring a lantern?" I stretched with my free hand until I found the tunnel wall. I shuffled toward her, trying to ignore the feel of slimy water—at least, I needed to imagine it as water—encasing my feet up to the ankles.

"Yes, but there is no need yet," she said. Reaching up past me, she pulled a rope I'd not even noticed, and the grill above us settled back into place. "It is not far. Come."

She strode forward, feet sloshing, as though she could see in the dark. Clumsy, I stumbled along a bit behind her, trying to imagine what we might find. Had Eliska somehow been using the sewers to sabotage the stability of the walls in the old city? With the bulk of the rebel force in the lower city, we'd lessened our watchfulness on the north and south walls as they had stopped attacking them. Had they been weakening from below without us knowing?

We stopped a short distance away. Hadrea dropped to a crouch, apparently unbothered by the mess it must be making of her skirts. "I almost missed this," she said. "I'd been following them, guided by the sound of footsteps, and then heard a clunk; suddenly, no more steps. I rounded this bend and there was nothing, no one left to follow. So I trawled about until I found this."

She tugged at my hand and I crouched, tentative, as she guided our hands into the slime. My groping fingers found a heavy metal ring. *Another entrance? To where?*

The ring opened a wide hatch in the floor of the tunnel. Water splashed down from our level below, and this time Hadrea swung easily into the opening and paused there.

"A ladder," I said, beginning to understand where we were going.

We'd speculated that tunnels under the lower city might mean similar ones existed on this side of the lake. But the Council had denied knowledge of such a thing, and we'd not been able to find records of any caves. I knew Hadrea had been looking for them; that was how she'd ruined her clothing and been forced into the Silastian dress that day. I tried not to think of that memory.

She climbed down first and I followed. The metal was good, built with non-corrosive orote, a slick, black metal used extensively in shipbuilding and plumbing. By the ladder was an alcove containing a tinderbox and lantern; Hadrea fumbled in the dark and then lit it, holding it aloft so we could look around.

"They met down here," Hadrea said, voice echoing in the eerie space.

These tunnels, I could see, were old and solid, better even than the ones under the lower city. The air was damp and heavy, old, like it wasn't quite suitable for breathing. Something scurried about outside the range of the lantern. It wasn't that I was afraid of the dark. I had paced and counted the length of my rooms, Tain's rooms, and most of the public spaces in Silasta so many times that my body knew their dimensions by feel and I could walk confidently without sight. But this was different. Untouched and un-known, the darkness here could hide anything. I shivered.

"I followed the light." Hadrea gestured to a corridor at the other side of the cavern. Then a scraping sound above us made us both freeze.

With swift fingers she shut down her lamp and pulled me against the wall. "The lamp," I whispered, and she fumbled around to find the little space to return it. Together we edged away from the ladder as another sound echoed above our heads. Footsteps. The sound of someone lifting the trapdoor. We risked a few more shuffles back to get out of the range of the lantern. Blood pounded in my ears, louder than the sound of the person descending. Hadrea pressed against me, her hair tickling my neck. Tension thrummed through her body as we squinted in the dark, waiting.

The figure disappeared into blackness as the door closed, but moments later the tinderbox clicked and then the lamp shed light over a woman—not Eliska—at the bottom of the ladder. We shrank back, but she only looked up at the ladder, apparently waiting.

Soon enough, the door opened again, and the woman's face broke into a smile as another pair of legs swung down into the hole.

"Darling," she said, and Eliska half-climbed, half-dropped the rest of the way down, squirming into the taller woman's arms like a child.

"Has it only been a day?" Eliska murmured, burying her face in the other woman's shoulder. I had to blink, watching her—she looked like a different person. Her hair, unbound from its usual tail, cascaded over her shoulders and her face looked softer, more feminine.

"I can't stay long, my love," the woman said.

"I know, it isn't supposed to be every night," Eliska replied. "I know it's a risk. But we have to try. And don't worry, I don't think anyone suspects anything of the loyal Stone-Guilder." Bitterness touched her words.

I'm glad you think so.

Together they walked in the direction away from where we hid. After the light bobbed away into the corridor, Hadrea and I slipped after them. She led the way, sure-footed. "They went in there last night," she whispered, her voice so soft in my ear it was like I felt the words on her breath instead of hearing them.

The light turned a corner and then disappeared. It was an alcove with a solid door. Through a crack we saw the light; they had stopped moving. We hovered outside. Soon telltale noises crept through the door along with the flash of light. I avoided Hadrea's face. "Is this what you saw last night?"

"*Mm.* Of course it is no crime, what they are doing. But Jovan, there is a shrine in there, a shrine to the great spirit of the lake. They are not merely enjoying each other, they are giving an offering. And asking a boon."

The words pierced my chest like darts. Eliska was Darfri, but had hidden it from all of us—actively hidden it, masking her own beliefs with faked anti-Darfri sentiment in Council. And now here she was, in full ritual practice in caverns whose existence we had searched for in vain, trawling through record and cellar alike. All that time, she had known. "What boon are they asking for?" Anger swelled inside me, anger and a fierce desire to act. I'd had enough of lurking in the shadows. But as I reached out toward the door, Hadrea caught my arm.

"No," she whispered. "We are not soldiers, Jovan. You do not know what these people might do if cornered."

I let her lead me back across the corridor. We fumbled about in the dark until we came to the next alcove, and there we waited. My anger boiled still, though I knew she was right; we could just as easily have Eliska arrested with the help of Order Guards. In any case, so far, all I could prove Eliska guilty of was failing to share her knowledge of caves, and hiding her religion. As Hadrea said, there was no crime in a romantic relationship, nor with being Darfri, even in secret.

Not long after, the woman pushed open the door. "I can find the way," she was saying as she left. "You keep the lamp."

She strode off, confident, into the inky blackness. I thought how well I knew my apartment from all of my pacing and counting; sight didn't matter if your body knew where to go. My guess was these caves were no new discovery to Eliska and her lover.

We heard the hatch clap shut.

Seized by the desire, once again, to stop lurking and do something, I took a breath and, dragging Hadrea behind me, stepped across the corridor and shoved the door open.

Eliska cried out. Half-dressed, her dress unbound and her hair disheveled, she was partway through retying her shoes, and she looked up at us in fear and shock as we burst in. One hand tried to gather her clothing around her, the other to block our view of the immense, elaborate shrine behind her.

"Don't move, Eliska," I said to her, my voice quivering with the anger bubbling up from within me. "Don't you move a fucking muscle."

Moonblossom

DESCRIPTION: Sunlight-sensitive vine with pale white flowers blooming only in low light (moonlight or heavily shaded areas). Small, glossy red berries are toxic.

SYMPTOMS: Stomach pain, nausea, diarrhea.

PROOFING CUES: Taste of berries is strongly sour and sharp.

24

Kalina

Until this desperate flight, until the nights lying huddled in inadequate shelter, I had never properly appreciated the relentless power of Silasta's famous winds. I tucked my legs closer to my chest, a pathetic ball, hair and clothes whipping about as I tried to sleep. Once, it seemed a lifetime ago, I'd loved the sound of the Maiso outside the walls. Now it was a curse.

The last few days were a haze of pain, sleep deprivation, and disorientation. I couldn't remember how many days I had traveled. Four? Five? More? The more tired I'd become, the less I'd been able to feel; all of the energy poured into worrying about Jovan and grieving for Tain had long dissipated in the endless fields and hills and the glare from the sun. My worry and doubt in myself had disappeared along with it. It had made me bold.

I snuggled tighter, rubbing my back into the warm, shaggy fur of the sleeping graspad. The strong smell of the animal no longer bothered me. I'd stolen it two evenings ago with a fearlessness that would have stunned my brother. The Kalina who'd agonized over that first oku, and frozen like a frightened rabbit in the face of the old man, would not have recognized the woman who had stalked the quiet village of Casperwan and taken the feisty little graspad. Riding it had taken some practice and I had fallen several times, but I seemed to have the hang of it now.

Today had been good. I'd taken advantage of the big steady paws of my new companion and traversed a more direct route south, away from the road and over the rocky hills. It brought me closer to the mines, but also made it harder to orient myself, especially in the middle of the day when the sun's position was of limited help. Alternating between walking and riding, I was traveling much faster than in those first few days.

I calculated that these were the Ash estates, but I couldn't remember the estate house position relative to the mines. It would be too dangerous to risk getting close given that it was presumably held by the rebels. Days ago, in sight of the road, dust clouds had alerted me to someone passing, and sometimes there had been signs of small groups in the distance, but the hills and fields lay bare and deserted.

Maybe I'll never see anyone ever again. I might die out here.

It was the kind of morose thought Jovan might have in one of his moods, and the melodrama of it gave me some weary amusement. My brother would have pictured his own demise in excruciating detail, but luckily I lacked both his intense focus and his imagination for inventing terrible scenarios with which to torture myself. Frequent tributary streams heading down to the river meant I was never far from water. There was no food left, but the Ash estates were kori country so there would be korberries soon, if nothing else. And I had made it this far. I tried to ignore the biting wind and relax. How could my body be so bone weary yet still resist sleep?

But I must have slept, because when I opened my eyes, there was someone standing over me. Too tired to even startle, I blinked up at the dark shape: a dream? When I rubbed my eyes the figure stayed there and as I tried to sit up a spear shaft dug into my side.

"Wake up." A shuttered lantern burst into light, revealing a man and a woman in army uniforms, their faces shielded behind conical leather helmets.

Relief made me laugh, though it came out a coarse choke. They stared at me, suspicion glittering in their eyes; I tried to stop but couldn't. The graspad awoke and swiveled its elegant neck.

"Who are you?" the woman asked, prodding me with the spear.

"What's wrong with her?" The man waved the lantern over me and clucked his tongue. "It's a woman. A Sjon." He squatted beside me and removed his helmet. "Are you all right?"

The woman moved the spear back, but kept it in hand, less trusting than her colleague. I tried to catch my breath and explain, but couldn't stop making the noise, or even tell if I was laughing or crying. *Scouts, they must be scouts. I've made it.*

"Aven," I managed to say between gasps. "I've come to tell . . . help . . . we need help."

"Who needs help?" the man asked. "What's your name?"

"Credola Kalina," I said. He whistled, looking to my covered upper arms. I pushed the fabric up, exposing my Family tattoo. "Please, I have to see the Warrior-Guilder."

He helped me to my feet. "Can you ride?" he asked. "We're a fair ways from the camp."

I nodded, my breathing finally stabilizing.

"All right, Credola," said the soldier. "You can tell me all about what you need as we ride."

My sleepy graspad gave a grunt of protest as I clambered on its back and wove my fingers through its long, knotted fur. The scouts had their own graspads, bigger than mine and better groomed, and they steered theirs with neat leather harnesses where I had just been directing my beast by tugging on the fur beneath its huge ears.

I'd done it. I'd found the army.

I let my head rest on the graspad's neck, and felt my body relax for the first time in days.

I woke in a tent, surrounded by purple-and-red striped fabric. I tried to stand, but dizziness forced me down again. I still wore my mismatched traveling clothes, but someone had given me a blanket. A plate of food lay beside the cushions: a leg of something—bindie?—a round of flat bread, and a small bowl of smoked vegetable paste. And tea in a metal cup.

I gulped some warm tea first, then hunger grabbed me and I was halfway through the glorious greasy meat before I became conscious of it and slowed my chewing. I needed to speak to Aven. But, oh, honor-down, I was so hungry. . . .

I ate the rest of the meat and a few mouthfuls of bread dunked in the paste, fighting not to eat too quickly and get sick. I finished the tea then, fighting the wooziness, and got to my feet, remaining bread in hand.

"Hello?" I called out, stepping to the tent flap.

The scout who had found me stuck his head in. He had a wide, pock-marked face with heavy laugh lines around the mouth and eyes, and a long crooked nose.

"You're awake," he said with a warm smile. "Here, sit. Finish your food. You must be hungry."

"Starving. I came from Silasta, and ran out of food a few days ago." Through a mouthful of bread, I added, "I'm sorry, but I need to speak to the Warrior-Guilder, urgently."

"You fell off your mount pretty hard, and you didn't rouse when we tried. Warrior-Guilder Aven told us to put you in here and get you some rest and food, and to tell her when you stirred. I'll send someone to let her know you're awake, if you stay and finish that."

I nodded. While he ducked back outside the tent, I secured another mouthful of delicious salty cheese.

He returned shortly, bearing a kettle of tea and more food. "You said you needed help," he said, frowning. "What's happened? Why do you need the Warrior-Guilder?"

"As far as I'm aware, messages for the Warrior-Guilder come to *me*, soldier, not you," a dry, raspy voice interrupted. Through the tent flaps ducked a tall, muscular woman in a military tunic and riding trousers. A snarled black plait snaked over her shoulder, and her arms bore both the Reed Family tattoos and the knife sigil of the Warrior-Guilder. "Unless you've had a promotion I've not heard about?"

The soldier scrambled to his feet, head bowed. "Apologies, Warrior-Guilder. I was just trying to get some food into her. She's half-starved."

Aven looked me over with a raised eyebrow. "So I see." I hastily swallowed my mouthful, feeling soft and plump and self-conscious under her hard gaze. "You can go, soldier." The man scurried out without a backward glance, and the Warrior-Guilder took his place, cross-legged on the floor in front of me with a rod-straight spine and a measuring look. Though I had seen her before, at the occasional demonstration or social event, we had never met, and I doubted she recalled my existence at all. "Now, little bird. What brings you to my camp in such a state?"

"Warrior-Guilder," I said, "you have to ready the army. Silasta's under siege."

Aven started to laugh, then frowned. "Siege? What do you mean?"

"There's been an uprising on the estates," I said. "Honor-down, I know this must sound insane. We've tried to get word to you for weeks, but they have us penned in. I don't know what's happened to the other cities. The Chancellor is dead, Credola, and"—my voice cracked a little—"the Heir too, the new Chancellor, Tain. They were both poisoned."

Aven's face grew still and her gaze narrow. "An uprising? The Chancellor murdered? I hardly think this would be the first we'd hear of it, if so. Is this some trick of the Doranites, to have us abandon the south? We've beaten them decisively." She leaned in, dark eyes glittering, menace emanating from her like a force. "You're not the first spy we've had at this camp."

I shook my head and blinked hard as tears of exhaustion and frustration built. "No. No, it's all true. Honor-down, I wish it were otherwise. But the estates really have risen against us. The Chancellor was poisoned and they marched on Silasta during the funeral. They killed our birds and then our messengers when we sent for help. We tried as best we could to hold the city but we had barely two dozen Order Guards and they built siege weapons. We collapsed Bell's Bridge and retreated to the upper city less than two weeks ago. We still held Trickster's and the Finger when I left, but we don't have long."

The Warrior-Guilder leaned in closer. She looked me over, her gaze merciless as a razor. "What's your name, little bird? I know your face."

"Credola Kalina. I'm Credo Etan's niece." This time the tears did break free, and I looked down at her hands, my voice dropping to a whisper. "He's dead, too."

Aven lifted my chin with a surprisingly gentle hand. "Honor-down. How did you get out of the city? And why send you as a messenger? Forgive me, but you don't seem an obvious choice."

Again, I shrank back into my own body a little, even though she was painfully correct. "I swam under the gate," I said. "They didn't send me. I just . . . The Chancellor wouldn't send any more messengers. The first lot, the rebels caught them and . . . and desecrated the corpses, terribly. Tai—the Chancellor, he wouldn't risk it happening again. Then he was poisoned, and I just didn't think we would last much longer if someone didn't find you."

Without another word, Aven stood, swift and graceful, and left the tent. I sat, feeling helpless, as Aven's harsh voice barked orders outside. Moments later, a great horn rang across the camp, three times. Then Aven came back into the tent. "We're mobilizing, little bird, packing up the camp right now. We'll be on the boats and back to the city before you know it."

"Thank you." The dizziness returned, dousing me with relief.

Aven smiled. It wasn't a pleasant smile. "Rebels, you say? Traitors, and a peasant rabble to boot. We'll pen them in the city they tried to steal, and crush them against the rock. We'll take Silasta back, don't fear."

Much as I resisted, it was impossible not to be impressed by Aven. The Warrior-Guilder was undeniably magnificent, striding around the place with such palpable authority that people reacted to her presence before they even saw her.

Though Sjon nobility by birth, Aven rejected all the civilized trappings of the Families. She was loud and ill-mannered, tolerated by the rest of the Council only for her undeniable skills in her Guild, and rarely publicly referenced by her own family—even Credo Lazar, who loved to brag about his family's accomplishments, rarely mentioned his cousin. Yet seeing her now, in her element, I understood Tain's infatuation. Aven was attractive in the rawest sense of the word, with an imposing presence and power that derived both from her physical prowess and her apparent lack of need for external approval. I could see now why Tain, surrounded as he was by willing partners who were clever and beautiful and artistic but nevertheless cut from the same cultured, pampered cloth, might have seen the Warrior-Guilder as someone refreshingly different and desirable.

It made me feel smaller than ever. A little bird, indeed. Aven had bidden me to stay in the tent and attempt to rest. It was the middle of the night after a hard day of riding and walking, and the cushions were inviting. Even with the lanterns off, I couldn't sleep, instead staring at the faint pattern of the tent roof lit by the moon above. Impatience rather than relief itched at me as the army packed up the camp. Perhaps once we were in the boats and on the way home downriver, I'd be able to sleep properly.

But even if the city is saved, Tain is still dead. My eyes stayed dry this time. I'd moved beyond tears.

"Not sleeping, little bird?" Aven's gravelly voice interrupted my thoughts. The Warrior-Guilder came inside as I sat up.

"I'm so tired," I admitted. "But whenever I shut my eyes . . ."

Aven nodded, understanding softening the sharp lines of her face. "We'll move within the hour," she said. "We've half-loaded the boats already."

"What about the mines? Will we lose them to the Doranites?"

The Warrior-Guilder shrugged. "I think not. We've beaten them decisively twice now. They don't have the men left to attack again. I'll leave a small group here to protect the workers, but I think this dispute's settled, for now." She sat down cross-legged beside me. "Since you're awake anyway, why don't you tell me everything you can about the rebel army."

When I grew hoarse, Aven finally took pity and ceased her relentless questioning. She surprised me with her gratitude. "You've been very brave," the Warrior-Guilder told me. "And you've probably saved Silasta. If you're strong enough, we'll get you to a boat, and I'll leave instructions that no one is to disturb you. I can see you're not well, Credola, and though you've not said anything about why, I can tell the difference between ordinary exhaustion and the kind that comes with a serious illness. Even the healthiest runner would need rest after what you've done. You've earned it."

"It's all right," I said. "I can help, if there's something . . ." I trailed off, embarrassed; of course she wouldn't need the help of a spoiled, wealthy invalid, the epitome of the Silasta she eschewed.

But instead of mocking, Aven patted me on the shoulder kindly. "You have helped, and you'll do more, but you have to rest first. I'll likely need more information when we get back to the city." She glanced out of the tent and dropped her voice. "We've already had more than one traitor in the camp, Credola. From what you've told me, it would be foolish to assume there is no one in the army involved in the plot. Only my most trusted men and women know the details of why we're returning. It would be safest if you spoke to no one."

"How long will the boats take?" I asked. "How soon will we be back?"

"We have the current," she said. "It'll depend on the wind. But we'll be back by the day after tomorrow, at latest."

"Tain want—I mean, the Chancellor wanted to negotiate a peace," I reminded her. "The rebels were provoked and manipulated, and he didn't want any more people to die. Could you just get them to surrender? Surely they won't try to fight once they have enemies on both sides."

The Warrior-Guilder looked me over for a long time. Then she sighed. "I will do what seems best. If they surrender, fine. It is no grand thing to slaughter our own countrymen. But you have to understand, Credola, my soldiers are patriots. Their capital was betrayed in their absence, and they will want to avenge it. We'll do what we can, but the Chancellor is not with us to negotiate anymore."

The dull, hollow place inside me grew a little bigger, but I pressed on. Aven was angry, and probably felt that she had been made a fool to be distracted by the Doran shenanigans, but I worried that those feelings would prevent her from seeing the rebels' side. "But someone will negotiate," I said. "The Council will probably have voted on a leader, at least until Tain's cousin Merenda can take over."

"If she is still alive," Aven said grimly. "If she wasn't in Silasta, where was she?"

I had no answer for that. Hopefully Merenda was safely in Telasa and nowhere near the Iliri estates. Bad enough that an untrained relative, not even a formal Heir, should become the Chancellor. But if Tain's cousin was dead, I didn't even know who was next in line. Merenda might have had a brother, but I couldn't remember. Casimira's scandalous exit from Silasta had dramatically reduced the viable number of Iliri heirs. Perhaps none of Tain's relatives had survived at all. Which of the scheming, self-interested Credol Families would replace the Iliris?

"It doesn't matter now," Aven said. "The Council will decide what to do once we've secured the city. But that is my priority, Credola: securing the city. If we have to carve our way through some traitors first, I can't pretend many here will lose sleep over it."

With that less than reassuring thought, Aven swooped out of the tent.

A short time later I was bustled from the camp and down to the river, where the large military boats awaited. My assigned guard was the scout who had found me. He told me his name—Garan—but admitted he'd been asked not to speak to me except as necessary.

"Surely the Warrior-Guilder doesn't think you're a spy," I said, as he showed me into a small cabin. After days of silence, I didn't much fancy the idea of having no one to talk to. The cabin already felt claustrophobic.

Garan leaned against the door. "No, but best to be safe, I s'pose. We already had a few incidents. I thought you were another Doranite spy, when we first saw you out there."

"So . . . you've found spies before?" I asked, hoping to keep him talking. Any conversation was better than none, even if we couldn't talk about what was happening in the city. The boat wobbled and I stumbled, then regained my balance. Military boats differed from the smooth, plump passenger boats I'd traveled on in the past.

"We've caught a few skulking around the camp since we've been here," Garan said. This time when the boat wobbled he was quick to offer a steadying hand. He gave me a shy smile. "The Warrior-Guilder trusted me to guard one of them, too. I—" He broke off, looking ashamed, as a group of soldiers walked past. "Sorry," he muttered. "Best take to your bunk and rest."

He shut the cabin door behind him, leaving me with nothing but the light of a small lamp and my thoughts. I explored the tiny cabin, but it was barely a few paces in total, windowless, just a box with a bunk and an empty chest. I sat down on the bunk. Even though the guard was for my protection, I felt rather trapped.

Poison rookgrass

DESCRIPTION: Fine-stemmed, attractive silvery grass, producing dry clusters of seeds in late summer. Seeds relatively harmless to birds, including bindies, but toxic to humans if consumed directly or through eating flesh of heavily affected birds.

SYMPTOMS: Extreme dryness of the mouth and throat, scarlet rash, dilated pupils, convulsions.

PROOFING CUES: Seeds carry a harsh, dry flavor. Affected birds, particularly bindies, demonstrate a yellowish tinge to the flesh and a pungent, enlarged liver.

25

Jovan

The Stone-Guilder stared up at us, eyes wide, mouth open, like a frightened child. The shrine behind her bore a sigil I now recognized as the mark of the lake spirit. It had been built with great love and care against the damp wall out of woven lockwort branches interspersed with bluehood and surrounded by little ceramic pots of scented oil. The floor was protected by reeds, and a well-made blanket covered the pallet. She had taken time with this place, used it the fortunes knew how many times, all the while pretending to know nothing of the catacombs.

"You know, you're quite the liar, Eliska," I said, and meant it. "All those times you pretended not to sympathize with the Darfri. You helped us when that boy was beaten but then you wouldn't back Tain in Council afterward. You pretended not to believe people when they said they'd seen Darfri magic at the siege. And all the while, here you were. Honor-down, you had us fooled."

Eliska didn't respond, just stared at us, stricken.

"There is no secret now," Hadrea said. "You had just as well finish getting dressed, and talk to us."

The Stone-Guilder dropped her head and cried.

Hadrea glanced at me, eyes narrowed with the same doubt piercing me. I'd thought of the traitor as a merciless killer; after all, they'd murdered the Chancellor and my Tashi, as well as several other innocent people. They'd helped orchestrate an attack on the city, destroying the lives and homes of thousands. They'd tried to murder Tain. I struggled to reconcile my mental image with the pathetic figure quaking before us. And yet, there was no good reason for what we had uncovered down here.

"Eliska, *why*? We trusted you."

She sobbed louder. "Please don't tell anyone," she said. She looked up at me with red eyes, her face streaked with tears and cosmetics. "You've no idea how hard I worked, Jovan."

I almost laughed, the comment was so absurd. "You want me to feel sorry for you because your scheme took a lot of *effort*?"

"What do you mean?" Then she clutched at me, eyes wild. "You don't think it was me? Who poisoned them? I'm not the traitor! Fortunes, I know this looks bad, but Jovan, I'm not the enemy, I swear to you."

I stepped out of reach. "Clearly you've been hiding your religion—you're down here performing some kind of ritual every night—what for? And where are we, Eliska? How did you know about these caves, and why didn't you tell us if you're not our enemy?"

She dropped her head in her hands. "I . . . I found them marked on an old map at the Guildhall. *Months* ago, Jovan, I swear, it has nothing to do with the siege. I was going to do a full exploration, but Chancellor Caslav told me not to."

I frowned. "You went to the Chancellor?"

"Of course! No one seemed to know about this place anymore—it predates the lower city. A lot of it's natural. There are bones down here, skeletons of some giant tunneling creature. But you can see on the map that some of it has been expanded or extended. I found the entrance and this part of the system seemed sound, but when I went to the Chancellor he told me it was dangerous and that he didn't want people trying to go treasure hunting and getting hurt. I put the maps away and didn't think about it again."

"You're saying the Chancellor knew about them already? Then why wouldn't he have—" I shook my head; it didn't matter. "You lied to my face. I asked you if the Guild had records of tunnels this side of the lake."

"I did." Her voice shook. "But I knew there was nothing down there. I got the maps out and checked; there're no exits from the city—it doesn't go anywhere near the walls—or passages to the other side of the lake. And the Chancellor was clear that it was unsafe. It was no use to the defense of the city. I only lied because it was my only private place."

Hadrea and I looked at each other. The trickle of doubt inside me wound its way deeper. Eliska caught the look and for the first time calculation passed across her expression. "I've seen you before," she said. Her gaze lingered on Hadrea's neckline and the charms hanging there. "You're Darfri, too."

But Hadrea offered no solidarity. "Yes. That only means I know perfectly well what you were doing here and who you were trying to summon."

Eliska dropped her gaze and clutched her clothing more tightly around herself reflexively. "Dara saw right away how ugly this was going to turn," she murmured. "I told her she was wrong—this is Silasta, by all the fortunes! I'd never advertised my beliefs because people look at you like you're an infant when you do, but I didn't hide them, and I've never had anyone be outright hostile. But as soon as we found out for sure this was a rebellion, Dara knew what would happen. She was right. I stopped wearing my charms." She touched the back of her neck where a necklace might lie, and I suddenly recognized the movement; I'd seen her do it a hundred times when she was anxious or under pressure. A nervous gesture. Fingers searching for jewelry that wasn't there. "Jovan, you don't know how . . . Everyone was so angry with the Darfri, saying the stupidest, cruelest, most absurd things about us. I couldn't see Dara in public or even in private. The other Councilors talk, when you're not there, especially, and you should have heard the vitriol. I was too frightened we'd be caught, and everyone would turn on me. I'd lose my position."

"And who is this Dara?"

A tiny smile brushed across her face for a moment, and her eyes took on a look . . . just a fraction of a moment, but that glimpse convinced me. Eliska loved this woman. "She's a carpenter in the Darfri quarter," she said. "She wanted to join the Guild, but no one in admissions would let her application progress. She had no one to vouch for her apprenticeship. But one day she found me in person, and shoved the most beautiful jointed toy under my nose and demanded to know why she could not get a place. I'd never met anyone like her."

"And then she told you about all the ways the city was mistreating the country people, and you sympathized." I kept my voice gentle. "And Caslav, Etan, Tain, the Darfri miner prisoner we had in jail? The murders were Dara's idea?"

Her head snapped up. "No! It's nothing like that! You have to believe me. Dara isn't . . . She just wanted to be with me. She loves the city. And we love each other." She slumped against the wall. "I grew apart from my Tashi—he's just an angry old man now, and I'm not close to my cousins. I wanted . . . *we* wanted, to leave our family homes and live together instead. I knew it would be odd, and I'd never have lasted as Guilder if people knew. Guilders have to be beyond reproach. If it meant we had to leave the city, I was willing. I've been saving for months now. When we had enough, we were going to rent a place on one of the estates and live there together as our own family."

"You know that would be just as unusual among the villages as in the city," Hadrea put in, regarding the Stone-Guilder with a softer expression. "There would be talk. Smaller villages can be vicious."

"Let them be!" Eliska cried.

"In that case, why skulk around in tunnels you've been told are dangerous?" I asked. "If you don't care about talk."

She shook her head. "They can talk all they like when I'm gone. But I wanted to help protect the city, and I'd have lost my Guild and been thrown off the Council if they'd known about this." Eliska looked between us. I realized I still held Hadrea's hand, and dropped it quickly. "Being Darfri, or loving one, doesn't mean you'd betray your honor or your home. Listen, yes, we were making an offering to the lake spirit. We want him to protect us, to end the fighting. He's very old and powerful, and he sleeps deeply, but is it not worth trying? We were all his people once—would he not protect us from tearing each other apart?"

Hadrea gave a bitter snort. "Or rise from the depths to destroy the city, which has ignored and shamed him," she said. "I can see why the rebels on the other side of the lake would be doing this."

Fresh tears welled in Eliska's eyes. She looked about fifteen years old.

"I'm not a rebel and I'm not a murderer. How can I prove I didn't do any of those things? What would convince you? You don't have any evidence against me. I love this city, I love my Guild, and I was always loyal to the Chancellor. Both of them." She wrung her hands together. "Please, Jovan. I would do anything to show you I'm not a traitor."

"It's too much, Eliska. Even if you're telling the truth, I can't risk it. You know Tain was poisoned—barely anyone knows that. It's too much of a chance, trusting you after all this. We're going to have to put you in jail until we can prove it one way or the other." I could not trust my instincts or my emotions when it came to this decision. "Do I need to call an Order Guard, or will you come along with us and preserve your honor for a bit longer?"

Eliska wiped her tears with the back of her hand and sniffed. She scrounged around for her dress's cording and wound it back on in silence. Only then did I dare look at Hadrea, who rocked on the balls of her feet, arms folded, frowning. "If you are not the poisoner, who is our enemy?" she asked Eliska.

The Stone-Guilder glanced up, straightening her hair with her fingers as she tried to reassemble her dignity. She looked at me, then back at Hadrea. "If you're convinced I'm your enemy, it doesn't matter what I think."

I shrugged. "And if you're not, you're a loyal Councilor I've just humiliated and accused of murder. Then you'd be reluctant to help me anyway."

She half-smiled. Clothing back in place and posture straight, she regained some confidence. "I've no head for intrigue," she said. "There are plenty of Councilors I don't like, but I've never thought of any of them as killers. I suppose I would just say what I told you the other day, Jovan. You seem bent on the idea that the poisoner is working with the rebels. And maybe they are. But they're no Darfri or rebel sympathizer, not truly. They killed your prisoner before he could tell you something that would help you understand the uprising. They murdered the only leader we had who didn't want them destroyed. Why are you so sure they care anything for those people out there?"

"A means to an end," Hadrea murmured. "Is that not your saying?"

My heart beat faster. The pieces that had been clattering around in my head, too jumbled to decipher, started straightening. Patterns forming. Images and memories—some my brain had been trying to draw to my attention for days, weeks even—began to make sense. Someone had incited the rebellion. If Tain and I had not returned unexpectedly early to the city, it would have been besieged while leaderless and absent its own army. Clearly the traitor wanted the city to fall. But Eliska was right: the traitor was using the rebels and the Darfri, shredding any chances for peace between the sides, murdering anyone who brought a chance of understanding between us, consigning both sides to massive losses of life. They'd tried to make us think our enemy was someone external to the Council; a rebel spy among the city Darfri, the Talafan visitors, a lone guard with a grudge. . . .

And my own brain had been trying to give me a clue for weeks. The petitioner who had tried to attract our attention the day we visited the hospital. His head had appeared in a sack days later; Marco told us the rebels had sent his head back with our runners', and the intelligence master had confirmed he was a spy working the southern border. But he had been trying to talk to Tain—not the intelligence master or Marco—in the *city,* not in the estates, and only just before the siege. He couldn't have been killed by the army outside.

"We never saw our own runners," I said aloud, barely registering the confused expressions of the two women. "He said the rebels sent our runners' heads back. But we only saw them wrapped up for burial." A spy who might have been trying to tell Tain something important—perhaps what was about to happen? "Tain would never even try sending out more messengers, not after that. And we thought they were such savages. Merciless. Killing our runners in the worst, most dishonorable way. . . . It just confirmed what barbarians everyone thought they were. Who would pursue peace after they'd killed our messengers rather than taking them prisoner? And taunted us with it?"

Eliska stared at me, her black-streaked face still and shocked. "They never did it?"

I shook my head, feeling on the brink of vomiting. "Maybe they killed our messengers, maybe they didn't. Our army never came, so I guess they didn't get through, either way. But they never sent those heads back. Marco killed the spy, a spy who might have been trying to warn us the rebels were marching. And Marco used the spy's head to harden us against the rebels and make sure we thought them cruel and honorless."

We looked at each other in the flickering lamplight.

Our enemy, our traitor, was the most dangerous man in the city. And fortunes knew how many of the Order Guards were working for him and not for us. How were we supposed to deal with him?

Eliska took us out a different route through the sewers. By now, I barely noticed the smell. Though my first impulse had been to charge off to do something about what we had just learned, it hadn't taken long to realize we had to be careful. We had to capture Marco without him realizing we knew he was the traitor, and I dared not use anyone to help except those I trusted. Which didn't leave me with many options for overpowering him physically.

Another failure to add to my list: I had likely witnessed Marco poisoning Caslav and not even noticed. I had seen Marco in his role as a bumbling, naïve temporary Councilor take the first bowl in front of Credo Bradomir, the most tradition-driven of all the Council, knowing he would be corrected for his error. A bit of sleight of hand, and a clear poison could easily have coated the inside of that bowl. But there was no point lamenting my stupidity now. We needed to tell Tain, and devise a plan to handle it. . . .

"Oh! Tain." I said aloud. Eliska and Hadrea stopped, water sloshing about us, and stared at me. "Eliska, you don't know. Tain's not dead."

The Stone-Guilder said nothing for a moment. Then, "Is this some kind of trick? I thought you believed me."

"I do." I ran a hand through my hair with a sigh. "It's because of that that you should know. He *was* poisoned. But we suspected either you or Marco, so we let you think the attempt had been successful."

She swore. Then, after a moment, she laughed. "Well, you know what, Jovan? That's the first good news I've heard in a while."

And I found myself laughing as well. It was a strange moment, standing in the half dark in a sewer, stinking of shit and slime and who knew what else, the three of us laughing like nothing had ever been so funny.

Eventually it dried up, and the gravity of the situation fell again on my shoulders. Eliska led us to the exit. Through the grate we could see nothing but darkness. "It comes out here near the north side of the lake," she said. "You can't get in from the outside, so Dara and I used it to leave."

"Yes," Hadrea said, calm. "I followed you out here last night as well."

Eliska ducked her head. "I thought I was being so careful. I never saw you."

I grinned. "No one ever does."

I followed the women through the grate. "We shouldn't go together to the Manor," I said, as Eliska closed it behind us. Aside from flickering lights on the far side of the lake, the night was quiet and still. "We can't know whether the Order Guards are loyal to the city or to Marco. He could have any number of them watching us."

"I'll go home," Eliska said. "I could use some time to digest this."

"If you come to the Manor tomorrow, on normal business, Argo will let you in. You can see Tain. And hopefully we'll have an idea what to do by then."

We parted ways there, Hadrea and I heading south, toward the bridge, and Eliska north toward the gate. The sense of companionship that had renewed itself between us spiraled away in the cool predawn air. Several times I tried to think of a way to start a conversation, but the longer I hesitated, the stonier her profile became. Inside the Manor, she stopped short of Tain's rooms and instead bade me a stiff goodnight before choosing the corridor that led to the rooms she shared with Davior and Salvea. She was gone before I could think of anything to say.

Dropping onto my pallet beside Tain's bed, I felt completely alone. He slept, mouth open, color good, looking relaxed. One good thing, at least, and the rest could wait until morning. While Marco thought Tain dead, he had no reason to be lurking about the Manor, waiting to strike again, and Tain needed rest more than he needed news of betrayal.

I woke to the sound of my friend snorting and grunting, then he sat up and peered down at me. "Jov?"

"I'm here." Blinking the sleep from my own eyes, I stretched and took a seat on the stool.

"You should replace that with something comfortable," Tain said.

"The discomfort keeps me awake. Well, that and your snoring."

He laughed, and the simple sound filled me with sudden emotion. It felt wrong to ruin the moment of levity, but I did it anyway. "Tain, Marco's the traitor."

"What?"

I told him everything. How Marco had managed the poisoning at the lunch. The spy who had tried to come to us. The rebel prisoner and the brutal execution of the jail guard.

Tain listened, stunned. Even more than me he had trusted Marco; he had a bond with the man from his tutoring even before he had become our invaluable adviser in the siege. "I can't believe it," he kept saying. "But he *loves* this country. You can't tell me he's still an agent of Perest-Avana after all this time?"

I didn't have an answer. "I can't tell you much of anything. But he's not working with the rebels to help them, and he's certainly not working for us."

Tain shook his head. "I'm still not sure I understand. Did our runners survive, then? And if that wasn't them we buried, who was it? They were real heads. I sang them the burial song."

I would never wipe that image from my mind. They *had* been real heads, I was certain; I'd smelled it even through the masking paste. But if they'd really been our messengers he'd have showed us one we knew; no need to hide the spy's head in plain sight.

But Tain answered his own question. "The missing street people," he said suddenly. "There's a streetwoman who's been trying to see me for weeks, claiming that Order Guards or dark spirits have stolen her child away. I've been getting letters. She said five men disappeared off the street in the night." I remembered, too; my sister had been accosted by the old woman on the same day as the secret burial. I had assumed the men she spoke of were just assigned duties on the walls, being relatively healthy and young. "Do you think he did . . . did that to them, just to fool us?"

"Who'd miss someone off the streets, especially now?" I muttered, extra guilt sinking in. "He probably figured we'd ignore it as unimportant, and he was right."

Honor-down, we had thought an impassioned army murdering messengers in such a horrific way was barbarous. How much worse that Marco could have done such a thing to five innocent strangers just to use their heads as convenient props in his gruesome play.

"How are we going to stop him?"

"I can't risk confiding in any Order Guards. They could all be working with him, for all we know. What if his allies volunteered to be the ones who stayed behind?"

Tain paused so long I thought for a moment he'd fallen asleep again. But eventually he said, "What about one of your concoctions? Could you knock him out?"

I nodded, thoughtful. "I don't want to risk any kind of altercation with him, but if I could dose his food or tea we could drag him to jail and we wouldn't need an Order Guard to watch him. Being a poisoner himself he's probably pretty careful, but if I choose something I'm immune to I can eat from it, too."

"Do it," Tain said. "I'm no use to you, weak like this. And Marco's a dangerous man. We need every advantage we can take."

I agreed, though fear chilled my veins. As Hadrea had been so quick to point out, I was no soldier. I wouldn't pit myself against *her*, a farmer, and Marco was a lifelong professional. What if I couldn't fool Marco? Would my fear and judgment show? I'd spent my lifetime hiding my role as a proofer. We would all just have to hope I could hide myself as a poisoner just as effectively.

The remainder of the day was spent in an endless game of dodging Councilors and searching for an opportunity to get Marco alone. I felt like a Muse piece, considering my every move to best avoid the most dangerous other pieces. I barely missed Bradomir, who was storming through the Manor gardens, prepping his excellent baritone for some shouting at Argo, and avoided too both Budua and Marjeta since I wished neither to reveal to nor conceal from them the truth about Marco. But as if he were playing the same game, Marco gave me no chance to talk to him in private, either. One minor crisis or another always interrupted us whenever I thought there was a chance. At least he was given no opportunity to cause mischief that I could see, since he was in full preparation mode for the inevitable attack on the bridge, managing the trenches and defense plans and conducting our last training of the people who would soon be our front lines. Eliska warned us grimly to get some sleep, because the rebels would not need much longer to prepare to take the bridge. It could be any time now.

I was meeting with the guards at the Finger, almost unrecognizable now with its additional fortifications, and the scouts on the southern wall when Nara and Lazar cornered me, both smelling suspiciously like kori. I told them Tain wanted a full Council meeting first thing in the morning. This time, I wasn't even lying.

"I was beginning to think he'd decided he didn't need a Council anymore," Nara told me, her peevish face even more pinched than usual. "Or he'd found a secret way out of the city and just left us here to burn."

Honor-down, sometimes I fantasized about slapping that expression off her face. "The Chancellor's working hard, Credola. He's done his best to keep the city running and he needs all of you to be pulling your weight, as well. What he *doesn't* need is his own Council spreading rumors like that to damage the morale of our people."

Lazar looked away, and the embarrassment on his face suggested he hadn't been keeping that particular suspicion to himself. I gritted my teeth. Nara lifted her chin a little more, looking me in the eye. "People are getting close to starving, Credo Jovan," she said. "Their Chancellor's lack of caring is the least of their worries."

I hadn't been to the stores in two days. I'd also barely eaten anything aside from portions of Tain's food. A sick knot twisted in my stomach. "What level are our supplies at?"

"We're out of oats and beans," Nara said, smug. The slapping itch in my hand returned. "There's enough rice for one serving a day at the ration stations, for perhaps another few days. Even with the nets out every day, there can't be enough fish for all of us. Fighting's breaking out. Are you blind, boy?"

I scanned the faces of the men and women loitering around the square. Listless, despondent. Thin. We had already cannibalized anything we could use for food; all the edible plants had long been stripped out of the gardens and used as extra fiber in the rations, and we'd eaten some dubious animals over the past few weeks, leaving only the ones that could supply milk. The rebels didn't even need to take the rest of the city by force. We'd all starve to death just as easily.

"They'll be eating each other soon enough," Nara said, voice dripping with scorn. "Little better than animals."

I did a much worse job of containing my anger this time; Lazar stepped back a little as my head snapped around. "You know, I've had about—"

But Nara had never been easily intimidated. She stepped up close enough to smell her sour breath. "About enough of these animals? Me, too. Perhaps you'd like to tell us what you know about my great-nephew? You know, I'm only an old woman, but I hear rumors, too."

Blood rushed to my face and I looked away from her accusatory eyes. Did she know what had happened to Edric, or merely suspect? "Tomorrow, at dawn, in the Council room," I muttered, and didn't bother with a farewell.

Since it was becoming increasingly clear I would not be able to separate Marco from his possible co-conspirators among the Guards tonight, the Council meeting it would have to be. The other Councilors might not believe that the Warrior-Guilder had merely fainted, but if all went according to plan, we would have the traitor incapacitated and we would no longer need to worry about their loose tongues. I returned to the Manor to prepare the teacups, nerves building. Would he suspect me? I tried to shut down the part of my brain that pictured all the ways it could play out if he did, because none of those outcomes looked positive for me. I just had to stay calm.

Fortunately, my exhaustion was greater than my anxiety this time, and it seemed like I had barely settled into my pallet in Tain's room when I was jolting awake again.

And then the city's alarm bells rang.

Darpar

DESCRIPTION: Dark brown crystal, hard but brittle, often found in conjunction with opal.

SYMPTOMS: Short-term, sudden increase in energy and strength, bad breath, developing into muscle tremors; longer-term weakness, memory loss, mental deterioration.

PROOFING CUES: Sweet, metallic taste and sickly smell on breath.

26

Kalina

A queasy belly woke me; I sat upright, retching, and cracked my head on a beam. Groaning, I swung my legs from the cramped bunk, clutching my head with one hand and my stomach with the other. A vaguely familiar tune ran through my head, a fragment of my dream. It took several breaths to remember where I was.

Outside, someone stopped whistling, and I realized the tune hadn't been in my head after all.

"Garan?" I called, trying the door.

He opened it, peering in with a furrowed brow. "Are you all right?"

"Sick," I managed, trying to step out. "Can I come on deck?"

He bit his lip. "I don't think . . . The Warrior-Guilder wanted you to stay belowdecks."

"You can see I'm sick," I wheedled. "Garan, don't make me throw up down here. It'd stink for you, too."

He looked back and forth down the corridor, wringing his hands. "I'm not sure . . ."

"We don't have to talk, and I'll keep a scarf up so no one notices me. Please?"

A moment's hesitation, then he relented. "Come on, then. But scarf up."

I unwrapped the sticky scarf from around my neck and threw it over my head like a hood, then followed Garan abovedecks. Late afternoon sun and lush green banks greeted me, and the freshness of the air filled my lungs sweetly. I sucked in several deep breaths, wondering how I had slept so long. Garan ushered me to the quietest part of the deck, looking nervous. *"I'm not the traitor, remember?"* I said, and he smiled in response, but his eyes still darted about as if expecting Aven to pounce on his disobedience at any instant.

"Where are we?" I asked, scanning the countryside. Our boat sailed along among dozens of others, a thicket of dark, quiet creatures making swift pace down the river. Unmarred green stretched away in both directions, giving no hint of our position.

Garan shook his head. "Not sure. I've been with you below, remember? But we look to be making good time; the wind and the current are helping us."

"Honor-down, I hope we're not too late." I stared north. We'd see the city long before we arrived; would it be a smoking ruin?

A burly wetlander striding past the other side of the boat gave us a sidelong look, and Garan took my hand. "Please, let's go below," he said, and I agreed, with another sigh. I didn't want to get my guard in trouble, but couldn't help dreading returning to the damp little box of a room.

Soon. Soon we'll be back, and Aven will save the city.

Garan shut my door behind me and I took a seat on the bunk. *As long as I don't go mad down here in the meantime.* I shut my eyes and lay there, listening to Garan's whistling and trying not to think too much.

False goaberry

DESCRIPTION: Fruit from the gravalana bush, often called "false goaberry" for its resemblance to the popular fruit, but distinguishable by the spiral pattern on the leaves.

SYMPTOMS: Contact with juice causes a burning rash on the skin, distinctive with large, hivelike growths, worsening with touch. Symptoms of consumption include burning sensation in mouth and throat, ulcers and bleeding from gums, internal bleeding, death.

PROOFING CUES: Intensely sour flavor, leaving the mouth dry; prickling, tingling sensation on tongue, cheeks, gums.

27

Jovan

It took me precious time to convince Tain to stay in bed. He staggered as far as his bedroom door, struggling to make his way in the blackness. "I need to be out there!" he yelled, some semblance of his old volume returning. But he was weak as a day-old kitsa, and it wasn't hard to wrestle him to safety.

"And how are you going to defend yourself in this state?" I demanded. "And how easy would it be for Marco to finish you off in a crowd?"

"If you gave me something—I know you've got things that perk you up, what is it, that mineral the javelin thrower was using a few years back? I could—"

"Darpar? No." I frowned. "It's a poison. Even if you were at full health it wouldn't be worth the risk. You need to rest. You're staying here with Salvea and Davi and I'll be back to let you know what's happening as soon as I can."

Salvea interrupted with a polite little cough before I could leave. "Credo Jovan, have you seen my daughter?"

"I'm sorry, Salvea, no."

"Oh." She twisted her hands together. At her feet, unusually silent, Davi leaned into her skirts and stared up at me, wide-eyed and accusing. "She wasn't in bed when the bell rang."

It wasn't even dawn yet; still dark and a fraction chilly. What nighttime explorations had she gone on this time? My heart grew heavy as I imagined her spying on Marco or something equally dangerous. "I'll look out for her down near the bridge," I promised.

The city was buzzing as people streamed in one direction or another in the moonlight, some running toward the lake and others away. It was a starry, bright night and as soon as I had a clear line of sight to the water it was obvious what had happened. The far shore crawled with activity; the rebels had built what looked like portable platforms which extended out into the lake, and onto them were being wheeled great catapults, now with an angle to the Finger. On the west half of Trickster's, a dark mass of troops advanced slowly. Out of reach of our torches and lit only by moonlight, I could barely make out their troops, shielded and in formation, presumably protecting further machines.

Their catapults were outside the range of the tower's archers, and they wouldn't risk advancing any of their soldiers across the bridge until they had done sufficient damage to the tower. They'd be open targets marching on the bridge, vulnerable to our archers from the shore and from the tower. By the time I reached the Finger, all the new archers' slots on the wall extensions were filled, and flaming, oil-filled basins stood at the ready. Across the water, drums and a droning chant echoed eerily. It was meant to intimidate us, and it was working.

I raced up the back stairs and to the top level. Marco showed me to the arrow slits so I could see the catapults being loaded. "They have reassembled their machines," he told me, grim. "That is what they have been waiting for. They will shoot at us from safety over there until they breach the gate."

"What do we do?" I asked. "We can't lead a charge over there; they've ten times the men we have, and it'd be us being picked off on the bridge."

He ran a hand over his head. "The Builders' Guild is bringing our other catapults down. We must destroy theirs before they destroy the tower. If their troops on the bridge advance, we will also need to be ready to meet them."

It was only then I remembered Marco was our enemy; in the distraction of the attack I'd dropped back into old patterns. As he left the room, already shouting orders, I shook my head. Some part of me still found it difficult to picture the humble and competent man as a villain. *Which is how he fooled us all for so long. But why?*

As I descended, the atmosphere among the men and women manning it was cold as the round stone walls. Everyone looked frightened.

"They're in place!" someone yelled, and I found a spot behind the new wall to hoist myself up to see. The different-colored stones had been cobbled together from an assortment of other buildings and remade into this fat, triangular extension to the tower; it couldn't compare to the strength of the city walls, but Eliska's Guild had done the best they could in limited time.

"Loooad!" someone cried. Our own catapult, the one built directly on the tower roof, was hidden by the lip of the tower; it now burst into action, sending a great chunk of rock hurtling over the water toward the opposing machines. Even their drums seemed to hold their breath a moment as the rock spun soundlessly in the air . . .

. . . and crashed short of the line of weapons, plopping harmlessly into the lake in a shower of white spray blossoming in the dark.

The rebel army cheered, a great roar of sound that drained my spirit. They retaliated immediately; fear drove me down from my perch on the wall as the stones sailed over the lake. The smash of stone on stone shook the structure with each deafening impact. From the sound of it, perhaps half of their shots had reached some part of the Finger.

"Five in the lake, Credo," Chen called down to me, her face oddly cheerful underneath her helmet. "Three on the bridge, no harm done there. Four hit us. No damage yet."

But they had our entire lower city to dismantle, and therefore an endless supply of projectiles. We wouldn't hold out forever.

A cheer from our side spun me around. Eliska led a procession of siege weapons across the grass, all on wheels. Some were catapults, but others I didn't recognize; low things like flat carts, loaded with massive metal javelins.

"Not much testing done on these yet," Eliska told me as I met her. "But they're more mobile than the catapults and we should be able to get them through the gate on the bridge and shoot at anyone approaching over it."

Behind me, another series of impacts and splashes signaled another round of fire. I suppressed a shiver. "Good luck," I said, moving out of her way.

I moved back out of range behind the trenches nearby with a crowd of others as the new machines rolled out onto the east side of Trickster's. Budua the Scribe-Guilder joined me there, gray like a ghost in the moonlight. We watched together, helpless, as the catapults exchanged fire. The rebels, cautious of our new javelin machines, were not yet advancing over the bridge. The first stone smashed into our makeshift wall and I winced as a spiderweb of cracks sprang out from the impact zone. Beside me, Budua didn't flinch.

"Credo Jovan!" A small voice came through the noise. Little Erel, Tain's messenger, had spotted me and scurried toward us. "I've been looking for you, Credo."

I glanced around me. Budua pressed her lips together, frowning; she now knew the truth about Tain. "What is it, Erel?" I dropped my voice, trying not to worry. Behind us another mighty crash shook the wall. Had Tain relapsed?

"Um, it's the lady. Hadrea."

My heart pounded a distracting rhythm in my head. "What's happened?"

"I've been trying to find you, Credo, but every time I go somewhere you've moved somewhere else." His tone rang with the exasperation of a twelve-year-old discovering the world wouldn't move in convenient predictability.

The crowd cheered suddenly and we all spun around to see that one of our catapult strikes from the Finger had successfully hit one of the extended pier platforms the rebels had built over the lake. The platform jerked and tilted and their catapult began to slide toward the water. I tapped Erel's shoulder and he snapped his gaping mouth shut.

"She left a message for you earlier. Before the bells rang. She said . . . um, that she was going to the Oll Woorin."

"To the what?"

More cheers as the frantic rebels lost control of the sliding machine and the floating platform tipped more dramatically, sending the catapult toppling almost gracefully into the silky waters of the lake. This time I had to gently take Erel's chin and redirect his gaze to me.

"Sorry, Credo. I think she said the Oll Woorin. But I don't know what that means. She didn't explain! She said you would know."

Another enormous crack split the air as our wall took a hit. Across the water, the rebels started up another chant, and unease spread around me, a palpable thing.

Frustrated, I shook my head. "I don't know what that means, Erel. She must have told you something else." *Oll Woorin*, I thought. The name tickled with familiarity. *Where have I heard that before?* My tired brain felt woolly as I scanned the lakeside blankly, trying to think. I couldn't remember where I'd heard the word.

"Os-Woorin, do you mean?" Budua said suddenly, and Erel nodded in relief. "Oh, yes, Scribe-Guilder. It could have been that, now you say it."

That I had *definitely* heard, but through the increasing pounding of my heartbeat in my head and the rising chant from across the water, I couldn't catch the thought. I looked helplessly at Budua, and the Scribe-Guilder cocked her head. "From the song, Credo. The children's rhyme. *Toil in secret/day and night/build it up/get it right/work so hard so we don't fall/the great Os-Woorin saved us all. . . .*"

"Old wooden, you mean. The great *old wooden* saved us all." Everyone knew that rhyme; the stacking game that accompanied it was played on every street corner and in every garden in the city. Falling from the top of the stack was the cause of many a childhood injury, but it never dropped in popularity.

Budua shook her head. "No. Oh, I know that's how the children sing it these days. Even in your day, I suppose. But they're not the words. Os-Woorin, not old wooden. What is an 'old wooden'?"

"What's an Os-Woorin?" I countered, but already my brain was tickling again. Os-Woorin. It sounded even more familiar, and it wasn't because of the rhyme.

"I don't know," Budua said. "But that's the right word, I'm certain of that."

Another crash and then a hush on our side. "Darfri magic," I heard someone whisper, and as if indeed the Darfri had summoned their spirits across the lake around their catapults a heavy mist was forming, obscuring our view of their machines. I shivered. The lake was often misty at dawn, but this was something different. Had they dropped some chemical in the lake that was reacting with the water? It was growing harder to disregard or explain away the strangeness.

And then my memory triggered. Of course; Hadrea had told me. The great spirit of the lake, that was its name: Os-Woorin. Our history books might have skimmed over the old religion but sometimes truth was buried in children's rhymes and stories. So Hadrea had gone to the Os-Woorin? What did that mean? Back to the shrine Eliska and her lover had built in the cave? Did she intend to try to ask a boon of the lake spirit herself? It hadn't worked for Eliska and Dara, and presumably the rebel Darfri would have tried the same thing. But I wondered; maybe Eliska had given her some other idea about how to contact Os-Woorin. I had sometimes suspected Hadrea knew more about Darfri magic than she was perhaps meant to. Did she know something Eliska did not?

I left Budua and went back to the Finger. The Stone-Guilder was on the roof with the catapult, wind whipping her hair, helping with adjustments to the machine. I dared a peek over the edge; the mist had hidden the rebel platforms entirely, but even as I watched a stone hurtled from the cloud and struck the base of the tower near the bridge, and we were all jolted by the impact. Someone beside me cried out as flying debris hit her in the face. I ducked back to safety.

"What is it, Jovan?" Eliska didn't even look up at me.

"You saw Hadrea yesterday didn't you? Did she ask you about the catacombs?"

She glanced up at that. "She took the maps. I brought them to you at the Manor yesterday afternoon and she said she'd pass them on." She pulled me backward and out of the way as the operators began loading another immense stone.

"I still haven't seen her. She was up before the bells this morning and I thought she might have gone down there."

Eliska dropped her voice, checking around her quickly for listening ears. "She was interested. There was a room on the map marked with the Darfri symbol for Os-Woorin, the lake spirit. I thought it must be an old shrine. That was what gave me the original idea to . . . well, you know. But it was well into the caves, probably right under the lake itself, so given what Chancellor Caslav told me, I never went there, and told Hadrea not to as well."

I almost laughed. As if Hadrea could ever be told not to do something she wanted to.

"Ready to fire!" someone called, and Eliska shook her head apologetically. "Jovan, I can't talk right now."

It was tempting to go the caves then and there, but I was Tain's only source of news of the attack on the bridge. I set back at a run, thinking hard.

"I told you, stop worrying. I'm fine. I'd be better if you gave me something—"

I looked up at Tain sharply. "I *told* you. These aren't substances to take lightly at the best of times. In your condition I don't know what they'd do to your body."

"All right, all right. I'm feeling much stronger anyway." Tain watched me, bemused, as I sorted through stacks of journals I'd brought from our apartments. The history of our family. These records predated Silasta and even Sjona, giving insight into our ancestors in the formative days of their reign.

"Is this just about Hadrea?" he asked as I flicked through the older hand-bound journals. "We don't even know she's down there. She could have gone anywhere."

"It's not just that. There's something about those tunnels, something about this lake spirit reference. We don't know much about it, but religion was important back then. Os-Woorin found its way into a children's rhyme that's lasted all this time. What do you think that means?"

"I've never thought about it," he said. "It's just a rhyme."

"Etan once told me there can be fascinating history in rhymes children sing," I murmured, turning the old pages carefully. The words ran back and forth in my head, mocking me. Was there some link between the rhyme and what Hadrea had told me about how the first Chancellor had summoned the lake spirit and blessed Silasta? Why weren't there any references in history books?

When children played the old wooden game, they formed piles, stacking on one another on the ground. The bolder ones sat on each other's shoulders during the "build it up" stage, and giggled as they wobbled, trying to stay up as they sang "so we don't fall." It was a song about building something, obviously, but not something wooden. "Are they talking about building the city?"

Here, this was the right era. My ancestor Tresa, the first proofer—though she had just been a close ally of the Chancellor with an interest in chemistry, then, not truly a proofer. I scanned. There wasn't much—innocuous notes about experiments, indecipherable comments about people I had never heard of. Some blank sections that looked like she'd started to take notes on something and never finished. The strange thing, the thing that bothered me, was why my own family's notes were so absent mention of spirits or ritual. If everyone was religious back then, even if it had fallen out of fashion and thus records over time, why had I no memory of Darfri beliefs in our own family journals?

"I guess it's just a song about the Os-Woorin blessing, then."

"Maybe." This next section had several blank pages. I stopped. Once or twice might have been an error, an unfinished task. But my family wasn't known for that. I smoothed the paper with my fingers. This journal was older than my family code. Sensitive information might have been conveyed another way.

It was still dark, and there were better lamps in the outer room. I left Tain on the bed and unpacked my pouches on the table by the door; both needed checking and refilling anyway. I took the jar of naftate, which I'd had out as a detector for manita fungus, and spread it thinly across the blank page, pulse thumping. Had Tresa known the trick with geraslin ink?

"Jov, what is it?"

The light still wasn't good; was that a glimmer of color? I laid the journal directly under the lamp and stared at the page, willing something to happen.

"Nothing," I said at last, returning to Tain, disappointment heavy in me. "I thought there might have been something important there."

"Mmm." His interest had faded. "I think I need to be down there."

I looked up from the journal. "At the front? Are you mad?"

"Tell me honestly, how's morale? Do the people still have hope?"

I dropped my gaze back to the book, avoiding his. The mood of the trenches had been apparent even from my short visit, and I wouldn't lie to my Chancellor or my friend. "People are saying we won't last the night. Some of our people have fled and are hiding in the city rather than wait to defend the bridge or the trenches. They're frightened. They think the rebels will use magic to defeat us." *Maybe they will,* I thought, my brain twitching with

unease at the clash between what I had observed and what I could ratio-
nally explain.

"And what are they saying about me?"

"That you're dead. Or that you found a secret way out of the city, and
fled." I saw his expression, and shook my head. "Unless we've found a way to
neutralize Marco before the night's out, you can't do anything about it. You'd
be the biggest target in the world if you went out there in this state. The
only reason we're managing to keep you safe now is that he thinks he already
killed you."

"I thi—" He looked up suddenly. "What was that?"

"What was what?"

Tain's head jerked to me and then back to the doorway, lost in darkness
outside the range of the small bedside lamp. "I heard something."

I stood. "It must be Salvea. Salvea? Is everything all right?"

The rustle of wooden beads marked passage into the bedroom. Then,
"Everything's just fine, Credo Jovan, Honored Chancellor," Marco said.

Petra venom

DESCRIPTION: Toxin extracted from the poison sacs of the venomous armored petra spider.

SYMPTOMS: When stung directly or poison is injected, intense pain and burning around sting site, followed by spread of stiffening and convulsing muscles, fits, breathing difficulties, coma, death. When ingested, immediate breathing difficulties, convulsions, and rapid seizures, death.

PROOFING CUES: None. Extracted venom is odorless and tasteless.

28

Kalina

Outside the tent, Garan was whistling again. The cheerful tune rankled, stuck as I was inside, hearing the sounds of the troops in the distance. We had pulled off the boats well north of the city, setting up a base camp out of sight of the rebels. A small contingent had been sent to the east bank to deal with the remaining rebel army guarding the south section of the old city; the rest were marching with Aven toward the main rebel army. I was stuck here.

"Don't worry," Garan had told me earlier. "We'll take the breach in the wall and trap the rebels between it and the lake. The day'll be ours in no time at all, and you'll be going home."

But he didn't seem to understand my distress at the idea. "They *attacked the capital*," he said, shrugging, as I tried to explain. "Whatever the reason, you can't expect there to be no consequences."

"They were forced into it," I argued. "What will it do to the country if we kill one another?"

My guard had simply shrugged and ushered me back into my tent.

Now I gnawed at my lower lip and wrung my hands, frustration eating at me. Stuck here in a dark, floorless tent, well behind the battle, I hated not knowing what was happening. Would the rebels surrender? Something about the tune Garan whistled irritated me more and more. It sounded familiar, but I couldn't place the song.

"Garan?" I tried. "Any word?"

He stuck his face into the tent, his expression a cross between exasperation and sympathy. "You'll know more when I do. Can't you just relax?"

I gave him a flat stare, and he grinned. "All right, you probably can't relax." He scratched his head with a sigh. "I know how you feel. Sometimes it's hard doing what I do, and being out of contact with everyone."

"Why're you stuck here with me? Is it because Aven didn't want to let anyone else know about me?"

"Partly. But guard duty's pretty common for me." He stuck one skinny arm through the tent door. "I'm not exactly first choice for the front line."

"You're a scout usually?"

He nodded. "I'm quick and I'm quiet, and I can track better than anyone else I know." As if embarrassed to be caught bragging, he ducked his head and added, "Least, that's what some people say. I'm not that great with a weapon, though."

"Do you get bored, guarding?"

He paused, then looked me over and grinned. "Guarding's not so bad, sometimes." As if he regretted saying it, Garan ducked back outside. Moments later, I heard the whistling again and smiled despite myself. Nothing could keep his mood down.

But I couldn't sit still for long. The song nagged at me. I hummed along, but no words came to mind. It was like picking at a scab. "Garan?" I called again.

"Yes?" He stuck his head in again.

"What's that tune? I know it but I can't remember from where."

"Oh." He frowned, then shrugged. "I'm not sure. It's been in my head for days."

I smiled. "Yes, I'd noticed."

"Sorry."

I settled back down on the single cushion, the only pretense of comfort in this plain little tent. Probably it wouldn't bother me so much if the situation weren't so frustrating. I picked at the grass, tearing the blades into pieces, and tried to think about something positive. Surely the rebels, if trapped in the lower city, would have to surrender rather than attempting to defend against a superior foe on two fronts. Aven's force was well trained and well equipped, and its members were motivated to save their home. The rebels couldn't hope to survive against them. And if they surrendered, Tain—no, not Tain, I reminded myself with a pang—the Council would hopefully work with them to fix what had gone so horribly wrong in our country. Maybe we could all look forward to a better future.

Garan stuck his head back into the tent. "I remembered," he said. "But you wouldn't know it. I was guarding the Doranite spy, weeks ago. The blasted fellow kept singing it."

"Oh." I frowned. "It just sounded so . . ." Suddenly, lyrics popped into my head. "Something about . . . seeing clearer . . ."

"Yeah!" Garan agreed. "Grant me just a moment's time, something-something . . . lips on mine?" He shook his head. "He was a traitor, but the song was catchy."

My heart beat faster and my mouth went dry. Suddenly I couldn't breathe.

"Had a beautiful voice. I didn't talk to him, of course," he said hastily, giving me a sidelong embarrassed look. "We put him down in a section of the mine, for safety. Don't think he even knew I was there. But he sang a lot. I didn't know the song, but it's a good one."

I found myself on my feet, clutching Garan's arm, breath catching in my throat. "You said he was a Doranite spy, but you called him a *traitor*. Was he from Doran or Sjona? Garan, what did he look like?"

He stared down at my hand on his arm as if not quite sure what to do about it. The possible impropriety of our conversation visibly dawned on him. Before he could pull away, I tightened my grip and leaned in closer. "It's important," I said. "I'm begging you. Tell me what he looked like."

"He was working for Doran, but he was Sjon," Garan said. "I don't know. Ordinary? Handsome, I suppose. Tall, sort of longish hair."

I squeezed my eyes shut. My chest hurt. "He was Sjon. Why did you think he was working for Doran?"

He stared at me, voice stiffening. "Warrior-Guilder Aven interrogated him. She concluded he was in Doran's pay."

"What happened to him? You were guarding him in the mine. . . . Where is he now?"

Garan tugged his arm free. "What do you want to know about a spy for?"

"He wasn't a spy," I said. The tightness in my chest made it hard to get the words out. "Honor-down, he was the last thing from a spy. *What happened to him?*"

The guard frowned, but when he saw the tears dripping down my face, he softened. "He was a traitor caught by the army. What do you think?" he said gently. "After the Warrior-Guilder finished questioning him, they hanged him, of course."

A half cough, half sob spasmed through my throat. Part of me knew what that meant, but surely, surely, it couldn't be true.

It couldn't have been Edric.

Because if it had been . . . I let go of Garan's arm and sank back onto the cushions. If Edric had made it through the rebel army after all, if his head hadn't been one of those in the sacks—then who *was* that in the sacks?— and if he had made it here, he would have gone straight to Aven as instructed. He'd have told no one else who he was; we had told the messengers not to risk the news to anyone else.

But Aven had treated him as a traitor. She'd "questioned" him, hanged him. And done nothing about the city. *Did she not believe him? Why not?* She'd acted like the news was a shock when I told her what had happened to the city.

"What's wrong?" Garan asked, after a long hesitation. "Why would you care what happened to some spy? Why would you think you knew him?"

I knew what it meant—what it had to mean—that Edric had been hanged and his story suppressed. "You have to get me out of here, Garan," I said. "Please."

The guard folded his arms, sympathy retreating. "I don't think so," he said. "Why don't you tell me what you know about this spy."

I pushed down my panic and studied him, evaluating his honest face with ruthless precision. Garan mightn't be the brightest man in the army, but he liked me. He'd talked to me even though he knew he shouldn't. His inclination was to sympathize, to help. Honor-down, I wouldn't get out of this camp without *someone's* help. I wiped my tears with the back of a hand and stood, trying to stay calm. "I can tell you his name was Edric Korantash

Ash," I said. "He was Credola Nara's second cousin. A rising musician in the Performers' Guild, and a competitive runner. And he came from the city for exactly the same reason I did: to warn the Warrior-Guilder what was happening to our city, and summon the army home."

Garan snorted. "He was nothing of the sort. He was found skulking around in the hills, spying on the camp. And I told you, Warrior-Guilder Aven herself questioned him. He wasn't a Credo. I saw his arms—no Guild tattoos, let alone Family ones. I doubt he was even from the city; probably just some estate worker who got tempted over the border." He tightened his folded arms, but said more kindly, "You're just mistaken. The man they hanged wasn't your friend Edric. I barely even told you what he looked like. Why are you so sure?"

"The song," I said. *Calm, stay calm. You can't look crazy.* "That song he was singing. You'd never heard it before because Edric only wrote it after the army left the city. I know, because he wrote it for me." I met Garan's gaze, pleased to see it troubled. "The only person who could have known that song at all—let alone known it well enough to sing it—was someone who was in the city right before the siege."

"Maybe I got the tune wrong. Maybe you don't remember it that well."

"It's called 'Kalina, Kalina'," I said. "Isn't that what he was singing? *My name.*"

He opened his mouth, his reaction betraying his doubt.

"And he *did* have tattoos; we just disguised them with cosmetics so that if he got captured they wouldn't know he was from Silasta. He must have told you that. He must have said all of this."

"I told you, I didn't talk to him." He shook his head. "Look, it doesn't matter. The *Warrior-Guilder* questioned him, I told you. If he was some messenger with word from the city, he'd have told her everything and we'd have been back weeks ago and none of this would have happened." He patted my shoulder. "You're tired and worried. You're not thinking straight."

I caught his hand. "Listen to me, Garan," I said. "*Listen to me.* Edric made it here, against the odds. You're right, he'd have told all of this to the Warrior-Guilder, because that's what the Chancellor told him to do. And the only reason Aven wouldn't have taken the army straight back after he told her was if she *already knew.*"

"That doesn't make any sense," he said. Now he looked afraid, and he tried to pull his hand away, as if I might be contagious.

"It doesn't make sense, you're right. Except if she's working with the rebels." My mind raced. Why would Aven have been lured to the rebel cause? She already held a position of great power, privilege, and wealth. But she didn't fit the mold of a Credola, either; perhaps her impatience and disdain for the city had indeed given her sympathy for the country folk. The army did spend more time out in broader Sjona than any of the other Guilds, guarding roads, dealing with bandits, and conducting training exercises. And perhaps Aven's betrayal of the city and Council wasn't so unexpected. Undeniably, hers was the least honorable, the least respected, of the Guilds. No one aspired for their child or Tash to end up there. Though Aven was on the Council, she was more tolerated than admired, and even Aven's own family considered her a vulgar necessity rather than a true equal.

"You're being ridiculous," he said. "Can you hear yourself? You told the Warrior-Guilder the same story, and she didn't throw you in a mine, did she? We're going back to save the city right now!"

True. Was she really planning to attack the rebels, though, or join them? The whole army couldn't be traitors or they'd never have needed a rebel army at all, and no matter how beloved Aven was as a commander, she could hardly just instruct the army to destroy their own city and hope for obedience. So what was her plan? What had changed? "Tain's dead," I murmured, more to myself than the horrified guard before me. "When Edric came, Tain was still alive. But when I came, he was dead." That didn't explain the *why*, but it might be significant. "Garan, you have to help me get out of here. I need to be able to warn the Council."

But the last trace of sympathy had disappeared, and now he looked at me with a mixture of revulsion and anger. "Credola," he said stiffly. "You're talking about the Warrior-Guilder. Your words are treason."

"I'm not talking against the country or the Chancellor," I snapped, desperation surging through me. "So it can't be treason."

"It is treason to me," he said. "I think the Warrior-Guilder needs to know you're throwing these accusations around. She can decide what to do."

The anger turned to icy fear so quickly I struggled to catch my breath. "No, please!" By the fortunes, what would Aven do to me if she knew I had guessed her secret? She hadn't hesitated to kill Edric. "Garan, *please*. I . . .

perhaps you were right before. I'm confused. I'm so tired." I widened my eyes, spreading my hands. Every part of myself I'd thought of as weak and pathetic, I summoned now. "You're right, of course you're right. Please don't tell the Warrior-Guilder I thought such stupid things, even for just a moment."

He frowned, looking me over. "Sit down and be quiet," he said at last. "I don't want to hear another word out of you." He stepped outside the tent and shut the flap behind him with a snap of fabric.

I swallowed, heart pounding. Aven was with the army, near the city. Even if Garan decided to tell her, he couldn't until she came back to camp. That gave me one brief opportunity. One last chance to save my city.

I dropped to my knees at the back of the tent, the farthest point from the door, and began to dig.

Graybore

DESCRIPTION: Crumbly mineral deposit found in veins of hard rock, generally deep underground. Dust caused by disturbing deposits is poisonous in large quantities (usually breathed in over time).

SYMPTOMS: Breathing difficulties, bloody cough, hair loss (from exposure over time).

PROOFING CUES: Insoluble, and dominating earthy flavor makes it difficult to include in toxic quantities in food, but has been used in perfumes to gradually poison the wearer. Visible as fine gray powder on release or cloudy residue in perfume bottle.

29

Jovan

We froze.

"I did wonder," Marco continued, voice lighter than usual, absent some layer of false humility, "why you would be running back to the Manor in a time of crisis, Credo, if there was no one here to report to." Behind my back, my fingers searched around for something, anything, to use as a weapon. My damn pouch of poisons was still in the outer room, utterly useless to me here. "And here you are, Tain Caslavtash Iliri, hiding away, breathing as ever."

I glanced around. There were daggers on the wall, mostly decorative. Hanging by the doorway—behind Marco—was Tain's armor and sword.

"Nothing to say, Honored Chancellor?" Marco asked. His voice grew closer until he stepped into our circle of light. He wore a breastplate and carried his great sword, which he hadn't yet bothered to draw; it swung by his side, menacing.

Tain's voice was calm and clear, but behind him his hands clenched into the bedding and I felt him pulling himself backward, just a fraction.

"What are you doing here, Marco? You have responsibilities down at the bridge."

"Well," the Warrior-Guilder said, stepping closer, "I just found out a job I thought completed was unfinished. And you know how I like the satisfaction of work well done. I came to fix that mistake."

Keep talking, I willed Tain, edging one foot off the end of the bed, getting ready to spring.

"You're really here to do this?" Tain asked, managing to sound cool and disappointed. "You're going to cut down the Chancellor in his bed? That's who you are?"

Marco smiled, a cold baring of teeth that made him look a different man. "I suppose it is," he said. "But be reasonable, please. I made every attempt to be subtle first. This is . . . messy. It is lucky most of the city already thinks you have fled Silasta." He glanced at me. "I didn't want to have to kill you, Jovan, or Eliska, but here we are."

"What's Eliska got to do with anything?" Tain asked, and this time his voice wavered.

"Do not think me a fool," Marco said. "You know the Stone-Guilder did not poison anyone. So chances are you told her the truth." He shrugged. "I will not enjoy killing her, but you know the dangers of battle. Anything can happen."

Anything can happen, I repeated to myself. And in the moment he stepped again toward Tain, I sprang off the far side of the bed, throwing myself into an awkward roll on the floor. I came to my feet by the ornamental daggers and had both in my hands by the time Marco caught up. I knocked his sword aside with one dagger—pitifully short by comparison to his blade—and lashed out with the other one.

Marco shifted his torso back and out of the way easily, bobbing forward again with the same cold smile. "You're brave, Credo. But you forget I taught you all those years ago. I've seen you fight. Or try to, anyway." He whipped his sword through my guard, easily parting my daggers, and only a last-minute dive to my side saved my throat from his blade. Unconcerned, the big man strolled after me as I backed away.

"You betrayed the city," Tain said, stepping between us. He carried his sword. Bile rose, bitter, in my throat. I'd tried to give him a moment to get out the door, and he'd chosen instead to go for his weapon. *Why didn't you run, you fool?*

Marco tapped at Tain's blade and laughed at the immediate wobble in the Chancellor's grip. "You can barely hold that up. The two of you drop those weapons and I will give you nice, clean deaths. Warriors' deaths."

Tain sprang forward, slashing down at the top of Macro's head. Marco blocked it easily. "We're not warriors," Tain said through gritted teeth. He pivoted and struck again, but Marco met his sword with lazy ease. I circled around, trying to get a clean angle at the Guilder, but he moved his feet and positioned his body effortlessly to keep me out of range. This time he sliced at Tain, and though my friend blocked it, I could see the strain it caused him, and knew he couldn't defend himself for long.

Marco knew it, too. His posture and expression were so relaxed he might have been eating lunch. We had to get out of here, or he'd cut us down without breaking a sweat. I looked at the doorway and circled again. Between the two of us we should be able to at least force him into moving out of the way of the door. If we could just get out of this space. . . .

"The door is locked, in case you are thinking about running," Marco said. He lunged forward suddenly, almost skewering Tain, who staggered back and hit the bed. Just as Marco struck down, I leaped in with a flurry of strikes, and though none made it through Marco's guard, it gave Tain time to right himself. Marco smirked. "I had to borrow the key off that old fool, Argo. He did not want to let me in."

Tain let out a hoarse cry and slashed out at the Warrior-Guilder. I lunged in, too, trying to time a gap, but Marco's agile body dodged and feinted to keep us at bay. After two steps back himself, he shifted to the attack and drove us back toward the window side of the room. A barely parried downward strike at Tain skidded down the outside of his shoulder, drawing blood, and I collected several long cuts down my arms that burned and drained my energy. Marco wielded his sword as if it were a toy, weightless, and drove us backward without effort. He seemed content to wear us out. Two of us, and it didn't matter. He was going to kill us both, just like he'd killed so many before. Fear drenched me, making me clumsy.

I weaved my way away from Tain and Marco, then made a run for the side of the bed.

"Not so brave now, then?" Marco called out.

I spun one of my daggers around and smashed the lamp with the hilt. The room went black.

I heard Marco's grunt of surprise and smiled in the darkness. I crossed the room silently. We couldn't defeat Marco, not even two to one, especially with Tain stripped of his strength. But we could tip the odds.

I heard a thud as Marco's sword hit the wall, and my smile widened as I realized Tain had moved away the moment I'd killed the light. Marco had incomparable advantage in sword work. But I had paced this room in the darkness, counting steps, so many times in my life, and so many more times in this last week, that I didn't need light to know its length and breadth. I knew where to step, how far, how many times, to avoid every bit of furniture. This was *my* world.

One, two, three steps, to the end of the bed. I let one of my daggers trail against the edge of the bedpost, creating a tiny slicing sound, then darted to the side as Marco followed the bait and lunged for the spot. I kicked out and knocked the stool by the side of the bed into his path. As he stumbled I leaped in, lungs too tight to breathe, and stabbed.

He roared with shock as much as pain as my dagger hit something hard, and luck more than skill saved me from his retaliatory swipe. My heart picked up the pace as I skidded backward to the wall near the door. I cursed in my head, my brief elation fading. That had been my chance, and I'd wasted it.

Swords clashed, and this time I almost swore aloud. Either Marco had found Tain or Tain had tried what I just had. I counted my steps forward and to the side, padding silently, moving around and around. Another clash, and footsteps, and the brush of warm air as someone rushed past me. Retreating. Tain?

I stepped back and to my right, counting in my head, picturing the lay-out of the room. The other person—this time I was sure it was Marco—followed the first, steps confident. Then a cry and a thump, and someone staggering up against the back wall. I swallowed my fear and tiptoed forward. *Don't panic now.*

"Come on, lads," the Warrior-Guilder said, his voice edged with irri-tation, as though offended that we had made his game unsportsmanlike. "Skulking around in the darkness? Come out and face me."

I heard the *whoosh* of his sword this time, but Tain must have moved

again, because it hit the wall and Marco swore in a language I didn't recognize. Now I was close enough to hear Tain's ragged breathing; either he
was too tired to keep quiet or too hurt from that last blow. Marco could
hear it, too; his voice moved as he did, and I knew then he'd done a pretty
good job of picturing the room layout himself. He was trapping Tain in
the corner.

"Where is the honor in this?" he taunted. "Honored Chancellor, hiding
in the darkness instead of facing his opponent? Credo Jovan, lurking about
instead of defending your friend and Chancellor? Where is your honor?"

I crept close behind him. My groping foot on the base of the curtain
exposed the tiniest breath of faint silver light into the room, so I could see
the rough shape of the Guilder as he raised his sword to strike Tain down.

"You know what?" I said, as I plunged my dagger into the back of his
neck. "Fuck honor."

Neither of us seemed to know what to say. We stood in the dark for a time,
Marco's body between us. The only sound to punctuate the darkness was
Tain's heavy breathing.

Then, "Is he dead?"

"I think so." I bent down and checked the pulse in his neck with hands
shaking like a seizure. His skin was warm. No heartbeat. I stepped around
the prone figure and fumbled in the dark to find my friend. He was slumped
in the corner, and when I tried to help him stand, his side was slick with
warm blood. "How badly are you hurt?"

"Not sure." Tain laughed, a bark devoid of humor.

I helped him to the bed then found and lit the main lamps in the room.
I tried not to look at the knife protruding from the back of Marco's neck.
There wasn't much blood; he'd died instantly. *Should have tried to knock him
out. Now we'll never know why he did it.* But there was nothing to be done
now. I'd killed him. I'd killed other people, but this was something I had
done to someone I knew . . . and had liked and respected. And I didn't feel
sorry about it: I felt nothing. No satisfaction, no regret. Just emptiness.

I checked Tain over. The main wound was a deep, clean slice to his side,
just below his ribs. "Put pressure on that," I told him, and he obeyed, eyes
dull. I didn't know how much blood he'd lost, or whether his stunned

silence was due to emotional shock or physical injuries. I sliced up a sheet with the spare knife and bound the main wound, then the smaller ones on his arms and shoulders. "We need to get you to the hospital."

He nodded, eyes already shutting as he sat back. *Or maybe I should get a physic here first,* I thought. *I could send Argo. . . .* And then I remembered Marco's taunt, and my throat clenched. "Argo," I said. A surge of hatred toward the dead man on the floor made my knees wobble. "Tain, can you stay here? I've got to go see if Argo . . . I have to check."

His eyes snapped open and he lurched to his feet. "I'm coming," he said, waving away my protests. "I have to get to the hospital anyway. If there's a chance Argo's still . . ." Neither of us wanted to say it aloud. "I'll follow. Go."

I ran. The route to the front entrance took me past Salvea's room and I thumped on the door. "Salvea! Tain needs help!" I didn't wait for a response, but hurried on. *Come on,* I thought, my steps feeling heavy.

I skidded to a stop in the main entrance hall. Argo lay slumped over the desk, his wrinkled brown head bare as a nut, his body motionless. My chest tightened. How many more innocent people had to die for Marco's insane war? Argo had never harmed anyone in his life. I reached for his neck, testing for a pulse.

And then caught my breath as I felt one. Weak but steady. "Argo? Honor-down, Argo, can you hear me?"

His eyes fluttered open. "Fortunes-damned upstart Guilder," he muttered, trying to focus on me as he raised his head feebly. "Tried to kill me. The Chancellor! Credo, the Warrior-Guilder's going for the Chancellor!"

"He's all right," I said, helping the doorkeep sit up. "Marco's dead, and Tain's all right." I touched his neck gently and the old man winced. "He choked you?"

Argo nodded. "Brash as could be," he said. "Said . . . said—" He broke off with a cough. "Said everyone would just think I keeled over," he wheezed. "Like I'm some kind of decrepit old thing, about to expire!"

I patted his back as he coughed again. "Thank the fortunes he underestimated you."

By the time Argo had found his feet, Tain hobbled into the entrance hall with Salvea's help. Davi followed behind, sucking his thumb, eyes wide. "Argo!" Tain staggered over and embraced the old man. "Honor-down, I'm glad to see you breathing."

"And I you, Honored Chancellor," he croaked, looking embarrassed.

"I want the physics to check you over, too," I told Argo. I tried to scoop Davi up to pass to Salvea, but the boy backed away, shaking his head, and I realized what a sight I must be, bleeding from small cuts and strewn with Tain's blood and my own. "Salvea, can you run ahead to the hospital and warn Thendra that we're bringing them in to check them over?"

"And you," Tain said. "You're hurt, too."

I tried to rub the blood away with a corner of my tunic. "I've got something else to do," I said.

Loaded with a good lamp and basic medical supplies from the hospital, where I'd made sure Tain and Argo were in safe hands, I went back to Red Fern Avenue and through the sewers into Eliska's tunnels. I tried not to think about what was going on at the lake. No further alarm bells had sounded, so I had to assume we still held the bridge. But I dared not wait any longer to find out if some harm had befallen Hadrea in the labyrinth below the city.

The caves lay silent and menacing as I descended. Calling out, I heard only my own voice, echoing back from the darkness. I tried not to think the worst. The system was huge; chances were she could be fine and still not hear me. She had moved confidently underground when she had followed me.

I found signs of her passage past Eliska and Dara's secret room, footprints in the dust and dirt visible with my lamp. They led deeper and lower, east toward the lake. This time I was prepared for any eventualities; my pouches were refilled and I had my supply of moonstone paste in hand to mark each doorway I moved through with a smear. Even if something happened to my lamp or I had to run back, the faint white glow from the moonstone would guide my way home. Sometimes Hadrea's tracks were heavier and deeper lines than normal footprints, and I wondered if she had been using a crude version of the same system, marking her way home. The air grew heavier, and the walls seeped liquid. When the ceiling started dripping heavy ice-cold splotches, I suspected I was under the lake itself. It didn't improve my feelings about the prospect of cave-ins. I called out again. Nothing.

The darkness seemed to thicken as I went lower and lower, as though my lamp's light couldn't match it. My breathing sounded louder and each footstep echoed, eerie. "Hadrea?" I tried again.

Was that something? I raced ahead, the lamp swinging wildly. "Hadrea?"

A sound, there was definitely a sound then. A cry? It sounded faint, weak. Was she hurt?

I rounded the corner, thrusting my lamp into each of the tunnel entrances I passed. In the third I thought I glimpsed something.

The light from my lamp spilled into the tunnel, showing a floor littered with rocks and dirt. The roof was bracketed and looked sound; no sign of a collapse. The rocks were spread out and, strangely, many were caked with dirt on one side and smooth on the other, with no discernible pattern. I had no time to puzzle that out, because moments later the edge of my light caught a brown sheen, and I leaped over the rocks to where Hadrea lay, her hair concealing her face, unmoving.

As I dropped down beside her, she propped herself on her forearms, easily tossing her hair back with a puff of breath. "You took a long time, Jovan," she said, and relief rendered me speechless.

She jerked her head behind her, gesturing to the pile of rocks covering her feet. "I was caught," she said. "It was clumsy, but I had been moving rocks for a long time. I was not quick enough."

"Are they pinned?" I asked, afraid of the answer. The lantern illuminated a pile of rocks at least knee height. If they had crushed her legs, they could have shattered her ankle bones. Not even the most talented physics could repair all the little bones in the feet or recreate a proper working ankle.

But she shook her head. "Just trapped," she said. "If only I had delicate little feet like your city women, perhaps I could pull them out."

I laughed, relief making the moment funnier. "Hold still." I moved rocks from the pile, taking care not to cause any falls. "What happened down here? I've been worried about you."

"There is a room here," she said.

"The Os-Woorin room. I know."

"Do you know what it is?"

"No," I admitted. "Is it a shrine, do you think? Did you come here to make an offering?"

She twisted over her shoulder to look at me. "You thought Os-Woorin speaking to us was just a story," she said. "But our ancestors were not such unbelievers. Perhaps they found some way to communicate with the spirit. We are under the lake, I think."

"I don't know what to think anymore." I looked past the piles of rocks. "Did you get caught by a cave-in before you found it?"

"It is not a cave-in," she said. "The room has been deliberately blocked off. The supports were destroyed and the tunnel brought down. Someone did not want that room to be entered."

Caslav had told Eliska the caves were unsafe. Had he known more, or had he simply heard that lie from his aunt before him? Was it a lie passed down through their line? I shifted another stone with a grunt. "So you tried to clear the rocks, by yourself? And you call me foolish?"

One more rock, and she let out a gasp of relief and wiggled free. I helped her to her feet and she stamped up and down across the corridor, stretching and shaking. It was strange seeing her in masculine farm clothing: long trousers and a vest over a shirt. She stopped and looked me over. She touched my arm. "Is that blood?"

"Oh. Yes." I told her what had happened, leaving out the detail of how Marco had died. Perhaps I didn't want to catapult it from the hazy, dream-like state in my memory to something real. The empty feeling inside made the retelling easier than it should have been. "The physics are with Tain," I finished. "And we don't have much longer to hold the bridge."

"You think we should go back up there and help."

I opened my mouth to agree, but instead fell silent, staring at the rocks spread out over the floor. The map lay beside my lantern. "No," I said, surprising myself. "I think we should keep moving those rocks. Whatever is in there, it might have helped the Chancellor hundreds of years ago. Maybe it can help again."

She smiled, and some part of me hoped I had made the choice for the right reasons. But that part shut up as she stepped closer. Blood pounded in my ears. "Hadrea," I said. It came out as a whisper. Honor-down, even sweaty and covered in dirt, she was so beautiful.

"I like the way you say it," she said to me, as she had once before.

For long moments I couldn't think, only feel, as her hands dug into my back and her breasts hardened against my chest. The salty taste of her made me dizzy. She backed against the wall, pulling me with her, one leg riding up to hook around my thigh. I wanted her so badly it scared me.

My hands shook as I broke the kiss and pulled back, putting some space between us. "What happened before . . ." I said, guilt at the memories breaking through my desire.

She scowled. "You could have died tonight, Jovan. And above us, the city might be falling. We might both be dead tomorrow in any case. So, what is that phrase you city people use?" With a jerk, she pulled me back in so close I could feel her lips moving against my cheek as she whispered, "*Shut the fuck up.*"

And I did.

We lay panting together afterward, silent, until the steady dripping of ice water from above drove us from the spot. I didn't feel hollow anymore, but full, too full, of emotions I didn't recognize. That had been something more than passion, something more than physical and emotional bonding. Something almost spiritual.

"Did you feel that?" she asked, as if reading my mind. She sounded tentative and her dark gaze searched my face as I considered my reply. I didn't know how to describe what I had felt.

"That was an offering," she said. "What you are feeling. That was you—us—opening to Os-Woorin, giving to it. It is here, do you sense it?"

I shifted, uncomfortable, but her words triggered a memory I couldn't suppress: the strange, echoey feeling of pressure in my head, of delayed response and blurred vision, almost like that sensation I had felt climbing the ladder back to safety when the Speaker woman followed me. I didn't know how to process the strangeness. Reason, logic fought against it. I cared about Hadrea, and I had never desired anyone, man or woman, in the way I wanted her. Perhaps this was just the heady sensation of infatuation.

"I care about you," I began awkwardly, and she laughed, a booming sound in the silent cavern.

"Jovan, you are very nice, too. But I was not fishing for a declaration of your affection. I was asking if you were too much of a wooden heathen to feel the *fresken*."

"I felt *something*," I admitted. "I don't know what, exactly, but—"

"You do know what," she said, clearly amused. "But if you would like to pretend that you do not, well and good." She stretched, and I felt the bumps on her skin under my hands and her tiny shivers. I found myself shivering, too, suddenly hyperconscious of the space—the icy damp air, the distant booms from far above. With reluctance we gathered our clothes from under us and dressed again. My stomach chose that moment to grumble, the hollow ache reminding me how long it had been since my last real meal.

Hadrea had already climbed back on the pile and was tugging at a large rock. I climbed up beside her and dislodged one myself, awkward. Mouth dry, I tried. "About earlier. I'm sorry," I began. "I shouldn't have said those things to you. I was—"

"I know what you were doing," she said, her tone resigned, not cold. "Blaming yourself. Punishing yourself. But you will not do it this time." She turned her gaze on me, and I found myself smiling. Who could argue with that look?

"I won't." This time, I wouldn't. Our world might, in fact, be ending, but I wouldn't regret one moment spent with her.

"Look!" she cried, and I scrambled up beside her, holding the lamp aloft. It shone through, past the rock pile, to the passage beyond. "We are nearly there."

Enthusiasm lending us greater energy, we cleared the rocks and rubble until we had exposed a hole big enough to crawl through. Far above, a boom sounded, and I eyed the roof nervously. Hadrea made to climb in, but I grabbed her arm. Eagerness aside, who knew how stable our little path might be? "Maybe we shouldn't do this? At least, not without someone else here who can help us if there's another collapse and we get stuck on the other side."

She wiped the hair off her face with a grimy hand. "Jovan," she said. "There is no time. Everyone in the city is busy either getting ready to fight for their lives, or hiding and hoping for the best. No one up there is interested in an old map and a Darfri spirit. But I can feel a connection to Os-Woorin. It is strong and still open. Perhaps you really cannot feel it, but it is there. I was not entirely honest with you, before. With anyone. Even my mother. We are not supposed to use *fresken* without supervision of a Speaker, but I was young and lonely and I thought . . ." She broke off, shaking her head. "It does not matter. What I am saying is there is some chance there is something here—something magical, I do not know, but something—we have to try."

Yes, it was madness to believe we would find the key to reaching some supernatural being buried in a room deep under the lake. Almost every part of me knew that whatever was in there, it was unlikely to improve our plight. But one stupid, senseless bit of hope remained that Hadrea was right. And, honor-down, I didn't want to return just yet to the disaster waiting for us above.

I went through first, feet first on my stomach, heading into the unknown. I shuffled backward, pressing my body over the rough stones and trying to calm the panic inside me at every tiny sound. I wished it weren't so easy to picture us being trapped, pinned beneath rocks here, left to starve or suffocate.

"Pass me the lamp," I said, coughing to disguise the squeak in my voice. "And my bag." I dared not descend farther without seeing where I was going.

This side of the tunnel looked much like the other. A cascade of rubble sloped down from a gaping wound in the ceiling, ending around knee height against a door. By the fortunes, I hoped that door opened inward, or there would be no chance of clearing a path to get it open.

Hadrea squeezed through next, and though it was wildly inappropriate in the circumstances, I appreciated her tightly curved backside leading the way. "You'll start a whole new fashion, walking around in those trousers," I muttered, helping her down the slope.

She grinned. "Keep your focus, Jovan," she said. "The door. Is it locked?"

"That's the least of our problems." I tugged out my small roll of tools from my bag. I could pick the lock, but it would do no good if the door opened the wrong way. I held my breath as I balanced on the wobbly ground and held the lamp up to the edge of the doorframe. No hinges, which meant it probably did open inward.

The lock was corroded, and didn't require much picking. I supposed whoever had last been here hadn't been worried about its integrity, since they'd planned to collapse the tunnel anyway. It didn't take long to deal with the lock, but it took both our full weights against the door to get it open—first pushing, then kicking, then eventually throwing ourselves against it—so warped had it become over the years in the damp.

We both fell in a tumble when it finally burst open, and I almost smashed the lamp. I picked it up, gave Hadrea a hand, and then, heart pounding, held the light up to illuminate the Os-Woorin room.

Silence.

Hadrea looked at me. "What is it?" she asked.

I held the lamp up again, mouth dry. "I have no idea."

By the time we reached the surface, the dull roar from above had grown to ominous levels, and without discussion we increased our pace. And as we came out of the sewers up near the north gate, fear solidified into a hard lump in my stomach.

Dawn had broken, and the Finger's gate had fallen.

Whether by the relentless force of their catapults, which we'd failed to destroy, or some other more direct means, like a ram, the gate and half the base of the tower were a crumpled ruin. The rebel army swarmed the bridge, fighting to get through the gate and out of the range of our arrow fire. Hadrea and I ran along the shoreline, half-deafened by the screams and cries of battle. Our soldiers clung to the remaining structure of the wall and tower, half shooting down arrows, some fiery, the other half hurling the miscellaneous contents of the great barrels stacked up behind the wall. The foul stench made me gag as we came closer. Order Guards yelled instructions to our troops in the trenches, preparing them for when the fighting moved to the shore. Among the rebels on the bridge I spotted several of the unarmored women adorned with symbols—Speakers?—their arms raised up and outstretched. Above them the wind whistled wildly, carrying dirt and rubble with it just as it had outside the walls. The maelstrom flew at our troops on the wall, knocking arrows out of their path and blinding them with debris as if the Maiso itself had come into the city and did the Darfri women's bidding. The screams of the fearful and the dying split the air. *This is it*, I thought, numb as I accepted a misshapen sword from someone. *This is the end.*

Then another, different, roar from the south made me turn. Our own men and women, cheering in defiance, for this short time drowning out the drums and the cries from the bridge and west shore. It took a moment to see why.

Tain strode along the river bank, dressed in ceremonial armor. He looked a magnificent sight, with his gleaming conical helmet, a bright cloak billowing after him and shining sword glinting in the dawn. No one would have known the armor and cloak concealed injury or that his poise masked his weakness. They saw him as a shining leader here to give them heart in the worst moments of their lives, and they did not care that they had not seen him for a week or more, or that only last night they had been muttering about him having fled the city. He was here now, and somehow his presence converted a scared rabble into a united force. I raised my hand and my voice as he came near, along with everyone else. Perhaps it was stupid, but whatever surged through the crowd surged through me, too. Maybe together we could get through this.

I turned to Hadrea. She had not cheered. She was looking at the clash of people defending the tower base, eyes wet. My brief burst of Silastian pride fizzled away with no more than a whisper. For Hadrea, this was no glorious defense of the city. These were her own people, perhaps even friends and family, dying for a war they had been pushed into against a population that had wronged them. If we saved ourselves today, what would be the cost?

And then Tain was upon us, tailed by Bradomir, Varina, and Javesto, even old Budua and Marjeta, all armored. I hoped the missing Councilors were engaged elsewhere and not dead or hiding. Even Lord Ectar, whom I hadn't seen in days, was here, with his servants, ready to fight.

"How are you—" But I broke off, already guessing what Tain had done by the wildness of his eyes and his quick, jerky movements. "You found my darpar." I shook my head; too late to worry about what it might do to him now. "Try the peace flag again," I begged, surprising myself with the strength of my desperation. "Before it's too late. The mercenaries in charge won't listen, but now it's face-to-face they can't shield everyone from your words."

He shook his head. Up close, there was no hiding the toll this performance was taking. His skin looked more gray than brown and his eyes were bloodshot. "We tried, Jov. They shot an arrow through it. They won't talk peace. They won't even take our surrender—I'm not too proud." He looked back to the bridge. "They're going to break through any moment. We have high ground but they've got the numbers."

"A lot of people are going to die today," Javesto said. His usually animated face looked dull and numb. I guessed he too saw the cost on both sides as a loss to all.

"Unless we can think of something to stop it," Tain agreed. He glanced at the other Councilors. "A moment, please," he said, and steered me away. From inside his breastplate he pulled my family's battered journal. "You left this under the lamp, Jov. Whatever you did, it worked eventually."

I took it, pulse thumping at the sight of the revealed words: pages of tiny, neat notes. "The heat, of course. It needed a bit more heat." I'd not factored in the age of the paper.

"Jov, did you and Hadrea find the Os-Woorin room?"

I nodded. "But it's . . . I don't know what it is. It's not a shrine. There was nothing Darfri in there. The whole room is some kind of machine." A great metal wheel, a sealed chamber. After all that digging, Hadrea and I hadn't come out with any understanding of what we'd found, or its relationship to the spirit of the lake. She had been disappointed but my disappointment had been mingled with some relief, as well. Perhaps I wasn't ready to be directly confronted with something that couldn't be explained. "I don't know what it's meant to do."

"Well, I do," said Tain. "Look at this. We—" He broke off as a horn sounded. "They're through," he said. "This is it."

Our people fell into place to meet the sudden rush of the enemy through the tower. We could no longer hold them off. My sweaty fingers clenched around the sword as I followed Tain into the throng. Then panic surged through me and I turned. "Hadrea!" I cried. She stood behind me, her long knife in hand, far steadier than I felt. "Get back to the city. The rebels won't hurt you and the rest of the Darfri. You'll be safe."

For a moment her face, wet with tears, stiffened. Then, instead of fleeing, she pressed in beside me and kissed me hard on the lips. "But you would not, without me. I have seen you with a sword."

It was like being at the bottom of the ladders all over again. My mouth was dry and I couldn't get enough air as the lines clashed together and the rebel army poured in. I joined the protective circle around Tain and only as a woman with a spear charged at me did I realize I hadn't taken a shield or even the crudest armor. I twisted to avoid the thrust, felt it catch in my tunic, and lunged back. As I did, the blur of Hadrea's shape caught my eye and I spun the sword at the last moment to hit my opponent with the hilt instead. *Idiot, idiot, you can't just knock them all out,* part of me shouted, but I knew, even as I ducked a swinging blow from a man with a hammer, that I was going to try. Unless and until it killed me.

The sword became my shield, for defense only. My free hand flung lava-bulb seeds into eyes. Beside me, Hadrea slashed and pivoted and darted in and out. I felt a clumsy animal compared to her; with every swing and parry I grew weaker. I could only avoid their relentless attacks for so long. I tired quickly, my movements slowing and my strikes weakening. A glancing blow from a club to my hipbone sent me staggering, and the club would have crushed my head if Hadrea had not suddenly been there, slashing at the back of the man's knees. He screamed and fell almost on top of me. I got out of the way just in time, wobbling to my feet.

I took another hit, this time a knife to the left shoulder, making me cry out in agony and lending a desperate strength to my right side as I smashed the base of my sword on the man's elbow. As he staggered back, I kicked him in the knee as hard as I could.

As we fought and struggled I became aware of a pressing sensation around my head and glanced at Hadrea; she was looking around wildly, obviously sensing it, too. I saw a Speaker approaching through the crowd, dirt and grass stuffed in her raised and outstretched fists. Her face turned to the lightening indigo sky and she chanted over the roar of the battle. Somehow she moved through the crowd undisturbed, never deviating in her path, a gliding water bird on a still lake. I ducked under a swinging shield and drew closer to her. I knew I shouldn't leave Tain's protective circle but my shaking legs shuffled forward almost of their own volition, compelled and repelled by fear and the memory of the gritty hand on my leg and the sight of the swirling mists and debris-filled winds.

The Speaker's head suddenly snapped down like a heavy lid closing. Her gaze moved over the crowd and she drew her fists in toward her bare chest as if pulling some great tense rope. The tight sensation around my ears intensified.

People behind me cried out simultaneously; I spun around. Great earthy ropes of grass and dirt burst from the ground and gripped Hadrea and Tain, along with half a dozen others protecting the Chancellor, pulling them to their knees like sentient vines. Hadrea clutched at her neck as the green-and-brown fingers tightened around her throat, and Tain coughed and beat at his chest as the ropy strands dragged over his shoulders. I started toward them but Hadrea's eyes met mine and instead of fear I saw resolution; she jerked her gaze sharply to a point over my shoulder. I nodded and pivoted, leaping toward the Speaker without much thought beyond reaching her.

We collided roughly; the last instant before impact I slipped sideways slightly so that instead of catching my arm around the Speaker's neck and barreling chest-to-chest as I'd intended, I struck her shoulder-to-shoulder. She stumbled back hard, losing one hand's worth of dirt and grass, but didn't fall. Her gaze snapped to me, crackling with rage. I had only enough time to stick my free hand into my pouch, for the next moment she thrust her arm toward me with a bellowed command, and grass and clods of earth sprang up from the very ground, pinning my arms and coiling around my torso like great snakes. The roaring in my ears intensified as the bizarre earth fingers tightened their grip.

I tried to back away but I was held fast, my sword flat and useless against my thigh. Inside the pouch my fingers scrambled around until they found a phial. Dangerous and foolish to attempt it, but I did anyway. With a series of quick, tiny yanks I got my hand out of the pouch and free of the bindings, the phial only just within my fingers' grip. Hoping the fortunes were on my side, I popped the lid of the phial with my thumb and flicked my wrist toward her as hard as I could.

The scream from the Speaker as acid splashed across her bare stomach reverberated in my skull. I, too, felt a burn like a hot needle driving into the side of my thumb where I had collected a tiny splash. But as the Speaker collapsed, still screaming, my bindings fell away to nothing. Relieved coughing sounded behind me under the howls and shrieks, and I almost cried with relief to see Tain, Hadrea, and the rest staggering to their feet as well. With my uninjured hand I struck the Speaker unconscious with the butt of my sword then hurried back to join my friends. Wary rebels now circled in once more. My heart felt heavy in my chest. Darfri magic was real. How could we possibly stand against something like that?

So loud were the rasp of my breathing and the hammering of blood in my ears that it took some time for the sound of horns to penetrate. I looked around, confused. What were the horns signaling?

Tain's voice cracked with disbelief. "It's the army," he said, then he shouted it again. "It's our army!"

Others took up the cry. All around us, men and women on both sides slowed and fumbled in their attacks, looking around in fear and confusion.

No one quite seemed to know what was going on. But the cheer picked up, louder and louder, until it finally sunk into my woolly head.

Aven had arrived.

Confusion reigned. Rebels on our side of the lake stopped pressing forward and instead worked to hold their ground as they peered frantically through the crowd, searching for instruction. None of the mercenary leaders could be seen amidst the mist rolling across the lake. Cynical, I doubted whether any had engaged in this first push across the bridge. Why should they when they could just send waves of our countrymen across to clear the way?

Eventually the retreat call sounded, and rebels fought their way, not forward into our territory, but back to the bridge. "Protect the tower!" an Order Guard screamed, and a surge of our own people thickened around the base of the tower to cut off the retreat. But Tain raced down the hill, leaving us scrambling to keep up.

"Let them through!" he bellowed. "Let them through!"

The Order Guard perched on top of the half-crumpled wall stared down at Tain as he charged toward them, head cocked as if not understanding what he'd heard. I puffed to keep up as Tain darted through the crush, fired by unnatural agility and energy from the darpar. Even unarmored it took all my effort just to keep him in sight while avoiding the desperate strikes of the rebels as they retreated to the tower.

"Let them through!" Tain yelled again, and this time the Order Guard repeated the cry.

"Clear the stairs!" someone cried from inside, and our people poured off to the side, allowing the retreating force to follow their comrades through the tower and over the bridge.

"What are you *doing*?" a rumpled and sweating Bradomir shrieked, catching up to us. "We can trap them here! Block the gate from this side and we can cut them off!"

Tain glanced over, his expression giving Bradomir roughly the regard he might have for a roach. "Aven's here," he said. "They're going to be trapped between us. Now's the time to finally secure a peace, not the time for more slaughter." He looked up at the Order Guard on the wall. "Make sure our archers don't shoot!"

"Are you mad?" Bradomir cried, reaching out with both arms as if to shake Tain. But before his hands came within reach, a wall of men and women stepped between them; among them, I saw with surprise, Varina. Bradomir dropped his arms, staring at them as if they didn't belong to him, and backed away.

The rebel force retreated over the bridge. I scrambled after Tain up the stairs and into the tower so we could see what was happening on the other side.

Clear of the mist, we saw the swarm pouring over the bridge and joining the great mass on the west shore. As we watched, the mercenaries on graspads circling the outer edges of the force began redirecting massive groups of rebels up into the city. Frustratingly, the Finger wasn't tall enough to see past the buildings of the lower city, and we could only speculate about what was happening on the other side.

"Aven must have attacked where they breached the walls," Tain said. "They're trapped."

The relief carrying me until now wavered. "We have to get them to surrender," I said. "If they fight Aven she'll plow through them to get to us."

"They'll be slaughtered," Tain agreed. He looked around the room and spotted an Order Guard emerging from the steps. "We need to get the peace flag back up. And we need to find some way of stopping the Warrior-Guilder from charging. Get me a messenger to the south gate tower; they should be able to see what's going on." He looked at Hadrea and me as he declared, "This war should be over. No one else needs to die."

While the Guard dragged out the arrow-torn peace flag, Tain, Hadrea, and I went downstairs. The shore that had been a battle zone such a short time ago now buzzed with confusion. Tain was pulled away to strategize with the Order Guards, and Hadrea and I joined in the people helping carry the wounded to the hospital. The battle on the east side had been short but brutal, and the inexperience and inadequate weaponry on both sides had left more wounded than dead.

I was bent over a woman bleeding from a massive sword wound to her arm, trying to stop the flow, when I heard, "Hey! Hey!" I looked over, searching in the dusky early morning light, and finally saw who was trying to get my attention. It was a Silastian man, propped up on his elbows, one obviously broken leg twisted out to the side. "What are you doing?"

Pressing a torn ball of the woman's shirt against the gaping wound and tying it down firmly with another strip, I squinted at the man. "Is it just your leg?" I asked. "Someone will be here to help you soon. We have to get all the critically injured people there fastest."

"But she's one of *them*," he said. "Help your own first!"

"I'll help whoever needs it," I snapped back, temper rising.

"She's a rebel! A traitor!"

"She's bleeding," I replied, looking back down at the unconscious woman. On a count of three, Hadrea and I hoisted her between us.

We made several trips to the hospital until I saw Tain.

"No response to the peace flag," he told me, grim. "The rebel force is split; some are trying to defend the breached wall against Aven." He swore, rubbing his grimy forehead. "I need to get her a message, tell her not to attack. But I don't know how."

We looked at each other, helpless frustration rendering us both speechless. Then Tain shuffled his helmet between his hands, looking shifty. "I . . . this is ridiculous. Stupid. But I don't know what else to do."

Someone called our names; it was Chen, approaching at a run.

"What's stupid?" I asked Tain as we made our way toward the Order Guard, who practically vibrated with urgency. *What now?*

"The Os-Woorin room," he said. "I want to use it."

Blisterbush

DESCRIPTION: Low-growing shrub, attractive glossy green trefoil leaves.

SYMPTOMS: Contact with leaves gives immediate reddening, then blistering of skin. Ingestion symptoms include intense, localized stomach pain, increasing in intensity and coverage over time, anal bleeding, painful urination, internal bleeding, death.

PROOFING CUES: Immediate blistering sensation in mouth, unaffected by cooking or masking flavors. Typically used as a surface poison only.

30

Kalina

Fingers aching and dirt caked under my fingernails, I held my breath and listened as Garan shifted around outside. Once or twice he had started to whistle, then stopped a few notes in. But no one else had approached and he had not spoken to anyone. He wouldn't believe me—it had been stupid to think he might—but maybe he wouldn't rush to give me away, either. Regardless, I couldn't stay in this tent.

I tested the hole. It was wide enough to fit my shoulders, but I couldn't tell if it was deep enough. We'd set up in the dark, so I had no idea what my tent backed onto or how exposed it would be out there. The camp wasn't exactly quiet, but the majority of the army was with Aven, marching on the city to prepare to take it back, not sitting around here waiting to spot a lone woman squeezing out of her tent prison. I could only be thankful Aven thought herself safe and had not considered me a threat. Otherwise I'd have been properly contained—or killed, more likely. Another "Doranite spy."

I stretched my sore hands. My body, still exhausted and damaged from the strain I'd put it through, hadn't enjoyed this new action. But physical weakness was nothing new to me. I took a breath. Time to try.

I lay out flat on the ground and stuck my head into the little trench, to be greeted with cooking smells and the light of the dawning day and, to my relief, not much more. The nearest people were around a campfire a distance away, their backs to me. Aven had set me up on the outskirts of camp, away from potential prying eyes. Now it made sense why the Warrior-Guilder had so badly wanted to keep me out of sight and out of contact. She hadn't wanted anyone to mention previous "spies," or fortunes knew what other clues that might have come my way if I'd been allowed to speak to the soldiers.

I wiggled quickly through the gap, trying not to disturb the tent fabric too much. One shoulder and arm came through, then the other. The hardest part over, I clawed at the grass on the outside and pulled up on my fore-arms to drag the rest of my body through.

If the rebels were negotiating a surrender, I could slip into the main body of the army and march into the city with everyone else. But what if Aven saw me? I had no idea how this would work, whether she would come back to camp before moving the army on, and check on her "guest." I cursed my-self for asking Garan for help. If I had just kept my mouth shut, let Aven and everyone else think me docile and grateful, I wouldn't have had to run. I'd made myself reliant on his silence.

Soldiers on graspads guarded the rear perimeter of the camp, so there would be no sneaking back south and hiding until after the surrender. My best chance might be to try to blend in with the army after all. I would need to leave camp fast, before Garan checked on me and raised the alarm.

I worked from tent to tent, avoiding the little knots of people still at camp. Some assembled supply wagons and loaded spare arrows and other weapons; others cooked in huge clay pots over campfires. The smells of simple food wafted over me as I darted about in the shadows, and the warmth of the fires only highlighted the unseasonable cold of the morning. A few camp followers lounged about the outskirts, chatting, paying me no atten-tion. I drew closer to the end of the camp, trying to figure out how to cross the gulf between me and the organized force ahead. Once I crested the slight rise I'd be visible from anywhere around.

A great horn blasted in the distance, making me jump. My stomach sunk into a tight ball as I realized what had happened.

The army was charging the city.

Though I couldn't see the breached wall from here, the roar of the army at its sudden push forward echoed over the land. There would be no surrender. My eyes burned again, anger, frustration, and confusion tearing at me. Aven wasn't joining the rebels. So what did she want? Not that it mattered right now. Whatever her reason, she was the city's enemy, not its savior, and there had to be some way of warning them.

But now that the army had charged the city, I couldn't slip in along with them; I'd be in the middle of the fighting. I had no illusions about my ability to survive that. Even if I got hold of a shield and somehow survived the arrow fire I'd never make it through the open fighting.

A figure burst through the distant mass, riding a graspad, bright red sash marking him as a messenger. I backed into the closest tent and ducked behind the door flap, heart pounding. My ill-fitting uniform and soft physique wouldn't stand up to close scrutiny. I waited until the big paws thumped past the crack in the tent, then, tentatively, peered through the gap.

The messenger cried out as he reined in his graspad, and people in the camp hurried over to hear the news. Fortunately, the man's voice carried. "The rebels have refused to surrender," he said. "The Warrior-Guilder has signaled the attack. We're taking back the city!"

A woman with thick arms and a hammer slung over her shoulder spat out of the corner of her mouth. "And what's our expected damage? We don't have siege weaponry."

"We don't need it," said the messenger, edging his graspad a little farther from the smith. "We're sending troops back to transport the rest of the weaponry and moving into full attack. They never repaired the breached wall. They'll not hold the pass for long."

A uniformed man with a long moustache nodded. "I suppose they'll do what they need to do," he said. "Mayhaps we'll be home by lunch."

The small group let out a raggedy cheer, but I found no heart in the words. I slunk back into the tent. If I didn't survive the day, no one would ever suspect Aven. Whatever her plans, she would have free rein at them, riding in to a hero's welcome. No one knew the truth but one woman stuck on the wrong side of two armies. I slumped back against a crate. All this way, and what had I achieved? I'd been nothing but a helpful cog in Aven's great machine.

The crate dug into my back. I shifted, trying to summon some thought or idea, but nothing came to me. I could just stay here, hiding in a tent full of spare arrows, and hope no one looked inside . . . except, I realized, I'd just heard mention of troops returning to collect additional weaponry, so someone would be back for these arrows to take to the battlefield, probably any moment now.

And then a germ of an idea wormed its way in after all.

Fingers trembling, I worked through the arrows, one at a time. The fletching was far superior to the ones we'd made back in the city; even, regular barbs, thick and straight. I counted carefully, mumbling as I broke the right barbs down.

It was stupid to think this would work. But I had no other ideas, and the arrows were right here, ready to be sent back out into the battle. My fingers were quick and sure; I'd always been able to trust my hands. Consisting as it did of only two symbols, Etan's code was simple to recreate in the fletching, but the chances of one of the arrows finding its way to my brother were so minuscule, and the chances of him recognizing it as a code even lower. . . .

Still, I counted and bent, hoping. If I didn't get out of this, at least there would be some possibility, however slim, that someone would find out what Aven had done.

The sound of approaching troops warned me. I scurried to the back of the tent, sweating despite the chill dawn air. *Stay or run?* I watched the tent flap, barely breathing, hating my indecision. Then I heard the cry, "Warrior-Guilder!" and my bowels turned to ice water. The shaking in my hands turned to a full-body shudder, and I wasted a few moments staring, paralyzed, at the tent flap, imagining Aven pushing it back, striding in. . . .

Move, you idiot! I shoved the back of the tent up off the ground, half-crawling, half-scrambling through the gap. I stumbled to my feet and looked around. Lighter than before, but still shadowy and gray. Around the edge of the tent the small group of men and women came by, followed by servants carrying dress armor. I caught a glimpse of the Warrior-Guilder's cloak flapping crimson in the breeze and ducked back again. Aven and her lieutenants were getting into full regalia to ride into the city. She would want to lead the heroic charge, no doubt. So I had two choices. Stay in the camp and hope she did not look for me, or make a break for it now and hope not to be spotted in the long stretch between here and the wall. And then hope not to be killed in the battle, of course.

The sick feeling inside me gave me my answer. I couldn't bear to hide here, waiting and wondering whether Aven would discover me missing. Better to take my chances now. I crept around the corner, and then, preparing to run, saw something that gave me a burst of hope.

My little graspad, separated from the others, had not been sent into the battle or used as a messenger animal. He was tied up not fifty treads away, distinctive with his shaggy, ungroomed coat and agitated pacing. On the back of a graspad, I would be faster and look more like a messenger and less like someone fleeing. I took a moment to force my curls into a rough braid and took a few steadying breaths. Keeping to the shadows and the shelter of the tents, I made my way closer to the graspad, not daring to look over my shoulder. I slowed, kept my head up, and strolled over to the little beast. My veneer of confidence wouldn't fool anyone, not with the sweat exploding from every pore and the shaking no amount of effort could hold back, but from a distance, hopefully, it looked like I was doing nothing unusual.

The graspad greeted me warmly, licking my hands and arms as I untied him, and swishing his heavy tail in pleasure at being free. They hadn't bothered to saddle him, but the bridle they'd used to tie him up would help me, at least. "We're going home," I told him, and found a note of hysteria in my whisper that turned into a giggle. "We just have to get through a few armies first."

I clambered on and the feel of his lean, bushy weight gave me a moment of true confidence. "Let's go," I whispered, and urged him forward.

But I was jerked off his back suddenly and hit the ground hard on my backside, too stunned to even cry out. A firm hand pulled me up by one shoulder, and I turned, everything moving slow and thick, as if underwater. Hard eyes unblinking, one hand gripping me and the other on her scabbard, the Warrior-Guilder smiled. I had never seen anything so terrifying in my life.

"And what are you doing, little bird?" Aven asked.

Her powerful hand around my throat, Aven dragged me onto the back of my raggedy graspad and wheeled away from the army, east around the broken wall. My spine bent backward across the animal's back and Aven's unrelenting pressure crushed down on my windpipe so that my struggles to breathe came from both my neck and my lungs. I was paralyzed, in too much pain and fear to cry out.

We rode to the river, out of sight, and she released me suddenly, letting my bruised body slide off the graspad and onto the marshy ground. I gasped desperately for air, lying on my side, my back in agony from the short, brutal ride. "You've made me angry, little bird," she said. "Your nose is entirely too much in other people's affairs."

"I'm . . ." My cry was a bare squeak. "I'm sorry. I just ran away because I was scared of the fighting. I'm not in anyone's affairs."

Aven shook her head, her manner suddenly maternal. The kindly side she'd shown me on my arrival played out again on her beautiful face. "I want to believe you, really I do." She squatted down beside me and I kicked away weakly, then more strongly as fresh panic burst free at the sight of the knife she had produced from her belt. I scrambled backward but she had my neck again in a moment, this time a vise grip from the back as she hauled me up, holding me in front of her so my feet dangled off the ground. "I was going to bring you with me, you know. We're about to ride into Silasta and I was going to present you to your brother as another example of my triumph. And now you've gone and spoiled it all. Now, did you share your little revelation with anyone? Anyone but your hapless guard, I mean. You know he was terribly sympathetic to you. He didn't like getting you 'in trouble.'"

I shook my head. Honor-down, I wanted to show some bravado, but I was crying too hard. "I didn't tell anyone else. I promise. And I won't. I won't."

"You know, I do believe you. But like I said, you made me angry." She bared her teeth and my tears stopped abruptly. I tried to say something, but no words came out. "A knife to the stomach is a bad way to die, did you know that? Excruciating." My whole body shook but I was frozen, unable to fight her off, unable to even struggle. The grip on my neck was paralyzing. She walked me into the water, striding into the marshes toward the channel, deeper and deeper, heedless of her clothes.

"Goodbye, little bird," she said. As if it had broken the spell, I screamed then, and twisted and bucked in her grip, but the knife went in anyway in a splitting, burning burst.

As she dropped me into the channel and the water rushed over my head, I almost couldn't feel the pain.

I just felt the cold.

Beetle-eye

DESCRIPTION: Powder ground from the carapace of the cave beetle; creates a glistening, fine black powder.

SYMPTOMS: In small doses, loquaciousness, excessive sharing of thoughts, lowered inhibitions similar to drunkenness; in larger doses, drowsiness, slurring of speech, coma.

PROOFING CUES: Mild "furry tongue" sensation increasing with dose, slight discoloration of liquids.

31

Jovan

"We're hauling them up safely," Chen told us as we arrived at the base of the southeast wall. Her urgent message had been the best possible kind; good news, for once. She had filled us in as we made our way to the wall where—it almost seemed impossible—soldiers from Aven's army had reached us at last. We raced up the steps behind Chen and she led us out onto the battlements, where two women in army uniforms leaned against the stone, talking quietly.

When they saw Tain, both visibly startled, and one blurted out, "Honored Heir! You're alive!" The other merely stared as we approached.

"Yes," Tain said, greeting each soldier with a grip of the shoulders, and smiling through his tired face. "You thought otherwise?"

"We had a messenger," the taller of the two said, looking Tain over and over as if he might be a hallucination. I jolted. One of our messengers had made it after all? Marco had faked the heads but I hadn't dared hope they had made it through the rebel army. But then why had it taken so long for them to return? She wiped sweat from her face with the back of her hand.

"We were told the city had been attacked and you and the Chancellor had been murdered."

"I fear it's true about my uncle," Tain said. "But I was luckier. And now, thanks to you, the city might yet endure."

But I had almost stopped listening. My heart felt like it stopped and then started again at ten times its usual pace. A messenger who thought both Tain and Caslav were dead? Not one of our original messengers, then. There had only been one person who had tried to leave the city after Tain's poisoning. "The messenger," I blurted, words struggling to escape my dry mouth. "Who was the messenger?"

Tain looked at me, catching up, my hope reflected in a rush of color to his face and the sudden clenching of his fists.

"I don't know, Honored Heir—I mean, Honored Chancellor," the soldier said. "A woman, I believe."

I squeezed my eyes shut, unable to breathe for the rush of elation that passed through me. *She made it?*

"I think she caught the deep-cold," the other soldier offered, oblivious to our reaction. "She swam out of the city, or something? The Warrior-Guilder was worried for her health."

I froze. *Fortunes, don't give me this hope and then take it away.* Kalina's health generally and her lungs specifically had always been poor. If she had the deep-cold, and she was stuck out in some tent in the open instead of being cared for in a warm hospital . . . But despite the fear, hope thrummed inside me still. No part of me had dared think she might have made it.

Tain took one of my hands and squeezed it. "She's safe with Aven now, Jov. No matter what happens here, we'll have her back soon." His optimism was catching; I returned his grin. "But we need to stop the attack," he said, turning back to the soldiers. "We need to get a message to the Warrior-Guilder to hold off the attack, and force a surrender."

The soldiers shifted, looking uncomfortable. "But, Honored Chancellor," one said, "the army is keen to defend the city and avenge its Chancellor. They won't want to hold back."

"*Listen to me,*" Tain said, his frustration showing. "Those people on the other side of the lake? They're our people. too. My uncle was their Chancellor, and they had *nothing* to do with his death. They are as much victims in this as we are—if not more so. I want everyone to walk away from this alive, do you understand? You have to make the Warrior-Guilder understand that."

The shorter soldier nodded. "We will tell her, Honored Chancellor." After a moment, her compatriot nodded, too, though she frowned as she did, and I wondered how well that message would go down with the troops.

"I'm sorry to ask you to do this, but I need you to deliver the message now," Tain said. "Every moment we delay . . ." He shook his head, looking back out over the lake, where the thick mist still rolled over the panicking rebels guarding their side of the bridge.

"Yes, Honored Chancellor," the taller soldier said. "But our boats are miles up the river. It will take us some time to get back across and reach the army."

"Then you'd best go, and my thanks and the fortunes with you," Tain said.

We stayed on the wall long enough to see them safely down the ropes again.

"Will they make it in time?" I asked.

"I hope so." Tain's fingers twitched, and we both stared down toward the lake, as if we could see through the ground to what waited below. The maddest of long shots, putting our hope in something that hadn't been used in hundreds of years. Yet what else did we have, if the army attacked before we could warn Aven to hold off?

We found Eliska directing repairs to the tower, one arm bandaged and her hair caked with dirt and blood, but otherwise unhurt. She followed us without argument back up the bank and listened as Tain outlined our plan, such as it was. She read the journal entries herself, mumbling under her breath, sometimes sounding incredulous and other times admiring.

"Is it even possible?" Tain asked, a boy again in his hopefulness.

Eliska opened her mouth, then shut it and shook her head, spreading her hands. "I just don't know," she said. "Tresa writes that this was probably the greatest feat of engineering in the known world. But they kept it a secret from half the new Council. It was a brilliant, cruel plan, and—"

She broke off and we jerked our heads back to the lower city at the sudden sound. Distant but powerful, the thunderous roar chilled me. We looked at each other. "They've attacked," Eliska said, sounding hollow.

And before we could even react, another sound came, this one closer, and it took a moment to register what had happened. Then Tain's whole body jolted and his eyes went wild. "No!" he shouted. "Stop!" He scrambled to his feet and took off down the slope.

"Tain!" I followed him, swearing.

As the horn faded, our soldiers poured through the remains of the Finger and across the bridge, swarming to engage the rebels from this side as well, trapping them between two fronts. Before he could get caught up in the crowd, I lunged with a desperate burst and caught Tain's arm. "Stop," I yelled, hauling him back out of the stream. "I'll deal with this. You go with Eliska—you need two people. If the Os-Woorin room is ever going to help us, now has to be the time and it has to be you. Go."

His face worked and his eyes darted between the bridge and me and back again, then he slumped and nodded. "You stop this," he said to me, as much a prayer as an order. Then he turned and ran back up the hill.

I let myself be carried as far as the tower, then threw myself up the stairs instead of streaming through onto the bridge with the rest of them. I burst out onto the roof.

Our peace flag lay trampled in a corner; in its place, the bright red of full attack billowed in the cold morning air. From here I could see above the mist to the chaos on the west shore. Our people were still outnumbered, even against the reduced force left to defend this side, but the suddenness and ferocity of our attack had put the rebels on the back foot. I tore down the red flag with clumsy fingers and fumbled with the heavy fabric of the green. "Who took this down?" I demanded, looking around at the frightened faces. Two children, not more than ten or eleven, raised their hands like scared schoolchildren. "On whose orders?"

"Cr . . . Credo Bradomir's." A fat lad with wild curls held aloft the horn with shaking hands, his eyes downcast. "He gave the attack order. We sounded the horn like he said."

I thrust the green fabric at the children. "Get this back up," I said. "You signal a retreat, and don't you stop blowing that horn until every man and woman is back over this bridge, or you run out of air, do you hear me?" He gave a quivery nod but I'd already run to the other side of the tower, taking care near the edge where a catapult strike had smashed the corner off. Behind me, the boys signaled the retreat as I craned, trying to see Bradomir's bright armor and cloak. *How long will it take this bloody mist to rise?* I spotted an Order Guard yelling commands from an arrow perch on the half-crumpled wall below me. "No one interferes with that flag," I told the group on the roof before I went back down the stairs. "Chancellor's orders."

I counted steps in my head on the descent and leaped off the landing, taking the two stairs at once, then skidded around, swearing, as the count finished uneven. *Just ignore it.* But that had never worked before, and whatever part of my brain governed my damn compulsions cared not for the urgency of the situation. I froze. A panicked sweat broke out over my face and neck. In the end it was easier to just go with it than to fight a pointless battle, so I hopped up the last two stairs on my right leg, then took the last two back down, one at a time.

I pushed through the clumps of men and women who had been heading out onto the bridge but who now milled about, confused, as the sound of the retreat horn penetrated. I sprang onto an empty weapons chest and bellowed at the crowd piling into the room. "Chancellor's orders! Get back and assist the wounded, all of you!" I pulled a burly woman up next to me. "You stay here," I said. "No one goes through in this direction, even if Credo Bradomir or anyone else challenges it. Call people back from the bridge and send anyone trying to go back to the field to help the hospital staff."

I peered past her out at the wide stone bridge. How long would Tain and Eliska take down under there? Would the machine even work? About to cross the bridge, I hesitated. I was wearing nothing but a filthy, damp tunic; I had no armor and no distinguishing clothing that would grant me attention from a distance. I needed help from someone with visible authority.

At the arrow perches on the wall, I hollered at the Order Guard. "Can't you hear the signal? Order the retreat!"

He looked down at me, frowning. "What? But we have them!"

"I need you on the other side of that bridge to get our people back. Chancellor's orders!"

He looked back over the bridge, one hand half-rising as if to point. Then he looked at me more carefully and dropped it. "Yes, Credo Jovan," he said, and he scrambled down the ruined wall to follow me. His distinctive bright uniform made him easy to spot, and he carried a small horn around his neck and a proper decorated shield over his back.

"We're going to need to sound that horn once we get over there," I said. "The people on the other side can't hear it from here."

"Yes, Credo," he replied, but shot me sidelong looks as he rebuckled his shield and unsheathed his sword. I took the horn and seized a shortsword from a passing man as we went back into the tower, heading for the smashed gate. Once there, I heard a familiar voice and anger raced through my veins.

"Wait here," I told the Guard, and stepped back outside.

Bradomir stood on the steps, cloak fluttering in the breeze, arms raised, yelling out to the people I'd just sent away. "Full attack!" he cried. "You cowards, we need to attack! Get back over there!"

I stepped down behind him and kicked hard into the back of his knee. Bradomir crumpled like paper and fell forward down the steps with a noisy cry and crash. He stared up at me, pain and fury twisting his handsome face. No remorse or pity tinged the contempt coursing through me. "Get up."

Torn between the indignity of lying at the base of the stairs and a clear desire not to do anything I said, Bradomir's moustache worked for a moment before he stood, wincing, and pulled off his helmet. He smoothed his hair and raised a shaking finger to point at me.

"You—" he began.

"You ordered the attack," I said. It wasn't a question, and he knew it; he regarded me with narrow eyes and a curl of the lip, but said nothing. "Against the Chancellor's direct instructions."

"Now is the time to strike," Bradomir said. "Tain is a green boy, swayed by emotion."

"That's your Chancellor you're speaking about," I reminded him, anger making me shake. "And he's trying to stop a bloodbath of our own people!"

"Rebels who killed his uncle and destroyed half our city," Bradomir countered with a sneer. "And you'd have them just walk away from here? But then you, *Credo,* you're swayed by something much baser, aren't you? You've forsaken your honor for some pathetic Darfri slut."

If he thought to wound me with a mention of Hadrea, it couldn't have been less successful. Instead, I thought of how much better, how much fairer and purer her concept of honor was than ours. I laughed and stepped down so we were nose-to-nose. I could smell the perfumed oil he'd still found time to wear. "I'm not sure you really understand what that word means. Anyway, you're about to get the chance to show just how *honorable* you are." I glanced back at the Order Guard, who stood, shifting between his feet, just behind me. "Help Credo Bradomir along. He's coming over the bridge to help us get our people back."

"Don't you lay one finger on me!" Bradomir spat at the Guard. "I am a Councilor and head of one of the most respected Families in this country. If you dare touch me . . ."

The Order Guard hesitated, then looked at me. Compared to Bradomir in his untouched armor, I must have looked a pathetic sight indeed; practically a boy next to the older Credo, filthy, sweating, holding a sword I barely knew how to use. The guard looked between us, then, with a grin and a sly salute, he raised his sword and poked Bradomir in the chest with it. "You heard the Credo," he said. "Get a march on."

Dignity forgotten, Bradomir fought and yelled as we dragged him into the tower. We went through the smashed gate, past my new gatekeeper, and ran out onto the bridge. Rebel catapult fire had damaged the stone in multiple places, and wide cracks and ragged holes zigzagged under our feet as we ran. Though I'd passed over Trickster's Bridge thousands of times, now its height above the water seemed precarious, and I found myself staring at the misty depths below.

"Down, Credo!" the guard yelled suddenly. He yanked me hard and I stumbled to my knees behind him as he knelt, propping up his shield. I pulled Bradomir down with me, and only a breath later, the shield shook as something pounded into it from the other side. To my right, another arrow hurtled into the ground and stuck in the crack between the stones. Heart pounding, I ran faster across the length, Bradomir forgetting to struggle or threaten me as he cowered behind his own small shield. I felt naked without any kind of shield or armor, running in a kind of partial crouch, ever aware that the arrow fire could take us down at any time.

We made it off the bridge and into the thick of it, and with shaking hands I raised the horn and blew the retreat signal as we joined the fighting.

The horn sounded pitiful in the roar of the battle on this side. I could barely differentiate between city people and the rebel force in the sweaty crush. I blew again. This time I saw some response; nearby Silastians looked over their shoulders at the bridge.

Slowly, the signal registered. More and more people backed away or even ran back toward the bridge. I felt a kernel of hope; maybe we could turn this around.

"We need to get back!" the Order Guard yelled in my ear. I looked back over toward the bridge, and the hope disappeared into a burst of fear.

The rebels had closed in behind us, cutting us off from the bridge.

Bradomir saw it, too; he stopped trying to lunge away and instead pressed back with the two of us, forming a tight little triangle. "What have you done?" he yelled, eyes wild. I'd never seen him without the veneer of calm, and it made him seem older.

I didn't answer. Couldn't answer. What had I done? I supposed I'd just consigned the remaining parts of our force to slaughter—I might have stopped the rebels being penned in but I'd done that exact thing to our own. At least I could see no Darfri Speakers among the force before us; it seemed less frightening, somehow, to be killed by natural rather than supernatural means.

As our scattered forces came together to form a rough circle, I blocked a spear strike, barely, and found myself thinking of Hadrea. I grabbed the end of the spear within my reach and yanked, and the man wielding it stumbled forward, losing his weapon. I kneed him between the legs, and tried to remember what I'd last said to her. *Stay safe? Be safe? Stay at the hospital?* Nothing profound to remember me by. I had barely any supplies left, but I sprayed some stingbark powder into the man's face and whirled around to face the next one. I knew what I should have said to Hadrea, and now I'd never get to say it at all.

The next strike was too fast, and though my hasty block deflected the sword, it cut into my other arm, a hammer of fiery pain in my forearm. My muscles already protested the action. All those soft years, and here I was expecting my body to put up with repeated fights on top of inadequate food, injuries, and general exhaustion. It wouldn't last much longer. *I* wouldn't last much longer.

Then a gong rang out, and another, and the rebels closing in around us began looking over their shoulders. The ferocity dropped out of their attack. It took some time before we realized what was happening; by then, the crowd had thickened and the surrounding rebels had ceased their fevered targeting of our group and were focused instead on the flood of people from the streets, retreating to the docks and riverbank to form one consolidated force.

Aven's army had broken through into the lower city. This was now a full battle, not a siege.

"Get to our army!" Bradomir cried. "We'll be saved!"

Off the docks and up into the buildings, we saw the first of them arrive, their uniforms and armor bright and matching, rendering the rest of us a childish mob. Relief and dismay warred within me. We might well be saved, but the rebels would be finished. This was not how it was supposed to go.

Then another sound penetrated the cries and clashes of weaponry.

A ghostly sound, but loud, so loud, and building with every moment; it reminded me of the longhorn at the Chancellor's funeral, but higher and colder. It rattled my ears, filling the air around us. Beneath our feet, the very ground seemed to shake. Men and women paused in their fighting, craning about. Fear and uncertainty bled through the rage. The sound was like a physical thing, seizing us all. Weapons ceased clashing and slowly the sound swallowed all others.

It came from the water.

Battle forgotten, everyone around me—rebels and Silastians alike—pushed and crowded to see the lake. The surface rippled, bubbled, like converging currents. Trickster's Bridge itself shook visibly, the stone groaning. People crowded tight on the docks, the sound binding us together. Though part of me knew what was happening, that rational portion of my brain was buried beneath the instinctive emotional response. And I gasped out loud with everyone else when something emerged from the eerie mist above the water.

Scatterburr

DESCRIPTION: Common, hardy weed with papery purple clusters of flowers, highly toxic to grazing animals such as oku and lutra; inhalation of smoke or contact with ash from burning scatterburr plants also toxic to humans.

SYMPTOMS: Chest pain, breathing difficulties, emotional distress.

PROOFING CUES: Smoke is heavy and smells sweet.

32

Jovan

Like a ghostly monster rising from the deep out of a children's story, something broke through the mist above the lake, its graceful motion accompanied by the wail that still resonated in my chest.

When its head first broke through, people around me screamed. A pulse ran through the crowd as we all instinctively drew back. Black and gray and dripping with water and slime that poured off it like long tendrils of fluid hair, it was immense, it was beautiful, it was . . .

"Os-Woorin," a woman cried, and as the great echoey noise quieted, the crowd on the west shore picked up that cry. The thing rose further, shoulders visible now, then its outstretched hands, somehow even more unnerving in silence. All around me, men and women dropped to their knees, some weeping. The Silastians crowded in our tight little circle remained standing, but just as frightened. Everyone seemed to have forgotten their weapons. Across the lake, it looked like every remaining person in the city had come down to the shore. I spared a glance over my shoulder and saw Aven's army and the fleeing rebels still moving in from the streets, but now crowding to see the lake rather than fighting. I even spotted the Warrior-Guilder herself, scarlet cape and ornate armor agleam, on top of a canal wall to observe. Others had clambered up on walls and buildings to get a view.

I turned back in time to see Os-Woorin—the statue, I had to remind myself, because the play of the mist and the wind moving the slimy fingers trailing from the stone gave the impression of the great thing breathing, moving, *living*—slide gracefully to a stop.

Then the creature spoke, and the screams and sobs in the crowd died away into a silence of terror too complete for sound.

"Stop," it said, and the booming voice carried a palpable chill. "This battle must stop."

It was at that point that I caught a glimpse of one of the mercenary leaders of the rebel army. A tall, orange-haired man built like a warehouse, his face carried no awe, and where many had dropped their weapons, he kept his up and craned about as though searching for a trick or a trap. I swallowed and tightened my grip on my own sword. "Hey," I murmured, squeezing the Order Guard's shoulder. His head spun about as if on a spring, and his eyes were wide with fear and confusion. "Listen. You have to get everyone, all the Silastians, to put down their weapons."

"But . . ." He looked back at the figure in the lake, shaking his head, and his voice came out high and squeaky. "What is that thing?"

"Just get everyone's weapons down," I said. "You have to. Now."

He stared at me, looked back at the lake, then back at me. Then he dropped his eyes and nodded. I patted his shoulder and worked my way through the gawking crowd toward the mercenary.

"This war ends now," Os-Woorin declared. By the fortunes, whatever amplification device that thing had, even our modern theaters could not compete. "No more death."

As I moved through the crowd, I heard the murmured prayers and quiet cries of people in every direction. But the tears and clutching hands, the bowed heads and frightened eyes, came not just from Darfri rebels. More and more people of city and country alike were dropping their weapons and falling to their knees. But the mercenary had obviously been paid well enough to ensure this war didn't end so simply. As I approached the orange-haired man tried to incite the people around him. "Get up, fools," he hissed. "This is some city trick. *Get up* and get your weapons." He kicked at a few nearby kneeling figures, but they seemed to barely notice.

I crept up behind him and clubbed him with the butt of my sword.

He fell in silence, half landing on two women beside him, but they remained transfixed by the figure in the lake and simply shook him off like an insect. I took his sword and moved on through the crowd, hunting my next target.

The pause stretched out longer and longer, and inside I wondered, *What is he going to say next?* Perhaps Tain himself didn't know. Speeches had never been his strength. But somehow, instead of making the crowd suspicious, the long silence intensified the atmosphere. Even the motionlessness of the great figure worked in Tain's favor, because the anticipation for the lake spirit's next words grew, even winding tight inside me in flagrant disregard for rationality. I hadn't truly believed this thing could be real, had not fathomed how it could have worked all those years ago. Now I understood.

I had just incapacitated the second mercenary when Os-Woorin spoke again.

"I speak to you with the voice of the great spirit of the lake, Os-Woorin," it said, and this time the east shore rang with cries of fear and confusion. Visible waves of reaction spread through the crowd there, the irreligious Silastians, after weeks of increasing rumors and inexplicable events, now faced with what appeared to be a giant supernatural being. I glanced up at the crimson-and-indigo-colored soldiers penning us in from the lower city, and saw much the same response there. *This is going to work,* I told myself. *Fortunes stay with us now, I think this is going to work.*

And then my heart almost stopped when the voice rang out again. "But I am not Os-Woorin."

Oh, shit. And it was going so well.

The murmuring started around me, confusion and distrust amidst the awe. I stared at the statue with everyone else, no longer knowing what Tain planned to do, hoping that at least *he* did.

"I am Tain Caslavtash Iliri," it said. "I am the Chancellor of this country, and I speak to everyone here as a plea for peace, a plea for forgiveness, and an acknowledgment of blame."

Anger, now, bled through the faces around me. Some rebels stood back up. Then people cried out anew as the back of the statue opened, a door in the thinning mist, and a figure stepped out to perch on an unseen platform. Tain, unarmored, bare-headed, carrying a speaking trumpet. Dwarfed by the giant statue, he looked almost pitiful. Frustration burst through me, hot and furious. He'd had everyone, on both sides, laying down their weapons. Why would he jeopardize that now, waste the last, desperate opportunity the submerged statue had granted us?

"The Credol Families, the Council, and the Guilds of this city have committed terrible injustices," Tain cried out, speaking through the trumpet. His voice was his own, now, not the eerie echoey voice of Os-Woorin, and though it carried well enough across the water, it lacked the power that had silenced the crowds. *He's going to lose them.*

"I know why our own people laid siege to this city, I know what drove you to it. It's not enough to say that I'm sorry, but I'm saying it anyway. Not all of us are Darfri. Not everyone believes in the old religion. But you don't have to be Darfri to see that we have at best ignored and at worst encouraged abuses of the land that we all stand on. Our land. That we have ignored or encouraged the disrespect and the denial from the majority of the Sjon people of the very privileges that were supposed to distinguish our society."

I licked my lips, unable to swallow through the dryness of my mouth. Muttering grew louder around me as more and more people stood, Silastians and countryfolk alike. Any moment, someone would swing a weapon again, and the mob would take over. And yet, I understood, and I loved him for it. To use the Darfri beliefs against them once again, even for the purpose of peace, would have been a further indignity, a stain on his offer of respect and equality. What peace could be built on such a further betrayal? Hadrea would approve. I was surprised to realize that I approved, too. Even if it cost us everything.

"These are transgressions spanning centuries. My ancestors built this thing you see, this fake Os-Woorin, to use the Darfri religion against its own followers, to give them unearned authenticity. They pretended they honored and respected the land and its spirits but really they were just greedy for the future they wanted and willing to go to incredible lengths to get it. The most elaborate lie in our history. Look at it! All of that engineering, all of that skill, that artwork, put to use for such a purpose. The Chancellors and the Council have been betraying their own people—our own people—from the beginning, in a thousand small ways and some huge ones. I am ashamed. Ashamed for me and for my ancestors."

Tain faced the west shore. "I'm here before you, unarmed," he said. "You can shoot me down. But you need to know I will listen and learn if you're willing to help me." He paused, and though it was too far to see his face clearly from this distance, I fancied I saw him lift his chin, shut his eyes, as though waiting for the arrows that must surely come. Silence stretched out around me, and though I looked desperately for the person who would start the onslaught, no one moved. Yet. "Sjona—all it was meant to be, all it *can* be—is for all of us. I don't deserve your help, but your children do, and their children. I think together we have to try." The words sounded familiar and I realized suddenly that he had drawn from my sister's suggestions after all. I fought down the hope and optimism at the thought of Kalina.

Then I saw the boat, just a small rowboat, moving from the east bank out to the statue. I counted two—or was it three—figures in it, but couldn't see who they were. Meanwhile, Tain stood there, exposed and vulnerable to our side of the lake and all the enemies that might lurk among us.

I sensed sudden movement from the crowd near me, and ran toward it without conscious thought. He was close, so close I could see the sweat beading on his forehead as he drew the bow back, but there were people in my way, I wouldn't get there in time. . . .

I lunged out, diving through a gap between two people, and slashed wildly with my sword at his bow.

The sword barely clipped the bow, but it was enough; the point caught in the limb tip and drove the bow down just as the mercenary released the arrow meant for Tain; it thudded harmlessly into the dirt and I was upon him, closing my elbow around the back of his neck and squeezing until he folded to the ground. I looked up to see three or four rebels staring at me. My breath caught in my throat. But then a voice rang out over the lake—not Tain's, a woman's—and all turned away from me, back to the lake. I craned along with them, fear redoubling inside me, a stone in my stomach.

I knew the voice before I even saw the figure.

"My name is An-Salvea EsLosi," she said, her rich, gentle tone reverberating through the speaking trumpet. "And I stand here with Tain, with my daughter and my son, because I trust him. I believe you can, too." My eyes fastened on the other figures: Hadrea, by the fortunes, Hadrea, and Salvea, and Davior, all standing there, with Tain, the last people in the world I could bear to lose. They crowded around the base of the great Os-Woorin statue, looking so *small*, water lapping around their legs. I could do nothing but stare, and hope.

"No one else needs to die," Salvea said. "No one else needs to be hurt. I am here for surety, with all the things that are valuable to me in my life. I make myself vulnerable to you just as the Chancellor has." She picked Davior up, clutching him to her hip. "Will not representatives for each region meet with us? Will Speakers not come forward and offer their wisdom?"

I looked around the crowd. Silence. But only for a moment; small, fierce discussions bubbled up between the rebel fighters in every direction, some erupting into larger arguments between the pragmatic and the passionate, the desperate farmers seeing a chance of going home and the true rebels, who would prefer to be slaughtered by Aven's force than discuss peace with the Council.

And then, "I will," someone called out. A round-bellied man with hair in a long tail down his back pushed out of the crowd, shoving to the front to stand on the docks by the lake. His voice rang out, unashamed. "We have no reason to trust the Chancellor or the Council, but I know you, An-Salvea, and I will take your surety." He looked back at the crowd behind him. "I have family back home. I would like to see them again."

Another person stepped forward, this time a woman, old enough that it surprised me to see her here, fighting. "And I," she said. "I will take this chance. We will see how well this Council listens."

The Es-Losis stepped back into their rowboat. At least a dozen rebels, clearly men and women of some influence, had come to meet them at the docks. Even several Speakers had emerged warily to join them. I could see no more mercenaries in the crowd, and no signs that the more zealous rebels would turn on their fellows rather than support negotiations. On the lake, where Tain lowered Davi down into his mother's arms. I dared to feel the tiniest glimmer of hope, and its reflection all around me, from Silastians and rebels alike. We just might have our truce at last.

And then, as though my foolish optimism had conjured disaster like Darfri magic, it all fell apart.

A deep rumble sounded first, like underground thunder, and then a tremendous *crack* from the lake. It took a moment to identify the cause of the sound, but then people began pointing and screaming: it was the statue, the fake Os-Woorin, rent with a massive crack from base to tip. As we stared in horror more cracks shot off from the initial fissure and the great face slumped suddenly as half the head compacted and began to slide downward. I found my voice as I pushed through to the shore, against the sudden flow of the crowd. "Get out of the *way*!"

Of course Tain couldn't hear me; he stood transfixed, staring up at the cracking, splintering statue, even as rubble rained down around him. Hadrea reached toward him from the wildly rocking boat, the screams of the crowd drowning out her yell, as if I watched a stylized silent play with actors in slow motion. I stumbled to the shoreline. Another huge crack made me jump. One of the Os-Woorin's arms split from its torso and thundered down toward the water like a great swinging hammer and Tain finally—finally— jolted to attention. He spun and grabbed hold of the stern of the rowboat but instead of leaping inside it he shoved it away from the path of the falling arm with all the force of his body, so hard it sent him sprawling face first into the water. My shout echoed Salvea's and Hadrea's, lost in the enormous splash of rock into lake. The little boat was flung away with the ensuing wave and Tain disappeared from my sight.

"Tain!" I bellowed. Frantically I scanned the shoreline but of course there were no boats on the west side. The force of the wave sent water spraying up as it hit the docks and rose the tideline dramatically; people shrieked and ran from the encroaching water. Back on the lake, the EsLosis' boat was still intact, Hadrea and Salvea soaking but upright, with Davi howling and clinging to his mother's shoulders, but it had been carried twenty treads from the Os-Woorin. The great statue continued to falter and fall in slumps and crumbling chunks, and still I couldn't see Tain.

"There!" Hadrea shouted, pointing with her oar.

Tain's dark head emerged from the churning water. Whether he heard my relieved cry to swim for the boat or not, he began stroking away from the collapsing statue to where Hadrea and Salvea frantically tried to fight the artificial tide being created by the heavy plunging stone pieces. But each collapse sent them farther and farther toward the docks. Salvea looked at the docks, then Tain, then up at her son on her shoulders, and the agony on her face cut me to the core.

"Bring Davi back!" I shouted, splashing into the water and loping toward them clumsily. "Get him safe!"

Then the very platform itself began to shift and tip, and the entire remainder of the statue plummeted into the water with a groan and a smash. The resulting wave spread so fast there was no time to get out of the way; I was knocked over and plunged underwater, spun about so I wasn't sure which way was up. I scrambled, twisting, until I found my feet, then stood and almost cracked my head on the EsLosis' boat. Hadrea was already leaping out beside me and together we dragged it back onto the shore. Davi jumped onto his sister's back and I helped Salvea out.

She stepped free onto the sand and as her hand dropped away I became bone-chillingly aware that something was wrong. More than wrong. This was not the crumpling of an ancient machine not used in centuries. Amidst the noise and the confusion I had missed it, but now I recognized the sensation in the air, the thickening, crackling pressure around my head.

I looked down the west bank to where the Speakers had gathered, already starting toward them, then stopped dead. When they had used Darfri magic—*fresken*—against me, they'd had a particular look: intense burning gaze, hands holding something of the substance they were manipulating, slow and controlled walking. Now, instead, the women had fallen to their knees and clutched at their faces and hair, crying. Whatever was going on, they were not drawing on the magic; it looked as if something were drawing on *them*.

Then the faces in the crowd around them changed, growing exponentially more fearful, and almost as one they started to scream.

I spun back to the lake. The water in the center was bubbling, spurting, raising steam in great clouds that surrounded a watery shape emerging, just like the statue had, from the depths.

But this time, it was no trick.

"Os-Woorin!" the cries picked up again, as they had before, but this time more terrified than awed. The thing rising from the depths was no static humanoid figure, graceful and mysterious, but rather a whirling, formless *thing* of water and rock and weed, its shape changing and expanding as it rose. Yet it did not resemble the maelstroms created by the Speakers during the siege, nor the earthy fingers that had bound me earlier this morning. It had presence: not quite a face, that I could identify, but a *sense* of one. And consciousness, and deep intelligence. And rage.

Mist thickened around the thing, swirling over the water in a wafting, spinning cloud. No, not mist, steam: the water was bubbling, boiling, and spurting around the creature. "We woke it up," Hadrea said, her eyes fixed on Os-Woorin. "Jovan, we're feeding it."

Spirits fed on emotion, she'd said, human emotion, and we had surrounded the lake with thousands of people in the heat and fury of battle, with surges of fear and optimism on each side when the army had arrived, and finally the infusion of hope and relief when we thought the fighting was over. And then we had convinced everyone around us that they were seeing the true Os-Woorin. We had made an offering, all right, but not the one we would have planned.

Os-Woorin roared, a terrible booming, gurgling sound like the crash of a waterfall. It turned, looking up at the old city on the east, where terrified Silastians cowered or ran. Part of its great, watery body extended toward the city, as if pointing. Then another deep rumble sounded from beneath the earth and a tower of water exploded out of the ground in the middle of the crowd on the shore, then another, and another.

"Honor-down, it's burning them," someone said, and my stomach turned over. It wasn't the force knocking people to the ground but the gushing, steaming water itself that burned them.

The voice of a man behind me cut through the screams. "Os-Woorin is punishing the heathens! The spirit-killers! They have brought it on themselves!" But even as he tried to rouse support in his peers, Os-Woorin roared again and this time its rage was directed at the western shore; a snaky "arm" whipped out of the surface and crashed back down on the docks, crushing and splintering everything—and everyone—in its path. Darfri or not, Os-Woorin was taking its revenge on the city and anyone unfortunate enough to be near it.

I looked back out to the lake, where Tain was swimming frantically away from the bubbling center, but making little headway. I jumped back into the boat. "I'm going to try to get him."

Hadrea fumbled in her sodden clothing and pulled out a handful of something green. She stuffed it into her mouth, then shoved the rest at Salvea. "Take it to the Speakers, Mother. Convince them to help." Then she took hold of the rowboat and pushed it out. I started to row, staring at her as she chewed determinedly.

"What are you—"

Then I realized. The remaining supply of feverhead . . . what had Hadrea called it when she saw the illustrations? *Babacash?* She had said it was sometimes used to aid in *fresken,* and I had noticed but not thought much on her interest in the plant during Tain's recovery. She had wanted it for herself, coveting the knowledge and power that had been denied her. She had brought it to the catacombs hoping to entreat Os-Woorin, but of course we had not found a shrine under the lake. She'd told me after our own small offering that she felt an open connection to the spirit and now she said it again to me as I pulled away from her.

"We are still connected! And I am going to stop this."

Then she stepped out of my reach and into the deeper water.

No, not into the water, *onto* the water, as if she climbed invisible stairs underneath the surface, and her cupped hands held water in front of her. I stared at her as I rowed back toward Tain, struggling to get a rhythm in the choppy waves, but she looked only at Os-Woorin, and her eyes and face took on the same focused intensity as the Speakers' had. She continued to rise as if on some platform until she walked on the very surface of the lake itself.

I glanced over my shoulder. Tain was treading water, captivated by the sight. I rowed harder.

"*Os-Woorin!*" Hadrea cried, and her voice carried over the shrieks and devastation, artificially loud. "Hear me!"

Os-Woorin, in the process of tearing the remains of Bell's Bridge apart, froze in its destruction. It turned slowly, forming and reforming as Hadrea drew closer to it. The water settled somewhat, the great waves caused by Os-Woorin's movements lowering into ripples. I checked on Tain again. He had seen me and started swimming in my direction, but his body was heavy and low in the water and his breaths more desperate than controlled. I tried to increase my pace, but my arms were so tired and my shoulder weak from the earlier wound; the sluggish haul of the boat seemed like it would never reach him.

Hadrea, by contrast, seemed propelled, gliding as she moved toward Os-Woorin, the water beneath her feet a platform. The crowd's screams gradually died down as everyone's attention fixed on the strange convergence of the woman and the spirit.

"Os-Woorin!" she cried again. "I entreat you: enough destruction. You have taken much power from us today. Do not use this against us."

It made a noise in response, a low roar, but this time somehow it conveyed meaning; as the sound hit me I felt infused by its sense of betrayal and fury. But then strangely, equally strongly, I felt a sense of apology and compassion, and I knew the author of those feelings all too well. Whatever power had clustered around the lake, Hadrea had found some way to use it, too.

"It is a balance," she was saying, and I could no longer tell if she was speaking aloud or not. "We share this power. It does not belong to you or to me. It is ours. It is *fresken*, and it is *tah*. We are bound together."

One more stroke and Tain was within reach. Half-sinking, exhausted, he must have swallowed too much water. I hauled him into the boat and he slumped against the edge, coughing up water. Back on the west shore Salvea was bent over the Speakers, shaking shoulders, and even from this distance I could understand her emphatic hand gestures as she entreated the Darfri for help. How they could, I wasn't sure. "Can you row?" He nodded weakly and I gratefully handed over one oar.

We turned the boat around and headed for the shore. Os-Woorin continued to morph and grow and shrink in turn, debris swirling around its watery form as if a visual representation of its thoughts. I could *feel* its consideration of Hadrea, its ancient indifference to this tiny person vying with its curiosity.

"What is Hadrea doing? How is she standing out there?" Tain broke off coughing to ask. "She can use Darfri magic?"

"She's asking the spirit to stop. Can't you hear her? Can't you feel it?"

He shook his head, looking at me like he'd never seen me before. "I can see it, but I can't understand what's going on."

If he couldn't, I didn't know how to explain. "Just row. I think she needs help."

Another roar split the air, and under it Salvea's heartrending cry as Os-Woorin blurred toward Hadrea in a sudden, immense wall of water that would surely crush her. I dropped my oar, heart in my throat. But instead of being knocked back by the force of Os-Woorin's blow, Hadrea seemed to slide through it; the water rippled and parted around her, splashing harmlessly ten treads from where she balanced, facing the spirit with deep calm. I *felt* her calm, and so, too, did I feel the confusion of the spirit as its rage rebounded without victim or recourse.

"This is a shared power," she said again, with more force this time. "We are connected. We are *sharing* the power, and we will not destroy each other."

It made another attempt, this time spurting geysers all around her, but once more, none of the boiling water touched her. This time I understood, because *it* understood. She had shared with Os-Woorin—we both had—and it was its power she was channeling; all the power that it had sucked up from the people around the lake was the same power that was keeping her safe. "We are the same, now," she said.

The spirit paused again, the geysers dying down. I felt a thin, fragile wavering, the edge of concession, and dared to hope.

But it darkened into rejection with the loudest, wildest howl yet, and the full force of the great thing turned on Hadrea like a concentrated storm. The Speakers on the shore—and others in the crowd—howled along with it, but our terror and hysteria was feeding it, making it stronger, and the invisible bubble of protection around Hadrea grew smaller and smaller until I could not see her in the assaulting waters, and could barely feel her presence.

"Help her!" I screamed at the Speakers, but they seemed incapable of responding. More and more Darfri in the crowd had come to the shoreline and were plunging their hands in the water beside Salvea, and I felt their efforts connect and grow. Os-Woorin could take power from us, but as Hadrea had said, it was a shared power. The miniature storm intensified, but then so, too, did Hadrea's protective barrier, and suddenly it was her control that was growing. I could see her small figure in the center of the flurry, her hands outstretched, and I felt her push back, and with it the water moved, and solidified, and compressed back against Os-Woorin until their two presences seemed equal. Two forces pressing on a sheet of glass that wavered and wobbled as they battled for dominance. And all the while I could feel her communication with it, as well, beseeching it. *We have wronged you, but there will be amends,* she told it. *The Compact will be restored.*

Tain's head ricocheted between the battle on the lake and the reaction of the crowd, uncomprehending, and it was his obliviousness to the true nature of the battle that triggered my memory. Hadrea had said *we* were connected. We had made an offering together, and somehow that link had remained. I wasn't Darfri and I didn't know how to help, not really, but I leaned over the side of the boat and plunged my hands into the water all the same, and tried to make myself open, to give her strength. As if that gesture sprang a trap in my mind, the tight intensity of the air broke into a million pieces and it felt easy and natural to pour into the whirlpool everything I felt for her and my home and my lost sister and uncle, and . . .

And the balance shifted.

The water started to tip away from Hadrea, back to Os-Woorin, and as I watched, my hope literally flowing into the maelstrom of power, she seemed to grow straighter and taller even as the spirit diminished. But she did so without aggression or anger, just calm determination and force of will. And empathy.

With a hiss like steam escaping a kettle, the tumult in the lake peeled back to calm, the geysers fell away to nothing, and slowly the creature's form sank back into the surface of the water. One last sigh, and all of the sucking, draining sensation of power in the air was gone, and the release was like waking from an intense nightmare, or breaking one of my worst compulsions. I gasped for breath.

Out in the center, there was one last splash as the power died away and Hadrea fell from whatever had kept her buoyant. Without a word, Tain retrieved his oar and I mine, and we set out to rescue her as she had rescued all of us.

Traitor's curse

DESCRIPTION: Toxin of unknown origin.

SYMPTOMS: Dizziness, followed by increasing swelling of the face and extremities, excessive perspiration, pressure sensation in the chest, difficulty swallowing and breathing, weak heart rate, heart failure.

PROOFING CUES: Unknown.

33

Jovan

As though the very weather celebrated the end of the war, the cold morning cleared to a bright day violent in color. The rich blue of the sky, the broken-mirror sparkle of the lake, the white walls and bursts of early autumn red and gold amidst the greenery made a glossy portrait of a city, painted over the violence and turmoil.

A weird dichotomy played between the rebels and the Silastians: deep relief at the end of the fighting, but inevitable distrust and suspicion as we came together. Nice moments punctuated the tension, though; families reunited between cityfolk and soldiers in the army and between some on both sides of the lake. The sight of them mingling on the shores that had so recently been a battlefield gave me heart. The hospital had become once again the busiest place in the city as hundreds of people who had fought for their lives now worked together to carry wounded from both sides.

Aven and her lieutenants marched across the bridge to applause from the city residents. The Warrior-Guilder strode first, magnificent in her decorated armor and crimson cloak, one arm held aloft to cheers. Tain met

SAM HAWKE

with her there on the bridge, clasping her shoulders and thanking her for her timely arrival in a voice rich with emotion. The army roared just as loudly for Tain as the residents did for Aven.

"By the fortunes, it's good to see you alive, Honored Chancellor," the Warrior-Guilder said, her face breaking into a rare smile. "We had heard otherwise."

Together they walked back across the bridge toward the upper city. The crowd between us swallowed whatever was said next, and hard as it was to wend through the throng to Aven, I got there in time to hear the information I most desperately wanted.

"Your brave little messenger," Aven was saying to Tain as they walked, shoulder to shoulder, heads bent close together. "How she made it through when no one else could, I just don't know."

"Lini," Tain said, his voice quaking. He saw me and gripped my forearm, pulling me in. I barely felt the slash of pain from my hastily wrapped wound. I stared at the Warrior-Guilder, waiting, hoping.

Aven directed her gaze to me. "I'm afraid I didn't get her name," she said. "But she bore your Oromani tattoos, Credo Jovan. . . ." The hard lines of her face softened as she placed a hand on each of our shoulders. The feel of her rough squeeze sent a frisson of shock through my body.

"Kalina," Tain said. "It was Kalina. Jovan's sister."

I turned my head, unable to look at her, unable to face the words I already knew were coming. "I'm sorry," Aven said gently. "We think she must have swum in the river to avoid the patrols."

"What happened?" Tain asked, though he must have known the answer, just as I did.

"The deep cold," Aven said, shaking her head. "She made it to us, and told us enough to send us back here, but she was barely conscious and coherent then, and she . . . Well, she collapsed and never woke again." I sensed her gaze on me. "I'm sorry, Credo Jovan. But your family should be proud. Your sister was a hero. We all owe the city's safety to her."

I couldn't handle the sympathy in her face, or my own grief reflected on Tain's, so I just stared at the ground. Though it had been barely more than a hope, I had secretly relied on the idea that my sister would come home with the army, and that I would retain some semblance of the family that had been my whole world at the start of summer. Now, after everything, it was just me.

They must have continued speaking, but I heard nothing as we made our way through the applauding crowd and toward the Manor, nothing but a high ringing in my ears and the distant babble of what might as well have been a foreign language. There wasn't enough air to breathe properly. All I could do was count steps and alternate squeezes of my hands, hoping the calming rhythm of the repetition would get me through this day. And the next, and the next? *Deal with them as they come.* The voice in my head sounded more like Etan's than my own.

Though the Council came together briefly, it was agreed that we would spend the day treating victims and cleaning up, with the Council and the representatives from the estates to meet to begin formal discussions first thing tomorrow. Perhaps it was relief, or perhaps a mark of how Tain's power and honor had grown, that none of the Councilors criticized the early ideas Tain put forward: financial and other reparations, immediate representation on the Council, new Guilds, mass schooling opportunities; even Caslav had been unable to voice such things. Now they offered no argument. Bradomir looked a different man, twenty years older, like someone had stolen the life force from him. Varina agreed forcefully with everything the Chancellor said. She nodded, eyes bright with focus, through Tain's heartfelt apology to the Darfri and other assembled community leaders. She, too, looked a different person, though perhaps that was through a lack of drugs more than anything else. I said nothing. Following even the vague direction of the conversation was like clutching at smoke. I wondered if the others could see what I truly was—an empty man.

Tain sent everyone off to their allocated tasks. Tomorrow the real work would begin. Rebuilding the city, repairing the damage we had done over centuries, reimagining the way people interacted, wouldn't be arranged in a single meeting. But it was a start, at least.

I looked up at last, thinking Tain and I were alone, and realized Aven, too, had hung back. She sat in the most relaxed pose I'd ever seen her, perched on the edge of the Council table, leaning back on one hand and shaking out her thick braid with the other.

"Honor-down, I'm so tired." She scratched her head vigorously and shook her hair out with her fingers.

Tain sat beside her, dropping his head forward. "Me, too," he said. "It's over, but it's not. There's so much work to be done, it's hard to even know how to start."

Aven nodded. With her hair down and lacking her usual rigidity, she looked younger. Almost vulnerable. Her voice even sounded softer as she put a hand on Tain's shoulder. "You'll do it because you must," she said. "And because you're the most honorable man we could ask to lead this country. No one else could have done what you did today, and stopped the fighting."

"I feel like I've failed," Tain admitted. The two of them seemed not to register that I was still there.

"Failed? You?" She laughed. "You succeeded where none could have expected you to. You survived, and in the end you saved a lot of lives. You'll be a Chancellor they'll write about, Tain."

Aven leaned closer, hand fluttering hesitantly and then, with more confidence, threading gently into his hair. And like a drowning man lunging for air, Tain kissed her, with all the hunger of months of watching and wanting her from a distance, and all the pent-up emotion of the day.

I stood and left the chamber.

I walked to the hospital, keeping to my most familiar routes, where I knew how to step to keep in perfect balance, and could walk over cracks in the stone with alternating feet, one of my favorite calming exercises. I didn't begrudge Tain finding something to hold on to in this maelstrom. But the sight of him finding it made me feel even lonelier and more lost than before.

So I sought my own anchor.

Hadrea was at the hospital, just where I thought she would be. Savior of us all, and yet there she was, her head bent over a patient, elegant long hands cleaning blood and dirt from around a wound. She looked up from over the table and her smile cut across the room, a crack of light in the darkness.

I threaded through the throng of physics, assistants, and patients, until I reached her side.

"Kalina?" she asked.

I shook my head.

Her response flashed across her eyes, but she said nothing, merely squeezed my hand. Grateful for the silence, I looked around to see how to help. I needed a distraction, something to make me feel useful.

"Here, give me a hand," a physic barked in my ear, and I followed her to the next bench, where a man lay groaning, his hands clutched around an arrow protruding from his shoulder. "Get some pressure around this, get the bleeding stopped. Don't try to move the arrow." She thrust a wad of bandages at me and moved on.

"Hi," I said to the man. "I'm going to try to stop that bleeding, all right?"

He stared at me with teary eyes and nodded. I had to pry his hands away from the arrow to press the wadding down on the oozing blood in a fat little loop around the arrow. "Help me hold this here," I told him, putting his bloody hands back in position. "Nice and hard. I'm just going to put a bandage around this arm and shoulder now."

Mindful of the physic's instructions, I worked carefully around the arrow shaft. The fletching tickled me in the face as I leaned over and worked the bandage around to hold the wadding in place. Then, stupidly, I found myself battling tears. Kalina had been helping with the fletching one of the last times I'd ever seen her. I realized then what lay ahead of me: I'd never be free of things that reminded me of my sister. We had grown up here, spent our lives together. Would there ever be a day where I wouldn't be surrounded by memories?

The worst of it was, she'd died thinking I thought her weak and frightened, someone to protect. I'd been blind to her strength, when she'd been braver than any of us. I'd never get to tell her that.

"There," I said, trying to keep my voice steady, as I finished tying the bandage. "The physics will get that arrow out when they can. You just rest in the meantime."

The group around me must have been the rebels defending the walls from our army, because most had arrow wounds of varying severity. I went between them, trying to steady the shafts and stop bleeding while the patients waited their turn with the physic. A small woman with a broad, flat face and the same brusque but kindly manner I associated with all physics, she raced between benches, seeing to the most severe cases as they arrived, and occasionally giving me instructions. "The heads are serrated," she said, showing me one that had been removed already. "That's why we have to cut

SAM HAWKE

them out so carefully." I took the arrow from her. The point had rough edges clotted with blood, and the fletching was damaged and shoddy. It was an ugly thing. I shuddered to think of its siblings, buried in flesh around the room.

I secured another arrow, this one part of a trio peppering the back of an ominously silent woman. As I wrapped and pressed, I found myself staring at the fletching. The one closest to me was damaged. And so was the one beside it. And now I thought about it, quite a few of the arrows I'd just dressed had had tatty fletching. The conscious part of my brain asked, *So what?* But another part, the part I'd learned to trust, niggled at me, pick-pick-picking away at my thoughts. The fletching wasn't tatty. It was missing barbs. A lot of barbs. *So the army used some inadequate feathers, just like us,* I thought. *Again, so what?*

I realized I'd been staring too long when blood leaked between my fingers through the wadding I held over the worst of the three wounds. I put extra on top, continuing to press, but my eyes locked onto the two damaged arrows, looking between them, something cranking along in my head.

I had to shift to avoid two men running past with a floppy body slung between them, and then, when I looked back at the arrows from a slightly different angle, I finally understood what it was.

The same damage.

Missing barbs, precise missing barbs along the length of one feather. It was the same pattern, the *exact* same pattern, on the two arrows. And when I looked down at the bucket holding my clean bandages and wadding, the arrow resting there that the physic had given me showed the same thing. Lines and spaces. Almost like . . . almost like lines and dots.

The part of me that processed patterns fired at last, and even as I scoffed at the idea—how could arrows be marked with a code only I knew?—I was fingering the barbs, counting, translating in my head, and I knew from the first few letters that the arrows were a message, not just any message, but a message to me.

The walls rushed in at me and my knees buckled. *Jov,* it said. *Beware Aven.*

I steadied myself on the edge of the bench. Only one person could have sent that message. The same person who had risked everything to seek Aven's help.

"Hadrea," I said, and she came over without a pause. "Help me?" I marveled at how she always knew what to say, or not to say. Despite the questions in her eyes, she helped me finish bandaging the patient in silence, waiting to let me speak. My voice sounded like another person's as I told her, "Kalina didn't die of deep cold. She was alive long enough to send me a message." I fingered the arrow, throat clenching. "And she was alive long enough to figure out who our real enemy was."

Hadrea frowned. "She did not die of the cold. But she is still . . ."

"I would say so." I could have choked on the stiffness of my words. No tiny sprig of hope worked its way into me, not this time. Aven had no reason to pretend Kalina was dead if she wasn't.

As we left the hall I thought I heard my name—a man's voice, amidst the chaos of the room—but when I craned around, no one was paying me any attention. I shrugged and continued out of the hospital. Inside, I was slowly turning to stone as my thoughts condensed into plans. I had supplies to pick up and preparations to make. It would be a long night.

I had still lost my sister. But now I had someone to blame.

They came in together, Tain with a kind of dazed swagger, Aven with casual confidence. I showed them in and bade them to sit with a cup of the finest Oromani brew, taking the seat with its back to the door.

Tain gave me a tired smile. "Why here?" What had once been his mother's sitting room, old-fashioned with fat, stuffy furniture unused for a decade and heavy velvet drapes decorating the walls, was over-warm and musty.

"It's private," I said. "There are so many people buzzing around the Manor, I wanted to make sure we could talk without being overheard."

"What is it?" Heavy lines crunched between Tain's eyes. I felt a surge of pity for my friend. He had lost almost as much as me, and I was about to rip those wounds wide open. I'd wanted to talk to him first, but he hadn't left the Warrior-Guilder's side since yesterday. It had to be like this.

"It's about the traitor on the Council," I said.

"Oh." Tain nodded, grave. "I've told Aven what happened to Marco, and why."

She nodded, giving me an approving look. "Tain told me of your bravery. You did much honor for yourself by killing that traitor." She sighed. "I can't tell you how ashamed and dishonored I am by having left him in charge. I never suspected him of disloyalty."

I stood, pacing around my chair, then stopped, looking at them in turn. The stone inside me hardened a little bit more. "Except he wasn't disloyal, was he?"

If I hadn't been looking for it, I'd never have seen the malice that flickered across her flat black eyes, so calm did she keep her expression. It didn't matter, though, whether she reacted or not. This was for Tain's benefit as much as hers. He frowned, lines in his face growing deeper. "What do you mean?" he said, a touch of impatience in his tone. "Marco was the traitor."

"Oh, he betrayed *us*," I said. "But he was never loyal to *us* in the first place."

Aven never blinked. Behind that cold, black surface, I fancied her mind turning, trying to work out what I suspected, what I *knew*.

I propped myself against my chair, holding eye contact. "I tried to reason out why Marco did what he did. What he hoped to achieve. The city falling? Then why work so hard on its defense? Killing Caslav and Tain? I suppose that was always meant to be the plan, but then Tain turned up early back in the city. What would have happened if we'd gone home with our planned transport? Bandits, I suppose? Well, he *thought* he'd finished the job eventually, though. And then, only then, did he send a bird."

Tain rose. "Jov," he said. "You're exhausted. It's been a . . . day. I think you need to rest. You're not talking sense."

"Oh, but I am," I said, eyes still fixed on Aven. "Sit down, Tain. Marco killed all of our birds, or released them with fake messages, but I'm guessing he had his own hidden. Because he needed to be able to tell his leader when things were prepared."

"In Perest-Avana, do you mean?" Tain asked.

"No. I said he wasn't disloyal. He swore his loyalty to his Guild and he kept that promise."

Tain laughed, a bark of incredulity, as he caught my implication. Aven just sat, silent, malevolence wafting from her like a smell.

"I thought at first you were just a straight-up traitor," I said. "Paid off by another country, some external enemy. But that wasn't right, was it? Or at least, it wasn't the whole picture. Too many things didn't make sense. Why bother with poisoning? If your goal was just destroying the city, Marco could have killed Tain any number of times. But he was trying to put the blame on Talafar, on Doran, to distract us from a threat much closer to home. He sent a bird after he thought he'd killed Tain because that was the signal for you to come home to save the day.

"It was almost perfect, wasn't it?"

Tain fell silent, his mouth open a fraction, looking between the two of us. Though she made no overt move, tension radiated from the Warrior-Guilder; she was a loaded spring. I should have been afraid, but emotion seemed beyond me now. "But it *wasn't* perfect. You wanted us desperate and leaderless when you rode in with the army and saved the day. You wanted the Council floundering, forced to vote on new leadership, and who would they think of but their hero—respected general, highborn. You wanted them to elect *you*." I laughed without humor. "That was the great, glorious plan. Aven rides in, clears the way to the city, then generously makes peace with the remaining rebels. I suppose the mercenaries were in place to make sure the peace deal happened at just the right time? Honor-down, you must have been *pissed* when you got here and found Tain alive and well, with you unable to remedy that, and the battle ending over something so completely out of your control you couldn't take credit for it."

"This is all very strange," Aven said at last, tone cold and even. "I'm not sure what I've done to offend you, Credo Jovan, but these sorts of accusations are not something I'm willing to have you repeat in public. My honor is at stake here."

"Honor?" I let my lip curl to show her my contempt, though inside I felt nothing at all. "You know, I've learned a lot about honor in the last few weeks. I suppose I see how you thought a great military victory would serve you well. But it looks to me like your backup plan was to ensnare Tain and take your influence over the Council that way, at least for now. If you can't have outright power, take it by stealth, right?"

"Jov," Tain said, confusion, shame, and anger warring for dominance in his voice. "Why are you saying this?"

"Because it's true," I told him. A stab of pity penetrated my shell for a moment, but only a moment. "Isn't it, Aven?"

"You've lost your sister," the Warrior-Guilder said. "So I assume you're not thinking clearly, Credo, and I'll overlook the insult. But you'd best stop now."

I leaned closer, clenching my fists around the edge of the chair. "My sister," I repeated. "I did lose my sister. Do you know why, Tain? How? Because my sister, my brave, brilliant sister, didn't die of the deep cold. She made it to Aven and she told her what happened here." I ignored Tain's falling face. "Somehow, though, Kalina figured it out. And she sent me a message." In my mind, I could still feel that feather, tickling my face. Kalina's last words, etched out in the fletching of arrows, a bare code. "Did you catch her sending messages? Is that why you killed her?"

Tain circled around behind me, hands opening and closing, seemingly unable to speak. Aven's silence stretched on, and Tain's manic pacing, and all the while I held her gaze, waiting.

Slowly, she started to blink. Her cheek twitched. I looked pointedly at the teacup beside her. "Have some more tea, Warrior-Guilder."

Beetle-eye had been used on prisoners long ago, before such things were frowned upon. It wasn't a truth serum, strictly, but it acted a bit like alcohol, lowering inhibitions. I'd have used something more debilitating but couldn't risk Tain ingesting anything else harmful after what his body had been through. I hoped it might loosen her tongue and possibly fool her into thinking she'd been poisoned. Poison had been part of her planning, but she didn't really understand my world.

Now conscious of the effects, rage darkened her expression. Then she smiled, the menacing baring of an animal's teeth, and spoke softly. "Such a clever family. But was it so clever to come alone? This one," she jerked her head at Tain, not even bothering to look at him, "is barely standing, and you're no fighter, Credo. You think the two of you are walking out of this room alive?" She laughed. "How did you picture this? Me confessing my wicked plans, and you two leading me out, chastened and chained?

"That's the problem with this city, you know. Soft and rotten to the core. Forgetting that the military is what gives a country its strength. Just like you two." She stood, graceful and sinister, a dark bird unfolding its wings. "I will have this city one way or another," she said. "I'd have settled for fucking a weakling in the short term, but I'll find a way of explaining your deaths, instead."

But I hadn't been so stupid, not this time.

Even as she reached for her sword, the heavy drapes around the room parted, and a dozen veiled Darfri stepped out, forming a circle around us, weapons drawn and pointing at the Warrior-Guilder. Hadrea, too, melted out from the shadows, her curved blade steady in her hand and half her face hidden by a dark veil. "I wouldn't move," I told Aven.

She did anyway, drawing her sword and lunging toward Tain in one agile explosion of muscle. . . . But I had come prepared for anything, this time, and she screamed and dropped the sword as the acid I threw dashed across her hand and arm. She fell to her knees with a guttural cry, clutching her burning flesh to her chest, and the Darfri were upon her in moments, hauling her back into the chair.

"Sorry, Aven, but no warrior's death for you," I said. "You'll be facing the determination council, and they can decide what to do with the rest of your life. And don't think we're foolish enough to rely on anyone in your Guild guarding you in the jail; you'll be guarded by people who know who you really are."

Aven looked over her Darfri captors with narrowed eyes. "And you're so sure your precious new Darfri friends will be satisfied with being ruled by a bunch of fat, rich sycophants?" She shifted her weight in the chair, adjusting her shoulders, and somehow she suddenly appeared more defiant queen than struggling prisoner. "I have friends, too, you know, who were rather keen on me playing the full revolutionary. You think the Darfri wouldn't join me? They were ready to tear you to shreds and feed you to their spirits about twelve hours ago." She smiled broadly at the man holding her left shoulder. "Wouldn't you prefer a real leader to a weakling boy?"

Tain, silenced by shock, finally moved. He stepped forward to the struggling Warrior-Guilder, taking an offered knife from the closest man. Darkness suffused him as he stood in front of her. "You destroyed our city," he said, voice hoarse. "You lured hundreds of people to their deaths, and tore the country apart. And you killed Kalina. You think I'm a weakling?" Here he leaned in so close she must have felt the breath from his half-whispered words. "Well, just you *watch and see*." Quick as a snake, he slammed the knife straight through her right hand and she howled an inhuman sound of rage and pain, pinned to the wooden arm of the chair.

Worried he might give her exactly what she wanted, I took Tain's arm and pulled him back. The muscles trembled beneath my hand and he stepped back as if in a daze, stunned by his own violence. "Don't worry," I said to

Aven, as her hoarse screams gave way to snarls. "Sure, you need all those bones and muscles to hold a sword. But you won't be holding one, ever again, so no harm done."

Hadrea pulled the knife out of Aven's hand and, after three others helped her bind the Warrior-Guilder's hands and feet, she wrapped a firm cloth around the oozing wound. "We will send a physic to see to that hand when there is one free. Though it might be a while."

"Please get her out of my sight," Tain said, and they dragged her out, hissing and spitting. Around her gasps of pain and aggressive curses, Aven looked back over her shoulder, not at Tain but at me.

"Don't think this is over."

I looked away as if the sight of her bored me. As my Darfri helpers left the room, the Order Guard Mago arrived. He moved out of the way of the struggling Guilder and her captors, looking alarmed, but saw our grim faces and did not comment. He cleared his throat. "Honored Chancellor, people are arriving for the meeting. Shall I allow them entry?"

Hadrea wiped her hands off and glanced over at Tain. "You had best go. You should not keep the elders waiting."

"Are—are you not coming?" Tain asked, his voice thin. Under my hand, his shoulder shook still.

"My mother will be there. I am better at pointing out problems than deciding on messy solutions. I will leave that to you." Hadrea smiled. "And hold you to account about it afterward."

"Jov?"

I squeezed his arm, but let him go. "You go. I need a bit of time to breathe. Start the meeting without me and I'll join you soon."

"I must care for my brother," Hadrea told me. "But I will find you after your meeting?" I nodded, unable to fake a smile, and the three of them left.

The truth was, I wasn't sure how to face them all now. It was a time for empathy and diplomacy, and I lacked the capacity for either at the moment. Scrubbed out like an old pot, nothing left inside me but scratches.

Tain would have to explain Aven and Marco's role in all of this to the others, which was difficult since we still didn't understand it fully ourselves. Though some of the mercenaries or "travelers" who had helped supply and ignite the rebellion had claimed to be disgruntled soldiers, Aven herself had never openly supported the rebels; she had never had any intention of helping them sack the city. She had simply used them for her own ends, not caring how many lives would be lost in the process.

Her cold eyes flashed before me again. I hadn't asked how my sister had died. What would she have told me? I began to pace. My chest burned with the effort of suppressing my imagination. If only I had done things differently. I counted my steps. *Mustn't think of Lini, must focus on the logic, the reasons.*

Though I understood why Tain had wanted Aven out of his sight, what I needed was more information from her. Certainly there was bound to be some crooked accounting in the Guild books, and possibly in the Reed family accounts as well, but she wasn't rich enough to have funded a rebellion on her own. And she had mentioned her "friends"; there were still enemies out there, wealthy ones. I wondered, though, what *they* had wanted. Aven had hungered for the Chancellery, but thanks perhaps to the beetle-eye she had as much as admitted she had used someone else's support of the rebellion to achieve her own goals.

I counted steps, following my thoughts around and around, skirting the edges of the painful ones. I needed to wash, and remove the small arsenal of things strapped around my body in preparation for this meeting with Aven: the remains of my poison supplies, the sedatives I'd spent half the night making, even the last of Baina's explosives. Aven was a warrior, and a cunning, intelligent woman; I had taken no chances. Yet in the end I hadn't needed much of anything. It felt almost anticlimactic.

My brain wasn't satisfied it was over. Something was wrong, something was missing. Yes, there were still enemies out there. We would need to have a longer-term strategy for guarding Aven, and some means of determining her loyalists in the army; we would be foolish to assume they had been limited to Marco. Aven had commanded deep loyalty and affection from her troops. Would her loyalists attempt to free her, try something new to destroy us, or simply fade back into the army, hoping never to be exposed?

Somewhere in the distance a faint rumble sounded; I jumped at first, thinking back to the lake, but realized it was more likely thunder. We were due some of our late-summer storms. It still felt odd, unreal, to think of something supernatural having a role in the weather. But no one in this city would be able to ignore the connection anymore, not after yesterday. I pushed back some of the heavy drapery at the edges of the room, letting some sun in, and peered out at the blue sky. No sign of clouds, but there was the thunder again.

I stared blankly at the sky, then started pacing again, trying to capture my disquieting thoughts. If Aven was in the employ of a third party, or at least had been funded by one, what would they do now that she had failed? Perhaps I needed to speak to the mercenaries. Their loyalty was, by definition, for sale, so perhaps we could buy information from them.

The distant boom was constant, now. Not thunder. I looked again out the window and this time saw smoke rising; something was happening in the city. Honor-down, could we not have one day of peace? I started down the hallway and heard a sudden burst of voices within the building—muted, probably from the business wing of the Manor. The meeting must have finished early. But farther along the spiral corridor the voices became clearer and my sense of wrongness intensified. Shouting, people were shouting. Had the meeting gone so badly?

Then I smelled the smoke.

I slowed my pace and softened my footfalls. Smoke in the city, smoke in the Manor. Aven had warned me it wasn't over. Padding closer, I listened.

". . . think because of a few words, that erases the past? I say this city is rotten to the core! Even the Chancellor himself admitted it was built on a lie." Cheers in response. I didn't recognize the voice—young, male—but chances were good we were dealing with some of the rebels who'd been shouted down at the lake yesterday. And an enthusiastic crowd of supporters, from the sound of it. "They took *everything* from us! Now we take everything from them!" This time amidst the cheers came thuds and crashes and the tinkle of breaking glass.

My insides grew cold.

Closer than the shouting I heard panting and footsteps. I ducked into an alcove, holding my breath. One of Tain's servants ran past, face wet with tears, looking over her shoulder as she ran. "Wait!" I stepped out and she jolted and drew in her breath to scream, but caught it in time with a shaking hand over her mouth.

"Credo," she whispered. "Credo, they've stormed the Manor. They—they've barricaded the Council chamber." She jolted again at another crash and skittered backward. "They're burning them alive!"

Tain. Salvea. Eliska and Marjeta and the innocent Darfri elders. "They've set the Council chamber on fire, and barricaded the door?" Too calm, I was too calm, and it was frightening her even more. She nodded, but took several more rapid steps from me.

"How many of them?"

"How many what?" She continued to retreat, eyes darting over my shoulder.

"How many people have they got? They obviously overwhelmed the Guards at the door."

She shook her head. "No, Credo. They *were* the Guards at the door."

Mago. Mago had seen us hauling Aven away. Had this been part of the plan all along, or was this revenge for us taking her down?

"Then more soldiers came up from the city and joined them. And some of the rebels, too, countryfolk, not many, but the ones who were still really angry. They're saying it's a revolution and the ones negotiating are betraying their cause . . . and they need to burn out the heart of the beast, and . . ."

"It's going to be all right," I lied. "Keep going down this hall. Do you think you can get out a window? There are small ones in the sitting room, through there. If you break the glass and climb out, do you think you can get out of the grounds unseen?"

"I don't know," she said, voice rising.

"It's going to be all right," I repeated. "It's not a big drop. If you can get to the Darfri quarter, raise the alarm there."

I didn't give her time to argue. Zealous rebels or Aven's loyalists or both, it didn't really matter. I couldn't get through ten people in time to save the people trapped in the chamber, let alone hundreds.

But maybe I didn't have to.

It took precious time to find the storeroom; several wrong turns and a few dead ends. Eventually I got to the one Kalina had mentioned, recognizable by the dusty cupboard with the carved doors in the corner. Up I scrambled into Kalina's little tunnel. It was ill-suited for my stockier form, and already thin lines of smoke wafted through its twilight length, but I wiggled along as swiftly as possible, trying not to think of my sister up here, trying not to think how I would get the more rotund of us through this tiny space on the way out. My shoulders jammed in the bends and my face grew hot as I drew close. I regretted the full pouches and supplies strapped to my body under my paluma, because they caught on every irregularity in the passage and I had no room to shed them. An eternity of shuffling, breathing, fighting down panic.

It was hot and dark in the viewing alcove, and smoke crept in from the room below along with the sounds of desperate coughing and wails of terror. On my hands and knees I fumbled with the viewing slit, trying to no avail to force it larger. The space was concealed behind the internal paneling, though, which surely wouldn't withstand a decent amount of force. I curled into a ball and rolled onto my back, spun around so that my shoulders were wedged against the back of the space, then kicked my feet as hard as I could at the viewing panel.

It popped out with a satisfying *crack*.

I scrambled onto my hands and knees and stuck my head in through the splintered wood. Below was a nightmare. They must have either rigged the room in advance or thrown some kind of flammable substance in before barricading it. The perimeter of the chamber crackled with angry orange flames, and two dozen–odd people huddled in the middle of the stone table, coughing and crying. Torn clothing masked their faces to shield them from the smoke, and those on the outer edges clutched water jugs and teacups as if the last dregs of liquid could fight the flames. "Tain!" I called, and through the smoke I saw his face turn up among the cluster. He had one arm around an older man who seemed barely able to stand.

"Jov!" He barked out a relieved laugh-cough and shoved his mask down for a moment. "Everyone, forgive me, but shut up and listen!"

Others spotted me, too; Salvea wept with joy at the sight. "Come on," I said. "Hurry." I had untied the knots on my cording before entering the tunnel and I pulled it loose from my body now, double thickness. But below me the flames licked up hungrily and I worried it would catch, too, if I lowered it straight down.

Tain followed my gaze. "Salvea, quick. I'll boost you." Together he and a burly Darfri man stood at the outer edge of the central table and made a stool of their arms. Salvea tottered up on it, her eyes wide with terror above her face mask. I threw her one end of the cording and she wrapped both hands tightly in the silky rope. Tain counted, "One, two . . ." and on *three* they hoisted Salvea like a pillar tossed at the karodee games up toward me. She hit the portrait below me with a squeal and I pulled her the rest of the way, bracing awkwardly in the small space, and soon had her forearms on mine.

She cried out as her arms caught on the splintery edges of the wood but made it up, fitting easier than I had in the space. "Keep going," I told her, squashed up as far as I could to let her past.

We got the smallest and the elderly in the room out that way: Nara, Marjeta, Budua, and Eliska, most of the rebel representatives, and Varina. But since I had burst the panel open another problem was presenting itself: the smoke, which was wearing down the remaining men on the table, was flooding the tunnel so badly now I could barely see through it. "They won't make it," I yelled to Tain between my own coughs. "They'll suffocate."

Tain looked at the barred door, now behind an impenetrable wall of flames. The portraits and other hanging wall coverings had caught, and a fair amount of the carpet. Even the treated wood paneling below me was starting to burn. Bradomir, Lazar, and Javesto all slumped on their knees in the central huddle, barely coughing anymore and almost invisible from my perch. Several of the Darfri leaders still stood, but the smoke was now so thick none of us would last much longer. Tain looked back at me, and his dark eyes were bleak. I fancied I could hear the sounds of fighting outside the door, but what good would it do? Even if loyal forces prevailed, they'd never get in here in time.

My friend gestured at the tunnel. "Go," he cried, and dropped to his knees. "Please, go."

But instead I looked up at the glass dome ceiling and had one final, dumb idea.

"Get me a fresh mask!" I called down urgently, and Tain didn't ask questions, just cut off another section of the base of his paluma, soaked it in the remaining teapot, and balled it up to toss to me. I wrapped it gratefully around my nose and mouth; the last one had already dried off in the heat.

I dug into my supplies one last time.

As I swung my torso out of the hole, I had a sudden and vivid memory of my uncle, standing in his workshop, beaming at me over a jar of silvery-white crystals we'd derived from bat dung. I could smell the caramelizing sugar and acrid chemical stench as the crystals turned purple in the flames, as richly as if he stood before me right now. His kind, wise eyes regarded me with approval and a dose of mischief. *I miss you, Etan,* I told him silently.

I took what grip I could on the ornate cornices, pressing my body tight against the hot wall, and wedged the last of Baina's devices into the space above the cornice. Then I lowered myself down carefully back into my hole, broke off a piece of the now-burning wood paneling, and held it at one end with a piece of my paluma, like a torch.

"Get low and cover your heads," I called down to those remaining on the table.

I lit the device, dropped the stick fuse, and squished back as far into the tunnel as I could get.

There was just time to note the flare of indigo before the dull *boom* and a splintering crash and then everything was heat and pressure and light, and I was falling, tumbling, landing hard on my back with a crunch.

I blinked. Light and sound came in waves; everything felt thick, like I was underwater. My body hurt, but I wasn't burning. I sat up and almost vomited. My brain lagged a hand's width behind my head and then ricocheted back into my skull moments later. I rubbed a hand over my head and found it covered with dust and shards of glass. I got my bearings: I hadn't fallen far, but part of the wall below the dome had been blasted open, exposing now-damaged stone behind the decorative paneling.

"Jov!" Tain's voice sounded distant, but his hands peck-pecked at me, plucking at my attention, and I turned my head—slowly this time—to see that he had climbed up the broken wall to me. Though his mouth and nose were covered with cloth still, his grin crinkled around his eyes. He gestured up, and I followed the line of the rising smoke out the massive hole in the dome. A rope fashioned from clothing hung from a distorted protrusion of metal at the edge of the blast hole, and the men were using it to help scramble up the rough ladder of rubble formed by the damaged wall.

Tain hooked my arm over his shoulder and put his around my waist. "Come on, my friend," he shouted. "We're getting out of here."

I went to see her one final time. She'd have heard the commotion, and presumably guessed from the fact that no one had come down here to release her that it hadn't gone as planned.

"It really is over this time," I told her wearily. My ears were still ringing and it was an effort not to cough. I would show her none of it. "I just wanted you to know. Your people are dead or arrested. There'll be no big rescue, no heroic escape. There's no revolution and certainly no military leader taking over the country." *And no more fears that her loyalists are hiding in the army.* "But we can make things more comfortable for you if you tell us who funded you."

Aven sat in the cell, her hand still treated only roughly with Hadrea's bandage and obviously causing her pain. She listened without speaking, then shut her eyes, took a breath, and relaxed in one fluid wave. I had to admire her sheer willpower as she took control of herself, almost as if she had switched off the pain entirely. Her eyes snapped open, seeking me out through the bars.

"Did you want to know how your sister died?" she asked, and aside from the extra throatiness to her voice, she might have been asking about the weather.

I said nothing.

"I was feeling a bit bad about it earlier," she said, her black eyes boring into me. It would have been the kind thing to do to just kill her cleanly. "I'd just found out our precious Heir was alive, and I'm afraid I might have taken out my frustration on your wee sister, Jovan. But now . . . well. Now I know she somehow managed to ruin everything so comprehensively, I rather think she deserved everything she got."

"I don't really care what you think about much of anything," I said, and hoped she would hear the flat honesty in my tone. I wasn't sure if I could care about anything anymore.

"Don't you want to know what I did?" Aven asked, a tiny, icy smile turning up the corners of her mouth. "I think you do. You gave me something in my tea earlier—I guess you must like hearing me talk. But you can't control what I talk *about*." She lifted her chin, somehow looking comfortable despite the indignity of her pose. "Such a pity dear Kalina was a little weakling, but she caused me so much trouble, I thought I might cut her in half." She grinned. I thought, numbly, that it was the worst thing I'd ever seen. "I was going to hack her little head off, but honestly that earther afterlife nonsense isn't worth worrying about. And anyway, I wanted her to feel pure terror before she died."

My hand gripped the bars. I realized my whole body was shaking. But inside I couldn't even properly feel the fury, the devastation her words wrought. I knew it was there, but it was like it belonged to someone else.

"Her body's at the bottom of the river now," Aven added. "There are all kinds of beautiful fish in there that would have loved eating out her intestines. Maybe she even felt their little teeth before she drowned."

One part of me wanted to respond, wanted to lunge, my animal to take on hers. The two guards to either side of me eyed me warily, perhaps contemplating stepping in. But in the end, the cold won. My eyes like sand and my throat a fraction of its normal size, I forced myself to meet her gaze without expression. "You know what, Aven? Dead is dead. She was too smart to fall for your lies, so you killed her. It doesn't much matter to me how you did it. She's gone either way.

"But it matters to *you*, doesn't it? You're still trying so valiantly to pick a fight. The big plan failed, and now you don't want to waste your life away in jail. But didn't you hear what I said earlier?" I dropped my voice and she leaned forward as if compelled to hear my words. *"No warrior's death for you.* No fight. No clean stroke of a sword. By the time you die, no one will be watching you, no one will care about you. Maybe no one will even remember you." I drew back. "You're going to lie in a jail cell, getting weak and frail and irrelevant. You might even live for years, like that.

"But death comes to us all. My uncle, for example, and the Chancellor, both died horribly. Without dignity, without comfort. *You* did that to them." I stood, letting my lips split wide into a semblance of a smile. "I have the last of Marco's poison now. I hope that'll help you enjoy your food and water in prison over the years. Anticipation . . . it's better than spice."

Then I turned and walked away.

My apartment was empty, all of my "guests" gone, just the debris of their passage to give sign of all that had changed in this house. I tidied up the rooms, one at a time, but took no comfort in the routine.

Our country would survive this. In the long run, it would be better for it. We had Aven and the surviving mercenary chiefs in custody, and we would work out who else was involved in her plan. We would untangle it all, and we would come out of this a better people. Tain had grown in this siege, nourished by the trauma, into someone new, someone stronger. I had confidence he would be the leader we needed.

I just didn't know where I fit anymore. This war had torn apart everything that had been important to me: my family, my job, my honor . . . maybe even my relationship with my best friend. I wasn't sure I could look at Tain without seeing, in all too graphic detail, what had happened to my sister. I had lied to Aven, of course. Dead was dead, but even thinking about the pain Kalina must have suffered at her hands was like tearing apart the edges of a wound. So I pressed the thoughts back into the cold stone and continued my tasks, wishing I could clean up the pieces of my life as simply as I could clean my home. The silence, broken only by my footfalls, echoed around me. Once a place of peace and warmth, now the apartments seemed big and cold. The war had taken my home from me as well.

But the war had given me something, too, if I was willing to reach out and take it.

She found me there, in Etan's kitchen—it would always be Etan's—and joined me in my cleaning without words. Sweeping the floor while I scrubbed the bench, we worked together in the silence for a while.

Then she stepped up behind me and slipped her arms around my waist. I froze. Part of me wanted to turn into her, to take the comfort she offered. But I just stood there, awkward, unable to respond, until she let go and stepped away.

Good, the cruelest voice in my head said. *You don't deserve comfort or peace.*

A pause. Then she slipped past and sprang up on the bench, facing me, legs dangling.

"When I was young," she said, "I was not the easiest child. I made up stories and talked to the spirits. I used *fresken* when I should not have. My eye even used to turn sideways sometimes, and people did not like to look at me. The other estate children, the girls especially, they tormented me. Little things, when we were small—tripping me behind corners, pushing me at the well—then more, as we got older. They knew I wanted to be a Speaker and they mocked me for it. They would cut my arms when I slept, or try to startle me when I carried hot water. And I grew up, but I carried it all still with me. For the longest time, I was . . ." She paused, looking distant. "Angry, yes, but mostly frightened. I swore no one would hurt me, and I took seriously the fighting games we used to play, so that I could protect myself. But I was so cold inside, Jovan. I was too frightened to let anybody close so they could not see how afraid I was of everything.

"And so I hid. I was cocky and brash, and quick to argue and fight, because I could use those things as a shield. I used the bruise inside me like that, giving it more relevance than it should have had. For a while, I let it be Hadrea. But it was not me."

She took my hand. Hers felt warmer than mine, firm and callused, as beautiful as the finest musician's or artist's. "You are hiding behind so many things. Your honor and your duty, which stopped you wanting things for yourself. And your grief for your uncle and now for your sister. You are using them as shields to protect you. But that is making those things define who you are, when they are not. They are parts of you, but they are not you."

I didn't let go of her hand. It felt like a lifeline. But the first emotion that cracked through the stone was fear. "And what if I don't know what else is there, when you take those things away?"

"Then we will find out." Hadrea smiled, and something warm buzzed between us. "Together."

Epilogue
Jovan

I woke in the middle of the night, disoriented, from my first dreamless sleep in months. I blinked, confused, and it took me at least ten breaths to realize the pounding sound hammering through my head was an actual sound, not merely a headache.

Beside me, curled against my back, Hadrea stirred. "What is that?"

I sat up. "The door, I think."

Scrambling to find a robe, I made my way to the front door, Hadrea trailing behind me, muttering blearily. A thick fog of drowsiness surrounded me. Irritation at breaking the first real sleep I'd had in a long time made me snatch the door open with a scowl.

"Credo Jovan?"

I blinked, bleary. The fog didn't lift. I didn't know the man standing at my door, disheveled and alone. He was young, early twenties at most, with a broad, plain face and big hands, twisting around and around each other in front of his belly. One of his arms was heavily bandaged and he had a healing wound by his left ear. "Yes?"

"Are you . . ." He spotted Hadrea over my shoulder and stopped, chewing his lip. His eyes darted about, and he looked over his shoulder.

I scowled, impatience increasing my annoyance. "Yes?" I said again.

Hadrea sensed it before I did. "He is afraid, Jovan," she said, a breath in my ear.

I looked at him, looked properly. She was right. Terror radiated from him. "What is it?" I asked, kindly this time.

"My name's Garan," he said, half in a whisper. "I'm . . . I was . . . a scout. In the army. I . . . I need you to come with me." He looked at me, eyes wide. "Please?"

"Where?" When he didn't answer, I folded my arms. "I'm not going anywhere unless you tell me more. What are you afraid of?"

He wrung his hands. "The Warrior-Guilder, Credo." He laughed, an anxious trill. "Honor-down, I know how that sounds . . . a lowly soldier like me . . . but I'm not making it up. I think she's going to try to kill me."

Behind me, Hadrea had already found cloaks for us both and was throwing mine over my shoulders before I could even respond. "All right," I said, following Garan out the door. "We'll come. And you should know, the Warrior-Guilder's in jail. And so are quite a few of her lieutenants. They attacked the Council, didn't you hear?"

His head snapped back over his shoulder, eyes glimmering like a scared animal's in the dark. "She's what? I've been in the hospital, I didn't hear. . . . Are you sure?"

"She betrayed the city," I said. "And she killed—" I couldn't even say it aloud. "She killed a lot of people. She's never leaving that jail, not ever."

Garan let out his breath and his whole body sagged, as though he'd been propped up by the air in his lungs alone. Hadrea caught his arm and steadied him. "Why did you think the Warrior-Guilder would try to kill you?" she asked.

He shook his head, dazed. "I was guarding your sister," he said, and if he said anything else I didn't hear it for the sudden rushing sound in my ears.

My heart started hammering as the emotion I'd suppressed burst through the cracks Hadrea had opened. Aven's cold eyes, the evil pleasure in her smile as she had taunted me, and her words, the terrible images she had used to try to unhinge me . . . This time I had no armor. I stopped walking, rubbed my hands over my face, trying to compose myself. "I can't talk about my sister. Please."

"She *told* me," Garan said, and though I couldn't see him, I heard tears in his voice. "She told me what she guessed about the Warrior-Guilder, and I didn't listen. I didn't believe her. I . . . What happened, it's my fault." He made a choking sound. "She escaped, but when the Warrior-Guilder came, I . . . I told her what your sister said. I didn't think . . . I only told her because I was worried Kalina might do something risky, run into the battle, and I thought we could help her."

Fury wormed its way through the pain, even though some part of me knew, looking at the poor scared lad, that I couldn't blame anyone but the monster responsible. Hadrea slipped an arm around my waist, and that calm contact drained my anger.

"It's not your fault," I said, and though my tone came out wooden, I meant it. "Who *would* believe a Councilor would do something like this. She was your Guild leader. You trusted her."

He dragged his fingers through his unruly hair, making it stick out even further. "There was something, though, something I didn't trust. I followed her. I'm good at following people," he added in a mumble. "Not much good at anything else."

I knew where this was going, and I didn't want to hear from another person how horribly my sister had died. It might make this boy feel better to share it with someone, but how would that help me? "I know what happened," I said. "I don't think I can hear it again, all right?"

But Hadrea's grip on my waist had tightened. Again, she read him better than I. "Garan," she said, and this time it was *her* voice that came out strange and tight. "Garan, where are we going?"

"To the hospital," he said. "I did my best, Credo, but I had to wait until the Warrior-Guilder was out of sight. Kalina fought so hard, but they struggled and she fell into the river. . . . Aven assumed she was dead, Credo, but she must have held her breath and dragged herself all the way to the bank."

As if all the air had been sucked from around me, my whole body tensed up. Moments passed in limbo, then I found my hands gripping the front of Garan's rough tunic, my face a handspan from his. "Is she . . ." I couldn't go on, just stood there holding him up like a schoolyard bully, unable to even ask, choked by hope.

Hadrea finished for me. "Are you saying Kalina is alive?"

Garan nodded, still looking terrified. I dropped him, shaking.

"Yes, but she's not in good shape, Credo. I grew up in Green Bend, by the river. I know what to do when someone's taken a lot of water—I got it out from her lungs, but her stomach . . . I'm no physic. The knife didn't land where it was meant to, but it was still a bad wound. I bandaged her up as best I could to hold it all together. I didn't dare ask anyone for help. I dragged her to the army in a body sling, and slipped in with the rest of the wounded. But I hid her tattoos and didn't tell the physics who she was, because I thought Aven might find out."

Kalina, I thought. And I ran.

The dark was no obstacle, not to me. Years of pacing had taught me the streets of the upper city; it mattered not that most of the lights had been out for weeks to conserve oil. The other two followed me as I raced through the city in a blur, fighting down the bursts of hope that both propelled and terrified me. I wanted to believe; honor-down, I had never wanted anything so badly.

It might have been midday, for all the activity in the hospital. Garan took the lead once we burst into the crowded hive of the main hall, and led us through the bustle. "Where is she?" I demanded, not caring how manic I sounded.

"Through here," he said, but I'd already seen her.

A tiny, pitiful figure on a bed; I'd have known her anywhere, even though part of me registered how alien she looked, how wrong, lying there so straight instead of curled up like a kitsa, the way she usually slept. Her hair was splayed over the pillow, a dark halo around a carving of a face. I knelt beside her.

"Lini," I whispered. I had to hold my hand in front of her nose to confirm she still breathed. That tiny puff of warm air was the best thing I'd ever felt.

"The physics already operated," Garan said, hovering behind. "But they don't know . . . there was so much damage."

"Who was the physic?"

Garan pointed him out; I recognized him as the physic who I'd helped with an injured soldier on the walls, weeks ago. He recognized me, too, and raised an eyebrow when he learned the identity of his patient. "It's a bad injury," he told me, pinching his nose. "We've repaired what we can, but it's going to be a waiting exercise now, I'm afraid, Credo."

Hadrea rested her chin on my shoulder, arms slipping around me. "We'll be here when she wakes up," she said, and I heard calm, not fear, in her voice.

"Yeah," I said. "Yeah, we will."

The physic shook his head, putting a hand on my shoulder. "I don't want you to hope unnecessarily, Credo," he said. "It will take real strength, a fighting spirit, and a determined body, to recover from this. You should know she probably won't wake up."

I sat beside Hadrea, feeling the warmth of her body against mine. I found myself smiling. "The hell she won't," I said. "She's the strongest person I know."

And we settled in together by the bed, to wait for my sister to come back to us.